W9-BUQ-838

PRAISE FOR ROSE TREMAIN'S
MUSIC & SILENCE

Winner of Great Britain's
Whitbread Novel of the Year Award in 1999

A critical triumph on both sides of the Atlantic

"Evokes a realm of candlelight, shadow, music, silence, castles, farms, dense forests, and perilous seas. . . . Tremain's prose style has an almost fairy-tale limpidity."

—*Los Angeles Times*

"Like Shakespeare—who is a recent playwright during the period in which the novel is set, and much admired by the characters—Tremain mixes history, myth, and invention, evoking the symmetries of fairy tales. . . . Tremain . . . uses the past as a fantastical world where the imagination has an almost hypnotic force. . . . She fills engrossing plots with odd details no one else could have thought of."

—*Newsday* (New York)

"Rose Tremain . . . has engineered a span between pop and art that's supported by each, yet marvelously out there in midair on its own. . . . Orchestrated more like a symphony than a novel. . . . Narratives keyed to different characters dip and soar around each other in surprising harmony, and one can't help marveling at what her dexterous technique lets the author get away with. . . . In the hypnotic state inspired by *MUSIC & SILENCE*, readers may find themselves not just distracted in entertaining fashion but inspired to the kind of emotional interaction that's increasingly rare in any kind of fiction these days. . . . Tremain offers a very great store of joy indeed."

—*San Francisco Chronicle Book Review*

"A magical novel . . . which offers great beauty, great ugliness, great wisdom."

—*The Spectator* (U.K.)

"Rose Tremain's . . . most successful fiction."

—*The Times Literary Supplement* (U.K.)

"Tremain's characterizations perform their own kind of magic as they effortlessly blend realism with the fantastic, leaving the reader dazzled and moved."

—*Chicago Tribune*

"Rose Tremain triumphantly returns to the fictional territory of history she covered so adeptly in *Restoration*. . . . Numerous shenanigans, machinations, and romantic twists and turns culminate in an uplifting resolution. Tremain's imaginative vision of history is a saga of grand themes, larger-than-life characters, and a sweeping, monumental narrative."

—*The Seattle Times*

"Striding over the hills and breaking them, like T.S. Eliot's Cousin Nancy Ellicott, comes Rose Tremain. Literary hills these, and gaudily flowered. Ms. Tremain, conjuring spells one moment and knocking them all of a heap the next, sows and tramples. . . . An unexpected loveliness that I doubt few writers other than Ms. Tremain could bring off."

—*The New York Times*

"Lyrical, voluptuous, and pictorially splendid."

—*The Sunday Times* (U.K.)

"Tremain's achievement in *MUSIC & SILENCE* is extraordinary. . . . She whips up a narrative world [of] vast, louring palaces, doomily dangerous women, crazed ambitions and, nestling miraculously at the fetid heart of all this, a tale of pure and courageous love."

—*The Daily Telegraph* (U.K.)

"Move over, Descartes. Sit back, Shakespeare. Rose Tremain is in your neighborhoods. . . . Settle in for a long, constantly rewarding, and enthralling read."

—*Milwaukee Journal Sentinel*

"Lush, dense and bittersweet, Tremain's novel . . . travels gracefully from castle to kitchen, equally at ease describing royal foibles and country wives storing pots of jam for the oncoming winter. . . . An engagingly intelligent novel of the impassioned politics of romance."

—*Star Tribune* (U.K.)

"When it comes to sheer, inventive, imaginative daring in fiction, Rose Tremain is just the best."

—*The Independent on Sunday* (U.K.)

"A superb novel, humming with music, real and imagined, literal and figurative . . . *MUSIC & SILENCE* is a wonderful, joyously noisy book."

—*The Guardian* (U.K.)

ALSO BY ROSE TREMAIN

NOVELS

Sadler's Birthday
Letter to Sister Benedicta
The Cupboard
The Swimming Pool Season
Restoration
Sacred Country
The Way I Found Her

COLLECTIONS OF SHORT STORIES

The Colonel's Daughter and Other Stories
The Garden of the Villa Mollini and Other Stories
Evangelista's Fan and Other Stories

FOR CHILDREN

Journey to the Volcano

For orders other than by individual consumers, Pocket Books grants a discount on the purchase of **10 or more** copies of single titles for special markets or premium use. For further details, please write to the Vice President of Special Markets, Pocket Books, 1230 Avenue of the Americas, 9th Floor, New York, NY 10020-1586.

For information on how individual consumers can place orders, please write to Mail Order Department, Simon & Schuster, Inc., 100 Front Street, Riverside, NJ 08075.

MUSIC & SILENCE

ROSE TREMAIN

WASHINGTON SQUARE PRESS
PUBLISHED BY POCKET BOOKS
New York   London   Toronto   Sydney   Singapore

For my daughter, Eleanor
Love always

The sale of this book without its cover is unauthorized. If you purchased this book without a cover, you should be aware that it was reported to the publisher as "unsold and destroyed." Neither the author nor the publisher has received payment for the sale of this "stripped book."

This book is a work of fiction. Names, characters, places and incidents are products of the author's imagination or are used fictitiously. Any resemblance to actual events or locales or persons, living or dead, is entirely coincidental.

A Washington Square Press Publication of
POCKET BOOKS, a division of Simon & Schuster, Inc.
1230 Avenue of the Americas, New York, NY 10020

Copyright © 1999 by Rose Tremain

Published by arrangement with Farrar, Straus and Giroux, LLC

Originally published in Great Britain in 1999 by Chatto & Windus, a Division of Random House U.K. Ltd., Great Britain

All rights reserved, including the right to reproduce this book or portions thereof in any form whatsoever. For information address Farrar, Straus and Giroux, LLC, 19 Union Square West, New York, NY 10003

ISBN: 0-7434-1826-3

First Washington Square Press trade paperback printing May 2001

10 9 8 7 6 5 4 3 2 1

WASHINGTON SQUARE PRESS and colophon are registered trademarks of Simon & Schuster, Inc.

Cover design by Brigid Pearson, front cover photo © Scala/Art Resource, NY. Caravaggio (1573–1610). Detail from *The Lute Player*. Hermitage, St. Petersburg, Russia.

Printed in the U.S.A.

CONTENTS

PART ONE

COPENHAGEN, 1629

Lilac and Linden

A lamp is lit.

Until this moment, when the flame of the lamp flares blue, then settles to steady yellow inside its ornate globe, the young man had been impressed by the profound darkness into which, upon his late-night arrival at the palace of Rosenborg, he had suddenly stepped. Tired from his long sea journey, his eyes stinging, his walk unsteady, he had been questioning the nature of this darkness. For it seemed to him not merely an external phenomenon, having to do with an actual absence of light, but rather as though it emanated from within him, as if he had finally crossed the threshold of his own absence of hope.

Now he is relieved to see the walls of a panelled room take shape around him. A voice says: "This is the *Vinterstue*. The Winter Room."

The lamp is lifted up. Held high, it burns more brightly, as though sustained by purer air, and the young man sees a shadow cast onto the wall. It is a long, slanting shadow and so he knows it is his own. It appears to have a deformity, a hump, occurring along its spine from below the shoulder-blades to just above the waist. But this is the shadow's trickery. The young man is Peter Claire, the lutenist, and the curvature on his back is his lute.

He is standing near a pair of lions, made of silver. Their eyes

3

seem to watch him in the flickering gloom. Beyond them he can see a table and some tall chairs. But Peter Claire is separate from everything, cannot lean on any object, cannot rest. And now, the lamp moves and he must follow.

"It may be," says a tall gentleman, who hurries on, carrying the light, "that His Majesty, King Christian, will command you to play for him tonight. He is not well and his physicians have prescribed music. Therefore, members of the royal orchestra must be ready to perform at all times, day and night. I thought it best to advise you of this straight away."

Peter Claire's feelings of dismay increase. He begins to curse himself, to berate his own ambition for bringing him here to Denmark, for taking him so far from the places and people he had loved. He is at the end of his journey and yet he feels lost. Within this arrival some terrifying departure lies concealed. And suddenly, with peculiar speed, the lamp moves and everything in the room seems to rearrange itself. Peter Claire sees his shadow on the wall become elongated, stretching upwards for a few seconds towards the ceiling before being swallowed by the darkness, with no trace of it remaining.

Then the end of a corridor is reached and the gentleman stops before a door. He knocks and waits, putting a finger to his lips and leaning close against the door to listen for the command from within. It comes at last, a voice deep and slow, and Peter Claire finds himself, in the next minute, standing before King Christian, who is sitting in a chair in his night-shirt. Before him, on a small table, is a pair of scales and by these a clutch of silver coins.

The English lutenist bows as the King looks up and Peter Claire will always remember that, as King Christian first glimpses him in this dark middle of a winter's night, there comes into His Majesty's eyes a look of astonishment and, staring intently at the lute player's face, he whispers a single word: "Bror."

"I beg your pardon, Sir . . . ?" says Peter Claire.

"Nothing," says the King. "A ghost. Denmark is full of ghosts. Did no one warn you?"

"No, Your Majesty."

4

"Never mind. You will see them for yourself. We are one of the oldest nations on earth. But you should know that it is a time of storms here, of confusion, of incomprehension, of bitter boiling muddle."

"Of muddle, Sir?"

"Yes. This is why I am weighing silver. I weigh the same pieces over and over again, to ensure that there is no error. No *possibility* of error. I am trying, piece by piece and day by day, to reimpose order upon chaos."

Peter Claire does not know how to reply to this and he is aware that the tall gentleman, without his noticing, has gone from the room, leaving him alone with the King, who now pushes the scales aside and settles himself more comfortably in the chair.

King Christian lifts his head and asks: "How old are you, Mr. Claire? Where do you come from?"

A fire is burning in the room, which is the *Skrivestue*, the King's study, and the small chamber smells sweetly of applewood and leather.

Peter Claire replies that he is twenty-seven and that his parents live in the town of Harwich on the east coast of England. He adds that the sea in winter can be unforgiving there.

"Unforgiving. Unforgiving!" says the King. "Well, we must hurry on, pass over or skirt around that word. *Unforgiving*. But I tell you, lutenist, I am tortured by lice. Do not look alarmed. Not in my hair or on my pillow. I mean by cowards, rascals, liars, sots, cheats and lechers. Where are the philosophers? That is what I constantly ask."

Peter Claire hesitates before answering.

"No need to reply," says the King. "For they are all gone from Denmark. There is not one left."

Then His Majesty stands up and moves towards the fire where Peter Claire is standing, and takes up a lamp and holds it near the young man's face. He examines the face, and Peter Claire lowers his eyes because he has been warned not to stare at the King. This King is ugly. King Charles I of England, King Louis XIII of France, these are handsome men at this perilous moment in history, but

5

King Christian IV of Denmark—all-powerful, brave and cultured as he is reported to be—has a face like a loaf.

The lutenist, to whom, by cruel contrast, nature has given an angel's countenance, can smell wine on the King's breath. But he does not dare to move, not even when the King reaches up and tenderly touches his cheek with his hand. Peter Claire, with his blond hair and his eyes the colour of the sea, has been considered handsome from childhood. He wears this handsomeness lightly, frequently forgetting about it, as though almost impatient for time to take it away. He once overheard his sister Charlotte praying to God to be given his face in exchange for hers. He thought, It is really of little value to me; far better it were hers. And yet now, in this unfamiliar place, when his own thoughts are so sombre and dark, the lute player finds that his physical beauty is once again the subject of unexpected scrutiny.

"I see. I see," whispers the King. "God has exaggerated, as He so often seems to do. Beware the attentions of my wife, Kirsten, who is a fool for yellow hair. I advise a mask when you are in her presence. And all beauty vanishes away, but of course you know that, I needn't underline the self-evident."

"I know that beauty vanishes, Sir."

"Of course you do. Well, you had better play for me. I suppose you know that we had your Mr. Dowland here at court. The conundrum there was that such beautiful music could come from so agitated a soul. The man was all ambition and hatred, yet his ayres were as delicate as rain. We would sit there and blub, and Master Dowland would kill us with his furious look. I told my mother to take him to one side and say: 'Dowland, this will not do and cannot be tolerated,' but he told her music can only be born out of fire and fury. What do you think about that?"

Peter Claire is silent for a moment. For a reason he can't name, this question consoles him and he feels his agitation diminish by a fraction. "I think that it is born out of fire and fury, Sir," he says, "but also out of the antitheses to these—out of cold reason and calm."

"This sounds logical. But of course we do not really know where music comes from or why, or when the first note of it was heard.

And we shall never know. It is the human soul, speaking without words. But it seems to cure pain—this is an honest fact. I yearn, by the way, for everything to be transparent, honest and true. So why do you not play me one of Dowland's *Lachrimae?* Economy of means was his gift and this I dote upon. His music leaves no room for exhibitionism on the part of the performer."

Peter Claire unslings his lute from his back and holds it close against his body. His ear (in which he wears a tiny jewel once given to him by an Irish countess) strains to hear, as he plucks and tunes. King Christian sighs, waiting for the sweet melody to begin. He is a heavy man. Any alteration of his body's position seems to cause him a fleeting moment of discomfort.

Now Peter Claire arranges his body into the stance he must always adopt when he performs: leaning forward from the hips, head out, chin down, right arm forming a caressing half-circle, so that the instrument is held at the exact centre of his being. Only in this way can he feel that the music emanates from him. He begins to play. He hears the purity of the sound and suspects that this, alone, is what will count with the King of Denmark.

When the song is over he glances at the King, but the King doesn't move. His wide hands clutch the arms of the chair. From the left side of his dark head falls a long, thin plait of hair, fastened with a pearl. "In springtime," Christian says suddenly, "Copenhagen used to smell of lilac and of linden. I do not know where this heavenly scent has gone."

KIRSTEN MUNK, CONSORT OF KING CHRISTIAN IV
OF DENMARK: FROM HER PRIVATE PAPERS

Well, for my thirtieth birthday I have been given a new Lookingglass which I thought I would adore. I thought I would dote upon this new Glass of mine. But there is an error in it, an undoubted fault in its silvering, so that the wicked object makes me look fat. I have sent for a hammer.

My birthday gifts, I here record, were not as marvellous as the givers of them pretended they were. My poor old Lord and Master, the King, knowing my fondness for gold, gave me a little gold Statue of himself mounted on a gold horse and bearing a gold tilting pole. The horse, being in a prancing attitude, has his front legs lifted from the ground, so that the foolish thing would fall over, were it not for a small Harlequin pretending to run beside the horse, but as a matter of fact holding it up.

And furthermore, I didn't ask for yet another likeness of my ageing husband. I asked for gold. Now I will have to pretend to love and worship the Statue and put it in a prominent place et cetera for fear of causing offence, when I would prefer to take it to the Royal Mint and melt it into an ingot which I would enjoy caressing with my hands and feet, and even take into my bed sometimes to feel solid gold against my cheek or laid between my thighs.

A message attached to this gift read: *To His Heart's Dearest Mousie from Her Lord, C4.* This I tore up and threw into the fire. Long ago, when I was his girl bride and I would tickle him with my small white fingers, he found this nickname "Mouse," it being at that time perfectly endearing to me and causing me to laugh and snuffle and pretend to do all manner of scuttling mousie things. But those days are past. They are gone so absolutely that I have trouble believing that they ever were. I no longer have the slightest desire to be a "mousie." I would prefer to be a rat. Rats have sharp teeth that will bite. Rats carry disease that will kill. Why do husbands refuse to understand that we women do not for long remain their Pet Creatures?

At my birthday feast, to which were invited a great crowd of the ambitious Nobility, most of whom ignored me utterly, I had some moderate sport by drinking a vast quantity of wine and dancing until I fell onto the log pile and then, finding the logs to be as comfortable as any bed, rolling around on them back and forth and laughing with the whole of my Being until I heard the assembled preening company fall silent and saw them all turn to watch me and begin murmuring evil words about me.

Then the King commands that I be helped to my feet and brought to his side and settled upon his knee, in front of all the jealous Gentlemen and their nasty Wives. He gives me water from his own chalice and generally makes such a fuss of me, kissing my shoulder and my face, to show the world that, whatever I do, they cannot plot against me to have me banished, because I am the King's Wife (even though I do not have the Title of Queen of Denmark) and he is still in slavish love with me.

And that he does this makes me bold in my ideas. It makes me wonder what I could do—to what length and breadth of wickedness I could go—and contrive still to remain here in Copenhagen, inhabiting the palaces, and keeping all my privileges. I ask myself what thing is there that would cause me to be driven away? And I answer that I do not think there is Any Thing that I could do or say which would bring this about.

So I go further and begin to wonder whether I shall cease to be so secret and furtive in my love affair with Count Otto Ludwig of Salm, but on the contrary make no bones about my Passion for him, so that I can lie with him whenever and wherever I choose. For why should I, who have never been accorded the Title of Queen, not have a lover? And furthermore, when I have been a few hours with my beautiful German man and he has given me those things I need so badly and without which I really cannot live, I do find my own behaviour towards the King and towards my Women and even towards my children to be much more kindly. But this kindness lasts no more than a few hours, or at most one single day, and then I become vexed again. And so it follows that if I were able to see the Count and have a little sport with him every day or night (instead of perhaps once in a fortnight) why then I would be always and eternally Kind and Sweet to everyone else and all our lives would go on much better.

But dare I risk confessing my love for Otto? Alas, upon reflection, I do not think so. He was a brave Mercenary soldier and fought in the recent Wars on the side of my husband against the Catholic League, and risked death for the Danish cause. He is a hero and much liked by the King. Such a man should be given all that he requests and all that he desires. But I do think that men give to each other only those Possessions that they are somewhat

9

weary of and do not fiercely love. And if or when they are asked to give away those things by which they set great store, they refuse and fly immediately into a fury. Which would be the case if now I should suggest that my lover be admitted here to my bed. And so I conclude that the very thing which makes me bold in my ideas of what I could ask—namely the King's love for me—is also the very thing which does prevent me from asking it.

There is but one course to follow, then. I must arrange matters so that, little by little, day by day and cruelty by cruelty, King Christian falls into a State of Indifference towards me. I must contrive it so that within a year or less my husband no longer hopes for nor expects by right or inclination any mousie thing from me as long as we both shall live.

THE CLOSED WINDOW

Denmark is a watery kingdom. People dream that it is the ships of the great navy which tether the land. They imagine hawsers ten miles long, holding the fields and forests afloat.

And in the salty air, an old story still drifts on the sea breezes: the story of the birth of King Christian IV, which happened on an island in the middle of a lake at Frederiksborg Castle.

They say that King Frederik was away at Elsinore. They say that Queen Sofie, when she was young and before she had begun her habit of scolding and cursing and hoarding money, loved to be rowed in a little boat to this island and there sit in the sunshine and indulge in secret in her passion for knitting. This activity had been proscribed throughout the land as tending to induce in women an idle trance of mind, in which their proper thoughts would fly away and be replaced by fancy. Men called this state "wool gathering." That the wool itself could be fashioned into useful articles of haberdashery such as stockings or night bonnets made them no less superstitiously afraid of the knitting craze. They believed that any knitted night bonnet might contain among its million stitches the longings of their wives that they could never satisfy and which in consequence would give them nightmares of the darkest kind. The knitted stocking they feared yet more completely as the probable instrument of their own enfeeblement. They imagined their feet becoming swollen and all the muscles of their legs beginning to grow weak.

Queen Sofie had, from the very first, transgressed the anti-knitting edict. Yarn was shipped to her from England in boxes labelled "goose down." At the back of her ebony armoire lay concealed a growing quantity of soft garments of many colours for which she knew that one day she would find a use. Only her maid Elizabeth knew her secret and she had been told she would pay with her life if it was ever revealed.

On the morning of the twelfth of April 1577, a day of pale sunlight and a tender blue sky, Queen Sofie, eight and a half months pregnant with her third child, set out at nine o'clock with Elizabeth to cross the lake and spend the morning knitting. Her chosen spot was a clearing in the woods, a little shaded by some hazel bushes and rose briars, where she would set down cushions on the mossy grass. Here she was sitting, putting the finishing touches to a pair of underdrawers while Elizabeth worked upon a sock, with the coils of yarn unravelling moment by moment between them, when the Queen felt a troublesome thirst come upon her. They had brought no provisions, only the secret knitting in a wooden box, and so Queen Sofie asked Elizabeth if she would row back across the lake to the castle and return with a flagon of beer.

And it was while her maid was gone that the Queen experienced the first pang of labour—a pain so familiar to her since the births of her two daughters that she paid it almost no heed, knowing the process would be long. She went on knitting. She held the underdrawers up to the sunlight to inspect them for dropped stitches. The pain came again and this time it was severe enough to make Sofie lay aside the drawers and lie herself down on the cushions. She still thought that many hours of labour lay ahead but, says the old story, Christian knew in advance of his being that Denmark needed him, that the kingdom was floating free at the mercy of the polar storms and the hatred of the Swedes across the Kattegat Sound and that he alone would be the one to build enough ships to anchor and protect her. And so he fought to be born as fast as possible. He kicked and struggled in his mother's waters; he headed for the narrow channel that would lead him out into the bright air that tasted of the sea.

When Elizabeth returned with the flagon of beer, he had been born. Queen Sofie had severed the umbilicus with a thorn and wrapped the baby boy in her knitting.

The story goes on. People no longer know what is true or what has been added or taken away. The Dowager Queen Sofie remembers, but the story is hers. She is not a woman who makes gifts of what she owns.

They say that Danish children born at that time were at risk from the devil. They say the devil, driven out of the churches by the implacable Lutherans, began to seek unbaptised souls to inhabit and that he flew round the crowded cities at night, sniffing for the odour of human milk. And when he smelled it, he would flit unseen through the window of the infant's room and hide in the darkness under the cradle until the nurse slept, and then he would reach out a long thin arm and with his threads of fingers find a passageway, via the little breathing nostrils, to the brain, at the core of which lay the soul, like a single nut of a pine cone. And he would gather it between his finger and thumb. With infinite care he would extract his hand, now slippery from its passage into a living organ, and, when the soul was out, pop it into his mouth and suck it until he felt arrive in his being a shuddering of ecstasy and joy that would leave him exhausted for several minutes.

Sometimes he was interrupted. Sometimes the nurse would wake up and sniff the air, and light a lamp and come towards the cradle just as the soul came out, and then the devil would have to drop it and flee. And wherever the soul landed, it would be swallowed by the matter around it and lodge in that place for all time. If it fell into the folds of a blanket, there it would stay, so that there were at that time a great quantity of children who grew up with no soul in them at all. If it fell onto the baby's stomach, in the stomach it would remain, so the infant would always and for ever have one thought, which was to feed the flesh of its hungry soul and so grow to a huge fatness ultimately fatal to the heart. The worst thing, so the women said, was the soul's falling onto the genitals of a baby boy. For then that child would become the very devil of a lecherous man who would in time betray his wife, his children and everyone who should have been dear to him just to gratify his soul's yearning for copulation and might in his lifetime commit infamy with more than a thousand women and boys, and even with his own daughters or with the poor creatures of the hearth and field.

Queen Sofie knew she must not let her son's little soul be stolen by the devil. They say that after he was rowed with her across the lake, and washed and laid in his crib (the bloodstained knitted drawers being consigned hastily to the fire), she ordered, all brilliant as the April morning was, that the window of his room should be closed and a lock be fastened to the casement so that it could not be opened day or night. The nurse protested that the baby Prince would suffocate for want of air, but the Queen would not be moved and so this one window in the castle was closed for six weeks until the child had been baptised at the Frue Kirke on the second of June.

And the King goes now and then to this room where he lay as a baby and looks at the window or at the dark night sky beyond and, knowing he is in possession of his soul, thanks God that the devil never came in to steal it.

It is also reported that, at the same time, King Frederik II and Queen Sofie sent for the great astronomer Tycho Brahe and showed their son and heir, Christian, to him, and asked him to make predictions concerning the future King's existence on the earth. Tycho Brahe consulted the stars. He found Jupiter ascendant and told the King and Queen the boy would have a fruitful life and be accorded honour and dignity throughout the world. He had only one warning: trouble and danger would arrive in 1630, the year following Christian's fifty-second birthday.

A TRAPDOOR

It is snowing at Rosenborg. The snow began to fall in northern Jutland and now it is blown southwards, carried on an icy wind.

Peter Claire wakes in a hard bed and remembers he is in Denmark and that today will be his first day as a member of the royal orchestra. He has slept for only three hours and the anxiety that accompanied his arrival seems scarcely to have diminished with the coming of the new day. He rises and looks out of his window onto the stable yard, where the snow is beginning to smother the cobblestones. He watches it fall, in gusts and flurries. He wonders how long this particular Danish winter will last.

Hot water is brought to him and, shivering in the cold room above the stables, he shaves his face and cleanses his skin of the dregs of its sea journey—of stale sweat and salt, of flecks of tar and oily grime. He puts on clean clothes and a pair of black leather boots made in the Irish town of Corcaigh. He combs his yellow hair and refastens the jewelled ear-ring to his ear.

Bowls of hot milk and warm cinnamon bread are served to the musicians in a refectory. Those already there, warming their hands on their milk bowls, turn and stare at Peter Claire as he enters: eight or nine men of different ages, but mostly older than he, all soberly dressed in suits of black or brown cloth. He bows to them and, as he announces his name, an elderly person with a quiff of white hair, sitting a little apart from the others, rises and comes towards him. "Herr Claire," he says, "I am Jens Ingemann, Music Master. Be welcome at Rosenborg. Here now, have your milk and then I will show you the rooms where we perform."

The King is out hunting. To ride in the forests, following the scent of a wild boar as the snow falls, is one of His Majesty's chief delights. "You will see," says Jens Ingemann to Peter Claire, "that when he comes in, he will be roaring with the rapture of it and ravening with hunger, and we will be asked to play for him while he eats. It is his belief that certain pieces of music aid digestion."

They are in the *Vinterstue*, the shadowy room where the lamp was lit the previous evening. Now, in the daylight, Peter Claire sees that what he took for plain wood panels on the walls are in fact oil paintings of sylvan scenes and sea prospects, framed in gold, and the ceiling above them is adorned with ornate stucco painted gold and blue. In a corner of the room is an arrangement of music stands.

"Well," says Jens Ingemann, "this is where we play sometimes. The days when we play here are good days, but they are few. Look around the room and tell me if you do not find anything unusual in it."

Peter Claire observes a fine marble fireplace embellished with the King's coat of arms, the silver lions which looked upon his arrival, a throne upholstered in dark-red brocade, two oak tables, numerous chairs and footstools, a line of bronze busts, a gathering of heavy candlesticks, an ivory model of a ship.

"No?" says Jens. "Nothing unexpected?"

"No . . ."

"Very well. We shall go on, then. Follow me."

They walk into the hallway and turn left into a stone passageway. Almost immediately Jens Ingemann opens a heavy iron-studded door and Peter Claire sees steps, set in a narrow curve, leading downwards.

"The stairs are dark," says Jens. "Take care that you do not miss your footing."

The stairs turn round a vast stone pillar. They end at a low tunnel, along which Jens Ingemann hurries on towards a distant flickering light. Emerging from the tunnel, Peter Claire finds himself in a large vaulted cellar, lit by the flares from two iron torches bolted to the walls. The cellar smells of resin and of wine, and visible now are hundreds of casks, lying like miniature ships in dry dock on curved wooden supports.

Jens Ingemann walks on slowly, his footsteps echoing slightly on the brick floor. Then he turns and gestures to the empty space between the lines of casks. "Here we are," he says. "This is the place."

"The wine cellar."

"Yes. There is wine here. And in a cage over there some poor hens that have never seen sunshine nor any green thing. Do you note how cold it is?"

"I would expect a cellar to be cold."

"So you will get used to it? Is that what you're predicting?"

"Get used to it?"

"Yes."

"Well, I don't suppose I shall be spending much time down here. I am not really a connoisseur of—"

"All your time."

"Forgive me, Herr Ingemann . . ."

"Of course His Majesty did not tell you. No one told you, or perhaps you would not have come. But this is where we have our existence. This—except for those few precious days when we are called up to the *Vinterstue*—is where we play."

Peter Claire looks disbelievingly at Jens Ingemann. "What purpose can an orchestra serve in the cellar? There is no one to hear us."

"Oh," says Ingemann, "it is ingenious. They say there is nothing else like it in all of Europe. I asked you if you saw nothing unusual in the *Vinterstue*. Did you not notice the two iron rings bolted to the floor?"

"No."

"I cannot remember if they had their ropes attached or not. Probably not, or you would have noticed them. Now, you see, we are directly under the *Vinterstue*. Near the throne, a section of the floor can be raised or lowered by means of the ropes. Beneath the trap is a grille and beneath that is an assemblage of brass ducts or pipes, let into the vaults of this cellar, and each one fashioned almost like a musical instrument itself, cunningly curved and waisted so that the sounds we make here are transmitted without distortion into the space above, and all the King's visitors marvel when they hear it, not knowing whence the music can possibly come and wondering perhaps whether Rosenborg is haunted by the ghostly music makers of some other age."

Jens Ingemann has walked on while talking, but Peter Claire stays where he is, looking around, noting that the torches are not the only source of light in the cellar, but that two narrow slits in the wall give out onto the garden at ground level. They are not windows, only reticulations in the brickwork, their spaces open to the air. And now, as Peter Claire stares at them, he sees a few snowflakes, like an errant coterie of summer gnats, come clustering in.

Ingemann reads his mind. "If you are thinking that we would be warmer down here if the room were not exposed to the outside world, then of course we all agree with you, and I personally have asked the King to have boards nailed across those apertures. But he refuses. He says the casks of wine need to breathe."

"And we can freeze to death, it's of no consequence to him?"

"I sometimes think, if one of us were to die, then he might be moved to rehouse us, but it is difficult to come by a volunteer for this role."

"How can we concentrate if we are so cold?"

"We are expected to get used to it, and I'll tell you something surprising: we *do* get used to it. For the Mediterraneans in our little company, Signor Rugieri and Signor Martinelli, it is the hardest. The Germans, the Dutch, the English and of course the Danes and Norwegians survive tolerably well. You will see."

BUTTONS

The child Christian, after his baptism, was taken away from his mother.

It was the custom of the time to put the baby into the care of an older woman—usually the mother's mother—because it was thought that older women, who had fought with their own mortality for a greater amount of time, were better prepared than their offspring to wrestle with death on the infant's behalf.

Queen Sofie was consoled by her two daughters and by her illegal knitting, but it is thought that the beginnings of her quarrelsomeness and her desire to amass a great and secret fortune of her own date from this time, when she was deprived of the baby son on whom she had already begun to dote.

For Prince Christian's little life was put into the care of his grandmother, the Duchess Elizabeth of Mecklenburg, at Güstrow in Germany. She hired two young trumpeters and positioned the boys, turn and turn about, outside the Prince's door. When the baby cried, they were to blow their trumpets and the Duchess or one of her women would come running. That the trumpeting disturbed the whole household counted for nothing with Duchess Elizabeth. "All that matters," she said impatiently, "is that the boy does not die. The rest of everything is chaff."

He was swaddled, with a wooden rod laid into the swaddling to force his back and his limbs to grow straight. Day and night he cried and the trumpeters blew. When one of the women suggested the rod should be removed, the implacable Duchess accused her of indulgence and mawkishness. Yet in her own kitchen she supervised the making up of an ointment from comfrey leaves to heal the tender skin where the rod had chafed it. And when the Prince's milk teeth began to bud she ordered that the gums should not be cut but allowed to be "pierced of their own accord, as the earth is pierced by the pale snouts of spring flowers."

When the swaddling was gradually loosened and the stout legs permitted to move and kick, and the plump little hands to explore the objects that lay within their grasp, the Duchess would often sit the child on her own lap and talk to him. The language she talked in was German. She told him about the way the heavens and the earth were arranged, with God and his saints high up in the vast blueness of the sky and all his angels floating among the white clouds. "And so you see," she explained, "because Denmark is a watery kingdom with a thousand lakes, it therefore follows that reflections of heaven are here more numerous than anywhere else on earth, and these reflections, being seen with the eyes of the people and kept in the hearts of the people, make them love both God

18

and nature, and so they are quiet, and when you are King you will be able to rule them and have their trust."

He would, while she talked, play with the tresses of her hair, which she unwound for him and wove into plaits. And some people whisper today that the King has confessed a strange thing: he believes he can remember the long golden plaits of his grandmother the Duchess of Mecklenburg, and when he is in a state of agitation he caresses his own plait, his sacred elflock, between finger and thumb, and this stroking of his own hair calms and soothes him. Yet no one seems to know whether this is true or, if it is true, to whom it was confessed. It might have been to Kirsten. Or Kirsten might have invented it.

He began to talk very early, but of course it was in German that he talked. He had a voice so loud that, when he cried out, the sound could be heard two or three rooms away, and it was thus soon decided to dismiss the daytime trumpeter, for whom there was no longer any need. The night trumpeter remained, however. Duchess Elizabeth was terrified of the power of dreams. If you did not console a child after a nightmare it would grow perpetually to confuse visions with reality and so fall gradually into a state of melancholy.

The night trumpeter was given a new instrument and a new set of instructions. He was not merely to blow if Prince Christian cried in the dark hours, but to play a sprightly melody to chase away the child's terrors.

And this, too, they say that Christian never forgot. Sometimes, at three or four in the morning, musicians are roused from their beds above the stables and summoned to the King's bedroom, where they embark upon quadrilles and capers.

At the age of three, talking constantly and unstoppably in German, interspersed with a little French he had picked up from his visits to the laundry room at Güstrow, where the French laundresses would pick him up in their hot, plump arms and smack fat kisses onto his cheeks, Christian was returned to his parents, King

Frederik and Queen Sofie, at Frederiksborg. He saw for the first time that his mother, too, had long golden hair.

To calm his incessant talking he was given red and black chalks, and encouraged to make drawings of the things which surrounded him: dogs and cats, wooden soldiers, statues, model ships, fire-irons, fountains and water-lilies, trees and fish. This skill he mastered very quickly, and so to the great store of chatter housed in his small frame was added yet another topic of conversation: discussion of his drawings. Nobody was allowed to escape the subject. Visiting nobility were shown sheet after sheet of scarlet soldiers and charcoal trees, and required to pronounce upon them. The King of France, on a sumptuous State visit, was amused to be addressed (in his own language) thus: "This is a picture of Nils, my cat. Does Your Majesty think it is a good likeness?"

"Well," said King Louis, "where is the cat? Bring me the cat and I will judge."

But the cat, Nils, could not be found. Hours passed, with servants calling its name from the gates and round the vegetable gardens, but still it could not be discovered. Then, in the middle of the State banquet, His Majesty of France suddenly felt a tugging at his embroidered sleeve. By his elbow stood Prince Christian, in his night-shirt, holding in his arms his cat, who wore around its neck a blue satin ribbon. "Here is Nils," he announced triumphantly.

"Ah, but alas," said King Louis, "now I do not have your drawing by me."

"You do not need the drawing," said the boy. "Kings remember everything. That is what my father says."

"Oh, yes, too true," said King Louis. "I had forgotten that we remember everything, but now I remember it. Well, let us see . . ." He took Nils from the boy and set the cat on the table between a bowl of fruit and a flagon of wine, and stroked it while the assembled lords and ladies smiled indulgently upon the scene.

"What I think," said the King of France, "is that the likeness is fair and correct in all but one thing."

"What thing?" said the boy.

"Your picture does not purr!"

The dinner guests laughed noisily at this jest.

That night, intent upon the King of France's observation and having no one with him, Prince Christian opened the door of his room and asked the trumpeter if he knew how one might make a picture that could utter sounds.

"Are you dreaming, Your Highness?" asked the young man anxiously. "Shall I play a jig?"

At the age of six Christian began to travel about the kingdom with the King and Queen.

He spoke Danish now, but had not forgotten his German nor his French. His memory for everything on earth seemed prodigious.

The travelling had two essential purposes: that the King might collect the tariffs and payments in kind from the fiefs and towns that resided on Crown lands, and that he might go freely about those towns, entering the places of commerce and manufacture to make sure that skills were being properly performed and goods made to a high standard. He told his son: "There is something we must eradicate from Denmark if we want to hold our heads high and trade with the world. And that is shoddiness."

The boy didn't at first understand this word, but its meaning was explained to him thus by his mother: "If you discovered," she said, "that the buckles of your shoes were of uneven size, when they were intended to be of the same size, you would conclude that the person who made them was guilty of lazy workmanship and this is what we call 'shoddiness.' You would be forgiven for tearing them off your shoes, or even throwing away the shoes altogether. We must have perfection here, you see. We must rival France and the Netherlands and England in all that we make and in all that we do. And when you are King you must take any shoddy thing to be an insult to our name and punish the persons guilty of its manufacture. Do you understand?"

Christian said that he understood, and it was not long before he came to believe that his parents had explained this matter to him because he had his own important task to perform with regard to it.

For whenever he now went into a workshop with his father, whether that of a glove maker, cobbler, brewer, engraver, carpenter or candle maker, he saw that he stood at precisely the right height to stick his head just above the work benches and so get a close and level view of the articles laid out for inspection—a view that was unique to him. Everyone else saw these things from above, but he beheld them face to face. He regarded them and they regarded him back. And his draughtsman's eye was as sharp as a new-minted coin. It constantly aligned, matched and measured. It sought out the smallest errors: loose threads in a bale of silk; a smudged rim on an enamel goblet; uneven stud work on a leather trunk; the lid of a box that did not fit perfectly. And then, quite unperturbed by the dismay on the face of the craftsman or merchant, he would call over the King his father, draw his attention to the imperfection no one but he had spotted and whisper solemnly: "Shoddiness, Papa!"

One day, in the town of Odense, the royal party visited a button maker. This button maker was an old man, known to the King since his boyhood, and he greeted the young Prince with an elaborate display of emotion and affection, and put immediately into his hands the gift of a sack of buttons. There were buttons made of silver and gold, of glass and pewter and bone and tortoiseshell. There were iron buttons and buttons of brass, copper, leather, ivory and pearl. And Christian was entranced by this gift of the button bag. To plunge his hand into it and feel the great quantity of buttons slip and tumble through his fingers created in him a shivery feeling of unalloyed delight.

When he returned that night to his lodgings in Odense, and he had eaten his dinner and was alone in his room, he placed a lamp on the floor and tipped out the whole contents of the button bag into the area of light. The buttons glimmered and shone. He crouched down and moved them slowly around with the tips of his fingers. Then he knelt very near them and put his face into them, feeling their cold, smooth surfaces against his cheek. He liked them more than any present he had ever been given.

It was only the following morning that he remembered the King's sacred command concerning shoddiness. In the cold white light of an October dawn in Odense, Christian spread the buttons in a wide arc over the floor, patiently turned each one of them face-side up and began to examine them.

He was shocked. For every perfect button—smooth-edged, evenly polished, showing no crack or chip, with its eye-holes symmetrically positioned—there were four or five or even six buttons which exhibited evident and undeniable defects. He felt sorrowful. The buttons seemed to look beseechingly at him, to beg him to overlook their individual imperfections. But he ignored their sentimental entreaty. He had been told that the future of Denmark lay in the eradication of shoddy work and he had promised his father to help root it out wherever and whenever it was discovered. He had discovered it here, and now he would act accordingly.

He made a pile of all the defective buttons, called for a servant and asked him to take them away. At some future time he would report to the King that the work of the old button maker was extremely poor and suggest that the man be deprived of his livelihood.

Back at Rosenborg a few days later, Prince Christian took out the button sack (which now contained only perfect buttons) from his trunk and plunged his hand into it. Because there were so few buttons left, the feeling of pleasure he'd got from this when he had first done it was entirely absent. From being the most marvellous gift he had ever owned, it had now become a thing of no consequence whatsoever and he soon laid it aside.

Yet he found himself very frequently thinking about it. It confused him. He couldn't find the key to it. He knew that what he had been given was nothing but a bag of imperfect objects and yet it had dazzled and excited him. He had *loved* it. This meant that what he had loved was flawed, a disgrace to Denmark. He knew that all this had to have an explanation, but he just could not perceive what it might possibly be.

One Birthday Gift I have not mentioned, because it has not yet arrived, is the one offered to me by my mother, Ellen Marsvin: she is giving me a Woman.

They like to be known as "Gentlewomen" or "Ladies-in-Waiting," but I do not see why any such Titles should be given to people who are in every way inferior to me and no better than Servants. So I refer to them merely as my *Women*. They have names, of course: Johanna, Vibeke, Anna, Frederika and Hansi. But I cannot always get these names into my head when I need them and so I say: "Woman, take this away," or "Woman, close the door," or another of the thousand and one commands I have to give them every day, many of which would be superfluous if they spent less time dreaming up wonderful honorary Appellations for themselves and more of it concentrating on the Tasks in hand.

Not long ago I decided to reclassify my Women's duties into new Categories. And I do believe that my Rearrangement is inspired. Each of them must now take responsibility for different parts of me, such as my hands, legs, head, stomach and so forth. Thus, to attire myself correctly, I need them all, which fact adroitly prevents them from being absent from my service on any day whatsoever. And this Constraint upon them gives me much satisfaction and secret mirth. My life is hedged about with Curtailments and the performance of certain Rites most odious to me, and I do not see why the lives of mere Women should be free of these things when mine is not.

When I mentioned my Reclassification of Duties to my Mother she, while finding it ingenious, did ask me whether I did not have more parts to me than there are Women. I answered that my Subdivisions had proceeded logically and that Johanna was now entitled Woman of the Head, Vibeke Woman of the Torso, Anna Woman of the Hands, Frederika Woman of the Skirt and Hansi Woman of the Feet. (These titles have the resonance of Guild Affiliations, and so I said to my Women: "There you are. You who are so attached to Nomenclature, take these designations and be happy with them.")

My Mother says: "But that is not *all* you are, Kirsten—legs and hands and so forth." By which of course she means that all mortals are Wondrous Creatures of curious complexity and that certain Needs and Feelings in us cannot be located precisely or entirely within the Categories I had listed, but may nevertheless need catering to by one of the Women from time to time. And so it comes into my Mother's mind to pay for me to have this Floating Woman, who may have no Guild Name, and is not assigned to any particular Part of me, but who will nevertheless be ready to serve me in any capacity at all times, day and night.

I think it is a Good Idea. And I heard today that such a woman has been found and will come to me from Jutland next week. Her name is Emilia.

In the winter, which is now, everything is pestilentially desolate here and the boredom I feel on certain days puts me into such a fury against the World that I long to be a Man and a Soldier like my lover, so that I could attack somebody with a lance.

Yesterday, there were some visitors here. Two of them were Ambassadors from England and the third was an Elephant. The Ambassadors were sickly-looking men who did nothing interesting and could barely speak any words of Danish or German. The Elephant, on the other hand, was most entertaining. It could kneel and dance. It arrived with a troupe of Tumblers, who stood on its back and its head and climbed up its legs, and I said to the King: "I want to ride on the Elephant!" and so the Tumbling People (who looked small but were very strong) carried me aloft and set me on the Elephant and I swayed around on it for a while, liking very much the sensation of being High Up, while they led it in a little circle, and I saw all the windows of Rosenborg filled with people watching me.

But of course after they had seen me on the Elephant, my Children one by one started a clamour to ride on it too. I forbade it absolutely and refused to be moved by their whinings and entreaties. This is the principal trouble with Children: they do not let you do one single thing but they must do it also, and this Habit of Copying does so grate on me that I declare I wish I had never had any Chil-

25

dren whatsoever because all they do puts me into an Irritation from which I cannot find any relief except when I am far away from them and in the Count's bed.

And alas, I have not been in that bed for a great while, but only in my own and dreaming of the other. To be on my own is sorrowful, but I can endure it in the expectation of my next meeting with my Lover. What I cannot endure any more are the Conjugal Visits of the King and I have now determined that I *shall* not endure them. So that when he came last night to my room and got into my bed, and tried to put his hand on my breast and press himself against me, I began a violent shrieking and crying, and said that my nipples were chafed and all my body sore and tired and could not be touched. I thought he would protest, for all men, when they are hot, care very little for the pain they may cause, but instead the King went away at once, saying he was sorry for my ailments and hoped that a little rest would cure them.

What he does not yet know is that no amount of rest will ever cure them. I could sleep until springtime and I would still feel as I feel towards him, and my only travail now must be to bring about his Indifference towards me.

This is all I want. I have decided that I do not care if I am sent away from Copenhagen or even if my quantity of Women is reduced. I do not mind if I never set eyes on my Children again. My future is with the Count. Nothing on earth but him brings me any pleasure or any joy.

THE TASK

Peter Claire and Jens Ingemann return to the refectory to await the first summons of the day. A second bowl of hot milk is put into the icy hands of the young lutenist.

Other musicians introduce themselves: Pasquier from France, a flautist; the Italians Rugieri and Martinelli, violinists; Krenze from Germany, a viol player. Pasquier remarks that he hopes Peter Claire will not run away.

"Run away? I have only just arrived."

"English musicians are fond of running away," says Pasquier. "Carolus Oralli the harpist and John Maynard—both ran away from this court."

"But why did they run away? What impelled them to do it?"

Rugieri joins in. "You will see," he says, "how we lead our lives, in the cellar, in the dark for most of the time. Today will be one of them. You cannot blame a man because he is homesick for the light."

"I do not really mind the dark," says the German, Krenze, with a slow smile. "I have always believed that life was merely a preparation for death. In the dark and cold, I think I am preparing more efficiently, no?"

"Krenze pretends that he does not suffer," chimes in Rugieri, "but we don't believe him. I look at our faces in the torchlight and I feel bound to this company of men, bound through suffering, because this is what I can see in every one of us. It's true, isn't it, Martinelli?"

"Yes," says Martinelli. "And we don't feel ashamed of this, because we know that even very great men like Dowland found these conditions difficult and how, when he was on leave from Denmark, he delayed his return. He pretended his ship from England had been driven back by wind and frost. He remembered what time consists of here . . ."

"He couldn't transcend his own pitiful life, that is all," says Krenze. "He wrote good music, but he could not make use of it, in his soul. In that respect his labours were pointless."

"Oh, come," says Jens Ingemann, intervening with flustered gestures, "why dwell on what is bad? Poor Mr. Claire. Why not describe to him what a very beautiful sound we make. You know even the hens are often quiet, completely quiet, as if in a trance, when we are making our music . . ."

"There should *be* no hens!" says Pasquier.

"True," says Jens Ingemann, "absolutely true, it is distracting to have hens with us. But this notwithstanding, I do think we are a very fine little orchestra. And to serve the King is a great honour. All our lives might have been passed in some provincial little town, playing cantatas on Sundays . . . You were in Ireland, in the house of a nobleman, before coming to us, if I remember, Mr. Claire?"

"Yes," says Peter Claire. "I was with Earl O'Fingal, helping him with composition."

At this moment one of the King's servants enters the refectory and announces that His Majesty has returned from his hunting and will take breakfast in the *Vinterstue*. He does not mention the cellar, but the musicians know that this is where they must go now.

They put down their bowls and, carrying their instruments, hurry out into the snow, which is falling fast.

A pair of fine virginals, which Peter Claire had not noticed earlier in the cellar, are unwrapped from a protective covering of velvet and Jens Ingemann seats himself before them, facing the semicircle. Krenze, the German viol player, walks round the music stands placing sheets of musical notation upon them. The first piece is a galliard by a Spanish composer, Antonio de Ceque. Rugieri, too, goes from stand to stand, lighting the candles affixed to them which, day after day, dribble lines of wax onto the scores.

They wait, tuning their instruments as quietly as they can, so that no discordant noise may be heard above. The torches burn brightly. In the chicken cage a brown hen is struggling to lay an egg. The snowflakes eddying through the gaps in the wall melt as they fall and create two puddles of icy water.

A noise is heard above: the trapdoor is opening. The tuning ceases. Jens Ingemann raises his hand to silence everything, but the brown hen is still ululating as the egg lodges half in and half out of her body. Pasquier hits out at the cage with his bow. The shock of this causes the hen to deliver the egg and run round the cage squawking.

Then, down the intricate assemblage of pipes, which debouch over the right-hand wall, is heard the King's voice: "Nothing solemn today! Are you listening down there? No fugues. No slow ayres. Play till the trap is shut."

They begin. It seems to Peter Claire as if they are playing only for themselves, as if this is a rehearsal for some future performance in a grand, lighted room. He has to keep reminding himself that the music is being carried, as breath is carried through the body of a wind instrument, through the twisted pipes, and emerging clear and sharp in the *Vinterstue*, where King Christian is eating his breakfast. He tries to imagine precisely how it must sound and whether his own part in it (this is a galliard where the flutes are dominant) can nevertheless be heard. He strives, as always, for perfection and, because he is playing and listening with such fierce concentration, doesn't notice the cold in the cellar as he thought he would, and his fingers feel nimble and supple.

He can hear, too, that the sound being made by this orchestra is one of great vibrancy, a generous sound, a sound, he decides, that no English ensemble would make. Ingemann leads it, nodding the beat with his head, but at the core of the sound is something new to him, a quality that he cannot quite define but which he knows arises from this particular composition of players from five different countries, each with his own and individual sensibility and mode of expression. Peter Claire has already seen that these are men of strong opinions who must surely disagree with each other for a great deal of the time, but now, huddled together in their dark domain, they seem to create a rich and faultless harmony.

After the galliard they embark on a saraband, also by de Ceque. Peter Claire has been told that His Majesty's meals, even breakfast, can be very long and that sometimes they play for hours on end with no break. But today is not to be one of them. When the saraband ends, just as they are turning their scores and preparing for the piece that will follow, the pipes suddenly fill with noise. It sounds like a sonorous belch.

Then the King's voice bellows: "That's enough! I'm getting indigestion. Mr. Claire, the lutenist, come up to my bedroom in half an hour." And the trap falls. It falls with a noise like thunder, sending a downward draught of warm air into the cellar, which extinguishes the candles.

Although it is only ten o'clock in the morning, King Christian has gone to bed. The drapes across his bedroom window have been drawn and lamps lit, exactly as if the night had come.

He instructs Peter Claire to sit near him. He says: "I wanted to have another look at you. Put your face here, in the light."

The King's eyes study Peter Claire's features once again with rapt attention, as though the lutenist were a work of art. "Well," he says after a while, "I was wrong. I thought I must have dreamed you in the night, but you are perfectly real after all. I thought I had muddled you with the angels I was encouraged to imagine when I was a boy, and also with . . . But never mind . . . This is very much how I used to picture the angels—with features like yours. My grandmother used to tell me they rode about on the clouds. At Christmas they would fill my shoes with gold and silver. I think I have been waiting for one all my life and none has ever appeared to me. But now you have come, you and your lute. So I have decided to give you a task."

Peter Claire says he is ready to undertake any task that His Majesty has in mind, but in the next minute the King falls silent. His eyes look tired and dreamy, as though he were on the edge of sleep, but after a few moments he rouses himself. He takes a sip of some white powder mixed with water in a glass. "For my stomach," he says. "Plagues me day and night. Won't let me sleep. A life without sleep begins to go badly. We lose the thread of things. This is what I always ask of music—to restore the thread to me. Tell me what you hope from it."

This is a question that no one has asked Peter Claire in all his twenty-seven years. He stammers that through his playing he believes he can express something of himself that would otherwise have no voice. The King asks: "But what is that *something*, Mr. Claire? Can you define it?"

"No. Perhaps I would say it is what is in my heart . . ."

"Deeper. The human heart has too direct a conduit from the senses. Far deeper than that."

"I don't think I know, then, Sir."

"Order. That is what we long for, in our innermost souls. An order that mirrors Plato's Celestial Harmonies: a corrective to the silent chaos that inhabits every human breast. And music comes nearest to restoring this to us. Even to a man who has not understood the nature of his own dilemma: in sublime music, he will discover that his strivings may be subsumed beneath a wondrous calm and he will feel at peace. Is that not true?"

"It may be, Sir, except that I know that there are men for whom music does not seem to be a solace . . ."

"Perhaps they have no souls? Perhaps the devil stole their souls away when they were born?"

"Perhaps . . ."

"Or they are still as children are, existing on the surface of the world and imagining there's nothing beneath?"

"Or perhaps it is that they have not heard music sublime enough?"

"I had not thought of that, but it's a reasonable assumption. Perhaps we should increase the number of public performances? Should we? I wonder if, in general, kings and governments are too stingy with music? I wonder whether we would have greater *external* order if the people could hear songs at the wash-house or pavans in the taverns?"

"You could experiment with that, Your Majesty."

"Yes, I could. Very many of our citizens are full of sadness and confusion. They do not know how to be in the world. They do not know why they are alive."

Peter Claire is not sure what he can say in reply to this. He looks down and his long fingers caress the neck and body of his lute. The King swallows the last of the white powder, belches loudly and puts down the glass. "I shall sleep now," he says. "I did not get any sleep last night. I went to my wife for comfort at half past four, but she sent me away. I do not know what we are come to."

King Christian still hasn't mentioned the "task" he has in mind for Peter Claire, and now, as he settles himself for sleep, Peter Claire gets up, thinking that this is a signal that he should depart and leave the King alone. He stands for a moment hesitating by the bed and the King looks up at him. "Here is your task," he says. "I want you to *watch over me.* I cannot tell you now if the task will be long or short, great or small, but I ask you this favour as I would ask an angel. Will you do it?"

31

Peter Claire stares at the King's large, ugly face. He's aware, in these moments, that something of great importance might be beginning, that perhaps, after all, he may not have come to Denmark in vain, and yet he does not know precisely what that something is. He longs to ask what King Christian means by the phrase "watch over me," but is afraid to appear suddenly obtuse and worthless. "Of course I will do it, Sir," he replies.

LAMENT OF COUNTESS O'FINGAL—FROM HER NOTEBOOK ENTITLED *LA DOLOROSA*

I was the eldest daughter of a paper merchant, Signore Francesco Ponti, and lived my life in Bologna under his kind protection until the age of twenty when Earl O'Fingal entered our house and fell in love with me at first glance.

I was dressed in white. My black hair hung about my face in ringlets. I held out my hand to Earl O'Fingal, who was at that time aged thirty-two, and, as I watched him press it to his lips, I knew what was in his mind. Within three months I was his bride and he brought me here to live at his estate at Cloyne in the west of Ireland.

Earl O'Fingal, ever known to his friends as Johnnie, was the most proper man and I must faithfully give account of his propriety and of his tenderness towards me. He spoke with a soft and pleasant voice and, during the first year of our marriage, gave me patient instruction in the English tongue, laughing sweetly at my mistakes, and in the evenings, when we had no company at Cloyne, reading to me from the sonnets of Shakespeare, so that many of these great works have stayed with me and now in this sad time bring me comfort.

> *When most I wink, then do mine eyes best see,*
> *For all the day they view things unrespected;*
> *But when I sleep, in dreams they look on thee,*
> *And, darkly bright, are bright in dark directed.*

That Johnnie O'Fingal loved me I never doubted, nor will I doubt it ever. Something of what he called his "vision" of me at Bologna remained always with him, so that even as I aged, I did not grow old in O'Fingal's mind. When I came to thirty I was still the white-clad angel he had seen standing before my father's fire, and my body, which by then had borne him four children, was still, to him, the perfect body of a girl.

But now I understand that in this affectionate delusion of his one may perceive the shadow or exemplar of the tragedy which began to unfold in the tenth year of our marriage.

Earl O'Fingal was twelve years my senior, but looked younger than he was. He was exceptionally tall, being, I think, about six feet and four inches, so that my father, while finding him an honest and charming man, did not particularly enjoy standing next to him and always preferred to conduct conversations with him sitting down.

He had most delicate hands. And these hands of his were restless and in a perpetual gesturing and folding and unfolding, almost as if they strove of their own accord to fly off his arms and have some other existence free of his body. His skin was very white and his hair not very abundant, but of a pleasing brown colour. His eyes were grey and lively. The people of Cloyne, because he was their Lord and Master, and because his father the late Earl had ever been a meticulous landlord and kept everything secure on the farms and in the cottages, would say to me, "And how does your handsome husband, Lady O'Fingal?" In truth, to my eye, "handsome" was not the correct word to describe Johnnie O'Fingal, yet for all that he was a moderately fine young man and, lonely as I was during my first years in Ireland, I grew very fond of him.

He was a kind father to our children, as patient with their lessons and with their childish ways as he had been with my instruction into the English language. Often, when I would sit at dinner with him in the lofty marbled room, or by the fire while he read the sonnets, I would find myself looking up at him and thinking that I had made a good decision in agreeing to accept him as my husband. I should here add another thing: Johnnie O'Fingal was possessed of a substantial fortune.

And now I must come to the great catastrophe. It began on a cold night of winter, when a storm swept round the house and I could hear the thundering of the sea very near us, as if it meant to come into our rooms and drown us all. Being afraid, I woke Johnnie, who rose up and lit a lamp for me and put a shawl about my shoulders. He told me that, as a boy, he often heard this same tumultuous sea, but knew that never in a thousand years would it reach to our doors, and so he calmed me and sat there in the lamplight holding my hand.

After a few moments he thanked me for waking him at that moment. When I inquired why, he told me that he had just had an extraordinary dream and that if he had slept through until morning it might have vanished away into that nothingness we call forgotten things.

Johnnie O'Fingal had dreamed that he could compose music. In this miraculous reverie, he had gone down to the hall, where resided a pair of virginals (of which he was an adequate player) and where we would sometimes invite the best Irish musicians of the day to entertain us and our friends with a concert, and had sat down in front of them and taken up a piece of my father's cream paper and a newly cut quill. In frantic haste, he had ruled the lines of the treble and bass clef, and begun immediately upon a complicated musical notation, corresponding to sounds and harmonies that flowed effortlessly from his mind onto the page. And when he began to play the music he had written it was a lament of such grace and beauty that he did not think he had ever heard in his life anything to match it.

I found this dream so wonderful that I immediately said: "Well, why do you not go down now this moment and see whether, when you sit at the instrument, you can remember the tune?"

"Oh, no," he said, "what we can achieve in our dreams seldom corresponds to what we are veritably capable of."

But I pressed him. Ever since that night I have wished that I had not done so.

Urged on by me, Johnnie descended to the hall and woke a servant to come and make up a fire. He remained there, sitting at the virginals, for the rest of the night and, when I went down at breakfast time, I saw him lit by a glance of sunlight falling from one of the high windows in the wake of the storm. His hair was wild. On the floor was a quantity of crumpled paper, scratched with lines and notes.

"Well, Johnnie?" I said.

He reached out and seized my hand. "Listen!" he said. "Listen."

He began to play a melody of strange and haunting sweetness, reminding me somewhat of music I had heard long ago in Bologna, composed by the great Alfonso Ferrabosco. I sat there in silent wonderment. When the playing ended abruptly I cried out, "Go on! It's beautiful, Johnnie. Play me all of it."

But he could not go on. He told me that these few miraculous bars had come to him within fifteen minutes of sitting down at the virginals, but that every attempt to progress beyond them had resulted in something mediocre, spoiling what had gone before. I told him that this was because he was tired and suggested that he return to bed and sleep for a while, and recommence when he was rested. I caressed his head, smoothing his hair. Two of our children had come down and were gazing in perplexity at their dishevelled papa. And then, much to their consternation—for this was a thing they had never beheld and thought perhaps never to behold in their lives—Johnnie O'Fingal put his face into his hands and wept.

EMILIA TILSEN

She was born in Jutland. Her father, Johann Tilsen, is a rich landowner with a passion for summer fruit. He felled forests of beech and oak in order to lay out plantations of blackcurrants and loganberries. Emilia's baby breath had about it the sweet scent of strawberry pie.

She is the eldest of six children and the only girl. On and on went the births of brothers. They exploded into the world, screaming and kicking. They fastened their gums to their mother's breasts and milked her so violently that she felt wounded and took to lying down on her linen-covered day-bed through all the hours between feeds, just to regain her strength.

Emilia would sit by her on the floor. She would sing her peculiar little songs of her own invention. *"What is the sky made of I do not know/Sometimes it is made of dancing snow."* She would lay kisses on her mother's hands.

And Emilia's mother, Karen, grew accustomed to her daughter's gentle, talkative presence and began to love her more than anything or anyone else in the world: more than her husband Johann; more than their fine house and the perfume of the fruit fields; more than the acres of beechwoods that remained; more than all her boisterous sons. Lying on the day-bed, she would look into Emilia's grey eyes and at her long hair neither dark nor fair and say: "We shall never be parted. We shall always sit like this together in the morning room. When you marry—for love, my darling, and not for money or land or title—we shall build a house for you and your husband within sight of this window and so we shall see each other every day."

So Emilia grew up in the shelter of Karen's love. They walked together on the beautiful land, going slowly, arm in arm and talking as they went, while the brothers ran and tumbled along ahead of them, drawn on by Johann's purposeful stride and by their archery games, and their dogs and their lessons in falconry. At bedtime, they brushed each other's hair and said their prayers side by side. *God, bless and keep from harm my beloved daughter, Emilia. God, please bless and keep from harm my beloved mother, Karen.*

But God did not hear. Or, if He heard, He did not oblige.

Two days after the birth of Marcus, her last son, Karen Tilsen died in Emilia's arms. It was a February morning and all the grey sky that hung above the world seemed on the instant of death to come pouring into the window in a never-ending, suffocating stream and enter Emilia's being and obliterate it. She was fifteen years old.

She is eighteen now. She is small and silent. A miniature portrait of Karen hangs on a velvet ribbon round her slender white neck, and this is the only possession for which she has any feeling.

The person she is fondest of is her youngest brother, Marcus. Very often she whispers to him: "You killed my mother, Marcus," but he still does not understand exactly what she means. He clings to her, hoping to find out, and she sits him on her knee and holds him close to her, because he smells like Karen, almost as if he were still part of Karen's body. She sings to him and takes him skating in the frozen winter. She informs him that Magdalena is a witch.

Magdalena arrived as housekeeper for Johann after Karen's death. She has dark hair and wide hips, and Emilia asks God to come through the window and smite her with swords. She imagines Magdalena's severed head bouncing down the wooden stairs and shattering on the flagstones of the hallway. She pictures black blood flowing out of Magdalena's eyes.

But Johann, from the moment he saw Magdalena, wanted to possess her. On her very first morning, some three months after the death of Karen, he followed Magdalena to the linen closet, bolted the door, positioned her wide hips over a linen chest and entered her from behind. She did not resist him but on the contrary murmured that she had never experienced anything she liked more than being taken in this way. When Johann had finished, even as he buttoned his breeches and was still staring with amazement at Magdalena's colossal arse, he said: "As your employer, I wish to do this from time to time. It will cause you no pain, I promise, but on the contrary become a pleasant part of your duties, and duty may in the end be transformed into something else."

Within a year, he married Magdalena. At the wedding, Emilia looked away from the couple and out at the grey sky that had come into the room on the morning of Karen's death and taken away her being, and she asked the sky to brew up a whirlwind to snatch Magdalena from the face of the earth.

But Emilia waited, and still she waits, and the whirlwind doesn't arrive. The years go on. The strawberries and the loganberries come into flower, and the summer rains fall and the fruit starts to swell and turn red and purple and is gathered, and the leaves droop and discolour and drop, and still no whirlwind pounces on Magdalena and hurls her into the clouds.

A baby boy is born to Johann and Magdalena and dies in hours. Emilia prays that Magdalena will die in its wake but, once again, her prayers are not heard. Johann's obsession with Magdalena's bottom knows no rest and he becomes careless of when and where he takes her, so that one hot afternoon, as Emilia walks with little Marcus by a lake, they suddenly come upon Magdalena bending over in the water, splaying her legs, then lifting her skirts to reveal her white moons of flesh, and then, as they watch, Johann wades towards her, naked except for his shirt and in a state of gross arousal. Three-year-old Marcus laughs and points. He does not know what he has just seen. Emilia covers his eyes with her hand. Magdalena and Johann turn and stare accusingly at the children, then squat down and hide the lower parts of their bodies in the water, Magdalena's skirts billowing round her, red as blood. "Go away!" Johann shouts.

That night, Emilia decides that her life has become unbearable. Inside her hatred of Magdalena, concealed from her at first but now becoming visible, something else is beginning to grow: a hatred of her own father. She thinks it may have no bounds. *No bounds.*

She falls asleep in a sweat of loathing and confusion, and has a gentle dream of her lost mother. She recognises this pattern of feeling: anguish followed by calm. She remembers that this was how she held to existence for fifteen years: ill or troubled, perplexed or sad, she would seek out Karen and Karen would talk to her and stroke her hair and hold her small hand in hers, and after a while she would arrive again at normality and serenity, and know that she could proceed with her life.

And now Emilia wakes weeping because the dream was so

fine and so real, and all through it she was skating with Karen, arm in arm, skating on and on down a long frozen river, and their two breaths made a single cloud that danced along in front of them, and the sound of their skate blades cutting into the ice was like a kind of singing. "Show courage, Emilia," Karen said to her.

What did this mean precisely? What kind of courage is her mother asking of her? Emilia lies in her narrow bed wondering. She cannot imagine any future in which she can be happy.

She decides it may be the courage to go to her father and ask him if some position might be found for her—as nurse or as companion or gentlewoman—in some household. All the while she is saying this, she keeps her eyes lowered, so that she cannot see the person to whom she's addressing her words, in case the hatred she has begun to feel comes into the room and lodges there, taking up all the available air and making it impossible to breathe.

"Look at me," says Johann.

But she can't. She will not. The knowledge that she despises her father is difficult to bear.

"Look at me, Emilia."

She feels her face becoming hot and red. She holds on to the locket on its velvet ribbon. *Show courage, Emilia.*

She raises her eyes and sees her father standing still and looking at her sadly. She tells herself that he is not a wicked man, that Magdalena has put a spell on him, that if it were not for Magdalena he would not be lewd and forgetful nor walk into the lake with his sex pointing to the far horizon.

"Now," he says kindly. "Tell me why it is that you wish me to find you such a position. I had always assumed you would stay here until you were married."

"I will never be married," she says. "I will never love anybody. I don't want to love anybody."

"Why do you say that?"

"Because it's true. I don't want a husband. I don't want anybody to touch me. I would like to take care of children or be a companion to a lonely person in some household far away, that is all."

A fine clock ticks in the room. Outside the window, snow is falling. *What is the sky made of I do not know.*

After a long moment of the ticking clock and the silent snowfall, and fragments of songs coming and going in Emilia's mind, Johann says: "I do not wish to be unreasonable. We will endeavour to find the kind of position you have in mind for yourself and we will place you there, but only for a brief time, and after that I shall order you to return. And when you do we shall give thought to your marriage. You must be married, Emilia, and that is that."

Emilia wants to say: Marriage is the angry mouths of babies suckling; marriage is dying on a February morning with no one to save you; marriage is Magdalena and her skirts like blood and her spells that can never be broken . . .

"I think that is a fair bargain," says Johann.

Emilia doesn't reply. She knows there are always ways to forestall the future. Some part of her believes in a heavenly place where Karen can be found, patiently waiting for her to arrive.

"Meanwhile," says Johann, "you will kindly show more affection towards your stepmother. She is generous to you and good-hearted, and you are unnecessarily cold and distant. You will be kinder to her for my sake."

Emilia looks out at the snow. She thinks it is considerate of Nature always to be moving and changing so that, when the mind is in pain, it is unfailingly provided with some kind of new entertainment.

FROM COUNTESS O'FINGAL'S NOTEBOOK, *LA DOLOROSA*

I must now mention my four children. At the time when our great tragedy began, the eldest, Mary (Maria), was nine, my two sons, Vincent (Vincenzo) and Luke (Luca), were eight and six, and my youngest babe, Juliet (Giulietta), was but four years old. Though I recognise that mothers very often seek to embellish the virtues of their children and even to endow them with gifts and attributes they do not really possess, I must ask any reader of this journal to believe me when I report that these children, brought up very kindly at Cloyne and with many learned, skilful and patient tutors and instructors employed to teach them philosophy and Latin, Italian and French, dancing, fencing, riding, poetry and embroidery, were growing into the most beguiling and beautiful souls that could be imagined.

When, with Johnnie and me, they embarked upon any tour of the estates, all the men—whether shepherd or pig-man, charcoal burner, mussel gatherer or poultry man—and their wives and families swarmed out to our carriages with gifts for the children. They would gaze upon them with great delight, and stroke Giulietta's hair and let her pick wild posies from their fields and gardens.

This love of the people for his children gratified and moved their father very greatly and he would often say to me that he believed that if a child is loved rightly by its parents and never hurt nor tormented by them, then that child will invite love wheresoever it goes and so will be at ease with love all its days—just as a man may be at ease in clothes that are comfortable and warm—and never competing for affection that it does not need nor striving for the worship of the whole world.

This opinion I shared and do share it still and, since the bad times came to us, I have tried to augment my love for Maria, Vincenzo, Luca and Giulietta in measure as Johnnie's tender care of them has diminished, so that notwithstanding all that has happened these beautiful children may still, in their future lives, be at ease with love and never ailing nor spiteful for want of it. But this task is hard. They loved their father and they saw him slowly, in the space of four years, sicken in madness and despair—in which state he could not love any living thing but on the contrary cast about him all the while for some breathing creature to wound, so that others might suffer as he did and know what he felt.

More times than I can bear to report it was upon the children that his anger turned, and he would scream at them and curse them and even raise his hand to strike them or snatch up some petty instrument of punishment such as a riding whip or a walking stick and attempt to beat them with this.

Time and time again they came to me and asked, "Mama, what is happening to Papa? What have we done to enrage him so?" and I would try to explain that it was not with them that he had begun to despair, but with himself.

If only he had not had that dream of sweet music . . .

I have often thought that this can by no means have been an ordinary dream because the life span of an ordinary dream is shorter than an instant of time or, if it should linger a while, may do so only for a single day and at that day's end will vanish with the dark. But the dream of Johnnie O'Fingal never left him. Yet if it was not an ordinary dream, then what was it?

When more than a week of sleepless days and nights had passed, I made him lie down with me in my bed, and I held him in my arms and said to him: "Johnnie, you know that this striving for your lost music must cease. You are tormenting yourself to no purpose. Look how pale and wan you seem. Remark how our children move so quietly in the house for fear of you, as if you had become a ghost. Hear me when I tell you, you must put this dream from your mind. You must forget it, my dear. For it has left you and will never return."

He looked at me with his exhausted eyes. "You do not understand, Francesca," he said. "If you had heard the song—the absolute *rapture* of it—then you would be with me, seeking day and night to recapture it. You must believe me that it was like no piece of music that I have ever in my life heard played. I know that the whole world would marvel at it, weep at it, feel it fill its whole being with joy just as it filled mine in the dream. And something as significant as that cannot be lost! Do not tell me that it is, for I refuse to believe it. I must be patient, that is all. We must all be patient, for I recognise that this search of mine has taken me away from you and the children, and from my duties on the lands. But I will soon return to you. The moment the song is rediscovered I will be my former self again and all will be mended and all will be well."

So adamant was his conviction that his reverie could in time become a concrete thing that I decided I should not chivvy and berate him, as I was sorely tempted to do, but stay silent and only try to care for him in his struggles, keep the children from him and undertake myself some of the tasks he should have been performing with regard to the buying of livestock and seed for springtime, the supervision of chimney stacks and roofs after the great gales and other matters needing his care.

I also instructed the servants to move the virginals out of the hall (where Johnnie's desperate playing could be heard all round the house) and into the library, where at least he could be alone with the door closed upon his terrible work. Privately to myself I pledged that I would let one month pass and then insist that Johnnie accompany me and the children to Bologna, where, in the altered environment of my father's house, his maddening dream might gradually float away and cease to torment him.

This month, marked only by vexation and unhappiness, was almost at an end and plans were already far advanced for our voyage to Bologna, when I was sitting by the fire one evening, reading aloud to Luca and Giulietta some of my favourite lines from Shakespeare's sonnets.

> O never say that I was false of heart,
> Though absence seem'd my flame to qualify.
> As easy might I from myself depart
> As from my soul, which in thy breast doth lie . . .

Suddenly Johnnie interrupted my recitation with the words: "Francesca, it is almost found!"

I laid down my book. "Almost?" I inquired.

"It is near! That's what I mean. I feel it coming. It's so near that I almost hear it . . ."

He then insisted that I and the children should go with him to the library. He made us sit in a line upon some chairs. Casting my eyes down our line, I saw that all the children, even my brave Vincenzo, looked dazed with fright.

A little playing followed: some chords in the key of D major. Then Johnnie began, one by one and slowly, to repeat the chords and in between each chord to babble some almost meaningless words that I cannot remember precisely but which ran something like this: ". . . and then it goes and soars and returns, a trill, a tender one-note trill, and then the valley or what should I call it but a place of echoes returning the melody to this . . ." and then another heavy chord and then more words: "and so it must be, must be in this key, the innermost echoing chamber, like the heart, like the human heart or like a crying on the hills or like this, this chord, like the sea . . ." and then another chord and another and so on, and then a sudden silence in which we all sat still and petrified upon our chairs, and Johnnie laid his head upon the virginals and seemed in an instant to fall asleep.

I rose and ordered the children to go to bed. Together I and the servants carried Johnnie to our room and laid him down and covered him. I sent for the groom and told him to ride to Cloyne to fetch Doctor McLafferty and, while I waited for him to arrive, sat watching by my husband, who was indeed sleeping, yet in his sleep crying out still, as though his searching was continuing and giving his mind no respite.

Doctor McLafferty, being told by the servants of Earl O'Fingal's strange condition, had brought with him a potion made of cloves, honey and cinnabar, which he told me would "soothe the brain of its trouble," and this he gently rubbed into the skin of Johnnie's forehead, but even as he administered it I saw some red patches as of a psora appearing on the skin and ordered him to stop. "No, Lady O'Fingal," he said, "begging Your Ladyship's pardon, but these welts are the very proof of the efficacy of my ointment. These lovely welts are the Earl's great anguish coming out of him, do you not see? Please have patience. Let his whole face be covered in lesions if need be; let them erupt and spew like volcanoes with foul matter and in a matter of days his mind will be as calm as a pond."

The doctor went away and I kept watch over Johnnie as he slept. To keep myself awake I read a little from the great tragedy of *King Lear* and prayed that the soothing sleep which, in this play, cures the old King of his madness would cure my poor husband of his. But he was not cured by any ointment of cinnabar. He was not cured by any tender sleep. On the instant of waking, he ran down to the library and began again on his demented search. "Recommence, recommence!" I heard him cry out.

The children and I travelled to Bologna. Though I entreated him on my knees and with tears and sobbing to come with us, Johnnie had refused. Once again, he had told me that he was "near, so very near" to achieving his desire and had come to believe that, in the silence following our departure, in the lonely state our absence would produce, it would at last be found.

I wrote many letters from Bologna, telling mostly of trivial things such as the purchase of fine Italian silk for some new dresses for the girls and the great delight my father took in spoiling his grandchildren, but received not one reply. Though sorely tempted to continue to reside with my father, where the children had returned to something like their former gaiety and sweetness, I knew that I had to go back to Cloyne. What I did not know was what I would find when I came there again.

What I found was a terrible quiet.

The virginals had been closed and locked with a padlock, and a tapestry cloth hid them from sight.

Johnnie O'Fingal, his face still infected with the psora caused by the ointment of cinnabar, yet with a deathly pallor spreading to his temples and affecting every part of his emaciated body, sat in an armchair, holding himself perfectly still and unmoving.

I ran to his side and put my arms round him and laid my cheek against his. "My dear," I said, "tell me what has happened that you are so thin and silent. Did my letters arrive? Oh, tell me what has occurred at Cloyne in our absence."

Johnnie did not speak, nor did his arms hold me to him. The children stood by, watching us, and Giulietta began to chatter in Italian, telling her father of the great adventures she had had on the ship that brought us home, but he paid her no heed and did not seem to hear her. "Oh, my husband and lord," I said again, feeling tears begin to start in my eyes, "it is your wife Francesca, and the children are here. See, they are by you. And we have missed you so. Will you not speak to us?"

He stirred in the chair. I felt his arm come up and I thought it was to draw me nearer to him. But it was not to draw me nearer. His hand crept upwards to my neck and encircled it, and I felt his fingers start to dig into my flesh and all the breath in my body begin to be squeezed out of me. I cried out and the two boys ran to my side and they prised the hand away from my neck and wrenched me from their father's grip. I stumbled and fell to my knees and the children clustered round me, terrified for their lives.

Johnnie O'Fingal sat silent and unmoving in the chair. He did not look at us, but seemed to rest his gaze on some far-away scene of his own imagining.

To recount these things is to make them live again. I see that my writing has become wild and very sloping on the page.

I note something more. Today is Giulietta's birthday. She is eight years old.

THE BOY WHO COULD NOT WRITE HIS NAME

They rose at dawn. They said prayers together in the lofty school hall as the windows slowly filled with light. King Christian still remembers that the old Koldinghus smelled of wood, as though one part of it were being sawn up to make planks with which to build another part. In summer, this wood smell became almost intolerably sweet. His friend Bror Brorson said one day: "To live at the Koldinghus is akin to living in a cask."

The boy Christian's travels with his parents King Frederik and Queen Sofie were over; the days of his drawings of Nils the cat and the golden fish in the lily pond at Frederiksborg were over; his nocturnal conversations with the boy trumpeters were over. He had known for some time that the day would come when these things would all be over and he would reside at the Koldinghus school, under the eye of his corrector Hans Mikkelson. But he did not like it. He told Bror Brorson: "The past is already filling up too quickly."

His companions, like Bror Brorson, were the sons of the nobility. Only high-born children were sent to the Koldinghus school. They were taught Latin, German, French, Italian, English, theology, physics, history and geography in the mornings. During lunch they debated in Latin and in one other foreign tongue. In the afternoons they fenced and rode and played ball games. They spent the evenings at prayer and they had no leisure. The days were too long and the nights too short. It was not unusual for a boy to fall asleep in the middle of an English lesson.

The time of day Christian preferred to any other was that moment when the activities of the afternoon were over and the boys would return to their dormitories to change their clothes before supper. It was not that he liked the dormitory or enjoyed changing his clothes before the unappetising supper that awaited him; what he savoured was the extraordinary feeling of physical strength—of mastery of himself—that he experienced in the wake of the fencing and outdoor games. It did not last more than half an hour, but while it was there it gave him profound satisfaction. And he decided, after some weeks at the Koldinghus, to put it to some use. For how often does a boy feel himself to be master of all that he sees and feels? To be a boy is to be very often most strangely amazed at the conjunction of every thing with every other thing or, to put it plainly, in a state of puzzlement with the world. But here, in the too slow progression of days, were moments when this future King felt at one with his role on earth, when he felt that he *could be King* or that *he was already King within himself.*

And so he contrived what he termed his "half-hour of absolute majesty."

He would take up a finely sharpened quill and a piece of vellum and, knowing his hand to be in perfect control of every stroke or loop of the pen and feeling the energy within him travel through him and emerge in its altered condition onto the parchment, he would write his name time after time in calligraphy of exceptional sophistication and beauty:

His Majesty, King Christian IV of Denmark
His Majesty, King Christian IV of Denmark
His Majesty, King Christian IV of Denmark

He would then embellish these repetitions of his name and title with renderings of the Latin motto he had already chosen for his future reign: *Regna Firmat Pietas* (Through Piety the Kingdom is Strengthened).

Regna Firmat Pietas
REGNA FIRMAT PIETAS

As the bell sounded to call him to supper, he would sign the page with a hasty but still perfect *CIV* or sometimes *C4* with the "4" resting inside the capital "C," like a child kneeling on the lap of its parent. He chose to see his own marvellous writing as a calligraphic expression of his innermost being and there was nothing flawed in it. There was no shoddiness about it. It was fine and complete.

Hans Mikkelson, the principal tutor, or "corrector" as he was officially known, was a man of strangely alternating moods. On certain days he could be patient with the boys, wrapped in his task of communicating to them his learning, as if that learning were a soft mantle that he patiently draped about their shoulders. At other times (and this was his more habitual mode) his thin face would wear a sour expression, he would be unnecessarily pedantic with his Latin corrections and he would make frequent use of a leather fly swat, slapping it viciously upon the boys' hands or upon the pages of their work and sometimes upon their ears. At least one pupil at the Koldinghus complained that throughout his life his hearing had been impaired by the terrible swiping of his ears by Hans Mikkelson's fly swat. Others would remember him with awe and affection, and fondly recall the affliction from which Mikkelson suffered: he had watery eyes.

This watering of the corrector's eyes was of great fascination to Christian. He attempted to determine what conditions caused the greatest amount of watering. He noted, for instance, that Mikkelson endured more trouble with his eyes in the mornings than in the evenings and that, if there was sunlight at the schoolroom window, the corrector had to position himself so that no scintilla of it fell upon his face. He likewise recorded that the teaching of Italian seemed to bring about abundant tears, as though the musical cadences of this language were so greatly at odds with his tuneless personality that some anguish was caused to him whenever he attempted to speak it.

If the lunch-time debate was in Italian, Mikkelson's dinner napkin would be a sodden rag by the end of the meal. History, too, appeared to cause him trouble, as did the singing of cantatas. But his eyes watered most of all when he was angry. As he walked about the room swatting and scolding, a veritable cataract of tears would course down his pale face, and Christian formulated the theory, expressed once or twice to Bror Brorson, that Hans Mikkelson had entered a profession about the value of which he felt an anxious ambiguity. Learning he loved, this was certain. It was the passing on of this learning that he did not love entirely.

Bror Brorson was Mikkelson's most detested pupil. He was the handsomest boy in the school, with a fine-boned face and eyes of a deep-sea blue and a thatch of thick blond hair. He could run very fast and ride well. Like Christian, he was physically brave. But what Bror could not do was write. It was not that he did not have in his mind the thing that he *intended to write*. He was no worse a Latin conversationalist, for example, than many at the Koldinghus. But when he came to transfer any thought, fact, or observation to paper, something impeded him from writing it correctly. What began in clarity ended in muddle. His work books were shameful. They might have been written by a child of four. And even his own name (easy as it was, with its satisfactory repetition) caused him difficulty. Sometimes, letters would be missing from it and it would appear as *Ror Brsen* or *Brr Rosn*. Most frequently all the letters were there but in some altered order, as *Rorb Sorbron* or *Brro Rorbson*.

"What is this?" Mikkelson would ask, swatting the word *Rorbson* as he stood by Bror's desk. "What foul chaos is here?"

A slash at the ear. A swipe at the errant hand.

"I'm sorry, Herr Professor Mikkelson . . ."

" 'Sorrow' we have already passed, Brorson. We are arrived at 'despair.' "

"I'll try again, Herr Professor."

"Yes. You will. But this time, you will write your name correctly."

My name si Rbor Sorren. Mye mane is Obrr Sorner . . .

A stinging slap of the cheek. A hard fist thundering down upon the desk. Tears filling Mikkelson's eyes.

"Get out of this class! You will go to the cellar. You will stay there till night, until your fingers are numb. Go!"

Bror Brorson began to spend so many days—and even nights, because Mikkelson's fury and exasperation with him increased with every day that passed—in the cellar that he soon appeared at lessons with a hurting cough so persistent that it interrupted the natural transfer of information from Mikkelson to pupils, whereupon he would be sent back to the cellar.

One night, Bror told Christian that he had begun to be afraid of the cellar. "I was not afraid at first," he said. "There are some mice down there, but I don't mind them. What I am afraid of is the place itself. I and the place are at war. Death is in it and wants to kill me, and I will not let it."

Christian loved Bror Brorson; he was his closest, most trusted friend. He went to Hans Mikkelson and asked him "as a favour to me, your future King," not to send Bror to the cellar any more. Mikkelson wiped his eyes, sighed and said: "I will cease sending him to the cellar when he ceases writing his name backwards. As my future King, you will surely understand the logic of this decision."

In the winter of 1588 Bror Brorson grew ill. He was taken to the sanatorium and given raw eggs to eat and hot balsams to inhale. Around his sea-blue eyes dark shadows had begun to spread. Christian visited him there every day and read to him from the Bible. Brorson told him: "The people I like the most in the Bible are the disciples. They are simple fishermen and would have difficulty with words." Both boys were eleven years old.

And then, as the class waited for Mikkelson in the schoolroom one cold February morning, some extraordinary news arrived.

Mikkelson entered the room and the boys stood, as was the custom. Usually, the professor sat down at his desk, facing them, but today he did not sit down. He stood very still, his eyes blinking as they always did when he attempted to control their vexatious watering, and then he spoke. "Word has reached us," he said, "that yesterday afternoon, in Zealand at Antvorskov, His Majesty King Frederik II, our beloved King, was taken suddenly ill and there, despite all efforts by his doctors to save him, passed away, God rest his soul."

Christian did not move. He put his hands round the edges of his wooden desk and held on to it. His first thought was for his mother and he wished he might be at her side, floating on the lake at Frederiksborg in a flat-bottomed boat.

"Kneel!" said Mikkelson.

All around him, the boys of the Koldinghus school pushed back their chairs and knelt, with their faces turned towards Christian. Then Hans Mikkelson knelt also and all the company put their hands together, as if in prayer. Christian knew he should speak, but all he could manage to do was to nod, acknowledging the salutation.

"Long live His Majesty King Christian IV!" said Mikkelson.

"Long live His Majesty King Christian IV!" said the boys, almost in unison.

Christian nodded again. Then he found himself staring at the desk in front of his, which was Bror Brorson's desk, empty of its occupant. He looked at Mikkelson, with only his head visible behind his enormous work table, and his eyes streaming with tears. "May I be excused from this lesson, Herr Professor?" he asked.

"Of course, Your Majesty," said Mikkelson.

Christian walked slowly, his head held high, and opened the door to the schoolroom. He passed through it into the passage and then he began to run. Running was forbidden in the corridors of the Koldinghus.

He ran like the wind to the portal that led onto a cobbled courtyard. The snow was thick on the cobblestones and Christian was wearing only his schoolday suit of dark-brown wool with its shirt of white linen. He sprinted as fast as he could go across the courtyard and in through the wooden door to the gabled annexe of the Koldinghus that housed the sanatorium. He did not stop or even break his stride when one of the nurses asked him what he was doing, but hurtled on until he reached the little room where Bror Brorson lay.

Bror was sleeping. The grey shadows round his eyes were darker than they had ever been. When Christian put out a hand to touch his forehead, it was burning hot.

Christian sat down on a wooden chair by Bror's bed. "Here," he said aloud, "I take up my station!"

He knew that he had come not a moment too soon. There was a fight going on in the room—death had come up from the cellar and was fighting Bror here in a little cell in the school sanatorium—and Christian had come to be on Bror's side.

Thoughts of his father's dying went from his mind. What he felt come into his being was a sudden rush of strength and power. In his mind, in the most beautiful writing he could perfect, he channelled this power into a rendition of Bror's name:

Bror Brorson

He said it, wrote it in the air with his hand, said it again, wrote it larger and larger with a more perfect flourish.

Bror Brorson. Bror Brorson. Bror Brorson.

He had two weapons and death had one. He had the new power of his kingship and his undeniably beautiful rendition of Bror's name. Death had only itself. He spoke to the sleeping Bror. "I am here now," he said. "Your King is here. You must rest and I will fight."

Word spread quickly round the school of the death of King Frederik, and the Sister, who was in charge of the sanatorium, came into Bror Brorson's room and knelt down by Christian and said: "Your Majesty must not be in the sanatorium. Your Majesty will, if it please you, leave this sickbed and return to school, where preparations are being made for your journey to Copenhagen."

"No," said Christian. "I have taken up my station here."

He did not know how long he would have to fight. He knew that whatever he had to do in Copenhagen could wait, but that his friend Bror Brorson could not. He asked to be left alone with his fight. He took up Bror's burning hand and held it in his. Then, with Bror's hand, he traced his invisible name. The boy's fever was intense and the little room smelled foetid, and Christian knew that death was crouching in the folds of the bedding, like the devil crouched over a sleeping infant not yet come to baptism, waiting to swat Bror Brorson's life away.

The short day's light began to fade and the snow fell unseen outside the window, but Christian did not call for a candle. He said to death and to the coming night: "I am darker than you. I am ink. I am pure and faultless calligraphy and there is no degree of blackness with which I am not familiar!"

The Sister came again to try to prevail upon Christian to leave, but he would not. Hans Mikkelson came, but he refused to let the corrector into the room and he knew that, now, he would have to be obeyed.

All night he fought death in the name of Bror Brorson. Death slithered from the folds of bedding and lashed the walls of the room with its tail. It breathed a mephitic stench into the air.

In the first light of dawn Christian felt a change come over the sleeping boy. The burning abated. But he knew that it must not abate too much, that he must not let Bror go cold. He called for a nurse to bring more blankets and these he placed over Bror, while death began its daylight cries, like a street trader tempting souls to pass its way. He said aloud: "This is the moment when all is won or lost."

Bror Brorson
Bror Brorson!

Bror opened his eyes just after the great clock on the Koldinghus tower struck seven. Finding Christian there, holding his hand, he said: "What's happening? Where have I been?"

"I do not know," said the eleven-year-old King.

Then Christian stood up and laid Bror's hand gently on his chest. "Sister will take care of you now," he said. "I must go to Copenhagen, to my father's palace, for since yesterday morning I am King of all the realms. I am going to give order that you travel to Frederiksborg when you are well enough. Will you like that? We shall ride in the forests and go fishing in the lake when the ice has gone."

"Will it be allowed?" asked Bror.

"Yes," said Christian. "An order is an order."

KIRSTEN: FROM HER PRIVATE PAPERS

As February arrives, certain Things that do please me excellently well have come to pass.

The King has gone away. That he should be gone is enough for me and I really had no desire to be told where he was going or why, but such is his habit to burden me with every detail of every Scheme that enters his mind that he bored me for at least an hour with some story concerning the discovery of Silver in the mountains of the Numedal in his Norwegian kingdom and how he must go there at once to find Men to hack and mutilate and blow up the rock to get all the Silver out of it.

I said to him: "Silver is very pretty, but I really do not wish to hear about hacked rock and men with gunpowder and picks; I prefer the Silver to arrive freshly polished in my room in the form of a hairbrush." Knowing how one comes by a thing, though it may be edifying, does not always make one feel merry.

I made this last observation also to my Lord and Master, but he, being a person who must always understand the How and Why and Wherefore of everything on this Earth, flew immediately into one of his rages with me. He called me a Vain and Shallow Vessel and a Bad Mother. He accused me of caring for no one and nothing but Myself. But I was not moved by any of this. I declared that I did not understand what my reluctance to hear about the dreadful workings of a Silver Mine had to do with my being a Bad Mother. And here I saw that I had for one moment got a little advantage over him in the argument, for he paused and shook his head and found no words for an instant or two.

And so I took the opportunity here to press home my ascendancy and cried out in a Pitiful Voice: "As to being a Shallow Vessel, women would not be vessels at all if men did not treat them as such! We would prefer to be Ourselves and Human, and no mere receptacle for men's lust, but what choice do we have? And if we are, in these miserable times, found to be Shallow, it is because we are filled to the brim with the products of men's licentiousness and cannot bear to take into us one single droplet more!"

Now I saw, to my satisfaction, that the King appeared a little discomfited. He knows how much I have suffered, bearing him so many children that the skin of my stomach is wretchedly puckered and my breasts, which once were as round as apples, do droop almost to my waist (so that when I am abed with the Count I must always keep remembering to position my body in such a way that the Droop be not emphasised). He knows, too, that I am in a state of great unhappiness in my life with him, but yet Denies this to himself, so that he is in reality no more honest than I, who cannot bear to look upon the toil of a Silver Mine, because he cannot bear to look upon me and see me as I am and know what I am feeling in my heart.

But this last I did not say, preferring then to go from the room and lock myself away in my chambers until he and his party (which contains every manner of Person from Cooks to Musicians) departed on the first stage of their journey towards the Numedal. I stood at my window, watching them go through the gates at Rosenborg, and no sooner were they out of my sight than I sent my Woman Johanna to the Count's house with the following message in the playful code Otto and I have adopted:

My Noble Count,
    Morgana the Queen begs to inform you that her Cat is missing and begs you to bring a big Mouse to amuse her while it is away.

No man in my life was like Count Otto Ludwig. Such is my delight when we are engaged in the Act of Love that I do not seem to take note of any time passing, but be in a World Apart, which world is composed only and entirely of his body and mine and the draperies and light of the room around us.

To sleep in his arms is very soothing and lovely. I do think that I have never known such a sleep as this. But immediately on waking, on discovering where I am, I do feel as naughty as a Vixen again. I cannot help it. I know that sometimes I should let him rest and not in a single afternoon insist upon more than two or three Moments—which I shall admit I do, because this is the only man I have known with whom I can have any real Moment at all and my health is suffering through a great lack of them, and why should I, who am the Queen in all but Title, suffer bad health through a sorry lack of Moments?

Yesterday afternoon, when I had had more than four or five Moments (and he but two), the Count suddenly complained that I was too avid for my pleasure. I did not like the sound of this at all. But instead of being angry with him I feigned some girlish tears and cried to him: "Oh, Otto, you are right! How shameful and lascivious I am! What a scarlet wretch you have chosen as your Mistress! You must punish me now, immediately. Oh, go to, with all speed, take up your belt or the curtain cord or any flagellating object of your choosing. And look, here I expose my naked bottom to its terrible lash. Delay not, but punish me without more ado!"

I need not set down the degree of alacrity with which the Count responded to my entreaties, for I do think all men love to chastise women and do get a great Excitement from it. And, although if the King or any other man were to beat me on any part or limb of my body I would detest it, and scream so loudly that all the servants at Rosenborg were woken from their idle beds, the passionate beatings given to me by the Count put me into a kind of delirium, and in this Delirium when I arrive at a Moment, it is of such intensity and long duration that I have begun to think the Count and I are still low down on the graph of Absolute Pleasure and that we could arrive, through experiment and invention, at a degree of Ecstasy that normal men and women never experience in their lifetimes, nor imagine to be possible.

So absolutely does my mind turn to Matters of the Bedchamber that I have cast about me, while the King is still far from Copenhagen and unlikely to return until next month, for every Means that I can devise to make the Count become more besotted with me, so that he be tied only to me with a knot of love and never look elsewhere for his pleasure.

Today—a day of sudden sun that began to melt the snow at Rosenborg—Herr Bekker, the Sorcerer, came to my summons and wrote down for me the ingredients of a Love Potion. He informs me that this Potion is very strong and I must administer it to my man (Bekker believes I am referring to the King, my husband) in small doses, "Or else, Madam," said Herr Bekker, "he could die of a surfeit of delight and this would be a black day for Denmark."

I made no comment on this last remark of his but ushered him speedily out in case he should begin upon some premature valedictory address to his Great Master. Alas, only after he had gone did I fall to reading the List of Ingredients and discover that one of these is a Thimbleful of Powder from the Grated Hoof of an Antelope. I do not think that any Apothecary in Copenhagen will have ready for me a convenient quantity of grated Antelope's Hoof, nor do I know how any Antelope can be found, to whose foot a grater may be speedily applied. From this it immediately became apparent to me that Sorcerers live in a World of their Own Invention and not in the Real World with the rest of us mortals. And this is profoundly irritating.

Feeling thus dejected by the impossibility of procuring the wretched Antelope's Hoof, I was about to summon one of my Women to go after the Sorcerer and inquire what he would have me do, if not voyage to the Plains of Africa or to the Mountains of Nepal in search of the animal, when I noticed that Herr Bekker had left his quill pen behind on my writing table.

I picked it up, thinking to return it to him with my Woman, and, when I held it in my hand, found it to be an object of startling and strange beauty with which, following a natural inclination, I began to caress my own cheek.

The quill feather is black, but with a sheen upon it the colour of mother-of-pearl and a bunch of soft feathers at its base that have arranged themselves into a little curl, like the curls on a baby's head.

The caressing of my cheek with the quill so lulled and soothed me that I quite forgot to send after Herr Bekker. And I decided that I would not return the quill but, on the contrary, pretend that it had never been left in my room, so that I can keep it for myself. For I think it has some magical property. The skin of my cheek felt very warm and a kind of happiness came into me that seemed to have its beginning there, in my face. When I heard a knock upon my door, I was startled out of my reverie and quickly secreted the quill in the drawer of my writing table, where I keep these papers and to which no one has any key except myself.

My Woman of the Feet, Hansi, entered then. With her was a young girl of very sweet and pleasing appearance whom I had never before seen. "Madam," said Hansi, "your new Woman is arrived, given to you by your Mother, and this is she. Her name is Emilia Tilsen."

"Ah," I said.

The girl, Emilia Tilsen, curtsied to me and bowed her head. I crossed to her and raised her up and bade her welcome into my service. Though the King calls me a Vain and Shallow Vessel and the Count, while he lashes my bottom with a silken cord, screams that I am a Very Vile Hussy, I know that I can still be kind and lovely when I am at peace with my life, and on the instant this girl Emilia engendered in me a feeling of gentleness and calm that was very marked and the like of which I had not felt for some time.

She has a pale, oval face and hair neither dark nor fair. Her smile is very pleasing and her eyes the colour of the grey sea. Her hands are small.

"Well," I said, "you have come from Jutland, if I remember, so I expect you are tired and would like to rest."

As I said this Hansi looked at me with amazement, she believing that, because I pay not the slightest attention to her Need for Rest, I am incapable of being considerate, whereas the truth is I can be exceptionally considerate and careful of others if I am *moved to be so*. The fact that I am so seldom moved is not my fault, but attributable to the fact that I am hedged about with gross and idle people for whom I feel not one jot of love.

"Oh, no," said this sweet Emilia, "I am not tired, Madam. If there is any task that I can perform for you, then please let me set about it."

She was wearing a little dress of grey silk. It was very plain, but it suited her well. Round her neck was a locket on a velvet ribbon. She had about her a fragile, pleasing perfume that reminded me of the smell of summer fruit.

"Very well," I said. "There is one small task that you might do for me, but first, if you are not tired, I should like to talk to you and hear about your life in Jutland, where I was myself born. So, Hansi, send for a little wine and some caraway cake, and Emilia and I will converse here for a while. Come here, Emilia my dear, and sit down on this chaise while we wait for the wine."

Hansi gaped at me. Never in her life had I spoken thus nicely to

59

her. She turned tail and went away, letting the door bang rudely after her.

I have now discovered that my sweet Emilia has had a tragic life.
She wears her Mother's picture in the locket round her neck and
says nothing will part her from this one possession.

I was very moved when I heard how her Mother died, ready indeed to weep—which thing I scarcely ever do, preferring to rail at
Life rather than snivel at it. "Oh, my poor girl," I said in a choked
voice, and took her in my arms, and laid her head on my shoulder
and stroked her hair. And together we cried, and after a few minutes of weeping, I said: "Let me tell you straight away, Emilia, that
I am also in an unhappy condition here at Rosenborg. You may observe my sumptuous rooms and count my great quantity of dresses
and furs, and all my golden ornaments and jewels. But for all this I
am a wretched woman. By and by, you will come to see why and to
understand how much I am despised."

"Despised?" said Emilia. "How could anyone despise a person as
beautiful and kind as you?"

"Oh," I exclaimed, "is this how you see me? Beautiful and
kind?"

"Yes. You are very beautiful. And look how, in my first hour at
Rosenborg, you have been so tender and gracious towards me . . ."

"I *was*!" I said, beginning to weep again. "I was both these
things when I was younger, before I was driven insane with carrying
children and pushing them out into a spiteful world. But all my
kindness was used up. And now I am so angry with my fate that I
would . . . I cannot tell you what I would do. I do not know what
terrible thing I am capable of doing!"

We sobbed a little longer. I had forgotten what a marvellous
thing weeping can be. Then I poured us some more wine and found
a kerchief with which to wipe our eyes, and I said to Emilia: "My
Mother gave you as a gift to me and I can see that she chose very
well. My other Women have specific tasks, but I will give you none
other than to ask you always to come when I call you and under-

take whatever foolish thing it is that has entered my mind. And I, in my turn, will try always to be gentle with you, as your own Mother would have been, and not ask of you anything that might cause you vexation or pain."

Emilia thanked me and promised she would do for me anything whatsoever that I asked of her and so I patted her small hand and we drank the wine and ate the caraway cake. Then I said: "Very well, Emilia. Now I want you to write a letter for me."

I then dictated the following:

Dear Herr Bekker,
    Upon perusing the List you put into my possession today, I do find that you have mentioned the words "Hoof of Antelope."
    Please be good enough to call on me tomorrow and explain to me how in the World I am to come by any such extraordinary Thing.
        Yours in expectation,
            Kirsten Munk, King's Consort

I noted that Emilia Tilsen's writing is round and neat. She did not comment on the words Hoof of Antelope, but only, when she had completed the letter, looked up to me with a little worried frown.

NORTH

King Christian's vast gilded ship, the *Tre Kroner*, travels northwards towards the ice floes of the Skagerrak. The *Tre Kroner* is the largest of the ships of the fleet. It weighs fifteen hundred tons. Its main mast is one hundred and thirty feet from main deck to crow's nest. Silk banners fly from the yards and the mast-heads, and billow in the wind. On the tall quarterdeck the royal coat of arms, painted gold and blue, catches the gleaming of the late winter sun.

With its fatness of sail and its mighty tonnage, this ship is more magnificent than anything ever seen on these waters. In all these ways, it resembles the King himself—exactly as he wished it to. To its Scottish builder, Christian commanded: "Give me bulk and bravery. Give me hugeness and a stout heart."

Now it ploughs towards Norway across the cold seas of the icy spring. Its cargo is barrels of gunpowder and the iron utensils for breaking rock and stone, together with ropes and tackle and chains. But when King Christian is escorted down into the hold to inspect these tools of the mine, it is not picks and shovels that he sees in the torchlight: he has already replaced them in his imagination with ingots of silver. And the barrels are filled with silver dalers.

The King's retinue is large, but this ship can accommodate one hundred and fifty souls. Cabins on the quarterdeck are given to the engineers, the people the King calls the geniuses of the mine, men who can look at a hill and know where the seams of precious ore are likely to run. The geniuses of the mine sit in a huddle on the lofty quarterdeck and fret and compare notes, and lay maps of the Numedal across their knees.

The King has included two musicians among the cooks, vintners, surgeons, apothecaries, geographers and launderers because he doesn't know how long he will be away from Copenhagen and he considers that a life without music—even life on a far-away hillside under a Norwegian sky—is a life where the cold indifference of the universe may hold absolute sway. And he is in no mood to hear its uncaring silence.

One of the musicians is his "angel" Peter Claire and the other is the German, Krenze, the viol player. Their quarters, shared with the surgeons, on the uppermost of the three gun decks are lightless and noisy, and as the ship passes Frederikshavn and begins to feel the west winds of the Skagerrak rouse the seas from their Kattegat slumber, the *Tre Kroner's* size affords her little protection from being hurled about in the angry water.

Krenze lies in his hammock, sipping ginger tea to ward off seasickness. Peter Claire's body begins to ache from the effort of trying to keep his balance, and it seems to him that this ache of his and the creaking and sighing of the ship confuse themselves and become one and the same. His world is shrunk to this, to bone and sinew, to wood and rope, all protesting against the inhospitable sea. It is only a few weeks since his journey from England and Peter Claire never expected to be aboard a ship again so horribly soon. He sleeps fitfully and dreams of his Irish Countess. "Gone," he says aloud, "and for always."

Krenze overhears this, but doesn't question or comment. Green-gilled, his thin hands nurturing his bowl of tea, he remarks acidly: "I am surprised His Majesty did not put us in the hold with the powder. What has become of his cherished concept of *underneath?*"

Peter Claire, his mind still filled with images of Countess O'Fingal, seeing in the tormented Skagerrak the slate-blue seas of the west coast of Ireland, says pedantically: "The hold is too deep. There are only two of us and, even on the main deck, he wouldn't be able to hear us."

Krenze smiles, despite his sickness. "You know we are a floating explosion?" he says. "One lick of fire down in the depths there and we will all be blown to hell."

"Why are you so sure it's hell, Krenze? Why should it not be paradise?"

"Look at us—how wretched we are! Foul weather at sea strips men of their dignity and makes them nothing. Hell is all we are fit for."

And so Peter Claire is silent and, not for the first time, asks himself what he is doing so far from his home and wonders, if he should drown in this freezing sea, what living souls would mourn him and what the sum of his life might be seen to be. He thinks of his kind parents, his father the Reverend James Whittaker Claire and his mother, Anne. He imagines them sighing for the loss of him, lamenting secretly that he had done so little with his life, only bind himself to a musical instrument and wander about the world—so far from his father's church of St. Benedict the Healer, so far from his mother's bounteous table—in search of new harmonies and strange company.

He knows they would pray for his soul, yet also find themselves wondering what kind of soul it was they prayed for. For all his life he has been quiet, secretive and solitary. As if he had been biding his time, always biding his time. Telling nobody what he hoped and feared because he knew that the things that he feared and the things that he hoped for were not the things that would come to matter. Something else waited for him. Something he could not yet see. But was it yet in sight? Peter Claire decides that, when or if they reach the Numedal, he will write his parents a letter. In it, he will say:

> King Christian has bound me to him more closely than I anticipated. He has acted out of superstition and not out of affection nor from any knowledge of who I really am. It seems, simply, that I resemble the angels he imagined as a boy. But I confess that I have been affected by this and do come to believe—or come to hope—that something of great importance will happen to me in Denmark.

Peter Claire watches the King. The King does not appear stripped of any dignity. On the contrary, his heavy frame seems to have acquired an agility it didn't possess at Rosenborg. And the workings of the ship are of eternal fascination to him. He doesn't stay in the fastness of the quarterdeck, but roams about the forecastle and the main deck, scrutinising everything and everyone. For minutes at a time he stares up at the topsails, his gaze resting on the midshipmen strung out aloft on the yard-arms—resting with an expression of awe, even of envy, as though in that universe of sky and sail there might be found a moment of release from all his earth-bound trouble.

"Oh, this is a wonderful ship!" he is heard to cry out, and at that very moment a mountainous wave comes rearing up at the *Tre Kroner*'s prow and water comes pouring over the gunwales, so that the King loses his footing on the deck. Men stagger to his aid and help him to stand, but he is not hurt, and once he is up again he refuses to go to his cabin. He holds fast to a shroud. Rain begins to beat down on him and the wind whips his elflock around his neck like a noose, but he pays none of this any heed. In moments, his gaze has returned to the men high above him. They are beginning to furl the topsail, dismantling their airy kingdom inch by inch. And when at last they climb down, some of them boys no older than twelve, King Christian holds out his hand to them in a gesture of admiration. And his eye scans the space of sky where the topsail flew and the rain clouds sweep in, billow upon billow.

With the coming of nightfall the storm dies down. A gentle wind from the south-west still ensures that the *Tre Kroner* makes head-way, but the seas are quieter and above the ship a thin moon slides into view as the clouds race away northwards.

Peter Claire and Krenze are sleeping at last, when one of the ship's crew wakes them and orders them onto the quarterdeck "by command of His Majesty." They struggle into their boots, Krenze cursing that the King is "a destroyer of a man's health and sanity," take their instruments out of their cases and hurry to answer the summons. They find King Christian, not in his cabin, but on the deck itself, out under the moon, seated in an elaborate wooden chair like a throne and wrapped in a sealskin coat.

He looks tenderly at his lutenist. "Nature," he says, "has given us a little respite, Mr. Claire. You and Krenze will now record the gratitude of the ship's company with some sweet ayres."

It is very cold. The musicians sit side by side on a wooden crate and begin upon a cycle of German songs—the very music with which, in his mind, Krenze has tried to console himself in his hours of sickness. As the songs start to be heard around the ship, more and more people emerge onto the quarterdeck to listen. The captain leans against some rigging and fixes his eyes on the moon and stars, but the geniuses of the mine gaze intently at Peter Claire and Krenze, as if the sounds they make contained some precious metal as yet unknown to them.

Now, with Emilia gone, Magdalena Tilsen rules over a house of men. There are six of them, including Johann, and Magdalena has come to recognise an extraordinary phenomenon: it is not only Johann who is in love with her, but also his two eldest sons, Ingmar and Wilhelm.

They have ceased, it appears, to pine for their mother. They are sixteen and fifteen years old, and Magdalena knows, from the way they cling to her and the habit they have adopted of asking her to kiss them good-night and then giggling as they both try to kiss her on the lips, that she arouses in them something more than simple affection.

The two boys next in line after Ingmar and Wilhelm are too small to be in love with her, but already Boris and Matti are, in their ways, possessive about her. They like to hold her hand. They like to take a furl of her ample skirt and enfold themselves in it, bound to her body, laughing. When she bakes cakes, they sit on the table and dip their fingers into the bowl and, when they have eaten mouthfuls of the creamy egg and butter mixture, persuade her to lick their little fingers clean. Sometimes they unbraid her hair and hold it over their faces.

She has converted them all. She overhears Wilhelm say to Ingmar that he envies his father and Ingmar whispers in reply that the smell of her "is fearful in that way." And the thought enters her mind that when the summer comes she may take Wilhelm and Ingmar to the woods that border the strawberry fields and show them everything they will ever need to know about a woman. Magdalena is from peasant stock. Her father's family motto (from whence it came, nobody remembers) was "Guiltless Are We" and all his clan took the words to heart in the way they arranged their lives.

Magdalena's uncle, a poultry man, showed her all the ways of pleasing men when she was a child of fourteen. ("There is no shame in it, Magdalena, but only a little learning.") Before she met and married Johann Tilsen, she still regularly slept with this uncle (of whom she remained extremely fond) and with her cousin, the poultry man's son. There was more than once talk of a child, but no child was ever born and now no one remembers what was said or done on the subject. *Guiltless Are We.*

So sure of her supremacy in the Tilsen house has Magdalena become that, relishing her many luxuries and satisfactions in this new life of hers, she walks about with an unsurpassed air of confidence. She reflects that it only needed the departure of Emilia to bring about this extraordinary augmentation of her power.

There is often a secret smile coming and going about her lips. And she's taken to spoiling herself with all the delicacies that can be procured in the neighbourhood, easily persuading her husband to purchase goose livers and cream, capons for stuffing, quail eggs, partridges, lambs' tails and pigs' trotters. Her flesh expands. Her cheeks are fat and rosy. That "fearful" perfume of hers seems to increase in intensity. She reigns and the men follow after, always yearning and then again yearning: *Touch my forehead Magdalena, kiss my lips Magdalena, lick my fingers Magdalena, wrap me in your skirts Magdalena, Magdalena come with me to the lake . . .*

But there is one exception. Marcus, the youngest boy, the child informed by Emilia that he had killed his mother, is apparently impervious to Magdalena's spell. When she picks him up he screams. He refuses to kiss her. If he goes to one of her cake makings, he holds his hands behind his back, so that she will not lick his fingers. And he is disobedient. Against all her orders he will go wandering away from the house on his own. He has been told that Emilia is no longer there, that she is in Copenhagen, but each time Marcus is brought back from his wanderings, when he is asked what he has been doing, his reply is always the same. He says that he has been looking for Emilia. Again and again it is explained to him that Copenhagen is miles and miles away, further than anyone is able to walk, further than the sea, further than the north star, but still he goes in search of her.

At night, Marcus cries. Often, he wets his bed and in the morning is treated, not to the beguiling touch of Magdalena's hand on his body that Ingmar longs for, but to a stinging slap on his legs or on his bottom. He lies in his damp cot with his face turned away from the room. He refuses to eat more than a few mouthfuls at mealtimes or to concentrate on his lessons. He is growing very thin and there are shadows under his eyes.

This obstinacy of Marcus's annoys Magdalena. Why, when with her irresistible smell and her buxom peasant beauty she has enslaved the entire household, must there be this one sorrowful little dissenter? There is no logic to it and this increases Magdalena's irritation. Marcus is the one child who never knew his mother and therefore he can feel no loyalty towards Karen, yet he it is who pushes his stepmother away.

"You must talk to him severely, Johann," says Magdalena. "We cannot have a child in this house who refuses to flourish."

So Johann (who does whatever Magdalena asks) takes his youngest son for a ride on his bay pony, leading him slowly and carefully along the lanes that border the fruit fields, and, when they come to a meadow, he lifts him down and lets the pony graze and they sit on the edge of a stone water trough still filmed with ice.

Johann looks at Marcus and sees in his small serious face the ghost of his first wife Karen. The other boys are growing up to look like Johann, with dark hair and sturdy countenances. Only Emilia and Marcus resemble Karen. And now, as Johann sits there on the horse trough, he wishes that they did not.

"Now, Marcus," says Johann, "pay attention."

The boy is examining the ice. He sees that there are things trapped in it: dead leaves and small sticks.

"Are you paying attention?" asks Johann.

"Yes," says Marcus. But his gaze doesn't move from the surface of the frozen water.

"Well, now," says Johann with a sigh, "you must tell me what is the matter with you."

He waits, but the boy doesn't answer.

"This running away and searching for Emilia. You know it is disobedient and very foolish."

Marcus looks up at his father. It is a sunny morning and Marcus rubs his eyes, as if the sunlight hurt them. He says nothing.

"Do you understand?" says Johann.

"Where is Copenhagen?" asks Marcus.

"We've told you: a long way away, across the water. Further than you have ever travelled."

"Magdalena could fly there. She is a witch," says Marcus.

"Stop that!" snaps Johann. "I will not have you say that! It was wicked of Emilia to whisper such a thing to you. Wicked. Indeed I am beginning to think she is a sinful girl and that it would be better that she stay in Copenhagen, so that we may all be tranquil here. So you must forget her, Marcus. You must forget her shameful lies and you must forget her. She will not come back to us. And Magdalena is not a witch. She is my wife and she is your *mother*."

"No, she isn't. I killed my mother."

"Another example of Emilia's disgraceful inventions! Upon my word, I thought her a good girl, but now I see how secretive she is. I believe I shall not permit her ever to return. And you, Marcus, if you don't cease these doleful ways you have and make progress with your work and begin to behave properly at mealtimes, why then I shall devise some punishment that may be cruel and which you will not like. Look at what you have: these fields and woods, your pony, a loving father, handsome brothers. You are the most fortunate of children. And you will from now on mend your ways or the consequences for you will be very disagreeable."

Johann expects Marcus to look frightened by now, but he does not appear frightened, only distracted, his large eyes staring at the sunlit meadow.

"Will Magdalena die?" he asks.

Johann's voice is loud and angry when he says: "Die? Of course she will not die! What thoughts are in your head? Whatever they are, they are not sensible and they are not good."

"I wish that she would die," says Marcus.

Now Johann feels a great torment come into him. He raises a hand to strike Marcus, but in that instant is aware of his youngest son as a pitiful creature, a ghostly soul adrift in his own confused world, a child without a future. He lowers his hand and, instead, picks Marcus up (how light he is, how small and weightless . . .) and sets him on his knee.

"I will forget," Johann says, "that you ever uttered those words, but you, in turn, must forget Emilia. You will never more go searching for her in the woods or by the lake or wherever it may be. And now you must promise me that all these wanderings are over. Promise me now."

Marcus, as if he were overcome with tiredness, leans towards his father and lays his face against his father's chest. Johann holds him closely and waits, but the only sounds that break the silence of the field are the scufflings of a bird among the old dry leaves.

"Promise," Johann says again, but Marcus neither moves nor speaks.

FROM COUNTESS O'FINGAL'S NOTEBOOK, *LA DOLOROSA*

While I and the children were staying with my father in Bologna the conviction stole upon Johnnie O'Fingal that I was the sole author of all his anguish. He reasoned as follows: had I been of a more courageous disposition and never woken him on the night of the storm, why then his dream of sublime music would never have risen to the surface of his mind. Thus, it was my childish weakness, my "womanish terror of nature's grandeur," as he put it, which had brought about our tragedy. I was entirely and only responsible, and the man who had fallen in love with me at first sight could now only look at me with hatred and barely suppress in himself a constant desire to do me harm.

The virginals had been locked and put away because Johnnie O'Fingal had renounced his struggles to recapture the lost melody, declaring that it had "gone beyond every reach of my mind and heart." With this renunciation he decreed that henceforth no music of any kind could be played in the house, not even by the children. Never more would there be concerts or any musical entertainment at Cloyne. "There will be silence!" he thundered.

And so silence there was. I and the children went about our lives—our lessons and pastimes, our walks and meals and reading and prayers—but we did all these things as quietly as we could and were by no means successful in including Johnnie in them, so that what came about in the month that followed our return from Bologna was no less than a separation between us on the one hand and him on the other.

He never came near my bed, but occupied a distant room that looked northwards towards the hills of Cloyne. He never visited the children's schoolroom nor talked to them at mealtimes nor took them out on any picnic or pleasing adventure. In the daylight hours he would either sit and gaze into the fire in his study or go about his lands all alone and often with no coat or hat, and walk for hour after hour until he grew tired and returned to sleep.

Seeing him wandering like this, with his wild, distracted look and his hair unkempt and thin clothes in winter and the psora un-healed on his forehead, his tenant farmers and peasants on the estate grew anxious for their future. Always, in the old days, he would stop at every cottage or dwelling and talk to the people there, but now he passed them by and did not return their greetings and when, as began to happen, they pleaded with him to set in mo-tion repairs to their roofs or barns, or to take note of the damp that had come into the church, or to pay Doctor McLafferty his annual stipend for the care of them and their children, he did not give them any answer, but only passed by, as though he had not heard them.

Naturally, I still went among them and when they saw me they would press their hands together or hold their heads, as if in pain, and say to me: "Oh, Lady O'Fingal, what calamity is come upon us? What has stricken His Lordship down?"

"It is a mystery," I would reply. "And I tell you truly that I do not know how it may be solved."

Then I would try to reassure the people that I would do every-thing in my power to find money for their repairs and to give the doctor his dues. But in a short time all the income to which I alone had any right or access was used up. I then went to Johnnie (though still afraid that his loathing of me might manifest itself at any second in some violent deed) and told him: "If you will not take care of everything on the estate as before, then you must give me the means to do it. You cannot let your people live in leaking houses or allow their children to sicken or die for want of the services of a physician."

"Francesca," he said, regarding me with the stony look of hatred to which I had now grown accustomed, "the plight of these idle peasants is of no interest to me. What do they know of suffering, compared with what I know? I have been face to face with the sublime and they have never come near it. I have heard the melody in the heart of the universe and then lost it."

"Oh, but, Johnnie," I said, "that you have *heard* it should make you the more inclined—and not less—to deal in all things like an honourable man. Surely I am right in this? What was revealed to you that night but a great beneficence to which you might aspire? And what prevents you from aspiring to it by means other than musical composition? You do not lack money. Only let me have the right to some control of the estate funds and I will aspire to do good in your place, and all will be well, and you will not be disturbed, I promise you, from your walks and reveries."

But he would not yield. He hounded me from the room. He declared that I, along with all members of my sex, was incapable of aspiring to anything noble for as long as I should live.

By the end of the year I had no funds whatsoever to pay the household staff nor the children's tutors. In shame and with fear and anguish in my heart, I rode to Corcaigh one day and pawned a diamond brooch Johnnie had given me for my twenty-fifth birthday.

I then, in despair, wrote to my father and asked him to make me a loan from his paper business. This he did straight away and, what is more, hearing of my plight and acting still as a most tender parent towards me, he informed me that as soon as time permitted he would make the journey from Bologna to Ireland and strive with all his might to set in train some resolution to the catastrophe that had come upon us.

It was Francesco Ponti who unlocked the key to the next chapter of our sad story.

For no reason that I could determine, other than that he was a man and a most clever and kindly person, the presence of my father in our house started almost at once to work some soothing magic upon poor Johnnie's exhausted mind.

He began to talk to him. I do not know what many things they spoke of together (and indeed it is true that my father does make many mistakes in English, so that it may have been some words muddled or confused with others that made to his listener a strange kind of logic) but after a few days I began to see a change in Johnnie O'Fingal. He appeared in his chair at mealtimes and would, from time to time, say some words to the children and let them tell him about their games or their work.

At lunch-time one day, while we ate a thin stew of lamb's neck, he suddenly embarked upon a discussion of the great matter of God and religion, his mind turning endlessly upon the question of how and when and in what manner we are afforded any proof of the existence of God. And my father, being a Roman Catholic but also a merchant and in no wise a great philosopher, answered him in a plain manner with a tale from his life as a man of commerce. He said God appeared to him in the guise of opportunity.

"You see, Johnnie," he said by way of explanation, "in whatever is *revealed to us*, there I see the hand of God. You understand me? For a saint, this revealing might be to go and make some conversation with the birds, or to give away golden things to a *mendicante*. You know my thought? But for me, I have a different revelation. I go to a city. It might be Roma or Firenze. It might be London. It could be Corcaigh. I visit a law man, an apothecary, an *ospedale*, a seminary. Many places. I do then talk to these people in these places and watch what they do. And then, little by little, God reveals it to me: where and how I can do business with them. I have in a leather box my samples of paper, all different qualities, and it is God who says to me, 'Francesco, show the Paper *Numero Due.*' "

I see that I have mocked my father's language a little here, but any reader of this notebook will forgive me, for this account does indeed give some flavour of the way Francesco Ponti spoke about the subject of God and opportunity. And what it procured that lunch-time, causing astonishment to me and all the children, was a thing we had not seen for very many months. And this thing was a smile on the face of Johnnie O'Fingal.

Some nights later my father came to my room after Johnnie had gone to bed and told me that he now at last understood how my husband might be rescued from the entrapment in which he found himself. With his simple logic, Francesco said to me that he believed the reason Johnnie O'Fingal had been unable to rediscover the music he had heard was that he lacked the professional skill to find it. He had proceeded "all on his own, without any qualified musician to help him," and so, of necessity, his endeavours had come to naught.

I protested that if a thing appears in a dream, then it is only the dreamer himself who has any hope of rediscovering it, but Francesco reminded me that Johnnie had "got very near" to playing the tune upon the virginals. If only some skilled composer had been by him to essay different melodies and harmonies, then it surely would have emerged at last and all our lives would have been glorified by its discovery.

Still I expressed my doubts, saying that I did not see how any man may hear what is locked inside another's heart, but my father then revealed that he had, on this very evening, put his opinion to Johnnie, who had listened attentively and said at last that he would now "endeavour to regain his strength to try again, with the hired help of some musical person."

I let a sigh escape from my breast. "Father," I said, "since you are come to us, Johnnie has by slow degrees begun to return to a little normality and kindness. And for this I thank you more than I can express. But please do not urge upon my husband any return to his search. For this will surely bring him again to absolute despair and misery. Only stay with us a little longer and continue with your conversations, and I entertain some hope that we can at length have something of our old life again."

My father laid his hand gently upon my head. "Francesca," he said, "this is a man who has seen paradise. You must not prevent a man who has been in this place from trying to go there again."

And so it was that, in due time, the padlock was removed from the virginals and a tuner hired to prepare them again to be played upon. The library was cleaned and repainted, and a great quantity of paper brought in by my father and laid beside a music stand. Upstairs a room was made ready and on the day that my father left us to return to Bologna a young musician by the name of Peter Claire arrived in our household.

How Can This Be So?

Kirsten Munk has always believed that the rooms inhabited by her women should be plain and simple rooms, unadorned by any luxury.

"Absence of luxury," she has told her mother, "is essential, if I am to retain control of them. Give them luxury and they will believe that this is a permanent condition at Rosenborg—as if feather beds fell from the air, as if ebony dressing-tables grew out of the floor. Whereas, when they see that this is not so, they will begin to ask themselves how they may get more things with which to warm themselves and embellish their ambitious bodies. And they will soon understand what the answer is: all luxury emanates from me! I can provide it and I can take it away. And so, comprehending this, they will always be striving to please me and always striving not to wake up my temper."

Thus it is that Emilia Tilsen lies now, on her first night at the castle, not in some spacious or comfortable room, but in a narrow bed in a high chamber with no fire to warm her, and a single candle to make a girdle of light against the Rosenborg dark. The sheets that cover her feel damp, as though they had never been aired in the sun, and Emilia is cold. She keeps the candle burning and lays her cloak trimmed with fur on top of the bedding, holding the fur against her face.

She is thinking about Marcus. She can imagine his face, as if he were standing there, in this unfamiliar room, just beyond the candle flame. His eyes are huge and shadowy, and he clutches some little piece of cloth against his cheek as a comforter. He begs Emilia not to leave him at home with his father and Magdalena, and his brothers whose fingers Magdalena is implored to lick when they've gorged themselves on her cake batter. He says: "I want it to be true that you never left."

But she has left. She is alone for the first time. Despite the cold of the room, despite her worrying for Marcus, Emilia now tells herself that she has been fortunate in being summoned here to serve in Kirsten's household. She is at the start of a new life. She has escaped from Magdalena and Magdalena's obscenity and spite. She blows out the candle and wills herself to sleep in the knowledge that tomorrow will be good.

Someone wakes her, calling her name.

Emilia has been dreaming about the strawberry fields and thinks at first that she is in Jutland. Then she sees a woman's face, frilled at its edge by the lace of a night-bonnet and lit by a lamp.

"Emilia," says the woman, "I don't know how you can sleep so soundly in such an icy room."

Emilia sits up. She is warm in the bed, but knows that the night chill is still in the air. The face in the bonnet belongs to Johanna, the oldest of Kirsten's women.

"Now," says Johanna, "before the day begins, I must warn you of all the things you do not know."

"What things . . . ?"

"Hansi and I are agreed: you are very young and we cannot let you go unprepared into the morning. I shall speak in a whisper, for Rosenborg is as full of spies as it is of spiders. But you must pay attention."

Emilia holds on to the fur of her cloak. Johanna seizes a hard chair and positions it by the bed. She sits down on it, placing the lamp on the floor, so that a tall shadow suddenly spreads itself across the wall, causing Emilia an instant of terror. Since the death of Karen she has not been comfortable with the way shadows in the lamplight move at such astounding speed.

Johanna lays a hand on hers which clutches the cloak. "Try to remember everything I say," she whispers.

And then she begins her recitation of the humiliations she and the other women endure in the service of Kirsten Munk. She tells Emilia about the "ridiculous nomenclatures" they are forced to suffer and the delight Kirsten appears to take in wounding their pride, so that each day contains "not one but very many vexing abasements of the kind we did not think would ever be put upon us in the service of the King's wife.

"My title," she continues, "is Woman of the Head. But my mistress always and eternally considers only outward things. My tasks are to dress and adorn her hair and to care for the skin of her face and the jewels she will wear in her ears and round her neck. She is not asking me to concern myself with the thoughts and schemes boiling inside her skull and indeed she does not imagine that I have any knowledge of these. But she is wrong! I have knowledge that could cast her out from the King's heart and throw her onto the street. And in time, I may use it . . .

"But, Emilia, this Woman of the Head is not so foolishly named. I was schooled by my father in thinking—quite by accident in that he had no sons and so he talked to me as if I might have been a man. He told me fables about good and evil, about wisdom and foolishness, and showed me how a fable can awaken the mind to the truth of what it perceives in the daily world. And so you see, I am aptly named and must take responsibility for all the women and try to help them and save them from cruelty, and this is why I am here, to tell you what a place of misery you have come to and implore you to try not to *feel* the insults that will be heaped upon you, but only take them into you as words that have no meaning, as if you felt nothing but the air upon your cheeks."

Emilia stares into Johanna's anxious face, at her forehead creased with worry under the white frills. She is about to tell her that nothing at Rosenborg can be more terrible to endure than the presence of Magdalena in the very rooms where her mother used to walk, but Johanna moves closer to her, so close that she can feel her warm breath in the cold air of the room, and continues in a voice hushed almost to ghostliness. "And for your own good," she hisses, "let me speak of things far worse than those we women suffer. Our mistress lives deep, deep in a deception that will soon come to light. She has a German lover, Count Otto Ludwig of Salm. When the King is away she is bold and careless. And sometimes we hear how they scream and cry out together. But we are sworn to secrecy—as she will make you swear. We have to act as if we are deaf and blind. We are threatened with death by drowning, far away in some lake in Jutland, if we make any reference to the Count or to the marks left on her skin when she has been with him. And so you must also become deaf and blind, Emilia. Blind and deaf and dumb."

Johanna draws back and looks at Emilia, as if watching to see what effect her words have had on the young girl who has been given no specific tasks but only the title of Floating Woman in this universe of shadows and secrets. Emilia appears calm. Surprised, of course, with her eyes very dark and wide in the flickering lamplight, but not yet afraid. Johanna opens her mouth to come out with yet more fearful revelations, but Emilia says: "She is unhappy."

"What?" says Johanna.

"Lady Kirsten. She told me she is 'despised.' "

"Of course she is despised! By almost everyone in Denmark. But not by the King. The King does not see her as she is. Yet I know that one day soon, he will wake up to what she is doing."

"People who feel themselves to be despised may do things they do not intend . . ."

Johanna laughs, then covers her mouth to stifle the sound. She rises then, picks up her lamp and moves swiftly to the door. "You will learn, Emilia," she says. "You will learn."

Emilia sits motionless in her bed in the dark. She hears Johanna's footsteps moving away down the corridor.

Then she begins to sift and examine the new knowledge that now seems to live and breathe with her in the small room, making some minute sound, disturbing the stillness of the air. To her lost mother she asks the question, How can this be so?

Karen looks at her gravely. After a while, she slowly shakes her head, telling her daughter that she does not know the answer.

TYCHO BRAHE'S RECIPE

Soon after the funeral of King Frederik, while the state rooms of the castle were still draped in black, Bror Brorson arrived to stay with his classmate at Frederiksborg.

Nobody at the Koldinghus school, not even Hans Mikkelson, had dared to return Bror Brorson to the cellar after Christian's vigil in the sanatorium and so the shadows around Bror's blue eyes had vanished, his face had recovered its healthy colour and Queen Sofie complimented her son for having as his friend such a handsome boy.

In the time of his recovery, Bror had also done battle with the writing of his name and he was now able sometimes to replicate a one-word signature, *Bror*, without experiencing anything more fearful than occasional confusion. And it was Christian's opinion that a one-word signature would suffice for Bror's lifetime. "As King," he said, "I will have a one-word signature, with just the little IV or 4 after it to distinguish me from my ancestors. So I have an excellent idea, Bror. Why do we not form a secret society, consisting only of you and me, to be known as the 'Society of One-Word Signatories'?"

Bror said that he liked the idea of a secret society, provided it did not have a written charter. But the utterance of the word "charter" woke in Christian an immediate longing for such a document and so he spent many hours compiling and perfecting it in his beautiful calligraphy, then reading it aloud to his friend and only asking from Bror his signature at the bottom of it. The final clause of the charter stated that

All Members of the Society of One-Word Signatories do hereby Promise and Swear upon their names to Protect each other Always and at all Times from Acts of Cruelty, wheresoever and whensoever such Actions of Cruelty shall be threatened against them, as far as human Endeavour and human Strength shall permit.

The signatures on the charter read

Christian   *Rorb*

Christian quickly rolled the document and tied it with one of the black ribbons with which his chamber seemed to be adorned since his father's death. He pronounced it "perfect."

The days that followed were filled with the sight of black-clad noblemen, members of the *Rigsråd*, or State Council, arriving to confer with the Queen, bearing sheafs of papers and running out again with their dark cloaks flying, as if time had been sewn into their garments and was now pursuing them up and down stairs, across courtyards and in and out of carriages.

Christian and Bror stood at a high window and watched them. "It seems," said Bror, "you have not yet become part of their arithmetic."

"No," said Christian. "It is stupid."

Danish law decreed that the dead King's son, though he might nominally use the title of King, could not be crowned until his twentieth year. Until that time the government of the country would lie in the hands of the flying noblemen of the *Rigsråd* and with the Queen. "It is short-sighted of them," said Christian. "We must find a way to ensure that I am taken into account."

So the two members of the Society of One-Word Signatories sought out Christian's grandmother, Duchess Elizabeth of Mecklenburg, her golden plaits no longer golden, but who in her old age could deny nothing to the grandson she had watched over night and day till his second birthday.

They found her in the castle kitchens, making jam from bottled gooseberries. When she was introduced to Bror she put down her slatted spoon and looked at him intently. "I am glad you were saved," she said.

They helped her measure the sugar and stir the fruit. When it was explained to her that the future King appeared to be forgotten, they saw appear, above her shining, bubbling copper cauldrons, a glitter of amusement in her eyes and a smile on her thin lips. "Forgotten?" she said. "How disgraceful. Forgetfulness we cannot endure by any means. We must draw attention to you."

She left her jam making to the cooks, and the One-Word Signatories followed her to the room she inhabited when she came to Frederiksborg. "Now," she said, "I have something that I have been saving against this day. It was inadvertently dropped by Tycho Brahe when he came here to make his predictions about your life. I should have returned it to him, but some feeling that it might prove useful one day prevented me from doing so. It is a recipe and I believe it might serve your purposes now, provided you are cautious and follow the instructions very carefully, so that you do yourselves no harm. You must bring to it all your skill and ingenuity."

Searching in drawers and cupboards, and sifting through papers and old pieces of knitting, she found at last a piece of parchment, worn a little as if by frequent perusal, and this she handed to Christian. He and Bror stared at it. On the parchment was a drawing of a skyrocket.

"Here you are," said the Duchess Elizabeth. "Now, Bror, I have heard that you are most excellent at practical things. You see here below the drawing is a list of ingredients and instructions for assembling the device?"

Bror immediately felt himself held by the image of the skyrocket's triumphant ascent into the clouds above Denmark. The ingredients and instructions, however, appeared to him as meaningless symbols.

Christian saw his friend's hesitation and at once began to read aloud from Tycho Brahe's faded writing: *Sal petrae, 70 parts; Sulphura, 18 parts; Carb. amorph., 16 parts.*

"That's right," said the Duchess. "The armourers at Slotsholmen will give you what you need. But you must weigh everything very carefully. And listen to me, children. Do not make it very large."

How large was very large? Christian suggested that it should be as tall as he was. Bror told him that such a rocket would blow the roof off the castle.

They decided in the end that it should follow roughly the measurements of Christian's leg, from his knee to his foot, its girth being that of his calf at its widest point. They agreed that such an object would not be too difficult to conceal "so that when we send it into the sky, there will be great amazement and wonder, mixed with a satisfactory amount of fear."

Tycho Brahe had specified for the housing "*a wicker Cage, perfectly turned at the bottom, so that only a small Aperture be left in the very centre, but making sure that a wicker Tail, to act as weight and conduit, be securely attached. This Rocket casing to have a pointed roof of excellently balanced construction. This Cage to be sewn entirely with a fine skin or supple parchment, so that no air be admitted to any part save the Aperture at the base.*"

Christian and Bror Brorson rode out of the gates of Frederiksborg, telling the grooms they were going to tease the wild pigs of the forest with a little archery practice. They made their way first to a basket maker recommended by the palace cooks and thence to a paper merchant, giving orders and leaving drawings and measurements as they went. They were on the road for Copenhagen, intending to be rowed from the city over to Slotsholmen, when the Queen's carriage overtook them. It was beginning to get dark, with the sky to the west full of snow clouds, and from deep within her fur coverings the angry Queen ordered them back.

"There is tomorrow," said Christian, as they turned their horses round. "Tomorrow has one word and it is mine."

The acquiring of parts and ingredients for the skyrocket and working for many hours together on its assembly made Christian and Bror secretive. Christian's young brothers, Ulrich and Hans, were prevented from entering their rooms or taking part in their pastimes. The Society of One-Word Signatories led its own enigmatic existence from early in the morning until late at night.

If the world had forgotten about Christian, so, too, had he momentarily forgotten about the world. And it was to him as if Bror Brorson had always belonged at Frederiksborg and would never leave it. In his dreams, Bror became a magical being. He conceived the notion that, as long as Bror was by his side, he could come to no harm. God and calligraphy had helped him to save Bror's life. Now Bror would watch over him.

When the skyrocket was complete it was smuggled into the Duchess of Mecklenburg's rooms, where she examined it for the smallest hole or rent and, finding none, set it upon a wide windowsill, pointing at the ceiling. "Fine workmanship," she said. "Your father the late King would have been proud of it. Now we are coming to the important moment, and do not think that I have not given it a great deal of thought."

The Duchess Elizabeth chose the date the thirteenth of April. On this day, the *Herredag*, the People's Court over which the future King believed he should be allowed to preside, would be assembling at Copenhagen castle.

"We shall take a closed carriage," said the Duchess, "and we shall order the coachman, though it be broad daylight, to light the lamps, so that we have fire for the taper."

As the day neared, the Society of One-Word Signatories, together with the Duchess of Mecklenburg, composed a declaration, to be read out by Christian in the moments after the skyrocket had disappeared into the ether, while the nobles were still staring with awe at the vapours of its fiery passage. This declaration bade the *Rigsråd* and the judges of the *Herredag* to *"remember their King, Christian IV, and henceforth to allow him Full Participation in the Affairs of the Country, so that nothing will be concealed from him and that he may learn how to arrive at Good Government before he is crowned."* It was set down by Christian in writing so exquisite that Bror, casting his eyes across it, declared it to be "like music."

Christian prayed for a blue sky for the thirteenth of April and his prayers were answered. Early in the morning the two boys, the Duchess, the skyrocket and an earthenware milk jar set off in a black carriage for Copenhagen with the coach lamps flaring in the bright sunshine.

Entering the courtyard of the castle, they saw to their satisfaction a great congregation of nobles assembling there. So excited did the Duchess become at this moment that she felt almost faint and had to fan herself with great vigour while Bror and Christian descended with the skyrocket wrapped in a velvet doublet. She called to the coachman to position the milk jar "a little way from the horses" and then to light a taper from one of the lamps.

Temporarily mistaking the taper for her fan, the Duchess waved it back and forth in front of her face, thus engendering a very lively flame within seconds and exclaiming in fright as she began to feel the heat of it coming near her fingers. Bror immediately understood the nature of the emergency and seized the taper from her while Christian, whose own heart was beating as if in time to a steady fast-paced march, carefully unwrapped the skyrocket and set it on the edge of the jar.

King Christian remembers that at this moment of setting the skyrocket on the jar some of the nobles turned and looked at him, and at Bror holding the burning taper. Then Bror plunged the taper into the jar and lit the fuse. The Duchess, standing near them, said in French, "Ah, bon Dieu!" and the milk jar filled with hissing flame as the fuse began to burn.

In the next moment, the rocket flew.

"Never in the history of time," King Christian is fond of saying, "has any object made by man gone into the space above the earth with such triumphant grace." And indeed, the rocket sped straight up, to where the birds turned on the springtime air, and then higher still, trailing its sulphurous smoke, until at last it exploded with a thunderous reverberation in the empty sky and slowly, like snow turned black to join the national mourning, pieces of charred parchment and tiny carbonated filaments of wicker came falling down upon the heads of the people and all the horses whinnied and reared up in the traces of the carts and carriages. There was gasping and screaming. Bror and the Duchess applauded.

King Christian unfurled his declaration and stepped boldly forward onto the steps of the Court House building.

CONVOY

The *Tre Kroner* is saluted by three guns as she sails into Christiania.

Commissioned by the King and designed by him with the help of Dutch architects, this new town deep in the fjords, at the furthest point of the Skagerrak's reach, is a source of pride to him. It was intended to be an *orderly* place and orderly it has remained. The streets are straight and the citizens, herded into the town from Otter Island, appear willing—as far as King Christian can ascertain—to walk upon the freshly laid cobblestones in straight, unintoxicated lines. The harbour is deep and the ships berthed there tidily arranged. Christiania smells of fish and of resin, and of the salt wind.

A great crowd of people gather around the King as he disembarks from his marvellous ship. The *Tre Kroner* will wait there to sail him home, while the geniuses of the mine supervise the extraction of silver from the hills of the Numedal. Then the ship will return to Christiania and wait a second time. It will wait for the silver to arrive. As the ore is stowed into the hold, soldiers will be put on permanent watch down there in the darkness. In Copenhagen the machinery of the Royal Mint will be oiled and repaired. A new likeness of the King (older, heavier about the jaw and with a look of increased anxiety in the eyes) will be struck, awaiting its impress on hundreds of thousands of dalers.

The people of Christiania press forward in the cold morning.

They want to touch the King. They hold up their children for him to bless. Some of them remember him coming to Norway as a boy with his father, King Frederik, and his mother, Queen Sofie, and visiting the craftsmen's guilds. They recall that the word "shoddy" became fearful and entered their nightmares. But they are impressed on this cold morning by the vastness of him. In his tall boots and his great brocaded cape, he seems like a giant out of the old legends. "Sir!" they call. "Sir! Sir!"

But Christiania is only an assembly station for the mine convoy. In covered wagons and on carts, the King's party now makes its way north-west to the rocky valleys of the Numedal. The two musicians travel in a draughty contraption, clad with canvas and drawn by mules. Krenze, huddled under sacking, remarks: "Winter had almost begun to recede in Copenhagen; that we have caught up with it again is intolerable."

Peter Claire doesn't answer. The German stares at him and under this relentless gaze he feels himself entering once more a state of melancholy, which thickens and deepens as the miles pass and the convoy begins to struggle through drifts of snow. So great now seems to be the distance between himself and his former life that he feels as though a return to it has become impossible. If something of his old longings and dreams remained with him in Copenhagen, here in Norway they have finally deserted him. A man can travel too far from his point of departure and become lost and never find his way back. All that remains to him then is to keep moving forward and pray that hope does not desert him too.

And so, as the mule wagon lurches towards the lonely outpost which is to become the village of the silver mine, and Krenze's unblinking eyes watch him from above the heap of sacking, Peter Claire understands that his life must be lived in its entirety without the love and companionship of his Countess. She will grow old in Ireland. Her daughters will grow up and inherit some of her beauty, but she herself—as she is and always will be in the mind of Peter Claire—will never again stand before him.

He tries to see her clearly, as if for one last look at her, before even the memory of her is snatched away by time. He lays her down beside him in the wagon and strokes her glossy hair, and hears her say, laughing, "Oh, Peter, what a lumpy bed you have brought me to!"

"His heart will burst, you will see," says Krenze suddenly. And the fragile vision of Francesca lying here on the sacking immediately vanishes.

"Whose heart?"

"The King's. For look at what he has to do: hire men; build a town; supply the town; explode the rock; extract the silver; transport the silver back along this infernal route. And then . . . the hardest thing of all."

"What is the hardest thing of all?"

"Ha! You don't know? You, who have been locked in your own reverie?"

"No, I don't think I know."

"Well, keep watch, lute player. You will no doubt eventually come to understand what it is."

"Will you not tell me?"

"No. I merely observe that the King is embarked upon a course which will be fatal to him. Perhaps we shall sail back to Denmark with his body in a casket in the hold of the ship? What do you think, Herr Claire? Then, no doubt, you would be free. Free to return to whatever or whomever it was you have been dreaming about."

"No," says Peter Claire. "I would not be free."

They journey all night, stopping once so that the mules and horses can rest while the cooks light fires in the snow and prepare a meal. King Christian now wears an enormous coat of leather, which creaks as he moves. He drinks three flagons of wine, declares that the snowdrifts illuminated by the fire resemble naked women crouched all along the route "and enticing me with their lovely hips," and has to be helped to his uncomfortable bed in the royal wagon, protesting that sleep no longer gives him rest from care. As he is borne away, Krenze spits into the slush.

Peter Claire is woken by the cart lurching to a halt and the driver shouting to the mules. Krenze also wakes and starts to mumble that there are fleas in the sacking and by morning they will both be plagued with flea-bites, when one of the King's gentlemen opens the door flap of the wagon and, holding a torch aloft, commands Peter Claire to bring his lute and follow him to the King's wagon.

Warm at last in the sacking and reluctant to leave this makeshift bed, Peter Claire nevertheless obediently tugs on his boots, picks up his instrument and follows the man out into the frosty night. Above them is a chill clustering of stars and under these cold heavens the bodies of the poor mules and horses steam, and ice gathers on the beards and eyebrows of the coachmen.

"His Majesty is not well," says the gentleman, whose speech is so perfectly articulated that it might be the voice of an English nobleman. "His stomach plagues him and he is much afflicted by small fears."

The royal wagon smells foetid and the King's breath, when Peter Claire comes near to the pile of brown furs from which His Majesty's troubled head protrudes like a potato from the earth, stinks of vomit. A bowl has been set near him and a servant waits with damp rags and clean cloths. Peter Claire feels his own stomach rebel at the thought of passing the rest of the night in this malodorous confinement, but he strives to master his discomfort and settles himself, as instructed, at the King's side.

"This is how my father died," says King Christian. "From a sickness of the stomach and bowel. I was eleven years old, so I did not witness it, but this is what the physicians told me." Then he takes a sip of water and adds: "Of course he did not have an angel to keep watch."

Peter Claire is about to reply that very few people have any power against disease or the slow failure of the body's internal organs, when the King says: "We are consoled as much by our delusions and imaginings as by any real or verifiable thing. Is that not true, Mr. Claire?"

Peter Claire thinks of the way in which—for a time—he deluded himself about the possibility of a future life with Francesca O'Fingal and says: "Well, Sir, my feeling is that all delusions, if they are to console us, must come in a kind of relay, one after another, so that we do not have to linger too long with one only, lest we suddenly perceive the stark truth of it."

The King gapes at him and a look of terror suddenly crosses his face. He swallows several times, as if mastering the rise of sickness to his throat. The servant offers the bowl to His Majesty and stands ready with his cloths.

But he seems to recover, enough to gesture at Peter Claire's lute, and the gentleman, crouched near them with a candle, whispers: "Play, Mr. Claire. Nothing fierce nor strained."

He tunes the lute, leans forward, as though he might be listening for a sound that is going to come out of the reeking darkness of the wagon, and begins upon an ayre by the German composer Matthias Werrecore. As he plays, he can hear the horses sneezing and stamping outside, but the convoy remains where it is on the road and doesn't move on, as if the whole company of men and mules had paused to listen to this song.

When the piece ends, the King nods and gestures for him to continue with something else. From his time at Cloyne he remembers an Irish pavan with which he used to comfort Francesca O'Fingal, but which he has not played since coming to Denmark, and he has already picked out the opening bars of this before he realises how greatly the sound of this melody is going to deepen his own feelings of melancholy. Held living and breathing in this music is the remembrance of the Countess's head, leaning upon her arm as she listens, and of her brown eyes, large and luminous yet heavy-lidded with desire, caressing him as they watch him play. So all he can do is surrender to this memory and, even as it engulfs him, swear to himself that this will be the last time he will ever think of her.

Just as the pavan ends, shouts from the coachmen and the jingle and chafing of harness are heard, and slowly the convoy begins to move.

To Peter Claire this night seems now to be frozen, not just in the empty spaces of the starlit Numedal, but also in a sudden immobility of time. And when the King pushes the bowl away from him, it is as if he is setting aside his own illness in order to understand what is happening in the mind of the man he has chosen as his angel. Peter Claire lets his lute rest at his side and the two men stare at each other, each with a quantity of questions forming inside his exhausted head.

Kirsten: From Her Private Papers

Since the King's departure into Norway, now that I can no longer see him, nor hear, nor smell him, my mind has felt a great and enduring Solace. In short, I do begin to thrive in his Absence, and when I contemplate my own Reflection in my new (more flattering) Looking-glass, I do see with much satisfaction that I am daily growing more beautiful.

I pray that he will be away for a long time. The digging out of a Silver Mine is a colossal Business (as he was at pains to explain to me) and my Husband—having the disposition to oversee and master everything in the Universe—will, I suppose, wish to stay to supervise the Miners and return with his ship so loaded with silver that it will be at risk from sinking in the Skagerrak.

Perhaps it *will* sink in the Skagerrak?

Perhaps I am to be a Happy Widow before the year is gone?

Oh, dear Lord, but it is not hard to picture the great weight and tonnage of the Silver Ore pulling like boulders at the keel of the ship, while the sails still strive to keep it flying through the wind, but yet they cannot and so the masts begin to tilt and the ship to list and the men below to feel the vessel going down and endeavour for as long as they have breath to take up the Silver and hurl it out into the water, but yet they cannot, they neither, for their breath is gone and they are drowned and white and floating in the sea . . .

Yet if none of this comes to pass, what am I to do?

Last night I had a dream that I walled myself up in a high Tower, with guards at the gate and stationed before the door of my chamber, and only those who knew my secret Password, which was *phantasma*, were admitted into my presence. But alas, everyone, Count Otto included, had forgotten the pestilential Password and could by no means bring it to mind, and so I was left all alone for the remainder of my life to grow old in unremitting Solitude.

(Dreams such as this one are utterly vexing and of no help to me in my predicament whatsoever.)

If only I could pass my days as I pass them now, left alone to do as I will, and every night visited by my Lover, then I should be content.

Otto and I, I here set down, have become so enamoured of Chastisement of each other while we are engaged in the Act that we are veritably addicted to these Practices and cannot resist them, even though our bodies are now showing secret signs of bruises and lacerations. Otto tells me that he can, when he is not with me, come to a state of brimming excitation just by the mere thought of the beatings I shall inflict upon him and he has commanded to be made for us a quantity of silken Whips (the curtain cords of my bedchamber and of its adjoining closet all being used up and frayed into pieces).

I know that when I shall see these lovely Whips I shall so pant to use them upon Otto that I may in my frenzy tear his breeches and find upon my lips some flecks of Foam, such as Mad People do give forth. And from this I see that my enslavement to Otto, and his to me, is indeed a veritable Derangement, as though we two were inhabitants of some Other World where no one walks but us and where no ordinary matters are considered, but only this one Thing, which binds us and which we cannot renounce for anyone or anything upon the Earth.

Our Flayings and Whippings are now refined and perfected further into Absolute Lust by the means of Words. I do not dare to set down what Insults we have screamed out to each other, only to record that if Otto accuses me of being "a verit. wh. & strump., a fornic. troll . . . etc. etc. . . ." these terms are quite habitual, even mild and courteous, and we are gone so far into Abuse of each other's Names that I do declare we need some Dictionary to help us come by some new terms that have not staled with use.

Ah, Otto, my lover, my Only Satisfaction, what is to become of us?

Shall we die from our heavenly Wounds?

When Otto is not with me I like to pass my time in Sleep or, for some part of each day, engage in some gentle Pastime such as Embroidery or games of Shove-Halfpenny or short walks in the gardens with my sweet Floating Woman Emilia.

Her alone, among my Women, can I endure for the reason that *she does not hate me*. I have come to believe that all my Nastiness stems only from this burden of Hate and that were I *loved* and *prized* by the Nobility and the Dowager Queen, and by my own Children, instead of being loathed and detested by every one of them, why then I would be Different and Good, and the name Kirsten would be associated only with Virtue.

For we are, in some measure, what others believe us to be. And because Emilia likes me and believes I am Honourable and Considerate, so then can I indeed be these things when I am with her and show towards her nothing but affection.

Lest her excellent opinion of me be disturbed by news of my Amours with the Count, I have sworn my other Women to secrecy upon this matter and, in giving her a chamber very far and distant from mine, ensured that she does not overhear any Noise which would betray to her what I was doing with the silken Whips and so forth.

My Woman of the Head, Johanna, was the most reluctant to swear, saying impertinently to me: "Madam, I do not see how we are supposed to keep secret a Thing which is not conducted in Secrecy," and this so enraged me that I took up the gold statue of the King on his Tilt-horse and only prevented myself from hurling it at her head by the sudden realisation that this might cause her to fall down utterly Dead. But I would not be surprised to find that she plots against me. I believe she is deluded into thinking, because her appellation is "Woman of the Head," that she is intelligent and cunning, but I do not spy any intelligence in her, only jealousy and spite.

During my embroidery hours with Emilia she has told me something more about the family she has left behind in Jutland and how all her brothers save one are caught in the spell of the vulgar peasant Stepmother Magdalena, and how she fears for Marcus, "the only one who is outside the spell," imagining his melancholy since her coming to Copenhagen. Emilia has such a tender heart that she is more moved by the plight of her brother than I have ever been by any plight of my own Children. And so I, in turn, do feel moved to comfort her. I put a kiss upon her soft hair and call her My Little Pet. And then we make plans together to buy some pretty bells and send them to Jutland for Marcus to put on his pony, so that he knows Emilia has not forgotten him.

And Emilia turns to me with a look of adoration in her grey eyes and says to me, "Madam, you are so kind and thoughtful, I do not know how I can repay you," and I am so astonished that I feel almost like weeping.

So agreeable do I find the presence of Emilia that I have lighted upon an Idea, which may be of assistance to me on that ill-fated day when the King returns from Norway. I have told her that there are certain nights in the month when cruel fears and hauntings do enter my mind and at such times I like to have near me some gentle person with whom, if it moves me, I can hold Midnight Conversations.

Thus, I have arranged it that, when I have my Menses and the Count does not come to me, a little cot is put in the chamber next to mine (through which all who wish to enter my own room must pass) and Emilia sleeps there at my door. I have told her to admit no one. I have said to her, "Emilia, you must promise me that not a soul in the land—not even the King, were he to request it—shall be allowed to come past you on these nights, because my mind is horribly discomfited and I cannot endure to converse with anyone in Denmark except you."

And so she brushes my hair and warms my bed with a warming pan, that the pains of the Menarche may be lessened by the soothing heat, and I see her arms going about these tasks so lovingly that I am moved to stroke them and find that her skin is as soft as a child's. "Emilia," I say, "I hope you will not leave me."

In the night, if I wake with my brain boiling with Terror, remembering anew my Great Predicament with regard to Otto and the King, I cry out and Emilia comes to me with a candle and we send for hot milk and hazelnut cake and build up the fire in my room and furl the drapes against the cold night air. Emilia, without showing any disgust, helps me to change my bloody rags. And then we talk of the Cruelties and the Nastiness of the world and how, in the corridors of this very palace, whispers against me may be heard passing from mouth to mouth.

An Ordinary Household

The herring fleet is going out.

Softly, into a calm sea, with the wind blowing from the south, the fishing boats set sail from Harwich quayside, where a few people, the early risers of the little town, stand and wave until the vessels are lost to sight in the morning mist.

The people wander away, each to his own house or place of work, each to his own task, until only one man is left standing there, as the sun rises higher and gulls begin to cluster and circle, following the boats, and the church clock of St. Benedict the Healer strikes seven.

The man is the Reverend James Whittaker Claire. He doesn't move, but continues to look out to sea, as though he planned to wait out all the hours until the herring fleet's return. But he is not thinking about herrings. What occupies his mind is the future. He is fifty years old and his hair and beard are grey. He has passed the night in a sleepless despondency that he did not anticipate and already he has been standing here for an hour, since well before sunrise, in the hope that the salt air and the banter of the fishermen would act as a balm upon his agitated spirits.

His wife, Anne, and his daughter, Charlotte, are at home in the vicarage and he knows that they will be going about their morning tasks, overseeing the baking of bread and the laying of the table for breakfast, calling to the hens in the yard and scattering corn. He understands that these women of his are happy and serene on this February morning and he longs mournfully to share in this serenity, but he cannot. He rubs his eyes and turns away from his contemplation of the sea. He begins to walk towards his church.

The previous evening Charlotte's suitor, Mr. George Middleton, had come to see the Reverend Claire to ask for her hand in marriage.

George Middleton is a Norfolk landowner with a large estate at Cookham, near Lynn, and an income of a thousand pounds a year. A boisterous man in his thirties with a loud laugh and rough handshake, he is a good match for the daughter of a vicar. What is more, Charlotte has declared that she loves him "more than any being in Norfolk or beyond" and when James Claire gave his blessing to the match, Charlotte flung her arms round his neck and declared she was "the most fortunate girl in England." Her cheeks were pink and her eyes shining. George Middleton whirled her, laughing, into his arms.

The wedding will take place in the autumn. Already, Anne Claire has begun upon a quantity of lists. The business of the wedding will occupy the minds of both women from dawn to sunset. And James Claire is happy for them, doesn't begrudge them one second of their contentment. Yet, in his own heart, he feels a misery so deep that, as he walks along, it almost causes him to stumble.

He has seen his future.

He has seen the mornings empty of Charlotte. He has seen the afternoons passing in unaccustomed silence. He has seen his congregation assembled at Evensong and, though he searches for his daughter's face among them, he knows that she is not there. He has seen himself grow old in mourning for his departed children.

While Charlotte remained, there was yet some distraction, some compensation for the absence of Peter. Sometimes James Claire has cruel dreams of his son lost in a storm, drowned in a frozen northern sea, or simply falling into an icy forgetfulness so that all memory of England and his former home seeps silently from his mind.

But, with his daughter near him, reminding him that Peter's love for music always did and always would triumph over his father's wish that he follow him into the Church, why then James Claire could endure his absence. Only now, in the certain knowledge that, when next winter comes Charlotte will no longer be part of his household, does the loss of Peter, stretching into a future the duration of which no one can predict, feel intolerable.

He and Anne will be alone with the hens and the apple orchard and their daily prayers. Charlotte and George Middleton will visit them from Norfolk from time to time, but the era of the family is past. Long ago, before either Peter or Charlotte was born, James Claire wept over a child which lived a single day and died without a murmur as night fell. Now, although he feels his misery to be a selfish, unwarranted thing, he cannot rid himself of the notion that a second dramatic darkness is about to fall.

With the bread baked and the butter and preserves set out on the table, Anne and Charlotte wait for James Claire to return from the quayside. They are hungry and their servant, Bessie, waits obediently by the stove, ready to coddle the eggs, but they do not particularly notice their hunger nor the time passing as they sit at a bureau and write the wonderful words *Trousseau List* on a plain piece of paper.

"Mother," says Charlotte, "when we have done this, you know we must send a letter to Peter informing him that I am to become Mrs. George Middleton."

"Yes indeed," says Anne Claire. "And I wonder if he will have leave to come home. That he should play at the wedding would gladden all our hearts, especially your father's."

"I hope he will like George," says Charlotte, "and that George will see eye to eye with him."

"Eye to eye," remarks Anne. "A strange choice of expression, my dearest, for do you not remember how Peter's eyes, so blue as they are, seem to reflect in them some other place, where it has always been hard to follow him?"

Charlotte thinks for a moment, imagining her brother, whose beauty she used to envy with ferocious pain, standing at the window, with sunlight falling onto his hair, and telling her that he was leaving for Ireland, and then later returning and announcing that his time in Ireland was over and now he was going to Denmark to join the royal orchestra.

At first she had been glad, then sorry at last, finding that she missed him. Later, after she had met Mr. George Middleton, she was indifferent to Peter's absence and all she hopes for now is that he will come home for her magnificent day. "Yes," she says to her mother, "of course I remember that. But it is only a look. It doesn't mean that he couldn't take part in a game of bowls with George on the lawns of Cookham, does it?"

Under *Trousseau List*, Anne Claire has already written:

12 pair silk stockings
12 pair linen thread stockings
5 plain linen petticoats
2 plain stuff jackets for morning wear

She pauses and says: "Bowls at Cookham? Why, no, Charlotte. Not at all."

From Countess O'Fingal's Notebook, *La Dolorosa*

On the day that Peter Claire arrived in our household I heard larks in the heather. I knew that spring had returned.

I had sent for a musician, following my father's advice, but the musician I imagined was elderly with a slow gait, wearing a black coat. When I saw Peter Claire standing in the hall, he took away all my breath.

It was as if he belonged to some world beyond time where all living things had at last attained perfection. At certain moments in my former life I had glimpsed other inhabitants of this divine place: a grey horse that stood in a meadow a few miles from Bologna; a ragged child watching me from behind a market stall in Florence; a young woman seated by a fountain, combing her hair. And I had always been certain that their habitation among us here on the earth would be brief, that God would be jealous of their absence and reach down His hand and take them to Him again before they had grown old or known unkindness or truly seen what alteration suffering can bring to a living countenance.

When Peter Claire had rested from his journey from England, I made known to him the bare facts of our tragedy. "Believe me, Mr. Claire," I said, "when I tell you that my husband was once a good and honourable man. Now he will appear to you as cruel, as violent, as a lunatic soul . . . Yet I cannot believe that the person he once was is lost for ever. He will return, if only you will be patient and help him with all the musical knowledge and skill I have been told that you possess."

Peter Claire looked at me kindly. This look of kindness was so troubling to me that I felt a blush come to my face and I lowered my head, pretending to search for my fan in the folds of my skirt, so that he would not see how much I was affected by him.

"Countess O'Fingal," he said, "I am more glad than you can know to learn of the task that I am to accomplish. Always, since childhood, have I loved music and yet I have never been able to say precisely *why* I feel this love. My father, who is a minister, tells me that what it expresses is a reaching out, in the soul of man—and in my soul therefore—towards God, and indeed it is this, I am sure.

"Yet the '*Why*' lingers. It is joined very frequently by a '*What.*' *What* is music and *Why* do I neglect all other things so that I may give my life to this alone? But now I see that if by some miracle I may return your husband to the paradise he glimpsed in his dream, then all my work until now will not have been in vain, but on the contrary will have been but a preparation for this extraordinary moment of revelation."

"Oh, pray," I said fervently, looking deeply now into the blue of Peter Claire's eyes. "Pray this may be so."

Hope is a strange commodity.

It is an opiate.

We swear we have relinquished it and, lo, there comes a day when, all unannounced, our enslavement to it returns.

So it was with Johnnie O'Fingal and with me.

On the evening of Peter Claire's arrival I persuaded Johnnie to go into the library, where he saw at once that the padlock on the virginals had been removed and the instrument cleaned and made ready to be played upon.

Without a word he sat down and I told him gently that there had arrived a young man who held the key to the ending of all our sorrows. "Tonight," I said, "he is going to play for us on the lute. We shall hear music again in this silent house! And then, tomorrow, you and he will recommence your work. Mr. Claire is very skilled at composition and he will be the means through which you are returned to happiness."

Johnnie looked up at me and it was at that moment that I saw rekindled in his clouded eyes the sudden flicker of hope. It trembled there. I stroked his exhausted head and laid his hands gently one upon the other in his lap. I sat beside him, and we waited while Peter Claire entered the room, bowed to us, paused to fine-tune his instrument and then began to play.

I do not know what song it was that he played. It was a fragment of great sweetness, seeming sweeter no doubt because of the quiet and loneliness in which we had existed for so long. Johnnie did not take his eyes from Peter Claire all the while that the song lasted, seeming transfixed by the sight of his hands that drew from the lute this patterning of sound for which, in nature, there is no equivalent or model and for the true understanding of which the young lutenist had told me he was still searching.

When the playing ceased, Johnnie sat very still. I saw that his eyes were brimming with tears. These tears he let fall, and did not wipe them away.

The following day the two men began work.

I gathered the children to me and asked for the pony cart to be brought. With Maria, Vincenzo, Luca and Giulietta, I set forth in the April sunshine to make a tour of the estates and tell the people that I believed their sufferings and ours would soon be at an end.

As always, the tenants received us with kindness, yet beneath that kindness I knew there was justifiable anger, for the ruin that we saw that day on the farms and in the dwellings was so very visible to me and to my children that, out of cowardice and fear, we abandoned the tour and drove instead to the river, where we ate the simple picnic I had brought for us and where we remained until evening, playing games with sticks and stones, telling stories, watching the moorhens at work upon their nests and the coots diving for fish, and the first gnats and flies of the summer hatch out among the sunbeams.

We returned at dusk. We crept into the house, listening for the one sound we longed to hear—an ayre so strange and magical we would recognise it as the divine composition of Johnnie's dream. But the house was as hushed as the tomb. We stood in the hall, not daring to go anywhere in case we might be disturbing that fragile moment of silence that precedes some great epiphany. "Mama," Giulietta whispered, "perhaps Papa's lost music is of the kind that no one can hear?"

I stroked her hair. "Perhaps it is, my dearest," I said. "I had not thought of that."

At this moment we heard the library door open. Giulietta put her hand in mine. Johnnie O'Fingal strode into the hall. On finding us there, he paused a moment to stare at us—as if we were visitors to the house that he had not expected—and then swept past us and up the stairs. We heard the door to his room open and close upon him.

Peter Claire told me that the morning had passed quite well. From the few bars of the remembered melody that Johnnie could play for him, Peter tried to hear in his heart the continuation that would be at one with the beginning. He arrived at length at three of these continuations. He made notations for them and played them both upon the virginals and upon the lute. Johnnie listened attentively. He knew that none of them corresponded to what he had heard, but he did not immediately reject them. He knew that the very *fact* that a continuation could exist was important and so he let the lutenist experiment with them for a while.

Then, in the afternoon, he grew impatient with them. He declared that all were "as cold as the moon compared with the sun that was in my mind" and refused to listen to them any more. He paced the library, tearing books from the shelves and throwing them to the ground. He opened the window and let out a wailing into the bright afternoon.

Peter Claire began to be afraid.

He started again—on a fourth continuation. Johnnie's anger abated. He sat still once more and listened. He picked up some of the books from the floor and returned them to the shelves. He admitted there was "some beauty" in this fourth continuation and thus began to copy it, note by note, upon the virginals, while Peter Claire struggled to find pleasing harmonies on the lute. They worked together until early in the evening when, at the moment of my return from the river with the children, Johnnie decreed that with each playing of it this fourth continuation grew more and more earthbound and stale. He ordered Peter to abandon it. By now, both men were too tired to go on.

In the space of one month, fifty-nine continuations were begun and abandoned. As time went on the number of hours Johnnie was able to work diminished. In mid-afternoon he would walk out of the library, go to his room and fall into a heavy sleep that would last until the following morning.

And so a new phase of our story had its beginning here. For, once the children had gone to bed, I found myself very frequently alone with the lutenist. I invited him to dine with me. After dinner, we sat by the fireside and I told him about my life in Bologna with my father the paper merchant and he told me about his childhood in Harwich and the sorrows of his father the minister at his son's refusal to follow him into the Church. The company of Peter Claire was so pleasing to me that hours would pass and seem as moments.

As the evenings grew lighter, we took to walking together after supper in the perfumed air of the Maytime dusk. We saw the apple blossom and the cherry blossom holding within themselves their white light in the diminishing day. We went down to the sea.

We discussed Johnnie O'Fingal's dream and the fragile chance that this riddle, which had caused so much suffering, would ever be solved. I told Peter Claire that I wished him to stay on, no matter how distant that solution might seem. I said to him: "My only hope is in you."

And so it was that, even as we talked about my husband's plight, with the waves breaking and gathering, breaking and gathering, before us and the colours vanishing from the world, we put our arms around each other and stood together, not moving, only feeling the heartbeat of the other and the welling up of a passion which we knew to be against all laws of loyalty and right feelings, and which must therefore never find its ultimate expression.

We did not even kiss. My longing to kiss and to be kissed by the exquisite mouth of Peter Claire (five years my junior and in my pay as teacher to my husband) was as great as any longing I had known in my thirty years on this earth. Yet I did not yield to it and nor did Peter force me to it. It was as if we both knew that with a single kiss our mouths would breathe the fatal syllables of the word "surrender."

Forwards into history went the story of the explosion of Christian's skyrocket in the courtyard of the *Herredag*. After it, the nobility did not dare, any longer, to ignore the uncrowned King. Indeed, so uncertain were they about what he would do next that they wanted to keep him within their sights at all times. In their jostling for power and aggrandisement, they now regarded him as a wild creature. They did not know which way he would dart, nor how many of them he might pursue into the briar patch of disgrace. For they had not reckoned with their future King's stubborn disposition and his troubling imagination that seemed at this time, since the saving of Bror Brorson's life, to take flight into realms where nobody could follow it. He did not appear to see the world as it was, but as his mind reconstituted it. One perspicacious member of the *Rigsråd* likened the boy King to "an artist who works upon an invisible canvas."

At one session of the *Herredag* documents known to be the work of a forger were shown to Christian. He was told that the date inscribed within the watermark pre-dated the founding of the paper mill from whence the document supposedly originated. Members of the *Herredag* prided themselves on thus revealing a forgery through their detailed knowledge of the nation's commerce and sat around the large table wearing smiles of satisfaction upon their faces. The forger, dressed in ragged clothes and with his hands manacled together, stood haplessly before them.

Christian held the forged documents up to the light. He let his mind float along the edges of the counterfeit watermark. He saw only its extraordinary perfection. He wished his father alive again so that he could show it to him as an example of supreme Danish craftsmanship, devoid of all shoddiness. He turned to the assembled nobility and said: "I find this work to be very beautiful and true." Then he looked towards the forger in his rags and said: "Punishment will serve no purpose. You have a skill, Sir, and will serve your country with that. A position will be found for you at the royal printers and you shall begin work there tomorrow morning."

These ideas, these fancies, these provocations: where did they come from?

Word passed among the nobles that Christian absorbed them from his friend Bror Brorson, who had no learning and could not write properly, and who saw the world through ignorant eyes.

Bror was still at Frederiksborg because Christian refused to be parted from him. Those courtiers who hunted with the boys marvelled at Bror's daring on a horse, at his perseverance in the chase, at his disdain of the scratches and wounds he sustained while in pursuit of the boar and at his extraordinary beauty. He now wore his fair hair long and, as he rode, it would fly out behind him. His skin was brown from the hours he spent in the open air. His eyes, once shadowed by illness in the cellar of the Koldinghus, now reflected the blue of the sky. But as time passed the whispering of the nobility against him grew louder. Bror did not hear it. Christian did not hear it. Yet it was in the wind.

And so another case came before the *Herredag* over which the young King-in-waiting presided. The accused man was a tailor's assistant. Over weeks and months this man had succeeded in manufacturing a lead stamp which could set down upon any paper a perfect rendition of his employer's signature. Making use of the stamp, the tailor's assistant wrote letters and despatched money orders to numerous cloth merchants, commanding bales of wool and fustian. The cloth he sold (at favourable prices) to a French seamstress making costumes for circus performers and travelling players. And with the money thus obtained he acquired, in secret, a wild Arabian stallion.

"A wild Arabian stallion?" said King Christian to the man. "How strange a thing to buy with ill-gotten gold. What can a man such as yourself, who has no park in which to ride it and no groom to undertake its breaking, want with such an animal?"

"Nothing," said the tailor's assistant. "I wanted nothing from it except to go and look at it. I have dreamed of Arabian horses all my life, not to ride them, but only to contemplate them, because they are beautiful."

Christian heard the members of the *Herredag* dissolve into spluttering laughter, but he himself let no smile pass across his face. "What is the name of your horse?" he asked.

"It has no name, Your Majesty," said the man. "I have tried to think of one, but no word in our language presents itself to me as fine enough."

"And if we send you to prison, what is to become of it? Who will feed it and care for it?"

At this moment, the tailor's assistant prostrated himself upon his knees. Would King Christian himself not take the beautiful creature as a gift and let it be schooled in the park at Frederiksborg and let it bring him honour and glory at the tilt ring?

The courtroom grew silent. The nobles of the *Herredag* stared at Christian in horrified anticipation that some new and ever more lunatic perversion of justice was about to escape his lips. And—as they perceived the matter—they were right.

"The name of the horse shall be Bror," announced the boy King. "Let him be taken to Frederiksborg this very day. And if you sign your promise to return the stolen money to your master, you shall be free."

The *Herredag* erupted in fury. It was almost as if a second sky-rocket had exploded in the grand hall, sending burning ash down upon every head.

The following day, very early in the morning, while Bror Brorson lay asleep, Queen Sofie entered his room. She jolted him awake. "Bror," she said. "Get up. I am commanded by Christian to tell you that you are to ride at once with the groom to Copenhagen, where a great surprise awaits you. You must not wake a soul, but go down into the yard where the groom is waiting. Put on your hunting clothes and take your whip and that is all."

Bror did not know what time it was, but only understood that it was very early because the sun was not yet risen above the lake.

He did as he was ordered and rode out of the gates of Frederiks-borg as the palace clock struck five.

On the road to the city, in the hamlet of Glostrup, his compan-ion the groom reined in his horse and Bror saw that one of the royal coaches was waiting there under the shade of a linden tree. The groom told Bror that this coach would carry him the rest of the journey, so the boy dismounted and got into the coach, and watched as the groom turned and led the two horses back in the di-rection of the palace.

But the coach never arrived at Copenhagen. It carried Bror Brorson back to his home in Funen, and many years would pass be-fore King Christian was permitted to see him again.

Letters were sent from Frederiksborg, an extraordinary quantity of letters in which Christian declared that he was lonely in the world "without my dearest friend and fellow One-Word Signatory, Bror." But no reply ever came. And Christian did not really expect one, knowing as he did that Bror was incapable of writing it.

AT THE *ISFOSS*

The convoy has arrived in the icy valleys of the Numedal.

Every house within five miles of the mine has been requisi-tioned by the royal party. The former occupants of these places now sleep in their hay lofts or in their barns with their animals. They puzzle over their fate. The King has promised them that they will share in the silver, which is to be hacked and blasted from the rock. Their dreams alternate between their shining future and their lost past.

The largest house, the one King Christian occupies, stands near a waterfall. But it is a waterfall that does not move. It is frozen. The King stares at this phenomenon. He tries to imagine in what pas-sage of time the alteration from roaring water to silent ice occurs. His mind wakes up the cataract and sees the unstoppable forward motion of the river, carrying everything with it as it reaches the lip and falls and keeps on falling. At this moment in its history it is as though the river will move and fall for ever.

Then Christian imagines tiny crystals forming on the surface of the water as the temperature in the air begins to drop and all along the banks the willow branches are furred with frost. The surface crystals become larger. They are like glass and they break into pieces in the downrush of the rapids and are thrown upwards for a second with the white foam, before falling back and being carried onwards by the lower stream.

Motion is slowed as the glass crystals expand and deepen, and icicles form at the lip of the fall. In the tiny icicles lies the coming metamorphosis of the waterfall into the frozen cataract, the *Isfoss*. They acquire thickness, length and weight. The water is transparent clay, moulding them, layer upon layer, and as the layers accumulate, so the sound diminishes. Now, in the surrounding cradle of hills, the roar of the river has become muffled. The human ear has to strain to hear it. And then, in the space of a single night, it falls silent.

All this Christian turns and measures in his imagination. Time after time he sets forth the sequence. And yet it continues to amaze him. There is a part of his mind which still cannot adequately explain it.

Krenze had remarked to Peter Claire that the King's heart would "burst" among all the travails that awaited him in the Numedal. And it has been true that since the arrival of the convoy he has scarcely ever been still, but always rushing from one place to another, supervising the hiring of men, the acquisition of timber and tools and horses, the design of new buildings, and the first encroachment of the life-blood of the hills, the cutting of the veins of silver ore.

Christian's hands caress and explore the rock. To the geniuses of the mine he remarks that "nature locks away her secrets like a courtesan, to tease us with longing" and to the miners with their picks and chisels he thunders: "Break up the mountain! Tear out its heart! I want the Numedal here in my arms!"

The King barely sleeps. At night he lies on a wooden bed and listens to the wolves howling, and feels intensely the pain of his love for Kirsten, which was once reciprocated and is no longer, and all that he can see in his future with her is sensual craving unsatisfied and affection tearing at his heart.

He does not know that Kirsten has taken a lover. The palace servants wish to protect him from unnecessary suffering. No rumour of the flayings with silken whips and the foul-mouthing of Kirsten by Otto and Otto by Kirsten has reached his ears. But he does not need to know these things to understand that Kirsten Munk has repudiated his love and is bound upon some other course. He wishes he were a wolf, with a wolf's habitation in a forest under the stars and the voice of a wolf to howl with.

He sends for Peter Claire.

The lutenist looks pale and does not sing well because he has a cold.

Like the King, Peter Claire stares at the *Isfoss*.

Unlike Christian, he can imagine it in no other way than in its present soundless and immobile form. To his lost Countess he writes an imaginary letter: *My dear Francesca, I have arrived at a place where time has stopped at winter and will never move on. I call it the Place of the Frozen Cataract. I do not know how long I shall survive here.*

He has dreams of his mother's baking in the vicarage kitchen, of the quayside at Harwich on a summer morning as the herring fleet comes in, of his sister's gaiety and fondness for dancing, of his father in his robes, moving towards his pulpit and looking down upon his congregation, and searching for his son's face and never finding it. And words spoken by his father return to him. "Peter," says the Reverend James Claire, "when you find yourself at odds with life, strive not to fight with fortune but fight instead with your own weaknesses."

And so he resolves to endure. He and Krenze try to warm themselves by playing jigs and capers, and moving in small circles as they play. The owner of the cottage where he sleeps likes these lively tunes and is amused by the sight of the German and the Englishman cavorting in his yard. Soon afterwards, he brings Peter Claire a coverlet of rabbit skins to lay upon his bed.

Not infrequently, his sleep is broken by a summons to the King.

One night he finds Christian alone and seated by a dying fire. His elflock has been unbraided and a few strands of limp brown hair hang down almost to his waist. As Christian talks, he runs his hands through the hair, combing it incessantly, as though this combing of his lock soothed his mind. "I sent for you because my head is boiling with confusion," he says. "So can you tell me . . . you who resemble the angels of my boyhood dreams, who resemble a friend once dear to me . . . can you tell me how confusion is to be unravelled in the mind of man?"

Peter Claire looks into the embers of the fire, like one expecting the answer to lie there in the ash. He knows that he must speak, but moments pass and he can find nothing to say and he feels the King begin to grow restless and cross. Then he remembers the King's lament that no great philosophers remained in Denmark and so he says: "If Monsieur Descartes were sitting with you now, Sir, he would say that confusion can be unravelled only by reducing the complex to the simple."

The King looks startled, as though, after all, he had not expected an answer to his question. "Ah," he says. "Yes. So he did say that. But his method: what was his method? I once knew it and now it has gone from me."

"Well, Your Majesty," says Peter Claire, "he suggests that we should reject as false everything that we cannot directly know. He had in mind those things we believe we have learned, but are unable to verify."

"Now I remember why I had forgotten the Cartesians! For what is truly verifiable, I ask you? Only mathematics! Two plus two will always and evermore equal four, but how is this going to resolve what boils in my brain?"

"It cannot. But if you can come by *one incontrovertible thing*, something with the manifest truth of two plus two or of the *cogito* itself, then, based upon this one incontrovertible thing and proceeding only from it, you might be able to find a pathway through what at present seems confusing."

There is a long silence in the low-beamed room. No wolf is heard, no cry of an owl, no human sound. The fire has lost all its former shape and structure, and is only a heap of cinders with a red glow at its heart.

The King turns towards Peter Claire and says: "The one incontrovertible thing is my love for my wife, Kirsten. Let us call it *Cogito ergo amo*. I first glimpsed her when she was seventeen, in church, and I asked God to give her to me and He did. I was thirty-eight. Her hair was the colour of tea and her skin was white and her mouth tasted of cinnamon. Danish law would not allow her to become my Queen, but I married her as soon as I could, and no man has ever had a honeymoon more sweet or more beautiful.

"I gave her twelve children. For fourteen years I have been faithful to her and, even in the darkness of my thoughts, mused only upon her. Today, when I see her, when I come to her room, I am as moved by her as I was before she became my bride. I love her like a child, like a dear mother, like a mistress, like a wife. I cannot number for you the times I have rejoiced that she is mine. When I run my hand along the silver veins in these valleys, it is not only Denmark's coffers that my mind replenishes, it is Kirsten's private treasure store. When matters of State do not occupy my mind, all that remains in it is my longing to be with Kirsten, not merely to hold her in my arms, but to set her gently on my knee, or walk with her in the orchards, or play cribbage with her or hear her laughter. And this longing never leaves me.

"But now the confusion enters in. For I know that Kirsten no longer has any feeling for me. No tender feeling. Only a mood of fury against me. She will not let me come to her. Sometimes, God forgive me, I take her against her will, reasoning that I am the King and her husband, and she cannot deny me. But that resolves nothing. It leaves a bitter gall. And yet my love for her refuses to leave me. My love, my passion and my longing. When the wolves cry in these hills, I hear this same sound in me. So tell me if you can, my friend, what I am to do."

The fire is grey, its heat gone. There is ice on the windows. Peter Claire shifts his position on the hard chair and says after a while: "My experience in the great question of love is very limited, Sir. But I do perceive that love and an answering absence of love are two elements in opposition. What my father would say, I believe, is that we should not strive to alter the opposing element, because this is futile. What we should strive to alter is the element that we ourselves are. Thus, if we discover, as seems to be the case with you, that our love is not reciprocated, we should cease to yearn for this reciprocation, but strive instead to dismantle the love in our own hearts. And then in time the confusion will be unravelled and on both sides there will be quietness."

The King stares intently at Peter Claire. It is as if, in the dim light of the low room, he is trying to ascertain that the colour of the lutenist's eyes is still blue. Then, after some moments, he says: "I believe I am calm now. I believe I am at peace." And he begins, very slowly and carefully, to replait his hair.

LETTER TO HIS DAUGHTER EMILIA FROM JOHANN TILSEN

My dear Emilia,

This day we received the gift of bells you sent to Marcus for his pony's bridle.

Though no doubt you intended a kindness to your brother, I must inform you that we cannot, as matters stand at present, let him have any knowledge of this offering and the trinket must remain hidden from him. It may be that, upon his birthday, it shall be given to him, but I shall then take the precaution of informing him that the bells are a present from me or from Magdalena.

If you are somewhat astonished by this and find it to have about it the smell of deception, let me explain to you that Marcus continues to cause this household a great quantity of displeasure and our patience with him is beginning to be frayed.

Though it has been explained to Marcus numberless times that you are in Copenhagen and that you will not be returning to Jutland, he stubbornly persists in wandering about the fields and woods of the estate, supposedly in search of you. Not merely this, but he seems so very distracted by this fruitless quest that he has become grievously inattentive to the life going on within this house and refuses almost all conversation with me, with Magdalena and with his brothers. He eats very poorly and has developed the distressing habit of vomiting up his food almost as soon as it is swallowed. Already, two servants have gone because they could not endure the odious task of incessantly cleaning up what Marcus has spewed out.

From this you will see that I have acted wisely in not giving any token from you to Marcus. I have told him that you pass your existence very far from this foyer, in what I have termed another world.

I have also informed him that if he does not begin to participate sensibly in the life of this family, he will find me unkind. Already, at night-time, we have had to take the precaution of tying him to his cot by means of a harness, lest he stray into the night and is drowned in the lake or mauled by a bear in the forest. I do not derive any pleasure from doing this, but I am a man driven almost insane by his youngest son and I must endeavour to bring matters to some sensible conclusion.

Please, therefore, send no more gifts or indeed letters or tokens of any kind to Marcus. I believe that he will only cease this search for you once he is convinced that you are too far away to be found.

Otherwise and in all respects, matters go well in your former home. Your elder brothers Ingmar and Wilhelm do daily grow into ever finer and more handsome young men and I am very proud of them.

Your dear stepmother, Magdalena, is with child again. I pray that this baby may be brought safely into the world. I ask God to give me a girl, so that when I am old I shall have this sweet young daughter to take your place.

From your affectionate father,
Johann Tilsen

Oh, Lord, but Men do Vex me and make me tear my hair with fury!

Do any—save my Exquisite Count—think aught of anything but their own Selfish Needs and Desires? Have any within them the littlest ounce of pure and tender kindness?

Were I a Real Queen, I declare I would occupy some Strategically Placed Castle and, from its safety, fire cannonballs upon each and every Man who attempted to come near me! And I do not jest. I declare I do despise them all.

Today, my sweet Emilia showed to me a letter from her Father that is the Vilest Document I have ever laid eyes upon. This treacherous and cowardly Father, all foolishly enamoured of his New Wife and being under her Spell, has been ordered to Cut Off his daughter and to pretend that she is no longer a part of his family. I would like to take the neck of Herr Tilsen and wring it with my bare hands! I would like to hurl him out of the topmost window of the Palace and see his heart split open on the cruel stone below! How can he treat Emilia so? And I am resolved: *He Shall Not.*

Immediately upon being shown the Letter and finding Emilia very white with terror and with grief, I held her to me and tried to comfort her and said to her: "Emilia, this sinful Father has reckoned without Kirsten Munk, and now he shall learn the folly of this. We shall today go into the City and purchase another set of bells. These I will despatch by Royal Messenger to your Father's house, with the Order that they be given, in the presence of the Messenger, to your brother Marcus, who is to be informed that they are from you."

Emilia attempted to speak, saying, "Oh, no, Madam, you must

not do this," but I cut her off and declared: "I shall do more! Every week from this time forth, we shall send a gift to Marcus. We shall send toys and hoops and learning books. We shall send kittens and birds and affectionate snakes. We shall send hats and buckles and clogs. No Saturday shall pass but there is a present from you and tender words from your pen to comfort him."

Emilia looked up at me, as though I might be some Wonder she had never before seen on this earth. She was lost for any word and so I continued to speak, finding my head very full and Brimming with Plans to punish her Father and show him that no man shall cast out a daughter in this way and not pay some price for it.

"I have another idea," I said. "My Mother, Ellen Marsvin, is a neighbour of your Father's and, indeed, it was she who found you and brought you into this position as my Woman—as you know. Very well, then, I shall command my Mother to be my Spy and yours in this matter. She shall pay visits to your Father's house and report to us how things go on and in what state of misery Marcus is to be found. And if it be discovered that things go very badly with him, why then we shall order that he be brought to Rosenborg and we shall nurture him here, with my own Children, and in this way you shall see him every day of your life and he shall be reassured that you are in This World and in no Other!"

I was so boiling with rage against this degenerate and loathsome Johann Tilsen that I felt faint and was forced to swoon upon my bed, where Emilia tried to revive me with a peach cordial. We wept together and lamented bitterly the Power that all Men do possess, and so we proceeded then to the other Matter that now concerns me and that is the King's return.

I am heavy with foreboding.

Such is the fragile nature of my mind that it contrives to put from it—as though buried under Snow—those things which cause it the greatest terror. In this way had I suffocated all thought of what shall become of me and of my delirium with Otto when the King has returned to Copenhagen. It is as if I had decided he would never return, but would remain for ever in the Numedal and there die in due time and never again come near me nor touch me nor say my Name.

But I was wrong. He will be home before the summer is truly come. And it is not only the dread I have of Otto's absence that fills me with anxiety. There is another more Grave Matter. The time of my Menses has come and gone, and there is no sign of them. I fear that I am carrying Otto's child. And if this be so, how shall it be squared with the King, who has not been permitted into my bed for many weeks and months? By the time the linden trees are all in leaf, I shall be Big. And so at last it must come to the King's knowledge that I have a Lover. And I shall be cast out. Or, worse than this, I shall come to a terrible end. Each and every Nobleman's Voice will be raised against me and a Petition will be got up that I be put to Death.

All this I decide to confess to Emilia.

I had not intended her to know about Otto, in case this knowledge made her turn against me and begin to Hate me, as does everyone else in this city. But I had to confess my fears to someone. And I reasoned that she, being a person of great kindness and loyalty, would strive not to condemn me, but rather remain by my side in my Trouble and try to bring me comfort.

I wept a great quantity of tears. "Emilia," I said, "do not harden your heart against me, I beg you! All mortals are weak when it comes to the great matter of Love, and I have been a loyal wife to the King and never strayed until this moment, but my Passion for Otto and his for me is such that we cannot subdue it by any means, and look how cruelly, now, I am to be punished."

Emilia's face was very pale. This second shock followed the other of her Father's Letter. And, seeing this pallor of hers, the idea came to me to conjoin the two Matters in one, thus binding her (quite cunningly) to me, so that we may each be constrained to succour and support the other.

I dried my tears. "I will do all that can be done for Marcus," I said, "and this I swear upon my wretched life. But so must you promise to help *me*, Emilia, for I have no one else here but you. You are my Woman and I your only Refuge, now that you are sundered from your family. Say that you will not condemn me and then we shall discover together some way out of this Maze of Sad Things."

She sat down upon a small chair. "Madam," she said after a little moment of quiet, with a worried frown coming and going upon her forehead, "whatever may befall you, I shall serve you."

"Do you speak true, Emilia?" I asked. "Swear to me that you speak true."

"I speak true," she said. "Upon my Mother's Life."

GUARDIANS OF THEIR TREASURE HOUSES

The Anti-Knitting Edict is a distant memory. The golden plaits are gone. Dowager Queen Sofie, mother of Christian, has shut herself up in Kronborg Castle at Elsinore on the Kattegat Sound, where she has only to raise her head and stare across the water to find Denmark's old enemy, Sweden, staring back at her. The stare is grey and unyielding. She knows that war will return.

But in her old age, what can she do about war? What can she do about anything in the world? For years, she has been accumulating her answer. It has been stockpiled in iron vaults deep underground, and every morning Dowager Queen Sofie takes up a heavy key and makes her way down, down into the darkness, and opens the door to her treasure house.

Gold has no perfume. Nothing of it escapes into the surrounding air. It does not wear nor spoil with time. And yet, as all the months and years pass, a change is occurring within it, a change so satisfying that the Queen never fails to marvel when she thinks about it: *it is increasing in value.*

It is stored in barrels (the coinage) and in piles of ingots (the molten metal refashioned to its most compacted form) laid one upon the other in clusters of six. Queen Sofie has lost all memory of what it once represented—in revenues, taxes and dues, in gifts and bribes, in forfeits and confiscations. She is no longer interested in any detail of that kind. All she knows is that a woman in her position, from whom power has slowly seeped away, must put her trust in wealth and nothing else.

Her daily visit to the gold vaults is always made alone. Not one of her servants is allowed anywhere near them, nor do they know where the key is kept. When she is inside the vaults, Dowager Queen Sofie bolts the door, shutting herself off from everything in the world but this.

In no other respect is she a greedy woman. On the contrary. She dines mainly on flounder fished from the Sound. In her cellar are some fine French wines, but she drinks them sparingly because she has seen what punishments to the body gluttony and inebriation can bring. She remembers only too well the repulsive sufferings of King Frederik, who corrupted his digestive system with liquor and game, and who died vomiting up his own faeces. She also knows that her son, King Christian, has this same frailty of the gut combined with a similar mania for rich meat and strong wine and, as she eats her quiet meals, prays that he will not die before her, leaving her at the mercy of a shiftless young grandson she does not love.

Queen Sofie's prayers have become more urgent in recent times. She has seen changes in Christian that appeared during his disastrous wars and which have not gone away. Something is going wrong in his life. His features—never clean and sharp like his mind—now resemble a collapsed cake into which misery has been stirred. This misery seeps out from his eyes. It oozes down the runnels of his cheeks.

The nobility and their wives, the few that Queen Sofie can be bothered to entertain at Kronborg, often murmur about the intolerable behaviour of Kirsten Munk and the extraordinary forbearance shown by the King towards this wife of his, who screams at her servants and is jealous of her own children, and falls down drunk in public and shows no shame. Queen Sofie shakes her head. "Yes," she agrees, "Kirsten does not comport herself well. It is as though she is searching, by one means and another and all of them disreputable, to understand why she is alive."

But privately she knows that her son's heart was given to this fiery Kirsten as surely as if she had cut it out and eaten it, and that however Kirsten may try his patience, he will never repudiate her.

Dowager Queen Sofie sighs, thinking about Kirsten's capriciousness and about the look of sadness and longing in her son's eyes when he reaches out for her to seat her upon his knee: "Come to me, my sweet Mousie. Come." She sighs because she sees there is nothing that she or anyone can do to alter this state of affairs. If a woman is weary of a man, then she is weary of him and will turn away from him to other things and that is that.

She herself, when she began in time to be weary of King Frederik's gourmandising, of the foolish nodding of his head when he was awash with wine, turned away from him and never again loved him with more than a few ounces of her being. And what was the thing to which she looked for consolation? She did not take lovers. She did not surrender herself to God. She began to hoard money.

Ellen Marsvin, mother of Kirsten Munk, now also lives alone—in Boller Castle in Jutland. The fruit fields of Johann Tilsen border her lands.

Like Queen Sofie, Ellen was, in her younger days, a beautiful woman. Now all that is discernible in an eye once bright with flirtatious fire is intelligence and cunning. She knows how, in a world entranced by youth and power, ageing women are neglected and despised. She believes that widows must be agile and shrewd if they are to survive. Her mind is occupied with the perpetual sifting and turning of plots and strategies.

Her treasure house is her kitchen. In summer, she lays down in sealed jars the great store of soft fruit she buys from Johann Tilsen: blueberries, junipers, strawberries, blackberries, redcurrants, blackcurrants, raspberries, gooseberries and sloes. In the winter she makes jam. And as she works with her sacks of sugar, with her boiling cauldrons, into her head (wrapped in linen to keep the steam from spoiling her hair) come pouring new propositions for her own survival. "Be vigilant" is her motto to herself. And she obeys it.

She knows the naked truth about her daughter: Kirsten is tired of the King and enamoured of Count Otto Ludwig of Salm. And this state of affairs is perilous. In her longing to be rid of her husband, Kirsten may put herself in grave danger—herself and her family, the Boller estate, her jewels and furniture: everything. It might all be lost, even the jam.

But Ellen Marsvin has risen far since her first marriage to Ludwig Munk and she does not intend to fall back into a mediocre life. Already she is trying to fathom how—if a separation between Kirsten and the King should occur—she may still make herself indispensable to Christian. There is a single key to her planning: foresight. In laying down her strategies, she knows she must always strive to see clearly not only what is, but what *will be*.

And so, upon receiving a long letter from Kirsten asking for a favour—a visit to the Tilsen household to ascertain how the youngest child is being treated—Ellen answers her daughter thus:

My dear Kirsten,
What! Am I to be your spy and Emilia's in the Tilsen house?
My dear, I am astounded that you should ask such a thing of me! But you have no doubt remembered that spies do not come cheaply and that if I am to carry out this visit as you request, why then I shall feel free to ask of you some good turn in recompense. The duties of a spy are most disagreeable and dangerous, and I hope you will not refuse me what I shall demand.

Then, revealing nothing more, she sends a note inviting herself to take luncheon with the Tilsen family. She tells Johann she will bring her order for next summer's berries. And she rides over on a spring morning, carrying a tiny silver pot filled with blueberry jam, intended for the child, Marcus.

There is no sign of Marcus.
The other boys look well and seem spirited. Magdalena Tilsen is huge with a coming infant. Johann is cordial. For luncheon a game pie is served.

When Ellen talks about her daughter's fondness for Emilia, all the heads nod their approval and Magdalena says: "It was Johann's wish that Emilia be parted from her family for only one year, but now that we understand how greatly the King's wife has taken to her, we are reconciled to losing her for longer than that."

"Yes," adds Johann, "we miss her, of course. But the honour she brings to us by being in your daughter's employ outweighs all other considerations."

When lunch is over, Ellen goes alone with Johann to discuss what quantities of fruit will be brought to Boller as the summer goes on. Over the making of lists, she produces at last her silver pot of jam and lays it on the table between her and Johann Tilsen.

"Ah," she says, "I had forgotten this. It was a little present for Marcus, but his absence from the table made it slip my mind. He is not ill, I trust?"

Johann does not glance up from the inventories.

"His table manners are bad, Fru Marsvin. We are trying to correct him, but without success. Thus, when we have company, Marcus takes his meals in his room."

"Oh," says Ellen, taking back the little pot. "I am so glad he is not ailing, for then I may see him before I go and give him this."

Now Johann Tilsen looks up at her. "If you give me the pot, I will make sure he receives it and is told that it is from you."

"No, no! You would not deprive me of a visit to Marcus, would you? When I have such a weakness for small children and their pretty ways."

"Marcus's ways are not pretty."

"Really? But I remember him with Emilia, so happy on his pony . . ."

"Emilia spoiled him. Now we are paying the price."

"Well, never mind his ways, Herr Tilsen. I should like to see him very much."

"I am sorry," says Johann. "It is not possible to see Marcus. He has a fever and is sleeping."

"A fever? And yet you said that he was not ill."

"A small fever. It will pass, but he must rest and not be disturbed. Your jam will be given to him when he is recovered."

So Ellen writes to Kirsten:

> . . . though I insisted as far as I could, Johann Tilsen would by no means let me have sight of Marcus and I did not see any sign of him about the house or garden as I left. I smell some secret. Is the child ill or not? Alas, on this visit I could not ascertain, but realising quickly that I must go there again so that I can uncover for you and Emilia what is being hidden, I pretended, all in the throes of compiling the fruit lists, that I had muddled them completely and ordered too many pounds of one berry and not enough of another and so forth. I snatched back the inventories, feigning a sudden flustering of my ageing mind and condemning myself for my dreadful habit of forgetfulness . . .

In the second part of this second letter, Ellen Marsvin defined for Kirsten the favour she had mentioned in the first.

She told her daughter that it had become impossible to find any diligent women of the wardrobe in Jutland and that she was therefore requesting that Kirsten lend her—until such time as some replacement could be found—her Woman of the Torso, Vibeke.

She signed herself *Your fond mother and spy, Ellen Marsvin.*

She was tired that night but could not sleep. Her brain brimmed with her hidden plans.

FROM COUNTESS O'FINGAL'S NOTEBOOK, *LA DOLOROSA*

My prayers to God asked: "How many continuations must there be before Johnnie O'Fingal can re-enter paradise?"

Peter Claire lost count of the number he composed as the summer passed. He told me that in each and every case there would be a moment when Johnnie would say, "We are near, Mr. Claire. Oh, I do believe we are near!"

But then, as the seventy-ninth or the eighty-second or the one hundred and twentieth continuation was repeated and modified, the veil of disappointment would once again begin to cloud my husband's eyes and he would put his hands to his head, covering his ears, and declare that the real music was lost for ever.

I thought that he would grow weary of the process and in a short time send Peter Claire away, but he did not. He told me that his work with the lutenist had given him hope: "Just enough of it, you see, Francesca, to make me believe that the search is not futile."

His health improved a little. The psora on his face healed up. He still kept to his room at nights and never visited me, but his behaviour could occasionally be tender, and I persuaded him to set in train the most urgent repairs to properties on the estate. And the people of Cloyne amazed me by their kind inclination to forgive him. "Oh, to be sure, he has been sorely ill, the poor man," they said to me. "But, God willing, everything will now begin to go better . . ."

One day in high summer, Johnnie announced to me that he was going to Dublin to visit his pipe maker. He would stay for one week. His pipes, in his hours of torment, had afforded him some small consolation, but by now he had sucked and bitten the stems all into pulp, and he wanted to put in an order for twelve new ones. It worried me that Johnnie—for so long a stranger to the city and to any great gathering of people—might become confused or lost in Dublin and I offered to accompany him, but he told me that he preferred to go alone. He would put up at an inn well known to him. He would see what concerts were being performed in the great churches of the city. He would dine upon oysters.

And so I let him go. As the carriage took him away, I felt that a burden had been lifted from me.

That same afternoon, a band of Gypsies came clamouring down the driveway. The children ran out to meet them and see what wonders and inventions they had brought. Giulietta was shown a hoop made of willow, so finely turned that it was impossible to discover where the join in the circle occurred. Maria seized upon a little watering pot no bigger than her hand. Vincenzo and Luca put on strange painted masks and ran about the garden shrieking at each other like devils and causing great mirth to the Gypsy troupe.

I found money for these objects and ordered that beer and cake be brought to the travellers, and I sat with them upon the grass while they brought out from their cart the creations of which they were the proudest and which they had saved until last, their trays of silver jewellery.

There were brooches, crosses, necklaces, bracelets and rings. All these things had been made by the man calling himself Simeon, who knew the blacksmith's trade. I regarded his large hands, very rough and with burn marks here and there on the palms, and marvelled that these hands could fashion articles of such delicacy.

I told the Gypsies that, alas, I had no money to spend on silver. I explained to them that since their last visit, trouble had come to Cloyne and that they found me in a state of some dejection. They looked at me with their black eyes. "Trouble and dejection," Simeon said. "These things follow us all our days, Countess O'Fingal, yet here we are, still. Perseverance is in the sinews of man. We are destined to go on."

I was silent as they began packing up their wares. I had enjoyed their company. And then, as they took their leave, Simeon pressed a tiny object into my hand. "Take this, Countess," he said, "and it will bring better fortune by the time we pass this way again."

I opened my palm. In it lay an ear-ring made of silver and containing in it a single jewel as small as a grain of sand.

That night, again I dined with Peter Claire. Our only companion was the sweet summer night, which crept in through the window and scented the room.

In this midsummer darkness, which was not quite darkness but only a luminous blue above the woods and fields, I felt as though I had begun to float—to float like a swimmer above myself and look down with pity and scorn on the great weight of propriety and resolution tethering me to the earth. I threw back my head and laughed at all these old burdens of mine.

"Why are you laughing?" asked Peter Claire.

"I am laughing," I said, "because I have decided to be free."

And so I took Peter Claire to my bed. We loved each other silently, in case any sound should wake the children, and when it was done, I looked at the young lutenist, deep into his eyes the colour of cornflowers, and knew that, after this night, my life would never be the same.

THE AMBASSADOR'S CONCERT

Towards the end of June, King Christian returns to Copenhagen.

Although he has tried, in the time remaining to him in Numedal (when the first silver ore is brought out and the King's party carouses joyously with the villagers of the *Isfoss* under the stars), to consign Kirsten Munk to that part of his heart which is indifferent to everything in the world, she keeps escaping from this confinement and returning to the place she has occupied for fifteen years—at the centre of the King's yearning. And even this (so perfectly in keeping with Kirsten's mercurial nature) amuses and fascinates him. The Kirsten that he loves is a woman who resists all attempts to imprison her. To Peter Claire, King Christian confesses: "Your counsel was good, but it is as if Kirsten *knows* I am trying to cure myself of my love for her, and she simply will not let me do it!"

It is night when the King's party arrives at Rosenborg. To Christian's astonishment, Kirsten comes to his bedchamber, blows out all the candles and lies down beside him. He can feel, as his hands hold and caress her, that she has grown fatter while he has been away but he does not find this displeasing and her skin is as soft as he remembers it. As he makes love to her, he whispers that when the first barrels of ore arrive from the mine, he will commission a statue of his beloved Mouse in solid silver.

"Oh," she says, "then I hope it will frighten all the scheming cats of the palace!" And she laughs her wild, cackling laughter.

Peter Claire is glad to be back in Copenhagen. He regains his room over the stables with something like happiness and he realises how deep into his consciousness had crept the idea that he would never return from the *Isfoss*. He stares at his hands, at his face in the looking-glass. He is alive. Premonitions can err.

A letter awaits him informing him that his sister Charlotte is to marry Mr. George Middleton in the month of September and begging him to make the passage to England for the wedding. This news raises his spirits still further, reassuring him that life in the Harwich household so dear to him is going on very well and that the sister everybody regarded as plain has found a rich and kindly husband.

Straight away, he writes to her: *My dear Charlotte, Mr. Middleton is the luckiest man in England.* And he sends her, upon impulse, a gift. It is the silver ear-ring given to him by Countess O'Fingal on the day he left Cloyne and which he has worn ever since. And when he has removed the little jewelled ring from his ear, cleaned, polished and wrapped it for Charlotte, he feels a satisfactory lightness of heart.

Christian sends for the musicians and orders them to begin practising for a concert to be performed in the rose garden for the English Ambassador, His Excellency Sir Mark Langton Smythe, whose visit to Rosenborg will take place at the end of the month.

Jens Ingemann bustles about in search of English music (ayres by Dowland, songs and pavans by Byrd and Tallis) and assembles the orchestra in a field, where, it is decreed, "all rehearsals shall take place, so that we shall adjust our sound to the vastness of the air and sky."

In the field is a flock of sheep.

"Sheep now!" snorts Pasquier. "As though chickens were not bad enough! Wherever we go, we are plagued by livestock."

"They will not come near us nor pay us any attention," says Jens Ingemann nervously, but this proves not entirely true, for from the moment the orchestra begins to play, the sheep raise their heads and listen, forgetting to graze for long periods of time.

But the playing is good, nevertheless. And once again, Peter Claire hears the sweet complexity of the sound made by this group of men. Thin and dry by comparison now seem his duets with Krenze in the Numedal. He is ready to swear that no other orchestra in Europe produces harmonies that teeter upon such perilous perfection.

Returning from the field one afternoon, towards an evening which has not yet announced itself by any noticeable diminution of the sun's brilliance, Peter Claire sees a young woman in the garden. She is gathering flowers. As the musicians come towards her, she raises her head and smiles at them, and Jens Ingemann and the other players bow to her and she nods to them and they walk on. But Peter Claire stops.

He stands by a sundial, pretending to read time from the shadow of the brass pointer, but in reality staying only that he may say a word to this person whom he has never before seen at Rosenborg. She wears a grey silk dress. Her hair is brown, neither dark nor fair. He notices that her hands are so small that she has difficulty holding the quantity of flowers she has gathered. "Shall I . . . may I . . . assist you?" he stammers.

"Oh," she says, looking up at Peter Claire and on the instant faltering as if she is taking in the striking beauty of his face, "no, there is no need."

But he goes to her side, lays down his lute, and holds out his hands so that she may give the picked flowers to him while she gathers some more. And so the flowers pass from her arms to his and he feels in their stems, where her hands have held them, something of the warmth of her.

He sees that he has caused her some confusion and that she is blushing, so, to calm her, he tells her about the concert rehearsal in the field and the way the sheep interrupt their grazing to listen to the music.

"Well," she says, "I have been told that the royal orchestra plays very finely. Perhaps the sheep had not before heard anything as excellent?"

That she should have the courage, in her confusion, to make a little joke moves him more than he can express. He laughs and then he asks her if she will be attending the Ambassador's concert.

"I don't know," she says. "Madame does not always like to attend public events."

"Madame?"

"Lady Kirsten."

"Ah," says Peter Claire, "so I work for the King and you work for his wife. Then perhaps we shall frequently be in each other's company?"

She hesitates, rearranging the flower stems. "I don't know," she says.

He longs to reach out and touch her, just touch her cheek or enfold her little hand. He senses that perhaps the moment has come for him to leave her, but he can't bring himself to do this. He has seen in her a fineness of spirit, a gentleness of heart, that he feels he has never before encountered. He is a breath away from telling her, there and then, that he loves her, but stops himself, realising just in time how utterly foolish this would make him seem.

He waits there, unable to move from his place at her side. To his delight, she raises her face and looks at him, and in that instant, as Peter Claire becomes aware that the shadows of the day have lengthened unnoticed while he has been with her, some understanding which neither can put into words passes between them.

"What is your name?" he whispers.

"Emilia," she says. "Emilia Tilsen."

Sir Mark Langton Smythe, as is the custom, arrives with a great quantity of gifts for His Majesty King Christian IV of Denmark from his nephew, His Majesty King Charles I of England. The gifts

127

are taken to the Long Hall and there offered to the King, seated on his silver throne with Kirsten beside him.

The presents include a fine oak dressing-table, an armoire made of maple and walnut, a tapestry footstool, an exquisite set of pewter drinking cups, a ship's model made of ivory, a longcase clock and a leather saddle. The last gift, however, walks into the Long Hall of its own accord and kneels down at the King's feet. It is a pair of Negro boys. This gift is wearing two jewel-encrusted turbans and two suits of coloured velvet, and when Kirsten sees it she lets out a cry of surprise and delight. "Ah," she exclaims, "slaves! How very excellent!"

Langton Smythe informs her that they have been given the names Samuel and Emmanuel and that they were brought to England by the owner of a cotton plantation on the island of Tortuga.

"Their trick, Madam," he says, "is to carry great weight—as it might be a sack of cotton—upon their heads."

Kirsten claps her hands and turns to the King. "I would like them to serve me," she says, "carrying the platters aloft on their turbans. It would make dinner so much more entertaining. Will you give them to me for this purpose?"

The King smiles. Since his return, Kirsten has visited his bed four times; the fires of his adoration have been stoked and fed, and burn with a jealous yellow flame. "Anything you wish, Mouse," he says.

"Oh, then I am happy! Do the slaves speak, Sir Mark?"

"Why, yes, Madam, they do. Their own language is peculiar—a singing kind of patois. But at His Majesty King Charles's court they have learned rudimentary English and I am sure you would be able to coax them to learn Danish words."

"I have an excellent idea. We shall permit them to play with my youngest children, who are never silent, but gabbling all the live-long day. Samuel and Emmanuel will learn Danish in the nursery and then they will be able to communicate with me."

The Ambassador's concert in the rose garden is to be preceded by a banquet. Fifty-two hens, nine swans and an ox have been slaughtered. Up from the cellar have been brought four barrels of wine.

Pregnant with Count Otto's child, Kirsten is prone to frequent bouts of sickness and does not wish to have any nausea brought upon her by the sight of the greedy nobles and their wives stuffing themselves with wine and meat. Yet she knows that the King likes to have her by him at such events and that her survival at the palace depends upon her behaviour towards him now. "What am I to do, Emilia?" she asks. "These banquets are like plagues, with all the air smelling of foul matter and foul mutterings against me. How am I to endure it?"

"All I can think, Madam," says Emilia, "is that you choose this as your moment to advise the King of your pregnancy, and . . ."

"No. It is too soon. I must conceal it for one more month, so that the dates realign themselves with what has occurred since his return."

"How are you to conceal it?" asks Emilia, looking at her mistress's body, which has expanded to a milky ripeness.

"I can," says Kirsten, "because the King sees what he wants to see and lies to himself about the rest."

So, on the day of the banquet, a dress of pearl-stitched satin is chosen, with a skirt very full and stiff, and Kirsten's body is pressed and squeezed into it and the laces pulled as tight about her waist as Frederika, Vibeke's replacement as Woman of the Torso, can draw them, and Kirsten, hardly able to breathe or walk correctly, is led into the Long Hall by her adoring husband.

She is seated next to Sir Mark Langton Smythe and they converse in German, which language Sir Mark has striven to perfect, liking as he does the way the verb withholds itself from its own completion until the last moment in almost every sentence, thus imparting to all linguistic constructions a hanging thread of mystery.

He finds Kirsten Munk mysterious, seductive, strange. She wishes to know about the island of Tortuga where Samuel and Emmanuel were born. As he tells her tales of beaches of white sand, bread trees, flying monkeys, witchcraft, and tornadoes lifting wooden houses into the heavens, he sees her become rapt by his words. What he does not know is that, as he talks about these far-away places, Kirsten has begun to be aware of something that she has never noticed before, and that is *the smallness of her life*.

As the stuffed chickens are served, she pushes the food away and begins to day-dream of a new existence, far from Denmark, miles and miles away from this ancient watery kingdom, in a new place where the sand is the colour of pearl, where animals fly over-head, where cinnamon cakes grow from bushes and where her only companions are her Otto and her sweet friend Emilia. Everybody else has been snatched into the sky by a tornado. Oh, thinks Kirsten, how beautiful this would be—how beautiful and how per-fect!

Ambassador Langton Smythe notices that his table companion has gone pale and he offers her a goblet of water, but his ministra-tions are too late. Kirsten feels herself begin to disappear from the banquet and arrive somewhere else. She does not recognise where this "somewhere else" might be, yet perhaps, she muses, she is float-ing on the clouds and is going to land in a bread tree? She can hear the wind sighing above her, or is it the sea that sighs underneath her, calling to her to come down?

She falls sideways, her head momentarily striking Sir Mark's el-bow, then hitting the cold marble of the floor.

Now the audience is assembling for the concert. They blink in the sunlight. They feel drowsy and full. Most of them know that once the music starts they will fall sound asleep, but still they bicker to get the best places, shouldering each other out of the way, spread-ing themselves and their belongings across whole lines of chairs.

Once seated, with the orchestra in place on a dais in front of them, they soon become restless. The concert cannot begin with-out the King, but the King left the banquet when Kirsten fainted and has not returned. His gilded chair in the front row is empty.

The audience yawns, stretches, gossips, admires the roses, yawns again and begins to doze.

Among the drooping and nodding heads, Peter Claire (who was not at the banquet and so did not witness Kirsten's collapse) is searching for Emilia Tilsen.

He supposes that Kirsten will make an entrance with the King and perhaps then he will see, in the shadow of the royal couple, the girl who, in a matter of a few minutes, has taken hold of his imagination.

He is tired because he has been awake all night in his room above the stables composing a piece of music. It is called "Emilia's Song." It's not yet finished, let alone perfected, but he thinks he has found a melody which is right for it: graceful and uncluttered. And words for the song have begun to come to him. They embarrass him, then delight him, then embarrass him again. He knows he is not a poet. What he feels, nevertheless, are sentiments that seem to crave some kind of expression more heightened and more true than ordinary speech can render them. This is the first time in his life that he has attempted to write a love-song and he suspects that the writing of love-songs is never the easy, effortless task that others such as Shakespeare contrive to make it seem. Indeed, *not being Shakespeare* appears to him, at this moment, as a not inconsiderable burden all Englishmen are forced to bear. And he wonders whether it would be better not to try to compose words to his song but merely to set to music some of the great poet's lines:

> *O how much more doth beauty beauteous seem*
> *By that sweet ornament which truth doth give.*
> *The rose looks fair, but fairer we it deem*
> *For that sweet odour which doth in it live . . .*

For these words surely express—far better than any of his own— the very thing that strikes him about Emilia Tilsen: that, although she is pretty enough, the real magic, the real fascination of her, lies in her nature, which, being serene, reflects back at those who love in her the traits in themselves which they most long to perceive.

While these thoughts meander round Peter Claire's mind, Emilia is sitting by Kirsten's bedside.

The pearled satin dress lies fallen across a chair. A compress has been applied to Kirsten's head and still visible among the mass of her chestnut hair is some dark blood. The scent of attar of roses lingers in the chamber.

Kirsten refused to let the King's physician examine her. He revived her with salts and was attempting to scrutinise her head wound when she fought him off and sent him away. She told him the heat of the hall and the strong smell of roast swan were quite enough to make any sensitive woman fall down in a swoon. Emilia made up the compress and helped her mistress into bed, where Kirsten remained awake until she saw the King arrive at the bedside, when she seemed to fall instantly into a deep sleep.

The King still stands there, looking down at his wife. He knows he is being impolite to the English Ambassador by holding up the concert, but suppose God were to take Kirsten away from him now, just as He seems to have given her back? Suppose the wound is deeper than it looks and her skull is broken? "Do not leave her for one moment, Emilia," he orders. "If her sleep begins to appear to you to be too deep, to have about it something not ordinary, send a servant to fetch Doctor Sperling and send another to fetch me. Do you understand?"

"Yes, Your Majesty," says Emilia, and then she adds: "I saw death come to my mother, Sir. I declare I would recognise it if it were anywhere near, but I do not think it is."

The King rests his bulky frame on Kirsten's delicate dressing stool. He sighs and passes a hand across his eyes, which look puffy and tired. "I fought with death once," he says. "Long ago. I saw it come into the room and it was black and had a sting like an adder. It almost took the life of my boyhood friend, but I fought it with its own weapon, with an answering inky blackness, and I won the day."

It is clear to King Christian that Emilia marvels at this story, but as soon as it has been uttered he regrets that it has come into his mind. The sad truth is that, as he ages, each and every memory of Bror Brorson creates in Christian a growing awareness of how, in a man's life, everything that is precious to him may little by little be lost and that, even as he believes himself to be embarked incessantly upon one accumulation after the other, he is in reality at the mercy of perpetual subtraction, so that when he looks about him in middle age he finds himself—to his own chagrin and surprise—in a grey desert where the horizon is unpeopled yet the ground is covered in shadows.

Emilia looks out into the sunshine and imagines the musicians on their stage and, among them, Peter Claire the lutenist. To evoke his face, his voice, makes her tremble. She remembers how, after Karen's death and the coming of Magdalena, any wish she might once have had to be loved by a man fell away from her so completely that she believed it was gone for all time. But, standing at the window on this summer afternoon, Emilia asks herself: "What is *all time*?"

And it is her mother's voice she hears in answer to this question. "At its moment of conception," says Karen, "*all time* is eternity. And only later, perhaps a long time later—on someday that no one had foreseen—does this eternity suddenly appear less infinite. And this is well known, Emilia dearest. Well known to those who have lived a little longer in the world than you."

CONCERNING CLOTH AND AIR

"Imagine," the King used to boast, "a spool of silken thread unravelling across Russia! Imagine the hills and valleys and towns, the rivers and mountains and cataracts, the seas of ice that it would have to cross! It was such a spool that was used to sew the coronation garments. Everybody in the country had new clothes in the red and yellow colours of the House of Oldenborg: soldiers, sailors, musketeers, wash maids, dancing masters, grocers, money lenders, midwives, children . . . everyone! It was my decree."

They say that tailors and button makers made more money in that coronation year, 1596, than they would ever be likely to make in the rest of their lives. Some worked so many hours at a stretch that they were stricken with temporary blindness and, when the great day came, couldn't see the King as he passed among them under his embroidered canopy. But at least they could get drunk in the streets of Copenhagen. On the King's orders, all the city fountains had been drained, cleaned and refilled with red and golden wine, and the citizens drank them dry.

King Christian had waited nine years to be crowned. He was determined that nobody living in Denmark would forget this moment in history.

A week before the coronation he sent for Bror Brorson.

Queen Sofie despatched a secret message to Bror's house in Funen ordering him not to come, but he arrived nevertheless. It was as if he had found the Queen's words entirely empty of meaning.

He had grown tall and his face was as handsome as it had always been, and his hair golden and wild. But yet there were changes in him. His legs were bowed from the hour upon hour that he spent riding—his only pastime. His walk, in consequence, had become awkward, almost foolish. And his blue eyes—his eyes the colour of the sky . . . there was something wrong with the way they looked at things. They looked and *did not seem to see.*

"Bror," said his royal friend, as he welcomed him to Frederiksborg, "I would like to know that you are happy."

Bror laughed. He flayed some dust with his riding crop. "Remember," he said, "Hans Mikkelson's fly swat?"

"Yes."

"That's where I would like to be—back at the Koldinghus

school. I wouldn't even mind being in the cellar, for I would already know that you were going to rescue me."

"But why would anyone wish to be back at the Koldinghus?"

"Only so that I could be a boy again."

Bror's body was restless, always shifting and moving like one constantly searching for something that he had mislaid, yet not knowing what the lost thing might be. Even in sleep, he fidgeted all the time and his bolsters fell to the floor, and his sheets were bunched and tangled. Queen Sofie warned Christian that his friend was going mad.

But King Christian wanted to believe, at this moment of his assumption of power, that everything in his previous life had some meaning and had been ordained by God. God had decreed that King Frederik should die young, knowing how strong was Christian's yearning to rule; God had decreed that his mind should be fertile enough to nurture within it five languages and so make himself understood and admired across Europe; God had decreed that Tycho Brahe's recipe for a skyrocket should be given into his hands by the Duchess of Mecklenburg and God had decreed that he should save Bror Brorson's life. Thus, Bror was part of God's scheme of things. He had been saved for a reason.

At dawn on the morning of the coronation, Christian woke Bror.

Outside, in the grounds of Frederiksborg, the lake still held on its surface the glassy stillness of the night. In Bror's wardrobe was hanging the suit of scarlet and gold he would wear on this day of days. In the state bedchamber were laid out the robes of white silk that would adorn the new King as he rode to church. On a velvet cushion in the vaults of the Frue Kirke sat the crown.

"Bror," said Christian, "we are going to ride towards the sunrise."

They mounted two headstrong horses bred from the Arab stallion once taken from a tailor's assistant in return for the pardoning of a crime. They rode east through the forests at a tearing gallop till the horses were white with sweat. They did not stop at any obstacle in their pathway, but jumped over it, and only when the sun was up and already hot did they stop and drink from a stream and let the horses rest in the shade of the trees.

"Now," said Christian, "we are alone. Nothing and no one is here but us and the horses and the forest, and you shall tell me now—before this day begins and my life takes a different course—what is wrong with you."

Bror bent down and immersed his face in the sweet water of the brook, and held it there for so long that it was as if he did not intend to surface. But then he raised his head and wiped the water from his eyes with his hand. The sun glanced on him through the branches of beech and dappled him with shadows. He did not look at Christian, but at some distant thing he seemed to have spied among the bracken. "I have come to the conclusion," he said, "that the human mind is like a piece of woven cloth. And my trouble is that mine . . . or so it seems . . . is all in threads . . ."

"You mean that you are confused?"

"Confusion usually *has an ending*. But these threads . . . I cannot seem to knit them back together . . ."

Christian said nothing, but only looked at his friend with a stern unblinking eye. Eventually he said: "Why has this happened to you, Bror?"

Bror picked out two stones from the water and rubbed them together in his hand, so that they made the strangely sweet piping sound of a skylark. "I do not know . . ."

"But there must be signs or clues?"

Bror returned to the stream, not to drink, but only to let the water trickle through his fingers as it bubbled onwards towards the wider rivers and the sea. "Perhaps," he said at last, "it is because I have never, since that day when we exploded the skyrocket . . ."

"Never what?"

"Never . . . since the Queen sent me away . . . found anything in the world to do."

Christian was silent. What went through his mind were the thousand sinecures he could bestow, yet he could not at that moment think of one which did not demand of its recipient the ability to read and write. He asked himself whether he should give Bror Brorson some menial occupation. Surely, he might make him a groom to care for his horses? But what would be the consequences of such an appointment? When he went by the stables, what would it do to him to remember that this was where his friend lodged now, in a room above the stalls?

Then it occurred to Christian that perhaps Bror's terror of written words and all his struggles with them might now be in the past. He picked up a twig from the dewy grass and in the dust of the pathway wrote his name, **Christian**, and handed the stick to Bror. Bror knew what was being asked of him and his eyes began a rapid blinking, as though some blinding light had begun to distress them. Then he bent low over the path and, with the earnest concentration of a child, he traced out a single letter that he followed with a full stop. The letter was not quite a "B" and nor was it quite an "R," but rather like an "R" that has repented of being an "R" and is in the middle of striving to become a "B."

Bror looked up at Christian and Christian looked down at the cross-bred letter, and the only sound was that of the river in its eternal travelling over the bed of stones.

"It doesn't matter, Bror," Christian said at last. "Today I shall find you something magnificent to do! You will take part in the tilting competition and I stake my life on the certainty that you will win it."

"I will try," said Bror. "I will try to win it, for your sake."

This was all there was to be done.

All his life, whenever the memory of Bror Brorson has surfaced to distress him, King Christian has repeated this sentence over and over again. On that day of the coronation, *this was all there was to be done.*

They say that even the sick and the dying of Copenhagen rose from their beds on that August morning. The streets were packed so tightly with people that, at times, it seemed that the air had nothing in it a man could breathe and some citizens began gasping and reaching up with their arms, trying to pull down towards themselves sweet breezes from the sky.

They moved and shouted as one scarlet and gold mass: the subjects of His Majesty King Christian IV, King of Denmark, King of Norway, King of the Goths and the Wends, Duke of Schleswig-Holstein, Stormarm and Ditmarsten, Count of Oldenborg and Delmenhorst. On his grey horse, surrounded by drummers, trumpeters and men at arms, with children throwing flowers in his path, he rode to the Frue Kirke under a scarlet canopy held aloft by four of the nobles, and the sound of human shouting and wailing with emotion followed him every step of the way.

And then he entered the church and—as Christian remembers it—the interior was cold and silent, with the people and their cries and flowers shut out, and solemnity reigned and voices were stern and there was the smell of sorrow in there, sorrow for all the dead kings passed away and sorrow for the smallness of man in the midst of all his colossal strivings.

And as the three bishops approached, to lay with their six hands the crown on the young King's head, it seemed to him that this was where the smell originated, in the vestments of the three bishops, purple and gold and white, and as he knelt before them and these vestments came round him and enclosed him, he had to fight against a feeling of repulsion and terror. For what the smell, by being all-enfolding and all-enclosing, seemed to negate was the very thing that was being bestowed upon Christian by the placing of the heavy crown on his head: earthly power. What the scent of the bishops' robes affirmed was his own weakness and impotence in the sight of God. Over his head were being whispered the words of the anointing. He had arrived at the most important moment in his life. Yet what was such a moment? Man at his greatest is still mortal. A nail in the sole of his foot can snatch his life away. Kings can never outlive their subjects.

It was the first time in his life that King Christian understood that God was pitiless. The weight of the intricate jewelled crown, when it fell on him from the bishops' hands, felt too heavy to be borne.

Then, at last, the service was over and he walked to the door of the Frue Kirke and once again out into the sunlight, where the crowds recommenced their cheering and, as the roar of their "Hosannahs" filled the air, he felt his melancholy pass and the crown on his head become light.

He looked above the people to the roofs of the houses and his eye rested there, and what it saw was a new skyscape of graceful towers, turrets and spires. Now that he was King, he would begin a programme of building such as Copenhagen had never seen. He would employ the best architects in the world, the most experienced craftsmen. Ingenuity and skill were the qualities that would count with him, just as they had counted with his father in his vigil against shoddiness, and into the cloudless air would rise a new city.

Somewhere behind him, wearing his red and gold clothes, stood Bror Brorson, ready to follow him to the coronation banquet, ready no doubt to beg of him a favour that would give some meaning to his restless existence. But Christian knew now that he could do nothing for Bror. He had been wrong to think that God—the cruel and pitiless God who had revealed Himself in the vestments of the bishops— had "saved" Bror for some future purpose. *Bror had no future purpose.* It was fruitless to think that a man like this, who could not even write his name, could have any important place in the new Denmark which he, King Christian IV, was going to create. In the battles to come, Bror Brorson would have to fight his own fight all alone.

Yet still King Christian wanted to turn round, to swivel his head, to catch Bror's eye just for a fleeting second, to see whether, by some look that would evoke the past, Bror would be able to make him change his mind. He wanted his decision put to the test. But at that moment the four nobles holding the canopy took up their places around him and the chancellor whispered to him: "Walk forward, Sir. Keep moving forward so that the procession can begin."

And so he could not turn. Instead, he walked into the arms of his people who threw roses at his feet, and Bror Brorson trailed along some way behind him, smiling his vacant smile and never knowing that he was slowly disappearing from the King's mind.

My dear Son,

I am commanded by Charlotte to thank you for your kind letter to her and your gift of the Gypsy ear-ring. I have told her she must write to you herself, but she begs me to tell you that she is entirely taken up with the buying of petticoats, silk stockings, pillowcases, ribbons and the thousand other artefacts seemingly necessary to a bride's future existence, and has no time at present to settle down to the task.

We are all glad to hear that you are returned to Copenhagen from Norway, and from the silver mine, which place did sound very lonely and where I would not like to have to picture you when—as happens very many times in a single day—my thoughts return to you. That the chestnuts are in bloom in Denmark gladdens my heart, for it means that summer has arrived there. In Suffolk, they have already blossomed and the blossom is fallen and the prickly husks of the fruit (which Charlotte used to describe as "tree furniture," as you will remember!) grow green and hard. From this you will see that we are a little advanced in the season compared with you, but do not infer from this that we have in any wise left you behind or permit our lives to go on as though you were not still a precious part of them.

And so this brings me to the news which your mother says I should not be imparting to you, but which—after very much thought—I have nevertheless decided to bring to your attention.

Our old friend Anthony Grimes, choirmaster and organist of our church, has died. We buried him last Friday morning and he is laid to rest within the sound of the bells of St. Benedict the Healer. He will be mourned by everyone in the parish and none of us shall forget him. He was a musician of rare talent and a soul so very gentle that merely to come into his presence always worked in me a feeling of sweet tranquillity. I know that he is with the angels.

I must immediately set about the task of finding some new and younger choirmaster, so that we may continue to enjoy sublime music at St. Benedict the H. But it is now that there creeps into my mind an idea. Why do you not come back to us, my beloved son, and take up this position? No one knows better than you what a high standard of musical excellence we have always maintained here and I can truly say to you that your talents would not be wasted. More than this, the stipend paid to the choirmaster is a good one and Anthony Grimes very frequently told me that he wanted for nothing in his life. More yet than this: I know how earnestly you wish to compose and not merely to play or sing. Well, my dear Peter, I can promise you firstly that time would be found among your duties for your own work. I would make you this sacred pledge. And I do not see why, with so fine a choir as we have, we should not try out your compositions during services and let the congregation of St. Benedict be your first audience.

In obedience to your mother, I shall by no means try to persuade you any further in this matter. If you do not wish to leave what is, after all, a royal position, then I shall understand and never mention it more. Know only how much my heart would rejoice to have you here, returned to the family and working within the sacred walls of my church.

Concerning other matters, let me give you a picture of Charlotte's fiancé, Mr. George Middleton. He is a fleshy man, but this flesh of his seems kind. He dotes upon Charlotte and calls her his "dear Daisy" (though I know not why). When he laughs, which he does not infrequently, his chin performs an amusing kind of wobble. We have visited his house in Norfolk and it is large and comfortable, and he breeds cattle there and grows marrows and all manner of other new vegetables brought over from Holland and France, and is manifestly liked by his neighbours. In short, he is a good man and I can see in Charlotte's eyes that she is hungry for him and hungry for his children and so I do believe that all of this will go on very well.

I shall hope to have some letter from you before the tree furniture has come to its last polishing and lies upon the ground.

From your loving father,
James Whittaker Claire

KIRSTEN: FROM HER PRIVATE PAPERS

I declare that no time in my life was as difficult as this is!

Small wonder is it that so many women exchange reality for the oblivion induced by strong liquor or—as I have heard is now the craze up and down the Kingdom—dance themselves to death. For a woman's life is for ever and ever hedged about with Complications and she must, through every hour of her waking, be attending to one or other of these and trying what solutions she can. There are days, I swear, when I am so Exhausted in my body and in my mind that I long to lay myself on my bed and never wake again.

Before the King's return from his Norwegian Mine, when I would open my eyes each morning and ask myself what Thing awaited me in the coming day, and then remember that I would spend some hours with Otto and be borne away once more upon the wild gallop of our passion, with my lover's member bucking into me in the manner of a Stallion rearing up and coming into a Mare, and the pain of the silken Whip lashing my buttocks, why then I would find the World to be a fine place. But alas, alas, that time is past! I am left with the pain and bloating of my pregnant state and with the terrifying need to disguise it from the King until sufficient time passes that I may pretend that the Child is his. The Child will be my excuse and he will have to honour it. He loves Children and has brought more of them into the world than I can count. That this Child will be a Rhenish boy with flaxen hair and golden skin, and a nature greedy for love, will make no difference. He will believe that it is his.

Meanwhile, the Count cannot visit me here and I dare not—lest all my plans are discovered and come to nothing—creep out of the Palace to any secret rendezvous with him.

Yet, we exchange letters. My old friend James, the Tennis Court Marker, who long ago stole an indecent kiss from me in the Summer-house and has therefore been in Thrall to me ever since, has agreed to be emissary and to travel between Otto's dwelling and Rosenborg with letters hidden in his work bag.

We write in a kind of code, muddling German, French, English, Italian and Latin words. The Names we have given each other are Stefan and Brigitte. Stefan's occupation is that of Jockey. (Oh, a Jockey, Otto, *mein lieber!*) Brigitte is the daughter of a Tanner. (Ah, and she knows how the hides are to be flayed, *mon très cher Comte!*) And between them both, in all the words that pour from their pens, there is not one sound grammatical construction. Brigitte and Stefan are, in truth, aberrant confectioners, making of language a cake that no one in the world finds beautiful but they.

Yet nothing much—aside from this correspondence—remains to give me any pleasure or mirth. The days pass, that is all. Summer brings its golden heat. I dream of Otto's mouth. I send Emilia into the gardens to gather flowers to scent my lonely rooms . . .

And nor do Matters with my Mother and Emilia's family go on quite as we would wish them.

Ellen Marsvin has visited the Tilsen household twice now and on neither occasion has she been able to set eyes upon little Marcus. Yet she has, notwithstanding her failure as our spy in Jutland, demanded and got from me my Woman of the Torso, Vibeke Kruse, to have as her own Maid of the Wardrobe. It is a Mystery to me why she wants this Woman. Vibeke is of a solid temperament and does not take offence when I berate her—as Johanna does—yet her duties in the Wardrobe are not performed so excellently that they could not be done by some Local Woman at Boller, and she is moreover very given up to her Love of Sweetmeats, so that she is to be found very frequently stuffing herself with sugared damsons and quince tartlets and spoonfuls of Apricot Cream. Thus, she is costly, and it causes me not the least disquiet to send her away. I marvel only that my Mother insisted so upon this subject and do begin to wonder whether she does not have some Secret Plan concerning this fat Vibeke.

But I do not miss her one jot. Truly, I am tired of all my Women, with their sulking and complaining, and whenever they come into my Sight I long to have them removed from it again. I would like to send them all away and keep only Emilia to care for every bit of me. Yet my clothes and jewels, being but fabricated and inert, do need this Coterie of the Disaffected to starch, iron, polish and steam some irritable life into them. There are days when I am laced into petticoats so angry and stiff that my feet could leave the ground and they would yet hold my body upright. My ruby necklace is put upon my neck still hot as blood from its furious shining.

To hell with the Women! At least God gave me Emilia, whose sweet disposition, I do swear, is a weapon against my encroaching Madness in the midst of all my deceptions and double-deceptions.

I try to comfort her on the subject of Marcus. I tell her that we must be patient. But one day she says to me: "Madam, I had a dream that he was found drowned in the Water Trough." And I can detect that she is distracted by worry for him. When she is reading to me her eyes will suddenly stray from the book. When we play cards she sometimes loses all account of who is winning.

I try to soothe her fears by taking her to buy presents for Marcus, just as I promised. So far, we have despatched a Mechanical Bird (which is wound like a clock with a key, and then opens its beak and lets forth an icy trill), a Sailor's hat, a pair of scarlet boots and a kitten. I have written to my Mother to tell her to inquire after these objects on her next visit to the Tilsen household and ask that they be brought to her sight. The kitten's name is Otto.

My one and only wickedness in this dreary month concerns my Slaves, Samuel and Emmanuel.

As requested, the King gave them to me, to serve me only and do my bidding and no one else's. That they are not paid, but do veritably live the life of Slaves—except that they wear fine clothes and are not Chained Up—wakes in me a peculiar excitement. That this feeling is a Reprehensible Thing, I am very sure. But yet I feel it. And I do believe that it has to do with the crude fact that I, in my duties as the King's Consort, do feel myself to be in the Position of a Slave, because I have no power of my own except what I can exercise through my body or through my Cunning.

This excitement of mine is a peculiar Phenomenon and I shall tell no one about it, not even Emilia, for I am sure she would not like to hear it. But I will now avow that, on Monday of this week, when I was dining quite alone in my chamber, and these two Negro boys were kneeling by my chair (Ambassador Langton Smythe has calculated that they are aged between fifteen and sixteen years) carrying aloft for me plates and baskets of delicacies, from which I could pick and choose with my slender white hands, there started to stir in me a little worm of Pleasure.

And I began a conversation with myself, one part of me saying: "Kirsten, are you not a Shameful Degenerate Person to feel such a thing within your body?" and the other part asking: "What is a Slave for, but to do your Every Bidding, Kirsten, no matter what that bidding may be?"

I rose to my feet and went to the window, drawing the thick drapes on the summer evening. Then I went to my door and locked it.

Speaking in English, which is the only language—aside from their own tongue, which is most strange and wonderful—that Samuel and Emmanuel understand as yet, I commanded the Boys to lay down their platters of food and to take off all their clothes. I said this very kindly, smiling at them all the while, lest they began to be afraid I was about to strike them or hurt them in some way.

They feigned not to comprehend what I was asking of them, but I repeated the command and sat down, waiting on my chair, while they slowly removed their velvet coats, their satin waistcoats, their jewelled turbans, their coloured shoes, their lace shirts and their silk breeches and stockings.

They stood there in their undergarments. As children, I am sure they had run naked in the wild surf of their island but, at the Court of King Charles in London, had been taught, no doubt, to cover themselves at all times and never stand unclothed in a room, not even when they were alone.

I indicated that they should remove their cotton pantaloons. And so they bent to do this and, when they stood up, were revealed to me in all their dark, shining beauty. I noted that their members were large and mannish, and a desire to reach out and touch them was so strong in me that I felt that ache which comes into me when I dream of Otto.

I knew that a Spirit of Wickedness was in the room. This Spirit has played with me all my life since I was a child. Through thirty years, it has played with me and taunted me, and does not let me rest.

I thought for several moments that it would again vanquish me. I knew that, whatever lewd command I might give, my Slaves would force themselves to obey me, through fear of being cast out into the world with nothing, and so for a space I let my mind boil in a magnificent stew of Carnal Entertainments.

But, in the end, I did not utter my thoughts. They were within a breath of forming themselves into words and something stopped them. And I declare it was Emilia who stopped them. For into me came an awareness of the shame I must later feel in her innocent company if I should trespass upon the bodies of my Slaves. And so

I stepped back from wickedness. I thanked Samuel and Emmanuel for showing me "this graceful form and shape of yours, such as I have not laid my eyes on before," and told them, with the gentleness of a Mother, to get dressed.

Not long after this, when I had unlocked my door and Samuel and Emmanuel had departed, Emilia came to me to ask if I wished her to play dice or cards with me before the night should come. Then she stared at my face and said: "Oh, Madam, you look flushed. Is there some fever come upon you?"

"Yes," I said. "I do believe there is. I am much given to these sudden fevers, but they pass. In a little time, Emilia, they always pass away."

A Small Square of Dust

Peter Claire walks alone in the streets of Copenhagen.

From the noisy commerce of the city, from the rattle of carts and carriages on the stone flags and the cries of the market traders and the flurrying of birds and the carillons of the church clocks, he is trying to pluck out answers to the hundred questions that occupy his mind.

He walks north-east towards the water. As always, people stare at him as he passes. The stares of the men are curious, confused; the stares of the women soften to entranced contemplation. It is not unusual for people to stop and try to hold him in conversation, pretending that they recognise him or mistake him for a friend they had once known. And today, as he meanders slowly through the crowds, a beggar woman claws him with her grimed hand and whispers in his face, "The lives of the Golden Ones are the shortest. Lay money down against your brief time." He gives her a coin, then quickens his pace as he hurries away.

Now he stands on the quayside and sees gulls circling the basin and a warm wind from the south setting the boats tilting and tugging gently at their anchors. He is reminded of Harwich: in the salt smell of the air, in the echoey cry of the gulls, in the slap of water against the wooden jetties.

But he does not think long about his family. His thoughts fold and refold themselves around Emilia Tilsen, yet do not arrive at any clear understanding nor any certainty. It is as though he has been set the task (once teasingly given to him by his sister Charlotte) of fashioning a table napkin into a water-lily, and indeed he can hold the image of such a lily in his mind, yet no one has shown him how this feat might be achieved. He folds, unfolds, refolds. No lily emerges.

Adhering to the Cartesian principles discussed with the King in the Numedal, he once again sets out the one thing of which he feels himself to be certain. He expresses it thus: *I experience an almost perpetual longing or fierce inclination to come into the presence of Emilia. Upon her approbation appear to rest all my hopes of future happiness.*

The gulls call to the clouds, the wind ruffles Peter Claire's hair and blows a few strands of it into his eyes. He asks: *What is such a longing? How may it be defined? Is it a true need or only a chimera or fantasy? Is it a longing of the body only, or of my whole being?*

What he seems to know is that it is a longing unlike any other he has felt. When he walked with Francesca O'Fingal by the sea at Cloyne he longed to possess her. But it is not mere physical possession of Emilia that he craves; it is something else, something more absolute. *It is,* he tells himself, *as if I believed that while I beheld Emilia, during every mote of time that I could capture her within my sight, nothing could harm me or bring to me any suffering. It is as though I imagined that, as long as I was with her, I would not die . . .*

Yet still no concrete revelation of any incontrovertible truth appears to him. Could it be that what he thinks he feels is merely a delusion born of his solitude and of his long separation from both his family and the Countess? Will he wake tomorrow, or the next day, to find that it has vanished?

He has encountered Emilia only once since the day when he talked to her in the garden. They came face to face in a corridor of the palace and they stopped, and Peter Claire reached out and took Emilia's hand. "I must speak to you," he said.

Emilia looked at him with her little worried frown and he could not tell what the frown signified. And having said that he wanted to speak to her, what was it, after all, that he hoped to say? Part of him wanted to tell her that he was writing a song called "Emilia's Song," but he found he couldn't bring himself to admit this—in case (as seemed to him very likely), when the song was completed, it turned out to be a hopelessly mediocre thing. So he repeated his one utterance again: "I must speak to you!" But having said this, he was at a loss. He felt himself to be incapable of following the single phrase with anything else. All he could do was press Emilia's hand to his lips and then turn from her and walk away.

Later, in his room above the stables, he despised himself for his faltering and cowardly behaviour. He sat down at his bureau and began to write Emilia a letter. But, like his song, he made no progress with the letter and soon abandoned it.

Emilia, who has never been vain, who has never thought to consider herself pretty, now spends long minutes staring at her face in the glass.

A small nose, soft grey eyes, a mouth of surprising sensuality, a pale complexion: what do these ingredients add up to? Is she ordinary? Or has she, without noticing it, become quietly beautiful? She moves her head this way and that, sees in her profile the profile of her mother and so concludes, "If I am like Karen, why, then, I am fair." But is this true?

She turns away from the glass. The hours that Kirsten Munk spends each day examining her own reflection have taught Emilia that when a woman keeps staring and staring at herself, she is trying to see herself *through the eyes of her lover*. If she finds fault, it is not the fault itself, but rather her lover's pitiless regarding of that fault that she sees.

So what is she, Emilia, doing wasting time gazing stupidly at her own features? She is behaving as though she had a lover, when the truth of the matter is quite otherwise. She passed a few moments in the garden with the handsome lutenist, and in a passageway, one day, he seized her hand and held it for an instant to his lips. Such fugitive encounters go on, no doubt, day after day and year after year inside the royal palaces. They signify nothing. They are fleeting abstractions that form in the rarified air and evaporate like the scent of the lindens.

Emilia remembers that, as she put her flowers into the lutenist's arms, she felt as though something—some understanding or agreement, something more than just the flowers—passed between the two of them. She finds this memory so thrilling that it almost makes her dizzy. But who, in reality, is to say that there was any such understanding? For what is life but successive alteration? Even those things which—like Johann's love for his wife Karen—have seemed to be *unalterably* so may in time appear never to have existed at all.

She tries to put the whole matter from her mind. She tells herself that a man such as this (who may also be vain and shallow and without any compassion) will fabricate a hundred "understandings" of this kind in a single year.

Emilia resolves that she will return to her former way of thinking about her own life, in which the love of a man played no part at all. She goes to the looking-glass one last time and covers it with a shawl.

My Dear Miss Tilsen [*says the note which arrives two days later*],

There are matters upon which I wish most urgently to speak to you.

I shall wait for you in the cellar where we play (below the *Vinterstue*) at seven o'clock on Friday morning.

Be assured how greatly I honour and respect you, and please believe me when I promise you that you have nothing in the world to fear from such a meeting.

Peter Claire, lutenist in His Majesty's orchestra

Emilia reads the note a number of times.

She then folds it and puts it away in the drawer where she keeps the laces and ribbons for her petticoats, and resolves to forget it.

After a few hours have passed, she goes to the drawer and takes

out the note and rereads it five more times. Again, she folds it carefully and puts it away, and closes the drawer firmly, as though with
this one movement she were locking it and throwing away the key.

That afternoon, Kirsten says to her: "Emilia, your thoughts are
not on this game. You have given away your jack of hearts when
you know perfectly well that I hold the queen."

And so Friday arrives.

Peter Claire longs for it to come and he also wishes that its
coming might be for ever postponed.

He is in the cellar at ten minutes to seven. He walks to the
open spaces in the walls through which the snow came sifting in
winter and looks out. The air of the early morning is gentle and
warm.

He then wanders about the cellar, breathing the resinous smell
of the wine casks and reading the marks and labels on them. No
sooner has he read them than these marks and labels undergo a
transformation and reformulate themselves into questions:

What shall I do if she does not come?

*If she does not come, am I to conclude that she feels nothing or only
that she is afraid?*

All year round, it is cold in the cellar, yet Peter Claire feels too
warm. He sits down on the chair that is habitually his when the orchestra plays or rehearses and tries to breathe slowly, so that when
seven o'clock arrives she will find him calm and serene. And then,
in the middle of the time when seven o'clock should still be some
way off, it arrives. The church clock strikes. It seems to Peter
Claire that the church clock has treacherously swallowed three or
four minutes of his existence in its haste to get to the hour.

He waits without moving. He is listening now for the sound of
the door. But there is no sound of anything, only the hens in their
dusty cage scratching and murmuring. He turns and looks at the
hens and notices that scores of their brown feathers lie around on
the earth, where they seem to search in vain for corn that no one
has remembered to scatter.

And then he hears it: the door opening and closing; her feet on the stone stairway. And she is there. She wears a brown dress with a black velvet ribbon at her throat.

Peter Claire gets up and moves towards her. He bows to her and she stops, staring in amazement at where she finds herself. He holds out his hand and, after a moment's hesitation, she takes it and he leads her to the circle of chairs by now so familiar to him and asks her if she would like to sit down. But she shakes her head and continues looking about her at all the unexpected things assembled in this shadowy cellar.

The lutenist notices how small his own voice has become. But its pathetic littleness only makes him laugh inside, because surely nothing matters now, not even the fact that he can barely speak, because she has come to him. She is with him and he is by her side and the thing that he has longed for is happening as the minutes pass. "Miss Tilsen . . ." he begins, his voice a little more firm. "Emilia . . ."

He wants her to speak, to help him, but she says nothing. And, in fact, she has barely looked at him. She is staring, with a look of dismay, at the chicken cage. He follows her glance and immediately feels he must apologise to her for having brought her to so peculiar a place, but before he can say anything about this, she asks: "Why do you keep hens down here?"

"Oh . . ." he stammers, "I do not. I mean, they are not ours, the orchestra's. It was not our idea. We would rather they were not here, because it is quite difficult to hear ourselves, our harmonies, sometimes because of the—"

"Do they have no water?"

"No. Yes. There was always water . . . in a little metal trough . . ."

"The trough is dry, Mr. Claire. Look."

He glances at the bowl and sees that indeed it is empty. He wishes there were a well or a water bucket down here, so that he could quickly refill the receptacle and turn Emilia's attention away from the hens and back to him. He looks around him, as if he hoped to discover some such well or bucket that he had never noticed before, when Emilia says: "Their whole confinement seems so dry, nothing but dust. Who cares for these creatures?"

"I do not really know."

"But I thought this was where you played every day?"

"It is. In winter, that is. Most days in winter, when the King is in the *Vinterstue* . . ."

"But none of you cares for the hens?"

"Emilia!" he wants to say, "why are you talking about these chickens? Why are you not helping me to find the words in which to declare that I love you?" But now he doesn't know what to answer. He curses himself for having arranged the meeting in the cellar. Why did he not choose the summer-house or the flower garden where they first met? He chose it, he supposes, because he wanted her to understand, by bringing her to this cold place where he's forced to pass so much of his existence, what kind of man he is— that he is a person capable of *making sacrifices*. And now, because of the wretched hens, all he appears in her eyes is neglectful and cruel. "Emilia," he says at last, "Emilia. We shall fetch water for the hens in a moment, but please listen to me . . ."

She looks at him now. She holds herself very still, yet he sees that she's trembling. He knows her thoughts to be flying between him and the hens, flying and returning and not knowing where to settle. She lowers her eyes as he blunders on: "When I saw you first in the garden and then in the passage . . . I felt something that is new to me, entirely new. I want to call it love. Love is the word which seems to fit it. But will you not tell me what you think it is? Will you not tell me what you feel?"

"What I feel? But I do not know you, Mr. Claire. What should I feel for someone I hardly know?"

"Of course, I should not ask these things so soon. Yet I know that there was some understanding between us. I know there was! So won't you tell me what you believe that understanding to be?"

She is shivering. Her small hands clutch at her dress. He chooses to believe that she does want to reply, that she has some reply to make, but she simply will not let herself make it. And her grey eyes will no longer look at him, but only at the square of dust on which the hens lead their monotonous lives in the near-darkness.

"I should not have come," she says in a whisper. "I'm sorry, Mr. Claire. Of course I should not have come."

From Countess O'Fingal's Notebook, *La Dolorosa*

On the night Johnnie was in Dublin, I recited to Peter Claire some lines from one of Shakespeare's sonnets that I remembered from long ago, when Johnnie was patiently teaching me English. I had learned these lines almost as mere words without meaning, but now I saw what depth of feeling was in them and, when I had said them, Peter and I lay together for a long time and did not speak, and after a while the first bird began to sing and we knew that the dawn was breaking and the night was over.

> . . .
>
> *Thy love is better than high birth to me,*
> *Richer than wealth, prouder than garments' cost,*
> *Of more delight than hawks or horses be;*
> *And having thee, of all men's pride I boast.*
> *Wretched in this alone, that thou mayst take*
> *All this away, and me most wretched make.*

Yet I did not know what degree of wretchedness was to follow.

On the following day, Johnnie O'Fingal returned from Dublin and had to be carried into the house by the servants, being discovered in the coach too ill and weak to stand.

We put him to bed and he fell into a deep sleep that lasted some twenty hours, during which he woke only once, to call for water.

Having watched over him for a long while, I at last went to my room to rest, but was awakened in the middle of the night by a strange feeling of coldness all over my body that I could not account for.

I looked down at myself and saw that all the bedclothes had been taken away and that I lay naked on the mattress. As I reached out to find the coverlets and draw them back to me, I realised that my husband was standing by me in the darkness.

"Johnnie—" I said.

"It was never mine!" he announced.

He held a corner of my bedclothes in a bunch in his hand and I could not pull them free, and to face him thus, unclothed and cold, while in another part of the house my lover lay sleeping, began to cause me some distress. I took a pillow from behind my head and laid it across my stomach. Still, Johnnie looked down at me, as if what he saw disgusted him, and my first thought was that his words *It was never mine!* referred to my body, with which I had betrayed him, and that this betrayal was now known to him.

Shivering and with my heart pulsing in my throat, I said: "Johnnie, tell me what you mean."

He then, like one so weary that he can no longer stand upright or summon any strength in his limbs, sat down on the bed. He put his head into his hands. I lit a candle and then I knelt and pulled up the bedclothes, both covering myself and bringing the blankets round Johnnie, as if they might help to soothe him in his distress.

And so he told me what had happened in Dublin.

On his second night in that city he had gone to the church of St. Jerome of Kilbride where the choir and orchestra were performing a concert of sacred ayres. He arrived early and so took a place near the front of the nave, from which he found himself staring distractedly at the musicians, as though they had no actual being but were conjured there by his mind alone.

He did not know what ayres they were going to perform but had a premonition that, as soon as the first note was struck, something fearful was going to happen. He was about to get up and leave, when the orchestra began to play. And what they played and what the choir then took up and made soar into the heavens was the very melody Johnnie O'Fingal had heard in his dream.

He sat on my bed and wept. "I thought that *my mind* had discovered this sublime sound," he sobbed. "I believed it had come from me, from my being, from my heart . . . but it was never mine, Francesca! The composer was one of *your* countrymen, Alfonso

Ferrabosco! So now I know that I am empty of anything noble, anything that transcends the ordinary and workaday. I have given up years of my life to this search and it has all been in vain. All that I have done is to make myself ridiculous and contemptible."

I took him into my bed and held him in my arms. My sorrow for him was indeed very great. How much he had suffered! How much he had sacrificed! The bitterness of this useless suffering conveyed itself to me with great force. And yet as I lay there, holding Johnnie's head on my breast, my thoughts crept from him and towards my lover and the passion we had known. And I understood that this was all that I would ever know of it. There would be no tomorrow. With his quest in ruins, Johnnie O'Fingal would pay the lutenist what he owed and send him away.

THE THOUGHTS OF MARCUS TILSEN, AGED FOUR AND A HALF, PLUCKED FROM THE AIR

Emilia.

She was my sister and she told me a rhyme. *What is the world made of I do not know, sometimes it is made of dancing snow.*

Sometimes it is made of darkness.

Then my father comes and says Oh, no, no, no, no, Marcus, I shall not tell you again we cannot permit this to go on. No, no, no, no, no. Counting them. Five. No, no, no, no, no, no. Six. Five and six makes eleven. And four before. Fifteen. And then my harness is put on with its straps and buckles, and I am tied to my bed and I cry. The straps and buckles hear me and they squeak. My cat Otto cannot hear. He is taken away and thrown out into the fresh air.

Otto, Otto, Otto! Three. Otto, Otto, Otto, Otto, Otto, Otto, Otto! Seven.

Out there where he is he cannot hear. Otto. One.

Emilia.

A messenger came with Otto in a basket. This messenger and the basket and Otto flew through the sky to me carrying her name.

Names can break you have to hold them carefully all the while you are flying and then you can speak them. E-M-I-L-I-A.

And Otto is like her, grey and white.

She told me I killed my mother and now my mother can see me from the cloud where she lies and when it rains on the water in the horse trough that is her crying for me just in that little place. My father says that water is not for you Marcus do not be so silly come away from the trough you will make yourself ill. I say yes it is for me it is my mother crying in this oblong shape and he says I do not know what to do with you Marcus I am in Despair.

Despair is a place quite near. Magdalena winds me round and round with wool so my arms are flat and she says it is a game Marcus what is the matter with you in the end you will drive us all to Despair.

I think Despair is a village. There is an inn and some houses there and an old man who sharpens knives.

The messenger came again the same one.

I heard his voice. I was tied in my bed with the harness of straps and buckles squeaking. The messenger said I have brought a lovely thing this time the wonder of Copenhagen but then there was no more sound so I called out messenger messenger messenger messenger! Four.

Messenger, messenger! Two. But Magdalena hid the messenger she is a witch and can make people disappear or make them be silent or make them fly away.

At supper I said I heard the voice of my messenger from Emilia and my brother Ingmar said Marcus is going insane and Magdalena said what messenger there was no messenger and you must come to an end of your inventions Marcus we are being very patient with you but our patience is running out.

Patience is made of wool. It winds me round and round and

round and round and round and round and round and round and round and round and round and round . . .

Now Magdalena has a bird. She says look Marcus it is not real but a mechanical bird and when I turn this little handle it sings for me and you can listen but you must not touch you must keep your hands away or you could break it. I said what is its name and she said I told you Marcus it is not real and so it does not have a name and please make sure your cat Otto does not come in here and mistake my bird for a living thing and try to eat it.

I say did the messenger bring this bird and Magdalena hits my ear and says very well that is all I am going to endure today.

Now I am talking severely to Otto in the meadow by the horse trough because he is trying to catch a bee. I say Otto do not be so silly or I shall take you to Despair.

THE SECRET MINT ROOT

On her journey to Jutland, Kirsten's Woman of the Torso, Vibeke Kruse, was seasick. She was not only sick during the wind-whipped sea crossings, but on the overland traverses as well, so that her coach had to keep stopping while poor Vibeke seemed to be vomiting up the dregs of every blueberry tartlet, every chocolate pie and every pot of vanilla cream that she'd ever eaten. Into the mossy floor of the great forests of southern Jutland sank these colourful remains of her gourmandising. She arrived at Boller in a state of prostration.

Ellen Marsvin had made ready for her a room of some elegance, the sight of which, when the other household staff looked into it and saw a Turkish carpet, a bed dressed with damask and a silver-and-ebony dressing case, caused them to experience one of those surges of jealousy to which they were all so prone. They began to gossip and whisper. They asked each other what Fru Marsvin could possibly have in mind for this unknown person.

But Ellen Marsvin said nothing. And when Vibeke stumbled out of the coach, whey-faced, damp and limp, Ellen merely ordered her to rest "until you are yourself again and I shall have the pleasure of showing you the Boller estate."

Broth was sent up and avidly drunk. A request came down for a mint cordial. Ellen Marsvin went herself to her herb garden and knelt to pinch out a little cluster of mint stalks. She marvelled at the way the mint grew, sending its purple roots far beyond its allotted territory, laying claim to soil that had once nourished sage or thyme, shouldering the other plants out of the way and springing up at distances so far from itself that it was possible to believe it intended to commandeer the entire garden. In a small conceit that suddenly pleased her very much, Ellen Marsvin whispered to herself, "Vibeke is my *secret mint root.*"

A week after Vibeke's arrival, when her face had assumed again its natural vividness of colour and she had been shown the woods and meadows of Boller, two seamstresses arrived to measure her for new clothes.

The seamstresses had particular instructions from Ellen Marsvin, which they had been sworn not to reveal to Vibeke. They brought with them bales of silk and velvet, knots of braid, cards of lace and boxes of pearl buttons, and they circled round and round Vibeke with their tapes while she caressed these things with her hands, which had never been slim and white but always rather rough and red, as though she had passed her life as a milkmaid. As they measured, Vibeke started to dream. She was beginning to get the feeling that some marvellous future awaited her.

Five dresses were commissioned.

So much braid and ribbon, so many small pearls, had to be attached to them and the lace for their ruffs put through so many starchings and pressings that three weeks would pass before the dresses would be finished.

It was the time of the beginning of the fruit bottling. Carts from the Tilsen estate arrived daily with strawberries and the first gooseberries. In the kitchen at Boller, the scrubbing of bottles filled the air with steam that took into itself the perfume of the fruit. To go down there was, for Vibeke, to descend into an ardent, scented paradise where the stomach could be soothed (and yet at the same time tantalised) just by breathing.

Volunteering to help stalk and wash the strawberries, she nevertheless let so many of the berries float up on the fragrant steam towards her lips and tumble into her mouth that the number of bottles filled eventually fell some way short of the total estimated by Ellen Marsvin. "How strange," remarked Ellen. "My calculations are not usually faulty."

When the seamstresses returned with the five new gowns and Vibeke stripped down to her petticoats to put them on, Ellen Marsvin stood watching her closely.

The dresses were very fine. As Vibeke drew the first one over her shoulders and felt the expensive silk caress her arms, her mind was again washed by a swell of dreams. She saw herself presiding over a sumptuous banquet. More marvellous yet than the dishes of pheasant, quail, partridge, beef and wild boar being held aloft for her inspection was the deference with which the guests appeared to treat her, with their smiles and their vigorously nodding heads and their approving laughter.

Oh, but then there was a sudden difficulty!

Vibeke felt her body being pinched—almost bruised—by the seamstresses as they attempted to lace her into the beautiful dress. They pulled and struggled. Ellen Marsvin looked on and showed nothing on her face but mild dismay. Vibeke's dreams unstitched themselves and all that remained was the reality of the too-tight dress and the sight of herself in the glass beginning to look as trussed up and foolish as a guinea fowl.

"I don't understand, Fru Marsvin," she said with a choking in her voice. "My measurements were taken, but now the dress does not fit me."

"No, it does not. I can see that. What a terrible shame," said Ellen. Then she turned to the seamstresses.

"Were Frøken Kruse's dimensions accurately set down?"

They nodded in unison. "Yes, Madam. We took very careful note."

"Is it possible that you could have miscalculated when you made up the dress?"

"No, Fru Marsvin. With material this costly, we would never make any errors."

Ellen Marsvin sighed and said: "Well, perhaps the others will fit. Try on the others, Vibeke."

The hooks and laces were undone and Vibeke felt the dress fall away from her. She watched as the seamstresses laid it aside and took out the second gown, a matchless confection of blue velvet, gold beading and satin bows. The mere touch of it, as she drew this second dress to her, woke in her a fierce longing to be returned to the imaginary banquet where she had been the guest of honour. But it was not to be. Vibeke's flesh could not—by any means employed by the seamstresses—be crammed into the beautiful gown and so this marvel, too, she saw snatched away from her.

When all five dresses had been tried and it was found that none of them fitted, Ellen Marsvin sat down and put her head in her hands. "Really," she said, "it is a great disappointment, Vibeke. The cost of these gowns is enormous and I certainly cannot afford to repeat it. Happily, you brought with you your own wardrobe, which must now serve you . . ."

"Oh, no!" said Vibeke. "It must only be that since coming to Boller I have let myself put on too much weight. If the dresses could only be kept for me then I will promise to curb my eating, which I know is a fault in me and one that I must address. I beg you, Fru Marsvin, do not give the dresses away! Let the seamstresses come back in one month and I swear they will fit me then."

"Ah," said Ellen, "but it is summer now, Vibeke, when the food at Boller is at its most plentiful, when the cream is thickest, when the mutton is at its most tasty and tender . . ."

"I know," said Vibeke, who felt by now that she would like to weep (but yet also, at the mention of "tender mutton," felt an involuntary pang of hunger). "I know, Fru Marsvin, but I swear I shall devise some regimen and keep to it steadfastly, if only these gowns can be mine . . ."

Ellen shook her head and raised her eyes to Vibeke sadly, as if to say, *You will not do it, you will be tempted from it and you will fail*, but then at last she turned to the seamstresses, whose faces betrayed nothing and were every inch as grave and sorrowful as Ellen could have wished, and said: "Let the dresses be kept for Frøken Kruse for six weeks. I shall send for you if her measurements show signs of alteration, but if I do not send, despatch the gowns to Rosenborg for one or other of my daughter's women."

A sound then escaped from Vibeke's throat. Ellen Marsvin will later liken this little sound of anguish to the cry of the blue marsh bittern, very rare in Jutland since the drought of 1589. "Whenever I hear the little shriek of the marsh bittern," Ellen will say, "I am reminded of the mint root and its secret ways."

THE ANNUNCIATION

It is July now, the month when King Christian expects to see the first ingots of silver brought down to Copenhagen from the Numedal mine.

The vision of silver in quantities so great that all his debts will soon be paid provides a safe haven for Christian's anxious mind. When memories of Denmark's defeat in the Religious Wars plague him with fury and remorse, he turns his thoughts to the valley of the *Isfoss* and the million upon million of dalers imprisoned there in the rock. He gives to these dalers (which he no longer sees as lumps of ore but as new-minted coinage) a consciousness and a will. He imagines them yearning to be free, yearning to arrive in his coffers, yearning to be sifted by his royal hands, yearning to serve him. On countless nights, he calls to sleep from the safety of this reverie of money and sleep almost always arrives.

Now, as July begins to pass and still no silver has arrived, Christian starts to fret.

He sits in his study, doing the nation's arithmetic and arriving always at a balance that brings on his indigestion. Everywhere he looks in the country there is need. He finds himself wondering whether there might be something else, some other commodity than hard currency, that could answer this need. But what might that "other commodity" be? Could dykes be constructed without earth and men to move that earth? Would men do this work if they were not paid? No doubt other kings had dreamed of a nation in which their subjects were content to gather up the leaves of autumn and call them gold. But in the end there is no remedy for need except money and more money after that—in quantities that are always and evermore increasing as time runs on and tomorrow's dreams become today's necessities.

King Christian writes out a list entitled *Extreme Measures in the Event of the Failure of the Mine*. These measures include the melting down of his private plate collection and the pawning of Iceland to a consortium of merchants from Hamburg. He also writes down the word "Mother." He adds several question marks after the word, but does not cross it off the list. It was Kirsten who once told him that the Dowager Queen was "sitting like a widow spider on a fat fortune at Kronborg," but Kirsten could give no proof of this, only "the common knowledge that it is true," and so he cannot know, given the long history of quarrels between the two women, whether this is a fact or a pure invention. Whenever he speaks to his mother about money, she always pleads poverty. "I have barely enough," she says, "to buy a basket of anchovies."

Kirsten comes to him one evening as he is doing his sums for the tenth or eleventh time. There is still light at his window and Kirsten places herself before him in such a way that this last golden radiance of the day falls across her face, turning her white skin to amber and discovering little coils of flame in her hair.

Christian puts aside his pen and replaces the stopper of the inkwell. He looks at Kirsten. He perceives no malice or fury in her, but a meekness that is almost tender and which reminds him of the early days of his marriage when she had been soft and malleable in his hands. "Well, my Mouse?" he says.

She sits very upright on the chair, with a smile just lifting the corners of her mouth. "Am I disturbing you?" she asks.

"Only from work that gives me stomach ache."

"What work is that?" she asks and now, for the first time, Christian notices that she seems nervous. In her hands she holds a little bottle of salts and this she keeps turning and turning in her lap.

"Accounts," he replies gently. "But all will be well when the silver arrives from the Numedal. What is the matter, Mouse?"

She lifts her head into the golden light. "Nothing," she says, "or at least I hope you will think it a 'nothing,' or rather something to gladden you, and this is it: when the winter comes, I shall put into your arms another child."

Christian finds that he cannot speak. The realisation that Kirsten still remains, in spite of all her tantrums and rejections, her sulks and accusations, her storms of weeping and her wild behaviour, his true wife and that her body could take his seed into it and let it engender a new life, thereby cementing again the bond between them, sends surging to his breast such an overflow of love and gratitude that he feels tears start in his eyes. In an instant, all his worries about the nation's precarious financial state fall away from him and are forgotten. He holds out his arms. "Kirsten," he says, "come to me. Let us give thanks to God, who brought us together in His house and holds you to me still."

The sun is moving very fast now towards its setting and the gold is gone from Kirsten's face and she is in shadow. She has opened her bottle of salts and is holding them to her nostrils, as though she felt herself about to faint. But then she seems to master the frailty that threatened to overcome her and she rises and comes to the

King. He reaches out for her as ardently as he had reached for her on the day when he first became her lover. He sits her on his knee and kisses her mouth.

King Christian has a private notebook in which he occasionally writes down the thoughts and meditations which seem to come into his mind *uninvited*.

These *Phantom Observations*, as he calls them, fascinate him far more than what he terms his "habitual mundane philosophising." Part of this fascination lies in the fact that he does not know where these things have originated nor how they have come into his head. Is the human brain like a plot of earth where crops, flowers, weeds and even the embryos of mighty trees could seed themselves according to the direction of the wind or the flight patterns of birds? If so, might it be overtaken by the random—as if by giant roots and thistles—so that reason has no space in which to thrive? Should a man strive, therefore, only to let in those thoughts which proceed logically from other thoughts and to protect himself from everything that had about it the *feeling of uninvitedness*? Or, might it be true that certain kinds of valuable perception only arrive as the wind-blown seed arrives in the water meadow, their provenance for ever unknown or unrecorded?

What absorbs Christian about all this is that he does not know the answer to any of it. It resists the definitive. But year by year, his notebooks fill up with these ghosts, these shadows, which, when he reads them again, sometimes seem to have no meaning at all, as if they were the jottings of a madman. One day, he tells himself, he will make a pyre of the notebooks and let all the thoughts and half-thoughts scribbled there rise up as smoke into the vacancy from which they have come.

Later on the night of Kirsten's announcement of her pregnancy, when darkness has come on and he is once again alone, Christian feels himself suddenly tormented by one of these uninvited ideas and this is it: *he has dreamed Kirsten's visit.* When the brain is over-burdened with worry—as his is now—it can start to see strange vis-itations, to conjure reveries, and this is one such insubstantial thing. The truth is that Kirsten never came into his room, never sat where the evening light touched her features, never spoke a word. The truth is that she *has never been there at all.*

Christian hurls his large body out of bed and takes up the lamp. He wakes no servant but goes alone and unshod over the cold mar-ble floors until he comes to Kirsten's rooms.

His knock is answered by the young woman, Emilia, and he can see that beyond her there are lights in the chamber, as though Kirsten had decided to stay up late, to play cards or gossip with her women. But when he pushes past Emilia he realises that the bed-room is empty. The bed has been made ready for the night, but it has not been slept in.

"Did she come to me?" asks the King.

Emilia looks confused. "Come to you, Sir?"

"Earlier this evening. Just as the sun was setting. Did she come to my rooms?"

"I don't know . . ."

"Where is she now, Emilia? Which part of the palace?"

Emilia holds herself very still but looks away from the King when she says: "She has gone out of Copenhagen, Your Majesty—just for the evening . . ."

"Gone out of Copenhagen? To what end? To whose house?"

"She did not say, Sir. She asked me to wait up for her, that is all."

King Christian walks to Kirsten's bed and stares at it. Then he reaches out and picks up the lace edging of the sheet and begins to fold it over towards the bed-head. He does this very tenderly, al-most as though he saw Kirsten asleep there, with her hair spread in a fiery halo on the pillow, and was trying to cover her from the night's chill.

Since his meeting in the cellar with Emilia, Peter Claire has felt himself to be living in a mild state of astonishment.

He finds it almost difficult to believe that what was said there can possibly have *been said*. He plays and replays the conversation, as though it might be a piece of music, the performance of which could be expected to undergo a gradual amelioration. Except that there is no amelioration. The stark fact remains: he offered his love to Emilia Tilsen and Emilia Tilsen refused him. In any version of the dialogue, however worded or reconstituted, her refusal is there and cannot be ignored.

It puzzles him more than it might puzzle other men because he is not used to being refused. In his twenty-seven years of life, women have behaved towards Peter Claire as the sea behaves towards the wind. His power to disturb their calm, to whip up their longings and even—at some ardent soirée in the early hours—to cause their mouths to be touched with a fleck of passionate foam, has never before deserted him. Yet now, when at last his feelings run deep and sure, when he seems to know that his future lies with Emilia and that a truly happy life would await him if his love were reciprocated, this one young woman appears as indifferent to him as stone. She was far more affected by the hens in their plight, by concern and sorrow for them, than by his declaration. She told him plainly that no understanding between them ever existed.

Yet she did come to the rendezvous.

In this one fact, Peter Claire chooses to see some reassurance. His note to her might simply have been ignored—as a thousand such hasty letters are glanced at and thrown away—and it was not. And Emilia seemed, as she descended into the vaults . . . what did she seem? Not quite, perhaps, the immovable stone he has conjured. Rather, a little like a tree, a sapling, that is too low to be rocked by the wind, but nevertheless finds itself in a small state of agitation.

And something else fills him with a strange wonderment:

Emilia's refusal has made her more beautiful to him. It has given her a mystery that she had not previously possessed.

He wishes that his sister, Charlotte, were here to tell him what to do next. Is he to take the refusal merely as a sign of Emilia's modesty and goodness, and so devise some continuation of his wooing of her that will nevertheless assure her how much he prizes these things in her? Or should he cease all advances to her, in the expectation that she might then regret her severity in the cellar and give him some sign that she would welcome their renewal?

Peter Claire sits in the refectory with Jens Ingemann and ponders these questions and, at last, asks the music master how he himself considers the great question of love.

They are eating herring with mustard. The quantity of mustard Jens Ingemann has spread around his herring is surprising.

"I do not consider the so-called question of love at all," says Ingemann baldly.

"You mean that you never think about it, Herr Ingemann?"

"I mean that I believe it to be irrelevant to any intelligent life."

"And yet—"

"There are no 'and yets,' Mr. Claire. What we aggrandise with the term 'love' is the selfsame involuntary thing that consumes the stench toad at the end of winter."

They eat the herring. Jens Ingemann swirls the salty fish in its bath of yellow and swallows it fast. After a while, Peter Claire says: "Did you believe this when you were young?"

"Oh, yes. That is not to say that I did not enjoy behaving like a toad. And it may be that toads experience rapture. Why should they not? And who can say, if toads had language, that they would not call it something else? Now, if you are asking me about the love of God, or my love of music, then I would give you a different answer."

"These are the things which bind you to the world? Nothing and no one else?"

"Bind me to the world?" Here, Jens Ingemann swallows his last morsel of herring in its mustard bath and lets a cold smile cross his features. "They do not bind me to the world, Mr. Claire. Far from it. They remind me that the world is a hideous and darkling pit from which I hope soon to escape."

He wipes his mouth with a linen napkin, then folds the napkin into a small neat square and places it beside his plate. Peter Claire finds himself transfixed by these actions, as though he expected them to reveal to him some important truth missing from the conversation. He knows that all they reveal, in fact, is Jens Ingemann's fastidiousness and passion for order, and that now, just as he does every mealtime, Jens Ingemann will close his eyes in a silent grace, then get up and return his chair to its rightful position in regard to the table, and walk slowly out of the refectory. But he wants, before he lets this happen, to ask the music master one last question, and so he puts out a hand to forestall the grace and says hurriedly: "Music Master, what do you say, then, about the King's love for his wife?"

Jens Ingemann's eyes, on the point of closing—as though the grace were a momentary sleep which overcame him every day at this hour—open reluctantly. "I say," he intones in a weary voice, "that it is the greatest misery ever to come upon him."

Peter Claire leaves the refectory at last and walks out of the palace gates and into the city, and loses himself in the crowds of the market-place. He does not know what he hopes to find among the shoe menders, the oyster sellers and the weavers, but to be here, to be in the world outside Rosenborg, always brings to him a familiar gladness of spirit, as if he were a child again and riding with his mother to see the fair at Woodbridge.

He pauses by a ribbon maker's stall and buys some white satin ribbons for Charlotte. When he holds them in his hands it is not Charlotte that he sees; his mind threads them into Emilia's brown hair and he imagines the scent of the hair and the soft warmth of the nape of her neck, and the silky ribbons falling down her back.

I am moving on a wire suspended above a chasm: this is how my Life appears to me. Will the wire break? Will I be cast onto the rocks of disgrace and misery? Or shall I continue to balance by some miracle in my world between the sky and the earth?

The success of my Announcement to the King (seeming to create in him not one whit of mistrust, but only the same innocent joyfulness with which he has greeted the news of the conception of all our many Children) brought to my breast such Relief that I was seized with an immediate Recklessness and did something which, I do declare, could have been my Undoing, had matters so conspired against me. I ordered a carriage to be brought to my door and, wearing a mask of feathers and carrying with me a riding crop, I fled in it to Otto's lodgings.

Now, I had sworn to myself that I would not weaken and visit my lover in Copenhagen until the whole matter of his Child had settled so deeply into its Coverlet of Lies that I was no longer at any risk from Accusations of Treason. But on that fine evening, in the wake of my excellent Performance as the King's loyal wife, my rage to mate with the Count was such that I could not master it by any means and do declare that I was in every particular no better than a mare in her Heat who, at the merest sniff of the stallion, reveals to him her inviting second Mouth, like a sudden vulgar pink orchid touched with dew.

Otto was with a group of Cronies playing cards. When the message that "Brigitte" awaited him was taken to him, he came at once into the room where I waited and said to me: "Alas, it is my turn to deal a hand. I cannot be absent from the room longer than three or four minutes."

"Well," I said. "Make haste, then, my dear Stefan."

He seized my arm and hustled me into a small chamber, really no bigger than a Closet, and I could not help but notice that a quantity of brooms and pails and feather dusters resided there, but I did not for long dwell on these, for no sooner had Otto's hand pushed up my skirt and begun to caress me than I came swiftly to my Pleasure. "Stefan!" I cried out. "Oh, let me die!" But Otto hissed at me not to scream for fear of discovery and then, while the Card Players waited downstairs and the minutes began to tick away, he pinioned me standing upright among the Cleaning Utensils, undid himself and took me in this way, with magnificent haste and brutality, while I thwacked his naked loins with the riding crop and he whispered, "Harder, Brigitte, harder!" so that all was over almost before it had begun and he fell against me gasping for breath. I felt his heart beating wildly against mine. I said: "Otto, my dearest lover, we shall never be free of each other. Never."

When I returned to Rosenborg, after ordering the carriage to drive in circles for some time so that I could recover my Composure, Emilia told me that the King had been to my chamber and discovered my Absence.

Once again, I felt myself to be upon my Wire and fancied I could hear the wind come round me and begin to cause the Wire to sway and move, and I could feel all the colour drain from my face and my legs grow weak.

I ordered Emilia to make haste to bring water and soap, and with this I hurriedly washed all traces of Otto from my body. Then I put on a clean night-gown and got into my bed. "If the King comes again," I said to Emilia, "let him come in. I will say that I went for a drive in the countryside to refresh my lungs. There is no Edict against breathing the night air."

He did not come. Emilia quietened my Anxieties by telling me that the King had seemed confused and that she supposed he had been drinking (as is his habit more and more) and then by reciting to me some sweet Stories about her dead mother, Karen, who used to dance with her on the ice in winter and in summer make for her a hammock of silk to be strung between two linden trees, and rock her there and sing to her.

I could clearly see that, in every tender particular, Emilia's Mother was a deal kinder to her daughter than I have ever been to my tiresome Children, and this observation might well have made me Hate Myself in the way that I am prone to do when I perceive my own Shortcomings. But I did not feel vexed, only sorry that I could not meet this dead Karen and by some miracle bring her alive again, so that she could return at last to the fruit fields of Jutland, to send the odious Magdalena flying back to wherever she came from, pursued by a swarm of bees.

In the early morning, I was once again put into a state of Terror by the sudden and unlooked-for arrival of Doctor Sperling. He brought with him his case of Instruments, the sight of which is enough to fill any woman's heart with dread, so cold and cruel do these things appear.

"Madam," he said, "I have been asked by the King to examine you. He has told me he believes you may be with child."

"May be?" I said. "There is no 'may be' in the matter, Doctor Sperling. I informed His Majesty last night that I will give him a new child in the winter."

The Doctor has small brown eyes that have no shine in them but seem quite dead, as if they might be stones. "Very well," he said. "If you would lie upon the bed, then I will verify how far advanced is your pregnancy so that we may know the date on which the infant is to be born."

For a moment I could not move, so great was my fear. But, as quickly as I could, I replied: "There is no need for any examination, Doctor. For was not the King away in the Numedal until the month of June? Thus, we can determine with great accuracy when the baby was conceived and we have only to count forward nine months to arrive at the date of its Birth."

"Nevertheless," said the Doctor, "I must make the examination, as commanded."

I let my eyes rest upon the Instruments. Feigning an even greater terror of them than I already felt, I let myself begin to swoon and fall. "No!" I heard myself cry out, "I cannot submit! I swear if you do this I shall miscarry . . ."

At this moment the King came in. Seeing me fallen in a faint, he ran to me and lifted me up and called for Salts. Knowing that all depended upon this moment, I pretended to be unconscious in his arms until I smelled the Salts under my nostrils. Then I opened my eyes and clung to my husband and said: "Oh, my dearest Lord, help me. Do not risk the life of the child by letting the doctor put any cold metal into my body!"

The King held me to him and said: "So I did not dream it, then?"

"Dream what?"

"Dream that you came to me and told me about the child . . ."

"Oh, no, the child is real and no ghost nor dream, but please, Sir, I beg you, send the doctor away!"

I hung about the King's neck as though I were his weakling Baby and he my wicked incestuous Papa. And in this mode I know that I can make him do almost Any Thing my heart can devise. In a very short while, I heard the doctor leave the room and close the door behind him.

And so the summer goes on in its heat and its plagues of flies. My belly begins to balloon outwards and my legs to ache. Were the child the King's and not my lover's, I declare I would seek out from Herr Bekker some deadly potion to rid myself of it. But, being Otto's, I cannot do it harm. It was made in a moment of Delirium and I imagine that it will fly out of me on trembling wings of blossom.

GERDA (1)

Emilia Tilsen stands in the cellar, staring at the hens.

They come clustering to her and poke their beaks through the wire of the cage. She can see a solitary egg lying in the dusty earth. She has brought grain and a pitcher of water.

She opens the door of the cage and goes in and begins to scatter the corn, and she likes the feeling of the feathered bodies round her skirt. It reminds her of going with Karen, as a child, to search for eggs laid carelessly here and there in the meadows and hedgerows, and of the joy of finding them and of Karen saying: "Well done, my peach."

These hens are greyish-brown and speckled, with white neck feathers. Jerkily, their heads nod in search of the grain and, her task accomplished, Emilia is about to leave when she sees that one of the hens has not moved, but only sits in the dust regarding her with a clouded yellow eye. Emilia squats down, folding her skirts round her to keep them out of the dirt, and stares at the bird. Once, long ago in Jutland, Karen nursed a sick hen back to health with boiled nettles. It lived for a while in the house and sometimes, as it began to recover, acquired the habit of flying up onto the dining-table at mealtimes. They called it Gerda. Johann warned it that the only chicken he wished to see on the dining-table was one that was plucked and roasted.

It is in memory of Gerda that Emilia, without hesitation, picks up the speckled hen, puts it under her arm and carries it out of the cellar. She takes it to her room—not to the chamber next door to Kirsten's where she often sleeps now, but to the high, sparsely furnished room she was given on her arrival at Rosenborg. She fetches a bundle of clean straw from the stables and makes a nest for the hen in one corner of the room. Compared with the cellar, the room is light and the bird keeps turning its head towards the window, as though the sky were a phenomenon it could not begin to understand. So touched by the sight of the hen's confusion does Emilia feel that she begins to stroke its neck. "Gerda," she whispers. "Gerda . . ."

And then she falls into a kind of dreaming. She is wide awake and can hear the sounds of voices far below in the courtyard and a restless fly bumping from surface to surface in the room, but her head suddenly fills with an imaginary future.

She has become the wife of the English lutenist, and she and Peter Claire are living in some green valley she has never seen. Their house is filled with light. Children cling, laughing, to her skirts, and she takes their hands and brings them to a fine room with a polished wooden floor, where Peter Claire and his friends are playing music so tender and melodic that the children become grave and silent and sit down on the floor to listen, and she sits by them and no one moves.

This dream is so extraordinary, so filled with marvels, that Emilia tries to prolong it. She imagines the music ending and the lutenist crossing the room towards her, and gathering her and the children into his arms. And Marcus is there! He is a little older— perhaps six or seven—and he turns a cart-wheel in the room before running out into the garden, where his bay pony is waiting with its bridle of bells. .

Death seems absent from this dream. What reigns in the house is order and harmony, and there does not seem to be any fear that these things will suddenly vanish. "But," says Emilia to herself as the dream begins to slip away, "it is not real. It is all sentimental delusion. It should have no place whatsoever in your mind."

And she gets up hurriedly and goes out into the park to search for stinging nettles.

But now, at night and at other times—in the middle of a meal or a game of cribbage—her thoughts return to what was said by Peter Claire in the cellar. He declared a feeling for her. "Love," he said, "is the word which seems to fit it." Why did she not stay to hear more, to try to see or read in his eyes and gestures whether he was sincere? Was not her immediate assumption that a man as hand-some as this must be a liar too hastily made and too unkind? Why did she force herself to be so curt to him, when everything spoken by him was courteous and tender, and she yearned to believe every syllable?

She disappoints herself. Truly, she has no idea what behaviour to put on. She is an ungracious, ignorant girl who knows nothing about the world of men and women except what she has seen in the Tilsen house and here at the court. In these places, lies and schemes fill up the very air of the rooms, but this may surely not be so in every household in Denmark? Why should a declaration of love *of necessity* be false? How would any wooing be able to progress at all if this were a universal truth?

Emilia stirs her nettle potion in a cup. She sucks a little of it into a dry straw, as she once watched Karen do, then opens the hen's beak and tips the dribble of liquid down its throat. She repeats this laborious procedure until half an inch of the nettle potion has been swallowed. "Gerda," she murmurs.

It is to Kirsten that Emilia eventually confides what took place in the cellar and how, in a moment of dreaming, she foolishly allowed herself to invent a beautiful future with the lutenist.

"What lutenist?" asks Kirsten crossly. "There was a lutenist here for years, but he was very elderly and I expect he's in his grave now. You don't mean him, I hope, Emilia?"

Emilia describes Peter Claire to Kirsten and sees her eyes begin to bulge. "Well," she says, "I haven't seen any such paragon at Rosenborg—not that I go to the concerts any more; they are too tedious and I only pretended to love music when the King was courting me. Are you quite sure you did not dream it all?"

"No," says Emilia. "I did not dream it all, only the part of it that did not happen . . ."

Kirsten gets up and looks out of her window. Her walking is beginning to be slow and she cradles her belly, as if it already weighs her down. When she turns round, she says: "Beware the beauties, Emilia. I have never known one who was not a dissembler. And as for the English: they have a reputation for coldness, but Otto has fought alongside them in war and he tells me they are the most devious fornicators of them all!"

"Well . . ." says Emilia. "I was very cool with him . . . I promise you that I did not give him any hope and yet—"

"Do nothing," says Kirsten. "If you should encounter him by chance, avoid his eyes. It would be intolerable that your heart should be broken, for what would you do then but leave me and go back to Jutland?"

"Oh, no, I would never go back to my father's house, Madam."

"Nevertheless, I cannot risk any such catastrophe coming to me, Emilia. I will find out what kind of man the English lutenist is. I will uncover his secrets and then I shall report them to you, and we shall determine how to proceed."

"FLYING TOWARDS RUIN"

No silver has arrived. Messengers sent to the Numedal have not returned.

King Christian lies in the dark and imagines he can hear his beloved country groaning deep in its heart, as though it were indeed a ship about to go down with all hands lost. And, on the horizon, an even blacker storm begins to gather . . .

He tries to understand how poverty has crept in where it should never have been. He berates himself for his mania—in his desire that everything in Denmark might be of the best quality and free from shoddiness—to employ foreign craftsmen. For now these same people grow rich and coffers of Danish silver and gold are shipped away to France or Holland or Italy, and only a poor fraction of it is left behind.

Yet all cannot be blamed on the foreigners. When Christian goes into the houses of the Danish nobility, what he sees is indulgence and luxury and waste on a scale so enormous that it takes his breath away. Men pick their teeth with silver and toss the picks away into the fire. Their rooms are lighted with two hundred candles. They keep llamas and ostriches in gilded cages for their amusement. They feed swan meat to their dogs. Their wives take up the new French fashion for wigs, and the French wig makers are become the new darlings of their world, and are paid with lascivious kisses and velvet purses full of dalers. The cribs of infants are fashioned from ebony . . .

All this must end.

King Christian gets up and calls for servants to light lamps, and he settles down at his bureau. He takes up his pen and begins to write.

He writes a momentous speech. The night has almost gone by the time it is finished. He intends to summon an Extraordinary Meeting of the *Rigsråd* and shock the self-satisfied nobility with the vehemence of his words. He will demand that every one of the nobles attend the meeting, yet even now, after his long hours of work, as he reads through the speech, he already hears in his mind the excuses of his chancellor: ". . . you know it is summer, Your Majesty, and somewhat close in Copenhagen. Many of our councillors are gone into Jutland for the cooler air . . ."

Christian feels anger in him like a sickness, like a physical agony that must rise up and come out. "I have called you here," the speech begins, "because I am in despair. I am your King. I am King of Denmark. But what is Denmark today? Where is it today? I tell you, my friends, that it is a sorry land. I tell you that it is flying towards ruin!"

But what will be the fate of these words? Who will hear them and take action? Christian imagines the faces of his councillors, like fat pink potatoes balanced on their starched white plates of ruffs. These men—those of them who will bestir themselves to come to the meeting—will listen to the speech, but no hint of worry or anguish will be visible on their faces; the universal patronising smile will quietly announce their knowledge of their own immovable power and their indifference to anything but their own comfort and their own arithmetic.

Always, King Christian has had to fight the nobility in the *Rigsråd* in asserting his power against theirs, but where once this battle—which began so long ago with the explosion of a skyrocket outside the Court House building—enthralled him, now it causes him bitter pain. For the truth is that these men no longer give him the respect he once commanded. His troubles with Kirsten, impossible as they are to conceal from the wider world, have belittled and weakened him in their eyes.

Choked by this knowledge, which will mean that his great speech will go unheeded and that nothing will be accomplished, the King imagines raising his wide fist and bringing it crashing down so hard on the council table that the papers he has brought with him lift into the air and a heavy gold and emerald ring one of the noblemen has taken off to relieve his fingers of its weight bounces upwards and lands on the floor. Immediately this man begins to scrabble after the jewel.

"Leave the ring!" King Christian shouts. "There shall be no more stooping after gems and riches! We are become a class of people enslaved to excess and every one of us should bow down to God in shame. But I am God's minister on earth and I hereby announce to you today that our vainglory has had its season and is past."

Here, the King takes a breath. Will he have the councillors' attention at last? He goes on. He warns them that a weak Denmark will no longer exist but only be "a nameless land under the sway of Sweden." He asks: "Shall your King rule over a desert? Is this the future that you would lead me to? Imagine this desert. If I were to pick up a handful of this desert soil, what would I find? I tell you that I would find the dust of regret, the sand of remorse. And no amount of weeping will make this desert flower and become what it once was. What it once was will have disappeared for ever!"

He pauses here. Will there be silence in the room? And if there is silence, what will the nobles be thinking? Christian puts his large head in his hands. He knows that his speech is doomed and will never be made. He was going to ask for a law to be passed against futile vanity, but how can he expect the *Rigsråd* to ratify such an edict when they know that Kirsten is indifferent to what she has called "the supposed poverty of Denmark," indifferent to how and where money is to be found to pay for her clothes and trinkets, her coterie of women, her suppers and entertainments? There will never be any such law while Kirsten remains at Rosenborg and this is the heart-breaking truth of the matter.

The King gets up wearily. He notices that the sunrise at his window is serene and lovely. Nature knows nothing of a country's ignominy.

He summons Peter Claire, who is still wiping the dust of sleep from his blue eyes.

The lutenist is ordered to play quietly and the King hears himself ask the young Englishman if he should sack all the foreign musicians and replace them with Danes.

Peter Claire looks at him with alarm, but then he recovers his composure enough to say: "This measure would save you money, Your Majesty, but I do not think that you would be happy with the result. The sweet complexity of sound made by this orchestra lies, I am sure, in the variety of our origins."

The King lies down in his bed. Already, with the music playing and with his angel by him, he feels calmer and, after a little time, he falls asleep.

When he wakes, he is told that his physician, Doctor Sperling, wishes to see him. Bread and cream are brought to him, but he has no appetite and sends the food away.

He has a longing to be out in the air and orders the doctor to walk with him in the park, where the day has continued fine and his favourite roses are still in bloom.

Doctor Sperling's expression is grim and yet at the same time his face seems to be struggling with a secret smile as he says: "Sir, unhappy as I am to trouble you with this matter, it has preyed so insistently on my mind that I cannot put it from me and so feel at last that I must speak to you . . ."

"Then speak to me, Doctor."

"It is a matter that concerns your wife . . ."

"If it concerns Kirsten," says the King, "then assuredly I must hear it."

They walk on. The scent of the roses reminds Christian of his mother, who, when she was young, liked to have a bowl of roses in her bedchamber.

The doctor's steps begin to slow and falter, and he masters his smile, to make it fade, as he says: "Sir, I must reveal to you that when I visited Lady Kirsten . . . although she would not submit to any examination . . ."

"Yes?"

"Well, Your Majesty . . . because she fell prone upon the floor and was wearing but her thin night garment, I was able to make . . ."

"Make what?"

"Make some anatomical observations, and I could clearly see . . . or so it appears to me . . . that the child shows itself already. And this I know, that no child in the womb makes itself plain in quite this way until approximately three months have passed, and thus I conclude . . ."

The King says nothing at all, only paces onwards with his long stride, so that Sperling now has to perform a little skittering run to keep up with him.

They have left the rose garden behind and are walking under an avenue of limes, in their wide shade, where the air is cool. The King does not look at Doctor Sperling but at the lime trees, seeming to examine them for signs of death or weakness. When they reach the end of the avenue he turns to the doctor and says: "Thank you very much, Doctor Sperling."

The doctor opens his mouth to qualify in greater detail what he has noted about Kirsten's pregnancy, but the King holds up a hand to cut him off. "Thank you for your observations," he says again.

Sperling looks confused (almost disappointed, as though deprived of the chance to recite some poem he had learned by heart) but he has no choice but to bow and retreat.

Christian waits until he is out of sight and then sits down on a stone bench that rests between two carved lions. He caresses his elflock. He looks back across the park to his beloved palace, his little Rosenborg, built for Kirsten, built in celebration of his love for her, and tears come to his eyes. He does not need to ask who Kirsten's lover is. He knows. He saw her dancing with Count Otto Ludwig at Werden, during the time of the wars. He saw the rapture on her face and that was all that he needed to see. He weeps silently at first, then feels his whole body give way to a terrible howling, such as he seems to have heard inside himself for days and months, and which at last comes out.

He is far from the palace and no one hears him. He tries to wipe away his tears with his sacred lock of hair, but the tears are abundant and the hair is beginning to grow thin. He remembers his great speech, lying on the open bureau. In his mind's eye he rolls it up, ties it with a black ribbon and lays it down in the musty depths of a closet he seldom visits.

GERDA (2)

Sitting down to compose a letter to his father and to Charlotte, Peter Claire unfolds the package of white ribbons and looks at them. One of the ribbons—the most costly of the purchase—has a gold thread running through it.

He knows, immediately upon taking up the ribbons in his hand again, that he is not going to send them to Charlotte. He arranges them carefully in the package and ties it up again. He has decided that the white and gold ribbons will be his messengers to Emilia.

He writes a simple note:

My dear Miss Tilsen,
　　These are the colours of my love.
　　Please tell me when I might walk with you in the park.
　　　Your very sincere
　　　　Peter Claire, Lutenist

He knows where her room is, in the highest storeys of the palace, and he plans only to leave the parcel with the note outside her door, arriving and departing when he knows she is not there.

In the late afternoons she is almost always with Kirsten. He has caught glimpses of the two women doing their tapestry in the garden, or sitting at an open-air table, playing dice or cards, or perched—in these latter days of summer—each of them in front of a small easel, trying to paint flowers. This flower painting touches him so deeply that he almost cannot bear to think about it.

He chooses a day when they are at their easels, frowning at the difficulties of their work, and climbs the stairs to Emilia's corridor. He tiptoes along it, hoping that no one will see him, and pauses outside her door. He can hear no voices or sounds except a dog barking in the courtyard and a few pigeons fluttering from turret to turret as the sun slowly loses its heat and starts to fall behind the west tower of the palace.

He is about to set down the little package of ribbons outside Emilia's door, when he hears another sound, which his long hours in the cellar enable him to identify easily enough: it is the noise of a hen coming from within the room.

Deciding that he has mistaken the room, but unsure whether Emilia must occupy the chamber to the right or to the left of this one, Peter Claire knocks tentatively on the door. Getting no answer (only a continuation of the hen's small murmurings, which sound to him always as if these birds are perpetually on the edge of a contented sleep) he opens the door and goes in.

The room is plain and bare—not unlike his own sparsely furnished chamber above the stables—but hanging from the door of the wardrobe is a grey dress he recognises as Emilia's and on a small dressing stand have been placed those simple articles of vanity that any young girl desires to own: a silver mirror and hairbrush, a cake of Spanish soap, a bottle of orange-flower water and a porcelain dish holding two or three silver clips and brooches.

On the narrow and tidy bed lies a small velvet pillow and on this Peter Claire sees the speckled hen sitting, as if upon a nest, and blinking nervously at him. In the far corner of the room he notices a heap of clean straw and a bowl of water. A few white chicken feathers litter the floor like blown thistledown.

Closing the door behind him, Peter Claire now allows himself to take in the place where Emilia sleeps and dreams, and has her private moments of washing and dressing. He stands absolutely still.

The presence of the chicken, though it makes him smile, only contributes, in him, to a growing feeling of enchantment. The room is warm in the late afternoon sun and Peter Claire has no wish to move a step from where he is. In the very air, in the shelter of the grey dress, in the quietude of the dressing stand, in the hen's own tuneless music, appears to reside the one element (that has no substance and no concrete form) after which the human mind yearns always and which it so seldom finds: happiness.

Peter Claire does not know how long he stays in Emilia's room. At last, he makes himself leave, places the gift of ribbons outside the door and goes back into the other world, where the day is coming to a clamorous ending and the dusk is descending, and the palace chefs are preparing supper.

Emilia does not return to her room that night. Kirsten is feeling restless and sick, and wants her to sleep near her in the next-door chamber. In the small hours of the morning she is woken by Kirsten's cries, which come out of nightmares Kirsten tells her are "more terrible than any I have ever had."

She orders Emilia to prepare a vomit. "By this odious means," she says, "we shall bring the terrors out of me."

Emilia mixes the powders as instructed and, as Kirsten retches into the bowl that Emilia holds, Kirsten clings to her arm and weeps. "Oh, smell the fear!" she cries. "Take it away, Emilia! I am poisoned with fear!"

The night is long. Emilia's head aches as the sun begins to appear at Kirsten's windows. Seeing her mistress peacefully asleep at last, as the Woman of the Head, Johanna, comes in to set out the combs and pins for Kirsten's hair and the ceruse for her pale cheeks, Emilia escapes to the stillness of her high room and to her morning task of dosing Gerda with the nettle potion.

While Gerda is cared for, the package of ribbons, unopened, and the note, unread, wait on the dressing stand.

But then at last she turns to them. She remarks for the second time that Peter Claire has beautiful handwriting. And the note has, beneath its apparent simplicity, an ardour which Emilia finds enthralling.

When she discovers the white and gold ribbons, her heart begins to beat wildly. Slowly, she picks up her silver mirror and, on hanging it on the wall, stares at herself. She knows now that *something has happened*. She begins to weave the white ribbons in and out of her brown hair.

LETTER FROM COUNTESS O'FINGAL TO PETER CLAIRE

My dear Peter,

I learn from your father that you are at the Danish court.

How splendid that must seem to you in contrast to your sojourn at Cloyne. I expect that all of what passed between us has been obliterated by those things that are happening to you now, but I still find myself wondering whether you ever think of me, as I think of you. You know that we women are such fools for memory; I declare we do walk backwards through life, with our faces turned towards the past.

One afternoon, in particular, I shall never forget.

It was a fine blue day and we walked on the beach with Luca and Giulietta, and found on the tide a quantity of pink shells like babies' toes.

And then you and Giulietta sped off over the sands with her hoop, each with a stick, and on and on you ran and the hoop sped before you faster and faster, but still you kept it bowling and still it did not tremble nor fall and you were like the flying spirits of the wind, dark and fair, against the blue sky.

Now I must tell you what came to pass after you went away.

My husband began to move towards death. And it was a death such as I pray never again to witness in my life.

Johnnie O'Fingal died by slow degrees. Day by dawdling day Death tightened its hold upon his voice and began to choke it, so that to make any word or sound come out, my husband had to summon all his forces and all his breath, and his eyes would almost seem to move forward under the lids (so that Vincenzo could not go near his papa without the terror that an eye would come out and lie suspended on his cheek) and the blood pulsed crimson in his face.

And it was not merely that language was leaving him. In this long-drawn-out strangulation of his vocal cords was a pain like fire.

"Help me!" he would try to say. "Help me!"

But there was no help. There was laudanum, that deadly ether, only that. And Doctor McLafferty said to me: "What do we hear along this path of life, Countess, but the eternally repeated cry, 'Help me, help me'?"

We did not know when death would come.

Maria who I do think loved her father most—his Sweet Mary—clung to me and cried, "Oh, Mama, the pity of it!" and said her prayers aloud with Giulietta. But the boys— when Johnnie's voice was quite used up and gone, and the breath in his body seemed to be no more than might keep a sparrow alive and he lay there in silence gasping for the sweet air—kept asking me: "Why did these things happen to him, Mama?" And I said I did not know.

"Is this what a man's life must be like?" they asked, weeping.

And I said I did not know.

He is buried at Cloyne.

I remember some words my father said: "Francesca, you must not prevent a man who has seen paradise from trying to go there again."

I pray that this is where he is.

I am alone with the children here. The estate passes to Vincenzo on his maturity, but I shall live in the house until that time and I have enough money to set all to rights among the farms and tenant cottages. And the people of Cloyne are good to us and I am not very often alone.

But I felt impelled to tell you what has happened in this household and to ask you, Do you still wear the ear-ring that I gave you?

Wherever you are, Peter Claire, know that I passionately loved you. I suspect that you do not particularly wish to hear this and that I am still looking backwards, as we women are so inclined to do. But for this fault, I ask your forgiveness.

Francesca, Countess O'Fingal

THREADS OF CRIMSON

Johann Tilsen notices that the flies and insects in Jutland, in this hot summer, seem to be more venomous than they have ever been. His neck is swollen and red where a horse-fly has punctured a blood vessel; at night, the infernal whining of mosquitoes seems to be part of a sudden feeling of apprehension that he cannot account for.

In the meagre portion of the bed left to him by Magdalena's voluptuous body he finds himself lying with his arms shielding his face. The mosquitoes feast on his elbows, where the sleeves of his summer night-shirt fall back towards his shoulders. The lumps they leave there (the pink and yellow colour of a strawberry before it is ripe) he anoints with vinegar, but the itching is brutal nevertheless. And while inspecting boxes of blackcurrants being sent over to Boller, he is stung by a wasp on his lip.

This sting is a final humiliation because he knows it makes him look ugly. To Magdalena he says: "I am being persecuted! God is sending me torments out of the sky."

But Magdalena is neither a sentimental nor a superstitious woman. "What a baby you are, Johann!" she says. "Nothing but a baby, with all your little needs and hurts."

The only place where the insects do not come is by the lake. In the hot afternoons, the boys Ingmar and Wilhelm, Boris and Matti swim here and Magdalena sits in a bower Johann has made for her out of wood and rushes, and watches them and smiles to herself, imagining the lessons she will one day give them in secret.

Marcus comes to the lake, too, but he does not swim, and Mag-

dalena does not look at him and he does not look at Magdalena.
He spends all his time staring down into the shallows.

Sometimes Marcus catches minnows in his hands and examines
their silvery bodies for a moment before throwing them back into
the water. He sees frogs and a black water snake, which he tries to
trap. The snake mesmerises him, as though it were a messenger,
like the one sent to him from Copenhagen. He imagines this thin
snake slithering down the cleft between Magdalena's breasts and
biting her stomach. To Marcus Tilsen it is as if the creatures of the
lake were all trying to talk to him and listen for his commands. He
counts them and whispers to them in a voice that no one else can
hear.

Then, one afternoon, while Ingmar and the other boys are
swimming far out towards a little island where willows form a cave
of darkness under their trailing branches, and while Marcus is
singing to a swarm of tadpoles, imagining them as a cluster of musical notes, Magdalena suddenly screams. Her body, in the bower,
goes rigid and then slack. On her face is a look of astonishment.

Marcus stares at her. He hopes that in a moment she will lie
completely still. Emilia told him long ago that people can die in an
instant, in the time it takes to count to two. After that, there is
nothing to be done except to dig a hole in the earth and put them
in it. Marcus muses that the hole someone would have to dig for
Magdalena would be very large and deep. It would be terrible to
have bits of Magdalena—a hand or a piece of skirt—still showing
after she was meant to be in her hole. But the earth of the fruit
fields is soft and digging there wouldn't be so difficult and then,
next year, gooseberries could be put in over the top of her and no
one would remember where she was or even that she had ever existed.

Magdalena is calling to him, but he has not heard. He turns and
looks out at the lake, and sees his brothers arrive at the island and
begin to climb out among the willow caves. They have not heard
her calling, either. Her face is bright red now and she is clutching

her belly and screaming again. She is no longer sitting on her little seat, but lying on the floor of the bower among the rushes. Her legs twitch.

"Marcus!" she screams. "*Marcus!*"

Now, he thinks, now, if I had that black snake, I would carry it there, stroking its head, and lay it down on her and it would disappear under her clothes like a trail of wet soot, and then in a moment she would certainly *stop screaming and be quiet*—just as she so often tells me to do when my harness is put on, or when Otto is thrown out of doors into the cold night . . .

"MARCUS!"

The rushes where she lies are wet, as his own cot is often wet in the darkness or in the daytime when he's there alone in his harness, which squeaks and cries.

"MARCUS!"

He looks back towards the island, but he can't see any of his brothers. They have disappeared among the trees. He begins to count. One, two, three, four, five, six, seven, eight, nine . . . Perhaps, sometimes, dying can take a while and you can probably still piss onto the rushes and cry out just before it happens. Ten, eleven, twelve, thirteen, fourteen, fifteen . . . But now, on the wet rushes, with her legs sticking upwards and her face turning scarlet and her eyes screwed into puffy slits, she looks so horrible that Marcus can't bear to watch her any more.

He splashes out of the shallows and begins to run. He runs right past the bower without looking at Magdalena. Even without his shoes, he can run fast because he is as light as the wind.

He hides in the stables.

His head fills with counting.

The bay pony swishes out at the flies with its tail and Marcus leans against its neck. The straw is scratchy on his naked feet.

The smell of the stables is so lovely that Marcus wishes he could sleep here instead of in his room where the walls are always dark in their corners and the damp-wool stench of his bed makes him long to fly out of the window and be with the owls under the stars and the moon . . .

When he wakes, he knows that whatever was happening to Magdalena must have ended because he has a feeling of something ending. Perhaps Johann has arrived at the lake, and Ingmar and Wilhelm are digging the hole in the soft earth and putting Magdalena in it, with nothing showing or sticking out? Perhaps, when Magdalena is buried and gone, there will be no more harness and Otto will sleep with him in his cot, and Emilia will come home?

Slowly, flitting from tree to tree, from hedge to hedge, Marcus makes his way back to the lake. On the mossy path he makes no sound and he stands by the bower like a ghost that no one sees.

Magdalena is no longer in the bower, where the rushes are shiny with blood. She is walking towards the lake. On one side of her is Johann and on the other side of her is an old woman Marcus has never seen. They hold Magdalena up. Her skirts are tied round her waist and her bottom and legs are bare and wet with blood.

She is led into the water. At the first lapping round of the cool water she lets out a kind of moan.

Marcus presses himself into the shadow cast by the bower, as the sun begins to turn fiery over the oaks and pines at his back. He tries to make himself as small as a dragon-fly.

The water is deep now, hiding Magdalena's legs, and Johann and the old crone gently lower her deeper into it until she is squatting down, and Marcus can see her straining, just as if she were doing her business right there where the silver minnows and the frogs like to play. She clings on to her helpers while the old woman reaches down into the water with her arm and suddenly seems to be exerting herself, pulling and wrenching, as though she were trying to pull some giant turd or thing out of Magdalena, and Magdalena screams again exactly as she did before in the bower.

She is not dead. She is laughing and crying both together. Then, she lies back in the water and lets herself float, and Johann and the woman wash her legs and her belly, and the place between her legs where the thing came out of her. And all three of them are happy now, you can tell, happy in the lake with the sun going down and Magdalena's skirts breaking free of their knot and ballooning out into the water. Johann kisses Magdalena with his lips still swollen from the wasp sting and the old crone laughs like a corncrake.

Dragon-flies can make a whirring with their lacy wings or they can be so still and transparent no one hears or sees them. And this is how Marcus is now, when Magdalena and Johann and the old woman return to the bower. Lying on the rushes, in the corner where they are still green and not stained with blood, there is a bundle wrapped up in some green cloth. Marcus had not noticed this bundle before, but now the woman picks it up and cradles it in her arms, and Johann and Magdalena bend over it.

"Ulla," says Johann.

"Ulla," says Magdalena.

When they have gone, when the sun is just a streak of red and the mist is appearing over the water and encircling the island, Marcus-the-dragon-fly steps out of the shadows and creeps down to the lakeside. His shoes lie on the bank and they are wet, and there is blood on the ground near them.

Slowly and carefully, he wades into the water, his hand searching among the bulrushes as he goes.

And then he sees what he is looking for. It begins as a stem, a cluster of crimson threads under the water, and the threads go upwards to the surface of the lake. And on the surface is the thing, like a blood-filled fungus, the thing that came out of Magdalena's body. It bobs and floats like a giant lily, and all around it is a frenzy of tiny fishes, nibbling at it and feeding. Even as Marcus watches, the thing begins to tear and break apart.

He wants to return to the stables, to stroke the bay pony and go to sleep again standing up against its neck. But he cannot move. He tries counting, but he cannot think of any single number. What he thinks is, I will see this thing in my nightmares. I will always see this for ever and ever in my dreams.

How I do loathe and detest Musical Performances!

For years, when I was still in love with the King and obedient to him in all things, and trying forever to please him, I endured these Tortures with as good a grace as I could muster. But now, except on State Occasions when my presence is Absolutely Demanded, I do not willingly go to listen to the Royal Orchestra. When the King devised his ingenious idea of letting the Musicians play in the cellar (and allowing their music to reach us only by means of ducts and tubes) I rolled around in a paroxysm of mirth and told him I thought this a Piece of Invention every bit as excellent as that of the Close-stool.

On Friday last, however, I forced myself to attend a Concert in the Summer-house. I know not what was played. The Ayres had something melancholic and English about them, every one. But then I was not paying attention to the music. I was there to observe the Lutenist.

Emilia was with me. I sat down beside the King, but he got up and left the moment he saw me, and the Performance went on without him.

Emilia sat to the other side of me and, although she remained as still as she was able, I who know her well could feel in her—at the sight of Peter Claire—an abiding anguish, a continuing Agitation of her spirit. And I here admit, I do sympathise with her state of discompose. For Peter Claire, this Lutenist who pretends to love Emilia, is without question one of the most Delectable young men I have ever laid eyes upon. Happily, I would take him to my own bed. Indeed, only thoughts of Otto—of the soft down on his belly, of the blond fur on his chest, of his silky Member and his exquisite tongue—prevented me from falling into a Reverie over this person and laying plans to lure him to my room. I am a fool for yellow hair. I do not know why I ever married this dark and mournful King— except that to marry the King did seem to me a most Miraculous Thing when I was young. Yet now I yearn for men who taste of sunlight, who have the blue of the sky in their eyes. And this Musician is just such a man . . .

"Emilia, Emilia," I said as we made our way back to the Palace, "oh, beware this creature! Promise me that you will do nothing, say nothing, and agree to no meeting nor Assignation of any kind until I have put in train my Investigation."

"Investigation?" said Emilia.

"Why, yes!" I replied. "For never in my life have I known a man as handsome as this who did not have three or four Amours going on all at one time. And alas, this may almost certainly be the case with your Lutenist. Do you wish to be the paltry Fifth Amour in a crowded and deceitful life?"

Emilia looked crestfallen as we made our way through the Rose Garden, but I took her hand and said gently: "Emilia, my dear, I am thinking only of you. How may one judge between Actual Sincerity and that which is False? A man such as this, whom women love at a glance, will be very practised in honeyed speech and lovesick poetry."

Emilia nodded sadly. When we were once again in my apartments I assured her that I would be her advocate and intercede with the King on her behalf. "By winter-time," I said, "perhaps you shall be a bride!"

And Emilia smiled and thanked me, and told me I was good.

I am not good. I lied to her about my advocacy.

The truth of the matter is this: were Emilia's suitor to prove worthy of her and love her to the ends of the world, I could not and would not let her go.

For I have come to believe, in my fearful life on the Wire above the chasm, that Emilia Tilsen is the only person who holds me aloft. Even Otto's absence I can bear if I am with Emilia. Even that. For her voice calms me, her drawings of flowers touch my heart, her ruses at cards entertain me and her very presence in my room engenders in me feelings of tender affection that I have not felt for any living being since I was a child and was given a white dog called Snowdrop which I carried about the house in my skinny arms.

How could I give Emilia up?

How could I bear to return to my former Loneliness among my angry and hard-hearted Women?

Must I see the autumn return and go alone to my dangerous Confinement?

Shall I endure the winter and not hear Emilia's voice in my room, nor see her sweet face? And know once again, as the wind blows from the north and the snows lie outside my door, that I am Hated and Detested, as I have always been Hated and Detested in this jealous world?

No. I shall not. I cannot let this happen to me!

Now, my Investigation has proceeded a little . . .

My loyal spy, James the Marker, having ascertained for me which room is occupied by the Lutenist, I waited until I knew the Orchestra to be embarked on some Repetition of their tedious melodies with Jens Ingemann and then brazenly took myself to the stable block, pausing not once to look to the left or to the right of me, but just Going On as I, as King's Consort, have every right to do.

No one stopped me nor asked me where I was going. I found the Lutenist's room, and quickly entered it and closed the door behind me.

My heart was beating fast, not from any fear of discovery, but from a delicious mounting Excitement, akin to that which I feel when I am journeying to visit Otto, and I do declare that, had I been born poor, I would have taken up the Art of Burglary right willingly—and may do so yet if my fortunes change.

With slow and careful Method, I searched the room.

It did not seem to me to be the room of a vain man. The clothes I found were simple and dark with not much embroidery upon them and this caused some small disappointment. (Vanity, in men, is such a strangely disarming and intoxicating thing.) However, there were several fine buckles upon the shoes and some leather boots made in London of such an admirable softness and I could not refrain from imagining Peter Claire's shapely legs inside them.

Sheets of music lay around, but I paid them scant attention. I have never been able to understand how anyone can conjure a tune out of black scratchings like mouse droppings upon paper. Perhaps, if the scratchings themselves were more pleasing, then the melodies would be better? Or perhaps it would make not the least difference? I admit that I know nothing in this whole tedious matter of Music.

I was looking for letters and at last, in a low drawer, I found one. But it was not a love letter, only a missive from the Lutenist's Father telling his son about the death of the local Choirmaster and begging him to come home to take up this lowly position. I mused for a moment upon what answer Mr. Claire had given to his parent. For who in the world will exchange a position in the Royal Orchestra of Denmark for that of Choirmaster in some provincial English see? I do declare the Lutenist's Father is a fool and has no knowledge of the world whatsoever.

I was returning this pitiful missive to its drawer, and beginning to feel disheartened that my Investigation had yielded me nothing of any use in my strategy with Emilia, when I noticed that beneath the bed, lying in the dust, as if hastily put there out of sight, was a second letter. Lifting it carefully and forcing myself to remember its exact position on the dusty floor, I took it up and began to read . . .

So now I have it.

Peter Claire was the lover of an Irish Countess. Recently widowed, she clearly wishes that he would return to her.

I took up a pen and one of the sheets of music from the bottom of a pile. I turned the sheet over upon its blank side and carefully copied out certain sentences of the Countess's, viz: *Do you still wear the ear-ring that I gave you?* and *Wherever you are, Peter Claire, know that I passionately loved you,* the while privately thinking how ordinary and dull the language of love so often sounds and glad in my Heart that Otto and I do not bandy these kinds of sentimental words, but instead trade the most delectable Insults.

But my thoughts run on. If I judge rightly, this Countess is a woman of some standing, left comfortably rich by the Earl and young enough to marry a second time. A man like Peter Claire, with his eye on advancement and fame, would do very well to put himself under the Patronage of such a person and so be free from all worries of a financial nature and free to play or compose wherever he will. (He will not stay in Denmark long. The English musicians never do. Something calls them home to their flat and misty isle.)

And so I conclude that this is what he will do. I have no need to invent any story whatsoever, for surely this letter that I hold in my hands sets out the Lutenist's future? Emilia Tilsen is a mere sweet girl whose looks fill him with tenderness, but before the year has turned he will leave her. He will return to Countess O'Fingal and make her his wife.

Choosing my moment with great care, I will in time show Emilia the sentences I have copied from the letter and inform her that Peter Claire's destiny lies not in Copenhagen but elsewhere, in a place that I have never heard of, called Cloyne.

The Quiet Soul

When King Christian is anxious, as he is now, he sees her in his dreams. It's as if she has understood the torments and humiliations Kirsten has made him suffer with her German lover and has arrived at his side to console him. Console him with what? She was pious and soft-spoken, and conversed more frequently with God than with him. She loved her pug dog Joachim. She was tall and sinewy and white, and sat very well on her horse. She bore him six children. She was his first wife.

Her name was Anna Catherine of Brandenburg, of the House of Hohenzollern. He married her as soon as he was crowned, when the two of them were twenty years old. Her title, Queen of Denmark, always gave her pleasure and made her smile, as though, whenever it was publicly spoken, someone had whispered into her ear a story that amused her.

At the time of the marriage there was plague in Germany, so Christian and Anna Catherine were married in Jutland, and the marriage was meant to be quiet and orderly, but a violent storm blew down from the Skagerrak on the morning of the wedding and the sky turned as black as night, and the air was filled with flying weathercocks and tiles and rain.

In the darkness of the palace at Hadersleben, the skin of the young Queen's face had a luminous white sheen to it. No more light fell onto it than onto the other faces, yet it stood out very plainly and Christian found himself wondering whether, in the very pitch of night, with the curtains of the bed drawn round them, he would turn and see this shining moonstone next to him on the pillow.

The Hohenzollerns fled from the plague and came flocking to Jutland in their wide capes and tall hats. The men were large and smelled of something strong and acrid, like gunpowder. They were proud and noisy, and roared at their womenfolk, but their womenfolk were like the sky which is impervious to the clamour of the thunder, like the sun which glitters in the water that the storm has left behind. And King Christian prayed that Anna Catherine would prove to be like that, with that kind of serenity.

On the wedding night, tired after the hours of feasting, the young King and Queen lay together with their hands lightly touching and talked until morning, and went to sleep in each other's arms.

Anna Catherine told Christian that she had a wanton fondness for pearls, that the forests of Germany held within them "a more beautiful silence than is to be found anywhere else on earth," that her little pug's name was Anders but that she called him Joachim for a reason she had not fathomed.

Christian talked about his programme of building, about his armouries, fortifications, palaces and churches, about his ships which kept the country afloat and about his dream of a great canal that ran from Rømø to the Baltic Sea.

Near dawn, when their eyes were closed and they were almost sleeping, he said: "We know that bodies fall towards the earth, but we do not know what is the nature of the thing called 'heaviness.' "

He said he wanted, in his great reveries of construction, to "defy this heaviness and let the cities of Denmark move outwards into the sky" and the new Queen replied that she considered this was a marvellous idea.

When Christian woke up, in the mink-dark of the curtained bed, he did not at first remember where he was nor who was with him. Then he saw Anna Catherine's face, very white and still, like an egg laid impertinently on the lace bolster.

Now, in his dreams, he is visiting the brickworks at Elsinore.

He is giving orders that more men must be hired, that production must be trebled, because he knows that all over the country his building projects are falling behind and his unfinished churches, warehouses and manufactories are being left roofless to the elements.

And then—as though he had suddenly become a warlock whizzing through stardust and landing on mountaintops or on the decks of his mighty ships—he is at Bredsted, where the dykes have begun to break up. He is staring at the sea, trying to match its fury with his own. Cartloads of rock are arriving and Christian begins to shout to the drivers of these carts, to the poor mules who struggle to haul them along over broken pathways, to the air that is filled with sea-birds and to the tumbling waves: "What the sea has taken, we shall reclaim!"

But he hears his own exhaustion in his voice. His tonsils are sore. He feels his own mortality in all his sinews, knows that the tasks awaiting him are always greater . . . just that small fragment greater . . . than his ability to solve them . . .

He expects to wake, then, with this familiar sense of things diving and falling away into ruin to haunt him through another day, but he does not wake. He flies off once more. He finds himself in the old nursery at Frederiksborg, where Anna Catherine is sitting with the two little Princes, Christian and Frederik, and the pug Anders/Joachim snuffles and sneezes by the fire.

Anna Catherine often visited the nursery. The love of her children did not wax and wane as Kirsten's did, nor ever dissolve into cruelty, but was an abiding thing, and to watch her there, holding the children on her knee and whispering stories to them in the candle-light, always calmed King Christian, and he would sit down beside her and listen to her quiet voice and know that *this* was a different way of talking to the world and that even a king can find instruction in a certain sort of quietness.

She asked him to build a fine observatory in Copenhagen. She said she had had a dream of a round tower, with an internal pathway of brick, wide enough for a coach and pair, spiralling round and round up to a platform at the top from which she could look at the moon.

"Why do you wish to look at the moon?" he asked.

"Everything that God has made I would like to look at," she said. "I have never seen a dromedary nor a volcano nor a tree of palms, nor a bird of paradise. If I should live long enough I should like to look at these things, too."

So the King began to commission drawings for the tower, liking the wild idea of the spiral road and already imagining the sound of the hoofs clattering and slipping on the steeply sloping cobbles.

But the architects puzzled over it too long. The weight of such a road, over such a width, they said, would always be too great for the centre-post to bear. He sent them back to their drawings. The word "always," he told them, was inadmissible. There was a solution to everything in the world and there was a solution to this.

But the years dragged on. Designs for flying buttresses came and went. The tower's circumference decreased, then expanded. Danish architects were dismissed and Dutch designers employed at twice the cost. There was demented Low Country talk of "narrow coaches" and "narrow horses." But each and every time, even on the smart Dutch drawing-boards, the mathematics came out wrong and King Christian had to inform Anna Catherine that the tower would not be yet.

"When?" she would ask politely. "When will it be, my dear?"

He wanted to please her because she made him quietly happy. He boasted everywhere of her good sense and her good nature. To her father with his smell of gunpowder, to her mother with her face like a bird, he sometimes wrote sentimental letters of gratitude that he did not send. But he could not, in the end, give Anna Catherine her round tower. She died in 1611, at the age of thirty-seven, and never looked at the moon from her observatory nor met a dromedary in the desert of her imaginings.

Christian wept for a long time over her death.

It was a death that seemed to come very slowly, for no reason. It began as a falling into melancholy, visible in her grey eyes, which acquired a haunted look. She renounced her riding and her walks in the woods at Frederiksborg. Then she started to grow thinner and smaller, as though all the Hohenzollern blood was gradually leaving her veins. She became strangely inattentive to her children's joys and woes.

Then, at last, she began to lean downwards. It was a perpetual leaning of her whole body towards the ground. And when Christian saw that she was doing this and couldn't make her spine straighten nor hold her head high, no matter how hard she tried to do so, he knew that the "heaviness" in the earth, which no one had ever truly understood, was drawing her back into itself.

The old pug, Anders/Joachim, wheezing now and smelly, and given to ever more violent fits of sneezing, which disturbed its own sleep, kept watch on Anna Catherine's bed and would not leave her. In death, her face was no whiter than on the day of the marriage, merely as pale and luminous as it had always been, as though, in compensation for the observatory that had never been built, the moon for ever lent it something of itself.

At Elsinore

Dowager Queen Sofie stares at her own face in a silver mirror. Her skin is hardening. There are ridges and patterns on it—patterns she would never have designed herself and about which she was never consulted. She applies a little ceruse to her cheeks, some white powder to her nose and her thin lips move silently, cursing time, the arrogant architect of her changed appearance.

Her mood was dark even before she looked in the glass. Christian had visited her for luncheon and the smell of roasted duck and frying cabbage had revived in her memories of King Frederik's fatal greed, which left her a widow too soon, with her Queen's crown snatched away. As her son's teeth tore the flesh from the breast and legs of the duck, she watched him in horrified silence.

And then out of his mouth began to pour a torrent of lamentation. He told her that a huge explosion had occurred in the Numedal mine, killing the engineers, the people he called the "geniuses of the mine," and scores of the miners, maiming others and halting indefinitely all work on the extraction of silver.

"The *Isfoss*," said King Christian, "is become a burial ground and the ore is still locked inside the mountain. Denmark's sufferings were about to end and now they are not ended. And what am I to do about the people of the *Isfoss*? I drank with them to the future. I told them they would have a share in the silver and now they have nothing—far less than they had before!"

Queen Sofie sat still, eating her little piece of flounder with its delicate bouquet of samphire. She made no comment on the deaths in the Numedal nor on the absence of silver, but waited, like one held by some peculiar enchantment, for her son to arrive at the reason for his visit. She knew that he had come to ask her for her gold.

Once the request was uttered, Queen Sofie felt a strange relief, of the kind that an actor feels when at last he is on the stage and the words of the play come easily to his mind. It was indeed as if she had prepared herself for this moment for a long, long while and now her performance would be faultless.

She took up the platter on which rested the flounder bones and held it out to him. "My dear," she said calmly. "This is what I live on—fish from the Sound. These waters of Elsinore keep me alive. But as to gold, I have none at all."

Christian looked down at the fish bones, almost as though he hoped to find something there, some sparkle of ore among the green samphire. His look became confused and he was about to speak again, when the Queen put down the platter and continued. "Most sincerely," she said, "would I like to help you. There are a few pieces of silver—mirrors and candlesticks and a samovar given to your father by the Tsar of All the Russias—that you are welcome to take, if these might help you out of your immediate discomfort. I will ask the servants to bring them to Rosenborg. But as to any treasure, would I be dining on fish if I were a rich woman? I have some jewels, of course, but these were gifts from your father and I do not think it right that you take these from me."

"I am not speaking of jewels . . ." said Christian.

"No, I did not think you were. You have made the assumption that there is some hidden store of riches at Kronborg. I suppose it was Kirsten who put about this story, but nothing could be further from the truth. I have only what was reserved for me, as the Dowager Queen, when your father died, and I must eke out my living with this small pension alone. Fortunately, I am not a person of expensive tastes nor appetites . . ."

"Mother," said Christian crossly, "I have heard it said that you alone could save Denmark from ruin, if you so wished."

"Save Denmark from ruin!" Queen Sofie let a rill of icy laughter escape from her throat and held out her thin arms. "If there is 'ruin,' my dear son, then it comes from within—in the habit of grabbing and spending that infects our times. Let the nobility look to their own recklessness and the burghers to their petty greed. Let the nation be shamed by its fat belly. Why do you not draft an edict against luxury? It is to the conscience of the elevated classes that you should be speaking, not to me, for I have nothing."

As soon as Christian had left, Dowager Queen Sofie took up a lamp and descended to her cellar. A chill of early autumn was in the house and the air of the dark store where her money lay was so cold that she could see her own breath as she prised the lid from a barrel and ran her hands through the gold coins brimming there.

In her gold lay all the passions of her past and all the consolations of her future. The soundless augmentation of its value was the only thing left on earth that could thrill her. She would defend her treasure with her life.

But now, as she stood there with her lamp and saw her own ghostly shadow on the wall, she knew, suddenly, that it was not well enough hidden from the world. Until today, she had thought it perfectly safe, but it was not. For if Christian so chose, he could send men to search the castle. With picks and axes they would break the locks on the cellar door and up into the pitiless light of day would come the barrels and the piles of ingots. She would try to preserve and defend them, but she would be told that they were forfeit, by the King's command. From that moment her existence would cease to be anything but heartache and terror.

So now, with her ceruse and powder on, she lies on a day-bed and dreams of a pit dug deep into the granite foundations of Kronborg. She herself, under cover of the long Danish night, would bury her gold there, ingot by ingot, sack by sack. With her own hands she would shovel earth over it and then command that it be filled in and covered over like a grave, and in time grass and weeds (and even trees) would grow in the earth and no one but she would know where the pit was nor what it contained.

Could anything or anywhere be more secure than a pit in the stony earth? "Only the sea" comes the answer. "Only a burial on the ocean floor," too deep for the fishing nets and the keels of the men o' war. But what good is a hiding place that she herself cannot reach? She imagines herself swimming down into the depths of the Sound, nudged by a shoal of flounder, without breath, without light, to haul a bag of coins back into the air and she shivers with dread. Yet even this, if it were humanly possible, she would do rather than let her life's hoard be taken from her. And with this determination visible upon her face, she falls into an anxious sleep.

The following day she gives orders for the digging of the pit. It is to be outside the battlements of the castle, within the shadow of a coppice of elm and oak.

She does not refer to it as a pit, but she orders that it must be deep. She pretends it is to house the foundations of a small summer-house, a bower where, in her old age, she will sit and knit—as she once knitted secretly with her maid on the little island at Frederiksborg—and watch the sun come up or go down as takes her fancy and slowly prepare herself to meet her God.

Her workmen tell her that a simple summer-house has no need of deep foundations and can be set upon the ground just as it is. For a moment, Queen Sofie looks at them in consternation, but quickly says in a strong voice: "The feet of my bower must reach down into the earth, to the place where all of us shall lie in due time." And they nod their heads and ask how deep it is to be, and Queen Sofie answers that it must be as deep as a man or woman standing upright, "so that they shall appear in my mind to carry the bower aloft upon their heads."

Work begins and will not be long to complete, but no sooner is it started than doubts about the pit begin to give the Queen nightmares. For how can a pit outside the battlements be guarded? She cannot put a guard upon an empty piece of ground without arousing suspicion. In the night the guards could bring torches and begin to scrabble beneath the grass . . . Word would pass among the burghers and peasants of Elsinore that the Queen's gold lay out under the open sky for anyone to take. One day she would go there for a bag of coins and dig down and down, and find nothing but the black earth and the worms.

Her mind is tortured by the impossibility of finding a true haven for her gold. The eyes of men see everything. Everything and nothing. Denmark's plight surely stems from their blindness and their wavering wills. Their own immediate longings and desires put them into a trance of irresolution.

Queen Sofie holds her head in her hands, feeling the bones of her skull. The keys to her treasure house are hard and cold against the puckered skin of her breasts, as cold and hard as her unyielding purpose.

Beyond the vegetable garden at Rosenborg stands the King's aviary. It is tall and airy, and made of iron. Golden pheasants perambulate round it, as if measuring and remeasuring its dimensions with their trailing tail feathers. High above them fly bullfinches, yellow-hammers, starlings and parrots. On the ornate roof flutters a flock of white doves.

It is here, in the lacy shadow of the aviary, that Emilia has agreed at last to meet Peter Claire. And so he waits, watching the birds, but half turned towards the direction from which Emilia will arrive. The afternoon has been warm, but now, at five o'clock, there is that faint, glittery chill in the air that warns of autumn, that speaks to the human heart of endings and departures.

And Peter Claire is filled with the certainty that no more time must be lost in his secret courtship of Emilia Tilsen. He knows now that he did not come to Denmark to play his lute, nor even to take on his role as the King's angel. He came to Denmark to discover his own worth, to understand what he might be capable of, and Emilia is the mirror in which he has set eyes on his own goodness.

The blue is being bleached from the sky, the circling doves an exemplary white against its aspiring whiteness, and Peter Claire is moved by the feathery beauty of these shapes and colours.

As for Emilia, this is the invitation—the summons—she has been waiting for.

In her walks and wanderings with Kirsten, in her submission to Kirsten's warnings about the perfidy of handsome men, her eyes have nevertheless remained alert for any passing glimpse of the lutenist and each sighting of him has reawoken in her precisely those feelings of agitation and yearning she once thought would always be absent from her life.

In obedience to Kirsten, she has tried to put Peter Claire from her mind, even to pretend that he had already returned to England and that she will never see him again. But he has refused to go.

And she has known that, before the summer ended, there must surely be one more conversation between them, a conversation in which something important will be said. The white ribbons have been eloquent and scarcely a day has passed when Emilia hasn't held them in her hands or pressed them against her face. But ribbons can say only so much. Emilia has begun to long for the words and the touch of the man.

Now, as she walks towards the aviary along the aisles of the vegetable garden with its borderings of box, its smell of fruit and earth, she is barely surprised by the daring she discovers in her own nature, by the speed with which she runs towards love. Everything that was meek in her and obedient and self-effacing seems in its turn effaced: the Emilia who moves towards Peter Claire is the Emilia who disobeyed her father, who refused to soften her heart towards Magdalena. It is the Emilia who skated helter-skelter on frozen rivers. It is the Emilia (even if she does not know this) whom Marcus sees in his confused head, the Emilia who sends messengers to him across the sky.

She has put the white ribbons in her brown hair. Kirsten is sleeping and will not wake till the darkness announces the nearness of supper time and the consolations of the evening. In this small gap of time, Emilia hopes that life will change.

When she arrives there, as the doves wheel and settle on the aviary top and look down on what is taking place, there is no moment of courtesy or chivalry, no hesitation nor sudden faintness of resolution, because the time for these things has passed. Peter Claire and Emilia Tilsen—dreamers in their separate rooms all summer long— meet as lovers at last, and when she feels his arm go round her waist and pull her to him, she knows he will kiss her and that she will not resist.

His lips are dry, hot as the burnished skin of his face. And when they touch hers, the kiss is like a sleep into which she falls and from which she would like never to wake, but only to go deeper and deeper into this repose. And the lutenist understands that this is what she wants, not a kiss of tenderness, not an insubstantial caress, but the kiss which is all-consuming, which marks an ending of all that has been and the beginning of all that is to come.

And when she breaks away and looks into his face the words come easily to him, so easily it is as though they were already half uttered and only needed the warmth of her body against his to come out. He asks Emilia to be his wife. He tells her it is for her that he has been searching, that he can imagine no future in which she does not play a part. Such is the passion of his declaration that it pulls her like a magnet towards him again, towards the blissful sleep of the kiss, and only after this, when breath and light return, does she say without hesitating: "Yes."

Then they stand just apart and stare at each other, and wonder whether they feel as Adam felt and as Eve felt when they contemplated themselves in paradise, and knew that, of all the wonders God had created, the man and the woman were the most extraordinary. They do not feel the shiver of autumn in the air. They are only distantly aware of the luminous sky and the white doves. One of the golden pheasants lets out a loud, irritable squawk (as though it thought that it, with all its superior finery, should be the object of their rapture) but they pay it no attention. They are face to face with all that they have longed for through the summer and they let it hold them perfectly still, as though caught in a trance, as though they might stand that way for ever.

THE FISHMONGER'S CART

In the night that follows this afternoon of the meeting between Peter Claire and Emilia, King Christian has a dream about the death of Bror Brorson.

This dream, which returns to him three or four times a year, always fills him with such horror that he finds himself almost unable to breathe. He has to get out of bed and light lamps and open the window onto the night air, and, after a while, the feelings of dread and repugnance begin to recede.

But on this night they do not recede.

Christian sits by a candle, unmoving. One window is open on the darkness and he finds himself listening for sounds from the park—for some nocturnal bird, for some breath of wind agitating the trees—to return him to normality and sanity. But the night is silent. It is almost as if there were no night, no park, no trees, no sky that will slowly lighten, but only the intimation of an absolute dark making its progress across time and drawing him deeper and deeper into itself.

He wishes he were a boy. He wishes he were riding with Bror in the woods at Frederiksborg. He wishes that he were not alive in this particular time.

An hour passes. Still the image of the dying Bror fills his head with terror. He wonders whether he will send for Peter Claire and see if music can comfort him, but on this night it isn't music that he wants. He wants Kirsten. He wants to lie with her as he used to lie and hear her laugh when he calls her his Mouse. He wants her to be kindly towards him, to kiss his head, to tell him that she loves him.

He gets up. He knows that she does not love him. He knows that the child she is carrying is the child of her German lover. These things are stored in his heart, waiting to overwhelm it, waiting for the moment when it says "Enough!" But still, as summer becomes autumn and the Count's child grows in her womb and the prospect of another winter stares before them all, his old longings for her are always with him, as though his body had not yet understood what his head understands. And tonight he wants her, not merely as his mistress, but as a child wants his mother, to soothe him to rest, to take away his nightmares, to tell him that all will be well. He feels that nothing and no one else is able to give him any consolation.

Moving slowly, as old men move, he takes up a lamp and makes his way to Kirsten's chambers. In the little ante-room next to her bedchamber he pauses, for he sees that a bed has been positioned across the door to Kirsten's room and that, on the bed, the young woman Emilia lies asleep. He stares at the bed and at the sleeping girl. Why has the bed been moved in front of the door?

He stands still, holding his lamp, and Emilia wakes and gasps with fright at the sight of his giant presence looming over her.

Then he hears Kirsten call her from within the room and Emilia stands up on the bed holding on to the door, blocking his way.

"Sir . . ." she stammers.

Still, he says nothing. Part of him yet seems to exist in his dream of Bror and is incapable—because of what he saw when Bror Brorson lost his life—of uttering any words.

Kirsten calls again and Emilia curtsies to him awkwardly, with her feet still tangled in the sheets, then she goes to open the door to Kirsten's chamber and enters. She closes the door. Christian can hear his wife's voice raised and now he knows why the bed is where it is. Emilia has been instructed to bar his way to Kirsten.

He puts down the lamp, stoops and, with one strong movement of his arm, lifts Emilia's bed aside. Then the door to Kirsten's room is opened again and Emilia stands there in her night-shift, babbling nervously about her mistress's "frailty," her mistress's "melancholy state." The King tells her he does not wish to hear one word more and moves forward to push past her. With a look of terror on her face she says: "You must not go in, Sir. I have been ordered to say that no one is to go in . . ."

He stares at her. She has a simple kind of beauty that reminds him of Anna Catherine and he does not wish to hurt her. But now it comes to him that *this* moment on *this* night, when visions of Bror's death are like a wound in his brain, is *the very last moment* in which he is capable of forgiving Kirsten.

Something of this resolution and intensity of feeling communicates itself to Emilia. She stares at his suffering face, at his eyes which have seen wars and piracy and drownings and the deaths of children and beloved friends. "Sir," she pleads, "I beg you . . ."

"No," says Christian.

And now he walks past Emilia into Kirsten's bedchamber, closes the door behind him and turns the key in the lock.

Kirsten appears terrified, as though he has come to kill her.

She screams and clutches the sheets to her, covering her pregnant belly. Her frizzy hair is wild and her face white, and her mouth is wide open.

Christian tries to comfort her. He calls her his "beloved Mouse" but she does not seem to hear this. He takes her hand and kisses it, and she snatches it away. When her screams subside they turn to pleading. "Don't hit me . . ." she begs. "Please . . ." There is sweat on her forehead. She says she will scream until the palace guards come running, till everyone at Rosenborg is awake, but still he tries to calm her, wiping away the moisture on her face, smoothing her hair. "I am your husband," he says. "And tonight you must comfort me."

"No!" she screams. "I shall wake the pastry cooks. I shall wake the stable boys. I shall wake the whole of Denmark!"

"Hush," he says. "Master yourself, Kirsten. I have come to love you, that is all."

But now her terror seems to turn to something else, to a fury so fierce that her hazel eyes bulge out of her face like venomous blisters. "You know that there is no love between us!" she yells. "Why do you persist? Why do you not leave me in peace?"

"Because I cannot," says Christian. "Because I must have a wife who is a wife and if you will not let me lie in your bed—"

"Do you threaten me? How dare you force yourself on me when I am not well! It is you who should master yourself and your desires. Have I not suffered them enough in fifteen years?"

Always, in her fury, she appeared beautiful to him and even now, when what she is saying insults and wounds him, he longs simply to take her, to spread her thighs and show her that for ever and always his strength will be superior to hers and that for ever and always his man's needs will find their satisfaction in her body.

He tries to prise the sheets from her grip. With his other hand he explores beneath them, finding her leg, moving his fingers slowly upwards. And in this fight with her he knows that already the dreams of Bror are fading, that the solace he sought is beginning to come.

He whispers her name: "Kirsten . . . Mousie . . ."

And then she hits him. Her balled fist slams into his head, just above his ear. He stares at her. Her face, in that instant of the blow to his skull, undergoes some alteration that he could never have imagined. Her mouth gapes, her cheeks are too fat, her breath stinks of cheese, her forehead is too high, too white, too stuffed with her wickedness.

King Christian recoils. His hand relinquishes her leg, knows that it will never again find its way to that private place that has tormented him for so many years. She is ugly and she is treacherous, and her body heaves with a German child, and he can no longer endure her.

Roughly, he pulls her to her feet. She shrieks for Emilia, whose small fists are beating on the bedroom door. "Kirsten," he says, "pack your things. You are leaving. You are leaving Copenhagen and I swear on the souls of my children that I shall never let you return!"

And suddenly she is silent. Her gaping mouth hangs there, wet and foolish. He knows that, for a second, she considers pleading with him, considers becoming what, in an instant, she can become—soft and seductive, turning him round her finger, making him light-headed with her words like honey—but then she decides against this. She turns away, her head held high. She understands that the time is over for these games and strategies. All that has passed between them is over. It is the dead of night in their dead love and there is nothing that she can do but gather her few precious possessions to her and go away.

King Christian wakes servants and goes down with them to the stable yard. He is about to rouse the grooms and the coachmen, to tell them to prepare two carriages, one for Kirsten and one for her women, when he sees a large covered cart standing in one corner of the yard, a cart such as tradesmen and farmers use for the transportation of goods and workers in the fields.

"What cart is that?" he asks and is told that it belongs to the fishmonger, a certain Herr Skalling, who is in the habit of visiting one of the chambermaids overnight. And Christian imagines this man, naked with the maid, coming to Rosenborg for his sport, just as Count Otto Ludwig of Salm came brazenly to Kirsten's bed, and he feels his anger harden and his disgust intensify.

He orders that the fish cart be requisitioned and that "four mis-matched nags" be found to pull it. Kirsten will be sent away in dis-grace, in a cart smelling of fish. And this will be his last sight of her, as the cart is borne away, as it shakes and rattles on the flag-stones, as the light comes up on its humiliating progress.

Grooms stagger out onto the cobbles, pulling on their clothes. Horses are brought out and given water and, as the commotion in-tensifies, lamps are lit in the rooms above the stables and heads lean out of the upper windows.

One of these watchers is Peter Claire. He sees the King, surrounded by servants clutching lamps, standing in the middle of the yard, shouting instructions for the four horses "of four colours" to be brought into the traces of the cart, and he hears the fury in the King's voice and knows that something unlooked-for, something terrible, is occurring. He dresses quickly and arrives in the yard as the horses are being brought towards the shafts of a ramshackle conveyance: a bay, a piebald, a chestnut and a grey. The harnesses rattle and clink, and the hooves stamp the ground, striking sparks from the stones.

The King's presence seems large, casting a wide shadow as the lamps move around. Peter Claire doesn't approach him, but asks a thin man what is happening.

"That's my cart," says the man. "The King has confiscated my cart."

"Why?" asks Peter Claire.

The man is small and sinewy, and has a face that seems worn down by weather and by care. "For his wife," he says. "He is send-ing his wife to hell in my fish cart."

As the cart moves towards the main entrance of the palace, Peter Claire follows it. He stays in its shadow, not daring to come to the King and understanding that no words of his will influence what is happening, but knowing beyond all doubt that if Kirsten is leaving then she will take Emilia with her.

Through his head race wild schemes of kidnap and rescue. But he knows that he can do nothing. Everyone and everything, on this strange night, is subservient to the King's design and nothing will prevent what is to come. Unseen, however, he goes into the palace by a side entrance and, as he approaches Kirsten's rooms and hears her screeching at her women, he calls Emilia's name.

But it is Kirsten who appears. She wears a black gown and, in the first light of day coming through the windows of Rosenborg, her face has the pallor of a spectre and in her hand is a silken whip, with which she hits out at the wall. "Lutenist!" she screams. "Go and fornicate with your Irish whore! Emilia is mine, and she is all that I have now and no man will ever take her from me!"

Yet still, in defiance of the wild woman and her weapon, and the spite in her voice, he calls to Emilia again and for a moment she is there: she carries an armful of Kirsten's clothes and she looks at him in the half-light but says nothing. Then Kirsten strikes his arm with her whip. "Go away!" she yells. "Go back to Ireland, for you will never see Emilia again!" The whiplash stings and Peter Claire clutches his arm and he feels his breath leave him for an instant, and when he looks up again Emilia is no longer there.

Just after five o'clock on this chill September morning, the fishmonger's cart, containing Kirsten and Emilia and such possessions as they have been able to assemble in the time allowed to them, is driven out of the gates of Rosenborg.

All the other women have been left behind and now stand in a shivering cluster by the gates, watching the cart go swaying down the drive and out of sight. When it has gone they do not move, but stare distractedly at one another. Not far from them, Peter Claire looks wretchedly upon the coming day.

But the King pays none of these people any attention and does not linger. For there now comes upon him a feeling of exhaustion, of tiredness in his whole being, such as he has never known. He goes directly to his bedchamber, closes the window and, still wearing his clothes, falls into a deep sleep, completely empty of dreams.

PART TWO

FREDERIKSBORG AND JUTLAND, 1629-1630

MARTIN MØLLER IN THE VALLEY OF THE *ISFOSS*

It is not that the cataract remains frozen. (Since April, the torrent flows and over its glassy lip the flotsam of summer falls with the white water—pollen and dust, mayflies and seeds. And now the first leaves of autumn float on the surface of the river.) But it is as if no one *hears* the sound of the waterfall.

They stand to the north of it, where the graves have been dug for the men who arrived from elsewhere, the ones who had nothing, no papers, no wives, no belongings to speak of, the ones whose bodies could not be returned to wherever they had come from because no one knew where they had come from. These were poor men who had heard rumours that there was work in the silver mine. They had walked through the snow and ice, and were hired by the engineers. When they died in the explosion, those parts of them that could be found were buried here at the *Isfoss*, in the rock that had killed them. Wooden crosses were bolted together by the coffin maker and planted round with stones, and inscribed with the names that people knew them by: *Here lies Hans, who died at His Majesty's mine on the second day of August 1629. Here lies Mikkel. Here lies Niels* . . .

Mainly, it is women who are seen on the hillside, staring at the fallen rock and at the mouths of the tunnels where the remains of the dead were at last brought out into the light. And what they hear is the deathly quiet all around them, which is the quiet of the vanished. They are the widows or mothers of the men from the Numedal. They stand motionless in their black clothes, remembering the day when the King arrived and told them they would share in the riches to come, and how these dreams of wealth took hold of their imaginations, and how they pressed their husbands and sons to abandon what work they had to become miners.

Visions of silver had illuminated the darkness of their low rooms. At mealtimes, silver was what they talked of. They examined the men's hands for traces of silver dust as they came home from the day's work. And there is scarcely one of them who does not possess a fragment of rock veined with silver ore, smuggled out inside a boot or even secreted inside a man's body, to be evacuated into a pot like a petrified stool.

The women held these fragments on their open palms.

"This?" they asked. "This speck of rock?"

"Yes," came the replies. "And I could be imprisoned for the taking of it, so keep it hidden out of sight and never speak of it until the mine is exhausted and all the engineers are gone."

The mine is not exhausted. This is one of the reasons why the widows and grieving daughters stand and stare at it. In the silence that is broken only by the cry of the eagles who sometimes turn in stately circles above them, they look at what cannot be seen, at the secret of the mountain. As winter comes on again the snow will fall and cover the place where the men went in and never came out alive. And the snow will freeze into a glacier and none of the few travellers who come this way will ever know what wealth is locked in there behind the sheets of white.

But the women know. They are the ones who made the exchange. They know what the men died for. And they want it all to come back again: the noise and magnificence of the mine. They want it to come alive once more, just as it was, with the shouting of the engineers and the whistle warnings of each explosion, with the hammer and shriek of the hundred picks at work and the songs at evening, and the tankards of ale in the rough hands of their menfolk, and the huge figure of the King passing among them and even sitting at their own firesides, talking of Denmark and Norway, and the great kingdom and all the prosperity to come.

They stand and listen, as though for some music emanating from the earth, which no one but they can hear. It was the music of the mine. It was the music of hope. They heard it for five months and then came the explosion, which happened with no warning. They yearn to hear it again, but know that it will never come.

The Lutheran minister who visits the widows and children of the miners is a man so thin and small that he has the nickname of *Rotte*, or "Ratty." His name is Martin Møller. In his wooden pulpit he has to stand on a footstool to look down on his congregation. And his sermons cause him anguish, week by week, for he is not a man who likes talking, except soundlessly to God. He often wishes that he did not have to preach or comfort, but only to *think*. When he is in a person's house he is often so quiet that the person forgets that he is there.

But these days, since the tragedy in the Numedal, Martin Møller has begun to talk a great deal. He understands that a terrible wrong has been done here and, instead of retreating into ever more implacable silence, he has given himself the role of spokesman for the bereaved and afflicted.

God tells him that it is not *just*, it is not *right*, that the King should let the mine be closed and forgotten, and the people abandoned to their grief and poverty. The villagers of the *Isfoss* were willing to re-imagine their lives for King Christian. Yet no reward except a few dalers of wages ever fell into their hands, despite all the royal rhetoric about riches and prosperity. And how are the widows to live now? asks Martin Møller of anyone who will listen. They try to grow onions and cabbages in the frozen earth. They go into the hills and gather firewood. Their children steal and beg. They have nothing.

And there is no word from Copenhagen; no representative. Every morning, Martin Møller looks out of the window of his house and hopes to see some stranger arriving, dressed in livery with boots of Spanish leather. And he also hopes to see, in that stranger's saddle-bag, a piece of paper with the royal seal upon it, on which there would be written some promise of compensation, or, better still, a heavy cart lumbering along in the representative's wake, filled with sacks of coins and with gifts of wool and cloth, of flour and wine, of oil and sugar.

"Ratty is deluded," say the mothers and widows among themselves. "No such person will ever come. The King does not care whether we live or die. If we were in Denmark itself then it might be different, but he is impervious to suffering in Norway."

But Ratty Møller is determined that these people shall be remembered. And who will speak for them if he does not? It is as if he has been saving all his words and all the breath in his small frame for this hour. Scuttling from household to household, his nose somewhat pink from the chill in the autumn air, he tells the daughters and the widows and the ragged waifs of children that he will travel himself to Rosenborg if the need arises (and this despite his terror of the sea) but meanwhile is finding some means to get a letter to the King.

And in this letter he pours out his heart. He describes the horrors that he witnessed at the mouth of the mine, and the misery and suffering that followed. He informs the King that a diet of onion soup induces melancholy and that melancholy leads in a short time to despair. *If you had not come here and given us hope, Sir,* he writes, *then surely we would have lived out our lives without any complaint. But you did come. You lifted us up. You gave us visions of what might be. And so, in our wretchedness, it is to you that we must make supplication . . .*

He begs the King to return to the Numedal. He describes himself at his window, waiting and watching for the man in the boots of Spanish leather, who never arrives. He speaks of his own smallness in relation to the window-sill. He says he is a nobody, a poor minister, a lonely man, a rat. *And yet,* he writes, *I dare to speak directly to my King and I dare believe that he will hear me and I dare believe that he will answer my prayer.*

The transformation of Martin Møller becomes a topic of conversation in the valley and his sermons are better attended than they have ever been. "Rats can be brave," some people say with a smile. "We should not forget that."

KIRSTEN: FROM HER PRIVATE PAPERS

We are at Boller in my mother's house.

Everything in the world can be endured except my Lover's absence. Otto has been banished to Sweden and there is nothing in my head except schemes and manoeuvres to bring him out of Exile and back to my bed or, if this is not possible, why then for me to leave Denmark for ever to join him in Stockholm. It is to these machinations that I give my days and my nights, my walks, my prayers and my dreams. When I am sewing, this is what I weave into my design—the flowers of my cunning.

I reason thus: King Gustavus Adolphus of Sweden, being my Husband's chiefest enemy, would pay dearly for any Intelligence relating to matters at the Danish Court and, in particular, any Disclosures or Revelations of the supposed poor state of the nation's Finances. And, knowing as I do that this accursed matter of Money is constantly on Christian's mind, I am certain there are in his possession Private Papers which pertain most interestingly to this subject and from which his Great Enemy could derive such advantage as he chose—in return for Otto's release into Jutland or my safe passage into Sweden.

But I am still at a loss as to how I am to procure these documents.

My Great Difficulty is that I can trust no one. The Danish Court is a cauldron of Venom and Spite, and I know that all who serve the King would, in their inmost hearts, like to boil me alive and melt down my bones for paste. It may be that even my erstwhile Messenger, James the Tennis Court Marker, though he once did everything at my bidding, is now also turned against me because I was expelled from Rosenborg in such a humiliating manner.

I dare not send any letter to him for fear that this is so. Indeed, it is possible to imagine that the very name of Kirsten has become a Forbidden Word in Copenhagen and that those who wish to speak of me must dream up some new Terms for me, such as "The Grand Adulteress" or "The Rhenish Count's Whore" or "She Who Fled Away in the Fish Cart."

I care not a jot for all this Gloating over my departure. What once could make me rage and weep now summons in my heart only a fine Indifference. I am glad to be gone from the Palace and to find myself in Jutland, which is a very silent place, with no Noise of people's churning and fury but only the wind in the trees at night to keep me awake. If I were not so lonely in my bed, I do declare I would be tolerably happy. Merely, I *must* discover some means by which I can barter with King Gustav for Otto. And I have told my Mother: "If my lover can come to me here, we shall have need of this house—for us alone and for our child—and you will have to remove yourself to some other dwelling on the Estate."

I inflame her by telling her I think a Cottage or Farmhouse quite sufficient for her needs and those of her Favourite Woman Vibeke. "Kirsten," she says, "Boller is mine and you shall not put me from it." But I reply that I am still, under the law, the King's Consort, which is to say Almost Queen, and that I can do as I wish and must be obeyed. And she flies into a temper and tells me that I was always Hard of Heart, to which I say only that, in this World, Women must be so, or perish. And to this, of course, she has no Answer.

The rooms I inhabit here are tolerably large and light, but there is by no means enough Furniture nor Objects of Value in them for my taste or Tranquillity of Mind, and so I have writ to the King asking him—who has treated me like a Common Harlot—to despatch to me "some few Articles of luxury, so that my Spirit be not so melancholy all the while." I have signed this note "Your Dear Mouse" in the hope that this alone will wake in him sufficient kindness to send me my ebony dressing case, my pair of silver mirrors, my

French walnut armoire, my golden Dutch clock, my oil paintings of flowers, my Flemish tapestries, my collection of fans and my bronze statue of Achilles.

I have also begged him to send me money, so that I am not "as a poor Mouse in my Mother's scullery" and—as an afterthought, which came on me in my solitary nights, with the wind sighing to me and some Bird far away imagining Spring and letting out from its breast its mating call—besought him to let me have my Slaves, Samuel and Emmanuel, at Boller. I have declared that I want them here "so that at least I may be served Nicely and hold up my head, now that I am brought so low." But I now confess that the reason for wishing them with me at Boller is that, if I cannot go to Otto in Sweden, then at least I shall have a little sport of Sex with my Black Boys.

I see no harm in this. My belly being already fat with Otto's child, I am at no risk from conceiving an infant who might be the colour of a walnut armoire. Kirsten cannot live unless her Desires be accommodated very *frequently*—she is made thus and cannot Help it and I do declare that it will ever be so. And these Boys, being from a wild, uncivil place, where they say men do keep female monkeys in cages and copulate with them for anyone to see, and where Magic Women do come as snakes to glide into the vulva of Young Girls to teach them what Pleasure is, why then I do not think that Samuel and Emmanuel would refuse to gratify the Almost Queen of Denmark. Indeed, I predict, rather, that they might prefer this particular Duty to any other.

Emilia has brought a hen with her to Jutland!

This hen, whose name is Gerda, was the scourge of our journey, constantly breaking away from Emilia's arms to flap round the Fish Cart, squawking and spattering us everywhere with its revolting grey Excreta. "Emilia," I said at last, "pray open the flap of this stinking cart and put that hen out into the night!" But she would not. She told me instead how she had nursed this Gerda back to health in her room—in remembrance of her Mother, who had once done this very same thing—and so did not wish to part with it "on some lonely road that it would not recognise."

"My dear," I said, "it is a *hen*! Hens recognise nothing! They do not know if they are in Odense or Pomerania! It will find grain and water, and that is all that a hen requires."

"No," said this sentimental Emilia. "Gerda knows me and she will die if I do not care for her."

Had anyone but Emilia chosen to bring a living Chicken on this long and terrible journey to Jutland, I would have taken up the bird in my hands and thrown it into the road, or I would have wrung its neck and plucked it and roasted it by the wayside. But there is something about Emilia's requests that I can never refuse. And so I endured the hen. I watched as Emilia stroked its neck to calm it. When we stopped to rest the horses, water was given to it. And for much of the time it lay asleep, wrapped in Emilia's skirts, quite as if it were a kitten or even an infant who finds itself at peace on the lap of its Mother.

Now it has a little house or Hutch of its own in the courtyard. But when Emilia and I go for walks, as we often do (for this is all that a person can *do* in Jutland: walk about it and look at what Nature has put here), Gerda accompanies us and steps along at our feet very daintily, never straying far from Emilia's side. It is so tame and Domesticated, I declare it would submit to being attached to Emilia's hand by a Leash. I think it has forgotten *what it is*.

We seldom talk about Peter Claire.

I brought with me the sheet of music on which I wrote down what was in the Countess's letter to him, but I have not made use of it yet. If it should ever come into Emilia's head to try to *leave me* and return to Rosenborg for the sake of the Lutenist, then I shall show it to her and inform her that she is cruelly deceived.

But I doubt that day will ever come. Emilia does not ask me what it was I screamed out to him on the night of our departure. I do believe she must have heard the words, but she is silent on the matter and so I respond with an answering silence.

The person we talk of most frequently is her little brother Marcus, who is tantalisingly near to us now and must be stolen away from Johann Tilsen and brought to us here. For Marcus, too, we have our schemes! I have decided that he will be raised as my Child and, when my baby is born, become its playmate and friend and be to it like a Brother. And when Otto comes to me, and my mother is sent away, my lover and I and Emilia and Marcus and the Child will be as some marvellous Family, which I shall keep always by my side, and I do declare that then, at last, I shall be happy and at peace.

THE BOUNDARY

The last stage of the journey to Boller, made as dawn arrived and the sun began to break through the morning mist, had taken Kirsten and Emilia along the edge of the Tilsen estate.

The fish cart had been exchanged for a rickety black coach, which smelled fusty and unfamiliar, like some forgotten parlour where the old had once lived and trapped mice, and sweetened their last summers with lavender.

From this carriage Emilia had looked out at her father's land and watched it slowly pass, and remarked to Kirsten that to find herself here in Jutland—in the very place she had left and thought not to see again for a long while—was so curious, so perplexing, that it was as though time itself were mocking her.

Kirsten had yawned and said: "That's time's chiefest delight, Emilia: mockery. If you didn't know this before, then now you do."

Along one side of the boundary ran a thick line of beech trees. Their leaves had begun to take on that elusive alteration which it is almost impossible to describe, and yet which is suddenly there in the September light and speaks of the cold winter to come. Looking at these trees, where the mist still lingered, unable to take her eyes from them, Emilia felt herself invaded by a memory so long buried that even as it surfaced in her mind some part of it remained obscured.

She is with her mother, Karen. They are walking along under

the beeches and it is the beginning of autumn, for Karen is wearing a woollen shawl and the colour of the shawl is grey. Emilia is small, perhaps five or six years old.

They have a destination and it is not far off. The destination is the largest of the trees. When they arrive there, Karen crouches down and takes Emilia's hand, and together they begin to sweep aside the new-fallen leaves until their hands arrive at the soft earth beneath. It is earth that is dry and light, and scratchy with the old husks of beechnuts. And in this place something has been buried. Karen whispers: "There!" and Emilia gazes down. Whatever it was that has been placed there gleams suddenly in the cold sunlight.

This was all that Emilia was able to remember. She tried concentrating very hard on the moment of discovery, as though by this means the object in the ground would suddenly become visible to her. She could see Karen by her side, hear her voice, even remember the soft grey shawl. But when she stared at the earth and the leaves pushed aside, she had no recollection of what had been there.

The room Emilia is given at Boller looks east—in the direction of her father's estate. Nothing of it is visible to her, but there is something fearful about knowing that where the park ends the Tilsen fruit fields begin. The horizon absorbs Emilia. She stares at it for hours, imagining the great trees as sentinels, keeping her hidden from the eyes of Johann and Magdalena. She feels that the very sight of them would petrify her, so that she would not be able to move or speak.

But Kirsten has told her that word of her presence at Boller will already have spread to Ellen Marsvin's neighbour. News, in Jutland, travels along the sandy paths with the tinkers, with the charcoal burners and with the blacksmiths. "And so," Kirsten has said, "the best course we can follow, Emilia, is to pay your family a visit. They will have to receive me! They would not dare to refuse. And you will be by my side as my companion. And then we can ascertain what is going on there and how things stand with Marcus."

To bring Marcus to live at Boller, to care for him and supervise his lessons, to take him away from Magdalena's influence, is a fine dream that Kirsten (who does not really like children, nor sympathises with their terrors) has dreamed for Emilia's sake. Emilia feels both gratitude towards Kirsten and apprehension on her own account. Anxiety about Marcus has tormented her ever since she left home. To have her brother here with her would be a joy and a deliverance. But to spirit Marcus away from his father and brothers appears to her as an impossible endeavour—as something which has reality only in Kirsten's mind, all cluttered as it is with never-ending plans and contrivances.

And there is something else. Emilia also knows that part of her has imagined a future far away from Jutland, a future as the wife of the lutenist. And how could Marcus Tilsen be made to fit into that? If she and Kirsten are really to become "mothers" to Marcus, then this is the way they must remain for ever. Could the day ever arrive when she would have to choose between Marcus and Peter Claire?

On the subject of Peter Claire she is silent, even to herself.

CONCERNING WHALES

A strange spectacle is taking place in the courtyard at Rosenborg.

The King has commanded that a large piece of stone be brought in there and propped against the fountain, which has been turned off. The servants complain to each other about the silencing of the fountain. The women lament the lost sound of the water falling and splashing, which "was a cheerful noise and could quite gladden your heart when the days were dark." Certain of the men simply grumble that "now there is nowhere to piss when you need to, returning late at night," and that pissing in doorways dirties the boots and attracts vermin and flies. They mutter that all the decisions made by the King these days are bad.

The King hears none of this grousing (or, if he hears it, is indifferent to it). Consulting with his Dutch stonemason, he has acquired a set of fine chisels. And now he is to be seen kneeling in front of the block of stone and laboriously carving letters and numbers upon it in a calligraphy quite as exquisite as anything he writes with a quill upon paper. And all the world seems to know what it is that he's writing: he is carving Kirsten's name and the date upon which she went away.

He doesn't like people to watch him at work. Servants bring him lemonade and retire. But he is observed from attic rooms, from half-open doorways. His own children stare out of windows and wish that he were not kneeling. Many of them are old enough to know that humiliation should be concealed, not blazoned, that unhappiness is best endured alone indoors or else in some wild place where the clouds pattern the earth, where the wind muffles all human sound.

King Christian speaks to no one and seldom looks up from his labour. He certainly does not see the children at their window. It is as though he were engaged upon a work of art, as though this carving of the stone were the only matter in the kingdom worthy of his time. But after several days he sends for Peter Claire and, when the lutenist arrives at his side, commands him to kneel down beside him. The King informs him that the task is complete.

Together, the two men stare at the stone.

"That is the sum of it," says Christian. "That is the ending."

Peter Claire nods. He does not say that the ending is his, too, that the loss of Emilia has deprived him of all his plans and dreams. What he says is that the stone writing is so fine that, were the King not the King, he would surely find a vocation carving headstones or Latin mottoes over the portals of institutions.

For the first time in a long while the King smiles. "Yes," he says, "if I were not the King!"

Then he lays the chisels aside. He dusts his hands, which are rough and blistered from the work. He looks around him at the sunshine falling on the cobbles and at the place where they are greenish, from where the water used to fall wider than the fountain bowl. He looks perplexed, as if he were seeing these things for the

first time, or else afresh and trying to remember what once they signified.

Christian keeps to his bed for more than a week. His clocks inform
him that time is passing, but he has no real sense of it doing so, for
every minute seems to him to be precisely like the one which preceded it.

Kirsten fills his soul. Where God once was, now there is Kirsten.

She laughs and dances; she carouses and shrieks; she rolls on the
log pile; she stamps and bellows; she bleeds into the bed. She is a
white breast, a rounded stomach, a crimson mouth. She is past and
present; she is loneliness and fever; she is solitude and sleep.

Food is brought to the King. He complains that he needs no
food. He is consuming Kirsten and Kirsten is consuming him. "And
at the end of all," he whispers aloud, "there will be nothing and no
one."

When he resumes his life (but only awkwardly, stumblingly, like an
invalid) it is to his want of money that his thoughts return. He has
been told once more that there is a great fortune to be made in
whaling ships, that the bodies of whales can be converted into so
many different commodities they could save the economy of the
nation.

And he remembers that three whaling ships were being built in
Copenhagen, but that now work on them has slowed or even
ceased altogether, because there is nothing with which to equip
them, nor to pay the shipbuilders. And the King curses and pulls at
his elflock and goes to his commode and strains to void a stool, as if
this might lessen the agony that he feels in his heart.

Seated there, ready to weep from the pain of his exertions, he
imagines the blue whales arriving silently in the waters of the
Skagerrak from the Norwegian Sea and being slaughtered by the
Swedes and turned into Swedish soap and candles, into Swedish
walking canes and corsets. And he damns these strutting Swedes in

their whalebone finery. He sends them to hell, to suffer for all eternity.

When the stool is out, he determines that the Danish whale boats will be finished and will set forth, and that the whales will come to Denmark's rescue, because something must happen soon, relief must arrive, life cannot go on as it has gone on this year . . .

King Christian goes down into the plate room. Out from their cabinets and cases he hauls a multitude of royal gifts dating back to the day of his coronation and his marriage to Anna Catherine of Brandenburg. He piles them up on the floor: silver soup tureens, samovars, slop bowls and fish platters, golden goblets, chalices, dinner plates, wine coolers and jugs. The piles topple and crash. Plates are accidentally kicked and go spinning across the floor. Christian no longer sees them as objects with any use or function, but only as currency.

Hearing a commotion, suspecting thieves, servants come running to the plate room. One of them points a musket at the King, who is wearing a brocaded gown and has no shoes on his feet. When the King sees this gun levelled at him over the chaos of the silverware, he flings wide his arms, like the God of old, like Moses on the mountaintop, and roars. Words come out of him like cannon fire. Denmark, he bellows, is sinking into the sea and he, her King, is falling with her, falling so deep into a stygian suffering that he feels he will never emerge again into the light. And why is there no one to save him and save their precious land? Why is he betrayed and let down at every turn? What climate of depravity reigns in the state that the King's wife commits treason with a German mercenary? Why does no one but he understand that honour is gone from all human dealings and has been replaced by covetousness and greed? How many times must he say these things before anyone begins to listen?

The musket is lowered and the servants stand gaping there. They feel that this volley of words might kill them, that their hearts might cease to beat, that they might never go from this room alive.

"Take up the plate!" orders the King. "Carry it to the mint and let it all be melted down! Dalers must be struck—as many as can be got from this continent of tableware! And I will go to the ship-builders myself with the money. And if any man steals so much as one sugar spoon from this store he shall be hanged!"

After this, King Christian goes to his rooms and tries to ascertain by arithmetic what sum can be realised from the plate and how many whales it might bring to Denmark's shores. Across the complex columns of the mathematics, he calls to the creatures who are not fish and are not animals, but some other thing that can live in cold and darkness and yet make fountains on the surface of the sea: *Come to me. Save my kingdom.*

But then there is the question of manufacture. Do Danish craftsmen know how to fashion stays and farthingales from bone? Will they be finely made or merely shoddy? Could these garments be sold in Paris and Amsterdam or would the French and the Netherlanders laugh at them and send their mockery echoing and tittle-tattling around Europe? *Ma chère, have you heard the finest jest? The Duchess of Montreuil is found not to be deformed after all. She was but wearing a Danish corset!*

These fears are interrupted by the arrival of a letter. The messenger tells the King it is a letter from the Numedal and, when he hears this, he forgets about the explosion there and imagines that the letter is going to announce the imminent arrival of a consignment of silver. But in the next moment he remembers the dead of the mine and the seams of ore buried under an unimaginable weight of stone.

He begins to read. He notes that the sender is a certain Martin Møller, a preacher, and this at first fills the King with weariness. He is about to lay the missive aside, when he notes that Møller's words are not feeble—as the words of so many preachers are feeble—but filled with the same passionate despair as that which he himself is feeling.

If you had not come here and given us hope, Møller writes, *then surely we would have lived out our lives without any complaint. But you did come. You lifted us up. You gave us visions of what might be . . .*

The King repeats this last phrase silently to himself, recognising that he finds in it a sudden consolation that he cannot explain.

Visions.

Visions of what might be.

The Thoughts of Marcus Tilsen, Aged Five, Plucked from the Air

Magdalena says baby Ulla is a little bit of heaven come down to us for we are good.

My father says now you have a new sister Marcus and you must be kind to her and love her and I say why didn't baby Ulla kill Magdalena when she came out of her and he slaps my eyes. I say I saw that red thing in the water that came out of Magdalena and that is dead eaten by the fishes and my father says there is evil in you Marcus and we shall bring a holy man to get the evil out of you and if it cannot be got out then we shall have to send you far away.

I wanted the Holy Man to come and be a messenger and bring me something from Emilia but he was old and thin. He said now Marcus we shall rebaptise you in the waters of the lake and cast out the devil from you and my father said we are Beyond Despair with this boy.

Beyond Despair is not a village. It is what Ingmar calls a wilderness he is learning about wildernesses and he says there are creatures there you have never seen.

I say to the old thin man if you take me to the lake I shall kill baby Ulla I will let her be eaten by fishes but my father whips me and I fall down. Otto I cry. Otto my cat.

In the lake it is cold as ice when the water comes over me.

Now they say Marcus we are waiting and praying that all the evil is gone from you and when we are sure that it is gone why then you shall be welcomed back into this family once again but we are not yet sure and so you must be locked away so that you do not harm baby Ulla.

My harness is put on and I am in my cot and the night comes. I am in a wilderness and I know what is in a wilderness now there are huge creatures called buffaloes and I have seen them in a picture. I say buffaloes come here at once do as you are bid and they are warm and they breathe like the cows breathe and I whisper to them good-night.

And when I am downstairs and my harness is off and baby Ulla is there in her cradle and Wilhelm says we are all watching you Marcus I am still with these buffaloes in my wilderness even though the morning has come. I am counting them.

Letter to Peter Claire from Countess O'Fingal

My dear Peter,

I do not know if my letter ever reached you.

That any letter—which is so insubstantial a thing—reaches its destination, when I consider what routes it must take and what weather may fall upon its bearers, does make me marvel.

When Johnnie O'Fingal once read to me the sad drama of *Romeo and Juliet* and I understood that all was lost because that Friar Lawrence's letter to Romeo was lost, I remarked to Johnnie that we are ever and always searching for ways by which we can be joined to those we love across the immensity of space and time, but that these ways are fragile and surely on the winds and tides must move a great quantity of lost things that will never be found.

I write, now, of a journey I am to make when Christmas is past.

As you will remember, my father, being a paper merchant, endeavours to sell his wares not only in Italy but across the further world. And it has come to his attention that there might be a great fortune to be had by the establishment of a paper mill in those northern countries that have a vast abundance of firs, which is the best tree for the manufacture of good paper. And from this mill, the paper of Francesco Ponti might find its way westwards even to Iceland and eastwards to the Russias, and this thought makes my father exceedingly content.

He is to travel to Denmark in the New Year. When I heard that it was to Copenhagen that he was going—there to get permissions from the King for the setting up of his mill—I asked him if I might travel with him, to assist him in all his negotiations, for as you will recall, he speaks very little of any language except Italian. And he is overjoyed that I should do this and says to me, "Francesca, you shall be at my right hand and together we shall see what is in this great kingdom of Denmark, and on this journey you will put from you all the sufferings of recent years and regain your joy in the world."

I did not tell him that you were in Copenhagen. In truth, I do not even tell myself that you are there, for it may be that you are no longer there but in some other court—in Paris or Vienna—but only, in the quiet of the night at Cloyne, ask God to let me see you once more and hear you play and, if I dare to speak such things, to hold you in my arms.

I shall come with my father alone. My dear friend Lady Liscarroll will take my children into her household and be as a mother to them. She is a woman of gentleness and kindness, and I have no fears that my Maria and her sister and brothers will not be cared for very well. And they, because that Lord Liscarroll's house is very magnificent and with an abundance of children there and toys and ponies, and even a falconer who may teach my boys how to command these birds, and a dancing master for the girls, say to me, "Oh, we do wish you to go, Mama, because you shall get well by this journey!"

I know, of course, that they are dreaming already of dancing, riding and falconry, and do not dwell so much on my melancholy as they pretend, yet also I find their concern for me very sweet and affectionate, and I tell them that in all my hours away from them they will be in my thoughts.

And so they will. Only if I should find myself with you again would all the world and they in it (upon their cantering ponies and calling to their falcons through the air!) disappear from my mind, which would have no room in it for anything but you.

My dear Peter, I know not whether this letter will come to you, or if it will be lost in the deep. If it does come to you, then pray forgive me all my boldness and want of scruple.

From your affectionate friend,

Francesca, Countess O'Fingal

A WALK IN AUTUMN

The lane is bright with sunshine.

Strolling arm in arm along it are the Reverend James Claire and his daughter Charlotte, and they have walked this lane so many times that they almost know how every stone of the pathway sits and where each tuft of ragwort grows and how the leaves will lie when they fall.

They stroll in the hope that the anxiety they are both feeling will be assuaged a little—by the fine day, by the gentle activity of walking—and that when they return to the vicarage they will be able to tell Anne Claire, who sits and sews in the parlour, that some altered feeling has risen up in them, that, after all, they have begun to believe that all is going to be well.

What weighs on them (on Charlotte most heavily, but on her father, too) is what has come about in the life of Charlotte's fiancé, Mr. George Middleton.

Ever a large man, George Middleton has, in the last two months, begun to lose his hugeness. Ever a loud man, this noisiness of his has begun to fade.

At first, Charlotte worried that some melancholy she could not account for had overtaken her future husband's mind. But she knows now that this is not the case. George Middleton is ill.

Being courageous, he has struggled to master his pain, but he has at last admitted to Charlotte that the agony in his gut is so intense as to make him feel faint and the Reverend Claire is privy to an additional suffering poor Mr. Middleton has not liked to mention to his future wife: he is plagued by an almost constant need to piss. He cannot lie in bed for an hour without the need to get up again. He can no longer go into company for fear that the room in which he finds himself be too far from a close-stool.

And so he has stayed at home in Norfolk, from where he has written letters to his "dear Daisy," telling her every morning and afternoon how much he loves and esteems her, and how he longs for their wedding. But the moment has not yet come, cannot yet come, because George Middleton is a sick man and, in this state, he cannot marry.

Now, on this fine autumn day, word has come from him that his physician has diagnosed a stone in his bladder. *This stone,* he writes, *might be the size of an apple and what is a whole apple to do in me but roll about as it will and so it brings me agony. Be gone! I tell it. Thou rotten apple, break and dissolve and pass through me and set me free.*

But it has not yet broken nor dissolved and George Middleton's life has been enslaved to it. And now, alone with his pain, waiting for the cutting, which will kill him or release him, he understands that the life he planned with Charlotte Claire may never happen. Even as he day-dreams of rearranging the rooms of his Norfolk house to suit her needs and fancies, he knows that such rearrangements may never come about, or if they come about that she may never see them; never entertain her friends in the small south-facing chamber that overlooks the rose garden, never see the name *Mrs. George Middleton* engraved upon a visiting card, never unbraid her hair in the soft candle-light of a shared bedroom.

And Charlotte and her father understand this, too: George Middleton may be going to die. How many men survive a cutting? They do not know.

The Reverend Claire wishes he were a physician and might perform the operation himself, so that in his safe hands would lie George Middleton's life, so that he would be prevented from dying by the sheer force of James Claire's will. As it is, all he can do is to pray. While he walks with Charlotte in the old familiar lane, the whimsical thought comes to him that the fairness of the autumn morning is such as to suggest that the great cloud they see on the horizon may not, after all, obscure their sun. "Charlotte," he says, "I do feel a sudden certainty that George will not be taken from you."

Charlotte says nothing. What loving father does not, in his eagerness for all to come to rights, offer hope as certainty? She tightens her grip on his arm, as if to say: "If he is going to die, then at least I am safe, at least I am protected by you. And for this I am grateful."

After a while, as they reach that part of the lane where their feet rustle the fallen chestnut leaves, James Claire says: "I have been thinking what strange pathways our minds do travel in respect of all that is dear to us. It is so often the case that those matters which at first cause us some anguish, when or if they are reversed, put us deeper yet into misery, so that the first 'anguish' does not seem as anguish at all, but as something else, which is more akin to happiness."

Charlotte smiles. It is well known among the congregation of the church of St. Benedict the Healer that the Reverend Claire sometimes finds himself tangled in some strange convolutions of speech. "What can you mean, precisely, Father?" she asks.

"Well," he replies, "when I heard that you were to be married to George, why then I saw as my chiefest sorrow the fact that you would be gone from the family and that when I looked down from my pulpit I would not see your sweet countenance looking up at me. But now I see that this was no sorrow at all, compared with the possibility now before us, that you may *not* be married to George! For in the future, when you are George's wife and in Norfolk with him and all is well, then I shall look down at the congregation and think, My beloved Charlotte is not here with me because she is with her husband and in her own house, and this is where I would wish her to be, and what I shall feel is happiness and no sorrow at all."

Charlotte laughs. At her feet, she feels something hard against her toe and they pause in the walk as she bends down and picks up the first of the fallen chestnuts in their green husks, the "tree furniture" she so loved as a child and used to polish with oil.

On the return walk, as both start to feel a pleasant hunger for their lunch, James and Charlotte's conversation turns towards Peter Claire.

A lively man by the name of Lionel Neve is now choirmaster at St. Benedict's. Peter's reply to his father's offer of the post was affectionate and complimentary about the quality of the music in this church, *yet please understand,* it said, *that my position here in Denmark prevents me from returning to England for some long while. The King has shown me great trust and favour and I must stay with him and fulfil my tasks, which are many, and not desert him.*

"He was right to refuse," says James Claire. "And I was wrong to ask this of him. What is a country church compared with a royal orchestra?"

"It is not that, Father," says Charlotte, "it is that Peter has not found the thing he is searching for. It might be the music inside him, or it might be something else, but I do believe he knows that he would not find it here."

The Reverend Claire nods. And he sees again that look in his son's eyes, which is like a staring out to sea, not to the grey sea of England, but to a blue sea that is far off, that has about it a kind of infinity, a sea that no ship could ever quite cross over to come again within sight of land.

Lionel Neve, on the contrary, is a person who seems entirely content with each day's modest curve. He darts about the place like a scurrying lapwing, with a tuft of black hair sticking up wildly in the middle of his bald pate. When he speaks about music, so distracted with enthusiasm and delight does he sometimes become that flecks of spittle appear at his lips' edge. His conducting is so energetic that it often lifts him clean off the ground in little jumps.

"Lionel was the right man," says James Claire.

"Yes," says Charlotte. "Lionel was the right man. What Peter is right for and what is right for him cannot be known yet."

They are at the gate to the rectory garden and they open it and begin to walk across the lawn. Of the single piece of "tree furniture" she has kept, Charlotte says that she will shine it and not let it grow dull, so that it will be like a light kept burning for George Middleton. She adds that she knows that this is foolish, but she does not care.

La Petizione

While the summer lasted, the royal orchestra played most frequently in the garden or in the summer-house at Rosenborg, but now, as the nights begin to draw in, the King goes back to the *Vinterstue* and the musicians go back to the cellar.

King Christian has told Peter Claire why he must insist that they remain there. He understands that it is cold for them, that the light is poor, that they might imagine themselves forgotten, "but this is what I always intended," he says, "that you *should be forgotten. That you should be invisible!* And then, when visiting princes and ambassadors arrive at Rosenborg and are seated in the *Vinterstue*, and lo and behold, there is music coming to their ears from they know not where, that is when I know how unique in the world this arrangement is. Because it makes people marvel! They look around them, asking themselves how it is that a pavan can float into the room from out of the bare walls. And then I see that, from that moment, they begin to think well of Danish ingenuity and so of Denmark. For this is precisely what people long for in a clamorous world."

"What do they long for, Sir?"

"To be filled with a sense of wonder! Do you not long for it also, Mr. Claire?"

Peter Claire replies that he had not defined this longing in himself, but nevertheless supposes that it is there.

"Of course it is there!" says King Christian. "But when did you last stumble upon the thing that satisfied it?"

The lutenist looks into the King's eyes that are puffy and red for want of sleep, that are marked so clearly with the imprint of anxiety and grief. He longs to reveal to the King that in the person of Emilia Tilsen he finds an answer to his yearnings, that she fills him with amazement and affords him a vision of the man he wishes to be. But it strikes Peter Claire as cruel, at this moment in history, to speak to the King about love. That Emilia is tied to Kirsten as surely as he is tied to Christian makes it impossible.

"I believe," he says carefully, "that when our orchestra is playing in absolute harmony, then I experience . . . for some moments at a time . . ."

"Wonderment?"

"Fascination."

"May these be one and the same?"

"Almost. I am drawn to such intense contemplation of the sound—seeming as one sound, but in reality composed of all our parts—that I am taken to some other part of myself."

"Wherein you feel hope or something akin to it?"

"Yes. Wherein I am no longer this habitual semblance of myself that walks about and eats and sleeps and is idle, but *myself entirely*."

At this last remark King Christian begins to fiddle with his elflock, for the observation has led him to see how very far, in his fruitless tolerance of Kirsten's wickedness, he has travelled from the man who once designed men o' war in his dreams, who saved Denmark's coastline from the sea, who gathered the vagrants of the city under the magnificent roof of the Børnehus and set them to work on spinning wheels and looms. "Ah." He sighs. "There's the trick: to find the way—whether forwards or back—to what we long to be."

For all Peter Claire's eulogies on the subject of harmony, recent rehearsals in the cellar have been marked by discord.

Jens Ingemann has had to keep tapping and tapping upon his stand: "Signor Rugieri, what is your sudden mania for fortissimo?

Herr Krenze, you are letting ugly sounds escape from your mouth and none of any beauty from your instrument. Mr. Claire, you are *behind*. Can you no longer keep time?"

It is as if the musicians are exhausted. When they congregate in the mornings, they barely speak to each other. They yawn. They stare out of their gloomy prison. In the absence of sunlight coming through the reticulated bricks, they see the long winter waiting just around the corner.

And then, one afternoon, when they have been playing for the King for almost four hours, and the light is fading and the candles are lit and dripping wax onto the sheets of music, Rugieri and Martinelli lay down their bows as the trapdoor above them closes at last and Rugieri stands up and his chair falls over behind him. "Gentlemen!" he says. "Martinelli and I have been *in conferenza*. We say that to endure another winter in these conditions is insupportable! We shall all die from the cold. From some consumption. From *sofferenza!*"

Martinelli runs his hands vigorously through his black, curly hair, as if to shake out such *sofferenza* as was already making its way into his head. "We ask what we have done," he says, "we who are among the finest musicians in Europe—to deserve to be put in this dungeon. If you can tell us, Herr Ingemann, then tell us, *per favore* tell us, *per favore* enlighten us . . ."

Jens Ingemann stares at the two Italians. He has ever been suspicious of them, fearing some such outburst from men who do not save their passion for their music, but who allow themselves to spend it upon ephemeral feelings. He does not answer them, but only glares at them, then lets the full iciness of his glare pass round the whole complement of players, so that all are held by its frozen grip. At this moment Rugieri takes out, from behind his music, a piece of parchment and holds it up. "*Una petizione*," he announces. "We drew this up last night. We ask the King to consider our situation. We ask him to imagine how much we suffer here, with the cold stones and the chickens . . ."

"Sit down, Signor Rugieri," says Ingemann suddenly and gives his music stand a swipe with his hand.

"No!" says Rugieri. "No, Music Master. We are not the only ones to dare to say we are badly treated. Herr Krenze and Monsieur Pasquier we know are on our side and will sign our petition. And if all shall sign—"

"None of you shall sign," says Ingemann. "There will be no petition."

Martinelli now lets out a noise that is somewhere between a sigh and a scream. Then, in a burst of Italian, he cries out that he is beginning to go mad in the cellar, that in his country only common criminals and the truly insane are put in such places, that the music itself, though he finds it beautiful, is not compensation enough, that he is not a cask of wine and refuses to grow old in a vault.

Krenze smirks. When silence falls after Rugieri's outburst, which not all have understood, the German viol player remarks that were he a cask of wine, he would be treated with a fine reverence, for the King prefers wine not only to music but to almost everything else in his kingdom. Ingemann snaps that he may have to report this observation to His Majesty. Pasquier, who has worn himself out learning Danish and refuses to embark upon Italian, inquires what Martinelli has said. Rugieri jabs his *petizione* and screams that King Christian is a man who has known suffering and thus can sympathise with theirs. Peter Claire, ignoring the cold fury that he sees rising in Ingemann's breast, asks for the petition to be read aloud.

The *petizione* is written in Danish, not entirely free from errors. Though Jens Ingemann pretends to block his ears, Rugieri begins to read it out:

To His Majesty the King,
    We the undersigned, his loyal makers of Sound, do beg him to hear our thoughts and this is they: that we are sad to be in somesuch cellar that we suffer so dearly from cold that our fingers have no blood in them . . .

"What pathetic fault-strewn rubbish is this?" interjects Ingemann.

There is a moment's silence before Rugieri, looking away from Jens Ingemann, continues:

And we do pray to His Majesty that he hear our praying to him in this our *petizione*, and that he do remove us to an elsewhere place . . .

"Enough!" shrieks Ingemann. "In all my life, I have not been among such idlers and fools. What are you made of? Milk? For what a stink you do make in your sourness, with your petty grievances and complaints. What a smell your want of resolution leaves behind it!"

"Hey-ho," says Krenze. "Now the morality. And trying to be poetry all the while . . ."

But Ingemann gives this no attention and continues. "Do you not know," he says, "that musicians from all over the world send letters to me, week by week, begging for places in this orchestra? Do you not understand that you can be replaced in a trice, in the time it takes to travel across the North Sea? And so you shall be replaced! Not one of you understands the *reasons* for our being below the State rooms, for none of you are men of intelligence or sensibility, so you cannot conceive of any reasons. And this I shall convey to the King: that his musicians have no understanding of anything. And you will be sent away."

Snatching up his sheets of music, Jens Ingemann marches out of the cellar. There is silence in his wake, broken only by the sound of his furious footsteps ascending the narrow stairway to the rooms above.

Later that night, King Christian sends for Peter Claire. "Lutenist," he says wearily, "I hear there is a mutiny."

He does not seem alarmed, nor even anxious, merely tired. It is as though, in comparison with the afflictions of his heart, this mutiny of the musicians is of no real consequence. Viol players and lutenists are replaceable; Kirsten is not.

Peter Claire is silent for a moment, then chooses his words with care. "Music Master Ingemann once told me that the cold in the cellar affected the Italians more than the others, because their blood is not used to it. Perhaps you may have some sympathy with this? And it is only this, Sir. That they fear illness as the winter comes on . . ."

King Christian is weighing silver, just as he was on the night of Peter Claire's arrival at Rosenborg. The scales themselves are objects of great beauty and the King has three sets of weights in Mark, Lod and Quint. The smallest weight, he says, can measure as little as one gram. And Christian's large hands, roughened by his hours out hunting, nevertheless manipulate the tools with surprising delicacy. "What about you?" he asks. "Have you forgotten your sacred trust to me? Angels should not mutiny!"

Peter Claire replies that he has not forgotten his trust and that he does not mind the cold in the cellar. Merely, he sees how others in the orchestra are beginning to suffer.

The expression on the King's face is blank. This blankness says: The word *suffering* is too strong to describe the habitual chill in the vaults. The King is suffering, the poor of the country are suffering, Denmark's reputation—in her descent into debt and poverty—is suffering! But what these querulous musicians describe is merely *discomfort* and they should not pretend otherwise.

But then he lays aside the weights and says, "Monsieur Descartes, as you once reminded me, tells us that when we are perplexed we should endeavour to reduce complex propositions to simple ones and then, from the simple, work our way, stage by stage, back up to complexity. Do you still believe in this method, Mr. Claire?"

"Yes, I think so."

"But when it comes to matters of *feeling*, how are we really to apply it? In the building of a whaling ship I could proceed thus. Ships I understand. But love is incomprehensible to me. For there is nothing in love that is *knowable beyond all doubt*."

"Imagine love as a whaling ship," says Peter Claire. "To build it strongly, you would begin with a strong hull. Ask, then, if the hull of your love was strong."

The King stares at the lutenist. Into his mind comes the old remembrance of the first time that he set eyes upon Kirsten Munk, wearing a russet dress, in a church pew. A smile passes fleetingly across his face as he replies: "No. I used to believe the 'hull' was strong. But now I think it was built upon a fancy, upon imagination."

"Imagination may also bring forth the design of a magnificent ship . . ."

The smile returns and then goes. Goes and returns. "True. But then must enter mathematical calculations. Then must enter some knowledge of future weight and stress, so that at sea the 'imagined' ship will still stay up and not founder."

"And in matters of love this *future weight and stress* is unknowable at the beginning?"

"Yes. It is unknowable—in all cases."

"Yet known eventually—at which point new calculations can be made and the ship modified if the need arises."

"Or scrapped. Or scuttled."

"Yes. If the original design is found to be faulty at its core."

"Yes. If, after all, it is faulty at its core . . ."

"And so, in discovering this, you have after all proceeded from the *unknowable* to something known."

The King is silent for a moment. Then he gets up and looks out of the window, where a waning moon is thin and cold in the sky. He stares at this moon for a long time before he turns and says: "Tell Jens Ingemann and the musicians that the mutiny is no longer relevant. The orchestra will not be in the cellar this winter, for I have decided to move back to Frederiksborg. There is no magical music there and nor will ever be.

"All this"—and here the King gestures round at the room, at his portraits and mementoes of Kirsten, at the gardens invisible in the darkness—"was born out of caprice, out of rhapsody, and I refuse to inhabit it any more."

THE VISIT

Vibeke Kruse has begun to lose weight.

This loss of fat from around her waist and stomach, from her thighs and arms, seems to have come about miraculously since the arrival at Boller of Kirsten and Emilia. And a few pounds, once lost, have inspired her at last to make the sacrifices Ellen Marsvin has been urging upon her: to forgo the cakes, tarts and puddings which so delight her, to refrain from heaping up by her bedside little baskets of sugared plums and raisins dipped in peach brandy to quench her pangs and longings in the middle of the night.

Now, she can allow herself to dream once again of the magnificent dresses she has never been able to wear, but which wait for her under linen wraps in Fru Marsvin's dressing closet. She is frequently to be found tiptoeing into this closet, removing the wraps and gazing at the beautiful garments. She runs her fingers along the lines of embroidery and caresses the clusters of velvet bows. She wishes the dresses were housed in her own room so that when a yearning for sweetness came over her in the small hours, she could get up and hold against her tongue the syrupy satin of a puffed sleeve, the frothy syllabub of a lace cuff.

But Vibeke consoles herself with the knowledge that the day is not far off when she will at last put on these marvels. And following on from that day, something else will happen—she knows this in the deepest recesses of her heart. Not a word has been spoken by Ellen Marsvin on the subject of this something else, yet Vibeke knows that it is coming. There is a *plan*.

As the days pass and the leaves fall and Vibeke Kruse feels the autumn brightness reflected on her complexion and in her lively eyes, so, in strange contrast, does Emilia Tilsen have the sense that she is sinking into an unstoppable drabness.

When she looks in her glass, she sees a face she almost does not recognise, that was not the face she saw at Rosenborg; her lips not those once kissed by Peter Claire; her eyes not those he gazed at. She begins to curse that fate that brought her back to Jutland. She has come to believe that only while Karen lived could she be happy in this landscape. Now the very sky oppresses her, the very scent of the forests, the very sound of the wind . . .

No letter arrives from Copenhagen.

To console herself, Emilia tries to imagine the time a letter might take to arrive here, in this place far from anywhere else. Through her mind rambles a picture of a slow, tired horse or mule, of a letter-bag leaking with the rain. She tries to believe that weeks—or even months—could easily pass before any words written at Rosenborg will arrive in her hands. And when Kirsten asks her, with a teasing smile on her lips, "What of the English lutenist, Emilia? What songs does he send you?" she replies simply that there are no songs yet.

" 'Yet'?" asks Kirsten. "What is this 'yet,' my dear Emilia? Is this 'yet' not burdened with a weight of expectation it really cannot carry?"

"No," says Emilia. "I do not think so."

For she does believe that something will arrive. Just as Vibeke Kruse knows that life has some marvels still in store for her, so Emilia Tilsen *knows* that what began in the cellar at Rosenborg, while the hens scratched in the dust, and continued out in the air by the flying birds of the aviary is not ended, cannot end like this in a slow fading to silence. Merely, she tells herself, there are moments in a life when patience must become the spirit's sole companion. If she sometimes composes letters to Peter Claire while she lies in her bed and listens to the white owls calling in the woods, she knows that she will not write them, or that if she writes them, she will not send them. She will wait. That is all. She will wait for Peter Claire to keep his promises.

Meanwhile, Kirsten announces to her that the time has come for a visit to Johann and Magdalena.

"We shall give them a little warning—a day or somesuch time—for that is only polite," says Kirsten. "But not so long that they can make any alteration to the household or conceal from us anything they might wish to hide. And so, in a very short time, Emilia, you will be reunited with Marcus and together we shall play with his kitten, Otto."

It is a cold day that Kirsten chooses.

Grey-upon-grey are the folds of the sky as she and Emilia set out in Ellen Marsvin's best carriage, with all the trappings of the horses polished and bright, and taking with them a gift of cherry jam in an ugly Flemish pot for Magdalena and a ball of scarlet wool for Marcus's cat.

Emilia has dressed herself in black. At her neck is her locket containing Karen's picture. On her forehead are visible the little lines of disquiet and suffering which wake in Kirsten a gentle tenderness towards her. And in the carriage, Kirsten (who is looking large and resplendent in a brocaded dress of green and gold, with her belly huge as a bell) picks up one of Emilia's diminutive hands and presses it to her powdered cheek. "We shall vanquish them, Emilia!" she says. "I am still the King's wife. They must do all that I shall ask."

And so, past the fruit fields, where the fruit is picked and gone, and the foliage turning to brown and red, the carriage goes forwards and always forwards until it arrives at the driveway to the Tilsen house. Emilia is silent. And it is silence that she hears, the silence of lost years that have no voice left in them.

When they go in, Emilia hangs back behind Kirsten, in her shadow, almost as if she believed she could slip in unseen and only watch and listen but not be required to speak nor feel her father's icy kiss on her cheek, nor catch the scent of Magdalena's body, nor the sour-milk smell of the baby.

The hallway is dark, as it always was, and so it is in the familiar half-light that Emilia sees them standing there in a line: Johann and Magdalena, then Ingmar and Wilhelm, Boris and Matti, and, beside Matti, baby Ulla in her cradle.

She looks along the line, notes at once that her brothers all seem larger than when last she saw them and that Ingmar is now taller than his father. But where is Marcus? Emilia lets her eye travel to the oak settle, behind which he often used to hide when strangers came to the house. She wonders if this is where he is. She wants to call to him, to tell him that she's arrived at last, that it's safe to come out. Yet she knows that she must hold herself in check on this most troubling visit, that neither her face nor her words must betray her feelings. "You are to be neutral, Emilia," Kirsten has said. "Do you understand what I mean by this?"

Emilia understands. Kirsten means that she must be allowed to work her own, long-perfected brand of diplomacy and that Emilia must act as if there were no whiff of cunning in the air, no transaction—spoken or unspoken—taking place. Kirsten has promised her that, at the end of the afternoon when they get back into their carriage, Marcus will be with them. He and the kitten, Otto. He and the mechanical bird. And his pony will trot behind with its bridle bells making music in the dusk . . .

But now there is only this solid line of the Tilsens bowing and curtsying to Kirsten. Johann is smiling, the brothers blushing. Magdalena squats in an obeisance so low that she is almost tangled in her red skirts and Johann has to steady her and push her up again from the elbow. Kirsten walks slowly down the line, holding herself very tall and aloof from them all, so that she seems to Emilia to have more majesty about her in this cold room than she ever possessed at Rosenborg or at Boller. Separate from the King, separate from her mother, she appears queenly, magnificent, a woman to be worshipped. And Emilia sees how the family is filled with awe, how every eye follows Kirsten as she moves from person to person, how Magdalena has become short of breath . . .

Then, swiftly, Kirsten turns. "In the carriage," she says, "we have some small presents for you, but here is the present I know you will treasure most highly: I have brought Emilia."

And so they have to acknowledge her now. They too, Emilia knows, would like to pretend she was not really there—this ghost of Karen they long to be rid of—but, in front of Kirsten, they have to show her some graciousness. Johann holds her awkwardly to him and lightly touches her cheek with his lips that are dry from the excitement brought on by Kirsten's presence. "You look well, Emilia," he says. But this is all. This is all he can find to say to the daughter he no longer wants in his life, who, until recently, was far enough away from it to let him believe she would never return.

"Thank you, Father," says Emilia. And she looks at him for a moment. His hair has become a little more sparse and she notices that his hands are trembling.

She passes on to Magdalena. She is drawn against her will into her stepmother's pungent embrace and gasps there for a few seconds, as Magdalena's arms encircle her, remembering how this smell of Magdalena always had about it something that sickened her, something from which she longed to escape. Magdalena, too, compliments her on her appearance and Emilia, in a voice that she can barely hear, congratulates Magdalena on the birth of Ulla.

Then she goes to Ingmar, who bows to her, as though she were a stranger, and kisses her hand. And the other brothers follow suit, bowing and hand-kissing—as if they imagined Emilia were not really their sister but some high-born gentlewoman of Kirsten's to whom they would pledge allegiance for a day.

Kirsten watches all this and then exclaims loudly: "Oh, my dears, you must not hold back your joy like this! You must behave to Emilia as though I were not here. Why do you not embrace her, boys? Herr Tilsen, why do you not take her in your arms?"

She waits just long enough to see the discomfort come into Johann's eyes, just sufficient time to read on Magdalena's face a sudden cloud of confusion, and then, before anyone moves, she says quickly: "Oh, but of course, it is your natural modesty and becomes you, and I should never have embarrassed you with such an observation! The King has always said I was too sudden in my utterances, and he is right! You will embrace Emilia in your own time."

She reads, correctly, the relief in Johann's look, in Magdalena's smile, and then rushes on, while they stand there captive in the hall, hesitating, not knowing whether there is, after all, some further gesture towards Emilia expected of them. "But now I notice something puzzling," she says, looking down the line of Tilsens. "Tell me, have I counted wrongly—for I was never as good at arithmetic as I would like—or is one of you missing?"

Nobody moves or speaks. Kirsten touches Matti's dark curls and turns to him. "Was it for you that we sent the kitten? Are you the youngest of all the boys, or . . . but no, no, now I remember that he is but five years old, the youngest. Is that not right, Emilia?"

"Marcus," says Emilia.

"Yes, that was his name," says Kirsten, her most formidable smile rearranging her features into a sudden alarming prettiness. "So where is Marcus? I must certainly be introduced to you all."

Magdalena looks at Johann. The younger boys look down at their newly polished shoes.

"Madam . . ." Johann begins.

"Perhaps he is out on his pony or playing with the kitten? Did he christen it Otto as instructed?"

"Yes," stammers Johann, "the kitten is Otto. But we were obliged to send Marcus—"

"Marcus will not do his lessons," says Boris.

"Only for a short while . . ." says Magdalena.

"Oh, dear," says Kirsten. "Now I am even more confused than I was. Do be plain. We brought a little ball of wool for Otto, did we not, Emilia?"

Emilia nods. She knows that she is about to be told something she will not want to have heard.

It is Magdalena who utters the words. "Alas," she says, "we tried all that we could try, as a kindly family, for Marcus, but we did not succeed in making him . . . amenable to the world. He is in the care of Herr Haas. We believe that through hard work and study, he will be cured."

"Cured of what?" asks Kirsten.

"Of his wickedness," replies Magdalena.

A silence falls. Kirsten looks at Emilia, whose face, turned imploringly towards Kirsten, is as white as moonstone.

"Oh, I am sorry to hear this," says Kirsten, with her beautiful smile vanished and gone. "I know from experience that children may sometimes be prone to dreaming when they should not, but wickedness—surely Marcus is not wicked. And who is Herr Haas? I do pray he may be a kindly person."

"Oh, yes," says Johann hastily.

"A schoolmaster, is he? Could he not come here to tutor . . . ?"

Again, a look passes between Johann and Magdalena. And now Emilia feels that her promise to Kirsten of neutrality is breaking apart and cannot be kept, and that there is no need to keep it because the things they came to remedy cannot now be remedied, nor may ever be. Her hands fly to her face and she cries out: "Father, what have you done to Marcus?"

"You heard, Emilia dearest," says Kirsten quickly. "Marcus is with a certain Herr Haas. But of course we must be told what manner of man he is."

Johann steps nearer to Kirsten, as if his words were for her only and not for Emilia, but he sees Kirsten reach out to Emilia and put her arm about her shoulders and draw her to her, as a mother might draw to her shoulder a darling child.

"He is at Århus . . ." said Johann.

"It is only and entirely for his own good . . ." says Magdalena.

"He would not do his lessons . . ." repeats Boris.

"Oh, but look," says Kirsten, "how Emilia is ready to weep! I hope you are not going to tell us that at Århus, in this house of Herr Haas, there is anything that would make her unhappy?"

At this moment, a single shaft of sunlight falls across the table laid next door for the elaborate luncheon Magdalena has prepared. And Magdalena turns her face towards it, knowing suddenly that Kirsten will not stay to eat it. "Marcus," she announces coldly, "has been sent to a house of correction. He will return when he has learned to distinguish truth from falsehood, but none of us knows how long that will take."

THE EXPEDIENCE OF DISGUISE

At the beginning of November, cold rains sweep down on Denmark from the Norwegian sea.

Dowager Queen Sofie walks out in the rain with her head wrapped in a shawl and looks down into the pit that has been dug to house her treasure.

Her eyesight is no longer good. She can see some creature trying to hide in the furthest corner of the pit and mumbles out loud, "What is that thing?" But it does not move and so she cannot tell what it is. She reflects that this is what happens when a woman grows old: she becomes incapable of seeing clearly what is going on right in front of her eyes. And so the people around her can take advantage. They can lie. They can say that a snake is a sliver of bark or a sliver of bark is a snake. They can pretend that everything is safe and in its place, when really, little by little, it has all been spirited away.

Queen Sofie can see, at least, that the pit looks desolate, even ridiculous. That she could ever have imagined bringing out her treasure and laying it down in this muddy hole in the earth strikes her as laughable, as the kind of idea a peasant might have. As she walks away (clutching the shawl round her chin, just as a peasant woman might clutch it) she wonders if she is becoming feeble-minded. "But how," she murmurs, "can the feeble mind recognise its own decline? If the mind can summon the thought that it might be growing feeble, is this ability alone proof enough that no such thing is occurring?"

She rages against these confusions. She rages against the freezing rain which shows no mercy.

Later that day, when she has rested, Queen Sofie goes down once more—for the tenth or twelfth time that week—to her cellar.

She has had a new idea. It was born out of the recognition that a queen might easily be mistaken for a serf by the simple wearing and clutching of a shawl. She has understood *the ease with which disguise can be achieved.* And this, she has now determined, is what is needed here. Her gold will stay in the cellar, but it will be *disguised* as something else. Certain small inventions—of marvellous simplicity—will deflect attention away from what it is to *what it seems to be.* Then, if her son should send men to search Kronborg for her hidden treasure, they will go down into the vaults and be as near to it as she is now, as she stands with her lamp at the door, but they will not see it. They will report that there is nothing there, only a few casks of wine.

She smiles. She has heard that the contents of the plate room at Rosenborg have been melted down. What more is there to melt now, save the crown itself? Yet the King is given up to his dream of the whaling ships, declaring that out of the sea in which Denmark is floating will come the creatures that will save her. If Christian will sacrifice the royal gifts of thirty years, including those that were given to him on his marriage to Anna Catherine, why then he will sacrifice *anything* for this and have no scruple about taking from his own mother all that she has left by way of consolation.

But now, it will not happen. If the Queen has worried that her mind is becoming feeble, at least she finds it still capable of invention. And with invention she will preserve her money store.

The following day she takes a carpenter and a bricklayer down with her to the vault. Into each of their hands she places a golden daler, then bolts the door, locking the three of them in.

Holding her lamp high, so that her lined face looks spectral in the darkness, she tells these men that she is about to give them certain orders, which they must obey to the letter and ask no questions. "And if," she whispers, "you tell any man or any child or woman or any mortal upon this earth by word or by paper what these orders are—and rest assured that I shall know if you do this, for there is nothing that blows on the air in Denmark that does not come eventually to my ears—why then your houses shall be burned and your families put out to beg on the streets and you shall be imprisoned here in the darkness for the rest of your lives."

The men gape. They clutch their pieces of gold. Both fear and excitement assail them and they pray there is no crime against God nor man about to be asked of them.

"Swear," says Sofie, "that you will do everything that I ask."

"We swear," say the bricklayer and the carpenter.

More gold is promised to them. They are told to begin work that night and continue without rest until their task is complete.

KIRSTEN: FROM HER PRIVATE PAPERS

In this miserable November, with the day not far off when my child and Otto's will be born into the World, I do find myself in a Horrible Dilemma.

I marvel that I can consider it a Dilemma. Were I to act in my

Own Interest and consider nothing but this, there would be no Dilemma at all, but rather and only a Piece of Fine Fortune and Luck, from which I would immediately seek to gain the great Advantage that I do spy in it. That the very notion of this wretched Dilemma comes into my mind at all does, I suspect, suggest that certain Changes have come about in me that I had not noticed until this moment, viz., I am becoming More Charitable.

The quandary is this:

—I have perceived at last how I can secure an Ally at the Court, who will help me in my dealings with my Husband's enemy, King Gustav of Sweden.

—I also perceive that I cannot make use of this Ally without causing hurt to Emilia.

What am I to do?

The predicament has been precipitated by the arrival of a letter.

It was addressed to Emilia and the bearer of it had come from Hillerød and so I knew, because the King has removed himself to Frederiksborg, that it must be from the English Lutenist.

With a sharp Silver knife given to me by Otto, I lifted the seal, taking care that it did not break in two, and began to read. It was night-time, with all at Boller (including the fat Vibeke, who goes wandering about the house at strange times of the day and night as though she were a Sow nosing about for Truffles) silent and in their beds.

My candle-light gave to the paper a kind of soft colour, as of honey, and to the words a black intensity, so that it seemed to me that I might run my tongue across the sentences and lick the words away and that to taste them would be marvellously sweet.

For this letter contained an outpouring of Love such as I once read long ago when I was seventeen and the King began to woo me by every Means and sent messages to me day and night and which, in their Degree of Longing, moved me first to laughter and then to weeping and then to an Answering Longing of my own. Because, in a bitter World, these feelings surely have a Rarity, like to certain species of birds that do hide themselves only in banana trees or in the freezing air above the clouds and are seldom seen. And so we listen and do hear their song and only afterwards—when all that they sang of is quite vanished and lost—do we wish we had not done so, for we miss it so.

The Lutenist declares that since Emilia's departure from Court, he does not sleep, but only settles

> nightly into a dream of you, which is not a veritable dream, but a waking reverie of all that I long for and all that my heart and mind can imagine. And in this reverie, my enchanted Emilia, you are my wife and I am your husband and together we walk into our future, and all that we take and all that we give makes us yet more fair in each other's eyes, so that the world, beset for always by cruelty and striving, by vanity and decay, does also show us marvels excellent and fair . . .

None but the most hard-hearted (among which I might once have counted myself) could fail to find some grace in these sentiments. And when I add to them the Remembrance of what a handsome Countenance the writer of them wears and how exquisitely yellow his hair does happen to be, I do understand that great good fortune beckons to Emilia, and that to withhold it from her is a Vile Act.

However, it is now that my Dilemma appears. For do I not have a Weapon trained upon the heart of the Lutenist? I am sure that no one knows of this letter except him and me and, most naturally, he will wish the thing to come at length to Emilia for whom it was intended and not stay hidden in my Dressing Closet. So I reason thus: would he not do Any Thing that I ask of him in order that this letter (and others that he may contrive to send) do reach their destination? And because he is much admired and trusted by the King, is he not my Perfect Man for the execution of my Plans regarding Otto?

All that I need to do appears before me with Perfect Simplicity. I must write a letter to Peter Claire. In this, I inform him that I cannot approve his love for Emilia, nor find myself willing to permit any word of his to reach her. I will say that she is my Woman

and must serve me for as long as I shall require and never Marry—
for this is her lot—and he must strive to forget her.

Only then, when he shall be wondering how he can vanquish
my stern ruling, shall I come to the Real Matter of my letter. I shall
ask him if he will find and send me, in secret, certain Papers from
the King's own bureau, in which are set out his fevered Calculations concerning the Finances of the Nation and which do, in their
desperation, reveal to all a Sorry State. And then I shall promise
that, upon receipt of these papers and if they be Satisfactory and
the Right Papers entirely, his own letter shall be given to Emilia.

Really and truly, this is an Excellent Plan. For with these papers
once in my hands, the day surely nears when my Rhenish Count
will be returned to me, or I allowed to go to Sweden to live with
him. For what would King Gustav pay for such knowledge? I know
I am not mistaken when I answer that he would think my Safe Passage to Sweden but a small price. And so my future becomes bright
once more. When I wake in the morning, I shall find Otto by me
and stroke his fair hair to set him prancing into the day . . .

Yet what if the Lutenist is obstinate and will not do as I ask? What
if his Loyalty to the King overrides his Love for Emilia, so that both
Loves are doomed and she has nothing and I have nothing, and we
are condemned to grow old in Solitude together at Boller, playing
Beggar-my-Neighbour?

How shall Emilia be comforted?

And how shall I find any rest or Consolation?

Oh, Lord, but I am tired and it is late! Late in this winter's night.
And the years turn and turn, and cannot be slowed or halted.

The rain has ceased.

The park at Boller has one great tree whose leaves, in late autumn, are purple and shine like precious stones in the sun.

257

And when I note the beauty of this tree, for all that the Winter begins to tear at it, I find my own passion for Life returning. And I know that I cannot waste my remaining years alone, but must go to my Lover. There is no future for me but this.

And so my mind devises a Good Stratagem. I shall write as I planned to the Lutenist, but I shall feel no Remorse or Guilt. For what did at first appear to be a Betrayal of Emilia, I do find, with thinking on it, that it is No Such Thing. On the contrary, by testing her lover in this way, I am rendering her a Great Service, for which she will sooner or later thank me!

For if Peter Claire truly loves her, why, then he will think nothing of taking from among the King's Papers a few pages of Arithmetic that His Majesty might never miss. He will but wait out the right time and then do what I ask.

Naturally, if he is an honourable man, the act may cause him some few hours of Anguish, but what is this Type of Anguish compared with that which accompanies the loss of the Beloved, for whom the World contains no replacement? It is as nothing. It is as the snow, which lies up in great heaps and valleys and then is gone in a single day.

And so I begin to write:

Dear Mr. Claire,

I write to inform you that your letter, intended for Miss Tilsen, was put into my hands by the Letter-Bearer from Hillerød. In no wise intending any Harm or to Spy upon another's words, but assuming only that any missive from the Court must be directed to me, the King's wife, I opened the letter and began to read it . . .

THE VISION

King Christian's rooms at Frederiksborg Castle face north.

As winter comes on and he looks out at the shadow of the great building (with his own shadow contained in it, yet invisible to him) falling across the lake, and feels the chill in the walls that no sun will dispel until summer returns, he asks himself: Why was it designed like this? He designed it. He had had a vision of what it could be.

He had looked at the old palace, built by his father, King Frederik, and at the water which flowed through canals and dams from as far away as Allerød to fill the lake, and at the miles of thick forest that surrounded these things and all the land that stretched over twenty-six parishes and seen that here, at Hillerød, he could build a universe in his own honour.

Taller than his father, larger, with a greater girth of body and spirit, Christian had always—since the days of the skyrocket—had a longing for things which were vast, which challenged the heavens, which could be seen from afar. And this is what he had dreamed of here: *a monument to hugeness.* On the great towers of his new palace he saw weathercocks, impossibly high and far away, turning on wings of gold.

He remembers now how his dreams for Frederiksborg preoccupied him. He remembers how, in a single night, he understood that the architecture must strive for order and unity, and proceed in a gradual way, like a piece of music, across the linked islands, towards a climactic structure, and how, at dawn, he woke his Dutch architect, Hans Steenwinckel, and showed him a flurry of drawings. "Hans," he said, "we must respect what the land is telling us. The logical axis, the logical *progression* of the buildings, is towards the north, and so this is where the climax must arrive. This is the place that the King must occupy. Beyond it, there must be nothing else; only the light on the water, the diminuendo and then silence . . ."

At Frederikssund, ships unloaded bricks from Elsinore, lime from Mariager, timber, limestone and marble from Gotland and Norway.

King Christian used to go down to the port and stand high up, overlooking the quays, and see the thousand carts and wagons waiting to carry the pieces of his vision to the place where it would begin to rise from the ground.

One afternoon he rode from Frederikssund in the back of a cart carrying sheets of copper. He lay down on the metal, still bright and unweathered, and stared up at the sky and imagined the rain falling on it, and the sun and the snow, and saw in his mind's eye the blue-green colour of the copper waiting within it for its private alchemy to begin.

This is how he arrived at the one idea that Kirsten had loved about Frederiksborg: its wild multitude of colours. To Hans Steenwinckel he said: "A castle is not part of nature. It must express not what is already there, but *what I see in my mind.*"

And the Dutchman had smiled and asked: "What *is* in your mind, Sir?"

A red that was not the red of the bricks, but something deeper, more scarlet or crimson, was there. Though he wanted the portals and niches to be graced with statues, he did not see them remaining white. "They will have struggled out of the stone, Hans," he said. "But that is just the beginning of their life."

And so Frederiksborg, as it rose in all its grandeur, had additional radiance gilded on every surface. The walls were the red of poppies, the creamy white of lilies. Golden monograms were sprinkled like pollen over doorways, windows and arches. And as for the statues: ambassadors from Italy, France and Spain all declared that they had never seen any cluster of figures so utterly fantastic, and the English Ambassador (accustomed as he was to the grey stone corridors of Whitehall Palace) admitted in private that he had to shield his eyes every time he walked past them.

For each one resembled a jewel. When the sun came round and touched the lapis lazuli blue, the emerald green, the topaz yellow and the ruby red, a blinding brightness shone from them—exactly as King Christian had planned—which spoke of something ostentatious and bold hidden in Denmark's character that had never been sufficiently perceived before. What this "something" heralded nobody could quite say, until one perspicacious ambassador from France declared at last: "What emanates from the lips—and even from the gilded arses—of these sculptures is the sound of rude laughter."

Now the King gets into a boat and rows himself out onto the lake and looks back and inspects his vision.

It took years to complete. Hans Steenwinckel died and was replaced by his son, Hans the Younger, who was quarrelsome and vain. The poppy-red brickwork still has to be repainted all the time to combat the enviousness of the winters, which prefer it to fade to what it once was.

Christian lets the small boat bob aimlessly on the wavelets. He stares at the great castle. Still, it is mighty. Still, its reflection in the water is breath-takingly deep. Still, its northerly crescendo touches him. Yet something has changed since those far-off days of his dreams and plans: he no longer knows what Frederiksborg is *for*.

He reminds himself that it was a vision within another vision— of Denmark's ancient head holding itself up, crowned with gold. But how does it sit now with that ideal?

He feels seasick. He feels that on the wind that troubles the lake there is the smell of death.

That night, as a northerly rain storm hurls itself against his window, the King works late, trying to bring order to his mind by answering letters that have been long outstanding.

Among these is the letter from Martin Møller, begging King Christian to rescue the people of the valley of the *Isfoss* before the winter. And Christian comes once more upon the sentence "*You gave us visions of what might be*" and is moved by it afresh, and falls into a contemplation of how the works of man, for all that he knows to what sad ends they may come in time, still enflame him with such a stubborn, unreasoning gladness—as though men were boys perfecting a beautiful calligraphy, as though they were the deer of the forests kicking up their hoofs at the smell of spring. He smiles at what Møller has written, then quickly takes up a pen and (in his still exquisite handwriting) begins:

Dear Herr Møller,

Oh, if I could return to the day when I met my Mouse, Kirsten!

Oh, if I could bring back into my heart that first vision I had of Frederiksborg!

Herr Møller, all life is an unravelling towards catastrophe. In our acceptance of that inevitable catastrophe lies our only chance that we may survive it, that we may move out from the great northerly shadow of all that we could not achieve into the clear water beyond. And so begin again. And always again . . .

The King knows that this letter is not finished, but these first few sentences seem to have exhausted him, as though the very phrase "begin again" had taken on shape and form, and become a hill that he could not climb or a glacier that he could not cross.

FRU MUTTER'S BED

The spirit of mutiny among the musicians has abated.

In Frederiksborg they are better housed, in slate-roofed buildings in the Middle Holm, where they have each been given two rooms instead of the meagre one they occupied above the Rosenborg stables.

They play mainly in the church, perched up on the gallery, where the winter light streams in through the tall, decorated windows, assembled round the fine organ made for the King in 1616 by his brother-in-law, Esaias Compenius of Brunswick. And it is as if the presence of this organ gives them legitimacy, as if they have at last come into a place where music is publicly honoured. The humiliations of the cellar begin to fade from their minds, and because the acoustics in the church are so fine, they are once more enraptured by their own sound.

Jens Ingemann, who has known many Frederiksborg winters, who has seen the Great Hall filled with people dancing and has conducted galliards for two Kings of France, likes the feeling of prominence that the gallery gives him. More visible here than at Rosenborg, he comes to performances looking smart in a new cambric coat and his white hair has been neatly cut. Though he keeps a stern eye on Rugieri and Martinelli, though he looks at Krenze with distrust, his habitual irritability has diminished. And like the musicians themselves, he recognises that, here, the playing of this little orchestra has about it an aching sweetness to which every listener is susceptible.

This is not a season for entertainments. The King is not in the mood for these things. But very frequently he summons the musicians late at night and they play for him alone, in whatever room he wishes to sit and hear them. And he congratulates them. He tells them that, if he is not mistaken, they are approaching some kind of perfection.

Peter Claire writes to his father, to tell him about the splendours of Frederiksborg and the sublime acoustics in the chapel (*which I do pray you could hear, Father, for I know you would marvel at it*) and to inquire after the health of George Middleton. Of Emilia he makes no mention, only adding, at the end of the letter, that *the King's wife is gone into Jutland and will not be seen here this winter.*

No reply to his passionate letter has come from Emilia.

Each day he hopes for an answer to arrive and each day he is disappointed. Yet he refuses to believe that Emilia's sentiments have undergone some terrible alteration now that she is away from him. He saw in Emilia Tilsen a person who would not be diverted from the course she believed to be right. He saw in her a steadiness of purpose, a fierce determination beneath the gentle exterior. Her behaviour with regard to the hen—taken from the cellar and nurtured back to health in her room—confirmed these things. And surely, if her heart were truly engaged, she would not betray it? He cannot imagine any other possibility. He is sure he is not wrong.

Yet still there is silence.

Meanwhile, a different letter has arrived—from Countess O'Fingal.

As Peter Claire reads of the planned visit to Copenhagen of Francesca and her father, he reaches up unthinkingly to his left ear, where he half expects still to discover the jewel bought from the Gypsies and given to him as a token of the Countess's love. And then when he remembers that he took it out and sent it to Charlotte, he feels relieved. Though his love affair with Francesca preceded his meeting with Emilia, he cannot prevent himself from feeling a kind of guilt about it, as though it were a betrayal and a costly one, which could, in the end, separate him from everything that he has planned.

Yet he also recognises that mingling with this guilt is a seductive memory of the Countess—of her large, supple body, of her wild hair, of her laughter hurled in the face of the wind, of the pleasures she chose to bestow. To all of this, he owes something of himself. He feels that he is in her debt and always will be, and that this must ever be recognised and acknowledged. Though his heart has led him elsewhere, he decides that he must not run away from a meeting with Francesca. He decides, in fact, that he must behave towards her as honourably as he can.

And so, one night, when he is alone with the King, playing his lute in the almost dark of the royal bedchamber, he begins to talk about paper manufacture and Francesco Ponti.

"I cannot afford Italian paper," says the King.

"Why, Sir? Because I have seen Signor Ponti's paper and I would say that it is the finest in Europe."

"I can afford nothing: no paper; no money for new mills. I can barely afford to entertain this Italian gentleman of yours to supper."

Peter Claire smiles and the King takes the smile for some kind of refutation. He gets out of bed and walks to his study next door, and returns with a sheaf of documents, which he throws down in Peter Claire's lap. "Read!" he says. "It is all set out there: what I owe, what I have lost, what I dream of and cannot have. No king was ever as humiliated by poverty as I have become. And from where will any help come?"

Peter Claire looks down at the papers, written in the King's own hand, and sees column after column of numbers. By each number is inscribed the name of a manufactory and the commodity that it produces: silk, linen, thread, buttons, lace, wood, paint, veneer, lacquer, ivory, wool, lead, slate, pewter, hemp, tar . . . and on and on, listing all that a country has need of if it is to thrive in the world of commerce. The list ends with an ornately inscribed minus sign against a sum of dalers so colossal that Peter Claire stares at it, finding himself wondering whether it really has a bearing on the list that has gone before, or whether it has not arrived on the page by a peculiar accident—from some other realm of mathematics which has perfected the feat of flying from one document to another by undetectable means.

The King registers the lutenist's disbelief and says: "You see? And now you want to add Italian paper!"

Peter Claire looks up. He is about to speak, when the King says: "In what were once my mother's quarters here, what we used to call *Fru Mutter's Sal*, there is a silver bed. It was her marriage bed when she married the King my father. And now I am going to have this precious object taken away and melted down and turned into coins. I am going to requisition and destroy the bed in which I was conceived! So you see to what desperate measures I resort. Before the wars with the League, there were more dalers in my treasury than Denmark knew how to spend, and now there is *nothing!*"

Both men are silent for a while, Peter Claire still contemplating the documents he has been shown. Among the conflicting thoughts that run through his mind is the possibility that the King will soon try to save money by sacking his orchestra.

When Peter Claire is dismissed at last and goes to his bed, he is unable to sleep, but sits awake by his candle. His thoughts thread in and out of each other like coloured veins through marble. He imagines a journey to Jutland and Emilia running towards him down an avenue of limes. He imagines a forest of fir being felled and a vast paper mill rising out of the sandy soil. He imagines Francesca walking on the beach at Cloyne. He imagines Emilia turning in the middle of the avenue and running away from him and never looking back.

The first frosts have come.

As Kirsten gets into the coach, she remarks to Emilia: "This air kills."

The coachman covers their laps with furs and they set off from Boller, travelling north, as a yellow sun rinses out the mist and reveals the clean, glittering whiteness of the woods and fields.

They are going in secret to Herr Haas's house, the house of correction, to look for Marcus. Though Kirsten usually likes to talk and chatter on journeys, to keep tedium and discomfort at bay ("because what is all travelling but a persecution of the bones and the stomach?"), she is silent on this icy morning, noting the beauty of the landscape through which they pass, yet understanding how spiteful is this December cold and letting this remind her of all, in a gilded life such as hers should have been, that is so very unkind.

Otto is still in Sweden and her plans to be reunited with him are not advancing as they should. Her letter to Peter Claire—which surely has reached Frederiksborg by now?—has received no answer. The idea that the lutenist may have shown it to the King leaves her feeling so terrified that she dare not even think about this.

Nor does she dare to send word to Otto. In despatching to her some (but not all) of the furniture that she requested from Rosenborg, the King has warned her that "all and every thing of yours shall be forfeit and you shall be cast into prison if any word from you reaches Count Otto Ludwig. You are to conduct yourself as if he did not exist in the world. You are to conduct yourself thus for as long as your life shall endure."

Her life endures. This is all that it is: an endurance. And when she thinks of how glorious it once seemed she feels a great welling up of rage which threatens to suffocate her. Then she howls and clings to Emilia.

And she knows this howling of hers is a terrible sound and that it frightens Emilia, but she cannot keep it down and she wonders if she is not beginning to lose her reason. "I am mad!" she wails. "Emilia, I am mad!"

But today she is quiet, lost in her contemplation of the frost, of the winter, which has begun to make her afraid.

The carriage jolts onwards, the horses sneezing and panting, the hands of the coachman numb, the wheels turning and turning, and all the landscape, as Kirsten perceives it, mute and indifferent to their passing.

In Emilia's mind is the anguished thought that everything is vanishing away: people; places; the things to which she clung. That which has not yet gone will soon disappear, just as the road on which they travel will vanish under the snow. If Marcus is not found today, in what place will he continue to exist? In memory. In some hoped-for future. But where *now*?

And her lover? For this is how she thinks of Peter Claire—as though she were his mistress or his bride, and had known everything that love could be. He is at Frederiksborg—or so she assumes—but to her he has gone into an empty space like a hole in the sky. And because no word comes from him she can't summon him to her any more. His features, all angelic as they are, are fading from sight.

She doesn't speak of him and nor does Kirsten. Sometimes she is tempted to ask: "Those words you said on the night we left in the fishmonger's cart. Those words about the 'Irish whore': tell me what you meant and what you know." But she doesn't ask, in case in them—in the answer that would come—there is finality. In Kirsten's silence on the subject Emilia has begun to read such an ending, but she refuses to let it be confirmed.

Now, as the coach bonds on towards Århus, she remembers her mother's injunction: *Show courage, Emilia.* She understands that, since the visit to her father's house, she has let herself become frightened. Only for Kirsten does she seem able to be courageous, understanding that Kirsten's troubles are as deep, as abiding, as her own and that, without Kirsten, she would indeed find herself in an empty world. Kirsten's will, she sometimes thinks in admiration, keeps them both alive. If all should come to rights some day, then Kirsten will have engineered it.

She will have conjured all the vanished people from wherever it is that they are hiding.

As the miles go by, the sun disappears behind a grey blanket of cloud and Kirsten and Emilia see that the frost is gone from the fields and a slow rain is beginning to fall.

Emerging from her silence, Kirsten says: "Now, Emilia dear, I hope you have our plan quite clear in your mind. When we arrive in the town, we shall stay inside the carriage and not show ourselves, and Mikkel our coachman will go on foot to inquire about Herr Haas and his loathsome house.

"Once the house is found, Mikkel will go in with the pretence that he has brought a message to Marcus from his father. And only then, when Mikkel returns to the coach to tell us that Marcus is quite definitely *there*, shall we appear and show ourselves. For who knows what lies Magdalena may have told about us? She may have said we are witches who do spirit children away and drop them to their deaths from the clouds!"

Emilia nods. "Magdalena is the witch," she replies.

"Quite so," says Kirsten, "and therefore is full of cunning and inventions of a fiendish kind. For in telling us where Marcus has been put, did she not foresee the day when we should go after him and try to bring him out? And do not tell me that she has not done her best to prevent us. We know not how she has done this, but only can guess that she has. So we must outsmart her."

Emilia nods again, and now they see that the coach is arriving at the edge of the town and seagulls stand perched on the roofs and chimneys of the cottages in the rain.

"Oh," says Kirsten, "look at those patient birds who do not mind the wet. They put me in mind of one advantage to this journey: at least we have not had your hen to contend with in the coach!"

The two women smile and then, without warning, Emilia sees Kirsten's smile become suddenly contorted, and she clutches at the furs and tries to speak, but cannot, and Emilia holds her and begs her to say what is happening, while shouting to the coachman to stop. Emilia hears him call in the horses, feels the coach skid and slide on the wet road, and then, in a great release of breath, Kirsten screams out, "The child, Emilia! The child!" And as she does so, Emilia feels a deluge of warm liquid falling onto her shoes and prays it is water and not blood, and some of the furs slide away and become tangled round their feet, and Kirsten kicks out in terror and in pain, and Emilia has to strive to hold her still.

"Don't fear . . ." she hears herself say. "Don't fear . . ."

The coach stops at last and Mikkel's face, red with cold, damp from the rain, appears at the door. He stares at Kirsten wrestling with her pain and at the water which carries in it flecks of blood, now spreading over the floor of the coach, and seems frozen, both by the cold journey and by the sight now confronting him.

Show courage, Emilia.

"Mikkel," she says, as calmly as she can. "Go into one of these houses, where the gulls stand, and tell them that the King's wife has need of a bed and of a midwife."

Mikkel doesn't move. Rain drips into his eyes and he doesn't wipe it away.

Show courage, Emilia.

"Mikkel," she says again. "Go at once. Ask that a bed be made ready and a midwife called."

He goes at last. He says nothing at all as he goes but only holds his back, where it seems to hurt him. When he reaches the door of the cottage, he takes off his hat and shakes the rain away.

The room is low and dark, lit by a smoky fire.

The bed on which Kirsten lies is not a bed but a structure made out of hay bales lashed together and covered with linen. At her head is a bolster filled with straw. "Every time I move my neck," she whispers to Emilia, "I hear a crunching. Will you verify, my dear, that there is no mouse nor bat nor anything eating my hair?"

Emilia reassures her, smooths the lumpy pillow as best she can. When the pain returns, Kirsten clutches Emilia's hand and her face contorts, as it did in the carriage. Yet between the spasms she returns to a self that is unafraid, almost sprightly, as though now that she is to be delivered of her baby her optimism is beginning to return.

She sits up and examines the room in which she finds herself, where water is simmering in a pot on the fire and where a peasant woman, whose cottage this is, is tearing a white sheet into rags and fussing with some winter roots to make an infusion. Several times, Kirsten apologises to the woman for interrupting her morning and reassures her that all her children "have been born in a trice, so that I will not inconvenience you for very long."

The woman is old, with eyes that look as though they are turning to milk. "The King's child!" she says. "My lady, I did not imagine the King's child would arrive in such a place . . ."

And Kirsten smiles at her and knows that this is why she has no fear; because the child is not the King's, because it is the child of her lover and will resemble him and be born swiftly, on the waters of desire. Indeed, she's excited, impatient to see it, talks to it as she sweats and strains: "Come on, my little Otto! Swim out of me. Swim into my arms."

The root tea is brought to her and seems to warm her body, right down to her feet. "Emilia," she exclaims, "this tea is quite a marvel. Note down the recipe and we shall make it at Boller."

On the straw bolster, Kirsten's hair unwinds itself, springing out from its pins and clasps, until it is like tangled golden thread heaped about her face, and Emilia looks at her and is once again struck by her magnificence. She resolves that she herself, from this moment onwards, will show more courage and endurance. Karen and Kirsten—two women so different from each other—have instructed her with their words and by example. She will not betray them.

Now Kirsten is trying to reassure her about Marcus, saying that today's journey has not been in vain, that they will return, that "nothing which is dear to you has been forgotten and Marcus must endure a little longer, that is all, just a little longer . . ."

At this moment the midwife arrives. She is stout and rosy-cheeked, her starched collar and cuffs only a little dampened by the rain. She curtsies to Kirsten, and without any fuss marches to the end of the hay-bale bed, takes hold of Kirsten's ankles and opens her legs wide. She bends and her head disappears under Kirsten's skirts, where she squints at the birth passage, then inserts her hand full in and Kirsten lets out a cry which is both a cry of pain and a cry of longing to receive her lover once more in this place.

The midwife's practised fingers measure the degree to which the portal of the womb is opening. She finds it wide and can feel the child's head pressing upon it, ready to be born. She extracts herself from the skirts and pushes them up, and Kirsten's naked legs kick and push as the pain comes once more.

The peasant woman brings the rags and a bowl of water, and lays them by the bales, made from grass cut in the hot summer of 1627, which is her only bed. And together she and the midwife and Kirsten and Emilia hold to each other's arms, forming a human shape like a boat, and this boat moves and rocks as the midwife begins a chanting, which is the rhythmic song, like a song of the sea, which she sings when she knows that the child and its mother are as one in their struggle, and that the moment is coming and will be easy.

The child is a girl.

It is cleaned and examined in the low winter light. It is swaddled in the rags and laid on Kirsten's breast.

"Emilia," she asks. "What name shall be beautiful enough?"

THE SHIP *ANNA-FREDERIKA*

It was a cargo vessel, built during the reign of Frederik II.

It had never lived up to its graceful name. It was heavy and lumbering; a ship that nobody had ever really liked. It might have been taken out of service and broken up long ago had King Christian's shortage of money not become so acute. Instead, its leaks were stanched and mended, its worn and faded decks stripped and revarnished, and it continued to plough its way across the Kattegat and round into the Baltic, ferrying wool and hemp to Finland and returning with copper and lead.

Early in November it had sailed out of the Horsens Fjord, bound eventually for Finland, with a cargo of sheepskins, rope and string, but carrying letters and packages as far as Copenhagen, where it would be reprovisioned for the first leg of its voyage through the Baltic.

As the *Anna-Frederika* set out, a moderate westerly was blowing, but the wind veered and the sails of the ship began to be tormented by a rough gale from the north. They were strong sails, made by men who had heard and heeded King Frederik's edict against shoddiness. The canvas bulged and strained, trying to contain the wind, but the ship became, in the words of the captain, "like an old drunk dame farting into her skirts."

As he gave the order to drop the topsails, he saw that the shrouds of the mainsail were frayed and torn. He swore under his breath and shouted for this to be reefed before its great weight began to uproot the main mast and send it crashing down upon the deck. "When we reach the sea of Samsø," he snapped to the boatswain, "you and your men will weave some new strength into these ropes and you will do it speedily, so that we can go on."

The ship surged forward, pushing at the water, trying to ride the swell, but it was as if the old, ungainly body of the *Anna-Frederika* was racked with so many pains that it wanted the sea to release it from any further endeavour; as if it was only waiting for a far-off towering wave to break over it and take it down into the calm and silent deep, to where the whales of King Christian's imagining lurked in the darkness.

The captain cursed his ship. He tried to stop his ears to its sighing and creaking. He did not want to die. In his rage, he ordered the boatswain down into the hold to "filch rope from the humdrum cargo for which we are all risking our benighted lives."

The darkness of the hold, and the cold there, and the feeling that it always had for the crew of being a place unfit for any man to be: these things impressed themselves more strongly than they had ever done upon the boatswain as he climbed down into it with his lamp held high.

But as he began to search for the bales of rope, he became aware of something else, something he had not anticipated: the cargo in this hold was stinking. It was a stench so foul, so suffocating and terrible that the man stood and held to a post, gripped by a sudden sickness. Sweat poured off his face and down between his shoulder-blades. He tried to master the sickness, but it would not be mastered. He vomited and his body convulsed, and his lamp fell from his hands and smashed on the floor.

He wiped his face on his sleeve. He spat into a tarred gulley where stale sea water from a hundred voyages had collected. He stood still, holding fast to the timber, trying to recover. He knew that the faint light still in the sky far above made it possible for him to move around the hold, to search both for the rope and for the source of the smell, yet his body felt so weak he could barely raise his arm or continue to stand upright.

He shivered. He made himself begin to grope forwards. With every step that he took he expected to find corpses. The ship continued to roll and lurch, and it seemed to the boatswain, as he staggered about, fighting to find air that he could breathe, that hell lurked down there in the *Anna-Frederika*, and that this hell had claimed him and that nothing in his life would ever again be sweet.

He tried to banish this feeling with thoughts of summer mornings off the island of Gotland, of the scent of linden trees in his childhood village of Vinderup, of his young daughter who smelled of linen still warm from the iron, but now he knew that he was losing his grasp of what was or what might be, that his steps were turning in a meaningless dance, that his daughter had vanished to a place he could not reach, that the light in the sky had gone out. He fell onto a pile of sheepskins and he felt the stink of them take him into itself and drown him.

Only when the northerly began to die down and the familiar shape of Samsø was visible on the horizon did the captain look round for the boatswain and see the doors to the hold still open.

With the dropping of the wind the smell began to seep upwards onto the deck and members of the crew stood at the hold mouth, covering their faces and looking down in confusion.

Two men were ordered to bring the boatswain up.

He was not dead, but his skin was the colour of lard and his pulse was so faint it was almost impossible to find it. He tried to speak, but his jaw was locked. On his clothes and in his hair the stench in the hold travelled up into the body of the ship.

He was laid in his bunk, where the captain stared at him, holding a handkerchief to his own mouth, cursing the storm, cursing the King for not giving him a seaworthy ship, cursing fate that had brought some unknown pestilential thing on board his infernal tub.

The boatswain died in the night. The hold was closed and padlocked, and covered with a tarpaulin roped to the deck. The torn shrouds were mended with odds and ends of cord and string. The *Anna-Frederika* limped on towards Copenhagen.

The following day, the two crewmen who had brought the boatswain out of the hold succumbed to death and the captain ordered that all three bodies be tipped into the sea off Hessel Island.

But he now knew that he and the *Anna-Frederika* were doomed. As he predicted, the ship was quarantined off Copenhagen. Those who survived the period of the quarantine would be taken ashore, but the *Anna-Frederika* and its cargo would be burned at sea.

In the days that ensued, watching his own body and those of his fellow officers and men for signs of sickness, the captain's restless and anxious mind sometimes turned to the sack of letters lying in the hold with the infected skins, and to their recipients who would never receive them now, and he wondered if, among all these papers, there were written any words which were not ephemeral and idle, but on the contrary of vital importance in a human life.

He meditated on the capriciousness of chance, which was as invisible as the wind and which, like the wind, could not be brought to any order, not even with prayer. In this, he thought, *all men are sailors, like us*. But the observation did not bring him any comfort.

And what the captain of the *Anna-Frederika* did not and could not know was that among the letters destined to be burned was the long communication from Kirsten Munk to Peter Claire in which she had tried to blackmail the English lutenist into becoming her spy. It had no destination now except the all-consuming fire.

HARD GROUND

George Middleton's submission to the surgeon's knife, and to the pincers which brought out of his bladder a stone so heavy it was as if some crystal from the earth had found its way inside him, was exceptionally courageous. The surgeon himself remarked on Middleton's stoicism while in the very epicentre of his agony and, when the operation was done, Middleton was sufficiently himself to thank the surgeon profusely for saving his life.

Then he lay in his bedroom at Cookham Hall and wondered if his life had been saved or not.

The continuing hurt to his stomach and to his nether parts, where the knife had filleted its way in between the anus and the cods, felt so great and the fever on him so capricious that he could not imagine ever rising from his bed. Indeed, the man that he had been—who rode every day about his park and his farms, who would dance a caper when guests and musicians came to Cookham—appeared to bear no resemblance to the man he was now, and to realign the one to the other seemed to him an impossible task. Part of him understood that he was dying.

He longed to see Charlotte. He longed to cram into an hour a lifetime of tender words. It did not matter if those words were not elegant nor very sensible. It did not even matter if, having found their way through the fog and damp of his fever, they came out in some kind of embarrassing confusion. What mattered was that they be uttered and that Charlotte hear them and remember them after he was gone.

He sent a coach to Harwich, and Charlotte and her mother Anne arrived at Cookham Hall on a cold December night.

When his "dear Daisy" came into his room and stood by his bed, holding his hand, George Middleton let out a sob of joy. And this sob, which was not so much a cry as a great outpouring of wonder at the sight of his fiancée, awoke in Charlotte such a storm of weeping that, as she laid her head down in the crook of Middleton's arm, both the sleeve of his night-shirt and the linen sheet which covered him quickly became limp and warm with her tears.

"Daisy . . ." said Middleton.

But she could not speak. Her heart told her that some things in a life are unbearable. If George was going to be taken from her, she knew that she would not be able to bear it.

"Daisy," said Middleton again, as he stroked her hair, "be brave, my dear darling thing."

"I cannot," she cried. "I cannot remember what bravery is nor how one goes about it."

George Middleton found himself smiling. He knew that part of his reason for wanting to go on living resided in his continuing wish to hear utterances of this kind. It was as if Charlotte amused part of him that had never ever been amused before. "See now, my dear girl, what a thing you have caused! I am laughing. Since you came in a mere few seconds ago, I declare my pain is on the run!"

She kissed his head and his face and his ear, and then his black moustache very lightly. Then she looked at him. She could see his pain and knew that what he said about it running was a lie. Even in the soft lamplight he looked pale, where before he had always looked pink and ruddy, and his eyes were as glittery as marbles, yet the lids appeared very heavy on them, as though at any moment he would slide away from her. "George," she said, "I shall not leave you. I will sit here until you are well and I do not care if I become part of the chair."

But he wouldn't let her keep a vigil. He said, "My dove, if you do this, we shall both become convinced that death is in the next room."

When he had told her, in words particular to him, to his boisterous heart, to his fondness for drollery, that she was the dearest, sweetest, most marvellous creature he had ever known or ever would know, he gave her a task. He asked her, on the morrow, to go into his park and into his garden, and tell him what she saw there and how it appeared to her, and what light or dark was in the sky and what wintry shadows lay on the land. He added that he would love to lie there and think of her in the gardens of Cookham— "where you shall soon be the veritable mistress and command what flowers are to be sown and how many rows of peas are to be planted"—and that if she should find anything in the park or garden that especially pleased her or amused her, she should bring it to him and he would be sure to smell in it the scent of the waiting spring.

Charlotte did not particularly want to walk alone in the cold outdoors while George lay in his room. She had very frequently imagined herself wandering in this green landscape where the sky was vast and the horizon low and dark with forests of oak, but George was always with her. Indeed, she *belonged* to George in her reveries; she was Mrs. George Middleton, and could not be anywhere but by his side.

Yet she agreed to go. She would ask her mother to accompany her and they would visit George's horse, Soldier, and the pig houses and the kennels, and skirt by the woods where winter feed was laid down for the game.

As they set out, each wrapped in a woollen cloak, Anne Claire remarked that the cold of December was "unforgiving in Norfolk," but Charlotte made no comment, only privately noted the hardness of the ground under her little brown boots and the stillness in the air.

When they arrived at the paddock where the horses still grazed, with woollen cloths on their backs, she called to Soldier. He was a large horse, black as the dark spaces under the trees of the forest, with a high neck and a haughty look, and no one but George Middleton liked to ride him, because of his strength and his hard mouth that never seemed to feel the pulling of the bit. "When you are married," said Anne gently, "perhaps you may insist that George ride one of the others . . ."

Charlotte stroked the horse's nose. "If I am married," she said sadly, "I do not think I will insist on anything except—privately to myself—that George continue to love me."

She found a jay's feather in the grass and picked it up, wondering if this was what he might like her to take him, but the feather was merely pretty and did not delight or amuse her, so she let it fall.

They looked at the pigs, huddled together in their barn for warmth, and Charlotte thought, The tail of a pig is a thing foolish enough to make a wounded man laugh, and wondered whether she might ask that a leash be tied to one of the sows and she would lead her up the polished stairs and along the landing to George's bedroom. But it seemed to her that pigs were too fleshy, their lives too brief, their behaviour too ugly, to be of consolation to George at this hour. And she did not want him to think her quite mad, only a little unique, only containing within her just that measure of the unexpected sufficient to make her irreplaceable.

She had no idea what she was searching for. She knew that in the shrubbery there stood a winter-flowering cherry that came into bud in December and that a branch broken from this tree might be the thing to lay on George's counterpane, but when she arrived at the tree it looked grey. The tiny buds were there, but they had not opened. There was nothing entertaining about it.

Then they arrived at the kitchen garden, laid out behind low hedges of box, and Charlotte saw rows of celery roots earthed up, onions dug out and laid to dry, apples fallen and discolouring to a mulch, leeks like low green fountains.

They were passing a bed of cabbages when Anne stopped. "I didn't know George grew these at Cookham," she said.

"What? Cabbages? I suppose that they grow in every garden, Mother."

"No," said Anne. And she stopped and peeled back the outer leaves of the cabbage and Charlotte saw at its centre, not the expected interleaving of the cabbage head, but a firm cream-coloured growth like a posy of daisies tightly packed and bound.

She stared at the strange vegetable. She had always loved nature's trick of concealing one thing within another, a thing you could not imagine until you had seen it, like a polished horse-chestnut inside its husk.

"Brought from France," said Anne. "They call them *choux-fleurs*: cabbage-flowers, and I hear that they are very delicate and good."

So this is what Charlotte took back to George Middleton.

He was sleeping, but she woke him and put the cabbage-flower on his rib-cage, where it balanced unsteadily, like a baby's head.

"Mama says," said Charlotte, "I should make soup from it for you, but I prefer it as it is."

George Middleton sat up. It seemed to him, unless he was quite mistaken, that since this last sleep of his, his pain had eased a little and his mind felt light.

He held the cabbage-flower in his broad hands, then lifted it to his nostrils and smiled at Charlotte. "Daisy," he said, "the scent of this thing is infernal!" And they both began to laugh.

Two Letters

As Peter Claire sits down at last to compose an answer to Francesca O'Fingal's letter, he reflects that a year has now passed since he left Ireland. He tries to imagine the changes that will have occurred at Cloyne: the quietly altered appearances of the children; the visits to the grave of their father; Francesca's assumption of all the duties of the estate; her wearing of mourning; her knowledge that life has played her a perplexing trick and that her future is unknown.

He wants to say to her that he can have no part in that future, but, as he takes up the pen, he hesitates. He cannot write what is in fact a reproach, a disparagement of her feelings, when what he feels for Francesca—for her daring as much as her beauty—is only admiration. He begins thus and hopes that, as the letter progresses, he will come by some formulation that will—without anything being explained—make known to her that their love affair is over.

My dear Francesca,
    You cannot imagine how greatly I was surprised by the disclosure that you and your father are to come to Denmark. It is as if I cannot envisage the means by which you will both be transported here, so vividly do I picture you in Ireland—or else in the elegant Bologna of my imagination.
    Let me prepare you a little for your voyage. Being once more in winter, we are held again by a great cold that is, in its intensity, more fierce than any I have known, whether in Harwich or at Cloyne, and you and Signor Ponti should not think light of it but come wrapped in furs and wool, and know that this is a cold one might die of.
    The King winters at Frederiksborg Castle (some few miles from Copenhagen, at Hillerød) and I shall endeavour to ensure that you are lodged here, for this is a very mighty castle with numberless rooms. Indeed, it is so vast that, as I walk about it, I do sometimes think that there may be souls lodged in the attics of the copper roofs of whose existence I am quite ignorant . . .

Here he pauses. His evocation of these small high rooms has brought into his mind the image of Emilia's chamber at Rosenborg, with her grey dress hanging on the armoire and the speckled hen roosting on her coverlet. This reverie fills him with such a wave of tenderness for her, such a yearning to put his arms round her, to become the proud provider of grey dresses or squawking hens or whatever it might be that she has set her heart on, that he lays down the pen and sits there, gazing vacantly at the wall.
    It is night and he can hear the wind sighing and he feels his new loneliness within the silence Emilia is imposing, this absence

which seems to have no end. It is a slow torture. Within it, his playing is suffering and it is he, not the Italians, whom Jens Ingemann rightly berates for his lack of concentration. Every day, day after day after day, he prays for it to be ended. He has imagined innumerable times the arrival of the letter-bearer and the words from Emilia that will, in the little space it takes to read them, lift all the weight from his heart.

How is it, he asks himself, that the human soul is prey to such absolute attachments and is so quickly made glad or filled with misery? Does the partridge mourn his lost mate? Does the wolf cast out from the pack feel sorrow of the kind that a man would recognise?

Peter Claire sets aside his letter to Francesca and begins to write:

Oh, Emilia, there is nothing good in your silence! Strive as I may to find a kind of grace in it, I cannot. It works in me nothing but discord and disorder, so that now in this night, I feel such agitation that I almost wonder if I am not beginning to lose my reason.

I beg you to write to me. There is no need of a long letter. Only tell me that I may continue to think of you as my beloved. Only say to me that we shall both work to find a way—within the great shadow of the King's separation from his wife—to forge a future together. For surely you shall not stay for ever with Kirsten, nor I with the King? But how am I to hope for any such future if my letters are not answered?

He finishes neither letter. He stares at the two beginnings, side by side. And then he sleeps. So wild and confused are his dreams that, when morning comes, he washes his face and flees his room as quickly as he can, for he cannot bear to think about them.

Later the following day, as the sky is once again darkening and yet more hours have gone by without any word from Emilia, he signs his name under the few lines he has written to her and seals this letter just as it is, knowing it to be petulant and boyish, but not caring, and pressing the seal into the hot wax with a fervour that is close to anger.

He lays it aside and after a while takes up his pen again.

Francesca [*he writes*], I must warn you and your father of another thing besides the cold. And this thing is His Majesty's troubles, that have come upon him in the year since I have been with him. His wife is gone away and this alone would cause him great heaviness of heart. Added to this, however, is another woe. And this is the King's want of money. When I talked to him of your visit, extolling the great virtues of the parchment and vellum produced by the Ponti manufactory in Bologna, he impressed upon me the impossibility of buying paper from Italy, and I am sure he has no dalers with which to build any paper mill where Signor Ponti might oversee the production of the fine paper to be made out of Danish firs.

Thus you will see that your proposed journey here might be all in vain and that your father might return empty-handed to Bologna and you would have had all the expense of it for nothing.

Naturally, I would be glad to see you at Frederiksborg, but I do not wish you to leave your children nor your father his work for any voyage that would not bring you what your heart desires.

From your affectionate friend,
    Peter Claire

Peter Claire reads this second letter several times before closing it. He notes what versatile things words may be and how, contained within them, can reside other words, nowhere set down and for ever invisible to the eye, but having an existence just the same.

My baby has been christened Dorothea.

Her head is covered with a blond down and her eyes are bright, and I shall always remember that, in the midst of pain, there was a kind of ecstasy in her delivery that I did not experience with any of my other Children. All that they gave me was pain unmitigated, and each one of them has caused me a grand quantity of Irritation ever since.

I am now endeavouring to love Dorothea. Each day, I pray that I shall not find her Irritating. But I observe that *of their nature* babies are bound to cause torment to all around them. They are worse than Emilia's hen, Gerda. The noise they make is infernal. The stench of them is scarcely to be endured, for they are ever spewing out strands of pearly vomit or straining till their eyes start from their heads to produce farmyard motions. Their talk is plain nonsense. At the least thing, they wail and scream. They have no teeth in their heads, nor any understanding of anything. In short, there is little in them to engender in me any feeling of Love whatsoever, and my affection, such as it is, for Dorothea rests only on the plain fact that she is Otto's child and therefore a Memento of my Lover.

I cannot bear to suckle an infant, so I have engaged a Wet-nurse. When she is fed and clean and not puking, I undertake to rock her in my arms and walk about with her, that I may be *seen* to love her, and my Mother says to me: "Why, Kirsten, I did not know you would ever show such tenderness towards any Baby of yours"; and I reply: "Why, Mother, if I have lacked tenderness towards my Children, then surely it derives from your example!"

And at this, she goes into a venomous mood, muttering all manner of accusations against me and insults to my character. But I tell her that I am perfectly Impervious to Any Thing that she can hurl at me. "I have," I remind her, "the *habit of submitting to abuse.* Nobody at Court was ever so snubbed and slandered as I was—and much of that in the open and to my face—so whatever you can dredge up against me is as a flea trying to bite the hide of an elephant and shall never bother me in the least."

And at this, she is quiet and skulks away.

And the longing grows in me hourly to turn her out of this house and send her and Vibeke to be eaten by Wolves in the forests.

Other matters conspire to vex me. Indeed, the number of Things designed to annoy me, upset me and frighten me as Christmastide approaches is miserably large and I declare that I scarcely know any hour when I am at Peace with the World or with myself.

First, and most gravely, I have no word from the English Lutenist.

Daily, I expect some reply to my Proposal, but he does not deign to answer it. Either he is already weary of Emilia and so does not care whether his letter reaches her or no. Or else, disdaining me quite and refusing to collude with my Plan, he has shown my letter to the King, thus putting me in the most grave and terrifying Jeopardy.

I curse him! I curse his lute! May his yellow hair fall out with the last leaves of winter and all his beauty be lost!

I dare not write to him again, for if my letter has been taken to the King, then perchance in his fondness for me and in memory of his "heart's dearest Mouse" His Majesty will set aside this one unwise communication or burn it and take no Proceedings against me. But if I should beg a second time for Documents with which I can barter with King Gustav, and this second letter should be shown to the King, so that he knows I am plotting against him in order to come to my Lover, why then I do believe he would send Soldiers to arrest me and I should be locked away in some Dungeon for the rest of my years, or else be burned as a Witch and a Spy.

What can I do?

When I reflect that I have no means (or none that I can perceive) by which I can be reunited with Otto, I find myself tearing at my hair and at my flesh, as though I would break myself in pieces and send me to him bit by bit. And only Emilia, who tries to hold me and calm me, does prevent me from ripping out my nails and scarring my cheeks, and, if it were not for her, I do not know in what state of Injury I would now find myself. In my Dreams, I am dead and laid in a cold grave in Finland. The snow and ice cover the place until it is invisible. And the seasons turn and no one comes near it, summer or winter.

Yesterday, to ease my fears, I decided to write to the King.

If his Reply be sweet, then I shall know that I am safe and there are no soldiers to be sent to take me away. If it be not sweet, or if no Reply comes, then I must consider whether I should flee with Emilia into hiding where I cannot be found.

I told my Husband of the birth of Dorothea—"your sweet child"—and asked him what other Names he would like to give her. I pretended her hair was dark. I said she had the cry of "a dear dove" and that she would grow up to resemble him.

All in among these lies, I begged him to send me some Money for Dorothea's care (for perhaps with Money I can find some means to come to an arrangement with King Gustav?) and also to despatch to me, as before requested, my two Slaves, Samuel and Emmanuel.

In some sport with these Black Boys lies the only hope of holding fast to my Sanity. I am still most horribly Fat after the birth of Dorothea and this fatness does disgust me and is a Stubborn thing that refuses to leave me, but clings to my waist and to my stomach, so that all my once-beautiful flesh now begins to fall in folds towards the earth. But on this matter, I reflect that Slaves are not supposed to utter any Criticism of their Mistress's body, or even to notice such things as Pendulousness. They must do my bidding and that is that. And so I shall have some Pleasure with them and then perhaps matters in general may go on a little better.

But in the case that they do not go on better, and I am to be Impeached or accused of Treason and thrown into a Prison for the rest of time, I have purchased from my Mother's Apothecary—at great and horrible expense—a little pot of Poison.

It is a white dust.

I show it to Emilia. I tell her it is my Vial of Death.

She stares at it, then at me and then at it again. "Madam," she says, "shall we die?"

I stroke her hair. "Emilia," I say, "I am not Cleopatra in her Monument with all her Women commanded to put the asp to their own breasts. If ever I should use this, it would be for me alone, so do not be so foolish as to think otherwise."

And then I see a solitary tear fall from Emilia's eye. And I know that this is falling not only at the thought of my death, but also because she feels herself to be betrayed by Peter Claire and, for a moment, I repent that I stole her letter, for I see that she is suffering and indeed that she is growing thin and that her hair, which was glossy, has become dull and her cheeks have no colour in them.

But I cannot give her the letter. Indeed, if any other letter should come, then I shall have to intercept this also. I am sorry for the hurt she is feeling, but I am certain her Anguish is as nothing compared with mine, and really I can only do as I have planned and not yield to any Sentimental Feeling. Because Emilia is my one and only Consolation and if she should leave me I know not what I should do.

"Emilia," I say, "you must forget your Musician and I shall tell you why." And then I go to my boudoir and fetch at last the sentences copied from the letter I found in Peter Claire's room. I give the Paper to her and she reads.

She does not move or look up, but continues to stand there, reading, as though the Paper were many thousands of words long and she could not come to the end of it, but must go on and on and on reading it until the light faded at the window and the owls began to call. So I reach out and take it from her hands and still she stands there, as if she had been made motionless by a Spell.

I let the Paper fall. I go to Emilia and try to put my arms about her, to comfort her as she comforts me, but she is stiff and rigid in my embrace, and then she turns away from me without a word and I hear her going up the stairs.

I allow a little time to pass.

Then I go to her room and knock upon the door, as if she were my mistress and I her Woman.

She calls to me to come in and I see her sitting by the window, with the hen, Gerda, on her lap. She is stroking the hen and the only sound in the room is the noise that the hen makes, which is low and murmurous, a little like the purring of a cat.

"Emilia," I say. "All men are liars. I know not one—including Otto who promised me more than he ever could give—who was not Perfidious. Only think of the way your Father has treated you and the cruelties the King has inflicted upon me. And so we shall live without them all! We shall be as we are: a Household of Women. No man shall cross our threshold any more. And I do declare we shall be happier than ever we were."

She makes no reply.

I pour for her a little glass of cordial and hold it out to her, but she pushes it away.

I wait in silence and the hen goes on with its own noise, while Emilia's small hands caress the feathers of its neck and back. I reflect that I have never before sat in a room without talking, listening to a chicken, and I have to cover my mouth so that I do not burst into a fit of Laughter.

And then Emilia says at last: "I shall try to forget everything. The only thing that I refuse to forget is Marcus. When shall we go again to Århus?"

I drink the cordial myself. The thought of another freezing journey in a coach makes me feel seasick. I pour a little more of the cordial and gulp it down. Then I promise Emilia we shall go to Århus in search of Herr Haas before Christmas. "And we shall bring Marcus out," I say, "and he alone will be the man in our household."

Among all these sorry things, one matter, at least, gives me some Entertainment. My mother's Woman, Vibeke, my former Woman of the Torso, has begun to appear at table and at other times in the day most gorgeously decked out in Expensive Dresses, as though she were Queen of Denmark.

These dresses are very tight upon her, for in truth she is as fat as I am and can only control her gourmandising one week in seven.

Yet I see that she thinks she is now a woman of Exquisite beauty on account of all these ruffles and bows and stiff petticoats and panels of velvet. It is as if she believed the dresses had transformed her Peasant's face. And this gives me a nice amount of Mirth and does make me forget for a moment—when I observe Vibeke strutting about like the Tsarina of All the Russias—my great store of sorrows and fears.

"Vibeke," I say to her one supper time, when she is shimmering at the table in golden Broderie, "from where have you conjured these extraordinary new Creations of yours?"

She looks hastily at my Mother.

"Vibeke had very few clothes," says Ellen. "And so I commanded some few new things to be made." But then she looks away, as though she is abashed by some Scheme that is in her mind and which she would not have me discover.

"How generous of you!" I exclaim. "It is merely a shame, when they must have cost you so much, that they were fashioned at least one size too small."

And I see the pain on her face and on Vibeke's, and this little visible Suffering of theirs, which they tried to conceal but could not, gives me an unexpected Gladness of Heart that lasts for several hours.

CONCERNING WHAT IS REAL

With the silver and gold dalers struck from the melted plate, King Christian has been able to pay for the completion and fitting out of three whaling ships. He tells himself that when these giants of the deep are found, the tide of Denmark's fortunes will begin to turn.

Counting and re-counting his coinage, he despatches some money to the preacher Martin Møller, in the valley of the *Isfoss*, and informs him that *a new company of specialists, possessing more knowledge than those who came with us before, will arrive next year and the mine shall be reopened and the silver shall at last be brought out.*

This time, the King will put his trust in Russian engineers. He understands that those Danes he once referred to as the geniuses of the mine are lost *because their genius was not sufficient to the task.* Now his chancellor tells him that only in Russia is "the secret of silver understood." It is understood because generations of tsars have willed it so, have built domes of silver, and spires and entire rooms. They have spun dresses and coats out of silver filaments. They live in a silvered universe. Next to God, it is in silver that they place their trust.

And so men are even now travelling across land from the Sayan mountains thousands of miles away, travelling in sledges and on snow-shoes to arrive in Denmark as the spring returns. And they will be taken to the Numedal as the cataract of the *Isfoss* begins to flow once again, and with their knowledge they will bring the mine back to life.

To Martin Møller the King writes:

All that remains to be resolved is the question of language. If you yourself, in your loyalty to your people and to me, your King, would find some means of learning the Russian tongue, then when these men arrive—if they are not blown into the sky by freezing winds or buried alive in the drifting snow— why then you shall interpret what they say and give orders to the miners who can be hired round about. And you shall earn my everlasting gratitude.

But still, with some dalers safely locked in his treasury and with his whale strategy and his new silver strategy being put slowly into place, King Christian's mind turns upon his need for more money and he cannot rid himself of the belief that at Kronborg, beneath his mother's State rooms, there is hidden a quantity of treasure so vast that, if he could only come by it, he would at a single stroke be released from his yoke of poverty.

The King arrives at Kronborg early in the morning, almost before it is light.

Queen Sofie, whose face has not yet rearranged itself to meet the day after a troubled night, sits by a silver samovar, drinking tea. The plaits of her grey hair have no spring nor shine in them and appear almost as though they did not grow from her head but had been attached to it by means of clips. Christian reflects that she is elderly and solitary, and should be left alone, and, for a few moments, he falters in his intention.

Then he yawns, as though he might be as tired as she, as though he has made the journey unwillingly, and says: "Mother, I am here because the time has come when we must all make sacrifices for Denmark. And so the moment has also arrived to relieve you of a treasure for which you no longer have any need."

She sips her tea. Her face betrays nothing. Her hands do not tremble as she holds the cup. "The story of my 'treasure,' " she says, "was put about by your wife and is her invention. I have nothing. I live on fish out of the Sound. I am surprised you are not more adept at recognising Kirsten's slanders, for you yourself have very frequently been the victim of them."

Though the King would prefer it if Kirsten were not mentioned, if her name and her behaviour would slip silently away from everybody's mind, he is able to control the small spasm of agony that this remark brings and to say calmly: "I know that there is gold at Kronborg. If you will show me where you keep it, I shall take only what is needed—for my whale boats, for my new expedition to the silver mine, for my unfinished buildings in Copenhagen—and leave you enough to last out your life."

Queen Sofie wishes to say that "enough" cannot be measured by anyone but her. "Enough" is presumed to be finite and is not. "Enough" is a mountain whose summit can never be reached.

But she keeps silent. She touches the samovar to see whether it has kept its heat and then she says: "Furniture and pictures I have. And tapestries. Is it these you are intent upon stealing?"

"No," says Christian with a sigh.

"Then what else? Spoons? Fans? My jewellery?"

King Christian gets to his feet. "I have brought men," he says. "We shall search your vaults."

"Ah, the vaults," says Queen Sofie. "You wish to take away my wine?"

It is dark in the vaults. It is a darkness by design.

The men hold high their torches and the King walks slowly along, examining the kegs of wine on their blocks, of which there are a great number. He pauses at random and orders that the tap on now this keg and now that be turned—to see that wine really does flow from it—and so the smell of wine begins to compete with that of damp and tar.

He pauses, takes one of the torches himself, as though only he could use it to illuminate the things he is certain must be there. He looks down at the floor. The dust and grime on it are thick, so that the bricks appear black. He begins to search for some trap in the floor—such as he has at Rosenborg in the *Vinterstue*—leading down yet further into the rock on which Kronborg was built, but through all the cellar there is no sign of one.

He sits down on a wine barrel. He wonders, for the first time, whether the story of the Dowager Queen's treasure was not simply one more falsehood with which it amused Kirsten to taunt him. He sends his men to search the rest of the castle, but he doubts that they will find any hidden treasure in bedrooms and closets, and he requests that they do not disturb too greatly the order of the rooms.

He is silent, gazing about him, warmed by the torchlight, aware of his own shadow on the wall. A hundred times he has seen the underground gold in his mind—the glint of it, its marvellous weight and solidity. But there is nothing here: only the dust of the years and a store of wine kept too long in the old kegs.

As the coach takes him back to Frederiksborg he considers how the lies told by his wife and by his mother have, over the years, competed with each other to confuse and ensnare him, so that, in very many matters, he no longer knows what is real and what is illusory.

On Christmas Eve, Kirsten says to Emilia: "I believe I shall put out a shoe for Saint Nicholas to fill! Grown-ups have a far greater need for gifts than children and I do not know why this is not more widely recognised. I shall ask the Saint to bring me Otto."

And the two women laugh at this, but then Kirsten announces that she is retiring to bed, to spend her afternoon dozing and dreaming, and Emilia is left alone.

The day is grey and cold. Emilia puts on a cloak and asks Ellen if she may ride one of the horses in the park. Ellen and Vibeke are playing cards and Ellen barely looks up as she replies: "Take the grey. The others will be too strong for you. Your turn, Vibeke."

Already, as Emilia mounts the horse, her spirits rise. She spurs the grey to an amiable trot and feels bright blood begin to come to her cheeks. She imagines the day when she will be riding away from Boller for ever, far away from the Tilsen fruit fields. And at the end of her journey her lover will be waiting . . .

For notwithstanding Peter Claire's silence, notwithstanding her knowledge of his former liaison with Countess O'Fingal, some part of Emilia's mind stubbornly continues to believe in the existence of his love for her. It just has not reached her, that is all. It has not reached her because it is somehow *confined elsewhere*. She cannot necessarily say where this "elsewhere" might be. Lately, she imagines that it is the cellar at Rosenborg, deserted now, as the King has moved to Frederiksborg, but containing in its darkness words and thoughts which will one day be uttered again. As time passes, the cellar becomes less and less a cellar in her imagination and more and more a chamber in the lutenist's heart.

She knows that all of this is whimsical, capricious. She knows it belongs to that side of her nature that Marcus shares—their tendency to dream and to invent—and which her father mistrusts and fears. For the hundredth time in her short life Emilia wishes her mother were with her. Karen would help her know what to believe and what to ignore or forget.

Emilia guides the grey horse into the forest, which runs along the boundary of Johann Tilsen's land.

She reins in the pony and dismounts. Then she leads him forward, under beech and oak, until she comes to the fence which divides the two estates. She does not pause, for she knows exactly where she is. She ties the horse to the fence and climbs over it.

It is as though her thoughts about Karen have led her here. It is almost as though Karen is with her and protects her or makes her invisible, so that were Johann or Ingmar or Magdalena to ride by, they would not be able to see her.

Emilia walks to the foot of the tree where, long ago, Karen showed her some object buried in the ground. She finds a flint to use as her trowel, kneels down and begins to dig among the fallen leaves and beech husks, down through the peaty earth that sends forth its scent of other seasons once witnessed and now past, until her hands touch something solid and heavy.

She digs more carefully now, more slowly. She is faintly aware of a light snow beginning to fall through the canopy of bare branches above her, but gives this little attention. Her knees are damp. Pheasants squawk from the Boller boundary. Rooks call and circle above their roosts. The sense of Karen sheltering her, smiling now at what she's doing, is so strong that she almost expects to raise her head and see her mother returned to the world.

Emilia lifts out the object, which is about the size and weight of a brick. The damp earth has coated it like a skin. She has to prise the soil away with her nails. And then, number by number, she sees a clock face appear: a casing that was once shiny brass; roman numerals in black enamel on a white ground. And she remembers . . .

She is four or five. Karen digs the hole at the foot of the tree. She is talking about time. She is saying that Emilia is too young to understand. And then she takes the clock and turns the hands, and shows Emilia where they are pointed and says: "This is the time that it will always tell."

The clock is placed in the earth and Emilia and Karen cover it

with handfuls of soil, and then with leaves and husks, and it becomes invisible . . .

Emilia stares at it. The clock is stopped at ten minutes past seven.
This is the time that it will always tell. But what does it signify? What
happened at ten minutes past seven that was so important to Karen
that she buried a valuable clock in the beechwoods?

Emilia continues to clean the clock face, using handfuls of dead
leaves, to bring the beginnings of a shine to the glass. And it is
only now, aware that a little unexpected moisture is helping her in
her task, that she notices the snow falling fast and laying a thin
white dust over the forest floor.

She stands up. She is poised between two resolutions: to take
the clock and keep it among her few possessions or to return it to
the earth. She cannot decide which is right, and it is as if the fast-
falling snow is warning her that she must hurry, she must replace
the clock or she must take it, but she must go back to safety inside
the Boller fence, find her pony and ride back before darkness begins
to creep on, before she loses her way in the snow and the fading
light.

And it is now, during these quickly passing moments of her in-
decision, that she hears a noise behind her. She does not turn at
first, because the noise is so fragile, so *almost not there at all*, that she
both does and does not notice it, and she is so preoccupied by the
clock and its significance that the sounds of the forest have no immediacy for her.

It is a whisper.

There has been no sound of any footfall, any scuffling of leaves
or breaking twig.

Emilia turns. She holds the clock to her chest. The ticking that
she hears is her own heart.

Someone was whispering her name. *Emilia.*

But she is alone with the tall trees, with the snowfall, with the
faltering light. Nothing moves.

Some way off, she hears the grey horse whinny. But she stays a moment longer, staring deep into the wood, clutching the clock, which she will take, yes, certainly take now, because it is something she can care for and cling to, her mother's clock, but intended to be hers, because no one else ever knew that it was there . . .

Emilia.

And then there is movement. From behind one of the stately beech trunks a thin figure creeps out. It comes towards her. It is so small, so light, that it seems to walk quite silently and to leave no impress on the ground as it moves. It is Marcus.

Emilia sets Marcus on the horse and wraps her cloak round him. Using the stirrup strap, she fastens the clock to the saddle, and they ride very slowly—so that neither they nor the clock shall fall—back to Boller. The snow keeps falling and is now lying thickly on the park.

Emilia talks to Marcus, telling him he is safe now, that whatever he has endured, it is over, he will not go back to Århus, to Herr Haas, to any house of correction, he will come to Boller and meet Kirsten and little Dorothea and the speckled hen, Gerda . . .

But Marcus doesn't reply. He says Emilia's name, over and over, in his small whispery voice, but this is all. He clutches the horse's mane.

From time to time, as the dusk comes on, Emilia looks behind them, half expecting to see, in the swiftly gathering shadows, the pursuing figure of her father. Once, she imagines she hears him—his big horse, the smack of his whip, his flapping cloak, his breath in the cold air—and urges the grey to a fast trot. But then the sounds vanish and there are only the rooks calling and the soft thud-thud of their own progress. "Boller is a wonderful place," she whispers. "In the garden are pools with coloured fishes swimming and in the larder are two hundred pots of jam."

Kirsten is still in bed when they return, but asks Emilia to come in. In a voice that is thick, as though she had been drinking, she says she has been playing with a magic quill given to her by a German sorcerer. "Imagine," she says, "that one's only pleasure is to be got from a feather!"

Emilia leads Marcus by the hand until they come close. Kirsten stares at him over her embroidered sheet and the furs heaped on the bed. "He is a wraith, Emilia," she says. "They have turned him into a ghost."

Marcus's face, like Emilia's, is heart-shaped and pale, but thin as a pauper's. His grey eyes roam the room, looking at Kirsten, then away from her, to her bed curtains, to her clothes hanging on an armoire, to the fire which burns in her hearth.

"Marcus," says Emilia gently, "this is the King's wife, Lady Kirsten. Will you bow to her?"

Emilia can feel his body shivering. His grip on her hand tightens.

"Oh," says Kirsten, still caressing her full lips with the black quill, "we are not at court now, God be praised. Bowing is for fools. But where is your cat, Marcus? Where is Otto?"

At the word "Otto," Marcus looks about him, as though the cat might be in the room. When he does not find it there, he shakes his head.

"Did the poor child run away from Århus?" Kirsten asks Emilia. "How could he have travelled so far?"

"I don't know," replies Emilia. "Or perhaps he was never there?"

"Never there? Well, good heavens, Emilia, have you considered how on earth we are to combat all their hundred and one deceits?"

Kirsten flounces from her bed then, in her petticoats, with her legs bare among the rumpled sheets, and begins brushing her wild hair. "You have given this insufficient thought!" she says crossly. "But, luckily for you, my mind is now beginning to work very fast. First of all, we must have the co-operation of my mother and Vibeke, and the other dim-witted servants. They must collude with us—with everything that I shall put in train—or else you know that your father will come and snatch the boy away."

"I expect he will try," says Emilia. "Unless . . ."

"Unless what?"

"Unless he sees it as a blessing: the last of my mother, gone . . ."

"Well, I do not think that we can rely on that. Now. You must do precisely what I say, Emilia. Marcus will sleep on a cot in your room and, if you want to keep him at Boller, you must not let the poor little ghost out of your sight!"

Marcus watches as the mattress and the bolsters are laid on the cot. Then he sits down on the floor and removes his shoes, beneath which his small feet are red and grimy. He takes off his brown jerkin, then goes to the cot and climbs into it.

"Marcus," says Emilia, "it is not night-time yet. In a while we shall give you some supper."

But he pays no attention to this. He lies down in the little bed and stares up at the ceiling. "*Emilia,*" he whispers again. "*Emilia.*"

The Thoughts of Marcus Tilsen, Aged Five, on the Eve of Christmas

Magdalena said if you are good the angels will come and fill your shoes with gold buttons when you are asleep but if you are awake and see them they will fly away at once and then in the morning there will be nothing only your empty shoes and what a shame that will be.

I went into the forest to see if the angels were waiting there drying their wings under the trees waiting to fly to me I hid in the trees and called angel are you there but not loudly in case my father could hear.

My father always said Marcus this habit of yours to go wandering away from the house we know not where or when is a wicked thing and one day you will be lost and we shall not know how to find you and what will become of you then.

He does not know that in the forest are voices they are everywhere in the leaves and in the wind.

I said where are the angels with their draggled wings and the voices said wait and hide and be quiet as a squirrel Marcus put your arms round the trunk of a beech tree and never move and you will see them and I said will they come in the night and fill my shoes with gold buttons and the voices said they did not know.

The snow began to come down once I asked my father where is it kept when it is not falling and he said you do not see the world properly Marcus despite all my efforts to teach you and this makes me very angry.

The angel was wearing a grey cloak and digging in the earth and then she turned towards me and the voices said she is not an angel she is Emilia she has been sending messengers from far away to find you but they have never arrived but now she has found you and you can run to her and she will take you away from Magdalena the witch and you will never come back you will never come back you will never come back.

My cat Otto is left behind.

I am in a bed in Emilia's room and my shoes are put outside the door for the angels and Emilia sits by me and whispers where have all your words gone Marcus have they gone up into the sky right up into the black sky above the snow clouds or did you leave them in the forest how shall we find them again and I reach up and touch her hair and she sings me a song about the snow.

Outside in the passageway the angels are arriving I can hear them they are not as quiet as they are supposed to be they are laughing as they fill my shoes and their wings brush against the walls.

MAGDALENA'S CHRISTMAS GIFT

Johann Tilsen and his sons searched for Marcus in the darkness until midnight. When the search party returned to the house, Magdalena made them drink hot elderflower wine to warm them and said: "Marcus will not be found until he wishes to be found, so why do you wear yourselves out so uselessly?"

Johann nodded. He had foreseen this disappearance of Marcus. It was as if it had only been a matter of time. Because Marcus was as fidgety as the wind, as a blown seed on the eddies of the wind. One day, Johann would look in all the places where Marcus hid but not find him. And after that he might never be found because this is what he seemed to want to do: put himself beyond everybody's reach.

Johann nevertheless announced that the hunt would begin again in the morning, as soon as it was light, and they would go on horseback and not only search in the woods and forests, and the fruit fields and along the lake, and on the island in the middle of the lake, but also ride over to Boller. "As we know," he said, "word that Emilia is at Boller might have come to Marcus by some means that we had not predicted."

They retired to bed. Weary as he was, Johann Tilsen felt an urgent desire to make love to his wife before he let sleep take him.

Now, on Christmas Day, a low sun comes up out of the landscape and coaxes a brightness that no one seems to have seen for a long while. And in this brightness, thinks Johann Tilsen, nothing can stay hidden. He imagines how the Christmas church-goers, dressed in black, would stand out against the blinding white ground, how the pheasants would appear feathered in a sleek new livery. And he tries to imagine Marcus walking towards him through the powdery snow, but the image is unstable; it comes and goes and, after a while, will not return.

Johann and Ingmar, with Wilhelm, Boris and Matti, set off towards nine o'clock, leaving Magdalena to supervise the roasting of the goose. Content in her kitchen, chivvying her maids for breadcrumbs and dried apricots and cloves, for chestnuts and pork dripping, Magdalena kneads the goose stuffing with her powerful hands and tells herself that perhaps today, Christmas Day 1629, one era is ending and another beginning.

Supplanting the dead wife, Karen, had not been difficult. Seducing Johann had been as easy as trapping a fly with treacle. That the four elder boys were all her captives she did not doubt. Magdalena reigned in the household, her own child was thriving on her abundant milk. For most of the time she believed that her future was assured and comfortable.

Yet now and then she was dismayed to see some vestige of Karen's power remaining, revealed to her by some look in Johann's eye, by some item of his first wife's clothing found and kept when it should have been thrown away, by some snatch of song remembered by one of the boys. And all of this Magdalena hated with such a passion that she could feel herself fly into an uncontainable fury within a few seconds.

Nowhere did that fury invade her more frequently than when she found herself with Marcus. For a long time now, she had wanted to be rid of him. Rumour that a house of employment and correction, modelled on the King's Børnehus in Copenhagen, had been set up in Århus inflamed her with longing to take the child there and leave him to his ghostly existence far from her sight. That Johann would not permit this felt to her like a betrayal, only mitigated a little when she was able to announce to Karen's daughter that this was where her brother was—because he deserved correction, because he refused to be happy, because he was lapsing into a silence that no one seemed able to break.

On the day of Kirsten and Emilia's visit, Johann had hidden Marcus in the cellar, for fear that he would beg Emilia to take him away.

"Let her take him!" Magdalena had said. "Let him go where he will!" But Johann had refused to yield. He, too, Magdalena clearly saw, was haunted by the child whose birth had been the cause of Karen's death.

And now, miraculously, Marcus was gone. He was gone to some place of his own choosing, where he might never be found. Magdalena sings as she fills the goose's rump end with the heavy chestnut and apricot stuffing. She pats the damp, pimply skin that will roast to a succulent amber crispness. She eats a pickled egg.

As the stuffed goose is being placed in a baking dish, Ingmar arrives in the kitchen.

He tells Magdalena that his horse has gone lame and that he has walked it slowly home while Johann and the other boys have ridden on towards the lake. So far, there has been no sign of Marcus.

Ingmar stands on the opposite side of the wooden table to Magdalena as she leans over the goose, still patting it and adjusting its limbs, then starting to rub them with salt. He does not move. He stares.

"A lovely big goose," Magdalena says as she works.

She knows Ingmar is staring not at the bird, on which they are all going to feast, but at her own breasts, still heavy with milk, still too plump for the dress she wears.

She reaches for another handful of salt. She leans even further towards Ingmar, her reddened hands working more vigorously than before, so that her breasts move from side to side. And she does not need to look up at Ingmar to know what he wants nor to decide that this is what she wants too. She had wanted it long ago when she let her uncle make love to her in one of the pigsties and understood, soon after, that where the father had been, the son yearned to go too. And then playing games with them both, tempting them, lying to them, chiding them, dancing in and out of their sight.

Power.

The older man kept in ignorance; his appetite fed by his own sense of his sin. The younger man kept in a state of wanting and waiting; his longing fed by the knowledge of what his father did.

Power which, once known, could never be matched except by repetition. Power that can now be replicated in this family. Magdalena knows that, for her, there is nothing on earth more complete than this.

She moves slowly, lingering in the kitchen, giving more orders to the maids, lifting the outer leaves of the red cabbages held up for her inspection and touching their succulent hearts, tasting dripping from the white bowl and giving Ingmar her finger to suck . . .

Then she unties her apron and moves silently up the stairs, tiptoeing so that she will not wake the sleeping Ulla, and Ingmar follows. Up above the bustle of the kitchen the house is silent, empty, with sunbeams glancing from the windows, a place of marvellous magic.

Magdalena chooses the linen closet, the very place where Johann Tilsen lifted up her skirt and took her without ceremony, without apology, asserting his self-appointed right as her employer to fornicate with her.

He thought he could do this and forget her. He did not know what power was hers. He did not know how cleverly she would use it.

And now, as she sees in Ingmar the same impatience, the same agony of need, she savours every second, ruffling his dark curls as she locks the closet door, then leaning against the linen shelves, against the piles of laundered sheets, and slowly unlacing the bodice of her dress and lifting out a breast whose nipple is hard and damp.

Magdalena knows that when Ingmar begins to suck, as the baby sucks, her milk will flow and that Ingmar Tilsen will drink. She will suckle him—her stepson—and he will for ever be enslaved to this one moment when events collide and the boy of seventeen drinks from the breast of the woman who haunts his dreams.

His mouth fixes itself to the teat. Magdalena cradles his head. Almost immediately he begins to cry, as a suffering child cries when comforted at last by its mother, his tears hot and copious, his arms encircling her body, drawing it to him, holding it as though he will never let it go.

Then she puts her mouth to his ear and whispers into it the very same phrases—dirty as potash—which once led her cousin to a madness of long duration, where thoughts of patricide were seldom far from his mind.

And all the while Magdalena is smiling. It is Christmas Day and a new era is beginning. It is starting now . . .

Later, as the bright day fades, the Tilsen family sit down together and the roast goose is brought in and set before them.

Johann and Magdalena are at opposite ends of the table and Ingmar sits next to his stepmother. He eats ravenously. His hunger seems to have no limit. Magdalena watches him and cannot get the smile to go from her face.

Johann tells her how he and the other boys rode over to Boller, rode boldly up the drive, only to find the house closed and every window shuttered. They knocked at the great door, but no one answered.

"It is strange, is it not," says Johann, "that no servant appeared?"

"No doubt Ellen Marsvin and Kirsten have gone away," says Magdalena.

"But Fru Marsvin wouldn't leave the house unattended."

"Perhaps it wasn't unattended. Perhaps the servants were drunk on Christmas wine! That is why they closed all the shutters. Did you hear any laughter or music or the sound of snoring?"

"No," says Johann crossly, "we did not."

"Perhaps the King has relented and called his wife and all her retinue back to Copenhagen?"

Johann shakes his head. Something in Magdalena's voice suggests that she is teasing him, but he cannot say why. "All of Denmark," he says, "knows that this separation is final."

They eat in silence for a while and the scent of the steaming goose and the mashed apricots fills the room and wafts out into the hall, and the little cat, Otto, comes to the door and sits waiting for a morsel of food to be thrown to it. Matti and Boris glance down at the cat. "If Marcus is never coming back," says Boris, "can Otto be mine?"

Johann Tilsen looks tenderly at Boris. "Nothing can be decided," he says, "until we know where Marcus has gone."

"He's gone into his world," says Boris.

"What do you mean?" asks Johann.

"There is a world where he goes. He told me about it before he stopped speaking. There are buffaloes there and a knife grinder."

KIRSTEN: FROM HER PRIVATE PAPERS

We spent Christmas in darkness.

I ordered that every door and shutter be closed and every curtain drawn, so that anyone calling upon us would think we were gone away to Arabia or drowned in the Sargasso Sea.

My Mother grumbled and protested, but I flew into a Rage with her, saying she would die a lonely Death if she could not be more considerate towards Other People instead of mired in her own little Universe of her Self and that this was the only way to safeguard Marcus from a wicked Kidnapping.

She retorted that Boller was *her* house and my arrival in it had constituted an *Invasion*, such as the Emperor's soldiers made into Jutland in the wars, so I said: "Very well, then, this is how I shall conduct myself, as your Enemy. And do not underestimate what this new Enmity will cost you!" And she on that instant took up a brass Measuring Rod and advanced towards me with it, intending to smite me, but I was nimble and avoided it, so her blow fell upon an oak table and the Rod bent itself almost in two. She looked mightily foolish holding the bent Rod in her hand and I laughed out loud at her, but I could see in her eyes that she wished me Dead and this observation discomfited me somewhat, because that she is my Mother and should love me, and does not, nor ever will.

I had my way nevertheless and Boller was closed and shuttered.

I prefer the darkness and the candle-light to the normal light of day. It is as though the entire scheming World has departed into the black sky and will come no more to trouble me. Even the wind can barely be heard. The fires burn more brightly. In the soft lamp-light I look younger. I hold Dorothea on my lap and see—by the candle flames that stand sentinel in my room and do not move be-cause there is no draught to move them—the features of my Lover. And I begin to compose a prayer (on this day when Jesus Christ was born) which asks for forgiveness of my Sins and the restoration to me of my child's Father.

On Christmas morning I said to Emilia: "Now I shall open my door and see whether anything has been put in my shoes by the Angels!" and she laughed at me, but then what do I discover in my shoes but two painted Eggs. And I know that they were laid by her hen, Gerda, and that she cooked and decorated them herself. And I do declare that I love these Eggs more than any Gold and shall keep them until they rot, because in them is all Emilia's sweet af-fection for me.

I show them to Ellen, my Mother. "What was the last time you made me any gift like this?" I ask her, but she refuses to look at them.

She is a Nasty Woman and Uncharitable as the sea, and I am amazed I have any Heart in my body, for I think there is none in hers.

And now—since her failure to smash me with the Measuring Rod—she has, as I predicted, thought up some marvellous Plan, about which she is devious and smug. (Lord, how I do detest the Plans of Others, which always have about them the unmistakable odour of cruelty!) All that Ellen will tell me is that, when the New Year comes, she and Vibeke are going to Copenhagen.

"Oh?" says I. "What for? To see the King?" But she will not say. Her lips purse themselves together like the petals of some old withered Flower.

This ugly pursing of my Mother's lips suggests, of course, that she and Vibeke may be planning some Foul Thing against me. Perhaps they will try to get the King to turn me out of Boller? But I do not think they will succeed in this, because the King is not cured of his love for me and would not see his dear Mouse put out into the cold. Yet, to be on the safe side, I have writ to him secretly to warn him against my Mother's Nastiness. I tell him I am happy at Boller and repeat that the child is his and lives and grows strong in the cold air of Jutland, and we two and Emilia should not be removed from here.

At the same time I have taken the dangerous step of writing again to the English Lute player.

Just before Christmas, some few days before Emilia found the boy Marcus, there comes another letter to her from Peter Claire and once again I was able to intercept it.

I declare this Lutenist is more foolish and Soft than I had at first assumed. This Softness of his may mean he is too cowardly to effect my intructions with regard to the King's Financial Papers, in which case all my Schemes fall to nothing. But I do so yearn for Otto, my beloved Stallion and Marvellous German man, I have resolved to try everything to come to him again.

The letter that the Lutenist sends to Emilia is full of sighs.

In the quiet of my room, I hear them. I imagine that is how England must be—full up with these sounds of Lamentation.

Peter Claire asks Emilia why she does not answer his first letter and begs her to say that she still loves him, because without her love he may be beginning to "lose his Reason." All lovers exaggerate and Peter Claire is no exception. Much to my vexation, he pretends that he and Emilia are innocent victims of the times and caught within what he calls "the Great Shadow of the King's Separation from his Wife," thus implying that if it were not for me, they could be entirely happy and free as larks. And this Distortion of Events helps me to harden my heart as I hide the letter. For I tell myself that I am saving Emilia from a man who may be somewhat Foolish and Sentimental, and not all that she believes him to be, and in any case what should she want with living in England with its exaggerated weather? Far better for her that she should stay with me here or come with me to Sweden and be part of the House I shall set up with Count Otto Ludwig of Salm. Perhaps there is some handsome cousin of the Count's whom she might marry? And in this way, she and I shall never be parted.

And so I compose a short note to Mr. Claire, reminding him of my previous instructions to obtain me "important papers showing how the King's Finances do stand, so that I may know what Future I can expect." I tell him that if these shall be quickly despatched to me, then I shall overlook his rudeness in pretending to ignore my first letter. I shall furthermore—at such a time—pass to Emilia those "words and sighs" intended for her, but if nothing comes to me directly from him, why then no letter of his will ever find its way into Emilia's sight.

In matters such as these it is best to be plain and concise. We are coming into a new year, 1630, when I shall be older than I was. I must play this card, for I cannot devise any other. Yet when I give my letter to the Bearer and see him place it in his bag, I do notice that my hand is shaking.

The great matter of Emilia's brother Marcus has taken a vexatious turn.

When, on Christmas Eve, she rode home with him and together

we outsmarted his Father and all the Brothers with our subterfuge of being absent from Boller, why then I was exceedingly merry and said to Emilia, "Everything shall come right now that we have found Marcus and made a Fool of your Father, and you shall see what a marvellous life we are going to have!"

But this "marvellous life" is not yet come. I do not know what I had imagined in regard to this child, but I do not think my mind had anticipated what a great Trial he would be to me. In truth, I have almost begun to wonder whether I can continue to have him with us in the house, so Strange and Irritating do I find him.

First of all, he refuses to speak. We do not yet know whether he was sent to the House of Correction or no, and whether it was from there that he escaped or whether he was never at Århus at all. Though I question him on these matters—very patiently—he will only gaze at me in bewilderment with his mouth hanging foolishly open and then, without warning, turn from me and run away and hide in all the most extraordinary places, so that for hours on end we cannot find him.

I tell Emilia that we must cure him of this Habit of Hiding, but she explains to me that it was from his stepmother Magdalena that he always hid and, until he is certain she is not here, he will continue with this practice. He is so small that he can hide in a drawer. Yesterday he concealed himself in an empty log basket. I never knew any person so ghostly.

And he clings to Emilia. He almost cannot bear to be absent from her and I now repent me that I warned her not to let Marcus out of her Sight, for she is forever lifting him onto her lap and cradling him like a Baby. I say to her, "Emilia dear, call one of the Servants that Marcus may be entertained in the kitchen or in the scullery, so that we may play our cards uninterrupted," and so she does this, but then Marcus refuses to go, breaking into tears and calling out, "Emilia! Emilia!" And so our Game is quite spoiled.

And all this tries my Patience. I have never been able to love children. They are barbarous monkeys. They make no attempt to learn any of the Rules by which Man endeavours to live.

But that I love the darkness of Boller as it is at present, I do de-

307

clare I would open the doors and shutters again, and if Johann Tilsen arrived here searching for Marcus, I would be seriously tempted to GIVE HIM BACK. For I cannot bear to see Emilia transformed into a Little Mother, when formerly her only concern was *my* welfare and *my* happiness, and I think lovingly of the hours we spent in the garden at Rosenborg, doing our water-colour painting together, without any of the present distractions.

Yet what can I do about Marcus, after all my promises to Emilia? I told her we would be a Contented Family. I said I would care for this boy "as my own Child." I said he would be made happy at last. But he shows no sign of being happy. At night, he cries in his bed and Emilia must forever be getting up to comfort him, and under her grey eyes are appearing dark pouches because she is so deprived of her sleep. Though he says a few more words than at first (one of which is "Otto") he comes no nearer normality in his speech or behaviour. He eats but little. He is afraid of me and will not take my hand. He pisses in his bed. And—worst of all—he has to be kept apart from Dorothea, for everyone can clearly see that a bitter Hatred of her appears in his eyes when he looks at her and I do declare he would like to smite her Dead with a fire-iron or kick her cradle down the stairs or set fire to her coverlet.

I have told Emilia that a Nurse must be engaged for Marcus and his own room found for him at a greater distance from mine. She, being so attached to this little wraith of a Brother, weeps at my sternness and begs me to have patience. "Emilia, dear," I tell her, "do not talk to me about Patience, for you know perfectly well that I have none."

Figure in a Landscape

The arrival of the new year, of the *new decade*, is celebrated in the streets of Copenhagen with flagrant pageantry.

Some of this has been arranged—musical capers, performing animals, tumblers and stilt-walkers—and some of it merely arises from the people's enthusiasm for the *idea of newness*, which in turn awakes in them an enthusiasm for liquor.

In this state of intoxication they become clowns, magicians and acrobats. They daub their faces with flour and mud. They conjure whores out of virgins and drabs out of old maids. They try to dance on the patient rumps of their cart-horses. They take it into their heads that they can climb to the high pinnacles of the city and fly.

And when the New Year carnival is over—or rather, when it is exhausted, for some obstinate minds admit of no "ending" to these wild revels—the streets are ugly with damage. The sick are dragged home. The dead are carried away. Broken tiles and chimney pots remain to silt up the already foul and choking gutters. And the citizens gaze out at the city and at the winter day, and crouch in their rooms and wonder why it is they are alive in this time and what it is that God conceals from them, and what it is that He will in time reveal.

Their King is also staring at confusion. He stares inward and he stares out. And in both places he finds destitution.

He longs for things he cannot name. Much of the time he translates this longing into a desire for food and drink. He orders his chefs to perfect new ways of cooking the wild boar he hunts in the forests at Frederiksborg. He drinks until he can no longer speak or stand and has to be carried to his bed. His servants notice that his breath is foul and that his gums are bleeding. His gut is like a barrel filled with damp powder; explosions gather there and cannot come to any release, and the pain of this sometimes causes him to snivel like a boy.

And in some ways he resembles the acrobat citizens—poised on a galloping horse or on a high gable, hesitating between the earth and the air, between opposing states and beliefs in violent opposition. One moment he is euphoric, optimistic, scribbling down ever more outlandish ideas for the salvation of his country, and the next cast into a gloom so deep that he prays to fall to the ground and die.

At these times he realises with dismay that his life these days is so mired in the physical and temporal that he is no longer able to feel the presence in his soul of the divine. He mumbles prayers and knows them to be futile. God is elsewhere and hears nothing. More and more, King Christian looks to his angel to watch over him and assuage his sadness with sad songs.

It is during this time of the New Year that a group of merchants from Hamburg arrive at Frederiksborg.

They are some of the richest men in Germany, holding between them a proportion of their country's wealth so far in excess of their rightful share that nobody can comprehend how such a fortune can be amassed by so few.

King Christian does not even seek to comprehend it. It is immaterial to his plans. He has invited the Hamburg merchants to Frederiksborg and now he lays before them a proposition: they are to act as pawnbrokers. He informs them, as they assemble in the Great Hall, where Jens Ingemann and his orchestra play portions of *Die Schlacht vor Pavia* by Matthias Werrecore, that the object to be pawned is Iceland.

No expression of surprise or agitation greets the King's announcement. These soberly clad brokers have perfected the ability to assimilate the unexpected while betraying no feeling whatsoever; that is an essential part of their skill. They do not even glance at each other.

"Iceland?" asks one. "With all rights and patents for mineral exploration?"

"With what proportion of its coastal waters?" asks another.

"For how long a term?" asks a third.

King Christian takes up a paper he has prepared in German and orders that this be read out to the merchants. They sit perfectly still and silent on their chairs as they listen to its contents. The paper sets out a demand for the sum of one million dalers. In return for this, the group is to be given *the land, its hills and mountains, its glaciers and valleys, its rivers and lakes and that girdle of ocean which* surrounds it to a distance of twelve miles, for a period of ten years, or until such time as the King of Denmark shall redeem the pledge and return the sum with all interest that shall be accruing upon that distant day.

The merchants rise as one, bow to the King and ask that they may retire to discuss "this interesting proposition." The King nods. The men file out to an ante-room and Christian orders the musicians to cease playing.

Peter Claire looks up. Nothing is heard, now, in the Great Hall but the retreating footsteps of the brokers. Nobody moves. The King sits motionless on his gilded throne with, at his feet, the two silver lions that appear to plead with him for their reprieve from the melting furnace. Jens Ingemann lays down his baton. Peter Claire notes that every face is grave. Only the German viol player, Krenze, is laughing silently.

Informed that his contract for the pawning of Iceland lacks sufficient detail and must be redrawn according to German law, King Christian is now nevertheless sure that the transaction will be completed and that the one million dalers requested will soon be his.

At first he feels exhilaration and a sense of wonder at his own daring. Why did he not think of such a plan before? Now, with this large sum of money, the new expedition to the Numedal can be financed, more whaling ships commissioned, more manufactories founded, more alms paid to the Børnehus, more streets and highways and fortifications repaired, more trading missions sent out to the New World. In short, the restoration of Denmark can now begin. Within a year he will once again reign over a prosperous nation.

He dreams of this time to come, when the flesh of the nobility is encased in whalebone, when the streets of Copenhagen are orderly and clean, when the silver from the Isfoss arrives at last. And then these dreams vanish without warning and are replaced by a new realisation: he imagined Iceland, where he has never set foot, as an almost empty landscape, and in this he is of course mistaken. There is no mention of the *people of Iceland* in the Hamburg document, yet people are surely there in considerable numbers, just as they are there in the valley of the Numedal. And what will happen to them when their country falls into the hands of the brokers? How will everything be altered?

He begins to set out a new clause, to be included in the agreement, which seeks to protect the homes of the Icelanders, their possessions, their fledgeling enterprises, their sea defences, their fishing fleets, but the wording—if it is not to put in jeopardy the dalers—is almost impossible to phrase and the King soon becomes aware of a returning darkness falling across his mind, like a shadow across the paper on which he writes.

He lays down his pen and calls for wine. He drinks until he falls asleep in his chair. The paper falls to the floor.

King Christian discovers himself in a dream of Iceland, where the sky is black above a shining white glacier and from all the surrounding hills the wolves are calling.

He is wearing snow-shoes.

His mission is to trudge on, until the glacier is crossed and the hills are reached. The wind howls in his head and his snow-shoes begin to split and fall apart.

And then he notices a figure ahead of him, small in the white expanse, alone like him, but walking towards him. And this sighting of the figure comforts and reassures him. They will meet and exchange a greeting. The stranger will tell him how to mend his shoes. He will share with him the thimble of schnapps he keeps in his coat pocket against the cold . . .

On he goes.

On and on.

Darkness begins to fall across the snow and the figure is almost lost to his sight.

Now, the King begins to call to the stranger, who should be near him by now, but no answering call comes. And it is at this moment that he understands who it is.

It is Bror Brorson.

Bror Brorson did not die at Lutter. Everything that was witnessed there and which has never been forgotten is now contradicted by the unalterable fact that Bror is alive and walking through Iceland under a black sky, and in moments he will appear by his side and the two men will embrace.

The King increases his pace. He is trying to run, even as his snow-shoes disintegrate further and splinters of wood pierce the snow crust and make him trip and almost fall. "Bror!" he calls louder. "Bror!"

But it is dark, too dark to see anything. And now a new understanding dawns in the King's exhausted mind: Bror Brorson was not walking towards him; *he was walking away from him.* And his pace is faster, was always faster and will always be, because Bror was a strong, athletic man, because his snow-shoes are not broken . . .

No matter if Christian walks all night, Bror will always be ahead of him and always unreachable.

The King wakes and sends for Peter Claire.

He describes the dream to him and tells him that, just before he woke, he heard Bror's voice saying to him: "Everything dear to us that dies, dies a second time."

"What does that mean?" he asks the lutenist. "Tell me what it means."

Peter Claire replies that he does not know, that it might refer only to memory, or it might suggest that man, in his search for love, will always make the same mistakes and therefore suffer the same derelictions.

The King nods and looks up. "I am tired of love," he says.

He shifts his heavy body in the chair, resumes his drinking, gulping the wine as though his thirst were unquenchable.

Peter Claire asks the King if he should play something, but the King ignores this and says in a low voice: "I have lost all sense of the divinity in things. When I was young, I used to feel it everywhere—even in my own handwriting. Now it is everywhere absent."

Servants have banked up the fire and the room is warm, almost hot. Seed pearls of sweat appear on the King's forehead and he wipes them away with his sleeve. Peter Claire says nothing, only tries to decide what he should play if he is requested to.

"We had your Mr. Dowland at court," the King says after a while. "And he was a man so full of his own importance that this great importance weighed him down and made him miserable. He made nothing but enemies here. Yet his music was sublime, was it not?"

"Yes," replies Peter Claire.

"Sometimes I used to talk to him, late at night, as I am talking to you. I was trying to discover the point at which he let his own importance be subsumed beneath the notes he heard in his mind."

"And did you discover it?"

"No. And yet it had to occur, did it not, that surrender, or the music would not have had that degree of perfection?"

"Yes. It had to occur."

"But I could not gauge it. I could not *see* it. Dowland was always and ever vengeful and jealous and puffed up. And only once did he say something to me which showed me a different side of him, and it comes to me now. He said that man spends days and nights and years of his life asking the question 'How may I be brought to the divine?'; yet all musicians instinctively know the answer: they are brought to the divine through their music—for this is its sole purpose. Its sole purpose! What do you say to that, Mr. Claire?"

Peter Claire looks into the fire. What he wants to say is that, in his recent life, he felt himself emerge out of confusion and enter a transcendent state of happiness that had something of the divine about it, but that his route to it was not his music. His route was his love for Emilia Tilsen.

But the King has already said he does not wish to talk about love, so the lutenist can only reply in terms more vague than those the King invites: "William Shakespeare says that 'the man that hath no music in himself, nor is not moved with concord of sweet sounds, is fit for treasons.' "

"Does he?" says the King quickly. "Well, there *is* something revealing. For you know my wife cannot abide music. She cannot hear a melody. She cannot . . . but there we are, at one blow, back upon the subject I can no longer discuss. This is how the human mind destroys itself—by turning and turning upon the one thing that gives it pain. I think this is what poor Bror meant when he said those words: that Kirsten is dead to me because I shall never lie with her nor love her any more, but in some way that I cannot foresee I will have to endure this dying a second time."

The King finishes his wine and calls for more. Then he requests that Peter Claire play "some fragment by that enigma, Dowland."

When the music ends, the King looks closely at his angel. "I hope you have not forgotten your promise?" he asks.

"No, Your Majesty," says Peter Claire.

"And, alas for you, you must keep it until you are released," says the King, as he rises and makes his way unsteadily to his bed. "Except that I shall not release you. There can be no leaving nor returning to England. You and I are alone on the glacier under the black sky and there is no escape. If you try to escape, the wolves that I heard will come down from the mountains and devour you."

The Cookham Revels

Of all the counties in England, the easterly county of Norfolk, with its forests and marshes, its slowly moving rivers, its acres of plough, its miles of swampy lowland uninhabited by anything except the newts, otters and water birds for whom it is an unchanging paradise, is surely one of the most silent in the country.

Yet on the eve of the New Year 1630, bobbing like a boat on this ocean of quiet, is a bubble of noise more bright and intense than anything witnessed since the time when Queen Elizabeth made a Progress here with a hundred courtiers in attendance, and plays were performed and great suppers were consumed and dancing lasted until dawn: Mr. George Middleton is giving a party at Cookham.

The night is cloudless, cold, full of stars and a big pale moon. But now, in room after room of the big house, beginning in the kitchen where the roasting spits turn, and moving upwards into the halls and receiving rooms where the fires are fed with apple-wood and the candles are lit, then upwards again to the bedrooms where the house guests are brought basins of hot water and begin to wash and dress themselves by lamp light, heat comes and laughter begins. The revels are starting. Down the muddy lanes, carriages make a slow progress towards them. The dogs in the hallway sniff the altered air and sense that something unfamiliar is occurring. This will be the party that everyone in this little corner of England will always remember.

As George Middleton, attired in a wine-coloured coat (with more lace at his neck and wrists than he would once have considered appropriate), descends his stairs, sees his house looking more splendid than it has ever done and hears his hired musicians tuning their instruments in the grand withdrawing-room, he is struck by a sudden feeling of joy so absolute that he has to pause on the bottom step and hold on to the banister. For he is an ordinary man, descended from ordinary men. He is not used to such overwhelming sentiments. He wonders if he may be about to fall over or whether, indeed, the scene before him is about to disappear and he will find himself to have been the victim of a grandiose dream.

At this moment a servant approaches him and asks whether he would care to approve the temperature of the wines, and taste the punch that is to be served upon the guests' arrival. No doubt George Middleton looks at the servant strangely—as he might look at a person who was not there at all—because the man asks anxiously: "Is anything amiss, Sir?"

"No," says Middleton. "Not at all. Nothing is amiss."

As he goes with the servant to taste the wines and the last of the tall candles in the silver candelabrum in the dining-room are lit and the complicated business of plate warming begins in the kitchen below, the musicians strike up a lively courante and the sound of this music finds its way into the room where Charlotte Claire, assisted by one of the Cookham maids, is entwining some expensive golden ribbons into her hair.

The women pause in their task and listen. It is as if this music finally wakes in Charlotte the understanding that the dark days are gone and that what lies waiting for her is of a different order of existence. That she will dance with her fiancé, in the company of all his Norfolk friends, that she will become the centre of everyone's attention, that she will witness George capering about the room like a man who has never been near to death, never suffered any agonies whatsoever, moves her to such a realisation of her own good fortune that she almost feels as if she might cry.

Yet what, she thinks, as the last of the ribbons is threaded through her dark hair, is one to make of life when it delivers such contradictory instructions? She had grown almost used to the idea that George Middleton was going to die and that she would spend the rest of her life in her parents' house, in mourning for what might have been. And now she must adjust once again to a future in which there is to be a spring wedding and she is to become the mistress of Cookham and, at some time in the years that stretch ahead, the mother of George's children.

She looks at herself in the dressing glass. Ever discontented because she did not possess her brother's beauty, Charlotte Claire, on this night of George Middleton's party, finds herself beautiful. As the laces on her dress are fastened and a simple rope of pearls put round her neck, she is overcome by a sudden urgent longing to be with George now, this minute, for the evening to begin, so that not a moment of it is missed or wasted. For what if it were—after all— to be the last evening of her life, or of George's? What if there was, in the end, no prolongation of her future beyond this one marvellous night?

She hurries now, inserting her feet into white satin shoes, snatching up her fan and, stealing one last look at herself, prepares to go down towards the music, towards the marvels that await her.

The hall is decked with garlands of holly and yew, and Charlotte's dress, made of satin and velvet (the kind of dress that this daughter of a country parson might wear only once or twice in her life), echoes the red and the green of the branches cut from the Cookham woods. These strong colours flatter her white skin and echo to advantage the darkness of her hair.

Though tempted to pause and show herself to her parents, who are putting on such meagre finery as they possess in the adjoining room, Charlotte doesn't stop to do this, because she must be at George's side now, she must be reassured of the living warmth of his hand, hear his voice, his laughter . . . She must make certain that he is really there.

He is just returning to the hall as she begins to descend the staircase. He stops and one of the dogs lollops to him and he scratches its neck as he stares up.

A woman almost devoid of vanity, Charlotte Claire now finds that this exquisite progress, down towards George's adoring eye, can be savoured like no other moment in her life, that each step she takes seems to enhance her awareness of her own perfection. She can only guess at what George Middleton is feeling and her assumptions, if the truth could be faultlessly expressed, in fact fall far short of the reality.

For George Middleton knows that whatever may lie in wait for them, he will remember this moment of Charlotte's descent of the staircase at Cookham for the rest of his days. "Daisy . . ." he murmurs. "Oh, Daisy . . ."

He holds out his hand and she takes it, and he holds her to him and whirls her round like a little girl, and kisses her neck and her cheek and the lobes of her ears. "How beautiful you are!" he explodes and holds her from him, at arm's length, like a painting that enraptures him. "No dress could suit you better. None. That dress has been waiting for you for twenty-two years."

Charlotte smiles and, still holding fast to his hand, looks approvingly in her turn at her fiancé's burgundy coat and his bold flourishes of lace.

George Middleton begins to laugh. "Daisy," he says, "I see from your gaze that you are a little astonished."

"Yes," says Charlotte, "but only because I am used to the everyday George . . ."

"Tell me truthfully, do I appear as though I had fallen through a hole in a white blancmange?"

"No!" says Charlotte. "Not in the least, my dearest. I would have said a queen of puddings!"

And they shriek with mirth and embrace each other as children sometimes embrace their toys, with an unfettered abandon.

For hour after hour the coaches wait out under the stars and the horses stamp, and even the creatures of the woods creep to the wood's edge to see what it is that disturbs the habitual quiet of the Cookham night.

Midnight comes and toasts are drunk, to the New Year, to the phenomenal success of the cutting for the stone that has saved George's life, to the skill of the surgeon, to the fortitude of the Middleton family, to God's kindness in sparing a precious life, and lastly to the future of George and Charlotte, to the spring wedding that cannot come too soon.

And then the music resumes and more wine is brought to the tables, and more puddings and sweetmeats and sugared plums, and the guests loosen their corsets and refill their glasses and their plates, and mop their brows and take their partners for yet another dance.

To the coachmen gathered in the kitchen, eating pies and drinking beer, the servants report that "nobody shows any sign of leaving," and so the party taking place down there becomes louder, merrier and more flirtatious. Impromptu jigs are danced in the pantry. The supplies of beer diminish. The carcasses of roast lamb and suckling pig are picked clean. An entire batch of mincemeat tarts, destined for the tables upstairs, is suddenly discovered to be missing.

George Middleton knows nothing of all this, but he would nevertheless approve it, because there is nothing, on this night, of which he is able to disapprove. Even those neighbours of whom he is not particularly fond. When he looks at them hopping in a jig or endeavouring to bow gracefully in a minuet, his heart forgives them their futile and irritating habits, their habitual disputatiousness, their past attempts to marry him to their ugly daughters. Indeed, he finds that he *loves* them. He even loves their *daughters*. He and Charlotte pass from table to table and hands reach out to them, and they seize these hands with an unconcealed show of affection. "Daisy," says George, "you have enabled me to adore the world!"

Enfolded in this wave of light, knowing few people but content to talk to whoever sits by them, the Reverend James Claire and his wife Anne are as happy as anyone in this company. It is as though these revels, in their magnificence (which is nevertheless a magnificence of a reassuringly plain and English kind), are, moment by moment, anatomising for them the person and character of their future son-in-law. They see that George Middleton has amplitude and grace. They understand that he has a gift for laughter. If they ever doubted his generosity they do not doubt it now. And what is the whole evening but an expression of George's love for Charlotte? James and Anne Claire, in seeing this love displayed before them, know at last that their second child, who always appeared to them less marvellous than the first, has arrived in her own time upon the threshold of a marvellous era.

But George Middleton has saved the most memorable moment of the evening until last.

Towards one o'clock, as the moon lies behind the tall cedars and the frost hardens the ruts in the muddy lanes made by the carriages, a painted cart pulls up in the driveway. Out of it climb five men dressed in the bright embroidered clothes and outlandish hats worn by the Romany Gypsies.

They do not go into the house but, seemingly oblivious to the cold, set up upon the stone terrace that skirts the south side of Cookham Hall a single music stand.

The noise and dancing inside the house are still loud and the Gypsies wait quietly, holding their stringed instruments, unseen by any except one or two of the coachmen who have come out to put blankets on their horses.

There is a pause in the revelling and George Middleton appears, shakes the hands of the Gypsy music makers, presents them with a thirty-shilling purse and a bottle of plum brandy, and goes back to rejoin the party. Almost nothing is said, because everything has been agreed in advance. And when George returns to the heat and noise of the withdrawing-room he merely sits down beside the Reverend Claire and begins a conversation with him about Peter and their shared hope that Charlotte's brother will return to England for the wedding in April.

Only very gradually then do the guests become aware of a new sound, a sound that floats into the rooms from the darkness outside, and slowly conversations subside and heads lift and ears strain to find the source of it. And people fall silent, listening to the playing of the Gypsies, and a different mood overtakes them, a mood of wonder and yearning, and they mop their faces and straighten their clothes, and discover that their bodies are tired, that they can barely move, and all they wish for is the continuation of this altered kind of melody which, after all the laughter and feasting, allows their hearts to leap up so that they almost feel they are no longer at a party but somewhere else, somewhere that transcends time and place, somewhere they have always longed to be and have never found themselves until now.

Charlotte, who is sitting beside her mother, drinking a cooling goblet of lemonade, puts a tender kiss on Anne's cheek, then gets up quietly and goes to where George is, and he takes her hand and, without speaking, the two of them go into the hall and then out into the night.

They stand by the front door, with the warmth and light at their backs and before them a terrace and garden, whitened by the frost but almost dark now as the moon falls behind the trees, behind the hedges, and vanishes. They take deep breaths of the icy night. They look upon a world suspended in a magical stillness, and the beauty of the old Romany ayres, that have crossed seas and empires to arrive in this quiet corner of England but still have in them the spirit of the Orient, fills their hearts.

STORY OF AN EXECUTION

Peter Claire stares at his own face in the mirror.

He is trying to see what others see there, to objectify his own features. The light on them is cold and hard.

His blue eyes, unblinking, are like the eyes of a map maker who, struggling to see in his mind the real plains and rivers, the real deserts and cities that lie behind his map, finds that it is far more difficult to recall them than he imagined.

Where is the truth about himself?

If King Christian chooses to see him as an angel, is it because there exists in him—within his nature, which is fearful and choked by an enveloping pessimism—something essentially virtuous? Can the King—with his store of years, with his long experience of men's good deeds and men's evil—see into his soul? Peter Claire moves his head, stares at his left eye, at his cheekbone shiny and pale on this January morning. When Emilia Tilsen remembers this face, what does she see there? The features of a vain seducer? To recollect that he once believed it was she alone who revealed to him his own best nature embarrasses him now. For what is she saying, through her silence, but that she has realised that she cannot love him? And if she cannot love him—she, who is loyal even to Kirsten, who can feel sorrow for a speckled hen—why, then, he is not worthy to be loved.

Peter Claire puts down the looking-glass and glances at his lute, propped against a chair. Before he met Emilia he knew himself to be happiest, most perfectly at peace with the world, when he was playing. Yet music is an abstraction. What does the lute player believe he is expressing? He struggles for precision, but is convinced that through that precision something of his heart can be heard.

How deluded is he on this matter? The heart of John Dowland was black. He was judged to be the greatest musician in England, but what filled his soul, by all accounts, was bitterness and loathing.

Peter Claire sits down and stares at the wall. For the first time in his life he feels that he would rather die than live until next week. He listens to the wind in the trees outside as though he hoped to detect in its sighing the stealthy arrival of an executioner.

She is pale from the long days and nights of travelling. She is taller than he remembers.

Francesca and her father look at him searchingly as in turn they take his hand, as if immediately trying to read what is in his mind.

With their eyes upon him he instructs servants to show the travellers from Ireland where they are to stay at Frederiksborg and explains to them hastily that the King, in this cold winter, is in poor health and often unable to grant the audiences he has promised. "He will see you," he says, "of this I am sure, but you may have to be patient for a few days."

"Of course we shall be patient," says Francesca. "And indeed, I think that a virtue can be made out of any delay. For while it lasts we shall have time to accustom ourselves to how life is arranged here. Isn't that true, Father?"

"True," says Ponti. "Truly."

"And more than this," Francesca goes on, "if the King is ill, then perhaps Mr. Claire's duties in the orchestra may be light and so he will be able to spend time with us . . ."

"Well . . ." begins Peter Claire.

"Also true," says Ponti.

They are following the servants out of the cold sunlight into the corridors of the palace. Peter Claire is about to explain that King Christian often has more need of his musicians when he is ill than when he is well, but cannot find the words, because he knows that Francesca will only despise them, seeing them for what they are— his excuse to neglect her, to flee from any association with her that might remind him of what he once felt. At this moment in their lives Peter Claire understands that Francesca O'Fingal can see deeper into his heart than anyone, including himself.

And all her looks affirm this. She flashes fire at him. She gives him one of her boxes to carry as they begin to climb the stairs. She is like a mother who has discovered that her favourite son is lying to her and will not set him free from her anger until the lie is out. And all Peter Claire can do is follow, carrying the box. He feels small and weak. Seeing her striding ahead, with her firm step, her flying skirts, her dark hair escaping from its braids, he knows that part of him is once again—in this matter of moments—in thrall to the very thing he feared: Francesca's power over him.

When they arrive on the top landing, not far from the room that Emilia once occupied, in which he found the hen and the grey dress, he dares himself to meet Francesca's eye. She smiles and the smile is triumphant and says: It is not over, Peter Claire. Men may imagine that their actions have no consequences, but it is not so.

The King, plagued by pains in his stomach, keeps to his room and receives no one, so Francesca and her father dine, that night, with Peter Claire and the rest of the orchestra.

Jens Ingemann is affable, praising to the Italian guests the "great feeling for music in the Italian soul" and smiling at Martinelli and Rugieri. And Peter Claire notes how every man in the room is affected by Francesca's beauty. They all know she is a widow. They wonder if she may remain among them here. None knows that Peter Claire was once her lover.

The conversation begins in English, eddies into Italian, thus disquieting Pasquier who tries French, to which Francesca can stumblingly respond, laughing at her own mistakes. Even Krenze, so often distanced from the orchestra's sociability, strains to find his way through these alternating languages so that he is not excluded.

Sitting some way from Francesca, Peter Claire watches her accept, as though it were the common currency of everyday life, this international adulation. She is gracious and witty. The smiles she allows herself are serene, rather than flirtatious. In the candle-light, wearing a dark-blue dress, her beauty seems to have arrived at a moment of perfection. And it is as though she understands this. How long, say her looks and gestures in his direction, can you resist?

He turns away from her and talks to Ponti about Denmark; about the great forests which grow, it is said, in Jutland at a faster rate than anywhere else on earth.

"Tell me," says Ponti, "how I am to win my concession from the King. What shall be my *strategia?*"

"Money," replies Peter Claire.

"Money?"

"This is all—apart from the separation from his wife—that is on the King's mind. You must offer as much as you can afford, Signor Ponti, for the acres of woodland and for the manufactory patents—money you will of course make back over time. And then you must demonstrate that the goods you produce will never be shoddy."

"What is 'shoddy'?"

"Flawed, inferior, imperfect. You must guarantee the same quality of paper that you make in Bologna."

"This I can. Shall I mention 'shoddy' to His Majesty?"

"Yes. Assure him you know his anxieties about it. And let him write on your vellum samples. King Christian has perfected an exquisite calligraphy and writing on good paper gives him pleasure."

Ponti smiles and nods. "I must know one other thing," he continues. "If my mill is to be in Jutland, what difficulties of transportation shall I encounter?"

Peter Claire replies that he has never been to Jutland. He does not say that he has imagined it a thousand times, this wide, unpeopled landscape where Emilia's footprints make patterns in the snow. He describes how it was occupied by Catholic soldiers of the Habsburg emperor for three years and how it is reported that the occupying armies built roads for their horses and cannon. "The soldiers are gone," he concludes, "but no doubt the highways remain. And there are many great houses in Jutland, such as Boller Castle, built by the nobility. And the Danish nobility like to know everything that is happening in the world, Signor Ponti, lest by some misfortune they are excluded from it. And so they would not let themselves be cut off from the routes of news and information."

Father and daughter retire to sleep as the church clock strikes midnight.

As Francesca leaves the room, she turns and gives to Peter Claire that same look that he recognises from their evenings at Cloyne. He has no defence against her invitation except to lower his eyes, pretend he has seen nothing, understood nothing.

And then, as the musicians fall to discussing the loveliness and intelligence of the Italian Countess from Ireland, he gets up and goes out into the cold night.

There is a powdering of snow on the cobbles, but the night is clear and he begins to walk away from Frederiksborg, in the direction of Copenhagen, but not noticing, really, where he is going, intent only on the activity of walking, of putting distance between himself and the evening that has just passed.

His head aches. He feels no love for himself, finds his faint shadow on the snow irritating, like a too-insistent companion. He wants to stamp on the shadow—obliterate it. He knows that with regard to Francesca O'Fingal he is exhibiting the same cowardice he sometimes showed as a boy, when he preferred to run away rather than to submit to his father's disappointment in him. He used to hide in the sand-dunes. He imagined the sand-dunes as a universe in which a boy might live for ever and never be found.

Now, as he trudges through the night, he imagines fleeing to the New World; just taking ship out of Copenhagen, retracing the first leg of his voyage to the Numedal and then in the Skagerrak seeing the ship turn westwards into the prevailing winds and falling southwards below Iceland into the Atlantic Ocean. He can form no picture of the New World, but only of the endless journey towards it. He can measure from this his own disinclination to arrive anywhere at all.

He does not know how long he keeps walking before a sudden tiredness overcomes him and he stops and looks up at the sky and the stars, which can guide mariners across the oceans but which are icy bodies in the black heavens, incapable of giving solace.

He notices then that, not far away down the road, is one of those small inns that never seem to close their doors and where men congregate, in these agitated times, to forget their poverty or keep at bay their demons, and he almost runs towards it, praying that somebody will be there at this late hour, that there will be a fire and a wooden bench on which he might lay down his head.

It is a low house, made of earth and bole wood, with a thatched roof. As Peter Claire goes in he smells pipe smoke and applewood, and sees the innkeeper in his apron talking with another man. Between them on the table stands a flagon of wine.

They turn and stare at him. They have heard no coach, no cart, no sound of a horse. The night has conjured the lutenist out of nowhere and the drinkers look startled.

Peter Claire apologises for the lateness of the hour, asks for ale "and a moment or two of rest by your fire," and the innkeeper gets up and pulls out a chair for him.

Immediately the other man, who has drunk his fill of the wine, begins to hold him in conversation. "You did not see it, then, Sir?" he asks.

He is elderly, with a creased and blackened face that looks as if it had withstood storms of dust and avalanches of ice.

"See what, friend?" asks Peter Claire.

"In Copenhagen today. At Gammeltorv. The execution."

The innkeeper, pouring the ale, looks over towards the table and comments: "Never will be such another, that's what they say."

Peter Claire holds his frozen hands out towards the remnants of the fire on its bed of soft ash. "Who was executed?" he asks.

"Young girl," says the wine drinker. "Died, she did, as was judged she must, but was a long time dying." And he shakes his head and takes another gulp of the liquor, and wipes his lips with the back of his hand. The innkeeper brings Peter Claire his flagon of ale, from which he drinks straight away. He does not know how far he has walked but, now that he is beginning to be warm again, he is suddenly aware how clamorous is his thirst.

"Do you know of Herr Bomholt?" asks the innkeeper.

"No," answers Peter Claire.

"One of the King's executioners." Then to the other man he says: "You tell the story. It's your tale."

The stranger rubs a grimed hand over his face, then fixes Peter Claire with a disconcerting smile. "Bomholt used to be good with the axe," he says. "One of the best. But you know the executioners are paid per capita: so much for a hanging, so much for a beheading, so much for a flogging, so much for a breaking . . ."

327

"A breaking?"

"Of the bones. Like when we eat a chicken, snap, snap! You eat chickens, Sir?"

Peter Claire nods. He drains his flagon of beer.

"Bomholt's greedy, then, you see. Wants his bagful of skillings like every other poor soul alive in Denmark today. Dreams of money and more money, and so he overreaches himself and damages a tendon in his arm. Spent the morning flogging whores. Eight of 'em, they say. Eight spheres of poxy flesh in one morning! And so his arm hurts. But he's greedy, just as I said. Wants his execution, doesn't he? Must have his purse for the beheading, his lovely beheading!"

The man pauses to laugh and his laugh turns to a cough. He spits into the sawdust. "And so," he goes on, "I witnessed this. I was standing in the front row of the crowd. The girl is brought out. To die for her lewdness, that she'd done the deed seven times with her brother-in-law! And lays her head down on the block. And all the crowd wait while the priest says a prayer. And then Bomholt steps forward with the axe. He tries to raise it high, to bring it down clean, first time. But he can barely raise it at all! He jabs it down and it cuts, but the cut isn't deep. So he tries again, tries to raise the axe, but cannot, and so it goes on, jab and jab, cut and cut, five or six times, but still the girl isn't dead. And what then, my friend? You know what happened then?"

Peter Claire shakes his head.

"Bomholt runs away. He drops the axe. And the girl is screaming like a corncrake. And people in the crowd were fainting . . ."

Peter Claire stares numbly at the man, at the smoky room. "What then?" he asks weakly.

"I finished her," says the man proudly. "One blow. Clean and sure. And got a purse for my pains." He slaps his knee. "One person's torture is another's gain, eh, Sir? We always knew the truth of that. Didn't we?"

When Peter Claire asks the King whether he will grant an audience to the paper manufacturer from Bologna, King Christian's weary brain finds a sudden unexpected refuge in a vision of impeccable calligraphy, the letters aligned in perfect symmetry. "Yes," he says. "Send him to me."

The King, seated in a chair by his bedroom fire, discovers that he is wearing his night-shirt beneath a cloak of leather. He cannot remember when he last ate or what it was that he was thinking about when the lutenist came in or whether any music has been played or not. He looks down at his legs and sees that they are bare and the veins in them swollen, as though worms writhed just under the surface of the skin. He asks Peter Claire to wait, to bring some furs to cover him, to comb his hair.

"What was I doing?" he asks as the comb begins to scratch his scalp.

"When, Your Majesty?"

"Just now. Before you mentioned the paper manufacturer?"

Peter Claire replies that he was listening to a pavan for solo lute by Ferrabosco and had declared that the piece reminded him of a voyage to Spain, where the evening light was the colour of jade and the women smelled of cloves.

Christian smiles. "I have lost my reason," he says.

When Francesco Ponti arrives, the King finds that a consoling normality still surrounds him and he asks him to be seated.

Signor Ponti executes a low bow and then turns and the King sees before him another figure, a dark-haired woman, who is introduced as Ponti's daughter. "Forgive me please, Sir," says Ponti, "but I have no Danish and my English is not exact. My daughter Francesca will be our interpreter."

King Christian looks at Francesca, who curtsies to him. He sees features he wishes to describe as "brave." He notes eyes of great intensity. He sniffs the air of his room, imagining that this woman must, like the beauties of Santander, smell of cloves or of some other lingering spice. And her presence reminds him that the world contains a diversity he had allowed himself to forget. He has been mired up in his fortress for too long. It is this imprisonment that has made his mind feeble . . .

Ponti has carried a large box into the room. From this he now takes out a collection of leather binders.

"My father would like to show you some samples of his paper, Your Majesty," says Francesca, who is nervous, but does not let this show in her voice, which is strong. "The manufactory Ponti is known throughout our country for the quality of its paper and parchment. From its inauguration, the manufactory Ponti has set itself against the production of shoddy merchandise."

The King nods enthusiastically. "Good," he says.

One of the binders is set upon a low table by the King's chair. It contains four sheets of clean, cream-coloured paper of an admirable smoothness and King Christian leans forward to inspect them, rubbing between thumb and forefinger a corner of one of the sheets. The touch of the paper is pleasing.

"My father has named this sample *Carta Ponti Numero Due*. It is not the finest, but it sells widely."

"Yes," says the King. "I like its cleanness."

"It is a very hospitable paper."

"Hospitable?"

"To the ink. A client of my father's, a cartographer, once said his pen was enamoured of the *Numero Due*, didn't he, Papa?"

"Yes," says Ponti and smiles.

And this notion of the amorous mapping quill amuses the King. He imagines the cartographer working on and on, barely stopping to slumber or to eat, his rivers and deltas ever more minutely etched, his renditions of ships and wavelets becoming ever more elaborate and fantastical. "This is what we need in Denmark!" he says. "For men to *love* their work once again."

A great variety of samples are laid before King Christian. His hands caress them. He brings them close to his face and smells them. He notes that Signor Ponti is deft as a magician, conjuring more exquisite binders out of his box than appear at first to be in it and snapping them open with a graceful movement of his hands. And Christian finds himself enjoying this, as he might enjoy some new entertainment, where the performers were well rehearsed. Indeed, when the box is finally empty and he has inspected all the different specimens of paper, he recognises that for a full half-hour his mind and his body have been at peace.

He calls for wine for his guests and for maps of Jutland to be brought, and these he unrolls before Ponti and Francesca. "Forests!" he announces, noting, as he runs his hand across the map, the lumpy quality of the Danish parchment, but nevertheless admiring the bright colours the artist has decided to use. "And much of these are mine: crown lands which the nobility cannot touch."

The Italians stare at the quantity of tiny emerald-coloured trees with which the map maker has covered almost half the land and at the abundant lakes and rivers which thread their way, like a tangled necklace of aquamarine, through the acre upon acre of bright-green woodland.

"Go to Jutland," says the King. "You will see how the terrain encompasses both timber and water in great quantities. I will send a surveyor with you. And then you will return and tell me if the *Carta Ponti Numero Due* and *Numero Uno* can be produced from Danish trees. I am interested only in paper of this kind of quality—with which my own calligraphy can become infatuated. If you can make this, I will give you the patents for your mill and we shall work out what profits shall be yours and what shall be mine."

Signor Ponti beams. Already, he allows himself to imagine the Ponti watermark surfacing on Danish documents of State, on almanacs and sheets of music, on handbills and architectural drawings, on the endpapers of learned books, on love letters and wills. He even contemplates the delicious notion that the word "Ponti" might become so synonymous with fine paper that, in due time, Danes would refer to it thus: "Bring me a sheet of ponti, Sir" or "The unhappy lover crumpled the piece of ponti and cast it into the fire."

And the King, too, is smiling. His brain feels clear. It is as though, on the clean sheets of paper, he has already begun to write down a future from which heartache and poverty are suddenly, unexpectedly, absent.

CHAMBERS OF SOLACE

Dowager Queen Sofie is in her cellar.

As always, she has closed the heavy door behind her and, with only a candle to light her way, she walks slowly down the line of wine casks, seeing whether she can memorise what lies concealed in each one.

Her coins were patiently sorted: golden dalers, golden rose-nobles, silver dalers, silver skillings. They were placed, in small quantities, in pigskin bags, tied up and sealed with wax. The bags were then immersed for a day and a night in basins of water, to ensure that they did not leak. Where leaks occurred the bags were opened and re-sealed, and afterwards placed, one by one, into the barrels.

Then came the moment of ingenuity. The casks were filled with wine.

Queen Sofie dared to let her coinage lie in soft sacks drowned in liquor, knowing that even if, over time, the skins might rot and the money tarnish, its value would remain. Moreover, the extent to which the skins were or were not decaying, the extent to which minute particles of the precious metal were or were not leaching out, could be measured simply by pouring off some wine and sniffing it. Queen Sofie has a nose so sensitive she had always been able to verify the late King's infidelities by a mere whiff. He'd had an aromatic beard. Proximity with it had always divulged to the Queen more secrets than Frederik II could ever have imagined.

So now Queen Sofie sets down her candle. She has brought with her a little cup and she stoops by the first barrel, turns the tap and lets a dribble of wine run into the cup. Then she plunges her nose right into the vessel and breathes in the bouquet, flaring her nostrils right and left, right and left. Wine cannot dissemble. It is tainted or it is not tainted and she is as good a judge of this as any connoisseur from Burgundy.

It has the scent of the forest in it and of summer fruit. It contains no less the scent of the lost past, when, at State banquets and religious feasts, men used to gaze with longing at her golden hair. And all these remembered smells are pure and not sullied by anything else.

The Queen tips away the wine and goes to the second barrel, pours and sniffs again. She tests five barrels, and the wine in all of them betrays not the mildest scent of degradation. From the last barrel, she pours a brimming cup and drinks this down. Her daring has worked. The bags lie in the wet darkness and are safe and intact.

Queen Sofie takes up the candle again.

She walks behind the casks and lifts down an iron bar from the wall. The candle is set once more on the tarred and dusty floor, and the Queen now begins to scrape carefully away at the tar, as though she were a peasant woman with a hoe and the cellar floor a plot of earth where precious seedlings grew.

She can hear a rustling in the cellar as she works and hopes that it is mice and not rats who have made nests in here for the winter. But nothing, today, makes her afraid. Her daring and resourcefulness have ensured her future peace of mind, and the excitement she feels when, after several minutes' hoeing with the bar, a miraculous gleam of gold appears beneath it is as intense as that which her lovers once felt when they touched her flaxen hair.

The tar and dust not only cover the gold ingots, but serve as the mortar that holds them together. Where once this floor was made of bricks, now it is made of gold. When King Christian came to search Queen Sofie's vaults for the treasure he knew was there, he was standing directly upon it.

The Queen digs up one gold ingot, cleans it with some rags and, hiding it beneath her skirts, scuttles up to her bedchamber with it and closes and locks the door. She lies down on the bed and places the ingot on her stomach and caresses it with her hand.

This action, this stroking of her gold, is so soothing that Queen Sofie quickly falls into a dream-filled sleep. Voices which she recognises but to which she cannot give names ask her what she will buy or get with her ingot and she replies that she wishes to buy happiness, but does not know the precise form and shape of it. "Is it possible," inquire the old, insistent voices, "that the precise form and shape of happiness is the ingot itself?"

And so she wakes and looks at her gold brick and understands—as, in all truth, she has done for some time—that there will never be anything that brings her more satisfaction than what lies heavy, here and now, on her ageing body. The time is past when gold can be exchanged for anything more marvellous than itself.

Meanwhile, seated at a French escritoire in her room at Boller, Vibeke Kruse, biting her lip like a child, labours to complete the calligraphy exercises set for her by Ellen Marsvin.

Ever ashamed of her handwriting, in particular her failure to make the letters *u* and *n* distinguishable from one another and to give any grace to her *g*'s and her *y*'s, she has recently been scolded by Ellen for this weakness and sternly told to correct it.

So she is doing lines of *n*'s, *g*'s that join and loop with each other, *u*'s that remind her of knitting unravelling. It is dull work, dull and difficult for her, but she perseveres because, at any moment, Ellen Marsvin is going to come in to examine what she has completed.

There is an ache in Vibeke's mouth. She would like to complain to somebody about this, but she does not, just as she does not complain about the calligraphy exercises. Because both these things form part of the great plan Ellen is making for her. The success of the plan depends upon silence.

Vibeke puts down her pen and probes her gums gently with a forefinger. What the finger finds there—the thing that is the source of the soreness that almost makes her weep—is a scattering of new teeth.

They are made of polished ivory. They lie in the gum sockets where her own teeth have rotted away and fallen out, and are kept in place by means of silver wire attached tightly to adjacent molars. The tooth sculptor charged Ellen dear for these adornments to Vibeke's mouth and so Fru Marsvin will not listen to any complaint about the discomfort they cause and what difficulties they create at mealtimes. Indeed, Ellen has snapped that this discomfort is all to the good if it means that Vibeke is afraid to eat. Let her not eat. Let her at last get thin! For only when she can go about with grace in her expensive new gowns, only when her handwriting has improved and her smile is once again devoid of gaps, can the plan at last be implemented.

Ellen Marsvin comes into Vibeke's room and closes the door behind her.

She crosses to the escritoire and stands behind Vibeke, looking down at her work, which still has a hopeless naïvety about it, as though Vibeke were learning to write her alphabet for the first time.

"Look!" says Ellen impatiently. "The heads of your *g*'s are all of differing sizes, when they should be of uniform size. Do another line."

Vibeke dips the quill in the ink and recommences so quickly and obediently that several *n*'s in the line above are smudged.

Ellen notices that the little finger of Vibeke's right hand is stained black. And though her struggles have something irritating about them, Ellen Marsvin nevertheless feels, at the sight of this ink-stained finger, a tenderness towards Vibeke that she can only express by laying a gentle hand on her hair. "It will come right, Vibeke," she says softly. "When the spring arrives . . ."

"I trust it will," says Vibeke, pausing in her *g*'s and turning round towards Ellen.

"We need a little more time. That's all. How are your teeth today?"

Vibeke wants to reply that the silver wire has been twisted so tightly that she fears it is cutting into the polished surface of her own undecayed teeth, and that the sockets where the ivories lie are red and sore. But she says only that she is getting acclimatised to these new sculptures in her mouth and that oil of cloves is effective against pain.

"Have courage," says Ellen, as Vibeke goes back to her writing. "Everything will be well in due time and when everything is well, then it will be very well indeed."

Liking the neat—almost poetic—convolutions of this last sentence, Ellen Marsvin looks round Vibeke's chamber with a satisfied smile. This room contains within its four walls all the secret "ingredients" of her plan. And in her plan a future full of consolations lies silently waiting.

JOHANN TILSEN'S DISCOVERY

As the cold of January deepens and ice forms on the water in the well, Johann Tilsen pursues his search for Marcus.

He rides out alone. He wraps a scarf round his nose and mouth, so that the freezing air is filtered by cloth, but his breath trapped inside the scarf condenses to water and the water turns to ice and the skin of his face begins to burn.

He is terrified of finding Marcus's body. He admits to himself that he is searching *in the hope that he will not find.*

He is almost grateful for the snow which has fallen, several inches deep, and which would freeze the corpse and even cover it sufficiently to hide it until springtime. Yet, where the snow has drifted and piled up, Johann Tilsen digs with a spade and with his hands, all the while praying that nothing will lie underneath the drifts but the fallen leaves and the earth.

As he continues his arduous exploration, he tries, now and again, when the agony of the search and the pain of the cold become almost too terrible to endure, to comfort himself with the idea that Marcus has somehow found the "other world" he used to speak about, that it exists somewhere—not merely in the child's confused head.

But Johann Tilsen is a rational man. He knows there is no "other world" this side of death. His visions of Marcus on some sunlit plain or prairie are mere delusions. On one of these icy mornings he will find him.

A lonely, hunched figure in the white landscape, Johann Tilsen looks at his life and begins to see in it signs that he cannot read. Until this winter, until the disappearance of Marcus, he always believed that he was in control of his own destiny, because he prided himself that he could see what lay in people's hearts. Now he senses—for no reason that he can determine—that this ability has deserted him. Under his own roof, in the thick air of the parlour, in the erotic darkness of his bedroom, something has changed or shifted, a "something" that he cannot precisely describe, but which is there nevertheless.

It has to do with Magdalena. Johann Tilsen stares at his wife— when he makes love to her and when she is sleeping—trying to see what it is that has altered, but it eludes him. Her behaviour is exactly as it ever was. She is tender towards him and ever concerned for his welfare. It is still easy to pleasure her. And in bed she continues to do whatever he asks, whatever his fancy conjures.

And yet, she is altered.

How can it be that alteration shows itself, but resides in no particular thing and cannot be defined?

"Magdalena," he whispers one night, as, with his member still inside her, he feels her drift towards sleep, "what are you hiding from me?"

She does not move. After a while, she replies: "You are my husband, Johann. You see all that I am."

"I *see* what you are," he says, "but I do not *know* what you are. And this has begun to torment me."

A candle still flickers at the bedside. Magdalena sits up, thus separating her body from Johann's, and blows out the flame.

They lie in the dark and she reaches out and takes his hand. "Johann," she says, "if you are tormented, it is not because of me. This search of yours for Marcus is doing you harm."

Johann is silent. There is some truth in what Magdalena has said; the hours he spends alone under the grey sky have certainly weakened him, both in body and mind. "Yes," he says, "but it is not this. Something has happened in this house. I feel it."

They hear the shriek of a night bird. Magdalena doesn't speak, so that Johann's last utterance and the shrieking of the bird seem to linger there together in the darkness for a moment and then die suddenly, as an echo dies.

"Magdalena . . ."

"Hush, my dear," she says. "Nothing has happened. Sleep the sleep of the just."

When he wakes in the morning, Johann believes he knows where Marcus's body can be found. A dream has revealed it to him. And the place was so obvious. It was staring at him all the time and he did not see it.

He says nothing to Magdalena. He goes out as soon as he has drunk his coffee, as the boys prepare for their lessons and Magdalena gives her orders to the kitchen maids.

He takes an ice pick with him, slung over his body. When he's fed and watered his horse, he picks up a blanket from the stables, one that Marcus's bay pony sometimes wears, and attaches it to his saddle. He rides eastwards, across all the strawberry fields, towards the summer pastures, towards a low, white sun struggling to climb above the skeletal oaks and beeches on the Boller boundary.

When he reaches the first of the pastures he dismounts and ties up the horse, and takes the blanket and the tools with him.

Now he stands, looking down at the water trough. He can hear Marcus's voice in his mind, fragile as a distant bell: *My mother can see me from the cloud where she lies and when it rains on the water in the horse trough, that is her crying for me just in that little place . . .* And he can hear himself scolding: *I do not know what to do with you, Marcus. I am in despair . . .*

The heart of Johann Tilsen is filled with terror as he scrapes the recent snow off the thick ice of the trough.

This ice is not transparent. It has thickened to solid whiteness. What lies inside it cannot yet be seen.

Johann shivers in the cold. He takes up the pick.

But then he pauses. What did he imagine he was going to do with the pick? Smash indiscriminately into the surface of the ice? The trough is deep, but the little body would have floated. Johann runs his bare hands over the ice. The surface is perfectly smooth. It is like a clean slab of cold stone. Though his hands burn, he keeps them there, as if in an attitude of benediction. What he feels is shame.

He remounts the horse. He will go back to the house and fetch more delicate tools—fine chisels and hammers—and with these he will uncover the body without damage to it. And then he will lift it out gently and wrap it in the blanket, which still smells of the bay pony, and carry it home.

The summer pastures are a long way from the house, and when Johann Tilsen arrives back there his feet and hands are so numb he decides he will warm himself by the fire for a few minutes before setting out again.

He walks into the parlour and sits down.

Damage.

The word taunts him. His own hypocrisies fill him with disgust. Marcus Tilsen was damaged long ago—by his own father's indifference. Nothing and no one else is to blame but this.

Johann stares at the fire. He is about to get up to go in search of the chisels when he becomes aware of the sound of weeping. He lifts his head. The weeping is coming from above him, from the room where he and Magdalena sleep. Yet he knows it is not Magdalena. Magdalena does not cry like this.

Silently, Johann Tilsen gets up and silently he goes up the stairs. In the time to come he will ask himself why he chose to walk so quietly, to tiptoe like a thief, and he has no answer except that this is what *he knew he had to do.*

As he approaches his bedroom, the weeping, he realises, is very loud, an abandoned, almost uncontrolled wailing. "Magdalena . . ." moans the voice. "Magdalena . . ."

The voice is Ingmar's.

Johann Tilsen opens the door and goes into the room. Magdalena is sprawled on the bed in a white petticoat that has been pushed up to her waist and its bodice opened. Ingmar Tilsen, naked except for his shirt, lies between her legs and weeps in his delirium, clinging to her like a man drowning, his dark head laid on her milky breasts.

The light is beginning to go from the sky when Johann returns to the water trough and the same bird that called in the night has begun to call again, more insistently, as though impatient for the darkness to come.

The air is so cold that every breath gives Johann pain. But he works on, almost oblivious to the freezing dusk, concentrating only on the task of chipping away at ice, fragment by fragment, like a sculptor who knows that within the block of marble the human form he has seen in his mind lies waiting.

The shards of ice bounce and fly. The sound of the chisel is loud in the silent afternoon. The horse sneezes and stamps.

Piece by piece, the oblong of ice in the trough is chipped away. Johann Tilsen finds acorns and leaves within it. He remembers Marcus staring at these floating things, prodding them with a stick, more intent on them than on the words Johann was uttering: *That water is not for you, Marcus, it is for the horses. Come away . . .*

Even when darkness has fallen, even when the ice is no deeper than a man's hand, Johann Tilsen keeps working. Not until his chisel strikes the stone base of the trough does he stop and sink down on his knees and rest.

ANGEL DESCENDING

In his new mood of strange optimism, due, it appears, to the arrival of the paper manufacturer from Bologna, King Christian has ordered Peter Claire to take Signor Ponti and his daughter to Copen-hagen to show them the buildings he is proudest of: the Børsen with its twisting spire, modelled on the King's own elflock, with stalls in it for forty merchants; the old smithy which became the Holmens Kirke for the sailors and ship workers of Bremerholm; his dear palace of Rosenborg, flower of his love for Kirsten.

The symmetry of these buildings, their impeccable brickwork, the delicacy of their spires and towers, have impressed Francesco Ponti. But the Italian notices, he says, some *contraddizione* between the King's unkempt and unhappy appearance and the neatness and optimism of his architecture. To Peter Claire, he asks: "What is this man?"

They have left Rosenborg and are in one of the buildings that form a protective wall around the Tøjhushavn, the deep-water har-bour, where the *Tre Kroner* now lies at anchor. They gaze down on the great ship, moored near a cluster of smaller vessels, and Peter Claire remembers the voyage to the Numedal and the music played under the stars on the quarterdeck. He gestures towards the *Tre Kroner*. "In some ways," he says, "King Christian resembles this ship."

"The large one?"

"Yes. It's the biggest ship of the fleet, as strong as anything you will ever encounter on the oceans. I have sailed in it and I know how mighty is its sail power and how strong its construction. Yet you see its bright colours and all the intricate gilt work? The King's desire for the golden things of the world sometimes obscures the strength that lies beneath it."

" 'Golden things'?" asks Ponti. "What is this?"

"Luxury," says Francesca.

"Not only that," says Peter Claire. "I mean that he is a dreamer."

There is a short silence before Francesca looks at Peter Claire and says: "A king should dream. Those who do not dream make nothing."

"I agree," says Peter Claire quietly. "But of course not all the King's dreams have been realised—and nor will ever be—and this is what makes him dejected."

Francesca doesn't reply. Their high view of the Tøjhushavn, with the swaying masts beneath them, has a strangeness about it that hypnotises them. It is as if they were not anchored to the earth at all but were balancing on the ships themselves, and yet securely, like birds, with their power of flight ready to save them if they should fall.

While Signor Ponti consults with His Majesty's surveyor, Francesca asks Peter Claire to take her riding in the woods of Frederiksborg. She tells him she has been in closed-in spaces—ships' cabins, jolting coaches, high lightless rooms—for too long and yearns to breathe "an air that is like the air of Cloyne, cold and beautiful."

He hesitates over this request, just as he has hesitated in his mind, since Francesca's arrival, between taking her in his arms and trying to find the words to tell her about Emilia.

And he knows that the Countess has noticed him hesitating, not knowing the reason perhaps, but has watched him move towards her and move back, take a breath to speak and then remain silent, catch her eye and then suddenly look away. Several times she has begged him to talk to her.

"Of course we must talk," he has said. "Only you must understand that my time is not my own, Francesca, music rehearsals are long and I am often called, at any moment of the day and night, to play to His Majesty alone."

"Why alone?" she has asked and seen him blush as he answered.

"The King has a nickname for me. He calls me his 'angel' . . ."

"His angel!"

"You may certainly laugh. Go on. The German viol player, Krenze, finds this exquisitely funny, and so does everyone else. And of course *it is*. But I cannot allow myself to find it amusing and nothing else. I made the King a promise and I have no choice but to keep it."

"What promise?"

"I can't tell you."

"And why have you 'no choice'?"

"Because I have sworn . . ."

"And when you have sworn, your word is your bond? What did you 'swear' at Cloyne, Peter Claire?"

"What did I swear, Francesca?"

"When we heard the owls calling. You said to me that if I should call to you, you would come."

Peter Claire looks at her. He cannot remember saying these very words, yet he can remember feeling some such thing, that he would always let her—the first woman for whom he felt an over-whelming passion—summon part of himself. So once again he has to look away from her, pretend he has been distracted by something outside the window, or recalled to his mind some errand on which he has forgotten to go. He knows that in all his dealings with her he is being cowardly. He wishes the days would pass and that she would be gone.

He agrees to the ride.

He agrees because he likes the idea of galloping fast through the Frederiksborg woods, to their limits and beyond, as if running away from his life. If he cannot escape to the New World, such as he dreamed of on the night he heard the story of the execution, at least he can ride until he's exhausted and find some kind of oblivion in that.

He chooses strong horses, giving no thought to how Francesca will manage her spirited mount, because in his imagination he has already left her far behind and is alone in his own part of the forest. And he rides on until he knows that he's lost. And in this feeling of being lost is a kind of rapture.

Francesca wears a riding cloak and hat of black velvet.

Under the lightless sky, her face appears pale, her eyes large, her lips dark. She instructs the groom to spread out her cloak behind her and Peter Claire notes the care with which the man accom-plishes this task, as though his hands had never touched velvet before, never saddled a horse for any woman as beautiful as Countess O'Fingal.

This beauty of hers—which she perfects first in the rearrangement of the cloak and then in the way she sits tall and straight and unafraid on her horse—Peter Claire sees as a studied reproach to him. It asks him how he can be so miserly as to resist her. It reminds him that enchantment very often triumphs over scruple and will continue to do so for as long as the world lasts.

They ride fast, just as Peter Claire had imagined they would, except that Francesca keeps up with him stride for stride, and when he glances at her he sees that she is almost laughing, and this remembered sound of her laughter is as potent as music.

So it is he who reins in his horse first and slows to a canter and then a trot. They are approaching a clearing, to which Francesca gallops on. She doesn't stop, nor even slow down, only calls to him to catch her up again. Clearly, the speed of the ride thrills her and she wants to go on at this daring pace.

And thus the gallop now becomes a kind of chase, in which Peter Claire has to use his whip, and it seems to him that Francesca, with her cloak billowing out in the air, is determined to outdistance him. For a moment, as the path turns northwards, he considers letting her go and idling here until she chooses to return, but pride forces him to keep following, pride and a kind of rising elation and a sudden insatiable curiosity, as though the Countess were leading him to some destination that only she is capable of finding.

His horse begins to sweat, but Peter Claire knows it will not falter when it starts to tire. These are the same Arabians the King uses for the tilting competitions, descendants of those he once rode in these woods with Bror Brorson. They are as edgy and strong as dancers, with sinewy hearts and delicate feet. They will let themselves be ridden until they fall.

And the woods themselves, so beloved by Christian for the wild boar hunts, spread out for miles around Frederiksborg. The paths go on and on. A man could ride in them all day and not reach their limit. So Peter Claire understands that there will be no reprieve— not yet—on this winter morning. There are only those things which define the moment, those things which play with time, giving it a frenzied, dreamlike acceleration: the spur, the whip, the pumping blood, the pursuit.

Then, at last, ahead of him as he turns a wide corner, he sees that the Countess has pulled up her horse and dismounted, and is unfastening her cloak and laying it on the ground. She stands, triumphant, waiting for him.

He leans on his horse's neck, trying to catch his breath. And, as Francesca seems to have predicted, he can't take his eyes from her. She removes some fastening from her hair and it falls free, just as she wore it at Cloyne, when they ran along the beach, following Giulietta's hoop.

Laughing, she says: "Did I tell you I had a suitor? His name is Sir Lawrence de Vere. Did I tell you that he is very rich and that I was thinking of marrying him?"

Perhaps it is the laughter or perhaps it is the mention of another man, but it is at this moment that Peter Claire knows that he has lost the battle to resist Francesca. He will go to his mistress now and she will be his mistress again and his desire for her will put everything and everyone else from his mind.

When he kisses her he knows that the kiss is a kind of submission. Peter Claire submits not only to Francesca's will, superior in the chase to his, but to the past. It is as though the intervening time between his departure from Cloyne and this moment in his second Danish winter had not existed or, if it had existed, had contained in it nothing of any importance.

When they return, in the early afternoon, and hand their horses to the grooms and part with a polite formality, Peter Claire goes to his room, banks up his fire and lies down, fully clothed, on the bed.

He closes his eyes and is asleep in minutes, but then, in minutes again, is woken by a knock on his door.

He can barely move.

He calls for the visitor to enter. A black-clad servant comes in, hands him a letter and withdraws.

Peter Claire stares at the letter. For one heart-stopping moment he wonders whether it is from Emilia Tilsen, but he quickly sees that the handwriting is of a sophistication he does not imagine her to possess and notices that the letter is bound by an elaborate seal, almost grand enough to be the King's own.

His tiredness is such that the task of lighting a lamp feels almost too difficult to accomplish. He craves a deep and dreamless sleep more than he has ever craved it in his life. He is nearly ready to lay the letter aside, to be read later when his head is clear again, when a little time has settled on the events of the morning.

Yet he does find the tinder-box and the taper, and puts the taper to the wick. Letters are like warnings of fire; the mind knows that it must attend . . .

Dear Mr. Claire [*he reads*],

What manner of man are you?

To whose letters do you make answer if you choose to disregard such an Important Communication from the *King's Consort?*

But let me remind you again of the ways in which you put yourself and your Aspirations in Peril if you will not speedily answer me, telling me that you will execute the Commission that I have given you. Indeed, I shall list the ways:

Your letters to Emilia Tilsen, my Woman, shall never be given to her. You may write Every Day and Every Day shall your Words be Intercepted, just as all those you have already set down, charming and ardent as they are, have been Intercepted and now moulder in an Iron Box and do not see the light of Day and are not heard and shall never be heard by Emilia unless perchance, when I am dead and she an old Crone, she may find them there and realise what her Life might have been, if only you had not proved so False and Full of Pride . . .

The Lutheran preacher, Ratty Møller, stands at his window.

His small house lies by a narrow road at the apex of a hill and every morning, as the steep road emerges out of the darkness, while Møller eats a bowl of bread and ewe's milk, he stares at it.

This staring at the road has become so ritualised a part of Ratty Møller's day that, very frequently, long minutes pass in which he forgets what it is that he is hoping to see. His bright, darting eyes contemplate that which is already there: the sparse trees petrified by the frost; the ruts in the snow and ice made by carts and wagons; a solitary bird turning in the stillness. And these things enter his consciousness and remain there, but they remain just as they are, without any addition.

Møller used, at one time, to put into the landscape a man riding into the village of the *Isfoss* wearing a brocaded cloak and boots of Spanish leather, but now he no longer remembers to imagine this person. He watches the road and the trees and the January sky, and this is all. His thoughts go elsewhere—towards some petty task awaiting his attention, or towards the words of a sermon half completed. The man in the leather boots has faded, vanished.

And so it is with astonishment—almost disbelief—that Ratty Møller sees approaching one morning just such a person, on a chestnut horse, and cloaked in red and wearing on his head a tall plumed hat.

Møller goes closer to the window. He rubs at the mist formed by his breath on the glass and back into his mind pour all his old hopes for the people of the *Isfoss*: that the King would return with everything necessary for the reopening of the mine, that the village would come alive again, that there would be songs at midnight and pigs roasted on the fire . . .

Behind the man in the tall hat two wagons appear. The carthorses strain and slip on the icy hill, and the wagons lurch. But they come on. And Møller, who lives these days on a diet of carrots, turnips and onions, augmented only sometimes by rabbit meat or a roasted mistlethrush, imagines the wagons filled to overflowing with smoked hams and live geese, fat squares of butter packed in ice, Portuguese lemons, dried flounder, jars of cocoa and cinnamon, sacks of nuts and grain.

Møller puts on his black coat and his scuffed black shoes, and goes out into the road. He raises his arms in a joyous greeting and the man on the horse removes his hat as a sign of salutation to the preacher.

"Welcome," says Møller. "Welcome, Sir."

Though the man's bearing is upright, he stumbles as he gets down from the horse and almost sinks to his knees. He says that the voyage has been long, that it sometimes seemed to him that the journey would have no end. And Møller replies that this was how it has seemed to them, the villagers of the *Isfoss*, that the waiting would never be over.

The man strokes his beard, to remove some of the ice crystals from it, and says: "The King's heart is as large as his kingdom. It is merely his purse that is small."

The wagons are parked in the middle of the village.

One by one, the villagers come out—men, women and children—to stare at them, and each individual begins to speculate upon their contents. If they all imagine a store of food to last the winter and bring to an end the hunger that snaps and claws at them even in their dreams, they also conjure from the silent wagons all the things they have ever longed for: bales of linen and coverlets of fur, pewter plates and jars of green glass, barrels of Rhenish wine and Spanish Alicante, bottles of ink, flintlock pistols, copies of Mercator's Atlas, pouches of tobacco, stringed lutes, cards of lace, balls and skittles, quivers of arrows, skates, monkeys that will dance on the end of a chain . . .

But what people long for is seldom what actually arrives. So of course there are no green jars, no wine, no lace, no capering monkeys. In fact, at this very moment, the King's representative, standing beside Ratty Møller's fire, is explaining how much—of all that the King commanded to be sent to the Numedal—has been lost.

"It is embarrassing to tell you this," says the representative, whose name is Herr Gade, "but when we set out, we carried far more than your people will find in the wagons now."

"Why?" says Møller.

"We had more than a hundred live pullets in wicker cages, but a fox got into the carts one night and killed thirty of them, eating only their heads and gizzards, which was all the beast could draw into his mouth through the basketwork. We packed the bodies in snow, but we had to throw them out. Even in this cold they began to stink."

"The waste . . ." says Møller sadly.

"And then, because the crossings were so hard and the journey so much longer than we imagined, some of the dalers and skillings intended for you had to be used to buy oats for the horses and summon blacksmiths to mend their shoes and to hammer rivets into the wheels of the wagons. There is a good supply of money left, but it is less than the King hoped to bring you . . ."

Møller nods. "And the corn seed?"

"Well," says Herr Gade, "again, because of the long passage of time from our starting out to our arrival, some of the grain had to be given to the remaining pullets, to keep them alive for you. If you seek to apportion blame, Herr Møller, blame the northerly winds, blame God who sent them."

"I am a preacher," says Møller. "I am not in the habit of 'blaming' God."

"No," says Gade. "No. Of course not. All I mean to emphasise is that the shortfalls are *not our fault*."

Ratty Møller goes to the window and looks out at the familiar road he has watched for so long. Bitterly he thinks, What are a few pullets, a few sacks of corn, a few coins, in return for the hope that was kindled and then dashed, for the lives that were lost? And now, nothing more will arrive upon that road until the winter is past.

"There is a little beer," says Herr Gade, "and cloth. Woollen cloth made at the Børnehus looms. Of a serviceable brown colour and quite warm."

"And silver needles with which to sew it, I suppose?" says

Møller bleakly and cannot resist turning to witness the representative's discomfort at his sour jest.

Herr Gade looks down, as if to inspect his boots, the soles of which are almost worn away from the pressure of his feet upon the stirrups. He takes a long breath before he says: "His Majesty told me to remind you that he is sending for engineers from Russia."

Ratty Møller looks up now at the King's representative, to whom, as the head of the community of the *Isfoss*, he must offer a bed for the night and food that he does not possess and courtesy that he does not feel. And he lets a sigh escape from his small person. Having longed so ardently and for so long for Herr Gade's arrival, he wishes suddenly that the man with the tall hat and the scarlet cloak would vanish away.

The cloth, the grain, the money and the pullets are counted and distributed among all the families. This arithmetic, however many times it is done, reveals that not one family is entitled to an entire pullet and so it is decided, once the representative and the wagon drivers have departed—back along the deserted roads, back towards the darkness of the sea—to pluck and cook all the birds on a vast fire out under the stars and hold a feast.

Tables are set in ten houses and the grain milled and bread baked.

The smell of the roasting chickens lures everybody outside, and the villagers warm themselves by the fire and drink the King's beer and begin to talk once again of the future the King will send.

This future, although it is not identical to the past, when the mine was working and when men secreted in their bodies pieces of rock shot through with veins of silver, nevertheless resembles it. And already the people of the *Isfoss* begin to imagine the Russian geniuses of the mine travelling towards them on elegant sleighs drawn by dogs like wolves, dogs with soft tails and yellow eyes, dogs which can move across the deserts of ice much faster than the speed of spring.

From that long afternoon when Johann Tilsen searched for Marcus's body in the water trough and did not find it, and instead discovered his eldest son in bed with Magdalena, life in the Tilsen household began to undergo a progressive alteration.

Ingmar was sent away. Johann Tilsen paid to have him apprenticed in Copenhagen to a friend of his own youth who made medical instruments. Ingmar was given no money and no provision was made for where he would stay in the city. "You have made yourself an orphan" was what Johann said to him. "So now you must fend for yourself."

Magdalena tried to intervene secretly and pressed a purse containing five dalers into Ingmar's hand, but Johann had foreseen this and made his son empty his pockets before the cart took him away. Johann threw the purse containing Magdalena's money into the fire. "This is whore's gold," he said, "and you shall not have it!"

The boy did not cry or complain or protest. His face was a white mask of anguish. As he sat in the cart waiting to leave he looked neither at his father, nor at Magdalena, nor at his brothers, who, in the case of Boris and Matti, did not understand why he was leaving and, in the case of Wilhelm, understood only too well.

Magdalena couldn't stop herself from sighing at the sight of the light snow falling onto Ingmar's soft brown curls, as the cart lurched off and disappeared down the drive. Of all the lovers she had known in her life, beginning with her uncle and her cousin, perhaps Ingmar Tilsen had moved her the most: the way he clung to her and cried, the way his lips fastened themselves on her breast, the way he smiled his secret smiles at mealtimes. And the thought that he would be cold in Copenhagen, and friendless, and have no kitchen to come to where he could lick sugar and butter from her fingers and when Christmas arrived be absent from the table when the goose was brought in made her heart break. "He's still a boy," she said to Johann. "With a boy's fantasies, that's all. You have been too severe."

"No," said Johann. "I have not been severe enough."

As for Johann Tilsen himself, such deep confusions and contradictions racked his brain and body on the subject of Magdalena that he began to wonder if he was going mad.

If his first thought had been to repudiate her and send her back to her family, this was swiftly followed by a desire to keep her as his wife but under a new regime of punishment, in which he would make her suffer so cruelly that her spirit would be broken and she would come to live in fear of him and think only of doing his bidding, day and night, whatever that bidding might be.

He burned her dresses. He took back all the gifts of silver he had given her. He drove her from their shared bed to a room in the attic, where the rain and the snow leaked through the roof. He beat her. He drew blood from her ear. He streaked her arse with purple bruises. And he believed that, in this way, he could continue to live with her, to salvage his wounded pride, to carry on.

But then he found to his dismay that her body still excited him. The beatings he gave it only augmented this excitement, so that, little by little, power and mastery of these moments leached away from him and passed to her once again. Because, once excited, he found that he could not resist her, and that once he was there, in the place where he had to put himself, his excitation only *increased* when he thought of her seduction of Ingmar, so that the very thing for which he was punishing her became by degrees an ingredient in his own ecstasy.

Magdalena knew exactly what was happening. "Johann," she would whisper, "what a man you are! As virile as your son . . ." And if at first Johann slapped his hand across her mouth when she uttered these words, she sensed that they nevertheless drove him on and that, just as she had tormented her uncle with the deeds of her cousin, so she would be able to reassert her mastery over Johann Tilsen by reminding him that his own son had spurned the young maids of the Tilsen estate to copulate with his stepmother.

When he left her, spent and tired, self-disgust would invade Johann Tilsen. He could feel himself stooping like an old man as he descended the attic stairs. Sometimes he locked Magdalena in the attic room and took away the key. At such times he wished her dead. He began to think that Emilia had been right and that Magdalena had a witch's powers.

If there was still daylight in the sky, he would saddle a horse and ride out into the woods and fields, and resume his search for Marcus's body. The idea that it was out there somewhere, undiscovered, frozen, pecked at by carrion, caused him such torment, such feelings of loneliness and self-reproach, that he often rode blindly, no longer searching the hedgerows or the thickets but letting the horse take him where it would and hardly noticing the dusk as it began to fall. At such times, part of him longed never to return to the house, but to die like Marcus in some other world of his own devising.

It was the key to the attic which ushered in the next phase of alteration in the Tilsen house.

One day, when Johann was out searching for Marcus, Magdalena summoned Wilhelm to her bedroom. She had Ulla with her and the baby was drinking from the breast when the boy entered.

"Wilhelm," said Magdalena, giving Wilhelm that radiant smile that used to haunt Ingmar's dreams. "Do you fear that your father might send you away from here to Copenhagen like Ingmar?"

"No," said Wilhelm.

"No." She smiled. "You are quite right, for it would not happen, for the arithmetic is not appropriate. How many sons can any father bear to lose?"

Magdalena lifted Ulla off the breast and laid her down on the coverlet beside her. Slowly, watching Wilhelm the while, Magdalena took the large white breast in her hand and inserted it back inside her dress.

She gave Wilhelm the key to the attic room and the sum of five skillings. She told him to take the key to the village blacksmith and have him copy it exactly and then return and hide the replica of the key in one of his own boots and say nothing to any living soul about it. Then she asked him to sit beside her and she stroked his hair, which was not soft and curly like Ingmar's but thick and springy like his father's. "Such lovely hair!" she said. "I have always thought how very pretty it is."

Wilhelm, aged sixteen, one year younger than Ingmar, the recipient of Ingmar's confidences, Ingmar having recited to him in the dead of night the details of his initiation and even told him that he should go to Magdalena, too, "for this is what she loves, that there be two or even three of us and she will enslave us all," took the key. He did exactly as he was told. He hid the key made by the blacksmith and waited until the next time Johann locked Magdalena in the attic and went out.

Then Magdalena called to him. He fetched the key from inside one of his boots, let himself into the attic and locked the door behind him. Magdalena lay on the bed with her skirt lifted to show a few inches of white thigh above her red stockings. She held out her hand to Wilhelm and told him not to be afraid.

But Magdalena, in her unstoppable greed for power within the household, now embarked with Wilhelm on actions so dangerous that even she, in the depths of the night, when the wind howled round the lonely Tilsen house, began to be frightened of what Johann would do if these things (which were not as tender as they had been with Ingmar, but more ugly and fierce) were revealed to him. Yet, the more vertiginous was her terror of Johann's wrath, the more inventive did she become in her enslavement of his second-eldest son.

And as for Wilhelm, he began to believe that his life was doomed. To his lost brother in Copenhagen he wrote: *Help me, Ingmar, for I am in mortal danger. I am doing what you did and I cannot stop. I want to stop, but I cannot, and I know that I shall die and go to hell unless I can be released from my affliction.*

At Boller, at the end of January, Kirsten Munk announces that she is tired of living in the dark, weary of the perpetual shadows and the dripping of the candles. She orders that the shutters be opened and all the drapes be drawn back. To Emilia she says: "We cannot live closed up like this any longer. If your father arrives, we shall have to hide Marcus in the cellar and that is the end of it. And we shall have no scruple about lying to Herr Tilsen, just as he lied to us."

Marcus no longer sleeps on the cot in Emilia's room. He has been given a small chamber "adequately far" from Kirsten's, so that she will not hear him crying in the night. And this chamber is one of the few at Boller left by Ellen Marsvin just as she found it. The room is so tiny it is almost a closet and might once have served as a place where clothes were kept or ironed. Its walls are covered, from floor to ceiling, by strange and beautiful paintings. No one remembers who the artist was or why or when these murals were commissioned, but what they depict is a bright, fantastical landscape of flowers and leaves, and in among all the foliage the eye soon discovers a multitude of insects, much larger than life, creeping, darting and fluttering everywhere, so that to enter the room is almost to *hear* the buzzing of the bees, the whine of the wasps and the whirr of the dragon-flies' wings.

When Marcus Tilsen first set eyes on these creatures, he appeared to forget on the instant his anguish at seeing his bed taken out of Emilia's room and began uttering little cries of delight. He went to one of the walls and investigated it gently with his hands. His fingers first explored a beetle crawling upon a scarlet leaf, tracing the contours of its blue-black body, then moved to a moth, depicted with its wings folded, like a speckled arrowhead, on a clump of moss, and then to a bee in flight against a brilliant patch of sky.

Emilia watched him. It had always been true of Marcus that certain phenomena absorbed his attention so completely that he appeared *lost* in these things, almost to *become* them—the water of the horse trough, the song of the mechanical bird, the antics of his cat, Otto—and Emilia immediately understood that this room was to Marcus like a kingdom entire, where his mind would loop and turn in a perpetually repeated journey of discovery.

He moved from creature to creature and started to murmur to them, a soft stream of words, words that he still refused to utter when anyone except Emilia talked to him, but which were there inside him, unforgotten. "Beetle," he said, "on your red leaf blue body bright red leaf in the forest moth much softer made of dust all you things stay with me and do not be disobedient and when the night comes still stay with me and bee yellow and black you stay but buzz very quietly when the lady is sleeping . . ."

He wanted his bed put close to the wall, within reach of the beetle, the moth and the bee and not so far from one of the dragon-flies that he could not stand on tiptoe on his cot and reach up and touch it. And the conversation with the insects that started the moment Marcus entered the room for the first time went on and on almost without stopping, so that he would wake and begin it immediately and fall asleep still whispering to them in the candle-light. He told them where to fly to and where to hide and whom to sting and how to search the sky for messengers. He asked them to hop off the wall onto his body so that they could be warm in his hand or make a nest in his hair. He counted them: one two three four five six seven spiders one two three four five six seven eight nine ten eleven ladybirds, one ant all alone.

Emilia said late one evening to Kirsten: "I shall use the insect paintings to teach Marcus arithmetic, and he and I shall make up stories about them, so that he will learn new words and new visions of what the world might be, and we shall make drawings of them with charcoal . . ."

Kirsten's expression was cross. "Emilia," she snapped, "you know that Marcus is quite simple and backward, and that with such children it is better to let them alone in their own world, for they will never amount to anything."

"Marcus is simple," said Emilia, "because nobody but I has ever tried to understand him, but why should he remain simple all his life?"

"Because that is his condition."

"But if I can start to teach him, then may not his condition be altered?"

"I do not think it likely."

"Nevertheless, I must try . . ."

"And when, might I ask, will you indulge in this orgy of teaching? What time is available to you outside that which, as my only woman, you are duty bound to give to me?"

Kirsten had begun to flounce about the room, anger starting to course through every vein in her body, right down to the soft blue veins of her delicate feet.

Emilia knew Kirsten well enough by now to recognise the visible signs—the flaring of Kirsten's nostrils, the intense brightness of her eyes, the strange gestures of her hands, which became like the supple, twisting and turning hands of an acrobat or a dancer. She looked at Kirsten calmly, pleadingly, and replied: "Early in the morning, before you are awake, or when you are resting in the long afternoons, then I will teach Marcus."

"That is all very well," snapped Kirsten, "but it might be that I wake early in the morning on the back or rack of some horrible nightmare and need you to comfort me, and then I shall call to you and you will not be there. And would this not be a dereliction of duty to the one to whom you owe so much?"

"I promise," said Emilia, "that I will not neglect my duty towards you. I swear you shall not even notice that I am not there—"

"Of course I will notice that you are not there! Why should I not? I will admit, Emilia, that you are small and sometimes quite like a shadow, but you have never been what I would term invisible to me. On the contrary, not only do I see you, but I also see all that is in you. Never doubt it. I have always, from the very first, seen inside your thoughts. And what I am beginning to perceive is that you care far more for your little ghost of a brother than you do for me!"

Emilia knew she could only protest that this was not so, but that all such protestation would be in vain, because Kirsten had decided to be angry, because she *needed to be angry*, and so the anger had to come out of her and run its violent course. The servants could hear her screaming at Emilia from two floors below and Vibeke Kruse was woken from a reverie of a pie-eating contest by Kirsten's tearful accusations of neglect and betrayal.

Emilia tried to pacify her with words, but the only words Kirsten required were those she herself commanded: "Say you will not do any teaching of Marcus! Say you will not go into that Insect Room to do drawing with him, when it is with me that you once used to draw when we were at Rosenborg!"

But Emilia would not retreat from her plan. So Kirsten began to sob, to pretend that she could not breathe, so horribly was she choked by her misery, and Emilia had to go to her and try to put her arms round her, to find herself pushed away so roughly that she fell backwards against a chest.

"Do not come near me!" screamed Kirsten. "For you are like all the rest of the world who hate and despise me and wish to see me ruined and dead! Oh, Mother of God, where is Otto? Where is the one and only living soul who can find it in his heart to love me?"

"I love you," said Emilia softly.

"But not enough, for then you would not have suggested abandoning me so that you may make pictures of wasps and stories of snails or whatever other horrible creatures slink and scuttle across those walls!"

Emilia waited.

At last, Kirsten said: "I was born with a demon. I was born a veritable insect. My sting will kill me."

Placing one of the servants in her room, in case Kirsten wakes and calls for her, Emilia rises at six, when it is still dark and before any fire has been lit at Boller, and takes a lamp and works with Marcus until the dawn arrives at the window and it is time to begin the normal routine of the day.

He doesn't complain at being woken so early. He does not even seem to notice that it is still dark outside. With his measuring rod, he calculates the distance between a butterfly and the branch on which it will alight, between an earwig and the trumpet lily into which it will crawl. He counts the stripes on the wasps and the spots on the ladybirds, the tracery of veins in the flies' wings and the number of legs on the centipedes. He lists the colours of the flowers and the different names by which they are known.

He begins to copy them, helplessly at first, seeming not to understand that his charcoal will very often make marks that he has not intended, that it is not enough for him to see a thing in his mind for it to appear on the paper.

But Emilia shows him how to proceed very slowly, looking constantly at the object, seeing it again and again and again, so that the eye guides the hand. And, after a while, his drawings take on an unexpected kind of beauty, so that a dragon-fly appears very vast and near, and the world towards which it is flying much smaller and further off, and a feeling of air and movement and space is by this means (all unintended as these means are) present in the picture.

Marcus talks as he works. He tells Emilia that at night he can hear the walls whispering to him and that he knows this is the language of the insects and that if a boy listens to the language of the insects for long enough then he will understand it. And when he can understand it, then the insects "will come to him and obey him."

"If they will 'obey him,' " asks Emilia, "what commands will he give them?"

"Be good. That is a command. And do not wake the Lady Kirsten. And do not dream."

" 'Do not dream'? What are these insects dreaming of, Marcus?"

"Of a plain dreaming of that plain."

"What plain?"

"My plain which is called Beyond Despair where the buffaloes are."

The lessons and the drawings and the voices that he hears in the wall, these things define Marcus's existence now. He no longer cries for his cat. If he wakes in the night, he talks to the insects until their answering whispers lull him to sleep again. He dreams he is a crimson leaf, a bud of blossom. The paintings are more real to him than what he sees outside the window and he is slowly coming to believe that, one day, he will "go into" the world of the insects and live there and be small like them, and shelter from the rain under a mushroom.

Whenever he is with Kirsten or with Ellen and Vibeke, he returns to his habitual silence, so that all three women complain about his continuing strangeness and no longer attempt to speak to him. They are almost as stern with him as Magdalena used to be. They wonder how much longer they can endure him at Boller. Indeed, their mutual detestation of Marcus's irritating ways seems, as the month turns, to create a diminution of the former antagonisms between Kirsten and her mother. Vibeke, tying and untying curling papers in her hair, remarks: "I don't understand why you are both so craven. Marcus Tilsen isn't our responsibility. He should be returned to his father without delay."

Kirsten weeps a little. She stares at her own face in the glass, white and fat and no longer beautiful. She weeps a little more. She brushes her hair so hard that thick strands of it are torn out by the brush. *All life is a torment of one kind or another.* The kernel of anger in her heart against Emilia begins to swell and harden.

It bursts open on a February afternoon.

It reveals itself in ways that even Kirsten did not expect.

Kirsten has closed the curtains of her room against the bitter frost that lingers in the air. She returns her bedchamber to its closed-in state, where no light exists except the firelight and the yellow candles, and in among the flickering shadows she lies down naked in her bed to contemplate the ruins of her life that has no sport in it and no excitement, and no wildness and no love.

She finds her magic quill and begins to console herself by stroking her lips and her nipples with this when there is a knock at the door.

360

She has a vision of her beloved Count Otto Ludwig entering her room, swearing and cracking his whip, and unbuttoning his breeches.

But it is Emilia who comes in and asks her tenderly whether she has need of anything.

Kirsten sits up in the bed. Her lips are wet and her nipples are hard and rosy in the lamplight, and her anger is as hard as the husk of a nut. "And if I have no need of anything," she says, "where will you go and what will you do this afternoon?"

"Well . . ." begins Emilia.

"Do not bother to tell me," says Kirsten, "for I know where you will go. You will go to that horrible Insect Room to be with Marcus."

"Yes," says Emilia. "But only if you have no need—"

"We shall hire some tutor for him! And you shall return to me and be by my side when I need you."

Emilia says nothing. She wears the grey dress she was once so fond of. She pulls a grey shawl round her shoulders.

"I do not sleep," says Kirsten, "so tormented is my spirit. Once you were my true companion, but now you have abandoned me. My hair is falling out of my head! I am in purgatory and you stand by and avert your eyes."

"No . . ." says Emilia. "I'm sorry for you . . ."

"I am not interested in your 'sorrow.' Of what good is that to me? You were 'sorry' for that stupid hen and I declare you lavish more affection upon it than you have ever shown to me!"

At this moment a voice is heard outside the room. It is Marcus calling to Emilia—his old repetitive cry that has never ceased: *Emilia, Emilia, Emilia . . .*

Kirsten Munk, King's Consort, Almost Queen, leaps out of her bed in all her magnificent nakedness, with her wild hair and her nipples like berries and her bush the colour of fire. "Go away!" she yells at Marcus. "Go back to your repulsive insects! Go and be the worm that you are! Emilia is my woman and she has no more time for you."

She slams the door. They hear Marcus begin to cry and Emilia attempts to move past Kirsten, to go to comfort him. But her way is barred.

And it is now that Kirsten feels her anger explode and break. She reaches out and takes Emilia by the shoulders and pulls her to her naked breast, pinioning her against her body and covering her face with kisses. Weeping copiously now, so that both their faces are wet, she tells Emilia that she was never the thing she was meant to be. Kirsten's sobs almost choke her, from so deep within her do they rise up. But she is full of words, too. She does not know what words, what caresses, what storms of tears are going to come, but she feels them all welling up in her and breaking, as a river breaks at the lip of a waterfall. And she knows that she has longed for days and weeks for this release and now it comes.

Emilia struggles to be free of the embrace, but Kirsten is strong and Emilia cannot be free of it, must endure the kisses and the torrent of accusations, must listen and not be able to stop her ears as Kirsten stammers that Emilia was meant to be her consolation for the loss of the Count. She was meant to be her woman and show her womanly love. At night, she was meant to sing her songs and stroke her head and lie down with her and hold her in her arms. She was meant to whisper secrets to her in the darkness and tell her wicked tales that women are not meant to know. She was meant to kiss her lips. She was meant to learn the secrets of the magic quill and what it could do to certain parts of the body. She was meant to bring joy and laughter and bright feelings of ecstasy and love, and all that she has brought is a winter of her own, a remorseless coldness, an insupportable *greyness*, an aura of death!

Kirsten lets go of Emilia at last, pushes her away so that her shawl falls to the ground. And the two women stare at each other. And the stare is such that both Kirsten and Emilia will remember it always, for as long as they live: it is a stare which understands that something irredeemable has been done, something that should never have happened, but which can never be undone and which has altered everything.

Later that afternoon a carriage containing Emilia and Marcus, and such belongings as they both possess, including Marcus's drawings and the speckled hen Gerda, makes its way down the drive and turns left at the end of it, going towards the Tilsen estate. Nobody stands at the door to wave them away and the carriage is soon swallowed up by the February darkness.

Of his lost kingdom of the insects Marcus says: "I was becoming small like them, Emilia, I would have lived under the leaves."

When Emilia and Marcus arrive at the Tilsen house, Johann is out on his horse and Magdalena and Wilhelm are alone in the attic.

Boris and Matti come out of the schoolroom and stare at Emilia and then at Marcus, as if both are ghosts.

Emilia kisses Boris and Matti. Boris says to Marcus: "Otto is my cat now."

"Where is my father?" asks Emilia.

"He thinks Marcus is dead," says Matti. "He searches for him in the snow."

"And where is Magdalena?"

"In the attic. Sometimes, Papa has to lock her in her room."

Emilia says nothing to this. She leads Marcus in, out of the cold, and they all sit down by the parlour fire. Marcus stares silently at his brothers and they stare back. Emilia asks one of the maids to bring hot tea, and when it arrives she warms Marcus's hands on the china cups.

Then, after some while, Wilhelm appears. When he sees Emilia and Marcus, he swears under his breath and goes running back up the stairs.

When Johann Tilsen returns to find Marcus alive and sitting by the parlour fire, he takes his youngest son in his arms and begins to weep, and this weeping of his goes on and on until Boris and Matti cannot bear it for another second and run out of the room. Emilia slowly approaches her father and lays a gentle hand on his shoulders.

Now, Emilia lies in her old bed in her old room and listens to the old familiar crying of the wind.

By her bed is the clock she found in the forest, with time stopped at ten minutes past seven.

She does not know why Magdalena was locked in the attic.

She does not know why Ingmar was sent to Copenhagen.

She cannot predict what world Marcus will enter now.

What she does know is that time itself has performed a loop and returned her to the one place she thought she had left for ever. It has stopped here and will not let her go. Kirsten will not come by in her carriage to beg her to go back to Boller. Emilia's foolish dreams of the English musician are all in the past. She will grow old in the house of her childhood, without her mother, without her father's love. She will die here and one of her brothers will bury her in the shadow of the church, and the strawberry plants, which creep further and wider each year, gobbling up the land, even to the church door, will one day cover everything that remains of her, including her name: *Emilia*.

MEASURING THE ICE

It used to happen when Christian was a boy and the lake at Frederiksborg froze in the heart of winter: the tennis court marker would be sent out onto the ice by King Frederik to measure its depth. He would bore holes in five different places, and Christian remembers watching this man inserting the measuring rod into the holes and then drawing it up and squinting at it, to calculate where the ice ended and the water began.

There was a formality about this measuring of the ice which used to create in the young Christian feelings of intense fascination and excitement, as though the tennis court marker were measuring time itself and would announce how much of it remained and on what day he would become King.

And then, if the ice was pronounced solid enough, the skating would begin. Everyone who worked for the royal household was permitted to join in. The stable boys would be seen dancing arm in arm with the scullery maids; the fencing master would perform a series of dazzling twirls and leaps; Queen Sofie's golden plaits would stream out behind her head; babies were pulled along on little sledges and dogs would try to follow the skaters and go slithering and sliding and rolling about in yelping confusion.

There were a few winters so mild that the lake never froze at all and everybody's skates would remain where they were, in drawers and cupboards, the leather unoiled, the blades unpolished. And at these times, the people of Frederiksborg would agree: "A winter without skating is not a winter. A winter without skating makes the spirit sluggish and brings in the spring too soon."

Now, on a February morning, in this winter of 1630, the King watches from his window as the tennis court marker walks out onto the ice, which has been forming slowly for a week, and begins to bore the holes for his measuring rod. The day is glorious, the trees dark and glistening as the sun melts the night's frost, the sky a soft and innocent blue. It is the kind of day on which the visibility of things makes the world seem as though it had been newly created. And the bright sheen on the silent, frozen lake makes King Christian yearn to be out there, moving and turning on the immaculate whiteness.

He has forgotten the pains in his stomach. And for one strange moment, as the marker walks from one borehole to another, the King can see Bror Brorson, dressed in brown velvet, a boy of twelve who skates with long athletic strides, who goes faster than everybody else, who never tires, who is still there, crossing and recrossing the lake when the sun goes down, when the dusk turns him to shadow and the night obliterates him . . .

"It is good ice," the King is informed. "It is as thick as four loaves of bread."

Christian lets out a shout of pleasure, orders that skates be found for everyone, including Signor Ponti the paper manufacturer and his daughter the Countess. While the King puts on the woollen bonnet he has always worn to protect his hearing from the cold, word goes round the castle: "The skating is going to begin!"

Jens Ingemann is summoned and told to make sure the musicians are warmly dressed, as golden music stands are brought out and set down in a line in the middle of the lake. Again, the sight of these music stands makes the King feel as contented as a child. He enjoys the way they appear to grow out of the frozen water, as though Danish ice had miraculous properties and could nourish music stands in its depths and make them sprout, like gilded saplings, in a single February morning.

Signor Ponti examines the skate blades on the boots he has been given and shakes his head. To Francesca he says: "No, no. To put all my weight on a little edge like this? I am a man of commerce, not a fool."

"No, Papa," replies Francesca, who, in the first years of her marriage, used to skate on the ponds at Cloyne with Johnnie O'Fingal, "you'll be surprised how well they will bear you up. You may hold on to me at first, until you're accustomed to it, and then you'll be off and gliding away."

But Ponti is not convinced. He says he will come and watch, and prays that his daughter will not fall over and break her leg or her ankle. He does not wish her to go hobbling into her future life.

As to Francesca, to skate on the lake within sight of her lover, while the sun shines, while she can feel her lover's eyes upon her: this prospect is so enthralling that she can barely wait to join the stream of people, led by the King, going down to the lakeside. She puts on her black velvet cloak, the velvet hat. As she looks at herself in her dressing glass, she wonders how much longer this beauty of hers will last.

But as she arrives at the lake, Francesca puts this thought from her mind. She is a woman who, since her sufferings with O'Fingal, has resolved to be happy. So now there is only the brilliant morning, the notes of music cascading into the air, the snickering of the skate blades on the perfect ice, the infectious laughter of the King, the beauty of Peter Claire, and a feeling of exhilaration as she moves and turns.

As he plays, Peter Claire notices how gracefully the Danes skate— as though the blades were part of their feet. Even the King's chancellor and the other elderly members of the nobility appear nimble on the ice. And the King himself, so heavy now and beginning to be sluggish in his movements, seems suddenly younger and lighter.

As the musicians came out onto the frozen lake, Jens Ingemann took from a pocket a folded square of cloth, snapped it open like a conjuror and set it down beneath his feet, so that he would not be standing directly on the slippery ice. But Peter Claire, Krenze, Rugieri and the rest have to manage as best they can on the unstable surface and Peter Claire notes the tension in all their faces. While the skaters seem as steady as dancers, the music makers are persecuted by a constant fear that they are about to fall over.

"There should be chairs," says Pasquier.

"And furs to keep our legs warm," says Rugieri.

But Jens Ingemann only scoffs at them: "Chairs and furs? What are you? A huddle of old crones? Even the pettish Dowland did not ask for a chair on the ice!"

So they have no choice but to play on, their legs stiff, trying to balance, and the sun climbs as high as it can reach in this deep part of winter, giving a clarity to the scene that hurts the eyes of Peter Claire. He wishes he were not here. He would like to exchange this too-bright day, in which Francesca glides in circles round him, for a different place: the place where Emilia Tilsen has her existence.

But how is he to arrive there? Though he has held in his hands the very documents Kirsten wishes him to steal and might even be able to write down from memory the complicated sum of the King's debts, he also knows that he is incapable of betraying the King to his enemies. He looks at His Majesty now, going round and round in his homely woollen hat, the dough of his face folded into a smile and two bright specks of colour starting in his cheeks, like sweet plums placed in the dough by some cook's affectionate hands. It cannot be done, he says to himself. Alas, it cannot be done.

March is come in and the snow has begun to melt.

Today I saw that some new little yellow flower had dared to open its head in the old, damp grass, but I do not know the name of it. They say it is from flowers that bees manufacture honey, but I refuse to tire my mind with worrying about how they do this. Some people, such as the King my husband, are forever asking questions about Nature, such as "What is the greatest distance that a Flea can hop?" or "Why is it that Owls can see in the dark?" But I see no gain to be had from burdening myself with any Knowledge that cannot be Useful to me. If someone could show me how to leap great distances or see when there is no light in the sky, why then I would be grateful, for these gifts might serve my Purposes. But Mere Understanding for its own sake only exhausts the Mind and I have noticed that in Denmark the so-called Scholars do seem to be the most melancholy people on this earth, which observation prompts me to think that all Useless Knowledge must fester in the brain and so bring in an Inevitable Anguish from which there is no relief.

But of Anguish I surely have my share?

I do not think I have ever known any Season as horrible as this one.

I am endeavouring to put Absolutely from my mind everything that I do not wish to think about, viz., the Departure of Emilia, and to concentrate only and utterly on securing for myself some Future which shall be more agreeable to me than this maddening Present.

No reply has come from the English Lutenist. I am surprised that he is so faint of Heart. I conclude that he cares nothing for Emilia. Indeed, he has perhaps found himself a New Mistress and put from him all thoughts of marrying a person who keeps a hen for a pet and who is tied by her heart-strings to her lunatic child of a Brother. And I would not blame him. The only Irritation is that, in consequence, I do not yet have in my possession those documents with which I can bring pressure to bear on King Gustav of Sweden and I do not see now how I am to get them, unless I go to Frederiksborg myself and pilfer them. Would I were a Flea and could become Small and hop there in a trice, or an Owl flying through the night and seeing everything there was to see in the sleeping world!

I have lived so long without my Lover now that I declare that there are days when I am almost Resigned to his Absence. But in between my bouts of Resignation, I am furious to hold him in my arms. I rage for his touch. I bite my pillow and mutilate my Sorcerer's Quill. And at these times I know that I must find some means—however devious—to come to him in Sweden.

And so I reflect that sometimes, because this Society is mired up in a slurry of Lies and Pretence, the most efficacious way of making a Bargain is to Pretend that one has in one's Possession that very Thing *which one does not have*. For People are no more suspicious than they are gullible. They can suspect that which is True and believe that which is False. They tend to see *that which they wish to see*.

Accordingly, and in a Mood of Bravery, I sit down at my escritoire and compose an audacious letter to the King of Sweden. I tell him that I hold in my hands "certain documents pertaining to His Majesty King Christian's Finances" which would no doubt be of great value to him, but that it is too dangerous to consign such Papers to any Letter-bearer, for fear that they fall into the maw of thieves. And I continue thus:

> If, therefore, Your Majesty would grant me Safe Passage into Sweden, where I would desire to live and have my Being, now that I am so much Reviled in Denmark, then I shall bring to you these Secret Papers, and I do declare that Your Majesty will live to thank me for what Things they shall reveal to you.
>
> Kirsten Munk, King's Consort

I am, on reflection, mightily pleased with this letter and I do not know why I did not think of this Stratagem before. For once I am in Sweden, then surely I shall find some way to remain there, with Count Otto Ludwig, even if, when I am at last in the presence of

King Gustav, I have no Secret Papers to show him after all. I shall
say they were lost in the Sound or that part of the ship caught fire
and burned them, or that they were stolen from me as I travelled
from Jutland. It makes no difference what I shall say. For I have
knowledge in plenty about the King my husband which shall delight the ear of his Old Enemy. And what I do not have, I shall
manufacture. I shall become a bee, turning useless little flowers
into Honey.

I am not the only one with recondite Ploys and Schemes.

My mother and Vibeke are so bursting with their Plan that they
walk about grinning and smiling and letting pass between them Secret Looks, which cause me such profound annoyance that I break
down at last and say to my mother: "What is this infernal Plan of
yours? For I do earnestly wish you would Get On With It instead of
skulking around this house like fat Vixens who have gobbled up a
Goose Farm!"

But of course, they will not tell me. They are enjoying their Secret too intensely. And perhaps they fear that I shall try to Foil
them—which indeed I would, if I could ascertain what Thing it
was they were about.

All I know is that Vibeke is being taught to master her new
Teeth, so that they do not click and clatter when she eats, nor fall
out into her pudding. And she is having Lessons of some kind, supervised by Ellen, who never was nor is now a patient Teacher, and
so I note that Vibeke arrives at supper very often with her eyes red
and her handkerchief wet, and sits silently at the meal or else answers with little answers when my Mother speaks to her. This
causes me some mirth and pleasure, but alas, these Moods of Misery
do not seem to last very long and the next day Vibeke's smile is
back on her face, as though it had never been off it.

Her efforts to become Slim have resulted in Failure. She is as fat
and greedy as ever she was; her flesh makes bulges in the dresses my
mother had made for her, and over her silver and gold necklaces
fall a quantity of chins. But nothing more is said about this. What

is more, I note that Other New Garments begin to appear on Vibeke's corpulent form—and these trimmed with Fur or Ornaments and costing my Mother great quantities of Money. "I am surprised," I say, "at the limitlessness of your Funds. And at the narrow way in which you choose to spend them. You know that I, too, should like some new dresses, but it seems you never think of me or make me any Offers."

But these words have no effect upon her. She tells me I have been "spoiled all my life" and that I have wasted all my Portion and let slip through my fingers everything that I once had. And the fact that this is True makes it no less hurtful to me. Mothers should not say such things to their Daughters, but rather strive to help them in their hours of travail. I tell Ellen she is a Wicked and Unnatural Woman and that the day is coming when I shall throw her out of Boller, just as I threw Emilia out, because I cannot abide to be near people who *do not love me*. But she only smiles her Vixen smile. "Do not fear, Kirsten," says she. "Vibeke and I shall leave for Copenhagen very shortly and then you will be Quite Alone."

This realisation of my coming Utter Loneliness engenders in me a most cruel Sadness.

I am a Person who cannot endure to be alone. I declare I was born crying out for Company and laughter.

What am I to do if King Gustav refuses me passage into Sweden?

I think that I shall kill myself. I have my little white pot of Poison, but I do admit that to take this makes me tremble because I do not know what shall happen afterwards or whether it be Fatal Absolutely or whether I might vomit it up again and lie on the floor in torment, only to be returned to Life after all. The risk of this might be great. I believe I shall have to go to some melancholy Scholar and ask him, whose Brain is stuffed with Knowledge-in-Waiting, what means have been discovered of taking one's own Life with Certainty but without the inconvenience of Pain and Suffering. I cannot quite imagine what these means might be. Except that I might shoot myself in the mouth with a Musket. But I wonder whether my arms are long enough, so that I can hold up the Musket and point it at myself and not inadvertently blast off my left leg or make a mighty hole in the wall? And I reflect therefore that although Death, in its Absoluteness, appears to us a Simple Matter, it may not be very simple after all, especially for those who seek it, because whatever the human heart craves and seeks, this very thing may be the one that is denied it.

And so I endure bouts of Pure Misery and Sorrow, such as I have never known in all my thirty-one years.

I find no consolation in my baby, Dorothea. For, although she resembles the Count in her colouring, she is not like him in any other way. She is merely Like All Other Babies, and that is: ugly, foul-smelling, cross-eyed, mewling, farting, uncomfortable, angry and Wretched. And when I declared before she was born that I would love and cherish her, I do think that I had temporarily forgotten what a Baby is and how my spirit is so vexed by every one of them that I could happily put them in a fish kettle and set them to boil on the range and afterwards eat their tender flesh for my supper.

I used to find consolation in Emilia—in her talk and in her Sweetness and in our little Pastimes together—but she is gone.

Last night, catching sight of the two painted eggs she gave me on Christmas Day, I took them up to cast them away with the waste paper and the spoiled writing quills and the dead ash of the fire. But then this act of throwing them out began to choke me, so that I felt sentimental tears come to my eyes, and so I only put them in a drawer, among our old paintings of flowers that we did at Rosenborg on summer evenings and which I saved, though I know not why.

Of course, I understand that, by this time, the eggs are rancid within the shell, but their putrefaction is still concealed by their sweet painted Exterior. And I wish to remark upon this to Someone and observe how the condition of the eggs resembles the condition of so many People, who may be beautiful of face, as I once was, and all corrupted within.

But there is no one at Boller to whom I can make such observations. Neither in my Mother's head nor in Vibeke's is to be found one grain of Philosophical Curiosity.

CONCERNING SHEETS AND DITCHES

At that moment when the winter is almost ended and the herons return to the lake at Frederiksborg, at that moment when spring sends one or two hardy messengers to announce its arrival, yet before it has quite arrived, King Christian likes to ride out into his kingdom to see what is happening on the land.

He travels beyond the regions owned by the crown (in which serfdom has been outlawed and the peasants are paid in money or in kind for their labour) into those great swathes of fields and forests still in the hands of the nobility, where landlords do as they please and reward their workers as the inclination takes them, so that on one estate men and women may thrive and be warm and on the adjoining land they may starve and have nothing.

King Christian would like to have passed a universal law against Vornedskab—the state of serfdom in Denmark—but his power is not absolute like the Kings of England; no law can become law until ratified by the Rigsråd. And it is the landowning nobility who sit in the Rigsråd and always contrive to remember, when such a law sits in draft form before them, the great quantity of dalers or the vast amount of corn or sheep or pigs they would be forced to sacrifice to keep in unaccustomed comfort men who were born to toil and suffer, and were docile in consequence, and who might now become demanding and rebellious. And so Vornedskab remains and all that the King can do is to make these yearly journeys to see how cruel the winter has been and to sprinkle skillings on the melting snow.

He takes only two or three in attendance with him and puts up

373

at small inns or in the houses of the clergy. In these places, in the smell of their low timbers and in their strange absence of light, he remembers travelling about the kingdom with his parents and looking in the workshop of carpenters, engravers and bookbinders. To those with him, he remarks: "Kings should travel and pry. They should be as inquisitive as rats. Or they will learn nothing."

This year, three men accompany him, and one of these is Peter Claire.

The days are bright. "In certain conditions of sunlight," the King observes one morning, "that which would trouble us attains a borrowed beauty."

He points to the thatch of a low cottage, the early sun on the damp reeds making them shine like silver. "Inside will be a floor made of mud," says Christian, "and a fire gone out, and every day shall feel like an eternity to those who dwell there."

"Shall we go in, Sir?" asks Peter Claire.

"Yes. We shall go in. We shall drop a stone into their pool of time."

No face appears at the small window as they approach the cottage, but they notice, at the turn in the road, a wooden crate set out and on the crate a little selection of objects marked *For Sale*. There is a broken pot, a wheel, the worn head of a broom, a stone pestle crudely made and a twist of string.

King Christian dismounts and picks up the wheel, from which one spoke is missing, and stares at it for a long time. Now, he thinks, the poor of Denmark have nothing complete with which to barter. They live from bits and parts of things. "And who," he says aloud, "ever passes this way to buy a broom head or a bit of twine?"

The cottage dweller is a man who lives alone with a cat. He grows turnips in the small plot of ground the landlord has given him, "for turnips grow economically, shoulder to shoulder under the frost, and every bit of them may be eaten." Then, with a smile, he says: "The cat belonged to my wife, who is in prison. She was a tabby cat, but grown quite white with the eating of the turnips!" And he laughs and the laugh turns to a cough and he spits into the embers of the fire.

The King sits down on the one chair, which is a rocking chair, and Peter Claire and the other gentlemen stand and blink in the low light, which every moment seems to falter, as though the sun were descending instead of rising to its noonday. The peasant apologises to the King that all he can offer him is water out of the rain butt. The King replies that water is the element in which Denmark floats and which gives him hope, and the man laughs again, almost doubles up with his mirth, and then coughs once more and spits once more and shakes his head, as though the thing which had been said might be the funniest jest he had ever heard told.

King Christian sips the icy rainwater from a wooden cup. He looks at the peasant's wrists and his hands the colour of bone protruding from the sleeves of a knitted jerkin so alive with holes the mice might still be scampering through the wool. "Tell me," says the King, "how your wife came to be in prison."

The man points to his bed, which is a pile of straw, no more and no less, and again this obstinate laughter of his wells up in him and sears his lungs. "Sheets!" He guffaws. "She stole sheets from Herr Kjaedegaard's laundry! Oh, but not to barter, Sir, not for any profit, but only to know what it felt like to sleep between them!" The King nods gravely as the cottar is seized by a violent coughing and choking.

Christian plucks at Peter Claire's sleeve and tells him to play something "soft and quiet for this suffering man," so he adopts his habitual leaning posture over his lute and begins a slow pavan, and the peasant, whose life has no music in it except the singing of the birds, stares at him in awe and crosses his arms in front of his chest, as though he fears his heart might escape through his rib-cage.

When the music ends the King rises and the peasant kneels, his lungs quietened by the pavan, and kisses the King's outstretched hand in its fine kid glove.

"Those objects displayed for sale on your crate," says King Christian, "will you sell them to me?"

A smile returns to the man's face, threatens to break into laughter. "What would Your Majesty need with an old wheel, a length of string?"

"Well, let us see. The wheel to remind me of destiny? The string to measure my own height and girth, to see whether I am grown larger in my kingdom, or begun to shrink?"

"Ha! That's a fine story, Sir. That's a piece of convolution."

"You do not believe me?"

"I believe you, Your Majesty. But only because I know what oddities lie in the mind. My wife was going to return the sheets, when she had had her night between them, but the justices of the *Herredag* did not believe her. But they should have believed her and then she would not be in prison and forsaking her cat."

Now it is the King's turn to smile. "What is her name?" he asks.

"Frederika Manders. And she slept on straw all her days and did not complain and now she still sleeps on straw in her dungeon in Copenhagen, but whether she complains or not I cannot say, nor whether she is living or not. This I cannot say either."

The King puts a purse into Manders's hands. He announces that his wife Frederika will be pardoned and sent back here to her plot of turnips, if indeed she is alive. And then, before Manders can stammer his thanks, the royal party walk out into the bright light of the March morning and the peasant watches, grinning, as the men take up the wheel, the head of the broom, the broken pot, the stone pestle and the piece of twine and stow these things away in their carriage, and then they are gone.

That night, by the fireside of an inn, where the rooms have a lingering smell of horses, which the King finds agreeable, and when everyone but he and Peter Claire and the landlord have gone to bed, Christian turns the stone pestle over and over in his wide hands. He has been drinking for five hours. "The pestle is quite large," he says. "Not as perfectly rounded as a grinding pestle should be. It might have served as a cudgel. Manders, for all we know, killed his wife with this and invented the story of the sheets."

The logs of the fire smoulder and fall and flare again. A clock ticks. The landlord wipes the beer slops from the table tops and begins to sweep the sawdust from the floor. This man longs to whistle, but knows he must remain silent until the King at last retires to sleep.

"Many times, you see," says King Christian, "I imagined putting an end to Kirsten's life. I could perfectly envisage taking her head in my hands and crushing it against stone . . ."

Peter Claire says nothing.

"She met her Count at Werden," the King goes on, "when we were still at war. I wanted her to be with me while I was fighting and so she was at Werden that night, when I had fallen into a ditch of thorns and could not get out, for I had broken my foot, and the ditch was deep so that I was concealed in it and not taken out of it until nightfall.

"Count Otto Ludwig fought on my side. Our army relied on German mercenaries, we had to pay with gold and silver. And he was one of them—who fought for gold and not for Denmark's dignity and faith.

"And that evening at Werden, I could not dance, because of the pain to my foot. And so my wife danced with the Count. And when I saw her dancing with this man, I knew that whatever she had felt for me was transferred to him—in that one night—and that where I had been rich an hour before, suddenly I was poor. That was when it first came to me—that I might kill her—and perhaps I should have done it then and spared myself four long years of pain."

The King is now half lying on a wooden settle. Peter Claire is perched on a stool not far from the King's knees. The King belches, then looks at him intently as he asks: "Must love always end in a ditch? What do you believe, Peter Claire?"

Peter Claire's mind conjures up Emilia Tilsen's face. "I believe," he says distractedly, "that it is constantly subject to change."

King Christian is still staring, without blinking, at Peter Claire, and the lutenist expects him now to question him on his own feelings (perhaps those for the Irish Countess who so lately charmed everyone at court?), but the King veers from this, gulps more wine and says: "Those sheets. When Manders and his wife lay down in them, did they turn to each other or were they each contented simply *by the feel of the sheets?*"

Peter Claire is about to reply, when King Christian cuts him off. "The answer is unknowable, of course."

The King closes his eyes, as if he did not wish to think about the great quantity of unknowable things in the world. Then he opens them again and says: "Kirsten has asked me to send her the black boys. I know why she wants her slaves. I see right through her, to the marrow of her bones. She wants to see what it feels like to sleep between them!"

The King's roaring laugh is hollow and loud, and startles the innkeeper out of his sawdust reveries. And, still shaking with wild amusement, His Majesty's huge body rolls slowly off the settle onto the floor, the wine spilling and splashing his doublet. He brings up a gobbet of spittle and aims it at the fire.

Peter Claire and the innkeeper help King Christian to bed, where he falls asleep at once.

The English lutenist goes to his own room, where the hard bed is too short for him, so that he cannot stretch out properly. He lies in the dark, with his knees drawn up to his stomach, thinking that for Emilia Tilsen this bed would be exactly the right size.

LIMBO

As the King continues to travel northwards, so Ellen Marsvin and Vibeke Kruse at last make their departure from Boller and begin their long journey to Frederiksborg.

In the jolting coach, Ellen looks at Vibeke, already pale with sickness, and wonders whether her plan will come to fruition or whether, after all she has expended in time and money on Frøken Kruse—on dresses and calligraphy lessons and ivory teeth—their combined hopes will be dashed.

But Ellen Marsvin is a woman of courage. The idea that the plan may fail and that she will then be forced back upon the meagre resources that she already possesses does not frighten her so much as *intrigue* her. Whatever hand life deals her, she will shape that hand to what advantage she can. Part of her longs to find herself, like Jesus Christ, in the wilderness, with nothing surrounding her but stones and scrub, and then, by her own resourcefulness, to find some means of survival—preferably that very means that nobody but she would have thought of. She would contrive to make jam out of bark. Her daughter, her servants and her friends would have imagined her dead, but she would not be dead. She would walk out of the wilderness and back into life as though nothing had happened at all.

It is Vibeke, not Ellen, who dreads humiliation and failure. And this anxiety, combined with the sufferings of her stomach, makes every moment of this voyage a torment to her. She stares up at the underbellies of the soft white clouds. She longs to unfasten her clothes, remove her teeth and lie down on a cloud and never wake until her marvellous future lies neatly spread out before her. She feels angry with Ellen Marsvin for having embroiled her in a scheme destined to falter and come to grief. She cannot remember ever having felt so wretched.

"Endure, my dear," says Ellen, as they board ship at Horsens. "No destination is ever reached without a little suffering."

But the crossing is rough and Vibeke watches the contents of her stomach float away on the black waves and feels her skin become old, like the skin of a corpse. She imagines dying in this cold sea world, in this salt limbo that divides one part of Denmark from another, and feels that this is where she has always been—in some interim place between departure and destination. She served Kirsten only in expectation of some better employment that never came. She submitted to Ellen's regimes only in the belief that Ellen's plan would make everything worthwhile, and now she does not know whether it will bring her what she hopes for or leave her with nothing. And in some corner of her being not preoccupied by bilberry cakes and vanilla syllabubs, she hoped for love. But on this subject, too, Ellen was always severe. "Vibeke," she would say sternly, "love does not enter into it."

The ship presses onwards, billowing in the westerly winds.

The sea-birds follow: a raucous, restless choir, grey-and-white against the white of the sky.

PART THREE

SILENT SPRING, 1630

KING CHARLES I OF ENGLAND MAKES A REQUEST

He enjoys standing still.

He likes to align himself at a certain window in Whitehall Palace, with the morning sun beginning to be warm upon the glass, and look down and watch the scurrying of the people in the court-yard below. Sometimes a man or woman will look up, because it has become known that this is how the King may be glimpsed, mo-tionless as a shadow in the tall window.

Conversations about this begin all over the palace all the time:

"Did you see him?"

"Once, I saw him."

"What is he thinking?"

"How can one know?"

He did not master the art of walking until the age of seven. Though now, at thirty, he holds himself graciously, there is in his walk some memory of those labours and humiliations of his child-hood, a kind of hesitancy that is not quite a limp but more a visible *disinclination* to put one foot in front of the other.

At the window, he does not move and he does not speak. The palace courtiers know better than to interrupt him when his back is so resolutely turned upon the room. They know that this condition of stillness and silence is consoling to his spirit. For just as walking remains uncomfortable to him, so expressing himself in plain words is very hard for him. It isn't that he does not know, in his head, what he wishes to say; it is simply that what he wishes to say is not what he is able to utter. He can talk to himself with absolute clarity and eloquence. And as with himself, so with God, whom he imagines as a near relation, privy to all the quirks and habits of his mind. But to express himself to his subjects—this is arduous. Sometimes, he will even stammer.

As to the thoughts, the aspirations, the endeavours or even the genius of ordinary men, King Charles I of England prefers to be shown the *fruit* of these—the perfected mathematical equation, the sonnet whose beat is as steady as a pulse, the portrait that is finished and complete to its last thread of imaginary lace, the musical performance that is devoid of all hesitation or flaw—rather than to witness the struggles of composition. A man's vision, before it has achieved its intended form, habitually expresses itself in confused strivings. And these the King does not wish to observe. He is able to admire only what has been distilled into art and set before him. Then, in silence, he will often marvel at what he sees or hears. His State rooms are filled with the works of the Renaissance masters. His love for the paintings of Caravaggio verges upon worship. He will sometimes point to an exquisitely rendered outstretched hand, the light upon a bowl of fruit, and, wordlessly, invite others to lower their eyes or bow their knee before this artist's genius.

In the swirling, chaotic world of London's streets and wharves, a world from which silence and stillness are almost entirely absent, copies of a Puritan pamphlet censoring *Nonesuch Charles squandering millions of pounds on vanities and old rotten pictures and broken-nosed marbles* circulate from hand to hand, but most of them are dropped by design or accident, and trampled into the mud or picked up by the breeze and blown onto the water, and so no whisper of their contents has yet reached this diffident, fastidious man, alone with his own divinity.

And it must be said that were it one day to reach him, he would consider it of no account whatsoever. It is his belief that a sovereign and his subjects are "clean different things," the one always unknowable to the many. He is King because he has been chosen by God and none can unsay this and none can criticise his actions. The actions of pamphleteers trouble him less—far less—than the few motes of dust he occasionally finds on the surface of his dressing glass. He dislikes dust. He tries to ensure that his fingers never touch it.

His gaze travels the length of his long nose and comes to rest on the courtyard, where a lime tree has been planted, where people pass and repass on errands of their own devising. He savours the moment. He wonders if he will not write an ode entitled "In Praise of Windows."

The man waiting to see him, on a morning in March 1630, is his ambassador to Denmark, Sir Mark Langton Smythe.

When King Charles at last turns round and re-enters a world in which it is called upon him to move and speak, Ambassador Langton Smythe is smiling and bowing. (The smile, the bow, the continual stretching of the facial muscles, the frequent bending of the spine and awkward extending of the leg: the lot of the subject might possibly be perceived as an exhausting one, thinks the King, if such perceptions were ever required—which they are not.)

He seats himself on one of his many brocaded thrones and invites the Ambassador to sit down opposite him. He remembers all at once that he likes this man, who was a favourite of his mother's, and so he feels his throat and his tongue relax and ventures a question, over which he does not stammer at all: "How is our uncle, the King of Denmark?"

Langton Smythe replies that King Christian is away from court, on his annual tour of the nobility's estates, and that he is still waiting for the merchants of Hamburg to pay him for Iceland. At which King Charles (who imagines Iceland as a desert of glass upon which snow falls perpetually, like dust) nods gravely and wonders aloud: "May this place be worth enough to pay all our uncle's heavy debt?"

Ambassador Langton Smythe shakes his head, saying that he doubts whether this money will ever arrive in King Christian's treasury, and he informs the King of England that this is why he is returned from Copenhagen: to plead for a little loan. "One hundred thousand pounds, perhaps?" he suggests. "To give your uncle some respite, Sir. To let him begin to put everything in order."

Langton Smythe understands how well loved, in King Charles's vocabulary, is the word "order" and that it might even have quasi-magical properties when carefully placed within a sentence. But now he sees the King arrange his long white hands into a thoughtful steeple in front of his face, and he does not know what this gesture signifies.

He dare say nothing more. Silence arrives in the room. The only sound is the crackling and spitting of the fire.

This waiting for the King to speak or waiting to know His Majesty's mind is a phenomenon well recognised by all who have dealings with him. Certain young courtiers are known to practise in secret, sitting for moments of long duration without moving, yawning, fidgeting, sneezing or letting escape from them the least sign of impatience. But all find it painful. "His dogs move about freely," the youthful Lord Wetlock-Blundall has remarked crossly, "but we are expected to turn into sphinxes!"

And it is perhaps three or four minutes now before the King makes a reply to Langton Smythe. In such a time a carriage might travel a mile, a musketeer fire and reload his weapon twenty-five times, a laundress lather several shirt collars and the moon change by a fraction its position in the sky. But of course, the Ambassador does not appear to fret. He merely waits and the waiting becomes his whole existence.

At last, the King says: "We are sympathetic. The fondness we have for the King of Denmark makes us so. But we are not, on this occasion, inclined to make any gift without asking for something in return. What do you think our uncle might be willing to offer?"

Langton Smythe had not anticipated such a question. Now it is his turn to plunge the room back into silence, while he searches hastily for an answer. For no reason that he can determine, his thoughts fly to the summer long gone and the concert in the garden at Rosenborg, the beauty of the music played there and King

Christian's pride in his orchestra, and so he seizes upon this. "It might be . . ." he stammers, "it might be that your uncle would lend you . . . or even *give to you* one or other of his musicians."

"His musicians? Are they renowned?"

"Yes, Sir. The sound they make has an excellent perfection which Your Majesty would instantly recognise."

King Charles fixes the Ambassador with a cold eye. "Such perfection must necessarily depend upon the entire *ensemble*. Are you telling us that our uncle would give me all of them?"

Langton Smythe looks helpless for a moment. "No . . ." he ventures at last. "I do not think he would, Sir. Yet there is one, a lute player, an Englishman, who makes a sound very pure in the solo . . . and he . . ."

"An English lutenist? Not kin to Dowland, we hope?"

"No, Your Majesty. His name is Mr. Claire."

At the word "Claire," something rare happens to the King's features: they compose themselves into a smile. Just as the word "Caravaggio" (in suggesting to him caravans and voyages under southern suns) seems perfect for the ultimate master of light, so, he thinks, does the word "Claire" (by its association with clarity, brightness and moonshine) fit a lute player admirably. "Very good," he says. "This is of interest to us. Shall you return to Denmark and ask our uncle if he will send us Mr. Claire, or shall we write to him ourself?"

Ambassador Langton Smythe feels suddenly uncomfortable in his chair. He is aware that perhaps he has suggested something foolish, something delicate that should never have been mentioned and which might even cause a rift in the friendship between the two kings. And in any quarrel of this kind he, the Ambassador, would be sure to be blamed and, if blamed, then sent away from office and be stripped of his annual stipend, his house and his allowance for claret.

He experiences a sudden flush of heat to his face and neck at the thought of these calamities. He wants to unsay what he has said. But it is too late. King Charles has risen, thus ending the audience, and is already crossing the room to return to his favoured

position at the window. He informs the Ambassador that he himself will write to his uncle "requesting the pawning of Mr. Claire to
us, for as handsome a sum of money as our purse can afford," and
then wishes him good-day.

FROM COUNTESS O'FINGAL'S NOTEBOOK: *LA DOLOROSA*

We have arrived in a land of forests.

I did not know so many trees could grow together so thickly for
so many deep, impenetrable miles. And the perfume of these firs as
the snow melts away from them and the darkness of them and the
blacker darkness underneath them makes me think them an extraordinary phenomenon, such as I have never before witnessed.

I tell my father that I am sure the air of these forests is the
sweetest air a man could breathe, but he is not interested in air.
What he sees when he looks at these dark woods is the most marvellous paper he has ever manufactured. He thinks only of his new
mill and how it may be the most productive mill in all of Europe
and how his *Ponti Numero Uno* will soon be the only paper used in
every salon from Copenhagen to London, from Paris to Rome, et
cetera.

The site where the Ponti mill will be established is so excellent
a place that it seems almost a pity that the mill is to become a real
entity there and not remain a vision in my father's mind. For I
know only too well that the vision of a thing is almost always superior to the thing itself because, in the vision, the thing is laid effortlessly upon what is already there and all the messy interim of its
making is conveniently put by.

The site borders a swiftly flowing river, going from the north to
the south, and the felled trees will be floated down to the mill
on the current of the water. I ask my father how they will float in
winter, when the river may be frozen, but he has already considered
this matter and replies that all the felling will be done in summer
and the tree trunks put into barns to be stored for the day when the

Ponti machinery grinds them to pulp and reconstitutes them as sheets of matchless paper. He speaks about this as though it were all to be quite soundless and easy, as though the fir trunks would slip into the river of their own volition and rise up again, like soldiers who sleep soundly in their barn billet, until called upon to sacrifice themselves for the great glory of the name *Ponti*.

But I do not make this observation to my dear papa. We stand together on the bank of this river, where patches of snow lie in wondrous separated crystals here and there on the grass, and I see a heron on the far bank, watching us. And when my father catches sight of this heron, he suddenly says: "The lutenist is charming, Francesca, but do not dream of marriage to him. Marry Sir Lawrence de Vere and you and the children shall be warm and safe all your days." And the heron flies away with a fish in its yellow beak.

We put up at a poor inn, where the wind comes through the walls and the beds are damp.

I cannot sleep for the cold and melancholy of the place, and think of my children, far away in Ireland with Lady Liscarroll and her falcons. And then I think of Johnnie O'Fingal lying in his grave and the sorrow and strangeness of his sufferings, which were more than a good man should have had to bear. And fear for the unknowable condition of life spreads through me like a fever in the darkness.

My thoughts return to what my father said to me on the riverbank and I confess that, in this cold and mournful place, I do find myself longing for some certainty, for some future that will not be snatched away from me.

Into my mind comes an image of Sir Lawrence de Vere, with his fields and woods at Ballyclough and his fine collection of Dutch clocks. Still handsome at forty-nine, he smells lightly of pepper and his hands are strong and warm, and I know that he yearns to be my protector. I confess I do not yet love him, but surely love may sometimes exist *in the future tense?*

I get out of my damp bed and light a lamp, and take up a sample of the *Numero Uno*. On this, in a careful hand, yet proceeding quickly lest I am tempted to change my mind, I write the following letter:

To Sir Lawrence de Vere
Ballyclough in the South of Ireland

My dear Sir Lawrence,

I am writing to you from the northerly part of Denmark, which they call Jutland.

I am encircled by forests. The great extent of these woods I cannot fathom, but they go on from horizon to horizon and the sun has a deal of trouble to rise above the tops of the trees in the mornings and, as the afternoons go on, seems to think always and only of descending into them again, as though the forests and not the sky were its preferred habitation, or else a cage where it understands it must for ever live.

In such a place, a man could lose himself and walk all his life and never be found. And it is this thought of how I myself might remain for ever encircled by these dark thickets if I do not follow the path laid out for me that prompts me now to write to you.

You did me the greatest honour in asking me to become your wife. That I requested a little time in which to consider my answer you will not think ill-mannered of me nor reflecting in any wise fears that I could not love you nor make you happy. I asked for time that I might savour your proposal in sweet secrecy while embarked upon my wanderings in Denmark, that I might wake with it at first light and hold it to me when my candle is blown out and I lie alone in the darkness.

And so it has been. Your proposal has been my dearest companion all the days of my travels. Indeed, were it now to be withdrawn, I would find myself returned to that state of solitary unhappiness it is so difficult for the human heart to

bear. And so I ask you, dear Sir Lawrence, do not withdraw
it! Rather, repeat it to me, that I may hear the pretty syllables of it a second time, and you shall have my answer and
my answer shall be yes.

From your admiring friend,
Francesca O'Fingal

After the letter is written, I feel a marvellous drowsiness coming
upon me and, in spite of the wind howling, I fall into a sleep so
deep that it is late before I can be roused from it. And I dream of
Ireland. I dream of the pink shells, like babies' toes, you find on the
beaches at Cloyne.

PICTURES OF THE NEW WORLD

No sooner is baby Ulla weaned than Magdalena Tilsen discovers
that she is expecting another child. She does not know whether its
father is Johann or his son Wilhelm.

She knows that she is at the very summit of her daring. With
Emilia and Marcus returned to the household, she can no longer let
Wilhelm come to her in her attic or anywhere else in the house,
not even the linen closet. But when she tells him this, he says that
if he cannot continue to fornicate with her he will kill her. He
owns a knife. He will plunge his knife into her breast.

He finds an old barn, beyond the fruit fields, where nothing is
stored any more and no one comes, and where rats screech from
under the walls. It is neither comfortable nor warm, but it is dark
and secret, and smells of the earth and the secretions of the rats,
and what occurs there with Magdalena is as thrilling to Wilhelm as
anything he has ever known or believes he will know. Yet afterwards he feels ill, a casualty of some external event in which his
will played no part. And it is true that he is growing thin. Johann
notices this and tries to make sure his plate is piled high at mealtimes.

As to Magdalena, she keeps the fact of her pregnancy to herself for the time being, fearing how Wilhelm might react to it. Johann no longer locks her in the attic and is grown kinder towards her than in the time immediately following Ingmar's departure. Yet she begins to sense that something else is occurring: Johann's passion for her is diminishing in ways which suggest not merely a period of diminution followed, as before, by a resurgence, but a cooling which will be final and permanent.

The signs are unmistakable. Where she could once call her husband to her with the merest word or glance or twitch of her skirt, now she watches him *turn away from these overtures*. His desire for solitude and separateness—always part of his nature—seems, every day, to be increasing. And when he is not engaged in some solitary task, where is he to be found but with Emilia and Marcus? The ghost of Karen has returned. With Wilhelm, Magdalena defies Karen. But Magdalena understands that her own ascendancy in this household has risen as far as it will ever rise and that now it has begun to fall.

In the night, while Johann snores beside her, she asks herself whether she should play one last card and let her husband discover her with Wilhelm—to inflict on him the final delirious torment that might (as he foresees his two remaining sons, Boris and Matti, going the way of their brothers in due time) put him in thrall to her for ever. But something holds her back. She thinks that to do this would be to open the door of a cage, not knowing what lay inside it, what venomous snakes, what vultures with heavy wings and vicious claws, what scorpions. And so she keeps silent. She walks to and from the rat-infested barn at least once a week. She goes on with her cake making, letting Boris and Matti help her and lick her fingers, just as they always did. She prays that Marcus will sicken and die. She listens to her body's alterations as it begins to nurture her unborn child.

Marcus sleeps in Emilia's room.

To her surprise, the boy seems strangely glad to see his father and begins to talk to him in the language he has shaped for himself, a language made up of different voices, as though he did not merely observe the things he talks about but *became them*. Sometimes, he is the rain.

Emilia explains to Johann: "Marcus sees the world from the inside out. He can imagine what it is to *be* a fly, a bird, a feather. This is why he cannot concentrate for long. He is always and always starting anew from the thing he has decided to become."

If this does not seem logical to Johann, he nevertheless decides to follow Emilia's advice that the way to help Marcus learn is not through written words or mathematical calculations on paper but through pictures.

In Johann's library is a big volume compiled by a Danish zoologist, Jacob Falster, who had travelled to the Americas and made drawings and engravings of the creatures he found there, and of their habitations. It is entitled *Pictures of the New World*. Johann lays the heavy book on his knee and draws Marcus to him and, in a new contentment, the two of them turn the pages and talk about what they find there:

"The Thylacine wolf. You see his bright eye, Marcus?"

Marcus nods.

"He lives in the mountains, called the Appalachian Mountains."

"What are those?"

"Mountains?" Johann raises both his hands. "Land. Rocky land that rises up, much higher than the hills, and where nothing grows and the snow falls all the year long."

"Cold wolf I am cold in those mountains."

"No, you're not. For you have this thick coat of fur, you see? Your fur keeps you warm."

Marcus snuggles inside his father's arm. He strokes the picture of the wolf with his finger. Then he turns the page.

"Grasshopper," he says.

"No," says Johann. "A locust. Like the grasshopper, but much hungrier. And the American locust travels in swarms, hundreds and thousands of them in a great green cloud. And then they may come down where a farmer has planted his corn or his beans. And what do you think would happen then?"

"Hopping and hopping in the beans . . ."

"Yes. And what else?"

"Making too much noise in the beans."

"Yes. Too much noise. But something worse. Remember how hungry the locust is? Do you not think he would be happy to have landed in a bean field?"

"Eating up the beans eating them all one two three four five six seven?"

"Yes. And so the poor farmer—"

"Oh, crying."

"Yes, crying. All the beans gone."

Marcus covers his face with his hands. Johann goes hastily on. On the next page is a picture of a salamander. When Johann tells Marcus that this is a lizard who can live in fire, he goes very silent and, holding him, Johann can feel the heat of his body intensify for a period of several minutes.

The American book preoccupies Marcus. He asks to see it every day. And with Emilia, he begins to make his own drawings, just as he did in the Insect Room at Boller, of the creatures that he likes the best—the bristle-worm, the ichneumon wasp, the stick insect and the scorpion. And the idea of the scorpion's sting seems to fascinate him more than almost anything else. He draws the sting as an arrow flying through the air or sometimes as a star. That he is told there are no scorpions in Denmark does not prevent him from searching for them. When he and Emilia go for walks in the meadows, to watch the spring arrive, Marcus is for ever looking for stones to turn over, convinced he may discover a scorpion underneath. And he calls to the invisible scorpions: "Come to me and be very quiet in my hand and I will take you there."

"Where is 'there'?" asks Emilia.

"Magdalena's eye," he replies.

Seeing the spring arrive reminds Emilia that, although her life has returned itself to the place where it started, time goes secretly on.

She can imagine the gardens at Rosenborg emerging from the long winter and knows how fast summer can follow spring, so that days identical to the ones she used to spend there with Kirsten could soon arrive and by the aviary other lovers might look at the darting birds and exchange kisses of the kind that are not easily forgotten.

She tells herself that if she is not to suffer beyond endurance, she must try to imagine that her time at Rosenborg did not exist. She must pretend that she dreamed it. For what, when a thing is past, differentiates it, in the reality of the present, from an illusion or fantasy? It had existence, *but has none now* except in memory. If the memory were to fail, then would it not be as though it had never ever been there at all? So this is what Emilia strives for—for her remembrance to fade, for everything that had to do with Peter Claire to grow cloudy and darken.

Her father is courteous to her, even affectionate from time to time, as he used to be before Karen died. And one afternoon, when Marcus is out riding with Boris and Matti, and there is no sign of Magdalena and Wilhelm, she takes her clock to Johann.

She keeps it clean and polished. It looks like a clock in perfect working order, except that the hands have not moved from ten minutes past seven. *This is the time that it will always tell.*

Johann looks at the clock and smiles and nods. Emilia waits. Then, in a hesitant voice, asks: "What happened at ten minutes past seven?"

"That is the hour," he says, "when you were born."

So then she thinks, It was *I* who was buried in the wood. Not out of any desire to remove me, but, rather, from my mother's will to keep me here with her for ever. She did not want time to take me away.

And so, a kind of acceptance of her lot begins to grow in Emilia. In her sleep, she no longer dreams of Peter Claire or of any future in which he is present. She returns instead to her dreams of Karen, and they are so real to her that when she wakes she can almost believe she is a child again, singing her peculiar little songs, while her mother smiles and puts a gentle hand on her hair.

What is the sky made of I do not know
Sometimes it is made of dancing snow.

KIRSTEN: FROM HER PRIVATE PAPERS

I am alone.

In the kitchens and corridors of Boller, the Servants scuttle about their tasks, but they are like Mice that the eye does not *see*, but only comes upon the things they have made or unmade, and so concludes that a merry Troupe of them has been secretly at work. Even those People who are visible to me, such as those who wait on me at table or upon whom I prevail with some futile Errand, do behave towards me like Ghosts, as though I had some Disease which could communicate itself to them just by being near me, and flee from my side as fast as they can.

And so I find myself in a House of Shadows, with only the Furniture to talk to, but even this, and all the World of Inanimate Things, seems to have risen up against me, to mock my plight and to vex me. The floors make themselves very Slippery, so that I have twice now fallen flat on my face at the entrance to the Dining-room; the fires begin to send out smoke into all the rooms to choke me and blind me. But Worst and rudest of these Things are the Mirrors on the walls. Whenever I pass by one, it contrives to Distort me, so that instead of seeing myself as I know I am—Almost Queen and Mistress of Count Otto Ludwig of Salm—what I am shown is a Scowling and Plump Object that I do not recognise at all. And my Dressing glass, a day ago, hatched a Treason so pernicious that I was forced to smash it to pieces with my bronze Statuette of Achilles. It revealed to me a Hair growing out of my chin. The Hair was black. Had I seen a Serpent on me, I declare I would have been no more Appalled than I was to see this foul Hair sprouting out of my Face. I screamed for a Maid and with some metal pincers she wrenched it away by the Root. But what if a Plague of these things should begin to sprout, as sometimes you glimpse on old wizened Crones near death? I declare, I am tortured by what shall now happen to my body. If I had never been Beautiful, then the Loss of it would be no Loss and I would not mourn its passing so. But my Beauty was a Thing that none could overlook. With it, I ensnared a king. In the garden at Rosenborg, he used to show me to the Flowers.

Now a letter comes from King Christian, saying that he wishes to Divorce me.

He declares that only his former Love for me prevents him from bringing me to a Trial for Treason and that there are many in Denmark who believe that I should be Bound upon a Wheel for my misdeeds.

He sets them out before me in his still-marvellous Hand (in case I had clean forgotten them), and to read the List of them, as though it might be a List of Filthy Garments to be delivered to the Washerwoman, discomfits me so far as to induce in me a heavy feeling of Shame. I have never understood why my Nature was so prone to wickedness. And always and still, I do not understand it. My Mother is a Schemer, but my Father was an honest man. Wherefore could I not have been like him and still Succeed in the World, and not lose all that I had and discover my hand empty of Every Thing except a Catalogue of my Transgressions?

And these are they:

That I betrayed the King my husband by fornicating with
     Count Otto Ludwig
That I baked Aphrodisiac cakes at Werden to lure the
     Count to my bed
That I gave away the King's Gold and the King's finest
     Linen to Count Otto
That I stole jewels belonging to the King's First Wife, to get
     money to purchase all manner of Gifts for my Lover
That I rejoiced when the King was ill

That I danced, once, when the King fell down with his
Stomach pains

That I was most frequently Blasphemous against the King
and rolled upon the Log Pile in the Hall at Rosenborg
calling out Obscenities

That I lied to All and Sundry about the Parentage of my
child Dorothea

That I treated my Other Children with cruelty and pulled
them about the Nursery by their hair

That by my Wantonness and Scheming, I brought the King
to a Great Melancholy, which did threaten His Majesty's
Life

And none of these Things can I deny.

Indeed, I could add More that the King does not include. But I declare I cannot, alone, be held responsible for these Crimes. Life itself brings us to Transgression because it is so very Bitter and Ugly and full of Sorrow. To stay Alive, we are forced to Scheme. To have any Joy, we must Steal like Magpies from the Pitiful Store of it. Were it more in abundance and God much more benign than He does seem to be, why then I think I should have been a Good Woman and in all my mirrors I would see the face of an Angel. But even God has been turned against me. The King reports that from all the Nation's Public Prayers, the name of Kirsten Munk is now excluded.

Where once I stood in wait, impatiently, for the Letter-carrier, now I pray that he does not come to Boller, but passes invisibly by, carrying all his Words elsewhere, to strike at other Hearts than mine. For I receive no Letter in this time that brings me aught but Fury and Disappointment.

Today, very fast upon the heels of my Husband's Letter, comes another from King Gustav of Sweden. And this Document is as a Prison that builds itself around me as I read. For it informs me that I cannot leave Boller to come to my Lover in Sweden, no matter what Papers I might come by nor what Intelligence of the King's affairs I might offer to his ancient Enemy.

I marvel at the cowardliness of King Gustav. Were his Seal not upon the Letter, I would think that Others had written it. For what inconvenience would my Little Presence in his Kingdom cause him when compared with the Great Advantages I offered him? But he repudiates me utterly: *I cannot so Offend the King of Denmark as to accord you any Safe Passage into Sweden.*

But Oh, the Hypocrisy of this! He (who has a thousand times "offended the King of Denmark" by complaining about the Sound Tolls and by waging bitter fights and Wars against this land) pretends he must remain white and unstained in this matter, but I say that he is not white, but Yellow, and I spit upon him. Were I the Absolute and not the Almost Queen, I would sell all that remains to me to buy ships and men, and I would begin a New War upon the Kingdom of Sweden and strive to take from Gustavus Adolphus all that he possesses, just as God took everything from His Servant Job, so that he might know what it is to be Scorned and to have Nothing, and know no Pleasure and be mired up in a lonely house with fires that belch and looking-glasses that break apart with laughter.

I have quite run out of Stratagems. Life is a blank, a nought, a minus.

I sit down at my escritoire and beg the King, as one last favour to me, whom once he called Mouse, to send me my Black Boys. For they know Magic, I am sure of it. They are the Children of Sorcerers. And this is all I can think of: that I may come to some Resurrection in the World through the dangerous study of Enchantment.

THE SEA-BLUE BOUDOIR

The date of Charlotte Claire's wedding to Mr. George Middleton has been set for the third of May.

Seamstresses are even now at work upon the wedding dress and upon the cloaks, dresses, petticoats and undergarments set out in the lists drawn up by Charlotte and her mother. To the items chosen by them, George has added the requirement of "one black mourning gown" and refused to be moved by Charlotte's protestation that nobody they knew seemed likely to die just at present. "Daisy," he said, taking her hand in his, "your 'just at present' is not a fixed entity. It is not the sundial, my dearest, but the moving shadow cast by the sun."

She goes frequently to Cookham, where the cold of winter still lingers in the morning frosts and in the furious winds that intrude upon the peace of the Norfolk night. She does not tire of walking with George round and round the house and its garden, its outhouses and its park. She feels—when she contemplates the fine arrangement of these buildings, the unimaginable expanse of green that surrounds them—as if she is about to become heiress to the whole of England.

Within Cookham Hall, a large upstairs room which looks west over the Cookham woods has been designated "Charlotte's Boudoir." Though she and George have laughed at the term ("Does it not mean sulking room, George? And wherefore should I have anything to sulk about?"), Charlotte is secretly enraptured by it and has no difficulty imagining herself within it, writing letters signed *Mrs. G. Middleton*, practising her dance steps, planning elegant supper parties, entertaining her friends or her mother to tea and cakes, or merely sitting and looking at the fire and dreaming of all the days and nights yet to come.

She has instructed the wall-painters to paint the boudoir blue. It is the blue of air and sea that she wants, which is neither deep nor pale, which is sweetly susceptible to light. And now this blue is going on, and Charlotte stands in the middle of the room and looks at it and discovers, in the midst of her enthusiasm for the choice of it, that it suddenly reminds her of her brother, of those luminous eyes of his which she has not seen for such a long time. And she feels her happiness falter.

Too content with her own lot to think of him very often, Charlotte Claire is now filled with an inexplicable panic on his behalf. Something desolate, something terrible, is about to happen to him. Of this she is suddenly certain. And so she cannot move. She clutches the lace at her throat. She knows why the black mourning gown has been ordered: it is for Peter.

The two wall-painters, seeing her go pale, set down their brushes and come to her side. The room is empty except for their ladders and she is helped to sit down on the low step of one of these, while Mr. Middleton is urgently sought.

He runs all the way from the stables and bursts in, panting. He kneels at her side and grasps her hand. "Daisy dearest, what is the matter? Oh, my darling girl, how pale you are. Charlotte, speak to me . . ."

"Oh, George, something has—"

"Is it the blue? Do you detest it after all? Only say and it shall be instantly altered . . ."

"No, not precisely the blue, but rather the thing which came to me when I contemplated the blue . . ."

The wall-painters, wiping the paint from their hands with rags, leave George and Charlotte alone, and his arms go round her and hold her tightly to him while she tells him now, on the instant, a certainty has invaded her: her brother is in danger.

If the admirable George Middleton has any faults, it is perhaps that he lacks curiosity and therefore has no tolerance for the things of the mind that he does not understand. The notion that his fiancée could "know" something that was occurring hundreds of miles away or indeed might not yet have occurred at all strikes him as so improbable as to be positively annoying and thus, without meaning to be harsh, he exclaims: "Tosh, Daisy!"

And this word "tosh" (that Middleton did not exactly intend to utter, but which came out all the same) is all that Charlotte needs to break down in tears. How terrible it is, she thinks, to live in a world where she can see tragedies and calamities in her mind, indeed *feel* the nearness of these things in her body, so that it grows cold and can hardly move, and yet not be believed by the man she loves. She pulls away from the warmth of George's arms and staggers to the window, where she lays her head upon the glass and sees, in the acres of parkland, only desolation.

Still kneeling by the wall-painters' ladder, George Middleton feels at a loss. He cannot leave his darling Daisy weeping at the window, yet what words can he find which will, at one and the same time, convince her she is deluded in her premonition and bring her the comfort that she needs? It is wretched, he thinks, when a person goes into realms of fancy. It disturbs the temperature of the air. It makes complicated things which should not be complicated. And he sincerely hopes that Charlotte will not do this very much once she is married.

But for all this, he is a kind and practical man. He straightens up and strides quickly to where Charlotte is standing, making the window-panes misty with her weeping. He lays a gentle hand on her shoulder. "I was too hasty with my 'Tosh,' " he says. "Yet I feel . . . doubtful on the subject of premonition, that is all. But listen to me, Charlotte. Let us go together now at once to my bureau and write a letter to your brother in Denmark, begging him to return for our wedding. Come, dearest heart. And then soon we shall have his reply."

For a moment Charlotte does not turn, but only continues her crying. For she knows that this fear of hers has found its way to a place very deep inside her, from which it cannot be drawn out except by the arrival of her brother, sound and well, in England. No writing of letters will assuage it. No feeling of George's that it is misguided will lessen its grip upon her mind.

But yet, the near presence of George, his tobacco smell, his largeness, always work a kind of magic upon her. She cannot not turn around and let him kiss her cheek and begin to smooth away her tears with the palm of his wide red hand.

And so she clings to him and the feeling of ice begins to leave her body, and yet she still murmurs, "Poor Peter. My poor Peter . . ."

"Hush, Daisy. All will be well."

"Oh, pray," she says. "For I could not bear it and Mama could not bear it."

"Nor your dear papa either. But it is not so. Nothing has happened."

He is wrong. Charlotte knows that he is wrong. But she says nothing more. She lets George kiss her salty lips and together they go down to the bureau, whose walls are certainly not blue but neatly upholstered with dark-brown leather. And the room smells of pipe smoke and paper and ink. It smells of men and all the rational, calm, unhurried business they undertake.

Charlotte sits down on an oak chair. She watches gravely as George begins to sharpen a white quill. "You write to him, George," she says. "For I cannot. Plead with him—as your future brother-in-law—to come home. Say he must do it for my sake."

A Prophecy Remembered

King Christian is trying to pray.

He kneels in his pew in the chapel at Frederiksborg, which he ordered to be decorated like a jewel box, with a balustrade and ceiling of ebony, embellished with silver and ivory ornamentation, and the side walls hung with biblical paintings mounted on copper plate. He has always found this sumptuousness useful in his communion with God. For his gaze is more easily lost in the contemplation of beautiful things than in that which is plain and of no account, and so his mind is thus "released into prayer"—or so he has often claimed.

For this reason—more than for any omnipresent worries about sacrilege—he has not pillaged his own pew, as he pillaged his plate room, for rendering into dalers. Indeed, he has left the entire church untouched. For when he raises his head and looks out and up, he wishes to rediscover all the splendours that he once imagined and let his eye meander there at will. What exists beyond the jewelled pew is as important to his concentration as that which is in it.

He is praying for God's protection. For in recent days the words of the old prophecy, the one made by Tycho Brahe when Christian was born, have returned to his mind and add themselves to the unease which comes and goes from him all the time.

It was foretold that at this age of fifty-three, in this year that has just begun, the King's life would be at risk. It was foretold that when this year ended, he might no longer be alive, and that such sorrows as Denmark had already endured during his reign might be magnified a thousand times. The King asks himself can prophecies, which derive from signs glimpsed in the stars, in the arrangement of the heavens themselves, be overturned by any human means? But not merely this: can God Himself, creator of the world, alter that which flies about the universe in showers of silver and may be the currency of the devil?

No answer comes. And Christian reminds himself that certain things—howsoever slavishly man might try to follow Cartesian principles in their analysis, however hard he struggles to dissect and realign them—are simply not susceptible to being known.

When the King walks from the chapel to his rooms, it is getting dark and he reflects upon the vain struggles of the March days to suggest the arrival of a new season when the night still seems to fall so fast upon the afternoon.

As he sips a cup of hot wine, King Christian is informed that Ellen Marsvin, Kirsten's mother, has arrived at Frederiksborg and is requesting an audience. He finds himself smiling. "Tell her," he says, "that no one can intercede on Kirsten's behalf. For not only have I despatched her from here, but I am beginning to succeed in banishing her from my heart."

Yet later he changes his mind and sends for Ellen. Ambitious and proud though she is, he always admired her, and her once-beautiful face, which wears the imprint of all her worldly strivings yet still has about it a fragile serenity, touches him more than it should—as though she might be a long-lost sister he had always liked.

And so they sit like old friends by the fire and drink the spiced wine. Neither the name of Kirsten nor the fatal syllables of the word "divorce" pass their lips. They talk about money and the sacrificing of Iceland, about the engineers from Russia who may surely be nearing the end of their long journey to the Numedal, about the preacher there and his letters, which mourn the absence of hope in the valley of the *Isfoss*.

And in this way the conversation turns towards the future and how it can be perceived when the duration of it—which once appeared so infinite—is now likely to be brief. Ellen tells King Christian that she will fight "to my last sigh, to my very last glimpse of any brightness" to stay alive and to hold on to what she has, and the vehemence with which she says this amuses him because it is exactly and precisely what he expects from her. He tells her that, if the prophecy of Tycho Brahe comes to pass, his own future "hangs by a little thread" and the tomb already stands open, waiting.

Christian has taken to drinking the waters from the well at Tisvilde, to try to cure the pains in his stomach and bowel. Great barrels of it are brought to the palace on carts and kept under lock and key, in case they should be tampered with and ordinary water substituted for the healing kind.

The King tries to imagine the "Tisvilde nectar" draining slowly through his body, carrying away with it the sources of his agony. When several days have passed without any sudden feelings of sickness, he declares that this is the thing that will make him well. "Perhaps," he adds, "Tycho Brahe foresaw the agitation in my gut and that it could be fatal. But now, with the magic of Tisvilde, I shall vanquish it."

A cup of the water is brought to him five times a day, the last before he goes to sleep. He savours its purity on his tongue, declaring he will drink no more wine, no more strong ale, but only this, until his digestion is comfortable once more. And in this fanatical observance of a routine devoid of any merriment he perceives a truth about himself: he has no wish to die. His work as Denmark's King is not complete and he does not want to desert his post.

One night, as he makes himself comfortable in his bed and is waiting for the water to be brought to him, he sees a young woman come into his bedchamber.

She is plump, with a rosy skin and dimples in her cheeks, and it is by these dimples that he recognises her as someone he once knew, but whose name he cannot remember.

She curtsies to him and sets down the water cup with a dimpled smile, and she comes near enough to King Christian for him to catch the scent of her, which is like the scent of plums or damsons, which once, when he could not find admittance to Kirsten's bed, made him think of visiting this homely girl and taking her in his arms.

And then it comes to him: she was one of Kirsten's women. She was known as the "Woman of the Torso."

She is about to leave, when the King calls her back. He says he cannot remember half of what he should remember in these recent times and one of these lost things is her name.

"Frøken Kruse," she says. "Vibeke."

That people disappear from a life and then one day are rediscovered, either they themselves or others very like them who are their *ghosts* or *substitutes of the mind*—this is a thing King Christian has ever been conscious of. And because these substitutions or reappearances have always seemed miraculous to him, he endows them with importance and is inclined to believe that God has sent them to perform some particular duty with regard to him.

Such is his feeling when he sees Vibeke Kruse standing in his room, when he smells her scent of plums and remembers her plump breasts, which he once strangely imagined as having the softness of feathers, as though he would be holding in his hands a pair of white doves and feel the beating of their hearts.

He invites Vibeke to sit down by the bedside. He asks her where she has come from and imagines some fanciful answer, such as *From an Aspen Tree* or *From the snows of Mont Blanc* or *From out of the sky*. But she says, simply, that she works for Ellen Marsvin now and has accompanied her here "to pay our respects to Your Majesty on our way to Copenhagen."

Strangely, it does not enter the King's mind that if Vibeke works for Ellen, then she is also in the household at Boller where Kirsten is still staying. Indeed, he gives no thought to Kirsten, but is entirely captivated by the presence of Vibeke, so much so that he forgets to drink the water, forgets that the hour is late, forgets everything but his desire to keep her by him.

He looks at her full lips, her comfortable chins, her wide haunches, her ordinary brown hair, her hands like the hands of a peasant girl, and says suddenly: "I am tired of pretence."

ROPE DANCERS

On a bright morning, Peter Claire hears the noise of heavy wheels on the cobblestones outside his window and other sounds—the playing of a little reed pipe and the jingle of a tambourine—that are unfamiliar. He looks down and sees a cavalcade of men, women and children running along beside covered wagons, and people from the palace coming out and greeting them like old friends, and pressing food and flagons of ale into their hands. And then a shout echoes round the courtyard and is carried inside the palace, and is repeated along corridors and bursts forth into chamber after chamber: "The rope dancers have arrived!"

They draw an instantaneous crowd to them—as though this moment had been anticipated for months, as though nobody at Frederiksborg had anything to do on that March morning but stand in a circle and stare at the new arrivals, and wait to see what marvels were about to be performed.

And already some magic is taking place. The children have begun tumbling, cart-wheeling and leap-frogging round the circle, fast and effortlessly, their limbs bending and springing to straightness again, like the branches of willow saplings. As they leap and whirl, wooden poles and planks, coils of rope, baskets of brass hinges and hooks are lifted out of the wagons, and a vast contraption, like the twin masts of a ship, begins to rise up in the great courtyard between the chapel and the Princess wing.

The King himself appears and stares at it. By his side is Vibeke Kruse, her hand held tightly in his, her face festooned in an enormous smile that reveals her new ivory teeth. These teeth shine in the sun. Not far from Vibeke, Ellen Marsvin silently watches and nods her satisfaction.

When another cart arrives, forth from which steps a black bear, to be led round on a chain, Peter Claire goes down to join the watchers, and in through the palace gates now come a great crowd of traders who have followed the performers all the way from Copenhagen with their baskets of cake and cheese, their tubs of oysters and whelks, their metal trinkets, their trays of bootlaces and knives. "Now," says Krenze's voice very near to Peter Claire, "see everybody scrabble for trash and suck oysters for breakfast! I ask you, how is mankind to be endured?"

When Peter Claire makes no reply, Krenze continues: "I should like to see the bear leading the little man by the chain. *That* would be an entertainment I should stay to witness."

Peter Claire turns to the German viol player. On his lips is some rebuke to Krenze's abiding cynicism, but the rebuke never shapes itself. Instead, Peter Claire recognises that he, too, is looking at the scene in a kind of misery, that he is indifferent to the cart-wheeling children and the sad-eyed bear, that even the great edifice going up by means of ropes and pulleys dismays him.

He says quietly: "Once the dancers are balanced on their rope, the crowd will long only for them to fall."

Krenze looks at him with approval mixed with surprise. "You are learning," he says. "I think at last you are learning more than angels are supposed to know."

Peter Claire is silent. But, now that he is talking to Krenze in the midst of this odd, noisy scene, there is something else that he wants to tell this stern, unyielding man, something else that has been coming and going in him for a while and which has begun to make him afraid. "Krenze . . ." he begins, but the German, thin and agile as an eel, is no longer there beside him and, when he looks all around for him, Peter Claire cannot see him anywhere. The crowd of traders and bystanders has swallowed him up.

Peter Claire's eye falls on the King, holding Vibeke's hand. He recognises Vibeke as one of Kirsten's women and wonders for a moment whether—if she is returning to Boller—she might be the means by which he could send a letter to Emilia. But this thought falters and breaks apart. For what is to be said to Emilia now? That his faith in her was always fragile? That, not trusting her love for him, he was lured without protest to the bed of his former mistress?

He begins to wander among the crowd, searching perhaps for Krenze or simply searching for *something* that will alter his morbid perception of the scene. He notices that the sun is almost warm. A girl in red offers him a dish of sweetmeats, but he passes on without stopping. He remembers the white ribbons, intended for Charlotte, and how, at the aviary, he saw them threaded into Emilia's hair.

And a new sound comes: two drummer boys, wearing frayed and tattered uniforms, begin a dry rat-a-tat, rat-a-tat, on small drums hung round their necks, indicating to the crowd that the masts are in place and the rope strung between them, and that the time is coming when the first of the dancers is going to step out into the void.

Now every eye stares up.

The dancers are silhouetted against the green copper of the steep roofs. Their feet, in soft slippers, are not as other feet but like gloved hands that can hold and cling. Their agility on the rope is such that *the rope is almost forgotten* and all the spectators see are the dancers pirouetting in the air.

Yet all Peter Claire thinks about is that they are perpetually poised in that moment before precipitation. The moment does not pass and vanish away but is constantly and always repeated.

And underneath the performers is nothing to break their fall: no net, no mattresses laid out, not even a heap of straw. The boy drummers beat out a fast roll. The reedy pipes are silent. The rope dancers spring onto each others' shoulders and the wind that turns the high weathercocks ruffles their hair.

Such bravery as this begins to work a subtle alteration in Peter Claire's mood. It is as though the daring of the rope dancers annihilated his own inertia by reminding him of what unexpected feats men can choose to perform, *if only they dare*. The sight of them begins to buoy him up and he turns his thoughts again to what hopes for happiness—if any—remain for him and Emilia Tilsen.

He has just begun to tell himself that these might rest absolutely and only upon his own courage, when the thing he was going to mention to Krenze occurs again: *the world goes almost silent*. The drums still rattle, the people gasp and cheer, the wind sighs round the steep roofs, but these things are barely present to Peter Claire. They have moved away, as though up into the sky, and what has replaced them is a sound *inside his left ear*, a noise like the tearing of rags, and with this internal sound comes a sharp and vicious pain.

The lutenist clasps his head in his hands. The pain and the sound of tearing intensify to a point where he wants to cry out—to beg someone to help him, to make the moment pass away. But it does not pass away. It goes on, as the rope dancers climb down and take their bows, and people begin to clap. He looks around wildly. He cradles his ear with his hand (the same ear in which he used to wear the Countess's jewel) and he remembers the silence which fell on Johnnie O'Fingal. He finds himself jostled as the people surge forward to lift up the dancers and carry them shoulder-high round the courtyard. No one pays him any heed. The bear is being led away.

Then the tearing sound stops and the pain starts to recede. Like a spring breaking and bubbling up out of the earth, the external noises in the courtyard come pouring forth again. They deluge the lute player's head: the bird notes of the pipe and the bell notes of the tambourine, the "bravos" of the crowd, the laughter of the dancers and the four-part laments of the street traders: "Cheeses! Oysters! Sweetmeats! Knives!"

Suddenly, Krenze is at his side again. The German makes no mention of the fact that Peter Claire's hands are still clamped to his head. "They were not bad," says Krenze, as the people sweep the performers on and on round the masts and back again. "Not bad. They knew their own capacity."

VIBEKE'S INVENTIONS

On her first night at Frederiksborg, Vibeke Kruse, recovering slowly from the journey, had carefully unpacked her wardrobe of sumptuous dresses and, as she smoothed out the creases, thought to herself: The secret of a successful life is not to die before one's death.

She admitted to herself that in her long war between her love of sweetmeats and her desire to be beautiful, in her struggles with the calligraphy pen and with the vicious silver wire of her new teeth, she had very nearly succumbed to a morbid perception of herself as a person of no worth, whose future could only be solitary and bleak, and who might as well die young. Yet she had managed to battle on and, now, here she was at last, at Frederiksborg, where Ellen Marsvin was already gossiping with the King and laying the foundations of the plan.

It was outlandish, Vibeke knew, Ellen's conviction that the former Woman of the Torso would be the one to supplant Kirsten in the King's affections, but then so were very many ideas (such as the notion that knitting had once corrupted the souls of women or that a hen could become as devoted to a human being as a dog, and yet both of these had been part of the life that Vibeke had seen) and thus there was no more reason to suppose that the plan would never come to pass than to suppose that it would.

In this mood of optimism, Vibeke had lain down to sleep. She had listened to the psalms of the carillon and heard someone singing beside the lake. She had kept a candle burning to reassure her, if she woke in the night, that she was on firm ground and not being tossed about on the angry sea.

When she had come, after a few days, into the King's presence, it was obvious to Vibeke straight away that the King remembered her and that he liked her. And what she had understood (perhaps because, by pure chance, the first task she was given was to bring him his cup of the healing water from Tisvilde?) was that here was a man who craved kindness. He needed someone who would care for him. His war with Kirsten had almost killed him. What he wanted now was to be saved from dying before his time.

And so Vibeke, instead of trying to seduce King Christian (for she saw that there was really no need of this, because he had already decided she would be comfortable in bed), tried to console him. She relinquished her efforts to be beautiful. She did not care whether her stomach bulged or her chins trembled or whether she ate too much or whether her teeth sometimes had to be taken out in the middle of a meal, for she saw that these things, which might once have been important to him, no longer were. What was important to him was her companionship and her affection. Vibeke Kruse would look after the King of Denmark and attend to his needs—including his need for laughter and his need for solitude—and in time, perhaps, if she was able to restore in him his appetite for being alive, her great reward would come.

She quickly formed the habit of vigilance over King Christian's sufferings. She noticed, for instance, that walking upstairs made him short of breath and even dizzy, and said to herself, Why should the King have to endure this when surely some means could be found to hoist him miraculously from the state rooms into his bedchamber? She remembered the clever trapdoor to the cellar at Rosenborg and the pipes and ducts that carried the sounds of the orchestra up into the *Vinterstue*. She reasoned that if music (which had no corporeal existence) could be made to travel so ingeniously, then surely some invention could be contrived to move the King's body from place to place.

Vibeke stood in front of one of the King's brocaded thrones and stared at it. She imagined how, if it were stone to be used in the building of a tower, it would be slowly hoisted into the air by the means of ropes and pulleys. She saw how light it was—even with the King seated upon it—compared with stone and how a very small quantity of ingenuity would be necessary to devise some means by which it could be lifted up and lowered down. She made little drawings with her calligraphy pen, showing a square cut out of the ceiling and the throne being swung aloft into the square, and when she had perfected these, to the point where she knew that at least they would *amuse* King Christian, she laid them before him.

He studied them with great care—with the same intensity with which he had once studied a quantity of buttons spread out on the floor and sheets of Italian parchment given to him for his inspection. Then he took Vibeke's hand and laid it against his cheek. "This is well done, my sugar-plum," he said. "This is very well done."

At night, when the King was asleep beside her, Vibeke Kruse began to stare at the spring moon through the gap in the curtains.

It struck her, as it had never struck her before, as an object of extraordinary wonder and magnificence. She knew that its radiance was borrowed from the sun, but did not understand how this could be so when the sun had disappeared from the sky. She put this lack of such understanding down to her own stupidity, yet she also decided that, at some future time, she would like to see the moon more clearly and so—by means of a telescope—pass *beyond her own limitations* to arrive at comprehension.

The idea came to her to ask the King to build an observatory from which he and she could look at the moon and stars. She imagined how, in summer-time, they two would be alone up there with the sky and how marvellous this would be.

But then she saw a flaw in her plan. An observatory would, of necessity, be a very tall building and how was the summit of any tall building to be reached except by a terrible quantity of stairs? Such stairs could kill the King. And so all that might follow of happiness—for her and for King Christian—could be sacrificed to this whim of hers to understand how the moon came by its own brightness. "And that is folly," Vibeke said to herself. "It is a folly such as Kirsten would have devised."

But still, Vibeke found herself staring at the moon, as it waxed and waned and waxed again. With its visible features, it was like some acquaintance from the past who kept reappearing out of the darkness because it had more to say to her yet.

The Whittled Stick

"No one knows," says Johann Tilsen to the doctor, "how the marks on her body came there, for she refuses to tell us."

Magdalena is lying in the bed. Blood flows out of her onto the white sheets. On the lower part of her abdomen are red bruises spreading slowly to purple.

The doctor looks from these to Johann's face and says again: "I know that sometimes a man . . . in a momentary loss . . . in a spasm of anger he did not intend . . ."

"I swear before God that I laid no hand on her," says Johann.

The doctor then speaks so quietly to Magdalena that Johann cannot hear what he is saying and Magdalena does not reply, only shakes her head. So the doctor replaces her coverlet and he and Johann walk out of the bedroom, which has a potent smell in it of Magdalena, as though there were ten or a hundred Magdalenas lying bleeding there.

They go downstairs and into the parlour, and the doctor stands in front of the fire and his face is the grave face of a man about to deliver an angry sermon. "There has without doubt been some hurt to her body," he says. "If she was not hit, then she fell from—"

"She was *not* hit!" declares Johann again. "I have sworn to you, I did not lay any hand upon my wife."

"Well," says the doctor, "whatever has occurred, she will miscarry."

Johann's hands are trembling. He runs his fingers through what remains of his grey hair. "What do you mean?" he asks distractedly.

The doctor stares at Johann Tilsen. He has known him for several years and has always considered him a good man. "She will lose the child," says the doctor again and, seeing Johann look bewildered and frightened, adds: "Perhaps she did not tell you?"

"No," says Johann bleakly. "She did not tell me."

"Well. There you are, Johann. Who can say why she did not tell you. But at all events, I am certain that the child will be lost."

The doctor leaves then, saying he will return.

Johann Tilsen sits down. He stares into the parlour fire, and Marcus comes to him, carrying his cat Otto, which he puts in Johann's lap, like a gift. Then he stands, holding on to his father's shoulder, and says after a while: "Is Magdalena going to die?"

The cat purrs softly. The flames of the fire are bright.

"I don't know, Marcus," says Johann.

After several hours, Magdalena's body yields up the tiny foetus and the thing is taken away by the doctor and put into a sack and buried in the ground.

But the bleeding does not stop. What quantity of blood, Johann asks himself, is in her, that so much can flow out?

Magdalena whispers in a fragile voice the things that are on her mind: she tells Johann that Ingmar should be brought back from Copenhagen, that he has been punished enough. She says that a kindly nurse must be found to care for Ulla. She asks Johann to forgive her.

"Forgive you for what?" asks Johann.

"You know for what," she replies and closes her eyes, effectively preventing him from saying anything more.

Though Emilia sits with Magdalena, even spooning broth into her mouth and undertaking the task of rinsing and replacing the saturated rags pressed between her legs to try to stanch the bleeding, none of the boys comes near her. Boris and Matti do sums at the schoolroom table, silently covering page after page with numbers, while Marcus lies on the floor beside them with his *Pictures of the New World*, drawing stick insects and moths, and stalks of Indian corn.

Finding them there, so good and quiet, so apparently engrossed in their work, Johann asks them where Wilhelm is, but they say that they don't know. His room is empty and he has not been seen since lunch-time, when he refused to eat, saying he had a pain "somewhere in me. A pain of sickness."

Johann goes in search of him and finds him at last, sitting on a step in front of the stables. Wilhelm does not look up when his father approaches him. He is intent on a task and his eyes never leave it. He has taken a long stick from the pile intended for staking out the rows of raspberry canes and, with a heavy knife, is carving simple patterns in it. His fingers are cut here and there, and a little blood seeps into the newly revealed white wood of the stick, but Wilhelm ignores this. And when Johann speaks to him he continues with this work of whittling the hard wood, fingering the grey-brown of the sections he will leave uncut, turning the stake in his hands, verifying that the patterns he is making run evenly around it.

"How's your sickness?" asks Johann. "Has it passed?"

"No," says Wilhelm.

"Then perhaps you shouldn't be out here in the cold?"

Wilhelm makes no comment. He merely goes on with his work, as though he were racing against time, as though the task had to be accomplished before the sun went down. And it is only at this moment and not at any moment before that certain thoughts enter Johann Tilsen's mind with regard to his second son, and he stares at Wilhelm, as he sits there with his knife and his stick, and he weighs up the consequences of putting to him a single question.

And it is as if Wilhelm can hear the question before it has been uttered, because Johann sees in his lowered eyes a sudden terrified blankness, so that he is sure that Wilhelm is no longer really looking at the length of wood in his hands, not even at the ground strewn with shavings light and dark, but is staring inwards, imagining the seconds which are about to arrive now and which, if they do, will alter both their lives for ever.

And so they are frozen just as they are: Johann looking down at Wilhelm; Wilhelm gaping at the ground. The seconds pass and gather into a minute. The minute passes and more seconds accrue. The day is silent and still, with not a breath of wind to move the trees.

Then, quite suddenly, Johann turns and begins to walk away. Over his shoulder, he says quietly to Wilhelm: "Don't stay out in the cold, Wilhelm. It were better that you came back to the house."

Only when Johann is completely out of sight, out of earshot, does Wilhelm plead with the empty air for understanding. "I did not mean to kill her," he whispers. "Only to *make some mark*—so that she would always remember *me*, above my father and above my brother. Remember *me*, Wilhelm. And say to herself that I was the one, the best."

Even baby Ulla is quiet. A visitor entering the Tilsen house on this day might never know that anything terrible was occurring.

Boris and Matti go on with their sums. Marcus converses with the stag-beetle he keeps in a moss-lined box. Otto the cat sleeps by the fire.

But in the room with its suffocating smell, where the doctor and Johann and Emilia wait, the agony of Magdalena is moving towards its inevitable end. She has drifted into a white sleep. When the doctor lets blood from her arm "to distract the flow from the womb and make it stop" she barely stirs.

For a while, Johann held her hand and stroked it or gently laid his palm on her cold brow, but now, as the day folds in upon itself and darkness comes, he retires to a little distance from her and only looks at her—just as if she were already dead and all that remained of her in the bedchamber were memories of her scarlet clothing, the sound of her night-time pissing into her pot that could sometimes arouse him, her legs fastening his body to hers, her dirty talk, her laughter, her pride.

And Emilia understands, by this discreet removing of himself from her, that Johann *wants* Magdalena to die, that at the age of forty-eight he is exhausted and longs now for a life in which he does not have to consider her.

Magdalena says nothing more to Johann. Noisy all her life, she drifts towards death with barely a murmur, and when the moment has come and gone, and the doctor has been paid and the sheet pulled up over Magdalena's dark hair, Johann and Emilia go down without speaking into the parlour, where Wilhelm crouches now, banking up the fire.

Johann sits down in his accustomed chair and the family gather round him. Only Wilhelm, preoccupied with the fire, remains a little apart, and Johann, when he looks at him, notices that he has chopped the whittled stick into three equal pieces and is feeding these to the flames. And the boy does this heedlessly, as though the stick were a length of kindling, as though all his work upon it, to alter it from stick to ornament, had never ever existed.

A ROYAL DILEMMA

April arrives.

Hoping for the scent of lilac, King Christian goes out into the gardens, but he sees that the cold still clenches the buds and he must wait a while longer to savour any real perfume of spring.

If this disturbs him, if the notion of a season unnaturally retarded by the weather makes him remember once again how this most dangerous of years might bring about all manner of things he did not expect, he does not let himself dwell upon it. Indeed, he has made himself a promise that he will no longer dwell upon anything that he finds troubling, because he has been made aware, in the days that have passed since the return to the palace of Vibeke Kruse, of an accumulation of pleasurable feeling in him which he can describe with only one word: happiness.

It is so long since the King has felt himself to be happy that he has almost forgotten how a man is to behave in this state without seeming foolish. He is tempted to forgo all other pleasures, to set aside all matters of business, in order to pass the time lacing and unlacing Vibeke's dresses, tickling her feet to make her laugh, summoning pots of cream to spoon into her mouth, letting her massage his aching shoulders, and his belly being slowly cured of its pains by the healing waters of Tisvilde.

But not only does Christian not wish to look foolish, he never again wishes to be a slave to love, and so he rations his time with Vibeke, letting her remain unvisited sometimes when he would like to go to her and—rather than spoil her as he spoiled Kirsten—contenting himself with the giving of occasional small gifts of no particular value.

Vibeke's delight at these objects, which might be a satin bow or a lace handkerchief or a little box of mother-of-pearl, touches him profoundly. To live (as he did with Kirsten for so long) with a companion who seemed never ever satisfied with anything except those commodities which had cost *too much*, for which the sacrifice—in money or in honour—had always been too great, now strikes him as a fearful thing. And so he hardens his heart still further against Kirsten, proceeding with the divorce and deciding, although the warm weather has not yet arrived, to return to Rosenborg, so that there, in the palace he built for Kirsten and which in his mind has always been synonymous with her name, Vibeke Kruse can replace her as his wife.

He summons Jens Ingemann and tells him to prepare the orchestra for a return to Copenhagen.

Ingemann bows, nods and then asks quietly: "Are we to be in the cellar again, Sir?"

"Of course you are to be in the cellar!" barks the King. "How else is the magical music to be achieved?"

"No. There is no other way . . ."

"And I wish the spring and summer to be filled with songs! Start practising pieces that are lively and gay, Herr Ingemann. No more sad ayres. Let Pasquier send to France for the latest dances."

"Yes, Sir."

Ingemann is getting old, the King reflects. Perhaps the damp and cold in the cellar give him rheumatism or catarrh? But this cannot be helped. The hidden music of the Danish court is a source of wonder to all who come to Rosenborg and wonder is a fugitive thing. Ingemann is about to leave, when the King calls him back and says: "One other thing, *Musikmeister*. If I am not wrong, something has happened to Peter Claire. He has moments of abstraction. What might be the cause of these?"

Jens Ingemann replies that he cannot say, that the English musicians have always been unfathomable to him and that this one is no exception.

It is in the King's mind to send for Peter Claire, when a letter from his nephew, King Charles I of England, is put into his hands.

Courteous and affectionate, this letter is nevertheless a teasing document. It offers King Christian the considerable sum of one hundred thousand pounds *to help Your Majesty in your continuing poverty since the wars*, but upon one condition. King Charles requests *the return to England, on perpetual loan or pawning to us, of your excellent lutenist by the name of Claire*. It gives no explanation, no embellishment to this request. It simply states that the money will be brought to Denmark *upon my having sight of Claire here at Whitehall* and looks forward to hearing the *sweet solo sound* he is reputed to make upon the lute.

King Christian sends immediately for the English Ambassador, Sir Mark Langton Smythe. "Ambassador," he asks, "how has this idea come into His Majesty's mind? Did you put it there when you were in London?"

The Ambassador replies that he only *mentioned in passing* the sweet sound of the lute player, thinking it to be of no account, and was surprised to find the King "so struck on the instant with the idea of having him at Whitehall."

The King sighs. "You must understand," he says, "that I cannot let him go. When I was born, it was prophesied that this year, 1630, would be the most dangerous of my life. I may not survive it. But I believe that I should keep about me each and every person who assists and does not impede my progression through the days. And Peter Claire is one such."

Langton Smythe gives the King a supercilious look, the weary look of the English rationalist who does not (or pretends that he does not) hold with distant prophecies and clumsy superstition.

"Dare I say," he says, "that large sums of money are likely to afford greater protection to you than a solitary lute player?"

King Christian ponders this, looking out of the window, where the sky is grey, where the lilac buds refuse to open, and says at last: "My nephew Charles has married a French wife and is disposed towards a Frenchified style. Why do we not offer him Pasquier?"

The Ambassador shakes his head. "I had the impression that he had set his heart upon Claire."

"Then I am in a dilemma." The King sighs.

Later that night, he asks Peter Claire to come and play for him and Vibeke.

Vibeke smiles all the while, showing her ivory teeth, and Peter Claire ascertains that she is a woman of little beauty, yet King Christian's restlessness appears miraculously calmed by her presence.

He embarks upon a love-song—the first he has dared to play since the departure of Kirsten. He notes that as the sentimental words come pouring out, the King reaches quietly for Vibeke's hand.

As the music ends and Vibeke retires, he is about to take his leave, when the King invites him to sit down beside him. With his habitual intensity, Christian examines Peter Claire's features. Then the King says: "There is something the matter, Mr. Claire. Shall you tell me what it is?"

If Peter Claire longs to confide in someone, to describe the sudden and inexplicable silences and the tearing pain in his ear, which afflict him without warning and during which he feels himself to be excluded not merely from any future in which he can be happy but from the world in its entirety, he nevertheless decides that to admit these things to the King is impossible. For what sensible man would continue to employ a musician who may be in the process of losing his hearing? "There is nothing the matter, Sir," he says. "Merely . . ."

"Merely?"

"I am sometimes haunted by . . . It is sometimes borne in upon me . . . that I have neglected certain people who—"

"You mean your family in England?"

"Yes. But not only—"

"They write you letters begging you to go back for your sister's wedding, is that it?"

"Yes."

"I understand that you should want to go to England. Why do you not ask your sister to postpone her marriage until . . ."

"Until, Sir?"

"Until . . . I have become sure that I no longer need you."

Peter Claire leaves then and the King goes into his bedchamber, where Vibeke waits, with her hair in thick plaits, rubbing oil of cloves onto her gums.

As they part, both men reflect upon all that might have been said in this recent conversation and yet was not said; and this knowledge of what so often exists in the silences between words both haunts them and makes them marvel at the teasing complexity of all human discourse.

ALEXANDER

He arrives at dusk, up the same road that Herr Gade, the King's representative, travelled with his meagre cargo of chickens and cloth.

His eyes are yellow and red, infected by the bitter cold and deprivation he has survived, and by all that he has seen on his journey through Russia. He stinks like the devil.

It is not Ratty Møller, this time, who is the first to see him. But the minute the people catch sight of him in the village, draped about with torn furs and with his hands bandaged, they guess who he is and lead him to Møller's house. For any such person, they firmly believe, is Ratty Møller's responsibility, not theirs. And all they can do is to wait to see whether Møller, with the few words of Russian he had managed to teach himself, can make sense of him.

His name is Alexander.

Møller banks up his fire, sits him beside it and takes the bandages from his hands, from which three fingers are missing, and cleans them and calls the doctor to examine him. Pus oozes from his eyes and down his cheeks into his thick beard. He has no word of any language except Russian and in Russian he cries out—for the pain of his eyes and his frost-bitten hands, and for the loss of his friends and fellow engineers who had started out with him from the Sayan Mountains and who did not survive.

The people of the *Isfoss* resign themselves to waiting. Will Alexander live or die? Will one solitary engineer have the knowledge required to reopen the mine? Will that knowledge remain tantalisingly locked away inside him because he has no way of explaining it?

Møller, who has to care for him, who is woken in the nights by his screaming, tells the people that he believes Alexander will not recover. His body is wasted. On a slate, the Russian draws pictures of dogs lying in the snow, of men hacking the flesh off the dogs and eating it. Among his few possessions is a silver cross, which he lays on his lips before he sleeps.

The preacher asks the people to bring whatever food they can spare, to trap birds in the forests so that he can make a nourishing broth of sparrows. The doctor mixes a paste of mercury to lay on his eyes.

Alexander's furs are taken away to be washed in the river and sewn together again. He is wrapped in clean linen, and as Møller performs this task he thinks how strangely the Russian's body and his thin face and dark beard resemble those of the Christ of his own imaginings. And so he begins to pray ardently for the man's recovery. That a kind of resurrection—one that would make good all the sacrifices made in the name of the silver mine—might take place there in his own house fills Ratty Møller with a sudden hectic excitement.

———

As the days pass, Alexander does become a little stronger. He is able to walk to the window of Møller's room and look out at the road. Yet the sight of the road seems to afflict him and the preacher gradually understands that it is not the road itself but the absence on it of his lost companions which torments him. Tears are mingled with the putrefaction that still leaches out of his eyes. He will smite his own head and his chest, and babble out his sorrows in an incoherent language Møller has no hope of understanding. And there seems to be a question hidden somewhere in all this.

"Tell me," Møller is able to ask in Russian. "Tell me what it is." Then Alexander will sometimes kneel at Møller's feet and even place his head on the stones of the floor, but all that Møller can comprehend is the Russian's agony of spirit.

One day, Alexander takes up the slate again and draws another picture of flesh being eaten. He turns the slate round and shows the picture to Møller. And the preacher who has struggled for so long to save the villagers of the *Isfoss* by bringing back the silver mine stares at this picture in horror. But then his look softens to one of pity, for now he has understood—on this cold April day in the year 1630—that the limit of that struggle has been reached. He lays his hand on Alexander's head.

Gently, with the help of the doctor, Møller leads the Russian to the church, where the sole thing of beauty and value is an oil painting of a crucifixion on the rounded ceiling. And Alexander, no longer weeping or crying out, kneels under this and Møller calls upon God to "forgive His servant Alexander for the means he had to use to stay alive and grant him rest."

Soon after this, Møller calls a meeting of all the people in the village of the *Isfoss*.

He addresses them gravely. He reminds them that before the discovery of the silver in their beloved mountains they were content. He says that he has come to believe at last, after what

Alexander has suffered, that the price already paid for the continuation of the mine is too high and that nothing more should be undertaken in regard to it. He says that certain dreams and longings can bring forth more suffering than they could ever cure. He says that it is now his opinion that the mouth of the mine should be sealed for ever and "any tree that will cling to the rock" be planted there, so that a generation from now no one will know, except by the graves round about, that anything was ever discovered there.

As the people begin to murmur and complain, as Ratty Møller knew they would, he says: "Consider now what the mine *is*. You will say that the mine is a stocked larder, the mine is a suit of fine clothes, the mine is the return of the King, the mine is companionship and revelry, the mine is music played under the stars. But since when was it these things?"

A shout of protest goes up. "It *was* these things!" insist the villagers of the *Isfoss*. "The moment of the mine was the greatest time we have ever lived through. And it will come again! It must come again!"

"This is exactly what I believed," says Møller calmly. "I lived from day to day in expectation of the moment when the mine would be reopened. But I was wrong to do so. We were all wrong."

The people mumble crossly among themselves. Then they ask: "What about Alexander? If today he is strong enough to walk to the church, then tomorrow he will be strong enough to start work, and by the time the weather is warmer—"

"No," says Møller. "I tell you that Alexander has done everything a man can do and he can do no more."

Still the people call out that Alexander is their last hope and that Ratty Møller has no right to deprive them of hope.

"I give myself that right," says Møller, still calm and unmoved by the shouting. "To weigh this man down with your longings for something that he cannot undertake is a cruelty and a sin, and I tell you we shall not commit it."

There is an uneasy silence while the villagers, sensing Møller's implacability, consider what he has said. They mutter among themselves: "What is the Rat talking about?" "Who gave Ratty the power to decide the fate of the mine?"

And then they shout it out: "By whose authority do you crush our ambition? By the King's? You're a poor preacher, no better than any one of us."

"I agree," says Møller, "certainly no better than any one of you. Much more culpable than you. For I was the one who wrote to the King! Remember that and never forget it. The mine would be slowly fading from your hearts, from your memories, by this time, and we would be returning to what we once were, if it had not been for my intervention. And I apologise to you for keeping alive this false hope. I ask your forgiveness."

When the meeting breaks up there is no agreement, no resolution. Feelings against Ratty Møller, as he makes his way back to his house at the apex of the hill, run high. He does not know how much or for how long he will have to suffer for what he now believes is right. All he knows is that he *has not erred in this judgement*. And when he sees Alexander, alive still, but with all his terrors and regrets held locked in his own language, and thus deprived of any true friendship and understanding, he tells him that he will not give way, that in this house the engineer can struggle to live or decide to die, just as he pleases, but that nothing more on earth will be asked of him.

"A LITTLE GOLD, A VERY LITTLE . . ."

Ellen Marsvin finds the former Woman of the Torso engaged on a homely task: she is mending a tear in the King's night-shirt.

"Vibeke," Ellen sighs. "You really must now put from you the habit of mind of a *serviteuse*. Let some washerwoman do this lowly task of sewing. You are to be the King's companion, not his maid."

Vibeke nods, but she doesn't put away the shirt, only spreads it out on her knee and caresses the soft fabric tenderly with her hands. "To mend the shirt gives me pleasure," she says. "So I shall mend it and that is that."

"No," says Ellen sternly, "that is not that. For in mending night-shirts and performing menial chores of this ilk, you will little by little become degraded again in the King's mind to a mere woman, and this was not the aim and object of the plan."

Vibeke raises a hand to her lips. "Fru Marsvin," she says, "pray don't make any more allusion to any plan. For when I think that . . . when I remember that . . . all these things might be perceived as mere *schemes*, I feel so ashamed . . ."

"What in the world can you mean, Vibeke?" asks Ellen. "For you know full well that a scheme is precisely what it was. And Good Lord but it has been a long time a-hatching and has entailed enormous expense—dresses and writing lessons and teeth—and even, I dare say, suffering on both our parts, and—"

"I know it," replies Vibeke, "but now I would like to unknow it."

"How peculiar you are! When there was never a plan that was so marvellously laid, so magnificently brought to fruition . . ."

"Please stop!" says Vibeke. "Please do as I ask and never more mention any word that has about it the idea of cunning and calcu-lation. For if it may have been these things which began it, it is not these things which carry it on. That the King should discover our scheming would be a sorrow such as I could not bear."

Going nearer to Vibeke and whispering, Ellen continues: "Whether he discovers it or not is up to you. It depends upon how well you are now able to play your part, Vibeke."

At which statement, a tear escapes from one of Vibeke's round blue eyes and begins to meander down her cheek. "It is not a *part*," she says sadly. "I thought it would be, but I was wrong." And she picks up the King's shirt again and holds it to her face. "He is good to me and I know that I make him happy, after all his sufferings with your daughter. And I would do anything for him, anything in this world . . ."

Ellen is silent for a moment, watching more tears roll down Vibeke's face, to be wiped away by the night-shirt. Then she begins to laugh. "Well, well, indeed, Vibeke, I don't quite know what to say."

"Say nothing, then!" says Vibeke passionately. "There is no need."

Ellen is still smiling to herself as she takes her leave of King Christian and orders her coachman to drive her to Kronborg.

Although Dowager Queen Sofie always detested Kirsten, or perhaps *because* she detested Kirsten no more and no less than Ellen detested her, and because she and Ellen Marsvin have always seen eye to eye in their belief that the King had to be *managed* if the women were to have lives they could bear to lead, she still regards the younger woman as an important ally. And when Ellen is announced at Kronborg, Queen Sofie goes down and greets her warmly.

The samovar is brought and the heavy curtains drawn against the darkening afternoon, and the two women sit listening to the sighs and gurgles of the samovar, and amusing themselves by chopping lemons into half-moons and star shapes, and setting them floating on their tea.

The servants are sent away and Ellen talks and tells the marvellous story of the plan, beginning at the very beginning, with the day when she decided to take Vibeke into her household at Boller and ending with the words she has recently heard from Vibeke's own mouth on the subject of devotion.

And Queen Sofie listens intently, congratulating Ellen from time to time "upon understanding so perfectly the importance of small matters, such as calligraphy," and eventually, when the story is concluded, pouring herself yet more tea and saying: "Now, at last, things shall go on better with my son, Fru Marsvin. I feel it will be so. And I shall be left in peace. And I tell you, my mind is much soothed by this, for you know the recent times have been very hard to bear, with the King sending men here and coming himself to search my vaults. There is nothing in them, of course. But it was once put about that I was accumulating treasure here . . ."

"Oh, yes," says Ellen. "I think it was my daughter who put it about. But she could never ever distinguish between truth and falsehood, not even to herself."

"Of course, I have a *little* gold, a very little. No woman should embark upon old age without something . . . in the case of emergencies."

"I agree," says Ellen. "How wise you are."

"I am, am I not? For even the mother of a king, in these restless times . . ."

"Yes, no. Exceptionally wise. And you must yield up nothing."

Then Ellen lets a long sigh, a deeper more mournful sigh than any produced by the samovar, escape from her and says: "You know, Your Highness, that all *I* possessed is at Boller. And now my daughter has turned me out of my home and usurped my furniture and my pictures, and I do not really know what is to become of me."

Queen Sofie appears shocked. "Oh, my dear," she says, "how very fearful. How could this possibly have happened?"

"I do not know. I suppose that everything moves in a circular way. The King threw Kirsten out, and with good reason, and so where can she go but to me? And because she is still the King's wife, she can do almost anything she pleases—or fancies she can. And thus I am homeless. Even my cellar filled with jam made by my own hands is commandeered . . ."

Queen Sofie looks aghast at this accumulation of horror upon horror. "Oh, dear!" she says. "Oh, especially the jam! Fru Marsvin, we shall act immediately. I was about to say that I will despatch men to put your daughter out of Boller, but instantaneously a better plan comes into my mind. Why do we not merely send for the jam and for such possessions as you dearly love, and house you henceforth here with me at Kronborg? I live very simply. I eat fish from the Sound. But perhaps you will not mind this, for I do not deny that I am often lonely . . ."

Ellen Marsvin protests just enough at this show of generosity to convince the Dowager Queen that she really is doing her ally the greatest of favours, but then agrees to everything that is suggested, and the two women sit back contentedly and listen to the breakers, lifted by the rising wind, beginning to batter the Kronborg shore.

"There will be storms, no doubt," says Queen Sofie after a while, "but here we shall be safe. Here, we can keep an eye on everything that happens."

And Ellen Marsvin agrees.

With the death of Magdalena, once her body has been taken away and laid in the ground, a feeling of calm descends upon the Tilsen house.

It is, thinks Johann, as though we have all gone through a peculiar illness, an infectious fever which agitated us, almost killed us, and now the fever has abated and we are convalescing. We are still fragile (Wilhelm and I, especially). We tire easily. We do not ride out as frequently as we used to do. We talk quietly at mealtimes. But we know that the fever will not return and that in time we shall be completely well again.

Wanting to eradicate the *scent* of Magdalena—from the bedroom, from the kitchen, from every bit of the house—Johann has packed a trunk with all her clothes and possessions, her scarlet skirts, her shoes, her book of recipes, her combs and brushes, her underwear, and despatched it by cart to the Børnehus in Copenhagen, to be disposed of among the poor as anybody sees fit. He has kept nothing, only her few jewels, to be given to Ulla when she is older and from which Magdalena's presence seems already to have been eradicated, as though the brooches and necklaces had been torn from her long ago or else had never truly belonged to her.

Now and then, Johann finds something that he has overlooked—a handkerchief, a ribbon—and these objects he simply throws away. Cakes are no longer made in the house, nor bowls of chocolate drunk in the mornings. The bower at the edge of the lake is torn down, plank by plank. The broken mechanical bird is reclaimed by Marcus. He lets beetles wander round in the cage, in case the bird should suddenly come to life and feel hungry.

Now, in late April, instead of fine warm weather, a grey fog descends upon eastern Jutland. It blankets the Tilsen house, so that it feels closed off from everything and everyone outside itself.

Emilia looks at this fog and feels a kind of gratitude for it. Because she no longer wants to inquire what is there in the wider world. She would prefer the wider world not to exist at all. She would like a rumour to arrive informing her that all the rest of Denmark had floated away into the sea.

She has a role in this house and on the estate now: she helps her father to organise the running of it. He and she sit at the parlour table, writing out orders and settling accounts. They do not talk about the past, nor of the future—neither of Karen, nor of Kirsten Munk, nor of Magdalena—but only of what occurs from day to day, from moment to moment. And the notion that anyone from another part of Emilia's life might find a way here through the thick grey mist seems at last so improbable to her that she no longer wishes even to think about it. That sometimes, in her dreams, she finds herself in sunlight by the aviary at Rosenborg is, she tells herself, just because the past can be stubborn and imperious, and refuses to let itself be forgotten down to its last dregs.

But even the dreams come less and less. And when she wakes in the mornings and remembers that Magdalena is no longer alive, that Marcus is making progress with his lessons, that her father is as kindly as he used to be long ago, that Ingmar is returning from Copenhagen, that she is as useful in the house as her mother would have wanted her to be, then she knows that life can be endured precisely as it is.

There is a kind of contentment in this, one that is affirmed by the perpetual presence of the fog, eclipsing both land and sky. And when Emilia's hen, Gerda, wanders away into this shroud of whiteness and is not seen again, she resigns herself to the loss of the bird with hardly a moment's regret.

Acceptance, she thinks, is the harshest lesson life teaches and the one most important to learn.

Johann Tilsen now decides that the daughter he has so much neglected should not pass the rest of her life caring for him and for her brothers; a husband should be found for her; she should be allowed a future of her own.

No sooner has this thought entered Johann's mind than he realises that he already knows the very man for her. He is a preacher called Erik Hansen, a courteous and kind person with long legs and arms, and wispy brown hair that blows straight upwards in the wind. Now aged forty, Erik Hansen is childless. His wife died in her twenty-eighth year. He has never had the demeanour of a man in search of a second wife, but Johann Tilsen feels certain that Emilia's gentleness, her quiet prettiness, will prove irresistible to Hansen and that, in their future life together, he would care for her devotedly.

He says nothing to anyone. He merely sends a letter to Hansen, inviting him to come to bless the Tilsen house, because he has "reason to believe that my dead wife's spirit might be lurking in some corner of it and become noisy, and prevent us all here from living together in harmony." He adds that, because Hansen's church is some way distant and because the "accursed murk and haze hangs everywhere around us" he would be welcome to stay a night, "or more than one night, if you can spare us the time."

So it is that Preacher Hansen arrives like a shadow one afternoon as Emilia is staring out of the parlour window. One moment he is not there and the next he is fully visible and close up, as though he had fallen out of the sky.

And Emilia is immediately horrified—that a stranger could appear like this without warning—and when she hears him knocking at the door, she remains where she is without moving, only turning her face away from the window. She hears the man cough in the damp air. And then she hears the servant opening the door and letting him in, and she hears his voice, which is light, and his footsteps, which are cautious, and she prays that this man may discover, after all, that he is in the wrong house, and get back on his horse and be gone for ever.

But he does not go. Johann Tilsen brings him into the parlour and Emilia sees his face, which is pale, and his eyes, which are small. He bows to her and she has to rise and acknowledge him.

Preacher Hansen. Herr Erik Hansen. Johann says his name more than once, seeming to make sure that Emilia takes it in. The stranger holds his hat in his hands, giving himself a penitent's air.

The buckles on his shoes are spattered with mud. He smells of leather and of his horse, and Emilia has to look away from him because he is part of all that should not be here inside this house; he is part of all that should have floated out to sea and gone down into the darkness underneath it.

His rituals are careful and tidy. He goes from room to room with his small cross made of mahogany. He kneels on the floor, in the very centre of each room, and prays silently, first with his eyes open and then with his eyes tightly shut, as though there might be something in the room which he had glimpsed and did not wish to see again.

He invites the whole family to go round with him, "to witness that there is no space unblessed," and when he has been everywhere—even into the room Emilia shares with Marcus, where his drawings of insects now cover the walls—Eric Hansen nods to Johann and declares: "I do not think that there is any unquiet spirit in here, Herr Tilsen. So you shall all live in peace."

"Where is that?" whispers Marcus to Emilia.

"Nowhere," says Emilia. "It is nowhere."

And Preacher Hansen overhears this, and turns to Emilia and smiles, and she sees that at least his smile is gentle and serene, so she supposes he can be borne for a day and a night, or however long it is that he must stay with them, if only he might scrub his body and put on clean clothes, so that he no longer smelled of his horse nor of anything living. She blurts out: "Now you should like to rest and to wash, Herr Hansen. Please let me show you to a room."

She sees her father nod and look at her approvingly. She glides away and up the stairs, and Erik Hansen follows her. And just as Johann Tilsen predicted, Hansen finds that he cannot take his eyes from her. She reminds him a little of his dead wife, who was graceful and quick in her movements, and whose hair was neither dark nor fair. And he understands on the instant that this is why Johann Tilsen invited him here: not because Magdalena's spirit was rattling in the rafters or billowing in the curtains, but so that he could be shown the daughter, Emilia. Catching sight of his face reflected back to him in a window, Erik Hansen smiles at himself. He sees that his period of grieving is at last going to come to an end.

He stays on.

Somehow, the men contrive it—that the preacher should discover that he has nothing in the world to do but to be the guest of Johann Tilsen for several days. They make the fog their excuse. They say the roads are treacherous, that collisions occur on the highways because the mist muffles sound as well as sight. "So," says Johann to Emilia, "Pastor Hansen will be made welcome here for a little longer and indeed I think his presence in this house at this time is beneficial to us all."

Beneficial. Emilia finds the word empty of meaning, almost preposterous. She knows that this is where life has arrived—in the place where it started. Only the impossible can alter it: the revelation that Karen had not died; the arrival out of the white landscape of a man carrying a lute. Otherwise, it must remain absolutely as it is, with precisely the degree of sadness in it that it contains now, no more and no less. To suggest that anything or anyone is "of benefit" to it is like suggesting that a bird, by landing in a tree, does the tree some fundamental good.

But she understands soon enough what the men have in mind and is not angered by it, because this is how these things go on, and is perhaps even a little touched by it—that her father should wish to find her a husband, that Herr Hansen should discover that he likes her. Merely, the men seem not to understand how utterly impossible it is. They are like innocent babes, knowing nothing. They make her smile.

She looks at Hansen, at his striding walk, at the pale skin stretched so tightly over his forehead and back across the dome of his skull to where the sparse brown hair so tentatively grows, and sees the stranger that he will always remain, the distance between him and her that will never ever be crossed. As a stranger he can be tolerated, but the idea that a proposal might suddenly, terrifyingly, come out of his mouth makes her feel sick. At all cost, she decides, this must be prevented.

She decides to take Wilhelm into her confidence. She doesn't tell him that she fell in love with a man named Peter Claire. What she says is: "Wilhelm, I prefer not to try to love any man. Will you go to Father and explain this to him?"

Wilhelm takes his sister's hand. She never knew about him and Magdalena, so it is the *original Wilhelm* that she knows, the Wilhelm who was a boy and innocent of any deception and any crime, and this fact alone makes Emilia precious to him. "I suppose you must marry," he says sadly. "Someday . . ."

"No," says Emilia.

"And what if you change your mind, Emilia? Then I shall have been your spokesman, only to look foolish in the end."

Emilia smiles and says quietly: "I shall not change my mind."

But this—despite efforts by Wilhelm which are valiant and stubborn on his sister's behalf—is exactly the opposite of what the men decide. As Erik Hansen gets onto his horse at last and rides away into the mist, both he and Johann say to themselves: "All things are susceptible to alteration. The day will come when Emilia Tilsen will change her mind."

What Happened at Lutter

The dream is familiar to King Christian.

It begins with the arrival of a ragged man he does not recognise, yet from whose blue eyes gleams out a fragment of the past, like a single shard from some beautiful mosaic whose overall pattern (into which the shard once fitted) has long been forgotten.

Christian stares at the eyes in a face which is brown from the weather, creased with time. The stranger says he works as a stableman. He wears a frayed leather jerkin and breeches. His arms are bare and his boots are worn. His fair hair is long and tied at the nape of his neck with a greasy ribbon. He says he has come to offer his services to His Majesty's army, to serve in a regiment of horse, because he knows horses as thoroughly as he knows his own name.

"What *is* your name?" asks the King.

There is a moment's hesitation, then: "Bror," says the stranger. "Bror Brorson."

With the uttering of these words, the King feels a violent heat come into his body, as though all that had happened through thirty years—all the marvels and all the sorrows—were being poured into him all over again, as burning oil and boiling water into a cauldron. He cannot move, cannot speak, cannot do anything but gape and nod, and then at last he holds out his hand and Bror takes it and kneels down and presses it to his lips.

It is at this moment in the dream that the King is sometimes able to wake up, while his army is still camped at Thuringia, before anything else happens, before the things that followed happen a second time. And on this particular cold spring night, in his room at Rosenborg to which he has returned with Vibeke, he wakes, very hot as he felt himself to be in his dreaming mind, and rouses Vibeke, who is lying quietly beside him, and whispers: "The dream was beginning again. It was beginning again . . ."

"What dream?" asks Vibeke gently, sitting up and taking the King's hand.

"Bror Brorson," says King Christian. "My dream of Bror."

Vibeke Kruse has never been and nor will ever be a sophisticated woman. Her refusal to aspire to any profound wisdom—a refusal much mocked and derided by Kirsten—stems from her unspoken belief that the kind of homely proverbs and axioms with which her mind overflows provide her with sagacity enough. Kirsten laughed repeatedly at these, but Vibeke didn't care and still continues to offer her sayings to those in need of counsel or comfort.

And this, now, she sees is just such a time, for the King is anguished and feverish. He asks her to stroke his head, from which his elflock has unravelled itself, so that a long damp thread of hair is wound about his neck like a black rope. Vibeke lifts the hair carefully and smooths it onto the King's shoulder. Then she says: "A dream told is a dream forgotten."

King Christian is silent. If he reflects, not for the first time, that women so often express things carelessly, seeming to have no conception of what might follow from the particular words they have chosen, he nevertheless soon passes away from this observation to something else, to something he would later identify as "a feeling of being tempted" or "a sudden feeling of longing to unburden myself of these terrors."

For he has never been able to talk about what happened after the arrival of Bror Brorson at Thuringia in his ragged clothes, after the kissing of his hand. It is as though he had never ever had the right listener or as though no listener had ever understood the real task, which was to ensure that the telling of the story did not hurt the King so fearfully that he would never recover from it.

He knew that Kirsten (or at least the Kirsten she had become by the time these things occurred) did not understand them. He had indeed wondered whether Peter Claire, the "angel" whose features resembled Bror's, might be the one to whom the story would be told and whether it would turn out to be this very duty and no other that he had in mind when he commanded Peter Claire to watch over him and not desert him. But somehow that day—that moment that would be like no other moment—had never arrived.

Now King Christian looks at Vibeke, feels her comforting hand on his brow. It is the middle of an April night, silent as the tomb. And it seems to the King as though everything is in suspension, as though Denmark were holding its breath, waiting for him to admit what he has never ever been able to admit except to himself in the dark recesses of his mind—that he was the one who was responsible for the death of Bror Brorson. Long ago, he and Bror, the only members of the Society of One-Word Signatories, had sworn to protect each other *always and at all times* from acts of cruelty. And then, when the time came, Christian discovered too late that his promise had been broken.

Vibeke lights a candle. "Thus," she says quietly, "Bror Brorson joined your army at Thuringia, before you went south to fight General Tilly?"

The King nods. A moment passes before he can speak. Then he says: "I commanded that he be given armour. I said he could not fight in a regiment of horse wearing those rags of his."

"No. I should imagine he could not . . ."

"He told me that he did not need armour. He said that death could not come to him if he was at my side, because I had fought death in the Koldinghus school, so that, with me, death was already dead. And he said, too, that God was on our side, that our war against the Catholic League was a just war and what did the just need with metal gloves, for God would surely protect his servants?

"But I could not bear the look of Bror in that jerkin with his bare arms and his boots all worn away at the heel, so I said, 'Bror, you cannot fight with me unless you wear armour.' And so he was given a back plate and breast plate, and a helmet and all the cumbersome metal covering of a cavalryman, and he was armed with a pair of pistols and a sword."

The King pauses here and Vibeke wipes the sweat from his brow.

"If only we had been as strong as I believed!" Christian cries out. "But my ally, Prince Christian of Brunswick, was weaker than he ever admitted. He himself was dying, of a great worm that gnawed at his bowel, and hundreds of his men were not even properly armed but had to fight with iron-bound sticks, and so his troops hung back while we went on, and the truth of the matter was that my army faced General Tilly almost alone, Vibeke, almost alone!

"I thought we could win the day, because Tilly had isolated himself from General Wallenstein, but Tilly somehow had word of what numbers I brought with me and so he sent a messenger to Wallenstein's rear requesting that eight thousand of his men turn and march north to face me as I came on. But I could not know this early; I only knew it late. And then I ordered the army to wheel round and flee back to where Brunswick was. And despite this, Tilly's forward guard harried my rear and we had to fight as we fled on, and I knew that sooner or later we should have to turn and face them and those coming to them from Wallenstein, and that a great battle would be fought."

Again, the King stops. He looks at Vibeke's face, softly lit by the candle, then beyond the candle into the dark of the room.

He goes on: "I took up a position outside the village of Lutter. I had high ground in my favour and woods where I could hide my cannon and my musketeers.

"Tilly marched on towards me. The date was the twenty-seventh of August 1626, and I can say that all the worst sorrows I have had to endure in my life began with that day."

Vibeke watches the steady burning of the candle and waits. The heat of the King's body is such that her own night-gown is drenched, where he leans against her breast. She notices that Christian's voice is becoming dry and rasping, as though there were insufficient spittle in his mouth, insufficient breath in his lungs. She wonders if he will end the story here, if he will decide that, after all, he cannot go on. "I know," she says gently, "that Danish lives were lost at Lutter . . ."

"Denmark was lost at Lutter!" says Christian. "All that it had been until then in prosperity, in esteem. For we paid dearly there, so very dearly . . ."

"And Bror Brorson was one who paid?"

"Bror should never have died! Our infantry were far outnumbered and I saw hundreds upon hundreds of our pikemen fall. But Bror should have survived, because the cavalry held on at the centre and on the left flank, and we regrouped and mended the broken lines and faced Tilly's onslaught three times, and at the third I cried out to the men that we could do it, that Tilly's cavalry were falling . . .

"But as we turned to go in for the third time my horse went down, shot from under me. You cannot know what sudden confusion and terror assails the cavalry soldier who finds himself on the ground, what helplessness and feeling of smallness! He knows that he is undone unless, by some flux in the battle, another horse, one that has no rider and gallops wildly about the field, comes his way. For battles are won by movement, by the forward push, and a fallen cavalryman, in his heavy armour, cannot move properly and feels that he will be hacked to death in the very next moment.

"And so I called out, to say that my horse was gone . . . and then what I saw . . . a cavalryman turned out of the advancing line, and came riding back to me and dismounted. The noise of the fighting was so terrible that at first I could not hear what he said to me, so then he thrust the reins of his horse into my hands and I understood that he wanted me to take his mount.

"And it was Bror. I said: 'I shall not take your horse, Bror! I shall not!' But he, even then . . . when I had seen already how he was . . . so thin that he looked almost starved . . . even then in spite of this, he was strong, just as he had always been, and it felt to me almost as though he *lifted* me onto his horse, and the next moment I seized the reins, just as though the horse had been mine . . ."

"By giving you his horse, Bror Brorson did no more for his King than any man would," says Vibeke, but Christian is not comforted by these words.

He is pounding the area of his heart with his fist. "As I rode away, I told Bror to go towards the woods, to take a musket from one who had died, but when I looked behind me he had not gone but was standing where I had left him, watching me ride away. I knew what he felt . . . how helpless and how his armour that I had insisted upon imprisoned him and prevented him from running to the safety of the copse. And yet I did not stay—I could not stay! I knew that all depended upon my cavalry and so I had to ride on, to rejoin the line, to urge them forward.

"The line was still holding. And I thought to myself how, in all probability, Bror had saved my life and how, with our cavalry, we would now win the day and ride back to Denmark bearing victory in our hearts and on our sleeves. And then I would rescue Bror! I was determined upon it, and how splendid it appeared to me! I would make amends for all my years of neglect and bring Bror to Rosenborg to care for the horses, and order that he be well housed and fed, and given the respect that he deserved—as the King's friend.

"But it was then that I saw, coming into the valley, the new men Tilly had held in reserve. I had not had them in my calculations. And they were a *wall* of men, numberless, or so it seemed, a wall that could never be broken by such of us as remained.

"When their musketeers began firing, I gave the order to retreat . . . This was my only tactic, for I saw that we were beaten.

"We wheeled round, some of those behind unseated by the sudden turning of the front line, and I cursed myself for my want of skill in the field, berated myself that I had led my soldiers here to this chaos, and imagined how I would never be forgotten for this and did not deserve to find forgiveness.

"We rode back across a valley of Danish dead, and the shame and sorrow of this I knew that I would always remember. But we could not stop to take them up and carry them with us. Our own cannon had been captured by Tilly's infantry and began to fire upon us as we fled.

"We rode through Lutter, northwards. And after a little time I could hear Tilly's army singing and cheering, and the sound of this froze my heart. Because I could guess how many we must have lost. And the folly of this—when I might have stayed in Denmark and never come into these Religious Wars at all—all the horror of this came into me, just as though I had been pierced with a sword, and I could feel my flesh go cold."

Again the King falls silent. Vibeke can feel, now, that the fever in his body has broken. He is shivering and his skin feels clammy, and she tries to pull up a coverlet, to wrap this more closely around him.

But he starts up, pushing the coverlet away. "Foul war!" he cries out, holding his throat, as though something were trying to choke him. "Worse than plague! War more terrible than all! For what men do . . . the things that they had never imagined . . .

"For I went back, in the darkness, with others, to find the dead and bring them back. And by moonlight . . . by the big summer moon, I came upon them, the dead and those who . . . I had prepared myself to come upon our dead, but those we had passed in our retreat had seemed like sleeping men and what I had imagined were souls at rest.

"But there was no soul at rest in the village of Lutter. Not one. Hell was come in and barbarity such as my mind could not comprehend. We had known that Tilly's men were lawless, that they dug up graves for gold, ransacked churches for treasure, raped the peasants' wives . . . but here at Lutter . . .

"They had taken out his eyes. As if his eyes had been precious stones. And he was . . . He had nothing to hold to or cling to nor any ground to lie upon, but he was *in the air*, impaled upon a stake, but not dead yet, Vibeke, not dead, not at rest, and his arms reached out and reached out—to hold fast to something, but there was nothing. There was nothing and no one. Only the empty air . . .

"And when I saw him, I called out 'Bror Brorson!' saying his name, just as I had said it in the Koldinghus school when I fought death at his bedside. I kept on and on repeating it, louder, louder: 'Bror Brorson! Bror Brorson!' as if that saying of his name could save him a second time. Until I understood that by the force of crying it out, it was itself changing and becoming some other word: *Rorb Rorson . . . Rorb . . .*

"And then I had myself lifted up on the shoulders of my men and I took him in my arms."

The King says nothing more. The story is told now. It is over.

He lies back against the pillow of Vibeke's breast and he is very pale, with, round his eyes, an area of bruising that Vibeke touches gently with her thumb.

CONCERNING TRUST

As April comes in, Charlotte Claire draws a picture of the days remaining until her wedding. Each day is represented by some object connected to the task of preparation for becoming Mrs. George Middleton: a satin shoe, a lock of hair cut off by a pair of scissors, a prayer book, a lace garter, a recipe for a syllabub, a posy of lilies, a knife. When Anne Claire asks Charlotte why she has included the drawing of the knife, she replies: "It is not a mere knife, Mother. It is a lancet. It is to remind me that George is mortal."

"We are all mortal, Charlotte," says Anne.

"I know," replies Charlotte, "but George is *more* mortal."

As each Monday, Tuesday, Wednesday, Thursday, Friday, Saturday and Sunday passes, Charlotte draws a neat line through it. And now only sixteen days remain. "I know," she says to her father, "that it is ungrateful to wish time away. When I am old or even a *little* old, I shall wish it all back, I am sure, but it cannot be helped."

George Middleton, of course, has not been shown Charlotte's picture of days. Though she wishes him to know that she ardently looks forward to her wedding, she does not wish him to know quite *how ardently*. He has no need to know this. It might make him complacent or too vain. But she thinks that she may keep the picture as a souvenir and, when she and George are ancient together, when their children are grown up and their grandchildren frolic on the Cookham lawns, she can dig it out from wherever she has hidden it and show it to him then, and perhaps a watery look—of tears or of laughter, it does not really matter—will come into his eyes?

In his turn, George Middleton looks forward to the wedding day. He tells his dogs that "soon we shall have Daisy here." And he has the feeling that, in a very short time, it will be as if Daisy had *always* been there. And this is exactly how the thing should be—conferring alteration upon the past by its absolute rightness.

Only one matter troubles him. A letter from Charlotte's brother has arrived at Cookham and George Middleton finds that he simply cannot decide what he should say or do about it.

The letter is courteous and friendly, but rather brief:

> . . . There are matters here in Denmark which prevent me from returning to England in time to see you married to my sister. I cannot describe to you what these things are, but must beg you to believe that they have an important bearing

upon my own future. Will you therefore explain to Charlotte that, though I shall think of you and even play for you some little song on the third day of May, and that I long to be told I am to be the uncle of some beautiful Cookham child, I cannot be at the ceremony?

Suggest nothing to her that will trouble her. Do not show this letter to her, George, but only send her my tender thoughts like doves to alight on her and murmur to her: "Charlotte Middleton, you shall be happy and you shall be blessed."

From your affectionate (about-to-be) brother-in-law,
    Peter Claire

George Middleton rereads the letter several times, as if hoping that it might contain hidden instructions that he had not at first perceived. He wonders whether, in failing to perceive them, he is being obtuse. For, knowing about Charlotte's feelings of foreboding concerning Peter, he is conscious of his duty to inform her immediately that her brother is well. But how is he to do this and at the same time distress her with the news that he will not be at the wedding? Furthermore, if he refuses to show her the letter, will she not believe, firstly, that something is wrong and, secondly, that he, George, is being secretive and cruel? Might it be possible to *read* to her only those small sections of the letter that will cause her no anxiety, such as the end of it? No, it would not. For she would not be content with this scrap; she would find some way to snatch the thing out of his hand. George Middleton sighs as he folds away the letter and feels cross that Peter has put him in such a predicament. It is all very well, he thinks, to give orders of this kind, but quite another thing to execute them.

The matter is much on his mind. He cannot forget Charlotte's sudden faintness in her blue boudoir when she believed that some calamity had overtaken her brother.

George Middleton plucks from his vocabulary (which is not as extensive as that of clever men, but serviceable all the same) the word "trust." He will resolve his dilemma by reminding Charlotte that mutual trust is one of the foundation stones on which good marriages are built and that, in this matter of her brother, she must *trust* him and not beg him to reveal more than he chooses to say.

He practises the sentences: "Daisy, my beloved, trust me when I tell you that Peter has his reasons for not returning . . . Daisy, my dearest heart, trust me when I say that, as a man, I understand certain things pertaining to Peter better than you . . ." And he hopes that this will be enough, that she won't pester him and will let the matter alone.

It is early evening on the day of Charlotte's arrival at Cookham. George has decided that the thing must be broached before dinner and so he knocks at the door to Charlotte's room, where with the maids, Dora and Susan, recently appointed to serve the future Mrs. Middleton, she is trying on the new petticoats and underbodices they have been embroidering for her.

He expects there to be a pause, while the maids fasten Charlotte back into her dress, but there is no pause, and it is thus that George Middleton finds himself (as if he had stepped into a tableau) in a room where Daisy stands with her hair undone and falling down her back, and her arms and legs bare, and all the rest of her adorned in a voluptuary of white linen and lacy threads. She and Dora and Susan are laughing—whether at him or at some private joke he cannot say—and Daisy's face is flushed, and she looks at him boldly, almost daring him not to retreat from the room.

He tells her that he has something of importance to say to her but that he will return later.

"Oh, no!" she says, reaching for a satin robe, which she puts on but does not wrap entirely round herself, so that her breasts above the bodice are still visible, "for I detest the postponement of anything important, George. Such things must be told instantly or else one may go mad with supposition and speculation. Susan and Dora will go out and you must tell me now."

He feels that he should protest, but he does not. The maids retire, each with her little charming curtsy, and Charlotte invites

George to sit down on a fragile-seeming chair not entirely designed with a man of his size in mind. He perches on the edge of it. The room smells of applewood and of something else which is no more and no less than the smell of his future wife, the smell that reminds him of daisies.

"Well?" says Charlotte. "Speak to me, George."

He clears his throat. He tries frantically to remember the exact phrases and sentences he was going to use, but finds that they have completely gone from his mind. The word "trust," however, lingers there, unconnected to anything, yet still insisting on its own primacy. He is dimly aware that it is a word too heavy for Charlotte's mood, which is the lightest, most teasing of moods, but it is all he can summon up, and so he begins: "I have been thinking, Daisy . . . pondering certain matters . . . and it has come to me how very important it is that we . . . how absolutely vital it shall be that we . . ."

"That we what, George?"

Charlotte sits on another chair, very near him.

He notices that her calves and feet are pink from the fire. He wants to lift her foot and take it to his lips and lick the delicate line of her instep. "Trust is the word I have come up with. In what I am about to say, I want to ask you . . . I want you earnestly to believe . . . that I would never . . . that I should never do or say anything which was not honest and which did not have your . . . your . . ."

"My interests at heart?"

"Yes! I want you to trust me, Daisy. Without trust, there can be no true marriage."

"I perfectly agree. But I do trust you. I know you would never . . ."

"What?"

"Never take any advantage of me in any way."

"No, I would not."

"Nor hurt me."

"Certainly not. Nothing could be further from—"

"So what have you come to tell me?"

Distracted, George Middleton is about to pull Peter Claire's letter from his pocket, but then remembers that he must not do this, that this is precisely what he *must not do*. But nor can he now, with Charlotte so near him in her petticoat and robe, embark upon the question of her brother's absence from the wedding, because he simply cannot remember how to convey any of these things. His thoughts wildly spinning, his face beginning to go red, he stammers: "It was . . . it was nothing, Daisy. I merely had a foolish longing to . . . to see you . . . to tell you before dinner that I love you and that you may always put your trust in me."

Charlotte stares at George for a moment. Then she gets up and crosses to him, sits down on his knee (thus putting, he notes, the survival of the chair into question) and wraps her arms round his neck. "How wonderful a man you are," she says. "How extraordinary that I am to be married to you!"

Then she giggles and bites his ear. The chair tips and his balance is almost lost, but he regains it precariously, and now he yields to the feelings that distract him and he kisses her mouth and her hair falls about his face.

Thirteen days remain until the wedding—with each one its own image in Charlotte's picture. But just suppose, Charlotte thinks now, something were to happen so that we did not get through those thirteen days and so I never experienced a kiss like this one ever again? Just imagine if I were never to know what it was to be in George's arms absolutely? And so she makes a decision and, when she whispers her decision into George's ear, all thoughts of his original mission regarding the letter fly out of his head and the only things that preoccupy him now are how fast he can remove his clothes and Daisy's bodice and petticoat, and how silently, when she is there before him on the bed, he can glide to the door and turn the key in the lock.

The following day, while on a walk to the kitchen garden to inspect this year's *choux-fleurs*, George Middleton tells Charlotte that Peter Claire is not coming to the wedding.

If he is surprised that she accepts the news quite willingly and does not press him to show her the letter (which he declares he has foolishly mislaid) it is because he does not fully know what she is feeling. He is a man and cannot entirely comprehend what it is, to a girl like Charlotte Claire, to savour her own power as a woman, with her wearisome virginity at last fallen away, and how the wonder of this is bound to obliterate—for the time being—all other concerns.

THE TWO SHADOWS

A few nights before the court removes itself to Rosenborg, even as the musicians prepare themselves for a return to the cellar, King Christian sends for Peter Claire.

He is weighing silver.

He looks up as the lutenist comes into the room and smiles, and asks him to play "the *Lachrimae*, the one you played on the night of your arrival."

When the music ends he is invited to sit down, and King Christian reaches out a hand and lays it tenderly on his cheek. There is silence in the room, broken only by the ticking of an ebony clock, and then at last the King says: "Well, I told you there might come a time when I would be able to release you from your bond. I did not know when it would arrive. But it has come. You are free to go to England for your sister's wedding."

Peter Claire looks up to see King Christian's face mould itself into a smile. The King removes his hand from the lutenist's cheek to slap his own thigh with it. "I am pawning you!" He guffaws. "You see what I am come to, when I find myself forced to sell my guardian angel!"

Not knowing how he is meant to respond, Peter Claire waits for the King's laughter to subside. He knows that such bursts of ostentatious mirth are often swiftly followed by a sudden return to melancholy. And, as expected, a different mood arrives as the laughter fades and the King looks sadly at the lute player. "Do not for one moment think," he says, "that I part with you willingly. But

I know that the English always yearn to return to their little island. And now . . . because my fortunes have turned . . . because Vibeke Kruse has enabled me to put the past behind me . . . why should I keep you? I must not keep you, Peter Claire. I must let you go."

Peter Claire waits in silence for a few seconds more. Then the lutenist says: "And if, in the night, you cannot sleep, who will play for you?"

"Yes. Who indeed? Krenze? Pasquier? I shall not find them as comforting as you. Perhaps I will wake old Ingemann himself?"

Peter Claire nods. Then the King declares: "One hundred thousand pounds my nephew Charles is paying for you! Could you ever have believed you would be worth so much?"

"No, Your Majesty."

"No. But imagine the things that you shall become in Denmark: whaling ships, dykes and fortifications, spinning looms, paper mills and counting houses. What an extraordinary alchemy! Perhaps, in the end, you will even become the Numedal silver mine? So if ever, in England, you are homesick for Denmark, think on that, my dear angel. Envisage silver ore in your veins. Remember the *Isfoss* and all our carousing under the stars! Imagine how, all over this land, you will continue to work a magnificent alteration."

Peter Claire's trunk is packed. He buys as gifts for all the other members of the orchestra new candles that burn brighter and more slowly, to light their hours in the cellar.

When he goes to say goodbye to the King, a linen bag tied with a velvet ribbon is put into his hands. "Open the neck and put your hand inside," says Christian.

He does as instructed and feels a quantity of small objects that might have been shells or coins but were not either of these.

"Buttons!" says the King. "I myself have assembled them for you. When you are agitated, let your hand wander in them and it may calm you. Some of them are valuable and some are worth nothing, so you may sell the bulk of them if you are moved to do so, but I counsel against it. For in their numbers they become something else, something greater than the sum of the constituent parts, and this is how I want you to remember me—as *something more* than I have ever seemed to you to be."

His coach is waiting. King Christian clasps him in a momentary embrace and looks, for a last time, into the eyes the colour of the summer air. "Rest assured," the King says, "that my stubborn belief in angels will persist!"

Now, a ship called the *Sankt Nicolai* is lying becalmed in the Kattegat, a few hours out from Copenhagen.

Peter Claire and the captain of the *Sankt Nicolai* stand side by side on the deck and contemplate the sky, listening and waiting for the wind.

"A peculiar sea," says the captain, "very black, the colour of a storm sea, yet almost perfectly still. I was told when I was a boy that understanding light was one of the first tasks of the good mariner, but now and then one comes across conditions that are difficult to read."

"And these are difficult?"

"Yes. What wind there is from the north, just a little scented with rain, but I do not really know what this north wind is going to do."

It is cold. Out of sight of land as they are, it feels to Peter Claire as if they had moved into a different season, as if winter had returned, as if this silent Kattegat might slowly turn to ice and make all further progress impossible. The ship rocks gently, the sails hang down like strange creatures of the air fallen suddenly asleep, the conversations of the crew seem loud in the absence of the wind.

The lutenist goes below and lies down on his bunk. The pain in his left ear torments him with its scratching and tearing. He wonders at the way pain hammers at thought, so that the brain seems incapable of holding to any one idea for more than a moment but is constantly in an agitation of unfinished things.

He falls asleep and has a dream of England. He is arriving at Whitehall Palace to take up his appointment with King Charles. He is brought into the presence of the King, who, he has been told, may sometimes have difficulty uttering the words he wishes to say. He waits politely, not daring to speak or move, while the King regards him, staring at his face in just the way King Christian stared on the night of his arrival at Rosenborg. And then he becomes aware that the King of England is struggling to speak or *is speaking*, but he cannot tell which because he can hear nothing. And the monologue or would-be monologue goes on and on, and yet the silence is absolute.

The ship is not sailing to England. The *Sankt Nicolai* is bound for Horsens in Jutland.

Peter Claire has one image and one only in his mind, and it is towards this that he is travelling: Emilia Tilsen.

She stands, not by the aviary with the sun on her face, but in the cellar by the chicken coop. She looks up from the starved hens scratching in the dust and lifts her face towards him, and her hair, which is neither dark nor fair, looks darker in the shadows that live perpetually there. And her look says: Peter Claire, what are you going to do about the world?

He does not know. But he believes that if he can only arrive at wherever she is he will know then, at that moment. And if he has lost her, then he will probably never know. He will live to be old, never ever knowing.

While he dozes on his bunk the north wind begins to rouse the sleeping sails and the captain orders the crew to scurry about the *Sankt Nicolai*, to bring her round into the wind. And Peter Claire, feeling the ship turn, and hearing the water pushing and slapping at her sides, thinks how, whenever he is on the sea, his mind seems perpetually dancing between expectation and dread.

It is almost night when the *Sankt Nicolai* enters the port at Horsens.

Suddenly worried that he might arrive too late—by a day or by an hour—and find Emilia gone away or married to some other man, Peter Claire informs the captain that his trunk is to be sent on after him and that he is going to set out for Boller straight away.

"Boller is not far," the captain says to Peter Claire, "but why don't you wait until morning when we can find a horse for you?"

"I prefer to leave now," he says. "In this way, I shall arrive with the sunrise."

The captain warns him that the roads in Jutland can be dangerous at night and suggests that it would be better to sleep on the ship, but these words vanish as a spell of deafness comes on and all that can be heard is the noise in the lutenist's head like that of tearing cloth. Peter Claire cradles his ear, fighting the pain, nodding at the captain, pretending to take note of what he's saying, then bidding him goodbye and setting out with no further ceremony through the dark streets of the little town.

As he walks, with the moon almost full and whitening the clouds the wind sends racing across the sky, Peter Claire tries to conquer the agony in his ear by humming quietly the tune of the song begun for Emilia and never finished. After a while he feels the pain retreat and the song emerge to make a sudden addition to itself, an addition without words but which seems to have an unexpected kind of beauty.

Peter Claire knows that he should stop to write down the music, but he does not want to stop. He is no longer cold. He has found a pace that does not tire him. He thinks about the miles that separated him from Emilia for so long, about that distance so much greater than itself which could not be crossed, even as words on paper, and how, on this moonlit night, it is being subdued, vanquished step by step by step, by his shadow and by his will. He almost dares himself—he who came searching for his future in Denmark—to believe that it is now within his grasp and that it will only take the coming of the day to reveal it. Without really noticing what he is doing, but filled with a determination to move more swiftly towards the sunrise, he begins to run.

He thinks later that if only he had not been running, if only he had just walked quietly on, then nobody would have heard his approach. He does not know what possessed him—when all the night lay ahead of him—to start running like a child. But no doubt it is the sound of hurrying footsteps that sends the two strangers out into the road. He sees them standing there, in front of their house, which is low, with a thatch of reeds. They stand and watch him come on and he slows to a walk once more.

In their shapeless garments, which might be night-shirts or cloaks of some pale material, they look ghostly, but their shadows cast by the moonlight are long and fall across the road. And this is all that Peter Claire can remember, that he walks on until he is almost level with the two shadows. He cannot properly recall the people, not enough to say if they were two men or a man and his wife, nor whether anything is said by him or by them. He feels sure, afterwards, that something must have been said, but knows also that whatever it was may never return to him. There are merely these things: his running, the sudden appearance of the strangers, and then the slow traversal of ground between him and the shadows falling across his path. And then there is silence.

KIRSTEN: FROM HER PRIVATE PAPERS

In this wilful Spring that is not properly a Spring, but a mere Extension of Winter with here and there some leaves and flowers shivering like girls in the bitter air, there is, I note, a great deal of Coming and Going at Boller.

These things happen one by one, in an Unpredictable way, so that it is impossible to perceive some kind of Pattern or Order at work, but yet when I walk about the house I do see that it is much changed from what it was but a short while ago, as though it might be some moving conveyance like a ship, from which both passengers and cargo arrived and departed all the while.

First of all, I have given away my baby, Dorothea.

If any should accuse me of Heartlessness, I shall defend myself vehemently, for truly I think what I did was a Kind Act and one that will earn me rewards in Heaven; and if people say otherwise, then it shows merely that they have no Imagination.

It happened in this way. A Friend of my Mother's, believing Ellen still to be in residence here, arrived last Tuesday with her daughter, whose name is Christina Morgenson and whom I have seen once or twice in my Life.

I did not truly wish to invite these Women in and give myself the Wearisome Task of making conversation with them, and indeed I was on the point of suggesting to them that they put up at some Convenient Inn, when—for reasons which I cannot determine—I changed my mind and made a Marvellous show of welcoming them to Boller and saying "Oh, please do be my Guests" and "Oh, what a Great Pleasure it is to find you here" and so forth. All of this was nothing but a Froth of Lies and I still do not understand why I came out with such Falsehoods, except that I have sometimes noticed how the Voice may occasionally decide, on a whim, to *Mutiny* against the Mind and to articulate all manner of rebellious Words that the Mind has not sanctioned, or which indeed it believed it had expressly Forbidden.

And so it was that I found myself Burdened with these People whom I had not invited and whom I suddenly remembered I did not like, but rather Detested and hoped never to see again in the years remaining to me. What an Utter Fool you are, Kirsten! I said to myself. What Insanity came upon you that you professed such Friendship for poor Christina Morgenson and her Insufferable Mother? And all that now preoccupied me was how quickly I might persuade them to leave.

It was during the evening of their arrival that a Beautiful Plan came into my mind. Christina Morgenson is my age and married to a Merchant from Hamburg but, through all the years that have passed since her Betrothal, has never given birth to any infant. In short, she is barren. And this Barrenness of hers is as a Wound to her, so that whenever the Subject of Children is mentioned she has the look of a person in great Pain and even kneads the area of her heart with her fist. And this kneading of Christina's heart first of all (kind-hearted as I am becoming as I grow older) made me sorry for her and then, almost on the instant, brought about the bursting forth of my Plan.

I ordered that Dorothea (who is now out of her Swaddling bands and does sit up a little and try to make sounds and blow bubbles out of her mouth) be brought into the Dining-room where we sat. I took the child, who in certain lights begins to look tolerably pretty, in my arms and then I rose and walked with her to Christina and laid her in Christina's lap, on top of her table napkin. I said: "Here is Dorothea. She has two Fathers, but no Real Devoted Mother. So why do you not take her, Christina, and call her Your Own? For I declare I cannot abide any Baby in this house, for I have had too many and am weary of them, and it will not greatly upset me if I never lay eyes upon Dorothea again."

I need not note the Quantity of Protestations that Christina and her Mother pretended to make: "Oh, Mercy, but we could never do such a thing!" and "Oh, heavens, but what Crime we would be committing to take away your child!" and so forth, la-la-la and tra-la-la. But I knew that these would run their course and end at last, for Christina's Countenance was quite Transformed when she held Dorothea in her arms, and the child in her turn reached out her arms to her New Mother and blew some of her famed bubbles into her face.

And when they had agreed, I said: "I merely think it is wise that you leave with Dorothea early in the morning, before I have woken, and in this way I shall not be tempted to change my mind."

And so when I rose on Wednesday there was no sign of my Guests and Dorothea was gone, and I felt much eased in my mind, as though some terrible Coming Event would now no longer be arriving.

Another much less agreeable Subtraction from Boller is the sudden Removal of a great quantity of my Mother's furniture.

Some Men arrived with carts, despatched by the Dowager Queen at Kronborg, and into the carts, despite my Protestations, were loaded tables and chairs, pictures, candlesticks, china, chaises, linen and even beds. The Larder was ransacked and all Ellen's pots of Jam taken away, so that not one remains, and this petty removal of the Jam (which was the only Sweet Thing my Mother ever manufactured) put me into such a Fury that I clawed the face of one of the Removal Men with my nails and, after this, they all fled away with their carts piled high and I stood at my door screaming Curses upon them and upon Ellen, who has never given me Any Thing except Life itself, but has rather sought to Take Away from me all that I possess.

I walked about the empty rooms, remembering how, when I was at Rosenborg, I could ask the King for any Object that my heart had set itself upon and he would give it to me and how, in this new and changeful season, it is to Vibeke's whims that he attends and I am forgotten. And such was my Melancholy that I could almost make myself believe I had been Happy all my Days with the King and never conceived for him any loathing whatsoever nor longed with a raging longing like a Thirst for my Freedom from him.

I sat down upon the floor in the room that Vibeke occupied while she was here and which now contains nothing except a carpet from the Orient and a large oaken chest in which Vibeke used to hide stolen food. I looked down at my hands (which I think are still soft and white and admirable) and saw Blood under my nails and thought to myself how even the drawing of Blood can sometimes avail one nothing at all.

But as the cargo of furniture leaves, as Dorothea vanishes out of my sight, so there are also Extraordinary Arrivals here . . .

Yesterday, in the early morning, I see a carriage coming up the drive and I recognise the King's Livery on the Coachman. I stand at a window, waiting and watching, and very soon do I spy, to my great Astonishment and Delight, my Black Slaves, Samuel and Emmanuel, descending from the carriage.

I go down to the door and the Coachman hands me letters from the King, which I know shall certainly contain Instructions about his Divorce from me, and so I lay them aside and go at once to

Samuel and Emmanuel, who do, notwithstanding their Blackness, look a little Pale from their journey.

I lead them into the house, holding each his hand in mine, the Black upon the White and the White upon the Black, and tell them how much I have looked for their Return to me and how, here at Boller, our hours shall be filled with stories of Magic and Spirits from their island of Tortuga and how, when we are weary of Tales, we shall devise our own Entertainments to while away the hours.

They smile at me. I notice they have grown a little since I last saw them and now seem not as Boys but as marvellous young Men, such as I never thought ever to see. And I cannot stop myself from yearning to touch them—their faces, their ears, their hair, their finger-nails like shells, their gilded uniforms—as though they were composed of some Other Substance than mere flesh and which would never change nor die.

On a whim, I lead them not to the Servants' Quarters but into Vibeke's former room, and tell them that this is where they will sleep—upon the Oriental carpet—and stow their few possessions in the oaken chest. And suddenly I relish the Emptiness of the room. I imagine that in such a space I shall, with Samuel and Emmanuel, create a Miniature Universe within the greater one and in this Miniature World become utterly lost.

So engrossed was I with looking at my Slaves and beginning to devise in my mind all manner of Wildness with them, that I did not realise until a little later, when the Coachman brought this to my attention, that there had been a Third Occupant of the Carriage.

It appeared that as the coach passed through the village of Høgel the Coachman came upon a Man lying in the road, across the path of the horses. The horses were pulled up and the Coachman descended and saw that the man was one whom he recognised—"One," he said, "who was part of His Majesty's Orchestra."

As he said this, my eyes grew large with Anticipation, for I knew that there was only one Musician who would be travelling to Jutland and that it must be Emilia's sometime lover Peter Claire.

457

And now he was about to fall, like a gift from the sky, into my hands entirely! I could not stop a little smile from creasing my face, for when the Truly unlooked-for Thing comes to pass, an irrepressible Excitement starts up within me, just as though I had been told that I could have all my life again.

"In what condition is this man?" I asked.

"Babbling, Madam," said the Coachman, "and in a Delirium, for he was hit about the neck and all his possessions taken from him, including his Instrument. But we took him up and set him in the coach with Samuel and Emmanuel, and they say that they talked to him in their language and brought down Spirits from the clouds to help to make him well."

Peter Claire.

There is blood in his fair hair. His blue eyes are closed. His body, which was cold when he was brought in, now seems to be heating up to a great Fever.

For him to die would inconvenience me, for who knows if some would not say that I had killed him? Moreover, now that I have him here, captive entirely, I also hold Emilia's Destiny in my hands and can do Any Thing it might please me to do to be revenged upon her.

Her absence, I confess, does weigh heavily on me, and when I sit alone by my fire I remember what a sweet Companion she was to me, one who—thought I—would do whatever I asked. But then I understood that Emilia *did not truly Love Me* and this thought makes me so furious that I can imagine beating her head against the wall. And why should this Girl, who only *pretended affection for me* and did not really feel it, be given some Marvellous Future with a handsome husband, when I have lost everything that was ever mine and may never see my Lover again as long as I live?

I order that compresses be laid on the brow of the Lutenist and a little blood let from his arm, to lessen the fever, and it is not very long before he returns to consciousness. He stares at me, wondering, I dare say, by what means he was transported here.

Then he looks around his room, craning his neck up from the pillow, as if to see whether his beloved is lurking like a grey hen under the chest or behind the curtains. And so I say straight away: "Emilia is not here. She left me. For there was a Great Quarrel between us, and therefore in truth I have no idea where she is gone."

"I must find her . . ." says Mr. Claire weakly.

"Well," I say, "I did hear some rumour that she was married and had gone away to Germany, but rumours in Jutland are like the wind, always whispering down our chimneys and through the cracks in our walls, so who knows whether this is true or no?"

Then it is as if my words have brought about a sudden Pain in the lute player's ear. He covers it with his hand and cries out, and because I am almost tempted to feel pity for him, I swiftly go out of the room, saying I will send the Doctor to him.

To cure me of my tender feelings I take up the King's letters, knowing how they will put me into a fine Rage. And they do not disappoint me in this respect. For I see from them how the King's heart has hardened itself against me so cruelly that no vestige of his former affection (not even the name "Mousie") appears to remain, and though he has sent me my Slaves he declares that this is the last thing that he shall ever do for me and that, even against my Will, I shall be divorced from him so that he can take Vibeke as his new Wife.

That Vibeke Kruse, with her fat arse and her clumping ivory teeth, should take my place and be Almost Queen of Denmark is a Thing so Mortifying that I declare I shall never recover from the knowledge of it! What I imagined when I left was the King pining for me and sighing for ever over the loss of his Only Mouse. But it is not so. And so I conclude that there is Nothing in this world that has Absolutely and of Itself the *power to endure*.

I go to Vibeke's former room, where Samuel and Emmanuel wait for me. I tell them that if they know the route to any Other Universe, then I should like to fly there on soft wings of blackest hue.

On the first day of May, Pastor Erik Hansen returns to the Tilsen house.

He had intended to wait until high summer before taking further his suit to Emilia, but now he knows that, in a short space of time, he has become accustomed to *think of Emilia as his future wife* and that therefore the gap between what is and what should be has grown intolerably wide. Disappointed that God took from him his first wife (whom he had loved very well), Hansen prays not to be cast out from happiness a second time.

To Johann Tilsen he confides that he will not demand any dowry for Emilia, that he will take her just as she is. He says: "I know that I am not a handsome man. I know that Emilia might prefer a husband with more hair on his head. But my very baldness she can take as proof of my honesty; for could I not cover it with a hat if I chose? And again, if she could see into my heart, I do think she would find there sentiments which might be described as handsome."

Johann looks at Erik Hansen. There is a touching plainness—or even colourlessness—about him, as though he had always lived in a landscape within which he had to remain concealed. His small eyes are bright and restless, his gestures eloquent. He appears in all respects what he is: a man who has glimpsed—beyond the featureless land where he has resided—a future more enticing than any he had previously seen.

"Emilia has told me," says Johann, "that she does not at present wish to marry. But she gives me no reasons, so we may perhaps assume that there are none—none specific that she can articulate—and that the 'wish' is no more than an indeterminate feeling."

"Or else it may be allied to her desire to keep house here for you and to take care of Marcus and Ulla . . ."

"No. I do not think it is that. I believe this disinclination has been part of her nature since her mother died, and it has never occurred to her to fight against it."

Pastor Hansen presses his white hands ardently together.

"I beg you, Johann," he says, "ask her to fight against it now! I would do everything a man can do to make Emilia happy. She would have servants enough and I would not burden her too heavily with church work, and she would have a little parlour room which was my wife's and would be hers entirely. This parlour is at present painted green, but if this colour did not please Emilia, why then—"

"You need say nothing more, Herr Hansen, for I am quite in favour of it," Johann announces.

"And you will speak to her?"

"Why do *you* not speak to her yourself?"

"Oh, no. I cannot. I am too agitated. I wouldn't know when to pause or cease. I might come out with a sermon . . ."

Emilia knows that Erik Hansen has returned. She sees his horse and hears his voice. She knows that it will not be long before she is summoned to her father and the wearisome question of this preacher's attachment to her once again laid before her.

She finds it all repulsive, fearful. It cannot be endured. She wishes there were no such thing as marriage. She wishes she were old and grey, and could be left alone.

She puts on her cloak and runs out of the house. Though the spring chill persists day after day in the northerly wind, there is sunshine falling on the fruit fields as Emilia crosses them and makes for the forest, where the beech trees are at last putting forth their showers of green.

She wants the forest to hide her. She would like to become small and ghostly, as Marcus once was—become so insubstantial that no man would ever again think of her as having any bodily existence.

She makes her way to the tree where she found the buried clock and sits down under it, wrapping the cloak round her so that she becomes a shapeless form, and begins to weep. Her weeping is silent. Such song as the birds are making goes on uninterrupted. Near her feet, a vole scuffles in the old dry leaves.

Show courage, Emilia.

Karen's voice now returns to Emilia in all its clarity, so real and near that it is just as if Karen were suddenly standing in the wood, looking down at her. And so she raises her head and looks up, then, feeling the sun on her face, tilts it and stares at the beech canopy which is still fragile as lace, with its glories to come. And it is in this contemplation of the arching trees, this patterning of the sky that speaks of spring and revival and all things returning and continuing, that Emilia at last understands what it is that her mother has always been trying to say.

Karen has never been talking about the kind of courage that has to be shown towards everyday worldly matters. She is not now, for instance, urging her daughter to show fortitude in the face of this new destiny as the wife of Erik Hansen. On the contrary, Karen alone has understood why this is impossible and why it cannot be allowed to happen.

If Karen bided her time, not calling too loudly but waiting to see whether what was begun at Rosenborg might lead to any beautiful future, then this is further proof of the message she was trying to give. For only Karen, among all the people that Emilia knows, understands fully why a human life led without love is not worth living. And so she will not allow her daughter to live it.

Karen is saying to Emilia: "Show the courage to come to me, to wherever it is that I am. Have the faith to know that I will be here when you arrive, that ever since I left you I have always been waiting for you."

Karen's nearness now is such that Emilia stops weeping and finds herself filled with a strange lightness of heart, an excitement almost, a feeling of pleasure and relief such as people feel when they have searched for something through great tracts of time and come upon it at last in their own orchard.

Show courage, Emilia!

Why did she not hear what was being said sooner than this? But now it is so miraculously clear to her, it is as though it were written down everywhere in the forest and etched in the pattern of beech leaves against the sky.

She will not be the wife of a preacher.

She will not grow old running her father's house and being a mother to Magdalena's child.

She will join Karen. It will be she, at last, and not the clock, who lies under the green canopy of the beech trees.

And it will surely be simple, in the end? It needs only the purchase of a little pot of white poison, such as Kirsten got from her apothecary. And then it will be like arriving on a frozen river all alone and skating on and finding, at the place where the river turns, her mother's hand held out, and taking the outstretched hand and then gliding away as they always did, the two of them together, arm in arm . . .

Later, when she gets home, she is summoned by her father.

"Emilia," says Johann, "I have given thought to the matter of Herr Hansen's proposal and I think that it is a good one. You believe now that you do not wish to marry, but examine your heart a little more minutely. I am sure there is a corner of it which would prefer to . . ."

"Prefer to . . .?"

"Capitulate. You have struggled against me for so long and I think you are weary of it."

Emilia goes to her father, who looks older now than he did when Magdalena first came into the house, and places a soft kiss on his cheek. "I will do whatever you ask," she says.

He holds her to him, his eldest child, who still reminds him of his first wife and even smells like her and has the same laugh. "Good," he says. "Then let me tell Herr Hansen that before the summer is over, you and he will be married. A June wedding would be fine, would it not?"

A June wedding. She sees the forest in her mind's eye: she wears some gossamer dress; she is lying under the canopy, which is a darker, deeper green, and her corpse is in shadow, from the ribbons in her hair to her shoes of white satin. A few leaves, disturbed by pigeons, come drifting and floating down on her body like rose petals scattered by the wedding guests . . .

"I will think about it," says Emilia. "I will think about a June wedding."

"Well, do not 'think about it' too long. Herr Hansen is an honourable man, Emilia. And when you are married, why then your own life will begin."

How strange, thinks Emilia afterwards, that this is what my father said—that my life would *begin*. How perverse people are in their thoughtless optimism. Only Karen sees everything clearly. Only Karen understands that the thing begun is going nowhere at all, but returning to the place where it first started.

This is the time that it will always tell.

"Some Long Way North of Here"

Peter Claire stares at the room.

Resting his body, down the whole length of it, where it aches and sweats, he is grateful to be in a bed with a warm coverlet, with the coming and going of servants who bring him refreshing cordials and morsels of food he cannot eat. He knows that, left out on the road where he fell, he would be dead by now.

But he is Kirsten's prisoner.

She has told him as much, laughing all the while. Too weak to move, to protest, he is at the mercy of her whims and desires, whatever these may turn out to be.

She visits him every day, sweeping into the room, smelling of some pungent spice, and laying her cool white hand on his forehead. "Exceptional!" she says of his continuing fever. "If they sent you spinning round the earth, you would glow like a comet, Mr. Claire!" When she leaves, she turns the key in the lock behind her.

He dreams of Emilia. Here at Boller, in the place where he thought he would find her, she returns to him as the dead return, confined to pathetic gestures of sadness or reproach, an insubstantial spirit who pales and fades with the coming of the light. And the idea that she might, in fact, be dead brings to him such a feeling of horror that he covers his face with his hands and finds himself praying: "Let anything in the world happen, but not this." For he is still moving towards her. This is what, in the depths of his fevered brain, he feels he is doing. The loss of his lute, the theft of his money and of the King's button bag, the pains in his body, his incarceration at Boller: these things constitute an interlude in his search for her. Somehow he will recover sufficiently to resume it.

But where is he to go? He knows her father's house is in Jutland and he asks Kirsten how near it is to Boller.

"Oh," she replies, "some long way north of here. I don't know precisely where. But anyway, I don't think she is there, Mr. Claire. Rumour had it that she was married, as I told you, and gone into Germany. Perhaps she is a little mother by now? She used to have a chicken for a pet, you know!"

He replies that he knows only too well, that he can never forget the sight of Gerda nesting in her room. And then he wants to say to Kirsten: Why did you hide my letters from her? What spite in you used innocent Emilia in your schemes of bribery? Do you not know how rare is love, that you could trample on it so? But he keeps silent. Kirsten shelters him in his weakness and now is not the time to find himself put out into the cold.

A doctor has dressed the wound on his neck and put his nose very close to the ear which now causes the lutenist almost constant torment and from which his hearing has almost gone. The doctor informs Peter Claire that he can smell something which he does not like. "Tell me what it is," says Peter Claire, but the doctor replies that he does not know but will try to "flush it out, Sir, flush it clean away."

Into the ear the doctor pours hot oil of cloves. It bubbles like a cauldron in the lute player's head and he cries out as his world begins to go dark. Then the cauldron settles to a manageable simmer and the doctor prods the ear with a reed and, as he withdraws it, remarks upon a gob of pus on the end of it. "Some foul infection you have, Sir," he says triumphantly. "Very choleric in appearance. I will consult my books as to how I shall make it yield."

The loss of the King's button bag begins to torment Peter Claire. To have stayed for so long at King Christian's side and now to find himself without any single possession by which he can be remembered strikes him as wretched. Already, during the voyage of the *Sankt Nicolai*, he had begun to form the habit of putting his hand into the bag and letting the buttons cascade through his fingers. This fingering of the buttons was oddly consoling. To feel how the precious and the valueless lost themselves in each other to form something else, upon which it was impossible to put any price, made him smile with pleasure. He determined that he would never travel without the bag, that this gift would be a constant reminder of the King who had mistaken him for an angel and who had always striven (despite every set-back and every disaster) to understand in what currency human happiness resided.

He remembers the stars over the Numedal; he remembers the songs played in the King's chamber as the dawn came up; he remembers the concerts in the summer-house, the half-told tales of Bror Brorson, the immoderate drinking and feasting, the weighing of silver, the discussions concerning Descartes's *cogito*, concerning the power of the sea, concerning betrayal and the obstinacy of hope.

And he understands that whatever his future holds, nothing in it will resemble his time with the King of Denmark. He thinks that, if it were not for Emilia, he would ask Kirsten to send him back to Copenhagen, where he would try to persuade His Majesty to despatch another of the musicians to the English court in return for the money promised. And then happily—if a lute could be found for him—would he go down to the cellar and play, in the knowledge that the man who listened up above, with his sad face, his faulty digestion and his bursting heart, was one of the few on this earth who understood the importance of music in human affairs.

But he cannot go back. While the tearing goes on and on inside his ear and his body's heat is such that he feels himself becoming thin as a reed among the pillows and bolsters, he is trying to assemble a plan. But what plan can a man make without money and possessions? He lacked the means of all persuasion. Surely, one of the servants might know where Emilia was to be found, but how was that knowledge to be obtained? And how, when he had no coat to put on his back and no horse to ride, could he travel the length and breadth of Jutland, or even make the journey to Germany?

Then, at last, he remembers his trunk. The captain of the *Sankt Nicolai* promised to send this onwards to Boller. In it are clothes and books, some silver boot buckles, a dressing mirror, sheets of music—a hundred small artefacts susceptible to barter. And so he waits patiently, immersed in his feverish dreaming, for the trunk to arrive, while the doctor wraps his ear in a poultice of buttercup root and he fancies he hears in the night a wild wailing coming from somewhere within the house.

The days pass. The sun at the lute player's window rises a little earlier each morning and is almost warm, now, on the glass. The root poultice lowers his fever just enough so that he can walk about the room.

He looks out of the window. He sees that all the beech trees in the park now offer to the wind branches heavy with green leaf, and this sighting of the spring in its flowering returns to him his sense of time: time beckoning him towards England; time taking Emilia further and further away . . .

When Kirsten visits him, he inquires after his trunk.

"Trunk?" she asks. "What trunk?"

"Sent here from the ship . . ."

"You expect such a thing to arrive? Have you not learned that there is no honesty on this earth, Mr. Claire? The contents of your precious trunk will long ago have been divided out, in the very port where you docked—or else, by some arithmetic that one cannot fathom, despatched to Turkey or even to the Caspian Sea! I should forget it if I were you."

Her laughter is as her laughter always was—loud and vibrant. He looks at her standing by the bed, her eyes very large in her white face, her abundant hair held up by a silver comb. He remembers the King saying: "To plead with Kirsten is futile. Only if you have something she wants will she yield."

"I regret the trunk," he says, "for there are documents in it that might be of interest to you."

"What documents?"

He watches her face. He sees her nose quiver for a moment, like a mouse smelling cheese.

"Those you once asked me to obtain—pertaining to the King's finances."

She hurls herself away from the bedside, taking out the comb to let her hair fall down her back, then gathering it up again in her hands. When she turns back to him she says: "The time for such an exchange has gone, Mr. Claire. Alas that it is so, but it is. Nothing in your trunk is of any value to me—and besides, I do believe you are lying. If you had anything worth talking about you would have whetted my appetite with it long before now."

She goes out, letting the door bang, then closing it with the key. The lute player ponders the notion that those who most unerringly detect lies in others are very often liars themselves and wonders what edifices of untruth Kirsten has built around Emilia. To see beyond Kirsten's constructions, he knows he must escape from Boller, but he cannot see, at present, how this is to be done.

He gets up unsteadily and walks again to the window, and looks at the sky, which is a blue so pale it is almost not blue, and at the feathery beeches fretting in the wind, and at the drop to the ground beneath the stone sill which seems too featureless and too steep even to dream of.

KIRSTEN: FROM HER PRIVATE PAPERS

I find myself turning the word SLAVE over and over in my mind.

There are people in Denmark who protest that the taking of Natives from Africa to work upon Cotton plantations on Tortuga, or to ship them as Ornaments to the Courts of Europe, is sinful; and so I think it is, for why should these people, because they are helpless, be made to travel away from their homes against their will and have wigs put on their heads or be scourged with a whip to gather the sticky puff-heads of cotton under a merciless sun? They might surely prefer to be left in peace, to sit in a Catalpa Tree or stroke a monkey or chew some magical root or just to *be* and not find themselves entirely at the mercy of Another's Whim?

But then I reflect that, because the word SLAVE is applied uniquely to them and to them only, an Injustice is thereby being perpetrated towards other groupings, categories and congregations of people. For surely the condition of Slavery is spread through and through our Society, except that it is not termed Slavery: it is termed Duty. And chiefest among those who live in a condition of Bondage and yet call their bonds by sweet names such as Fidelity and Hope are Women. For are we not owned—as Drudges or Ornaments or a combination of both—by our Fathers and Husbands? Do we not labour and bring forth children and get no reward for this except the reward of the mewling child itself, which is no reward at all? Might we not as well pick cotton in the heat of midday as lie on our backs with our legs spread open to the branding iron? What wages have we deserved in all our terrible work and pain of the bed alone, and never got?

These thoughts, which on occasion in the course of my Life have made my blood boil with Fury, are now most useful to me, for manifestly they contain more than a grain of Truth and so they ease my Conscience in all my dealings with my Black Boys. I embellish them further. I ask myself: "Is not the Servant (underpaid and enjoying no luxury whatever) Slave to the Master? Is not the Infant (racked by his wooden swaddling bands) Slave to Pain and Ignorance? Is not the Carriage Horse Slave to the whip? Is not the Body Slave to Mortality? Is not the bright Day Slave to the coming Night?" In each and every case, the answer is Yes. And so I see that all the world turns on a Prevailing Condition of Slavery from which there does not seem to be any escape. And this comforts me much. For, when I ask certain Things of my dear Samuel and Emmanuel, I am surely not—if my Thesis be followed to its Conclusion—committing any Wickedness whatsoever, but only being borne along on the great tides of Custom and Observance which have always and ever flooded the Earth and will do so long after I am dead and gone.

And indeed, in the matter of my Boys, it is surely I who am becoming Enslaved and they who are becoming Free, for with them lies all the power of their Magic.

They wait for me in their room (where all Vibeke's dresses used to hang), which I have furnished with a hundred cushions, and they feast there on fruit and sweetmeats, and plump woodcock from the forests. They can weave spells by calling forth their *Lwa*, or Spirits, and I say to them: "Oh, my dear Children, my Beautiful Ebony Boys, my Handsome Young Stallions, do whatever you will! Do whatever it may please you to do with a woman who was Almost Queen, for truly I tell you that I am Weary of Everything in the World."

And their eyes bulge with excitement and out of their throats come the strangest ululating sounds and songs, and their members grow so stiff that they can lift me up and I can balance my body upon them, upon their two members and upon nothing else, so that parts of me are anchored to the earth and other parts of me do seem to Float in the air. I have never experienced any such thing before, and when I float there I am in Ecstasy—more than ever I was in with Otto and his silken whips. And I know that this shall be the nearest I shall ever come to veritably Flying.

I could spend all day and all night in this room. The Magic is so strong that I never weary of the Feats we try.

To give my attention to the things of the World—such as the King's letters and my need for money and furniture and jam, and the predicament of the English Lutenist—causes me great Irritation. I declare I am no longer interested in Any Thing which, formerly, I might have found Amusing. To have played a Game with Emilia's would-be lover, who fell so marvellously into my net on his broken wings, would, before my Introduction into the Black Magic, have given me hour upon hour of mirth and delight. But really and truly, now I can't be bothered with him. For what is he but a Slave to his love for Emilia? And how pathetic I do find this! I have it in mind to tell him that Emilia is Incapable of Love for Anyone except her dead Mother, but even to say this wearies me.

And so I come at last to a Resolution. I shall let the Lutenist go.

Let him find out for himself what Slavery to Love becomes! Let him see for himself what it is to be bound in Perpetuity to Another, from whom there is no escape—except in Deception and lying. Let him discover what Marriage is and how it may be a Stone chained to one's ankles (once admired as delicate and curving in a sweet arc over a satin shoe, but now thickening and bleeding as the Chains chafe and bite) which in due time drags one down and down into the freezing darkness.

The Musician's famous Trunk arrives at last, but I don't even bother to ransack it to see what it contains in the way of Papers. I merely command one of the servants to take out of it a new suit of clothes and a coat, and give these to Mr. Claire and tell him that he is Free.

I then order that a horse be given to him. (I do quite Draw the Line at giving him a Carriage, so he must lump what possessions he can upon the horse's withers and think himself lucky.)

He is grown very thin indeed, so that his clothes hang poorly upon him. His head is bandaged, keeping the Poultice in place over his suppurating ear. And there is, I must admit, much human sadness in the sight of this bandage, so that I do think that, after all, it was my Kind Heart, touched by this Unexpected Pitiful Thing, and not any Nastiness or Vengeful Feelings in me on the subject of Marriage, which decided me to end Peter Claire's Misery and lead him to his Heart's Desire.

He is almost at the end of the drive when I open the front door of Boller and run after his horse. My hair escapes from its clip and billows about my face, half blinding me in the wind. I catch the reins of the horse and hold it still. Then, when I have recovered my breath from my Burst of Running, I say: "She has not gone away, Mr. Claire. She is at her Father's House. Ride east through the woods over there and you will find her."

He gazes at me, quite stupidly, as though he cannot bring himself to believe me. And I don't blame him, for I have told him so many falsehoods; so I smile at him and add: "I had it in mind to play a long Game with you—to its bitterest end. But I find simply that I no longer have the stomach for it. So God speed you, Peter Claire, and will you tell Emilia that, in spite of all, I have not thrown away the painted Eggs?"

The Voice That Cannot Be Heard

Emilia has her pot of poison now, white as snow. Unable to pay the money demanded by the apothecary, she has given him, in exchange, the only thing of value that she owned: the stopped clock. The apothecary, so accustomed to working with his scales and measures, held the clock in his hands, as if the value of all things could be measured in weight alone. Then he wound it up and shook it, and this shaking of the clock set it ticking and the hands moved on from ten minutes past seven.

Everything moves on; always, on and on.

The air has begun to smell of early summer. Erik Hansen has been told by Johann that Emilia has agreed to become his wife and keeps asking when the date of the wedding is going to be set. "Emilia will set it," replies Johann, "as soon as she is ready."

As soon as she is ready. As the days have passed, taking her forwards, hour by hour, towards her only destination, Emilia's dreams and reveries of Karen have increased and Karen has moved nearer to her, always nearer, away from shadow and silence, taking on colour and substance and voice, so that now she no longer seems ghostly but just as she used to be when she was alive and lay on her day-bed in the afternoons, listening to Emilia's songs.

Emilia settles herself there, on the floor near the day-bed. She closes her eyes. She asks Karen to give her courage. Because when she looks at the poison, she feels afraid. To imagine her own heart stopping and all the world that she knows going on without her is still a fearful thing. So she whispers to Karen: "You must help me. You must be the one to tell me when the day, the hour, has arrived . . ."

One morning, Emilia is alone in the schoolroom with Marcus. Johann and the elder boys (including Ingmar, recently returned from Copenhagen) are out working in the strawberry fields. Half completed in front of Marcus is a charcoal drawing of a striped lynx and Marcus tells Emilia that he is pleased by the way this drawing makes the animal look real. He has named the lynx "Robinson James" because, although it is there on the schoolroom table, he knows that it really lives in America and might therefore have an English name. "Robinson James," he says to Emilia, "was in the New World before anyone knew."

"Knew what, Marcus?"

"That the New World was there."

Marcus talks all the time now, as though endeavouring to make up for his years of silence. Little by little, he is emerging from his locked-in world, where Despair was a village, where Beyond Despair was a wind-swept plain. His harness is a memory and that memory itself is beginning to disappear—as if the harness might never have existed and the sounds it made, the chafing and squeaking, might have come from somewhere or something else. All that separates him from what Johann calls "an absolute normality" is his stubborn, continuing ability to hear the whisperings and mutterings—inaudible to everyone but him—of the creatures of the fields and forests. When he lays his head on the earth it fills up with sound. He cannot let it lie there for too long, for then he feels himself begin to lose hold of his thoughts and to imagine himself perched with a starling on an elm twig or burrowing with a mole into the crumbly earth or even flying with a bee in circles above the white-currant flowers. And it is difficult to get back from these places. When he returns from them he feels as feeble and small as a glow-worm facing out the darkness with its miniature light.

Looking at Marcus's drawing of the striped lynx, at its eyes, which in nature would be yellow and bright, Emilia understands suddenly that it is staring at her with impatience, that the world is getting weary of her procrastination, that the time has come.

She takes up Marcus's hand and kisses it. She wants to whisper some final words to him and is considering what these words should be when she hears the sound of a horse approaching the house. Marcus hears it, too. He scrambles down from the work table and runs to the window. He tells Emilia that a man is riding into the yard.

"I hope it isn't Pastor Hansen," says Emilia.

"No," says Marcus. "It is a wounded man."

The wounded man dismounts and looks around him. Marcus sees him look up at the schoolroom window and raise a hand in a greeting, and Marcus waves back.

Emilia has not moved. She wills the stranger—whoever he may be—to turn round and ride away. She thinks: How black my heart has become, blacker than stone. Such a heart must be made to stop.

But then she hears her name called out. Her name comes echoing in from outside, from the air which was silent.

"Emilia!"

She remains absolutely still. The heat of her body increases so swiftly, violently, that she puts her hands to her face, to cool her burning cheeks.

Marcus says: "He is calling you."

She says nothing. For what is there to say when she refuses to let hope return? Refuses utterly.

"He's calling out, Emilia, Emilia . . ."

She will not look up or move or do anything except lay her burning face in her hands. Nothing and no one shall turn her aside from the future she has planned. Nothing and no one. *Show courage, Emilia.*

Marcus sees her obstinacy, her immovability. He hears the horse sigh, hears the sighing and desperation in the call of the wounded man. And so he runs out into the sunshine, to bring him in, to ask, in the voice a doctor might use towards a patient: "Would you like to see my picture of Robinson James, the striped lynx?"

And the man says: "A striped lynx with an English name?"

"Yes," says Marcus, "because he is in the New World."

And the man replies: "I am from the Old World, but I too have an English name. I am Peter Claire."

Emilia waits alone. She does not straighten the folds of her frock nor smooth her hair. She is still moving, moment by moment, towards her solitary bed in the forest and will not be turned aside by this, which might be only an echo, a chance resemblance to something she knows is past and gone.

And when she hears the man come into the hallway and approach the schoolroom, she feels herself trembling, that is all, just trembling a little for fear of what happens to the human heart in certain conditions, if its defences falter, if courage fails . . . but only shivering very slightly, shivering in this great surge of heat, her mind and body host to sudden contradiction . . .

Marcus leads him by the hand—as if he had known him all his life. "There is my lynx. And here is Emilia."

Only now does she look up.

The face and body are thinner. The bandage flattens the abundant yellow hair. He carries no lute.

"Mr. Claire," she says at last in a whisper. "Some hurt to your head . . ."

"No," he replies. "My ear is damaged a little, that is all. Nothing compared with the pain of losing you. Nothing."

Marcus now watches as the wounded Englishman crosses to Emilia, who has at last stood up, and puts his arms round her. He expects his sister to draw back from him, as she always draws back from Herr Hansen when he tries to embrace her, but she does not. She lets herself fall towards the wounded man and lays her head on his breast.

Marcus Tilsen prefers this man to Pastor Hansen, much prefers him, not just because he is tall and is far younger than the pastor, but also because what he can hear now is a voice inside the man whispering to him (to him alone, to Marcus Tilsen) as the vole and the beetle and the butterfly whisper to him on summer days, and the voice is agitated and frail. It is the first time that this has happened, that a voice has come to him *from inside another person*, and Marcus knows it must be important.

Marcus runs out towards the strawberry fields. The pigeons gossip in the trees; the frogs chatter from the brimming ditches.

When he finds his father, he tells him that a new husband has arrived for Emilia, a wounded husband with an English name and a voice that cannot be heard—not even by the man himself—but he, Marcus, hears it and knows that he will be able to talk to it and hear it answer.

"Marcus," says Johann, "what in the world are you talking about? You are making no sense, boy. Slow down. Tell me again what has happened."

But all Marcus can find to use are the words he has already said. The only witness to the arrival of Peter Claire, he has seen the truth of what this stranger is: he is Emilia's husband. No other possibility but this exists and this is the only way he can explain it.

So all Johann Tilsen can do is to call the other boys to him, and they return together, half walking, half running, like a posse of men in pursuit of a thief. And they come clattering into the schoolroom and see Emilia and Peter Claire standing hand in hand before the fire.

"Emilia?" begins Johann. "What is happening?"

But then he stops and stares at his daughter. For it seems to him in this instant that it is not Emilia's face that he's seeing; it is Karen's face. It is Karen's face looking up at him as she looked up on the day of her wedding.

And perhaps Ingmar and Wilhelm and the other boys see this too, this sudden resemblance to Karen, for all of them are quiet, as though brought under a sudden spell, while Emilia and Peter Claire explain to them how each believed that love was lost, but that it was not lost after all, and the last of the afternoon sun shines through the window onto Emilia's hair, making it seem more fair than dark.

In the night, Marcus wakes his sister and says: "The voice is trapped in Peter Claire's ear."

Emilia doesn't question her brother. She lights a candle and together she and Marcus go to the room where Erik Hansen was lodged when he came wooing and where Peter Claire now lies with the window half open upon the summer night.

They kneel by the bed, and Peter Claire takes Emilia's hand, and it is Marcus who unwinds the bandage from around the Englishman's head.

Now that the coverings are gone, Marcus can hear the voice much louder than before and he thinks it is a voice in agony, a trapped voice, the kind of voice a creature would have if it were chained to a cot in a harness all alone in the darkness.

He puts his ear to Peter Claire's ear and listens. Now he can hear a tearing sound, as though the creature were biting the harness, trying to sink its teeth into the leather straps.

He sees the wounded man tighten his grip on Emilia's hand. And Marcus understands that there is no time to be lost. He lays his hands on Peter Claire's shoulders and puts his mouth very close to the ear and begins to whisper into it.

The musician can at first only feel the boy's breath on his cheek, but then he becomes aware of a minute sound, wordless, the faintest pianissimo sending an almost musical reverberation into his head.

The three stay absolutely still, heads close together, as though a secret were being passed around and around.

After some moments Marcus stops, listens again. His face is pale, even in the warm candle-light, and there is sweat on his lip. "Deep . . ." he murmurs. "Lost . . . But I shall keep calling . . ."

Now the sounds Marcus makes are louder. "I have found it!" he says at last. "It has heard me!"

And what Peter Claire begins to hear is a commotion like the bubbling of a river, and out along the current of this river the slippery, shiny body of an earwig is carried and falls into Marcus's mouth.

Marcus feels it land on his tongue, the creature trapped in the dark, trying to eat its way out, the creature nobody could see and nobody could hear except him. He reaches up and calmly takes it out of his lips and holds it in his palm for the others to see.

There is blood on its carapace. Its gossamer antennae search the air for direction and light. Emilia and Peter Claire stare at it in amazement and wonder. Then Marcus moves to the window and holds out his arm. "Earwig," he says, "go out into the night." And when it has crawled away, he turns to the lutenist. "Your wound will heal now," he says.

But Peter Claire barely has time to thank him, for straight away Marcus lies down where he is on the hard floor and falls asleep, like a child who has spent his night walking miles and miles under the moon.

Emilia takes a blanket from the bed and covers him, but she cannot bring herself to leave the room. She tells herself that she must watch over Marcus and the lutenist agrees; Marcus Tilsen, worker of the strangest wonders, must be watched over until morning.

And so Peter Claire and Emilia lie down side by side on the bed and wait for the coming of the dawn. He tells her that when they are married they will travel to England and sail into Harwich, where his father and mother long for his return. He says the chestnut trees will be in bloom in the lane that leads to the church of St. Benedict the Healer. He says: "There is a last sea journey to be made, Emilia, but I know we shall arrive."

The chestnut candle flowers are blooming now as George Middleton travels in an open carriage towards his wedding. Looking at these heavy white flowers, at the green gloves of leaves, he thinks how, year upon year, in their exaggerated show, these trees have seemed to invite some response from him and how he has never found one. But he has it at last. To Colonel Robert Hetherington, his best man, who rides with him in the carriage, he says: "Well, Hethers, the simple answer is Yes."

Colonel Hetherington is about to inquire what this floating "Yes" is attached to, but decides not to bother. All men are a little peculiar on their wedding day and George Middleton, formerly so dependable, so entirely at home as the bachelor of Cookham, has proved to be an utter fool for love. Not only does he tell a story about being restored to life by the placing of a cabbage on his stomach by his fiancée, he calls her "Daisy," when her name is Charlotte, he has spent more money redecorating her boudoir than restocking his woods with game, he has said that no one in the world makes him laugh more than she and, for her sake, once summoned a troupe of thieving Romany Gypsies to play at his soirée. Eventually, thinks Hetherington, he will revert to what he was, but, for the time being, George Middleton is quite mad.

If George Middleton could know to what extent Colonel Hetherington mocks him he would not greatly care. He would willingly admit that lovers are foolish and that the world, which pants so relentlessly after amusement, loves to make buffoons of them and see them toppled from their clouds and fall to earth, like Icarus, with an ungainly splash.

But like all who believe themselves enamoured, he imagines that his love for Charlotte Claire will last for ever. Marriage, he thinks, is not an end but a beginning. Still to come are the thousand nights of rumpled tomfoolery with Daisy, the hundred summer picnics at Cookham, where, round and round the green lawns, first a clutch of elegant baby carriages will be wheeled and then, as time passes, children's voices will begin to be heard calling in the Norfolk air: boys running after ball and hoop, girls tangling their petti-coats with skipping ropes . . .

George Middleton can see all these things as clearly as though they had already happened. As the carriage draws up outside the church of St. Benedict and he shakes the hands of the cluster of friends waiting for him, he is wearing on his round face a smile of such ridiculousness that one of the group, Sir Lawrence de Vere (recently married, himself, to a widowed Italian Countess, now pregnant with her fifth child), bursts out laughing and says: "I am glad to see you find it funny, Middleton, for of course it is!"

And then, in the shadowy church, cool in its body of stone, there is Charlotte, lifting the veil from her face and turning to-wards her "dearest George." Invited by her father to take up his bride's hand, George Middleton seizes it almost roughly in his de-sire to press it to his lips and a noise like a cry escapes from him, a noise no one (not even he) has ever heard him make before. He sees Hetherington turn worriedly towards him, and even Charlotte, who is seldom surprised by any word or exclamation of his, casts him a look of shock. And he thinks, God only knows exactly what that was, but it felt like my heart shouting.

Some weeks later, describing the wedding to Charlotte's brother Peter and his wife Emilia, both George and Charlotte will say that they remember little of the ceremony itself—only this peculiar noise which George made and which has never been heard since.

But they remember walking out into the May sunshine, where the guests showered them with flower petals, and how, at this mo-ment, a breeze sprang up and the drifts of falling blossoms from the chestnut trees were blown onto them too and joined the soft cas-cades of the thrown flowers.

Each to each, they recall it: "Do you remember, George . . . Do you remember, Daisy . . . it felt as though we were walking through scented snow?"

To my dear Nephew,

Today arrives in a Spanish chest the one hundred thousand pounds in gold so kindly given to me by Your Majesty in exchange for my lutenist, and I send you the deep gratitude of a loyal uncle.

While I admit that I have found no satisfactory replacement for the lute player and that, in consequence, the harmonies made by my orchestra seem to me less sweet than once they did, I nevertheless wish you joy of him and pray that, if any trouble come to Your Majesty, his playing may temper your anxiety or soothe your sorrow—just as it sometimes did for me.

And I shall admit, I did like Peter Claire very much, not only for his playing but for that he reminded me of my childhood, when I thought that angels would fill my shoes with gold and when my friend Bror Brorson rode with me in the forest of Frederiksborg.

Yet let me say at once that this very good sum of money brings more consolation to me than you can imagine, so that my head is straight away boiling with new schemes and plans for my continuing restoration of Denmark to her former glories and beyond.

And I shall describe to you which scheme I love the most. It is my plan for a great observatory to be built here in Copenhagen.

It was suggested to me by my wife, Vibeke. She said: "Oh, why do you not build a tower, higher than anything that stands hereabouts, and put at its top a large telescope, so that we may go there together to regard the unchanging order of the heavens and listen to the music of the stars and discover for ourselves how the moon comes by its brightness?"

I said: "Of course these are the things we long for, to comprehend what the moon may be and to hear the one sound from which chaos is absent, which is the sound of the universe itself. Yet, Vibeke, imagine all the stairs that we shall have to climb to reach the summit of such a place! I am too old and fat for so many stairs!"

But Vibeke declared that she too had a detestation of stairs and was not thinking about any stair whatsoever, but was dreaming of a fine curving carriageway, moving upwards, round and round, but gradually, so that horses and carriages could ascend it, and we ride in comfort in those carriages and are brought without any effort to the very top.

And it was then, my dear Charles, that I remembered how my first wife, Anna Catherine, had once asked me to make this very same thing, this internal pathway to the heavens, and how I had tried with all my might and main to get it built, but how the designers could never arrive at a plan by which it could be safely held up and endure the passing of time.

But time has moved on, and with it man's cunning and skill.

Today, I have been informed by my architects (who are Danish men of ingenuity) that if the central pillar be of sufficient strength, then there is no reason why such a masterpiece could not be built and endure. And so I have commanded that new sketches be made and all the new mathematics of the scheme be put in hand.

And when at last this tower is completed, then I think people shall come from all over the world to see it and to note how, in Denmark, we build structures that have nothing of shoddiness or weakness in any part of them.

When I was a child, the astronomer Tycho Brahe prophesied that this year 1630 would be a year of danger for me and that I might not survive it. And, I shall admit, there are some dark nights—when my digestion plagues me with its old pains—when I almost feel that death might creep unseen into my room.

But yet not many such moments. And rather, it steals upon me that what I have endured in recent years, both in the wars and in the battles with my former wife Kirsten, was a true trial of my strength and my will, and now this time of misery is replaced by a time of grace.

History teaches us that all such feelings of good fortune should be treated with suspicion and are but interludes: brief moments between one winter and the next, between the wars that are past and all the wars yet to come.

But Vibeke tells me that I should not torment myself with this observation, but rather go forward as if this cessation of sorrow were destined to endure through a fine variety of changing seasons. And I do think that she is right.

I do not know how long it shall take to build my observatory. But when it is finished you shall visit us here, and with Vibeke and your Queen we shall ride to the top of the tower and there dine upon the sky—upon the dusk the colour of blueberries and upon the full moon, like a sweet round pot of cream.

From your affectionate uncle,
Christian IV
Rosenborg, September 1630

KIRSTEN: FROM HER PRIVATE PAPERS

Last night I had a dream.

I was standing in the pew of a Church. Some Choir was singing, but I paid little attention to the Music. All that I could feel and know through every pore and hair of my Being was the gaze of my lover Otto, which, from the opposite Pew, fell upon the white skin of my neck and on my milky breasts above the lace of my russet gown. And what I felt was such Wonder at my own Power over this man that I thought I would fall down in a faint.

But only then did it come upon me in the dream that the man

was not Otto, the gaze was not his: it was the King's. And so I woke myself in horror. For I saw that I had confounded one Love with Another, so that the two were indistinguishable, each from each.

And therefore where, I ask, is any Truth or any Absolutely Known Thing in all the Universe, if two feelings held in Implacable Opposition in my heart (the one of Yearning and the Other of Loathing) can merge and become one and the same in this dream of mine?

Can it be that Time unfolds upon us such a Relay of Wonders that they constantly overtake each other in our Memories? Or is it, rather, that those things we termed "Wondrous" never were any such thing, neither the first Wonder nor the second, nor Any Thing which came afterwards, and all that we veritably inhabit is Fold upon Fold of Desolation?

I know not the answer to this. They say that Music, to reach into a Human Soul, depends upon Expectation born of Memory— that certain notes will follow in sequence after certain others—and so we hear the thing we call Melody flowing through Time. And if Memory be faulty—as I do think mine must certainly be—then we shall remain all our lives Indifferent to Music.

I am not merely Indifferent to Music; I detest it.

When I was at Rosenborg, if the Orchestra was playing beneath us and the King left our State rooms on some Matter of Business, why then I would walk immediately to the trapdoor, through which the droning sounds of strings and flutes came surging up the ducts and pipes, and with my vengeful foot kick it shut.

And so I imagined with great Relish and Satisfaction that with the downward draught of the heavy closing trap the candles set upon the music stands in the cellar would be blown out and the foolish Musicians would find themselves, on the instant, in silence and darkness. And I would smile.

But I do also see that this Fault or Weakness within my Memory may be the Thing which leads me perpetually into a very lamentable Confusion. And I feel this Confusion spread to all Things upon the Earth, so that that which was once Inimical to my soul is confounded with all that dazzled it and I know not where to go or what to seek after, nor whither my Life is headed.

All I can do is to return to my Boys, Samuel and Emmanuel. They are the Children of Spirits and not tethered by any Expectation to this Loathsome World.

I take their hands in mine, the Black upon the White and the White upon the Black, and I say to them: "Give me the Wings of Angels, the Wings of Demons. Lift me up and let me fly."

MUSIC & SILENCE

ROSE TREMAIN

A Readers Club Guide

ABOUT THIS GUIDE

The following questions and author interview
are intended to help you find interesting and
rewarding approaches to your reading of Rose Tremain's
Music & Silence. We hope this guide enriches your
enjoyment and appreciation of the book.

For a complete listing of our Readers Club
Guides, or to read the Guides online, visit

http://www.SimonSays.com/reading/guides

A Conversation with Rose Tremain

Q: **What is it that drew you to Denmark and the reign of Christian IV as the occasion and setting for *Music & Silence*?**

A: In 1990, while in Denmark on a journey from Copenhagen to Elsinore, I was first told about King Christian's device of housing his musicians in the cold wine cellar underneath the state rooms, so that the music they made would arrive invisibly, in a magical way.

These images struck me immediately as vivid and cinematic: the artists in the dark and cold, struggling to produce a beautiful sound; the Man of Power by his fire in the well-lit room. I could see that inherent in this strange arrangement was the idea of polarity we recognize as being present in all human endeavor. But I knew that to do these images justice, I would have to explore the ideas of some complexity in relation to states in opposition—love/hate, loyalty/betrayal, music/silence— and, as you can see, several years passed before I was able to begin this book.

Q: **Shakespeare's words play a significant role in the emotional lives of Christian, Peter Claire, Countess O'Fingal, and other characters in your novel. Had Shakespeare's dramas and poetry, in fact, become widely known and produced outside of England by the 1630s?**

A: I don't think Shakespeare's plays would have been widely known in Denmark in the early 1660s. It is, in fact, Peter Claire, the English lute player and Johnnie O'Fingal, the Irish Earl, who quote from Shakespeare, not the Danes nor the Italians in the story. But this is Shakespeare's time, and I felt that his poetry had to be part of the fabric of this book. And of course Shakespeare understood, better than any other writer, the immensity of what lies underneath what is visible and it was this BIG understanding of his that urged me on.

Q: Along with being a powerful presence in the lives of your characters, Shakespeare's influence also seems to bear directly upon the structure and character of your novel as a whole: *Music & Silence* falls formally in the line of Shakespearean romance. Like *Twelfth Night*, your novel follows a richly episodic form, interweaves multiple plot lines, mixes realism with suggestions of magic, mines a range of interconnected themes, and ultimately resolves itself with a series of apparently happy love couplings. Of course, Shakespeare's influence can probably be read into virtually every novel ever written, but did you explicitly look to Shakespeare as an antecedent in the planning and writing of this novel?

A: I don't think any contemporary writer would admit to trying to emulate Shakespeare, but perhaps, because he has played such a part in our education as writers, we unconsciously do so. Certainly, in *Music & Silence*, I wanted to find a complex, multi-voiced 'Shakespearean' form, in which many and various component parts add up to a coherent whole.

As my life as a writer has gone on, I've striven more and more to explore the kind of timeless themes that so enthrall us in Shakespeare's plays. Novels which may be set in a particular period and do their best to evoke that time for the readers, can also, if the arguments and interweaving plots are both universal and compelling, transcend time and still speak to readers many years from now.

My novel *Restoration* is now twelve years old and still sells well in several countries. I think it was in that novel, in 1988, that I began to paint on a much larger canvas than before and decided that, for me, the novel wasn't worth writing anymore unless it had satisfactory internal complexity.

Q: As *Restoration* did, *Music & Silence* succeeds wholly in capturing all the textures of life as it was lived hundreds of years ago. Tell us about your research.

A: I have very strong opinions on how the novelist must work with history to produce something distinct, original and timeless. I believe that research should be done in a scholarly way, through reading, looking at paintings, visiting buildings and landscapes, handling the fabric, utensils, and ornaments of the period.

However, once the months of research are complete, they should be followed by a time of quiet thought, in which the fictional characters and their story will be murmuring up and the researched data will be fading away into the unconscious. Only in this way can historical fact be alchemised into something new and living.

Q: One of the novel's most fascinating aspects is its exploration of the tension between notions of the divine and of the secular, which is a tension that colors much of the literature created during the English and Italian Renaissance's. Are music and silence metaphors for the divine and the secular, or is this too reductive?

A: *Music and Silence* are metaphors for the Divine and the Secular. They are also metaphors for Creativity and Ignorance, for Order and Confusion, for Love and Indifference. The novel is a meditation upon human life's arrangement above a great precipice of alternating states. It also suggests the paradoxical discovery that many of these polarities are not as absolute as one first believed them to be, that Kirsten Munk, for instance, for all her professed indifference, is capable of kindness and occasionally shows extraordinary courage as in her dealings with Emilia's family.

Q: Conditions for women in 1630's Denmark, England, and Ireland left much to be desired. Your female characters contend with their difficult situations in a variety of ways. Kirsten Munk, Almost Queen of Denmark, is certainly the most reactionary and subversive of these characters. Was Kirsten's voice a challenge? What sorts of reader responses have you gotten about Kirsten?

A: Women in the early seventeenth century had no power. They were "owned" first by their fathers and then by their husbands. Their only serious weapons were their beauty and their sexuality, and I'm quite sure that they understood this.

The history books talk about Kirsten Munk as a "shameless" woman, who enthralled King Christian for years and years. And what I wanted to create was a character who is stupendously indifferent to what the world thinks about her—thus giving her leave to behave in any way she chooses. I'm also aware that readers love wicked characters. Even in the novels of Jane Austen, we adore the schemers and manipulators. To write the Kirsten sections—once I understood what Kirsten was capable of—was pure entertainment, and I was very sorry to say goodbye to her. Judging from my letters, I think a lot of readers felt the same way.

Q: The novel is full of allusions to the magical power women possess over men. But at the same time, women are portrayed as slaves, as property, as helpless pawns in a man's universe. How was this paradox perceived in the 1630's? Was Kirsten's clear-eyed view of gender and power all that rare and revolutionary a perspective at the time?

A: No doubt, many women did not perceive their subservience, or, if they perceived it, saw it as protection rather than enslavement. Ceilia in *Restoration*, for example, is happy to be the King's plaything—provided it's with her that he plays. Emilia, in this story, aspires to liberation from her father, but only because he's indifferent to her and allows Magdalena to treat her badly. She will happily become Peter Claire's wife and submit her own yearnings to his, if that is asked of her. In contrast to Emilia, however, Kirsten is a woman who completely understands both her own enslavement and her own source of power. She schemes to get her way until the very end, when she sees that she can go no further and flies off into a realm of madness and magic.

Q: Ellen Marsvin is a fascinating creation: unshakably resolute in her goals and void of self-pity, she seems to approach life as if it were a work of art that she aims to render with bold, unsentimental strokes. Her personal refrain in life seems to be, "Endure, my dear." Even the specter of utter failure "does not frighten her so much as intrigue her." So is it fair to call Ellen the most courageous, self-aware, and evolved character in the novel? And what of her blunt declaration that "love does not enter into it." Is this hard-bitten view part and parcel to her general pragmatism, or is it the legacy of a broken heart?

A: Kirsten inherits much of her courage from Ellen Marsvin who, in real life, was more beautiful than her daughter and no doubt used her beauty to her own advantage for as long as she could. When we meet her here, her beauty has gone, but Ellen has understood enough about the way power works and where influence lies to continue scheming successfully to the end of her days.

She and the Dowager Queen are the cynics of this tale. Both are hard-bitten but stoical. I don't think either of them are as evolved as the characters of Kirsten and King Christian, but like the chorus in a Greek tragedy, they know exactly what the action signifies and who is heading for favor or disgrace.

Q: You are already renowned for your skill in crafting intricate and densely packed narratives. But *Music & Silence* is, if anything, your most expansive and complex work to date. How did the writing process differ for this novel?

A: At the center of this story is the orchestra. What I wanted to create in this novel was an "orchestral work" where theme and melody are repeated, echoed, underscored and subverted. To achieve this, I had to introduce a variety of "instruments" in the very differing characters and voices. I also had to be aware of pace and coloration, following a fast-paced "movement" with a slow section—and so forth. The plotting of this book is so complex that there were days when I felt bewildered, but most of the time, it was fascinating and seductive to write. When it was finished, my world fell very silent.

Q: What do you most hope a book group will come away with after reading and discussing *Music & Silence*?

A: I hope readers will feel that this book is absolutely *itself*, not precisely like any other novel, but something else, that perhaps resists genre classification. I hope that it may have made them think about certain aspects of life—the connection between music and tranquility, for instance, or the link between fine calligraphy and understanding—in a way that they hadn't anticipated and which would be new to them.

Q: Where, and to what time period, will you be taking your readers next?

A: I am going forward two hundred years, to the 1860's. The new novel will be about a woman in her thirties who finds herself in the bitterly harsh man's world of the New Zealand gold rushes. It will be a novel of the wild, of endurance, and of a struggle to the death for the getting of riches.

Reading Group Questions and Topics for Discussion

1. In the award-winning *Music & Silence*, Rose Tremain treats us—by way of an exhilarating series of interwoven plot-lines— to a uniquely ambitious and often sly inquiry into humanity's endless endeavor to find order in life: to wrestle reason from chaos, consolation from melancholy, music from silence. At one point, the whole town of Copenhagen collectively wonders "why it is they are alive." Clearly, these are not the thematic concerns of your typical historical romance. So to what degree does Tremain redefine this genre? In recommending this book to a friend, how would you describe it?

2. Discuss Tremain's writing style. How does her deliberate, three-part structure highlight and even reinforce the tone, rhythm, and narrative arc of *Music & Silence*? What particular techniques does the author use to establish the novel's moral murk and its alternately haunting and comic moods; to develop and distill her myriad themes even as she continually propels her story forward; to develop her characters' ambiguous motives; and perhaps even to dare us, like so many King Christians, to will some sort of order upon the teeming universe of this novel?

3. Even as Tremain so vividly renders the psychological textures of seventeenth-century Denmark, many reviewers have suggested that she also manages in *Music & Silence* to speak meaningfully to the conditions and uncertainties of our own time. Do you agree? Explain.

4. Rose Tremain has said elsewhere that "the seventeenth century is filled with extraordinary colors in my mind." Discuss Tremain's descriptive talent for bringing these colors to life in this novel. What colors and scents are introduced and then tellingly recur throughout the novel?

5. In the particular emotional realm of *Music & Silence*, the meanings and consequences of dreams are omnipresent and enduring. To King Christian, without dreams, whether they are dreams of architectural transcendence or abundant silver or musical wonder, life is meaningless. By contrast, Ratty Moller in Iceland comes to the devastating conclusion that "certain dreams...can bring forth more suffering than they could ever cure." How do dreams feature in the lives of Tremain's other characters?

6. At one point, during a description of the New Year's celebration of 1630 in Copenhagen, Tremain's narrative takes an unusual step back, recedes from the immediacy of the raucous carnival and, with the panoramic scope of a movie camera, delivers perhaps the most resonant lines in the novel: "And the citizens gaze out at the city...and wonder why it is they are alive in this time and what it is that God conceals from them, and what it is that He will in time reveal." Discuss the ways in which this universal condition of uncertainty and confusion, of walking through life in darkness without a fixed destination, plays out in the lives of each of Tremain's principle characters.

7. What is the nature of power in *Music & Silence*? Discuss how Tremain illustrates and subtly comments upon the undercurrents of power that pulse through every relationship and situation in this novel: the power of men over women, of women over men, of kings over musicians, of love (and life) over death, of music over silence.

8. Who ultimately wields his or her power most successfully? Ellen Marsvin? King Christian? Kirsten Munk? Magdalena? Queen Sofie? Explain.

9. How have the moral, political, sexual, and artistic codes and contradictions which Tremain brings to life so vividly in seventeenth-century Denmark and England evolved across the centuries? To what degree have conditions regarding personal expression today changed or remained the same?

10. Confronted with the list of crimes and misdeeds committed against King Christian, Kirsten is uncharacteristically stoic: "None of these Things can I deny." At the same time, she suggests that her "Transgressions" are a natural product of her life as a woman. "To have any Joy...we are forced to Scheme." In the realm of *Music & Silence*, how much truth lies in this assertion?

11. Does the outcome of the novel's various plot lines support the truth of Kirsten's cynical statement in the previous question? Why or why not?

12. One of the most poignant moments in the novel occurs as Dowager Queen Sofie comes to terms with the essential nature of her "treasure house." Emerging from a dream, Sofie strokes her gold ingot and realizes something which, on some level, she has long known about her obsession with hoarding: "There will never be anything that brings her more satisfaction than what lies heavy, here and now, on her aging body." Does this idea, that the value of a life's quest, whatever the quest may be, lies always and exclusively in the quest itself and not in its reward, seem to soothe or trouble Sofie? Explain.

13. To what degree do the other characters in *Music & Silence* contend with and arrive at Queen Sofie's realization above? Do any characters find that the opposite is true? Consider, for instance, the life-quest of Peter Claire.

14. Describe the extreme change King Christian undergoes over the course of Tremain's novel. Would you say he is redeemed by his love for Vibeke? Why?

15. Does Tremain encourage a traditional 'good-and-evil' reading of her novel? For a woman in the seventeenth century, what does it even mean to be good? For a man? Explain.

16. Discuss the complexities of Kirsten Munk. What was your reaction to Kirsten, and how did your reaction evolve as you read? In Kristen's Private Papers throughout the novel, we come to see a woman every bit as capable of expressing astonishing venalities and overwrought displays of self-pity as she is capable of poignant revelations and (perhaps unique among all of the novel's characters) a penetrating and lucid perception of the nature of life. In light of all this, try to construct an argument that identifies Kirsten as the tragic heroine of Tremain's story. What is the nature of this tragedy?

17. How would you describe the other characters in this story? What are the motivations underlying their choices and actions?

18. What does Peter Claire mean when he dreams of "becoming"? Discuss the interconnectedness of identity, fate, and free will in *Music & Silence*.

19. On the final page of the novel, Kirsten muses, "They say that Music, to reach into a Human Soul, depends upon Expectation born of Memory....And if Memory be faulty...then we shall remain all our lives Indifferent to Music." What is Tremain up to here? Reread the final entry in Kirsten's Private Papers. How does this passage speak to and even resolve Tremain's rich exploration of binaries and thematic opposites through the course of the preceding story? Can music, in the end, actually emerge directly from its apparent antithesis, silence? Can light come from darkness? Understanding from confusion?

20. Alongside Kirsten's musings in the previous question, consider the hopeful resolutions of each of the novel's couplings—Peter and Emilia, Christian and Vibeke, George and Charlotte, even Sofie and Ellen. How do these happy endings complement or contradict Kirsten's final thoughts?

W9-BTF-541

COMPLETE
Houseplants

CREATIVE
HOMEOWNER®

COMPLETE
Houseplants

FEATURING OVER 240 EASY-CARE FAVORITES

Jack Kramer

CREATIVE HOMEOWNER®, Upper Saddle River, New Jersey

COPYRIGHT © 1999, 2008

CRE▲TIVE
HOMEOWNER®

A Division of Federal Marketing Corp.
Upper Saddle River, NJ

his book may not be reproduced, either in part or in its entirety, in any form, by any neans, without written permission from the publisher, with the exception of brief excerpts for purposes of radio, television, or published review. All rights, including the ght of translation, are reserved. Note: Be sure to familiarize yourself with manufactur- r's instructions for tools, equipment, and materials before beginning a project. Although ll possible measures have been taken to ensure the accuracy of the material present- d, neither the author nor the publisher is liable in case of misinterpretation of directions, nisapplication, or typographical error.

Creative Homeowner® is a registered trademark of Federal Marketing Corporation.

COMPLETE HOUSEPLANTS

MANAGING EDITOR	Fran J. Donegan
EDITOR	Lisa Kahn
FIRST EDITION EDITORS	Miranda Smith, Nancy Engel, Heidi Stonehill
GRAPHIC DESIGNER	Maureen Mulligan
PHOTO RESEARCHER	Robyn Poplasky
DIGITAL IMAGING SPECIALIST	Frank Dyer
JUNIOR EDITOR	Jennifer Calvert
EDITORIAL ASSISTANTS	Nora Grace
INDEXER	Schroeder Indexing Services
COVER DESIGN	Maureen Mulligan
ILLUSTRATIONS	Mavis Torke
FRONT COVER PHOTOGRAPHY	David Van Zanten
BACK COVER PHOTOGRAPHY	*top* David Van Zanten; *bottom left to right* Friedrich Strauss/Garden Picture Library; David Van Zanten; Friedrich Strauss/Garden Picture Library

CREATIVE HOMEOWNER

VICE PRESIDENT AND PUBLISHER	Timothy O. Bakke
PRODUCTION DIRECTOR	Kimberly H. Vivas
ART DIRECTOR	David Geer
MANAGING EDITOR	Fran J. Donegan

Current Printing (last digit)
10 9 8 7 6 5 4 3 2 1

Complete Houseplants
Formerly published as *Easy-Care Guide to Houseplants*
Library of Congress Control Number: 2007933863
ISBN-10: 1-58011-397-4
ISBN-13: 978-1-58011-397-7

CREATIVE HOMEOWNER®
A Division of Federal Marketing Corp.
24 Park Way
Upper Saddle River, NJ 07458
www.creativehomeowner.com

Metric Equivalents

All measurements in this book are given in U.S. Customary units. If you wish to find metric equivalents, use the following tables and conversion factors.

Inches to Millimeters and Centimeters

1 in = 25.4 mm = 2.54 cm

in	mm	cm
1/16	1.5875	0.1588
1/8	3.1750	0.3175
1/4	6.3500	0.6350
3/8	9.5250	0.9525
1/2	12.7000	1.2700
5/8	15.8750	1.5875
3/4	19.0500	1.9050
7/8	22.2250	2.2225
1	25.4000	2.5400

Inches to Centimeters and Meters

1 in = 2.54 cm = 0.0254 m

in	cm	m
1	2.54	0.0254
2	5.08	0.0508
3	7.62	0.0762
4	10.16	0.1016
5	12.70	0.1270
6	15.24	0.1524
7	17.78	0.1778
8	20.32	0.2032
9	22.86	0.2286
10	25.40	0.2540
11	27.94	0.2794
12	30.48	0.3048

Feet to Meters

1 ft = 0.3048 m

ft	m
1	0.3048
5	1.5240
10	3.0480
25	7.6200
50	15.2400
100	30.4800

Square Feet to Square Meters

1 ft² = 0.092 903 04 m²

Acres to Square Meters

1 acre = 4046.85642 m²

Cubic Yards to Cubic Meters

1 yd³ = 0.764 555 m³

Ounces and Pounds (Avoirdupois) to Grams

1 oz = 28.349 523 g

1 lb = 453.5924 g

Pounds to Kilograms

1 lb = 0.453 592 37 kg

Ounces and Quarts to Liters

1 oz = 0.029 573 53 L

1 qt = 0.9463 L

Gallons to Liters

1 gal = 3.785 411 784 L

Fahrenheit to Celsius (Centigrade)

$°C = °F - 32 \times \frac{5}{9}$

°F	°C
-30	-34.45
-20	-28.89
-10	-23.34
-5	-20.56
0	-17.78
10	-12.22
20	-6.67
30	-1.11
32 (freezing)	0.00
40	4.44
50	10.00
60	15.56
70	21.11
80	26.67
90	32.22
100	37.78
212 (boiling)	100

Safety First

A ll projects and procedures in this book have been reviewed for safety; still it is not possible to overstate the importance of working carefully. What follows are reminders for plant care and project safety. Always use common sense.

Always consider houseplants poisonous to eat. Some parts of plants are always poisonous to people and pets, while others may be poisonous, or at best cause indigestion, in people and pets. If there is a chance that children or pets will eat parts of houseplants, be sure to position the plants safely out of reach. The author and the publisher accept no responsibility for injury resulting from ingestion of any plant mentioned in this book.

Always consider the possibility that houseplants may cause skin reactions in people with allergies. Some plants, such as those from the euphorbia genus (including poinsettias) give off a milky sap that can cause skin problem sand eye injury. Also it's wise, especially for beginners, to exercise caution in handling unfamiliar plants. Gloves can provide protection, although glove exteriors will likely continue to be contaminated. Washing your hands after plant care helps prevent transmission of plant substances. The author and the publisher accept no responsibility for any injury resulting from the handling of plants mentioned in this book.

Always ensure that the electrical setup is safe. Be sure that no circuit is overloaded and that all power tools and electrical outlets are properly grounded and protected by a ground-fault circuit interrupter (GFCI). Do not use power tools in wet locations.

Always read and heed tool manufacturer instructions.

Always wear eye protection when using chemicals, sawing wood, drilling wood, and using power tools.

Always consider nontoxic and least toxic methods of addressing plant pests and diseases before resorting to toxic methods. When selecting among toxic substances, consider short-lived toxins, which break down quickly into harmless substances. Follow package application and safety instructions carefully.

Never employ fungicides, pesticides, or other chemicals unless you have determined with certainty that they were developed for the specific problem you hope to remedy.

Always read labels on chemicals, solvents, and other products; provide ventilation; heed warnings.

Always wear appropriate gloves in situations in which your hands could be injured by rough surfaces, sharp edges, thorns, or poisonous plants.

Always wear a disposable face mask or a special filtering respirator when creating sawdust or working with powdery gardening substances.

Contents

Introduction to Houseplants

ouseplants are beautiful on their own, and well-placed houseplants can transform a room's decor into something extraordinary. Besides their beauty, plants add oxygen and humidity to room air, while also cleansing it by absorbing common household pollutants. And some plants have a lovely fragrance.

In addition, these wonderful life forms possess something akin to personalities. In fact, many indoor gardeners insist that plants respond well to affection and are good listeners. If you've ever observed people caring for houseplants, you may have overheard an exchange resembling an intimate conversation.

Thus, factors of aesthetics and plant nurturing combine to provide profound enjoyment that nourishes the psyche. Indeed, houseplants bless those who tend them, as well as mere onlookers.

Origins & Growing Conditions

In centuries past, houseplants originated in the wild in various parts of the world. Although many of today's houseplants are pure descendants of their wild parents, countless others have resulted from human matchmaking.

Of the more than 400,000 native plants in the world, houseplants represent a small portion. Although there are more than 35,000 native species of orchids and more than 9,000 ferns, the number of newcomers cultivated by man defies calculation. We present about 240 of the most popular houseplants available in North America. The featured plant families and groups include traditional houseplants, as well as newcomers, and all are generally available.

People often assume that houseplants come only from tropical climates, where humidity and heat are intense.

Although many popular houseplants did originate in the tropics, others evolved in cooler regions. And although many cacti and succulents occur in deserts, others live in tropical rain forests.

Whether growing naturally from wild seed or from one of the many methods of cultivation, houseplants do best in growing conditions similar to those in which their progenitors thrived. Even so, you don't need to transform your home into a jungle or desert to ensure that plants from those climates survive. Most of today's houseplants can adjust to a range of indoor conditions.

Plants can be propagated by various means, including leaf cuttings, as shown here.

How this Book is Structured

Chapter 1 presents the characteristics of the main families and groups from which houseplants come. This first chapter also lists plants profiled in the second part of the book. Chapters 2 through 6 discuss decorating with house plants, choosing plants and containers, caring for plants, and propagating them by various means. Chapter 7 covers diagnosis and environmentally friendly solutions for plant problems, including diseases and insects.

Part II features photos and descriptions of the most popular plants. For more on using the plant profiles, see page 111.

In this book, all plants are listed by common name and scientific (botanical) name. One disadvantage of relying on the common name is that it's not the most accurate way to find the plant you want. This is because many plants are known by more than one common name and because some vastly different plants share a common name.

To ensure accurate identifications, botanists have adopted a world standard for names. They've assigned plants to family trees based mainly on similarities of their reproductive structures. The scientific names are rendered primarily in Latin. So if you know a plant's scientific name, it's easier to obtain the plant you want.

This book employs the scientific names used by the Royal Horticultural Society's *Index of Garden Plants*, as well as older scientific names that are still widely used in houseplant catalogs. When the scientific name has changed, you'll find both the new and old names listed, with one of them noted in parentheses and an "aka," short for "also known as."

When a houseplant has no common name, the scientific name is coined as the common name, such as in guzmania.

Family. In this book, the family is the largest grouping of plants sharing common characteristics. The scientific family name is written with an initial capital letter, as in Begoniaceae, and is not italicized.

Principles of plant naming are illustrated in the name of this plant. Its common name is Camille dumbcane, while its scientific name is Dieffenbachia picta 'Camille'.

Genus. Normally, the next smaller grouping of plants within a family is the genus, which is written with an initial capital letter and is italicized; the plural for genus is genera. The genus name is usually the first word of a plant's scientific name, as in *Guzmania lingulata*.

Species. The second word in the name indicates species, which is a group of related plants that are alike except for small variations. The species name is italicized.

Variety Vs. Cultivar. Scientists take nomenclature further by assigning a name if the plant is a variety (a variant of a species that occurs as a result of natural mutation) or a cultivar (meaning a *culti*vated *vari*ety, resulting from human intervention).

The terms *variety* and *cultivar* are commonly used interchangeably, even though there is a technical difference. A cultivar will be listed with single quotes, (as in the label for the photograph above). When a cultivar is used as part of the common name, as in the example Camille dumbcane, above, single quotes aren't usually used.

Hybrid. A hybrid is a plant that results from the breeding of two genetically different parents. Often written with an ×, a hybrid may differ in significant ways from its parents and even from its siblings. A hybrid is listed like this: *Begonia* × *hiemalis*.

CHAPTER ONE

Foliage, Flowers & Families

Broadly speaking, there are two categories of houseplants—those prized mainly for their foliage and those valued primarily for their flowers. Within these two categories are plants of every size and description, from miniatures and dwarfs to tree-size specimens, from compact bushes to trailing vines.

The foliage plants include many traditional houseplants. Their leaves may be deep glossy green, rich emerald, light springlike chartreuse, or combinations of green and other colors. The realm of flowering plants is even larger and more diverse. Flowering plants offer glamorous color accents that can harmonize with a room's color scheme or add new tones.

LEFT *Combine foliage types* to create an interesting display of plants when grouping them together.

ABOVE *A corsage orchid* adds a note of elegance to any room.

Foliage Plants

Foliage plants are grown primarily for their leaves because they don't bloom under average home conditions, or if they do, the flowers are not showy. Many foliage plants can tolerate low light. For example, philodendrons, snake plant (*Sansevieria*), and cast-iron plant (*Aspidistra*) are long-time favorite houseplants because they can survive the dry conditions and low light levels of most homes.

Following are profiles of the families that contain many well-known foliage plants traditionally grown for their foliage, plus listings of family members profiled in "Plant Profiles," page 108.

Begonias, orchids, and African violets

Houseplants grown for their foliage display an amazing variety of shapes, textures, and color combinations. Today, you don't need to settle for just a Boston ferns or parlor palm.

Acanthus Family (*Acanthaceae*)

Although this family contains a number of fine flowering houseplants, including zebra plant (*Aphelandra squarrosa*) and firecracker flower (*Crossandra infundibuliformis*), it is most famous for its foliage plants. The leaves of an acanthus plant inspired the carvings on Corinthian columns in ancient Greece. Acanthus family members are found in Mexico, South America, India, Madagascar, and Asia. Especially attractive foliage plants in this family include the polka dot plant (*Hypoestes phyllostachya*) and the striking metallic-purple Persian shield plant (*Strobilanthes dyerianus*). See their profiles on pages 112–117.

Acanthus

- Zebra plant, yellow plume plant, (*Aphelandra squarrosa*)
- Firecracker flower (*Crossandra infundibuliformis*)
- Nerve plant (*Fittonia argyroncura*)

Polka dot plant (Acanthus)

Persian Shield Plant (Acanthus)

- Mosaic plant (*Fittonia verschaffeltii*)
- Acanthus (*Heimigraphis repens, Ruellia colorata*)
- Polka dot plant (*Hypoestes phyllostachya*)
- Shrimp plant (*Justicia brandegeana*)
- *Sanchezia speciosa* (*S. nobilis*)
- Persian shield plant (*Strobilanthes dyerianus*)

Aralia Family (Araliaceae)

A diverse group, the Aralia Family includes trees, shrubs, and vines, as well as herbaceous plants (which die back to the ground each winter in their native habitats). Aralias that are popular houseplants include the canopy-like umbrella plant (*Schefflera actinophylla*), which has big, bright green compound leaves that emerge from their stems like fingers on a hand; oriental-looking false aralia (*Dizygotheca*), with its slender serrated leaves; the frilly Balfour aralia (*Polyscias scutellaria* 'Balfourii'), with its small scalloped leaves; and pretty Ming aralia (*Polyscias fruticosa*), with leaves that

English Ivy

are crinkly and heart-shaped. The familiar English ivy (shown below) is also a member of the Aralia Family, profiled on pages 120–122.

Aralia

- Finger aralia, false aralia (*Dizygotheca elegantissima*)
- Ivy (*Hedera canariensis*)
- English ivy (*Hedera helix*)
- Swedish ivy (*Plectranthus fruticosa*)
- Ming aralia (*Polyscias fruticosa*)
- Ginseng (*Polyscias guilfoylei*)
- Balfour aralia (*Polyscias scutellaria* 'Balfourii')
- Variegated umbrella plant (*Schefflera actinophylla* 'Variegata')
- Lollipop plant, yellow shrimp plant (*Pachystachys lutea*)
- Purple Spike (*Porphyrocoma pohliana*)
- Chocolate plant (*Pseuderanthemum atropurpureum*)

Arum Family (*Araceae*)

This comprehensive family, generally known as the aroids, includes many favorite indoor plants, such as philodendron, anthurium, Chinese evergreen, pothos, alocasia, spathiphyllum, syngonium, and dieffenbachia. These beautiful foliage plants generally grow in shady, humid locations in South America, near the equator, and in Central America. They come in a range of sizes from small to large, and many have variegated foliage that is splashed, splotched, streaked, or mottled with creamy white, golden yellow, or even red or pink.

Germanic folklore held that arums, particularly philodendrons, brought good luck. But indoor gardeners appreciate the members of this family primarily because they provide beautiful green accents. See their profiles on pages 123–134.

Arum (aka Aroid)

- Chinese evergreen (*Aglaonema* cultivars)
- Shield plant (*Alocasia* × *amazonica*)
- *Alocasia* 'Black Velvet'
- Copper alocasia (*Alocasia cuprea*)
- Green Goddess alocasia (*Alocasia* 'Green Goddess')
- Flamingo flower (*Anthurium cubense*)
- Tailflower (*Anthurium hookeri*)
- Flamingo flower (*Anthurium scherzerianum*)
- Fancy-leaved caladium (*Caladium* ×

Camille Dumbcane (Arum)

Black Velvet Alocasia (Arum)

Satin Pothos (Arum)

Variegated Umbrella Plant (Aralia)

hortulanum, Caladium hortum hybrid)
- Hilo Beauty colocasia (*Colocasia* 'Hilo Beauty')
- Dumbcane (*Dieffenbachia* species and cultivars)
- Pothos (*Epipremnum* species and cultivars)
- *Homalomena rubescens* 'Emerald Gem'
- Swiss cheese plant (*Monsteradeliciosa*)
- *Nephthytis* hybrids

- *Philodendron* species and cultivars
- Domino peace lily (*Spathiphyllum* 'Domino')
- White-flag plant (*Spathiphyllum floribundum*)
- Arrowhead plant (*Syngonium podophyllum*)
- Angel's wings (*Xanthosoma lindenii*)
- *Zamioculcus zamifolia*
- Calla lily (*Zantedeschia* cultivars))

- Hart Leaf fern (*Himionitis arifolia*)
- Strap fern (*Microsorum spc.*)
- Fluffy Ruffles Boston fern (*Nephrolepis exaltata* 'Fluffy Ruffles')
- *Nephrolepis exaltata* 'Timii'
- Button fern (*Pellaea rotundifolia*)
- Cabbage head fern (*Polypodium vulgare*)
- Cretan brake fern (*Pteris cretica*)
- Leather fern (*Rumohra adiantiformis*)

Cabbage Head Fern

Ferns (Various Families)

Ferns comprise a group of leafy plants from several botanical families that share the characteristic of reproducing by means of spores instead of seeds; ferns do not bloom with flowers. These lush plants have graced North American homes since the Revolutionary era. Most ferns come from shady woodlands and are valued for their divided, often delicate leaves (called *fronds*) and their lush, graceful forms. They offer distinctive leaf shapes ranging from stalk-like (such as those of the cabbage head fern) to fishtail, to ruffled (like those of the Boston fern). Some ferns have small, round leaflets, like those of the lovely maidenhair (*Adiantum*) and button (*Pellaea*) ferns. Easy to grow in low light, ferns are outstanding performers indoors. See their profiles on pages 158–164.

Ferns
- Lacy maidenhair fern (*Adiantum tenerum*)
- Bird's nest fern (*Asplenium crispum, Asplenium nidus*)
- Tree fern (*Blechnum gibbum*)
- Holly fern (*Cyrtomium falcatum*)
- Rabbit's Foot (*Davalia trichomanes*)
- Japanese shield fern (*Dryopteris erythrosora*)

Lily Family & Relatives (Liliaceae & Other Families)

The large Lily Family is best known for the many kinds of trumpet-shaped flowers grown from bulbs in outdoor gardens and greenhouses. But a surprising number of foliage houseplants, such as spider plant (*Chlorophytum*) and foxtail fern, also belong to the Lily Family. Healing aloe (*Aloe vera*), dracaenas, and cast-iron plant (*Aspidistra*) are also members of this clan. The plants in these families come from several continents—Africa, Australia, and China. See their profiles on pages 171–178.

Lilies & Related Plants
- *Aloe bellatula*
- Healing aloe, medicine plant

Japanese Shield Fern

Healing Aloe

Mulberry Family (Moraceae)

When you think of the Mulberry Family, you probably think of it as the source of purple tree fruits that birds love or the leaves that were once fed to silkworms to produce the fiber that became the most luxurious of textiles—silk. But some classic foliage houseplants also belong to this family. The handsome ficus, or fig, trees are part of this clan. The diminutive creeping fig (*Ficus pumila*), the graceful weeping fig (*F. benjamina*) in all its variations, and the boldly dramatic braided fig all make excellent houseplants. See their profiles on pages 179–181.

Mulberries

- Weeping fig, aka banyan tree (*Ficus benjamina*)
- Braided fig (*Ficus benjamina*)
- Ficus 'Silver Cloud' (*Ficus benjamina*)
- Variegated fig (*Ficus benjamina* 'Variegata')
- Burgundy rubber plant (*Ficus elastica* 'Burgundy')
- Variegated creeping fig (*Ficus pumila* 'Variegata')

Spotted Ox Tongue Plant

- (*Aloe vera*, aka *A. barbadensis*)
- Foxtail fern (*Asparagus densiflorus* 'Myersii')
- Cast iron plant (*Aspidistra elatior*, *Aspidistra* 'Milky Way')
- Bottle plant, ponytail palm (*Beaucarnea recurvata*, aka *Nolina recurvata*)
- Variegated spider plant (*Chlorophytum cosmosum* 'Variegatum')
- Orange stem lily (*Chlorophytum orchidearea*)
- Ti plant (*Cordyline terminalis*)
- Dwarf pineapple dracaena (*Dracaena deremensis* 'Compacta')
- Red Wine corn plant (*Dracaena fragrans* 'Red Wine')
- Rainbow dracaena (*Dracaena marginata* 'Tricolor', aka *D. cincta* 'Tricolor')
- Spotted ox tongue plant (*Gasteria bicolor* var. *liliputana*)
- Silver squill (*Ledebouria socialis*)
- Song of India (*Pleomele reflexa*)
- Spineless yucca (*Yucca elephantipes*)
- *Dracaena* 'Janet Craig'
- Variegated dracaena (*Dracaena warneckii*)

Braided Fig

Burgundy Rubber Plant

Palm Family (Palmae)

Palms were a symbol of riches in ancient cultures. Considered sacred to Apollo, palms were said to have been introduced to Greece by Hercules. During the 1800s, palms were fixtures in parlors and conservatories, but they eventually fell out of favor. They were later grown mainly as outdoor plants in warm climates. But palms are again becoming popular as indoor plants, and with good reason. They are generally undemanding, and many do well in low light. Notable examples include lady palm and bamboo palm. A large, leafy palm can be a striking presence. See their profiles on pages 188–191.

Chinese Fan Palm

Butterfly Palm

Spiderwort

- ✖ Brazilian wandering Jew (*Callisia repens*)
- ✖ Moses-in-a-boat (*Rhoeo discolor variegated, Rhoeo spathacea*)
- ✖ Purple heart plant (*Setcreasea pallida,* aka *Tradescantia pallida, Setcreasea purpurea*)
- ✖ Wandering Jew (*Zebrina pendula*)

Purple Heart Plant

Brazilian Wandering Jew

Palms

- ✖ Fishtail palm (*Caryota mitis*)
- ✖ Bamboo palm (*Chamaedorea erumpens*)
- ✖ Butterfly palm (*Chrysalidocarpus lutescens*)
- ✖ Chinese fan palm (*Licuala grandis*)
- ✖ Lady palm (*Rhapis excelsa*)

Spiderwort Family (Commelinaceae)

The Spiderwort Family is the source of some favorite houseplants. Generally having smooth, pointed leaves, the plants often have a trailing habit, as exemplified by the basket plants known as wandering Jew (*Zebrina* and *Callisia* genera). Some family members have green foliage, but the leaves of others are colored purple or bronze, or striped in silver, green, purple, and even pink. Spiderworts rarely bloom indoors, but some will flower if given bright sun from a southern exposure. See their profiles on pages 192–194.

Spiderwort

Flowering Plants

Most plants flower, but the plants grown primarily for their showy blooms are the ones we call flowering plants. In the past, most flowering plants were grown mainly in greenhouses and conservatories because they generally demanded more sunlight and humidity than the average home could provide. But newer home heating and cooling systems, with better temperature and humidity controls, have made it possible for more flowering plants to thrive in houses and apartments. In recent years, even orchids—long considered difficult to grow in homes—have become some of the most popular of the flowering houseplants.

Flowering houseplants come from many families. Gesneriads and begonias contain hundreds of available cultivars. And exotic plant families such as gingers and bromeliads bring brilliant color into the home.

Two other huge "groups" of plants that bloom indoors are cacti and succulents. These groups are usually lumped together because they generally grow well in arid conditions, although some cacti are native to jungle habitats and need more moisture than their desert-dwelling relatives. Succulent plants are able to store water in their tissues. Both groups include plants that are grown for flowers as well as foliage, including the crown-of-thorns, orchid cactus, and ever-popular Christmas cactus.

Amaryllis Family (*Amaryllidaceae*)

The plants in this family grow from bulbs or corms, and most come from South Africa, the Mediterranean, or South America. Many lovely houseplants belong to this clan, including amaryllis (*Hippeastrum*), fireball (*Haemanthus*, aka *Scadoxus*), Amazon lily (*Eucharis*), and Kaffir lily (*Clivia*). These plants are related to the Lily Family, as their trumpet-shaped flowers attest. Plants in this family also have long, strap-shaped leaves. After blooming, these plants need a rest period before they will flower again. See their profiles on pages 118–119.

Amaryllis

- Kaffir lily (*Clivia miniata*)
- Amazon lily (*Eucharis* × *grandiflora*)
- Fireball, Catherine wheel (*Haemanthus katherinae*, *Scadoxus multiflorus* ssp. *katherinae*)
- Amaryllis (*Hippeastrum* cultivars)

Begonia Family (*Begoniaceae*)

This enormous family consisting of one genus from South America contains thousands of species and cultivars, ranging in size from a few inches to several feet tall.

Begonias are divided into groups of plants based on appearance and growth habit. This book organizes the genus into five major groups, as follows:

Angel-wing begonias are mainly fibrous rooted, with cane-like stems that may stand up straight or cascade when grown in a hanging basket. The leaves are wing-shaped, with one lobe larger than the other. Leaf colors range from apple green to greenish brown with dots and spots of silver or white. Flowers in shades of pink, red, salmon, and orange bloom mainly in spring and summer.

Hirsute (meaning hairy-leaved) begonias have leaves flecked with short hairs. Their bearded flowers are white or greenish white to pink. Blooming times vary but occur mainly in fall and winter.

Rhizomatous begonias may have round or star-shaped leaves that range in color from plain green to variegated in fancy

Kaffir Lily

Picotee Begonia

patterns. The rhizomes store moisture for the plants.

Semperflorens (meaning everblooming), or wax begonias, are compact plants with small glossy leaves that may be solid green, variegated with creamy white, or reddish bronze in color. They bear small flowers in many warm colors.

Rex begonias are grown exclusively for their patterned foliage that shimmers in combinations of silver, metallic green, and purple. Hundreds of cultivars are available. Rex means "king," and many of these plants are so exquisite they are fit for royalty. See their profiles on pages 135–139.

Begonias

- *Begonia* 'Cleopatra'
- Reiger begonia (*Begonia* × *hiemalis*)
- *Begonia* 'Kewensis'
- Red-leaf begonia (*Begonia* hybrid)
- Angel-wing begonia (*Begonia* hybrids)
- *Begonia* 'Iron Cross' (*Begonia masoniana*)
- *Begonia* 'Picotee'
- Rex begonia (*Begonia* Rex-Cultorum hybrids)
- Wax begonia (*Begonia* Semperflorens-Cultorum hybrids)
- Maple-leaf begonia (*Begonia superba* 'Rana')

Bromeliad Family (*Bromeliaceae*)

Perhaps best known for one family member, the pineapple, bromeliads are beginning to rival orchids in popularity. There are more than 2,000 species, both terrestrial and epiphytic (growing in trees), mainly from South American rain forests. Bromeliads are prized for their colorful bracts, which come in shades of red, rose, orange, yellow, purple, and pink-blushed white, and for their exquisite foliage, which may be banded, striped, or splashed in combinations of green, silver, pink, red, purple, yellow, black, or cream. Bromeliads are nearly indestructible. See their profiles on pages 139–146.

Yellow
Poker Plant

'Orange Star' Bromeliad

Bromeliads

- Silver urn plant (*Aechmea chantinii* hybrid)
- Urn plant (*Aechmea fasciata*)
- Variegated pineapple plant (*Ananas cosmosus* 'Variegatus')
- Fantasia bromeliad (*Billbergia* 'Fantasia')
- Earth star (*Cryptanthus* species and hybrids)
- *Guzmania lingulata* 'Orange Star'
- *Guzmania lingulata* 'Rana'
- Poker plant (*Guzmania zahnii*)
- Striped neoregelia (*Neoregelia carolinae* forma *tricolor*)
- *Neoregelia* 'Royal Burgundy'
- Blushing bromeliad (*Neoregelia* hybrid)
- Fingernail plant (*Neoregelia spectabilis*)
- Plume bromeliad (*Tillandsia cyanea*)
- Tufted bromeliad (*Tillandsia ionantha*)
- Yellow poker plant (*Vriesea* hybrid)
- Flaming sword (*Vriesea* × *poelmanii*, *Vriesea splendens*)

Crown-of-Thorns

Aechmea chantinii

Cactus Family (*Cactaceae*) & Succulents (various families)

All cacti are succulents, which are plants with swollen fleshy leaves and stems that can hold water for long periods. Even though all cacti are succulents, not all succulents are cacti. Even so, catalogs and retail outlets tend to group cacti with other succulents. Usually thought of as desert plants, many cacti—such as the Christmas cactus (*Schlumbergera × buckleyi*)—live in rain forests. They require almost as much water as other plants, although many are accustomed to dry dormant periods when little or no rain falls in their natural habitats. See their profiles on pages 147–155.

Easter Cactus

Crepe Paper Flower

Cacti and Succulents

- Desert rose (*Adenium obesum*)
- Peanut cactus (*Chamaecereus sylvestrii*, aka *Echinopsis chamaecereus*)
- Jade tree (*Crassula ovata*, aka *C. argentea*)
- False rose (*Echeveria* hybrid)
- Orchid cactus (*Epiphyllyum* spc.)
- Crown-of-thorns (*Euphorbia milii*)
- *Gymnocalycium baldiana*
- Felt bush, velvet leaf (*Kalanchoe beharensis*)
- Starfire kalanchoe (*Kalanchoe blossfeldiana*)
- Dinner-plate kalanchoe (*Kalanchoe thyrsiflora*)
- Globe cactus (*Mammillaria celsiana*, aka *M. muehlenpfordtii*)
- *Pachyphytum* species
- Ball cactus (*Parodia penicillata*)
- Crown plant (*Rebutia* hybrid)
- Easter cactus (*Rhipsalidopsis rosea, Hatiora rosea*)
- Pencil cactus (*Rhipsalis* species)
- Christmas cactus (*Schlumbergera × buckleyi*)
- Thanksgiving cactus (*Schlumbergera truncata*)
- Donkey's tail (*Sedum morganianum*)
- Starfish flower (*Stapelia gigantea*)
- Torch cactus (*Trichocereus candicans*, aka *Echinocereus candicans*)

Torch Cactus

Euphorbia Family (*Euphorbiaceae*)

This is one of the world's most diverse plant families. Its members range widely in appearance and include spiny succulents, flowering plants, and plants grown primarily for their colorful foliage. All members of this family have a sticky white sap that bleeds out when the plants are cut. This sap can irritate human skin and eyes upon contact, so wear gloves when pruning the plants. One of the most popular euphorbias is the poinsettia, which is now available with white, pink or two-tone leaves. See their profiles on page 156–157.

Euphorbias

- Chenille plant (*Acalypha hispida*)
- Snow bush (*Breynia nivosa*)
- Croton (*Codiaeum* hybrid, *Codiaeum variegatum* var. *pictum*)
- Poinsettia (*Euphorbia pulcherrima*)

Gesneriad Family (*Gesneriaceae*)

Gesneriads come mainly from South America; some family members are from Africa. Most Gesneriads have flowers that provide vivid fall and winter color. And some, such as Cape primrose and African violet, flower for much of the year. The African violet is available in many sizes, from miniature to dwarf to standard, and it blooms in shades of purple, blue-violet, pink, and deep red, as well as white. The flowers may be single, double, star-shaped, fringed, or edged in white. Family members too often overlooked include the flame violet (*Episcia*), with its ornamental foliage and brilliant red flowers; the goldfish plant (*Nematanthus*), which bears small orange flowers that look like tiny goldfish; the Cape primrose (*Streptocarpus*), with clusters of pretty tubular blossoms; and columneas, trailing plants with flowers in shades of yellow and orange. See their profiles on pages 165–168.

Poinsettia

Gloxinia

Gesneriads

- Lipstick plant (*Aeschynanthus* species)
- Button columnea (*Columnea arguta*)
- Flame violet (*Episcia cupreata*)
- Goldfish plant (*Nematanthus gregarius*, aka *Hypocyrta nummularia*)
- African violet (*Saintpaulia* cultivars)
- Gloxinia (*Sinningia* hybrids)
- Temple bells (*Smithiantha speciosus*)
- Cape primrose and *Streptocarpella* Cape primrose (*Streptocarpus* hybrids)

Ginger Family (Zingiberaceae)

From Malaysia and India, gingers have only recently become popular houseplants. Butterfly ginger (*Globba*), Resurrection lily (*Kaempferia*), and several other members of the Ginger Family are adding their tropical elegance to

more and more interiors. These striking plants have elongated leaves and spikes of fragrant flowers in warm shades of yellow, gold, apricot, orange, coral, red, pink, and white. With their unusual and stunning color, they create a bright ambiance. See their profiles on pages 169–170.

Gingers

- Orange tulip (*Costus curvibracteatus*)
- Crepe paper flower (*Costus cuspidatus*)
- Siam tulip (*Curcuma alismatifolia*)
- Java tulip (*Curcuma* species)
- Butterfly ginger (*Globba winitti*)
- Resurrection lily (*Kaempferia rotunda*)

Orchid Family (Orchidaceae)

In the wild, orchids inhabit almost every corner of the globe. There are at least 35,000 wild species. In North America, orchids are the top-selling houseplants. With retail sales exceeding $100 million per year, they have surpassed even African violets in popularity. These plants are enjoyed as houseplants both because they are beautiful and because they can tolerate neglect. The flowers of many orchid genera, such as *Oncidium*, *Cattleya*, and *Phalaenopsis*, last for weeks or even months. Orchids offer a dazzling array of flower forms, sizes, and colors. Some are fragrant as well. Given the right growing conditions, orchids bloom reliably year after year. See their profiles on pages 182–189.

Orchids

- Stefan Isler orchid (× *Burrageara* 'Stefan Isler')
- Guatemalan orchid (*Cattleya guatemalensis*)
- Corsage flower (*Cattleya* hybrid)
- Wildcat orchid (× *Colmanara* 'Wildcat')
- Jill Katalinca orchid (*Cymbidium* 'Jill Katalinca')

Orange Cattleya Orchid

- Stars 'n' Bars orchid (× *Degarmoara* 'Stars 'n' Bars')
- Antelope orchid (*Dendrobium antennatum*)
- Topaz dendrobium (*Dendrobium bullenianum*)
- *Epidendrum stamfordianum*
- Dancing lady orchid (*Oncidium maculatum* 'Paolo')
- Sharry Baby orchid (*Oncidium* 'Sharry Baby')
- Lady slipper orchid (*Paphiopedilum insigne*)
- Red Sky lady slipper orchid (*Paphiopedilum* 'Red Sky')
- Lady slipper orchid (*Paphiopedilum sukhakulii*)
- Moth orchid, dogwood orchid (*Phalaenopsis* hybrids)
- Orange cattleya (*Sophrolaeliocattleya* Hazel Boyd 'Sunset')
- Orchid lily (*Spathoglottis plicata*)
- Winter orchid (*Zygopetalum crinitum*)

Stars 'n' Bars Orchid

THE LATEST PLANTS

As is the case with fashion, paint colors, and celebrities, houseplants fall in and out of favor and new ones come on the scene from time to time. Listed here is a group of plants that have become popular over the past few years. Check your local garden center for availability in your area. You'll find more information on these plants in the "Plant Profiles" section beginning on page 108.

Panama Hat Plant

Botanical Scientific Name	Common Name
Selaginaella kraussiana	Spike Moss
Lantana camara	Lantana
Ipomeae batatas	Sweet Potato Vine
Celosia plumosa	Red Plume
Gynura sarmentosa	Velvet Plant
Alternanthera hybrid	Joseph's Coat
Carludovica palmate	Panama Hat Plant
Torenia fournieri	Wishbone Plant
Coleus hybrid	Flame Nettle
Cuphea hyssopifolia	Cigar Plant
Asplenium crispum	Bird's Nest
Hemionitis arifolia	Hart Leaf Fern
Soleirolia soleirolii	Baby's Tears
Nephrolepsis	[no common name]
Pteris cretica 'Lemon Tree'	[no common name]
Crassula spc.	Stonecrop
Cissus rotundifolia	Kangaroo Vine
Lysimachia nummularia	Creeping Jenny
Calathea (Maranta) roseo picta	Prayer Plant
Allamanda nerifolia (dwarf)	Trumpet Plant
Huernia kewensis	Dragon Flower
Musella lasiocarpa	Flowering Banana

Baby's Tears

Red Plume

GIFT PLANTS

Calla Lily

Although gift plants come from many different plant families, they have become so closely associated with holiday and seasonal giving, that they deserve their own special category. At Christmas, the most popular gift plants are the ones you would probably guess: Christmas cactus and poinsettia. Next come Easter cactus and Easter lilies.

Gardenias are especially popular for Mother's Day. Greenhouse growers force hydrangeas into bloom for sale in spring. Elegant calla lilies are widely available in spring and summer.

There are many plants, including chrysanthemum, Thanksgiving cactus, amaryllis, and florist's cyclamen, that thrive in the cool autumn weather.

Available throughout the year, gloxinias, are especially nice in winter and spring. And there are orchid cultivars in bloom almost every month.

To make gift plants last, keep the soil moderately moist, but do not fertilize. Keep the plants in dappled sunlight, and maintain moderate temperatures. Keep daytime temperatures no higher than 78°F because heat quickly desiccates these plants. Pick off dead leaves and flowers as soon as you notice them.

Keeping Gift Plants Growing. Unfortunately, it is difficult or impossible to get many gift plants, including chrysanthemums and hydrangeas, to grow well or rebloom indoors, so they are not profiled in this book. Enjoy them while they are blooming, but you will be forced to discard them when they are finished.

Other gift plants can be grown as houseplants. Bulbous plants, such as cyclamen, can be kept, as can nonbulbous orchids and Christmas cactus.

When bulbous plants finish blooming, repot and grow them in fresh soil as you would other houseplants. Stop watering bulbous plants when the foliage dies.

Then unpot the bulbs, and store them in a cool, dry, dim place for six to eight weeks. Then replant the bulbs in fresh soil, and water only sparingly. You'll soon see new growth, at which time you can water to keep the soil evenly moist. If all goes well, a new crop of flowers will appear.

Hydrangea

Cape Jasmine Gardenia

Easter Lily

Chrysanthemum

Cyclamen

HANGING PLANTS

Plants trailing from hanging baskets are popular, and it's easy to see why. Hanging plants with cascading leaves and flowers look graceful and draw the eye. Today there are many kinds of containers available for hanging plants. The lavish growth and handsome foliage of new varieties of favorites

Goldfish Plant

Swedish Ivy

such as pothos make it easy to create a lush, plant-filled paradise in your home. The wax plant, a popular old-fashioned vine, is now available in many cultivars. Some have striped or mottled leaves, and the clusters of waxy white or pink flowers are sweetly fragrant—a cherished asset in a home.

Trailing angel-wing begonias are resplendent with color. They have lovely, silver-spotted leaves with a shape resembling angels' wings. However, their flowers are small. These plants grow easily in normal home temperatures.

The Gesneriad family presents fine red-flowering lipstick plants and the aptly-named goldfish plant, with its puffy orange blossoms. Another relative, the columnea, is dainty and pretty.

For best results, choose a container that has an attached saucer so that you can water without fear of damaging floors and furniture. (See pages 58–59 for detailed information on these containers.)

Also, examine the hanging device, usually a wire or plastic hook, to ensure that it is sturdy enough to support the weight of the basket. Most important, install ceiling or wall hardware securely enough to support the weight. Hanging baskets full of damp soil can be quite heavy and make an awful mess when they come crashing down. In most cases you will need to add extra support to the overall structure or attach plant hangers to ceiling joists. See pages 60–61 for guidance on hanging containers securely. For a more complete list of trailing plants, see "Plants for Hanging Containers," on page 54. For more information on caring for specific kinds on hanging plants, consult "Plant Profiles" beginning on page 108.

Lipstick Plant

Button Columnea

CHAPTER TWO

Decorating with Plants

Houseplants can do a lot to improve the decor of your home, including enhancing the overall ambiance of the space, cleaning the air, and providing visual accents and focal points. And don't forget the intangibles of houseplants. Imparting a gardenlike setting, houseplants also can give solace and brighten your spirits.

You can place your houseplants for different purposes: decorating windows, adorning tabletops, creating cascades from hanging containers, hiding unattractive walls, and enlivening plain interiors. Large plants can serve as screens, room dividers, or other architectural elements.

Windows are logical locations for houseplants because they let in the light that plants need to grow. Whether on shelves, on windowsills, or in hanging containers in front of windows, houseplants soften hard, structural lines and provide welcome texture and color. You can position large plants on either side of a window to frame an attractive view—or hang basket plants at different levels before a window to create a living screen rather than resorting to curtains or blinds. Even skylights can admit enough light for some plants to grow.

Houseplants add color and style to an ordinary table. Shown here is a mix of flowering and foliage plants, including orchids, ferns, and alocasias.

RIGHT *Houseplants* dress up a plain corner. Railings and furniture combine to create visual boundaries.

BOTTOM LEFT *This window greenhouse* results in a rainbow of color. Shown here are coleus, cyclamen, and begonia.

BOTTOM RIGHT *This outdoor garden room* springs to life with plants, including gingers and orchids, that thrive in diffused, sunny locations.

Decorating Techniques

Decorate with houseplants that will draw and hold the viewer's attention. Your goal should be a pleasing composition that contributes to the style of the room, not a haphazardly arranged jungle. Orchids, angel-wing begonias, and episcias are just a few of many sun-loving plants great for a position near a window or below a skylight.

Another technique employs plants to create a transition between an indoor room and the outdoors. If you have sliding glass doors or a large bay window, place houseplants inside that resemble—or are related to—plants growing outdoors. In the Southwest, for example, an outdoor garden could be echoed by potted cacti and succulents indoors. In the Southeast, palms and gingers can create a continuous tropical feeling, both indoors and out.

Preventing Water Damage

It can be a challenge to prevent water from dripping onto woodwork and floors when you water houseplants close to windows. To avoid damage, either place plants over flooring impervious to water (such as tile), carry plants to a sink to water them, put waterproof saucers under the plant containers, or use containers that have attached saucers. Water the plants slowly so that the water doesn't spill over the container edges and is not too much for the saucers to handle.

Another option is to place pots atop a layer of pebbles in cachepots, most of which do not have drainage holes. Cachepots are decorative pots that hold a plain pot in which a plant is actually potted. The pebbles prevent the bottom of the inner pot from staying constantly wet, thereby helping prevent root rot. Be sure that the drainage water in the cachepot does not rise higher than the pebbles and flood the inner pot.

Displaying Plants

You can display houseplants in myriad ways for special effects. A single specimen on a table or mantel will add a burst of welcome color. You can group plants on shelves or racks, or turn a favorite specimen into a focal point by displaying it on a stand or pedestal.

Bring the outdoors inside with an arrangement of potted plants. The vertical cactus anchors the scene and adds drama, while the varied leaf shapes of the other plants provide eye-catching texture.

Houseplants can make dim corners inviting, especially when you place them in attractive ceramic containers or on stands. Orchids and gesneriads displayed this way are particularly breathtaking. In fact, they can be more striking than traditional cut flowers, and they usually last much longer.

With adequate lighting, larger plants can fill unused corners or stand near a chair or couch to bring the outdoors into the room, lending a green feeling. Large houseplants mounted on dollies can be moved about according to whim—perhaps positioned to frame a doorway or to serve as a green sculpture or accent in a room. A large spot-lit specimen plant can be a dramatic focal point.

Practically every room in the house offers places for plants. (See "Plant Placement" on page 35.) Even kitchens and bathrooms can be decorated with houseplants. In fact, these rooms tend to have good light and humidity, two elements on which most houseplants thrive. In the kitchen, houseplants lend a cozy feeling. And plants in bathrooms soften what otherwise tend to be hard-edged, utilitarian lines.

RIGHT **This tropical oasis** *includes simple elements: a white chair and shades, and houseplants that contrast with them.*

BELOW **This gloxinia's bright red flowers** *and glossy green leaves shout for attention when situated near these cobalt-blue glasses. An asparagus fern, at left, softens the edges in this bold tableau.*

Elements of Design

As with antiques and artwork, you will get the greatest impact from houseplants if you arrange them according to established aesthetic principles. Balance, proportion, and harmony are important. One houseplant in a room can look lonely and out of place, but a well-balanced grouping of three or five plants can become a synchronized team in harmony with its surroundings. Similarly, a 5-foot dieffenbachia on one side of a room and a 5-inch begonia on the other side would be out of balance, but repeating these same plants together in other areas of the room can create a sense of rhythm and proportion.

Try to give some thought to plant arrangements, placing them with the same amount of care as you would furniture. (See "Plant Placement," page 35, for more details.) After choosing locations for your plants, stand back and survey the overall arrangement. Does the picture say what you want it to? If not, keep moving and arranging plants until you achieve the desired effect.

Grouping small plants. Smaller plants gain visual impact when you group several together. When grouping plants, aim for a variety of sizes and a range of textures. Arrange the plants so the change in height or texture is gradual, rather than placing the smallest plant next to the tallest one or placing the boldest, coarsest plant next to one with the smallest, most delicate leaves. Also, try to create some depth. Set some pots in front and others in back instead of lining them up like a row of soldiers.

Containers

A well-chosen container displays the plant to its best advantage and becomes a decorative element. Select containers that are in proportion with the plants they display. Also, the texture of the plants should be compatible with nearby plants and the room's decor. For example, a cachepot looks more formal than a wicker basket, and a terra-cotta pot looks more natural than a colored plastic pot. When in doubt, it's always safe to use a white ceramic pot, which complements almost any decor and houseplant.

Consider, too, that extra height adds to the importance and grace of a houseplant. Most houseplants look best when elevated slightly, on a dolly or display stand for example. Even a saucer can give a plant a little lift.

See Chapter 4, beginning on page 52, for detailed information on the types of containers available for houseplants.

Form and Mass

One of the most important design qualities of a houseplant is its form, or shape. For example, plants such as schefflera often have a canopy shape. Other plants may appear fountainlike, rounded, rosette-shaped, or trailing. Leaves can be oval, round, elliptical, lance-shaped, straplike, or delicate and feathery. You can achieve spectacular results if you use one form to echo another in a room—by placing a tall, arching palm in front of a tall, arching window, for example.

Yet a contrast of dissimilar forms can be equally pleasing, such as a columnar cactus against the horizontal lines of walls and furnishings. You need to decide

ABOVE *When grouping small plants,* use different heights to promote interest. The poinsettia on the floor anchors the stage for the angel's wings.

LEFT *Classic elements* of design are at work in the range of sizes and textures in this eclectic room. Some of the plants here include ferns, bromeliads, and dracaena.

ABOVE **Columnar plants,** *such as these cacti, add sculptural accents and a Southwestern look to this room.*

where and when you want such accents. Tall, columnar houseplants can serve as bold sculptures—aralias (*Polyscias*) are among the best plants for this effect. Other good vertical plants include palms, dieffenbachias, tall dracaenas, weeping fig, and columnar cacti.

A group of forms or shapes creates *mass*, another important aspect of design. Masses of low, bushy plants look best softening the hard edges of furniture. For this, ferns are ideal low-growing plants, as are calatheas,

orchids, and Chinese evergreens (*Aglaonema* species), especially when set off by beautiful plant stands or pedestals, as shown on page 27.

Texture and Scale

Texture describes the surface quality and visual weight of a plant. Scale is the relationship of one object to another. When these two qualities are well considered, houseplants can greatly enhance a room's decor.

Texture. Plants considered to be coarse-textured have bolder leaves and more dramatic proportions. Fine-textured plants have small, delicate leaves and slender stems.

You can use texture and scale to change the perception of space in a room. For example, a fine-textured plant such as a small-leaved creeping fig (*Ficus pumila*) positioned at the far end of a room will fool the eye as

RIGHT **Form and mass** *here create a balanced display. Shown left to right are a vertical fig, a bushy fern, and for accent, an amaryllis.*

FAR RIGHT **The flowering** *tuberous begonia is always elegant and looks at home atop this ornate table pedestal.*

PLANT FORMS

Canopylike

Spreading to Fountainlike

Rosette-Shaped

Trailing

Treelike

A few fine-textured plants unite this room. The plants are in scale with their settings, from the tall tree in the corner to the short, bushy plants near the chairs. Note the trailers atop the cupboards.

you enter, creating the illusion that the plant is farther away, making the room seem larger. On the other hand, placing a bold, large-leaved plant at the far end of the room can help make the space look smaller, more intimate, and more inviting.

Scale. The scale of plants in relation to one another and to the room must be appropriate. Visualize an overgrown palm stooped against an 8-foot-high ceiling. The bent plant, searching for light, would look restricted and awkward and make the whole room feel uncomfortable. Similarly, a small African violet on a grand piano would become lost in the piano's mass.

Color

Houseplant colors can affect a room's personality. Color perception is determined by the light that strikes and reflects from surfaces or is absorbed by them. Each color has value, that is, lightness or darkness. Also, a color can be warm, such as red, or cool, such as blue.

Leaf textures of various houseplants include (left to right) begonia, pilea, and plectranthus.

Colorful indoor flowering bulb gardens *create an early spring. Narcissus, crocus, tulips, and muscari bloom here.*

The color of foliage *appears to change in different light. The leaves of this Chinese evergreen are beautifully highlighted in the afternoon sun.*

Color and Light. Houseplants are seen in either natural daylight or in artificial light. The type and quality of that light affect how colors are perceived. Sunlight from a southern window appears warmer than the cool light entering a north window. Day and night also affect color perception, and so do the different types of artificial light. For example, incandescent lamps cast a warmer light than fluorescents.

First, you need to decide what times of day are most important for viewing your plants. Determine whether your rooms are visually warm or cool at those times before you consider the colors and color values of your

RIGHT **This color wheel,** *made of a sampling of the many colors of houseplant foliage and flowers, demonstrates that nature starts with the primary colors of yellow, red, and blue and combines them for endless variations. Colors opposite one another are complementary. Neighboring hues tend to harmonize.*

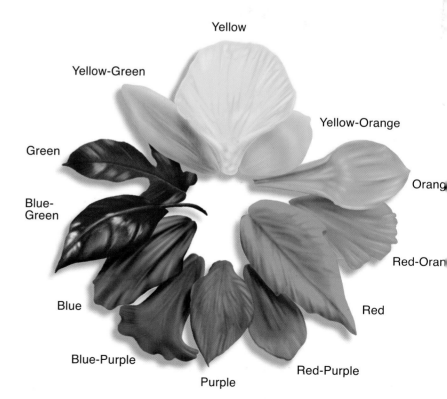

Yellow

Yellow-Green

Yellow-Orange

Green

Orang

Blue-Green

Red-Oran

Blue

Red

Blue-Purple

Red-Purple

Purple

ABOVE *Create a mass of texture and color* by grouping foliage and flowering plants together. Shown are mosaic plant, poinsettia, begonia, and arrowhead plant.

RIGHT *The airy, yellow flowers* of this orchid stand out against the deep red wall, providing subtle pyrotechnics and lightening the weight of the heavy furniture.

Color differences exist even among cultivars of the same plant, as illustrated by these crotons. Some are green, others variegated. With so much choice in plants today, you can choose colors that harmonize with the room.

houseplants. For example, a plant is not just green. It may be dark green, like the leaves of a rubber plant, or light green, like the fronds of a lacy maidenhair fern. Also, the rubber plant's leaves are leathery and almost opaque, allowing no light to pass through the leaves. So the plant appears dark and heavy. On the other hand, the delicate fronds of the lacy maidenhair fern allow light to pass through them, giving the plant a pale, airy look.

Beyond Green. Colors besides green are important, too. Variegated leaves are marked or margined with a color other than green. And flowering plants also contribute color. When adding plants to your decor, choose colors that echo, harmonize with, or contrast with the colors in the room. If your furnishings are of darker wood tones, use dark-valued plants—dark green, purple-green, and blue-green—to create a harmonious look of dark on dark. A burgundy rubber plant (*Ficus elastica* 'Burgundy') or a multicolored maranta would be a good choice. Then you could create dramatic contrast by adding a few light green plants, with yellow-green or apple green foliage, or variegated plants, such as dracaena or coleus. Refer to the color wheel on page 33 for a visual example of complementary colors.

Plant Placement

Considering basic design elements, you can use plants to bring out the latent beauty of a room. The living room is usually the most formal room in a home, and often it's also the largest space. So a living room tastefully decorated sets a tone for your house. However, if your living room contains only furniture, the room can lack warmth and impact. Plants, with their color variations, personality, and character add a dimension of vigor, color, and texture.

Here's an illustration of the basic principles of designing with plants: consider the usual rectangular shape of most living rooms. The sofa, which is usually the starting point for the positioning of other furniture, is one large mass. The sofa is usually placed against a long wall because the wall can handle the sofa's mass. But suppose the sofa or sofas were instead perpendicular to the wall—far enough from the wall to allow space for an end table or two with a lamp on one end and a passageway on the other. To balance the mass of the sofa, you could place next to it a large plant or several smaller ones or even mass the plants. Such an arrangement could provide contrasts in texture and value—and enhance balance as well.

Matching Plants to Rooms. When choosing plants and their locations, try to match the visual mass and weight of plants to the size and proportion of the room. For example, it's usually better to use bigger, bolder plants in a large room. Also, group plants of different sizes to create visual interest. For added height, try placing a small plant on a plant stand or pedestal behind a larger plant on the floor. If you have a number of smaller plants, place them on shelves or on a tiered plant stand to create greater impact.

Symmetrical, well-trained plants with large, smooth-textured leaves, such as *Dieffenbachia amoena* and corn plant (*Dracaena fragrans* 'Massangeana'), are highly appropriate for formal rooms. They are often best centrally positioned in front of a large window and become an important design element when repeated. In a large, open, L-shaped room, consider the space carefully and try to imagine groups of plants from all sides. If the room has beams or cornices that make strong horizontal lines, consider a row of plants to carry through the horizontal

Correct plant placement, using balance, form, and texture, is represented in this living room. The fig tree in the corner sets the stage for the other plants, which accentuate, rather than compete with, the green upholstery.

motif. Rooms with slanted or hipped ceilings look best with groups of plants. If the ceiling is vaulted or cathedral-shaped, you can plant cascading or fountainlike plants, such as philodendrons or arching palms, in hanging baskets to create a harmonious look.

Accent Lighting

Today, you have many options for accent lighting with attractive, easy-to-install fixtures. Lamp manufacturers and home-improvement centers offer many accent lamps—both floodlights and spotlights—specifically designed to feature plants and to help them grow indoors.

Floodlights are most suitable for accents because they can light almost the entire plant. With floodlights there is no sharply focused beam pattern. Instead, the most intense light is at the outer limits, and the illumination drops 10 percent of the maximum at the center of the beam. For information on growing plants under artificial light, see pages 56–61.

Track lighting has evolved as well. The track is a strip of hardware mounted on a ceiling or wall. You can attach contemporary lamp fixtures to the track at any given point and angle them in various directions. Display-lighting tracks can be used in straight lines or in various patterns to cover almost any desired plant or portion of it.

CHAPTER THREE

Choosing Houseplants

M any people buy houseplants on impulse, choosing in a moment's fancy. Yet when selecting plants, it's wise to consider their future as well. For example, consider a plant's growth habit and its eventual size and colors. Some plants look far different young from the way they do when they mature. Some become slender and graceful. Some begin to cascade. Others develop a broad, bushy habit.

Plants can remain small (less than 18 inches), or become medium size (19 to 36 inches), or grow large (taller than 36 inches). Foliage can become almost any shade of green or perhaps reddish, golden, purple, or variegated (with two or more colors).

LEFT **Tall, imposing plants** can benefit high-ceilinged living spaces. The plants visually lower the ceiling and divide the open space, changing a utilitarian space into inviting living quarters.

ABOVE **Young and mature plants** can be displayed using a tiered plant stand. As plants grow, they can be moved to different shelves.

Also consider a plant's needs in relation to the environmental conditions in your home. Some plants require lots of sun; others prefer dappled light; and still others tolerate shade or dim light. Some won't tolerate drafts or nighttime temperatures below 55°F. (See the plant profiles, beginning on page 108, for information on the needs of individual plants.)

Before you buy, try to locate a garden center, nursery, or other source that supplies high-quality plants. And no matter where you buy, examine each plant carefully for problems, as discussed on page 43.

Size of Plants

Most rooms have space for at least two plants, but not every room has space for two large plants. Large, treelike houseplants grow 4 to 8 feet tall. In retail outlets, these larger plants are often called specimen (or select) plants, meaning that they are already mature and at the peak of their form. Specimen plants can cost $150 or more.

Medium-size plants generally cost $15 to $25. If your space and money are limited, you can buy medium-size plants and treat them as specimens by elevating them on pedestals or tables. Small plants in 6-inch pots can be suit-

Small- and medium-size plants *at all levels provide a cheery note of welcome in this sunny entryway—without blocking traffic.*

able, too, and allow you the joy of watching them grow and mature over time. These small plants are usually classified as starter plants. Usually neither too large nor too small for most rooms, small plants are good choices for beginners. Caution: beginners should avoid plants in 2-, 3-, or 4-inch pots, because these are just past the seedling stage and are not yet strong. To survive, such seedlings need more care and coddling than plants well established in larger pots.

Shape & Growth Habit

Again, some young plants look far different from the way they will look when fully mature. When young, dragon tree (*Dracaena concinna*, aka *D. marginata*) has one or two nondescript branches. But at maturity, dragon tree bears large, thrusting branches, each crowned with a cluster of dramatic-looking, red-edged spear-shaped leaves. Butterfly palm (*Chrysalidocarpus lutescens*) grows into a fountain shape. Lady palm (*Rhapis excelsa*) stays low as it matures but becomes bushier. When young, bamboo palm (*Chamaedorea erumpens*) is a slender stalklike plant; it becomes somewhat bushy at maturity.

Without the gracefully mature palm *at right and the compact fern in the next room, this room setting would lose much of its charm.*

***The vertical sansevieria** breaks up the strong horizontal lines of the fireplace. The caladium adds balance and stretches the scene while focusing attention on the hearth.*

***This trailing succulent** will never outgrow its space alongside the stairway, where it diverts attention from otherwise uninspiring structural elements.*

The characteristic growth pattern of a plant is called its habit. Houseplant habits are generally classified as shrub-like, treelike, fountain-shaped, canopylike, rosette-shaped, or cascading. For the best visual effect in a room, try to select plants with lines that will contrast with the dominant lines of the room. Thus, to soften the hard lines of a room, use fountain-shaped or canopylike plants. Or if you prefer, exaggerate the linear space of such a room using large, vertical, treelike plants. Of course, always keep in mind your home's space restrictions. Avoid overwhelming a room with too many plants or with specimens that are too large for it. Otherwise, the space will feel crowded, even junglelike.

Leaf Size & Shape

The size and shape of a plant's leaves can determine, to a large degree, that plant's character. Individual leaves can range from tiny to quite large. Foliage can take many forms, from straight and sword-shaped to many small leaflets, such as most fern fronds.

Smooth, pointed leaves can make a plant look majestic and elegant. Plants with this type of leaf are ti plant (*Cordyline terminalis*), yuccas, and dragon tree (*Dracaena concinna*). False aralia (*Schefflera elegantissima*)

CHARACTERISTIC PLANT SHAPES

Here is a small selection of plants that illustrate differences in shape.

Shrublike Plants

Alpinia purpurata (red ginger)

Dracaena surculosa (gold-dust dracaena)

Monstera deliciosa (Swiss cheese plant)

Philodendron bipinnatifidum (fingerleaf philodendron)

Radermachera sinica (China-doll plant)

Treelike Plants

Araucaria heterophylla (Norfolk Island pine)

Cordyline terminalis (ti plant)

Crassula ovata (jade plant)

Dracaena fragrans (decorator plant)

Ficus benjamina (weeping fig)

Ficus elastica 'Decora' (rubber tree)

Fountain-shaped Plants

Beaucarnea recurvata, aka *Nolina recurvata* (ponytail plant)

Cycas revoluta (sago palm)

Dieffenbachia amoena (dumbcane)

Guzmania lingulata (bromeliad)

Neoregelia spectabilis (fingernail plant)

Canopylike Plants

Polyscias fruticosa (ming tree, ming aralia)

Schefflera actinophylla (umbrella tree)

Schefflera elegantissima (false aralia)

Rosette-shaped Plants

Asplenium nidus (bird's nest fern)

Dracaena deremensis 'Warneckii'

Neoregelia carolinae (blushing bromeliad)

Cascading Plants

Aeschynanthus speciosus (lipstick vine)

Asparagus densiflorus (emerald fern)

Begonia cultivars (angel-wing begonia)

Chlorophytum comosum (spider plant)

Epipremnum aureum (pothos)

Gynura aurantiaca (velvet plant)

Hedera helix (English ivy)

Nephrolepis exaltata 'Bostoniensis' (Boston fern)

Saxifraga stolonifera (strawberry geranium)

Setcreasea pallida (purple-heart plant)

Syngonium podophyllum (arrowhead vine)

Zebrina pendula (wandering Jew)

One specimen plant, like this ficus, often is all that's needed to make a room feel more inviting. This plant's position near the window forms a connection with the greenery outside.

has an Oriental feel—its serrated leaves resembling the delicate brush strokes of Japanese painting or calligraphy. The large agaves and Trichocereus, or Echinopsis, cacti are dramatic living sculptures. Swiss cheese plant (*Monstera deliciosa*) brings the jungle indoors, and Chinese fan palm (*Licuala grandis*) is formal.

A plant with large leaves can look bold and make a dramatic statement. For example, rubber tree (*Ficus elastica*) and fiddle-leaf fig (*F. lyrata*) need to be displayed in a large room. In a smaller room, a plant that has more slender leaves, such as butterfly palm (*Chrysalidocarpus lutescens*), with its airy, fountainlike fronds, is more appropriate.

Plants with scalloped leaves, such as some philodendrons, are often more decorative than plants with straight-edged leaves because scalloped leaves tend to look more graceful. Yet scalloped leaves can sometimes look too fussy, so choose plants in accordance with the formality of the room. Small-leaved ming aralia (*Polyscias fruticosa*) looks quite frilly. Palms, which are so often associated with tropical designs, are more versatile, blending beautifully with both contemporary and traditional settings.

Leaf & Flower Color

In addition to shape and size, consider foliage color. There are many shades and tones of green. For example, decorator plant (*Dracaena fragrans*) has foliage that is almost apple green; the cultivar 'Massangeana', known as corn plant, has yellow stripes down the center of the leaves. Dark-leaved plants (look for varieties named 'Burgundy' or purpurea) tend to look heavy and massive, whereas plants that have light-colored leaves, such as arrowhead vine (*Syngonium*), look quite graceful and airy.

You can go a step further and choose flowering houseplants that coordinate with a room's color scheme.

LEFT *Sizes, shapes, and textures* are carefully blended here, creating a pleasing harmony of green.

ABOVE *The arching fronds* of butterfly palm seem suited for the old-fashioned motif established by the antique rocking chair and the teddy bears.

The gold and yellow tones in the foliage of these plants would add zest to any room. The flowering bromeliad (top right corner) has three distinct colors.

Look for plants with flowers that match, harmonize with, or contrast with the colors of carpets, drapes, and upholstery in a room. For example, in a room with a yellow color scheme, you might choose houseplants with flowers in harmonizing shades of gold and orange. Yet a spot of bright red could add a striking accent. If you'd prefer a lively, contrasting approach, choose blue and purple blooms for the yellow room. For a quieter, more unified look, choose flowers of a yellow shade

The deep-green leaves of this ficus tree add warmth to this formal room. The tree also lends elegance to the table setting while making the space cozier.

that's close to the other yellows in the room, perhaps augmented with light-green foliage. An elegant, formal room done in white and neutral wood tones would be enhanced by deep-green foliage plants and perhaps blue or white flowers.

Buying Plants

Houseplants can be purchased almost anywhere—florists, nurseries, garden centers, mail-order companies, home-improvement centers, and supermarkets. If you know what to look for and select carefully, you can buy healthy plants from each type of supplier.

Retail Outlets

Florists sell premium plants such as large philodendrons, ficus trees, cacti, and orchids in bloom. They also sell plants associated with the holidays, such as those described on page 22. Although plants from a florist tend to be more expensive than plants sold elsewhere, they will usually be of high quality, and reputable florists will often replace a specimen plant if something goes wrong with it. Also, staff at florist shops tend to be quite knowledgeable and are usually able to recommend plants for your needs.

Nurseries, garden centers, and patio shops carry houseplants, and also stock outdoor plants, such as annuals, perennials, trees, and shrubs. These sources usually carry table and desk plants such as begonias, small bromeliads, a few palms, and some ferns at moderate to high prices. They also generally offer a good selection of hanging plants. These suppliers specialize in all kinds of plants, so if you shop there ask to talk to someone on the staff who is particularly knowledgeable about houseplants.

Mail-order companies offer a good selection; they will ship even the largest plants. However, shipping costs are usually high. Also, you may need some acquaintance with scientific (botanical) names to be sure you are ordering the exact plant you want. To help you in this regard, the Plant Profiles, beginning on page 108, list both scientific and common names.

Supermarkets, general merchandisers, and home-improvement centers often have a fairly large assortment of

LEFT *This florist's collection* of orchids allows you to select blooming plants without waiting for them to flower. Florists often sell blooming houseplants and gift plants.

BELOW *A wide assortment* of houseplants, from flowering gems to foliage plants to hanging baskets, can be found at supermarkets, home-improvement centers, garden stores, and florists—and even through mail order.

foliage and flowering plants, and sometimes staff there can offer good advice. If you know what to look for, you can get good buys and healthy plants. Most mega-stores receive new plants from their suppliers twice a week—Mondays and Thursdays. For the best selection, try to shop as soon as a new shipment has been stocked. Import stores sometimes have nurseries, but care and quality vary from store to store. Wherever you shop, consider that some plants sit so long in the store that they have cobwebs, and sometimes you'll even find plants infested with ants or other pests.

Examine Closely

Before you buy a plant, inspect it carefully. Plants that have been force-fed to grow quickly usually die quickly, too. Avoid plants with wan or limp leaves. You want perky, bright-green foliage. Stems should be solid and firm, not limp. Be sure the plant looks fresh, not bruised or off color. Using your finger, check to be sure that it is potted in soil and not a soilless mix that is mostly filler material. The pot should feel fairly heavy, not light as a feather, when you lift it.

It is vital that you inspect for insects and disease. Examine both tops and bottoms of leaves and the leaf axils (where leaves attach to stems). Brown or white streaks on leaves can indicate rot or plant disease. Chewed leaf edges mean that insects have been at work and might still be in the soil. Shake the plant gently; if

whiteflies are present, the disturbed insects will fly around the plant like a cloud of tiny snowflakes. Never buy a plant if you see signs of insects or disease. Also, check the soil; avoid plants that are growing in dry, caked soil because they are usually drought stressed.

Indoor Conditions

Successfully matching plants to room conditions can mean the difference between a healthy plant and one that must be discarded after a short time. Conditions in the average home or apartment vary from room to room and from daytime to nighttime. Temperature, light, and humidity are key factors. Consider the various room environments in your home, and try to determine which plants will work best in each.

Halls and Entryways

People form their first impression of your home inside the entry, but in many homes this is hardly a hospitable place for plants. If the space is large enough, a plant on a pedestal can lend an elegant look. If there is a reception

SMART TIP

Before You Buy

Examine plants carefully for signs of pests, disease, or stress before you purchase them.

The roots *emerging from the bottom of the pot indicate that this plant should have been transplanted into a larger container; these roots have been exposed to the air and have probably dried out.*

The white stains *are signs of fertilizer salt buildup. This plant may be stressed; look for another.*

RIGHT A specimen bird's nest fern *takes center stage in this showroom. Be sure to inspect plants closely for pests and diseases before you purchase them. To be safe, you can quarantine new plants for a few days and then reinspect them before placing them with your other plants.*

FAR RIGHT Do not buy a plant *with limp or yellow leaves. The leggy growth with long stems and few leaves is another sign of trouble.*

Large potted plants transform this functional space into an inviting transitional area. Here, large jars and the sand-colored tile floor convey a Southwestern feel.

table, use a small plant such as prayer plant (*Maranta*) or a small colorful bromeliad such as Cryptanthus.

If the hall is barren, think about using a single large plant in place of a piece of furniture. Cascading plants placed on tables or shelves in halls will soften the sharp lines of furniture and hardware. Always use appropriate mats, saucers, or other protective devices so that water leaking from drainage holes does not damage furnishings.

Drafts and Light. The hall or entry may have temperatures of 65° to 75°F. But doors opening and closing allow cold drafts that cause problems for some plants. In winter, an open door can give plants an arctic blast, which can kill or severely damage any but the toughest plants. Often, halls and entryways have little natural light. In this case, choose plants that tolerate low light levels. Yet even these plants may need more light.

To give plants more light, you can install ceiling lights aimed at the plants or move the plants to brighter locations periodically to help them regain their strength. You

The plants give this dramatic stairway a more appealing, less formidable scale. They also break up the plain expanse of hallway behind the stairs.

can also put the plants outside in summer to replenish their vigor. The "Smart Tip," below, lists some plants that will survive the ins and outs of halls and entryways.

Living Rooms and Dining Rooms

These generally large rooms tend to be bright with natural light and usually have even, moderate temperatures of 65° to 75°F. These conditions make most living rooms good places for plants. Plants can contribute to living rooms and dining rooms in a number of ways. Large plants, thoughtfully placed, can lend a sense of organization to the space and direct the flow of traffic. Small plants can accent the decor and provide their own interest. Study the light levels in different parts of your living room or dining room to see where plants could thrive. Then think about the plant forms that would complement the architecture, space, and furnishings. With all this in mind, you can begin selecting plants. (See "Shape & Growth Habit," pages 38–39, for information on plant forms.)

Large plants are generally well suited to spacious living rooms and dining rooms because the plants don't look out of scale there. If the room is long and narrow, choose an upright plant with slender branches, such as a specimen dragon tree (*Dracaena concinna*). If the architecture is modern and the decor contemporary, consider a large, sculptural cactus. Such plants are especially striking in modern interiors.

Color Considerations. When plant color contrasts with wall color, the plant draws the eye, often making a large room feel smaller and more intimate. Consider the drama created by a cascading, brightly colored

This dining area needs the low planter near the expanse of windows as much as the flowering plants themselves need to be positioned near the light. The attractive planter does not obscure the view.

A single arching palm can work wonders for an otherwise sparsely furnished living room. This palm fills the gap between the two sofas, echoes the green in the large painting, and—not least—brings nature indoors.

❧ SMART TIP ❧

Plants for Halls and Entryways
Aspidistra elatior (cast-iron plant)
Begonia, rhizomatous types
Chlorophytum comosum (spider plant)
Dieffenbachia (dumbcane)
Dracaena
Ficus (fig trees)
Fittonia verschaffeltii (mosaic plant)
Maranta (prayer plant)
Philodendron
Syngonium (arrowhead vine)

When plant colors contrast with walls*, they help make large rooms more intimate. The plants at the far end of the room add a bright highlight to muted walls and furnishings.*

If you have limited floor space*, look up. Here, a trailing plant is displayed beautifully atop a corner curio cabinet.*

gesneriad, such as Episcia 'Flame', against an off-white wall. If there is no nearby window light, install a spotlight or track lighting. (See "Light," page 60, for more information on artificial light.)

Conversely, for a small living room, select plants with leaves similar in value and color to the walls; plants that echo room colors make a room seem larger. Another way to create the illusion of greater space is to group plants toward the center of the room. Avoid blocking the traffic flow.

Tight Space. If your floor space is limited, consider hanging baskets of ferns or tropical trailers from the ceiling. For greater impact, try positioning the baskets at three different heights. To break the monotony of walls that are mainly windows, use medium-size plants, perhaps in groups of three, to bring color and life to the blank area. Such plants will benefit from the excellent light.

Plants as Accents. If you have a fireplace, you could set a few plants on the hearth to draw attention to this feature of the room. However, because of the heat and dryness created when a fire is burning, it's essential to remove the plants then. Another likely place for plants in living rooms and dining rooms is behind a table and chairs, to supply vertical accents. Instead of placing a long table behind a sofa, try a row of identical plants in identically colored containers. Install lighting fixtures to ensure that the plants receive sufficient light.

Once the large plants are in place, add a few complementary table or desk plants to pull the room together. The goal is to balance the large plants with smaller plants placed around the room, not to make your living room look like a plant shop. You can move the small plants around from time to time to change the look of the room or to balance sunlight intake.

Plants in bedrooms improve the air quality while creating a tranquil atmosphere. The fern and the palm in the bedroom lend a sheltered, cozy feel to this space.

The ficus tree in this more traditional bedroom adds needed color and visually raises the wall height.

Bedrooms

There was a time when people didn't keep plants in their bedrooms because they believed the plants would deplete oxygen levels and make breathing difficult. Actually, the opposite is true—plants give off oxygen during the day as a byproduct of photosynthesis. Plants also improve air quality by absorbing pollutants, while creating a relaxing ambiance. Graceful palms or ferns on bed tables or in hanging containers are especially fitting.

Contemporary bedrooms are often designed for both living and sleeping. In a bedroom divided into sleeping, dressing, and sitting areas, you can use plants in imaginative yet functional ways to create the feeling of an indoor garden. For example, you can place about three tall plants in a row to create a divider or natural screen between the different parts of the room. Keep a watering can in a nearby bathroom so that you can water the plants easily.

Bathrooms

Today's newer homes generally have large bathrooms. These luxurious rooms—often a cross between a spa and a traditional bathroom—need plants to soften the hard look of tile, chrome, glass, and marble, and to make the space friendlier.

Bathrooms can be excellent locations for plants. In fact, many plants grow better in bathrooms than in any other place in a home. The warm, humid conditions there help make tropical plants grow well. Also, many bathrooms have frosted or patterned glass windowpanes, which provide diffused light that is neither too bright nor too dim—exactly what most plants prefer.

Decorating Ideas. Floor plants are ideal for a large bathroom, and there is usually ample space for them. Smaller plants, such as orchids and bromeliads, can

Well-selected plants can thrive under bathroom skylights. And the daily higher doses of humidity in the bathroom can complement good lighting to provide excellent growing conditions.

suggest the tropics. Vanities and tables offer innumerable places on which plants can be displayed.

If your bathroom is small, consider placing a hanging fern or other basket plant near the window or installing glass shelves across the window to create platforms for small plants. Another option is to place a vertical plant stand or plant pole in a bright corner to accommodate several smaller plants on different levels. In a bathroom without windows, plants can thrive if placed close to fluorescent lights that are kept on 12 to 16 hours a day.

Even though tropical plants are particularly well suited to both the environment and style of many bathrooms, you should be bold in trying all kinds of plants there, including those that aren't doing well elsewhere. Plants really perk up in the brighter light and higher humidity of the bathroom. The only plants to avoid placing in bathrooms are those that prefer drier conditions, and many of the plants with fuzzy or hairy leaves.

Kitchens

Modern kitchens tend to be large, natural centers of activity often located near a recreation or morning room. There is usually plenty of bright light from windows or skylights and ample humidity from cooking, so plants can do well in kitchens. There, your favorite plants can lend a personal touch and extend a cheerful, colorful welcome to all who gather.

Shelves, cabinet tops, and windowsills are all prime places for small potted plants. Flowering plants such as

African violets, geraniums, and miniature begonias grow luxuriantly in bright, humid kitchens. Dozens of medium-size foliage plants, such as prayer plants (*Maranta*), arrowhead vines (*Syngonium*), and peperomias, also do well. In a large kitchen where you want a green look, consider a floor plant such as a large lady palm (*Rhapis*) or sago palm (*Cycas*).

White and yellow are two favorite color schemes for kitchens. In a white or yellow room, plants with apple green or variegated foliage look splendid. For a unified look, put all the plants in pots of the same color.

LEFT ***The warm, humid conditions*** of bathrooms help tropical plants thrive. The plants shown here soften the hard edges of the tile and help transform this oversize bathroom into a spa.

BELOW LEFT
The upper tier of plants benefits from skylighting, and the flowering plants benefit from artificial light.

BELOW RIGHT
Kitchens become more inviting when decorated with plants. The ficus tree enjoys window light, while anchoring the dining area.

GROWING CULINARY HERBS INDOORS

If you're looking for compact plants to grow on a sunny kitchen windowsill or under lights, consider culinary herbs. Their flavor will be milder than that of herbs grown outdoors, and their leaves will be smaller, but you can still use them to perk up midwinter recipes.

Recommended indoor herbs include basil, chives, bay, mints, marjoram, oregano, rosemary, and parsley. You'll need several pots of the herbs you use most.

The best indoor location for herbs is a warm, sunny south- or west-facing window that receives a minimum of six hours of sun a day. Turn the pots every day or two so the stems grow reasonably straight. If you grow herbs under fluorescent lights, keep the lamps 5 to 6 inches above the tops of the plants, and leave them on for 14 hours a day. (For more on artificial lighting, see pages 60–61.)

Plant herbs in 6-inch pots with a porous, all-purpose potting mix that is equal parts potting soil, sand, and peat moss. Start new plants from seeds or cuttings, as explained in Chapter 6.

An abundance of herbs thrives in this sunny window. Herbs need at least six hours of light a day.

Fertilize the herbs monthly with an all-purpose liquid fertilizer. Avoid overfertilizing, or your herbs will grow too quickly and have poor flavor. Herbs don't like soggy soil. So let the soil dry slightly between waterings, and then water when the soil feels dry just below the surface.

Most herbs thrive in temperatures of 65° to 68°F indoors, with a slight dip at night. Plenty of humidity and good air circulation are also important. If your herbs are on a windowsill, move them back from the glass during very cold winter weather.

To use herbs in cooking, wait to cut their leaves until the moment they are needed.

LEFT *Herbs grown* in the kitchen provide the indoor gardener with satisfying plant work and the cook with wonderful flavor enhancers.

ABOVE *Leafy culinary herbs* in matching hand-painted pots please both the eye and the palate.

Gallery of Herbs

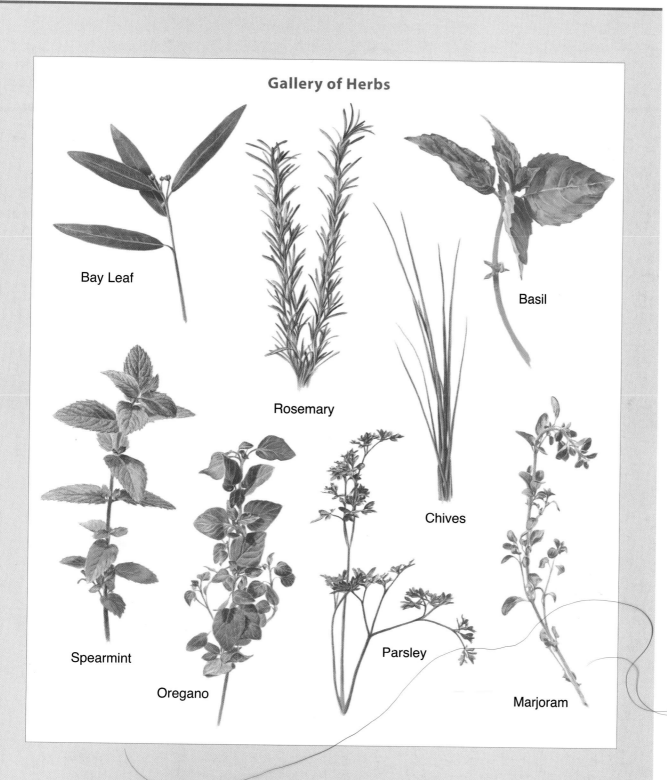

Bay Leaf

Rosemary

Basil

Chives

Spearmint

Oregano

Parsley

Marjoram

CHAPTER FOUR

Houseplant Containers

Virtually any vessel that can hold soil and allows drainage can be used as a plant container. Baskets, tubs, terra-cotta pots, decorated pots, glazed ceramic jardinieres, Victorian-style urns, wine casks, boxes, terrariums—the list goes on. You can also use decorative containers, called cachepots—pots without drainage holes—to hold smaller planted pots that have drainage holes.

When selecting a houseplant container, be sure to consider its appearance, its proportion in relation to plant size, and the material from which it is made.

LEFT *This shallow glazed pot* houses a colorful cymbidium. Here the low pot perfectly suits the plants, though it conceals an inner pot with necessary drainage holes.

ABOVE *Hanging in a window*, this flowering lipstick plant eliminates the need for any other window treatments.

RIGHT *A hanging basket* filled with variegated ivy trails is positioned over small plants to create depth.

Hanging Containers

Hanging pots and baskets come in many sizes and are made of various materials. There are slotted redwood baskets, in which you place a potted plant; woven baskets lined with plastic; plastic pots with hangers attached; and wire baskets meant to be lined with peat moss or sphagnum. There are also ceramic hanging pots—some decorated, some plain—with attached saucers. In addition, there are simple, attractive wrought-iron hanging containers. Whichever type you choose, be sure the container has the means of catching excess water that will drain from the soil.

Hanging Hardware

You also need some means of suspending a container from a ceiling or a wall. Chains are usually the most attractive answer; they come in different sizes and colors. You can also use sturdy wire or clear monofilament fishing line. For an informal look, try woven and macrame hangers to convert conventional pots into hanging containers.

No matter what kind of hanger you use, be sure it can support the weight of the plant and pot. An 8-inch diameter container filled with damp soil can weigh approximately 50 pounds.

For ceiling attachments, all you need is a screw hook. When you install the hook, embed it into a ceiling joist or a structurally strong surface, such as wood, so that the screw threads have a firm hold. Even with lightweight plants, it's unwise to depend solely on the structural integrity of gypsum or acoustic ceiling panels. (See "How to Install Supports for Hanging Plants" on page 60.)

Although you can grow almost any plant in a hanging container, cascading or trailing plants look better in hanging motifs than upright plants.

Plants for Hanging Containers

Acalypha hispida (chenille plant)
Aeschynanthus (lipstick plant)
Begonia, angel-wing types
Chlorophytum comosum (spider plant)
Columnea (columnea)

LEFT *Hanging containers* hold plants that add beauty and color at eye level. This Congo fig combines a trailing habit with upright growth— an interesting choice to hang.

Epipremnum aureum (pothos)
Episcia (flame violet)
Ferns
Hoya (wax plant)
Nematanthus (goldfish plant)
Philodendron (philodendron)
Sedum morganianum (burro's tail)
Zebrina (wandering Jew)

FAR LEFT *These* **containers** *include a plastic planter box (top left), simulated concrete (top right), an orchid pot with slots (lower right), and a shallow bulb pot (far left).*

LEFT *This* **three-legged urn** *is an elegant container for Paphiopedilum orchids. The simplicity of the container suits the plant well.*

Pots

Pots can be made of unglazed terra-cotta, glazed pottery, or various kinds of plastic.

Terra-Cotta Pots

Simple terra-cotta pots are available in diameters of 3 to 24 inches and in a range of depths. These pots are inexpensive, and their earth tones complement practically all plant colors. *Note:* soil dries out quickly in terra-cotta pots because their walls are porous. But this can be a plus because it prevents plants from becoming waterlogged. Soak all types of terra-cotta pots overnight before planting in them—otherwise the containers will absorb moisture that the plants need from the soil. You can find terra-cotta pots at nurseries and garden centers, in the

plant section of general merchandisers, in supermarkets, and at many florists.

Variations of the classic terra-cotta pot include cylindrical containers, strawberry jars (which have small planting pockets on the sides), pots shaped like animals and birds, and shallow azalea or fern pots. The basic

Pots and plants *of various sizes and shapes sometimes look best if the pots are of a uniform color. Here, the terra-cotta color helps showcase the whole composition.*

ABOVE **Glazed decorative pots** *set off these colored flowers without competing with the blooms. To avoid water damage on furniture, it's best to water plants on a separate trolley or at the sink.*

ABOVE RIGHT **Glazed ceramic pot** *complements narcissus and pansies. Colors, shape, and scale combine to make this arrangement perfection-in-a-pot.*

RIGHT **A terra-cotta pot** *with a raised relief design is a classic choice. Terra-cotta (literally earth-fired) complements almost any plant color or decorating style.*

LEFT *Cachepots* are made of various materials. They are usually used to hold planted pots set on a layer of pebbles or shard to aid drainage.

BOTTOM LEFT *A shallow terra-cotta pot* is ideal for this dish garden of succulents and cacti.

BOTTOM RIGHT *A glazed cachepot* planted with a bromeliad makes a lovely centerpiece on the table. The pot is just tall enough to hide the base of the plant.

cylindrical pot is available in three sizes, with a maximum 14-inch diameter.

The azalea pot is squatty, three-quarters as high as it is wide, and 6 to 14 inches in diameter. It often looks to be in better proportion to plants than the typical narrow clay pot.

Italian terra-cotta pots can have rims of varied shapes— a tight lip, a round edge, a beveled edge, or a wavy edge. All of these variations can be attractive. Venetian pots are barrel-shaped, with a band design pressed into the sides. These formal-looking containers are sold in 8- to 20-inch sizes. The graceful Spanish pots have outward sloping sides and flared lips. Their walls are heavier than those of conventional clay pots, and diameters range from 8 to 12 inches.

Three-legged pots are bowl-shaped and raise plants up, putting them on better display. They are 8 to 20 inches in diameter. Bulb pans or seed bowls generally are less than half as high as they are wide. These containers look rather like deep saucers; they are sold in 6- to 12-inch sizes.

Glazed Pots

Glazed pots are usually used to impart a more formal and elegant look to plant displays. But you cannot plant directly in most glazed pots because they have no drainage holes. To use your favorite glazed pot, put a plain plastic or unglazed terra-cotta pot with a drainage hole inside the decorative container.

Plastic Pots

Plastic pots are lightweight and easy to clean. Because plastic is not porous, be careful not to overwater; water-logging the plant can cause root rot. Also, because of their light weight, plastic pots may become unstable and tip over when planted with heavy specimen plants.

Cachepots

These decorative containers usually hold plain pots with drainage holes. Place the planted pots atop a layer of pebbles or gravel into which excess water can drain. Porcelain cachepots may be splashed with flower or fruit designs, often with gold accents. Brass or copper cachepots are rich looking and not overly expensive. Mahogany and teak cachepots provide a unique look, but are expensive. Some cachepots are hexagonal-shaped, with footed bases.

A simple glazed pot *is an effective container for this casual collection of plants.*

The wooden plant stand, *elevates plants to table level. The plastic saucer on wheels is one type of plant dollie that is used to move plants around. The waffle grill and round disks protect furniture from moisture damage.*

Tubs and Urns

Tubs can be round or hexagonal and made of wood, stone, or concrete. The best wooden tubs are durable, rot-resistant redwood or cypress. Stone or concrete tubs can look good indoors in a sunroom. Japanese soy tubs are inexpensive and appropriate for informal family rooms and dens. They are widely available. Blue-glazed Japanese porcelain tubs are formal and rich-looking, especially when they contain small, treelike plants such as jade plants (*Crassula ovata*).

Urns come in a variety of shapes and sizes and usually have a pedestal or footed base attached. They may be made of fiberglass to simulate stone, bronze, concrete, or other materials. Urns look best when viewed at eye level, such as at the end of a sunroom shelf. Flowering houseplants look especially attractive in urns. Although pedestal urns are handsome, there is a drawback: their large size can make them appear overpowering in a small room, so reserve their use for large spaces.

Boxes

Small indoor trees and shrubs look especially good in simple wooden boxes. The wood complements the stems and trunks of the plants, and the solid structure of the box provides a visual base for the plants. A layer of moist unmilled peat moss, or sphagnum, on top of the soil lends an airy touch to the container, keeping it from looking too heavy. Because a wooden box filled with soil and plants can be quite heavy, keep wheeled trolleys (sometimes called dollies) under these containers so you can move them easily.

Choosing Containers

Select a container that complements the plant's appearance and growth habit. Bushy, round plants are often complemented by bowl-or dish-shaped pots. Tall vertical plants often look best in cylindrical containers.

Also consider pot depth. Some plants have shallow roots; others have long roots. A plant with an extensive root system needs a deep container, while a plant with few roots, such as a bromeliad, needs only a shallow pot. The pot should comfortably accommodate the plant's roots but should not be so big that the plant looks lost in it. Besides, too much "unused" soil tends to get soggy and rot the roots.

Container color is another important consideration. When in doubt, opt for understated colors. Bold colors clash with most home surroundings, while white or dark green are generally complementary to furnishings. Terra-cotta blends beautifully with most interiors.

When growing potted plants on windowsills, tabletops, or other furniture, protect the surfaces from water stains. Buy plastic or terra-cotta saucers to match the pots. Saucers are available in diameters from 4 inches to 28 inches. Many terra-cotta saucers are unglazed, so moisture still seeps through if it is left in the saucer. Look for saucers with glazed bottoms, or put a cork mat or felt protector under the saucer. This is certainly important when you place plants on fine furniture.

Pedestals, Stands, Trolleys

You can buy an array of plant stands, pedestals, and other decorative display furniture to show off your plants. Most stands are made of wood, wrought iron, or plastic and raise plants nearer eye level. Besides making plants look attractive, a grate-like stand or platform can help air reach plant roots. Elevated stands, actually pedestals, vary in height from 12 to 60 inches and generally support a single plant. There are also wrought-iron stands designed to display six or eight pots and fitted with iron rings to hold plants in place.

Plant trolleys (sometimes called "dollies") are wooden platforms with wheels or large plastic saucers with wheels. These movable "stages" offer a good means of moving big plants around to change the look of a room. (*Note:* you need to move plants to the sink or put a saucer underneath them when it's time to water.) The units also raise plants off the floor and thus help prevent water from staining wood surfaces.

HOW TO INSTALL SUPPORTS FOR HANGING PLANTS

Although it's important to position hanging plants where they will be most attractive, it's more important that they be securely hung. These pages show how to find structural support and install hardware. Note: rot-weakened wood won't be a reliable support, and some plants greatly increase in weight as they grow.

Attaching Hooks to Ceiling Joists

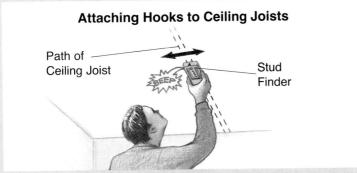

Path of Ceiling Joist

Stud Finder

BEEP!

1 To locate ceiling joists or wall studs, slide the stud finder perpendicular to likely supports, and lightly mark exact edges. This lets you drill holes into exact centers of supports for maximum holding power.

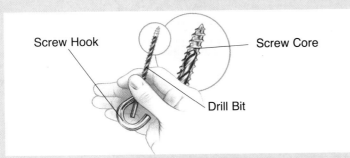

Screw Hook

Screw Core

Drill Bit

2 Predrill the hole. Compare the diameter of the screw shaft with that of the drill bit. The bit should be smaller than the screw.

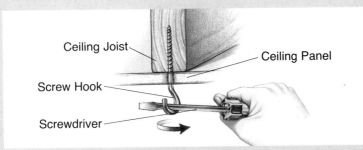

Ceiling Joist

Ceiling Panel

Screw Hook

Screwdriver

3 Install the screw. You may need to use a screwdriver as shown to complete the installation. All of the threads should bite into solid wood.

Installing Bridging

Ceiling Joist

Solid Bridging

Screw Hook

Ceiling Panel

If ceiling joists are not directly above the point where you wish to suspend a plant and you have access to the joists from above, you can create solid wood bridging before driving the screw hook.

Attaching a Base Plate

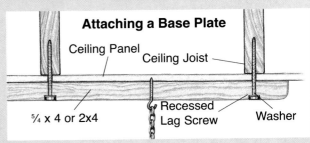

Ceiling Panel

Ceiling Joist

⁵/₄ x 4 or 2x4

Recessed Lag Screw

Washer

If you don't have access to the joists from above, you can create a solid base for screw hooks in various positions by attaching a thick wooden plate to two or more ceiling joists. Fasten the base plate to the joist by means of recessed lag screws and washers.

Installing a Hanging Pole

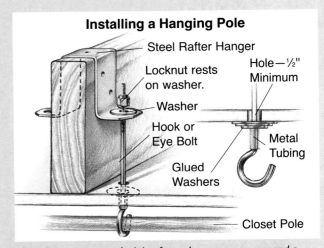

Steel Rafter Hanger

Locknut rests on washer.

Hole—½" Minimum

Washer

Hook or Eye Bolt

Metal Tubing

Glued Washers

Closet Pole

If you have access to the joists from above, you can suspend a closet pole perpendicular to ceiling joists with steel hangers and hook or eye bolts. This assembly allows sturdy support, and it lets you slide plants along the pole.

DECORATIVE CEILING HOOKS

Decorative ceiling hooks sometimes come in packets with an optional screw and toggle bolt. Caution: Packaging on smaller hooks (screw threads a mere ¾ inch long) may suggest that the hooks can support up to 30 pounds, but this assumes ideal installations.

Installing a Decorative Hook. A toggle bolt has more holding power in gypsum ceiling panels than a mere screw, but its effectiveness depends on the support of weak panels, which could become even weaker if damp. If you employ this light-duty assembly, follow manufacturer's installation instructions, but use plants weighing no more than 5 pounds (no heavier than a half gallon of milk). Installation steps:

Decorative Hook

Small Hook with Screw. Never drive a decorative screw hook into unsupported drywall (gypsum) panels. Such an installation allows only a few turns of the screw thread to bite into flimsy support material. See proper installation below.

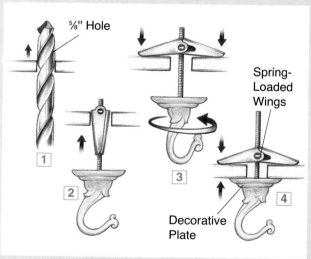

⅝" Hole

Spring-Loaded Wings

Decorative Plate

1 Drill a hole just large enough for the folded wings of the spring-loaded toggle, usually ⅝ inch or larger.

2 Insert the assembled toggle bolt.

3 Pull gently downward on the spring-activated wings so that they bite into paneling as you turn the hook to drive the threaded portion of the bolt upward.

4 Stop when the wings and plate are snug.

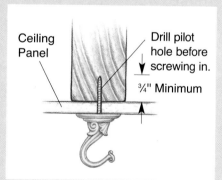

Ceiling Panel

Drill pilot hole before screwing in.

¾" Minimum

Instead of driving this screw hook into unsupported ceiling paneling, drive the screw through the panel into a ceiling joist so nearly all screw threads bite into wood. (See "Attaching Hooks to Ceiling Joists" on previous page. When selecting a drill bit, follow the manufacturer's recommendations or use the technique illustrated in Step 2 on the previous page.)

WALL BRACKETS

Wall brackets for lightweight plants come in assorted shapes and sizes. Attach them to wall studs. For guidance on finding wall studs, follow instructions on the opposite page. Packaging usually includes screws of suitable length for the bracket size and plant-carrying capacity.

Swinging-Arm Brackets

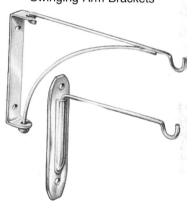

Fixed-Arm Brackets

CHAPTER FIVE

Growing Houseplants

It takes more than sufficient light and good potting soil to grow healthy plants. Other cultural needs, such as fertilizer, water, temperature, humidity, and air circulation, must also be met. Each of these factors in a plant's environment is affected by the others. Although it's not necessary to provide perfect conditions for a plant to thrive, you must provide a reasonably appropriate balance among the various factors so that plants will prosper and reward your efforts with beautiful foliage and flowers. This chapter explains good growing conditions and how to optimize them.

LEFT *Cool, indirect light* from a north window is perfect for the fern and the Chinese evergreen.

ABOVE *Houseplants outgrow* their pots, making repotting part of their care. Generally, plants this size and smaller should be put into pots one size larger, every year—larger plants, every two years.

Light

Without light, plants will die. Light is necessary for photosynthesis, the production of sugar and starches from carbon dioxide and water. How long a plant is exposed to light each day—the daylength, or photoperiod—determines the amount of food that the plant manufactures and whether the plant grows well and produces flowers.

Daylengths

Some plants, called short-day plants, will not bloom unless they receive enough hours of darkness each day.

DAYLENGTH NEEDS OF PLANTS

To determine the amount of artificial light a houseplant will need, it is helpful to know how much natural light a plant receives in its native habitat. Most plants are day-neutral, meaning they are not too particular about the daylength. However, some plants need sufficient hours of darkness and bloom naturally in the winter when the days are short and the sun is low. Others need the long days and strong light of summer to bloom. Short, long, or neutral daylengths can all be approximated with artificial lights alone or in combination with natural light.

Short-Day Plants:

Begonia Rex-Cultorum hybrids (rex begonia)
Cacti, many types
Euphorbia pulcherrima (poinsettia)
Kalanchoe
Orchids, many fall-blooming types
Schlumbergera × *buckleyi* (Christmas cactus)

Long-Day Plants:

Orchids, many spring-blooming types
Pelargonium (geraniums)

Christmas cactus, which flowers in winter, is a good example of a short-day plant. Long-day plants, on the other hand, need long days to set buds. Summer bloomers, such as most of the familiar garden annuals and orchids, are long-day plants.

Other plants, such as African violets, are considered day-neutral, which means they are not particular about daylength and will flower at various times of the year. If you want to grow flowering houseplants under artificial light, you can use their daylength needs to determine how many hours a day to keep lights on for them. (See "Daylength Needs of Plants," at left.)

Window Light

The amount and intensity of light entering your windows depends on the exposure and whether the light is obstructed.

Southern. A south-facing window is brightest, and plants on south windowsills may receive direct sun for much of the day. South light is too intense for many plants, and some will sunburn—you may notice a darkening or "burning" of their leaves. South windows are also hot, so be sure not to let plants growing in these windows dry out.

To soften the light from a south window, place a sheer curtain between the pane and the plants. Good plants for south windows include cacti and succulents, amaryllis, geraniums, and many other plants grown mainly for their flowers.

Eastern and Western. East windows are the next brightest and an ideal location for many plants. An east window gets cool, bright morning sun and indirect light in the afternoon.

West windows are reasonably bright but can become quite warm when lit by the hot afternoon sun. The best plants for west windows are those that can tolerate heat.

Northern. A north window receives indirect light all day, and is the coolest, dimmest exposure. Not many flowering plants will thrive in a north window without supplemental light, but plenty of foliage plants will do well.

Flowering plants and those with variegated leaves need the brightest light, while foliage plants and ferns

The strong heat and light of a south-facing window are well suited to this cactus container garden.

need the least. Many houseplants are native to jungles and rain forests, where the light is filtered through the trees. For these plants, sunny southern windows can be fatal.

Intensity. From all exposures, light levels decrease dramatically the farther away from the window you go. In the center of a room, light may be only half as intense as the light on a windowsill. You can increase light for plants if you have reflective surfaces nearby.

Too Much or Too Little Light

Most houseplants thrive where they receive bright or dappled light from a window, without direct sun. Learn to observe your plants for signs that they're getting appropriate amounts of light.

Plants that aren't receiving enough light respond by "reaching" toward the light source. Their stems grow long and spindly and often curve in the direction of the nearest window. Also, their leaves will be fewer and smaller than normal and spaced farther apart on the stems.

Plants receiving too much light often turn pale green and eventually yellowish, a symptom that can be

mistaken for lack of nutrients. The leaves may curl downward, which might look like symptoms of underwatering.

If you see such symptoms in your plants, consider all of the elements of their environment—including light—before attempting to adjust the conditions.

Artificial Light

Plants evolved in nature in response to the sun's spectrum of wavelengths, so artificial lighting tends to increase in effectiveness the more it emulates natural light. Try to choose plants that will do well in the natural light of your home, and then supplement with artificial light as needed.

The important factors are the duration and intensity of the light, and the spectrum wavelengths present. Plants need the blue, red, and far-red wavelengths of the spectrum to grow normally. Blue enables plants to manufacture carbohydrates. Red controls assimilation and affects a plant's response to the relative length of light and darkness. And far-red controls seed germination, stem length, and leaf size.

If the duration and light levels in your rooms are insufficient, you will probably need to provide supplemental light. This is especially important if your windows face north or if tall buildings or trees block light for part of the day.

Incandescent Light

Incandescent light bulbs can help plants grow somewhat, but they emit only the red-orange part of the spectrum and thus aren't sufficient on their own. And about 70 percent of their energy is wasted as heat. As an alternative, incandescent floodlights have built-in reflectors that concentrate light more efficiently. Yet like standard bulbs, they provide only the red wavelengths. And if placed too close to plants, their heat will dry out both the plants and their soil.

As supplemental light, incandescents can be useful during the shorter days of winter. In this case, a 200-watt floodlight placed 2 to 3 feet from a foliage plant supplies needed light without overheating and drying the plant.

How to Build a Knockdown Growing Stand

DIFFICULTY LEVEL: Difficult

TOOLS: Screwdriver, framing square, wood rasp, drill with ⅜-, ¼-, and ⁷⁄₆₄-inch bits, and one smaller bit for the screw hooks you select

This stand supports an array of containers for raising seedlings under three fluorescent shop lights. For storage, the stand can be quickly disassembled.

You don't have to own a saw to make this stand. A home-center employee can cut the plywood for you, and you can probably borrow a handsaw there to cut the 1×2 lumber and closet pole. The cut wood fits into a midsize car for transport.

Designed by Rita Buchanan
Illustrated by Steve Buchanan

Materials

Lumber: As shown below and right
Lights: Three 48-inch fluorescent shop lights with hanging chains
Fasteners: As shown in photo below

2	3" × ¼" carriage bolts
8	2" × ¼" carriage bolts
4	1½" × ¼" carriage bolts
16	¼" wingnuts
4	1" screw hooks or cuphooks
16	#6 × 1" flathead screws

Cutting and Assembly

(All wood dimensions are shown right and opposite.)

1 *Cut a ⅜-inch sheet of plywood for the two shelves and the bottom brace.*

2 *Use four 6-foot lengths of 1x2 lumber for the legs.*

3 *From four other 6-foot 1x2s, first cut the four 60-inch shelf supports and then the eight 6-inch stop bars.*

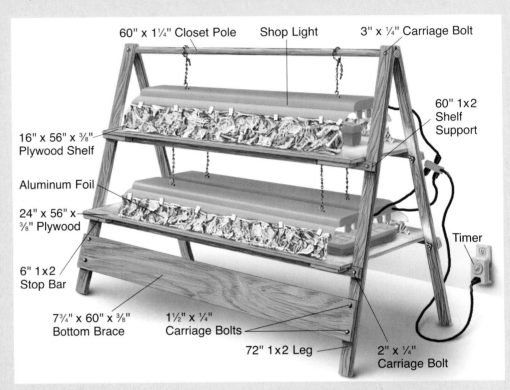

60" x 1¼" Closet Pole — Shop Light — 3" x ¼" Carriage Bolt

16" x 56" x ⅜" Plywood Shelf

Aluminum Foil

24" x 56" x ⅜" Plywood

6" 1x2 Stop Bar

7¾" x 60" x ⅜" Bottom Brace

1½" x ¼" Carriage Bolts

72" 1x2 Leg

2" x ¼" Carriage Bolt

60" 1x2 Shelf Support

Timer

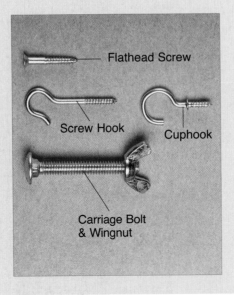

Flathead Screw

Screw Hook

Cuphook

Carriage Bolt & Wingnut

⅜" Plywood Cutting Diagram

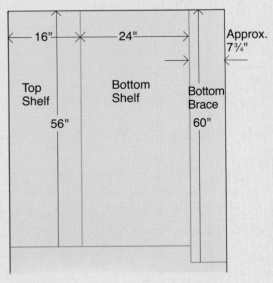

16"   24"   Approx. 7¾"

Top Shelf   Bottom Shelf   Bottom Brace

56"   60"

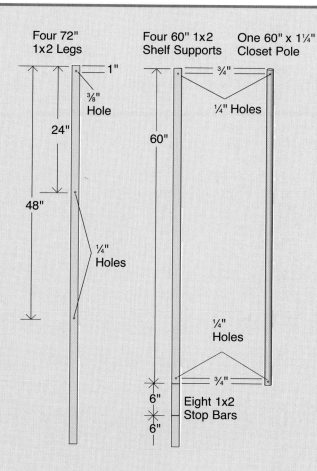

Four 72" 1x2 Legs

1"

3/8" Hole

24"

48"

1/4" Holes

Four 60" 1x2 Shelf Supports

One 60" x 1 1/4" Closet Pole

3/4"

1/4" Holes

60"

1/4" Holes

3/4"

6"

6"

Eight 1x2 Stop Bars

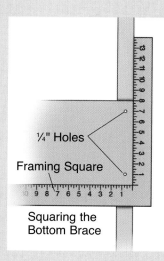

1/4" Holes

Framing Square

Squaring the Bottom Brace

this allows the legs to swing open without binding.

8 Place two legs on the floor, parallel and about 60 inches apart with the rasped indentation down, and place the bottom brace on the legs about 10 inches from the leg bottoms. Use a framing square, as shown below, to align one end of the brace with that leg. Then, with scrap wood underneath the leg, drill two 1/4-inch holes through both the brace and the leg. Repeat at the other end of the brace. Then insert four 1 1/2 x 1/4-inch carriage bolts through the holes, and tighten the wingnuts to fasten the brace to the leg.

9 Lean the leg and brace assembly against a wall, and fasten the two shelf supports by means of 1 x 1/4-inch carriage bolts and wingnuts.

10 As in the preceding step, lean the remaining two legs against a wall, and fasten their two shelf supports.

11 As shown at right, sandwich the closet pole between the rasped indentations at the top ends of mating legs, and fasten with a 3 x 1/4-inch carriage bolt and wingnut.

4 Cut a 60 x 1 1/4-inch closet pole, and drill 1/4-inch holes 3/4 inch from each end.

Legwork

5 Drill 3/8-inch holes 1 inch from the top of each leg.
6 Mark and drill two 1/4-inch holes in each of the four legs and shelf supports as shown on the previous page.

7 Using a wood rasp, carve a shallow indentation near the top of each leg to accommodate the closet pole (see the photo, right). Note: extend the indentation farther above the hole (toward the top of the leg); after assembly,

Shelves
12 Position stop bars under the corners of each shelf, flush with the shelf edge. Drill a 7/64-inch hole through the first stop bar into the shelf, and fasten with a #6 x 1-inch flathead screw. Drill and fasten a second screw before repeating the process at each corner.

Putting It All Together
13 Using a drill bit no larger in diameter than the solid core of your screw hooks or cuphooks, drill and then screw the hooks into the bottom of the top shelf supports, about 10 inches from the ends.

14 After spreading the legs approximately as shown in the drawing, place the shelves on their supports. Hang the bottom shop lights, and tie the top one in place.

15 For waterproofing, apply paint or wood sealer.

Growing seedlings under shop lights.

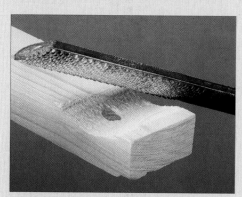

Carving Indentations Using a Wood Rasp

Sandwiching the Closet Pole

Artificial lights, used in a combination of spectrums, enable houseplants to thrive in the absence of sufficient natural light.

Fluorescent Light

Fluorescent lights are more popular for houseplants than incandescents for many reasons. First, they burn cooler and can be placed much closer to plants. Also, they give more light (lumens) per watt than incandescents. Fluorescents are available in an array of sizes and configurations, and as special grow lamps that resemble incandescent floodlights. In addition, fluorescent lights are available in various wattages, as well as in various wavelengths that allow you to use them in combination or singly to approximate sunlight.

Types of Fluorescents. For houseplants, there are three main types of fluorescents to consider:

❋ Cool-white tubes, which have enhanced blues
❋ Warm-white tubes, which have enhanced reds
❋ Special growing lamps, which emit a broad range of wavelengths, including blue, red, and far-red. (These may be advertised as wide spectrum or full-spectrum lamps and provide more red and blue than standard fluorescents do. They screw into regular sockets, but they emit unnatural-looking light.)

Combining Lights. For a pleasing look, you can combine cool-white fluorescents with warm-whites. Or you can combine cool-white fluorescents with incandescents, thereby providing a relatively full spectrum and good looks. But position the incandescents farther from the plants.

The necessary distance between fluorescent lights and plants varies with the type of plant and its stage of growth. Some plants need to be 3 inches from the lights; others, 12 to 15 inches.

Give germinating seeds and cuttings 10 lamp watts per square foot of growing area. Most foliage plants need 15 watts per square foot. High-energy flowering plants need 20 watts per square foot. If you supplement fluorescents with incandescents to get the vital far-red wavelengths, use a 4:1 ratio. Thus, if you are providing 200 watts of fluorescent light, add 50 watts of incandescent light. Temper these guidelines with common sense. Move plants farther from the lights if the leaves look burned or if colors fade. Move plants closer if growth is spindly.

Note: Because fluorescent lamps gradually lose their effectiveness over time, it's wise to replace them annually even if they look okay.

Metal-Halide & Mercury-Vapor Lights

These high-intensity, expensive lamps provide relatively full-spectrum light but tend to be used more by professional growers. Be sure to follow the manufacturer's suggestions for their placement.

🌿 SMART TIP 🌿

Lighting Rule of Thumb

If your room lacks sufficient natural light, keep artificial lights on for 12 to 14 hours a day for foliage plants and 16 to 18 hours for flowering plants. Automatic timers are handy for ensuring that plants are getting enough light and for the right amount of time.

This full-spectrum mercury-vapor floodlight *delivers a balance of the blue-red and far-red wavelengths.*

Soil

Unlike most garden plants, houseplants are in containers and cannot send their roots far down through the soil to seek water and nutrients. So it is up to you to supply the right balance of nutrients and moisture by providing the plants with good-quality potting soil. Make sure the bag contains only soil.

Bags labeled as potting or planting mixes are often peat based and may contain little soil. While soilless mixes can work well, they contain no nutrients, so plants growing in them need to be fertilized more frequently. Standard all-purpose houseplant soil works fine for most plants. You don't need to buy plant-specific soils.

You can purchase potting soils in 2-, 5-, 10-, and 20-quart (dry) bags. A 2-quart bag of soil is sufficient for three or four plants in 6-inch pots. A 5- or 10-quart bag will provide enough soil for at least a dozen 6-inch containers. For pots 10 inches in diameter, start with 20-quart bags.

At the nursery, test the packaged soil by squeezing the bag. It should feel soft, pliable, and slightly moist. Avoid dry, caked, or sandy soil. Look for soil that is a rich black

The ceiling incandescent lamp is an attractive means of displaying and providing growing light for this lush fern.

ABOVE *Before potting,* cover the bottom of a clean container with pot shards and horticultural charcoal. The shards improve drainage, and the charcoal helps drainage and sweetens the soil.

LEFT *Most repotting jobs* can be done with two trowels—one wide, one narrow. The wide blade is useful for scooping large amounts of soil into pots. The narrow blade works better for backfilling and working with smaller plants.

POTTING MEDIA

Fir Bark

Pebbles

Sand

Charcoal

Perlite

Pot Shards

Peat Moss

Humus

Soil

REPOTTING

First choose a container. If the plant needs a larger pot, find one that is two inches deeper and wider than the original. Disinfect any containers that were previously used by soaking them in a solution that is one part chlorine bleach and nine parts water. Rinse with clear water. Put a piece of mesh screen over the drainage hole so the soil doesn't wash out. Cover the screen with a layer of pot shards and then a layer of horticultural charcoal.

Note: If you are repotting a large plant or indoor tree, ask someone to help you by supporting the plant while you adjust the soil level. Two pairs of hands make it easier to properly center a large plant.

Crown

1 After removing the plant by tapping the bottom of the pot on a hard surface, grasp the plant by its crown, and gently tease it out of the pot. If the plant won't budge, slide a butter knife between the rootball and the pot, and slice around the inside of the pot.

2 Use your fingers to crumble away the old soil, and remove dead, brown roots. If the roots have taken on the shape of the container, use a fork to pull them straight or a knife to slice through them. Make three or four vertical cuts from the crown to the base.

3 Holding the plant in one hand and a trowel in the other, scoop fresh, moistened soil into the bottom of the pot. Position the plant on top of the soil. Then adjust the soil level until the crown of the plant is just above the edge of the pot.

4 Center the plant in the pot. Add soil to fill the space between the roots and the pot and to cover the roots. Press soil firmly with your thumbs to eliminate air pockets. Keep the soil level 1/2 inch below the pot rim to prevent overflow when watering.

5 Water the plant thoroughly in its new pot. After a few minutes, water it again. Wait 10 minutes, then discard any water sitting in the saucer. You may want to cover the plant with a plastic bag to retain moisture and lessen the chances of transplant shock.

color. Reject soil that looks old or gray; it's probably low in nutrients. Also, buy a small bag of compost (humus).

Soil Recipes

To make a good, all-purpose potting medium for most plants, thoroughly mix the contents of a 5-quart bag of potting soil with 2 cups of compost in a bucket.

Cacti, Succulents, and Flowering Plants. Substitute 1 cup of sharp sand for the compost. Avoid fine powdery sand, salty seashore sand, and sand with debris. For flowering plants, add 2 tablespoons of bonemeal to the basic recipe.

Gesneriads. Blend equal parts potting soil and fine-grade fir bark. Some growers prefer to raise gesneriads in a soilless mix of peat moss, perlite, and vermiculite, but you may find that the blend of soil and fir bark works better.

Orchids and Bromeliads. Grow orchids and bromeliads in fir bark, not packaged soil or a homemade mix. Of the three grades, or sizes, of bark—fine, medium, and large—medium is best. It is easy to work with, and orchids thrive in it.

Note: Soil keeps well; just store what's left over in a tightly covered container or closed plastic bag. Place the bag in a cool location.

Potting

Many plants are sold in a mix that is mostly filler and contains little soil. If you purchase one of these, you can wait two or three weeks, if need be, before you repot the plant into good soil, but do plan to repot it eventually. Soil fillers may be sand, wood shavings, or crushed gravel, all of which furnish few if any nutrients to plants. A container that feels light, even when the potting mix is moist, probably contains mostly filler. Before you buy, ask a staffperson what kind of potting mix was used. If the plant is potted in mostly filler, gently remove as much of the original potting mix as you can. Replace it with the appropriate soil mix described under "Soil Recipes," above.

Drainage. Be sure that any container into which you are potting has drainage holes to prevent water from standing in the container. Standing water can cause stagnant and waterlogged soil. Soggy soil may eventually lead to root rot.

Plants should be repotted into larger containers as they grow. Here, copper pans disguise plain pots with drainage holes. Although these plants are all about the same size, you could display a small plant on the top step in the smallest pan, a full-grown plant on the bottom in the largest container, with the other transplant sizes in between.

Basic houseplant-care equipment includes (clockwise from left) a mister, a watering can, some twine (for staking), a sieve (for soil), and stakes and dowels (for support and to poke pilot holes for fertilizer).

RIGHT *Never leave plants* in standing water. If the roots stay wet, they won't get enough air. Root rot and plant death will result.

BELOW RIGHT *A moisture meter* can help you determine if it's time to water. Or you can simply push your finger slightly into the soil. If the soil doesn't give, that means it's dry and in need of water.

Sprinkle some horticultural charcoal chips in the bottom of the container to keep the soil fresh and help drainage. In small containers—6 to 10 inches in diameter—use 1 tablespoon of charcoal chips; in large containers, use 2 tablespoons. Horticultural charcoal chips are sold in boxes or bags at garden centers and nurseries. *Warning:* Do not use barbecue briquettes.

Repotting

Even established plants need to be repotted periodically because their roots can outgrow the containers and the soil may accumulate toxic salts from fertilizers. Established plants in containers up to 10 inches in diameter should be repotted annually. Plants in larger containers should be repotted every two years.

Plant Removal. It is easier to repot a plant when the soil is slightly dry rather than wet. Wet pots are heavy and messy to handle. As shown on page 70, begin by tapping the side of the container several times against the edge of a countertop or table. Tap firmly, but not so hard that you crack the container. That should loosen the ball of soil enough so you can remove the plant without

harming the roots. Crumble away some but not all of the old soil, and trim off any dead roots.

Container Preparation. The new container should be clean. Soak a terra-cotta pot in water for a few hours before potting so that the clay will not absorb water from the soil. Disinfect reused containers by soaking them in a solution of one part chlorine bleach to nine parts water. Rinse well with clear water. Center the plant in the soil; then fill in and around the plant with soil.

Finishing Up. Firm the soil in place with your thumbs. This pressure should help to eliminate any air pockets in the soil. Roots need the air in the tiny spaces between soil particles, which are not removed when you firm the potting mix.

After you have firmed the soil, add more soil until its surface is a ½ inch from the pot rim. This reduces the probability of overflows when you water. Now tap the bottom of the container on a countertop or table again to settle the soil; firm the soil one more time; and then water the plant thoroughly. After a few minutes, water the plant again, and discard any water standing in the saucer after another 5 or 10 minutes. Label the container with a tag that states the name of the plant and the date of repotting.

Care After Repotting

Repotting is a shock for plants, and newly repotted plants need a period of recuperation. Do not expose them to sun immediately because the roots are not yet up to their full strength and cannot absorb moisture readily. That's why it's important to water plants thoroughly after repotting them. A bright location that does not receive direct sun is fine. Then water plants as needed to keep the soil evenly moist but not soggy, and watch the plants for about a week to see how they are doing. If you notice that the leaves are limp (indicating insufficient water) or brown and soft at the edges (indicating too much water) adjust watering accordingly. (See "Poor Care: Symptoms and Causes," page 102.)

Some plants have a bit of trouble recovering from repotting. Good humidity usually eases the recovery process. You can help retain humidity by covering each plant with a plastic bag. Remove the bag periodically and whenever condensation appears on the inside. You can consider the plants ready to be moved back to their regular locations when they begin to show some new growth.

Water

Although watering is easy in itself, watering at the proper times and in the correct amounts seems to be the greatest challenge. In fact, overwatering and underwatering are the chief causes of houseplant death. Yet if you follow the guidelines below, you'll do fine.

You can water at any hour in the daytime, but avoid watering at night, which can cause fungus. Treated water out of the tap is fine for houseplants—chlorine, fluoride, and all.

What is most important is the water temperature. Cold water can shock tropical houseplants, making water absorption impossible for their roots. So always use tepid, room-temperature water.

Water plants thoroughly, because an insufficient amount of water will create dry pockets in the soil; when roots reach a dry spot, they stop growing. To be sure the soil is completely saturated, water your plant, and then rewater with the excess water that drains into the saucer. Throw out the excess that drains the second time. If standing water remains in the saucer, it will keep the soil in the pot too

PLANTS THAT DISLIKE DRY CONDITIONS

The plants listed here prefer relative humidity of about 50 percent. If your growing area is especially dry, mist these plants occasionally, or place them on pebble trays to add some humidity in their vicinity.

Lacy maidenhair fern (*Adiantum tenerum*)
Lipstick plant (*Aeschynanthus speciosus*)
Anthurium species
Yellow plume plant, zebra plant (*Aphelandra squarrosa*)
Bird's nest fern (*Asplenium nidus*)
Rex begonia (*Begonia* Rex-Cultorum hybrids)
Earth star (*Cryptanthus* 'Tricolor')
Sago palm (*Cycas revoluta*)
Florist's cyclamen (*Cyclamen persicum*)
Holly fern (*Cyrtomium falcatum*)
Dendrobium species
Flame violet (*Episcia cupreata*)
Cape jasmine (*Gardenia augusta, G. jasminoides*)
Flame-of-the-woods (*Ixora coccinea*)
Goldfish plant (*Nematanthus* species)
Boston fern (*Nephrolepis exaltata* 'Bostoniensis')
Dancing lady orchid (*Oncidium* species)
Moth orchid (*Phalaenopsis* hybrids)
Philodendron species
Cabbage head fern, polypody (*Polypodium vulgare*)
Ming aralia (*Polyscias fruticosa*)
Balfour aralia (*Polyscias scutellaria* 'Balfourii')
Brake fern (*Pteris tremula*)
Moses-in-a-boat (*Rhoeo spathacea*)
Leather fern (*Rumohra adiantiformis*)
African violet (*Saintpaulia* hybrids)

Gloxinia (*Sinningia speciosa* hybrids)
Peace lily (*Spathiphyllum* species)
Cape primrose (*Streptocarpus* hybrids)
Tillandsia species

Leaf edges of this plant have turned brown and crisp in response to insufficient humidity in the room. Plants listed in this box require higher humidity levels than would be comfortable in most homes.

soggy, a condition that can cause root rot and plant death.

Keep the soil evenly moist for most houseplants. (Many cacti and succulents are exceptions, although they do need moisture.) Because large containers hold water for longer periods, you need to water plants in large containers less often. Water evaporates from terra-cotta containers faster than from glazed or plastic pots, so water plants in terra-cotta more often. If the soil gives under the pressure of your finger, do not water. You can use a moisture meter, as shown on page 72, but using your finger can be just as reliable.

Overhead Watering

Use a metal or plastic watering can with a long spout that allows you to reach through foliage to the soil. The spout should have a rose (resembling a showerhead) that releases a gentle spray of water rather than a concentrated flow. Another good way to water plants is to set the pots in a sink or tub and turn on a gentle shower of tepid water. Water slowly, gently, and deeply.

Overhead watering is good because the water falls on foliage as well as the soil, and most plants like water on their leaves. However, avoid getting water on the foliage of African violets, cyclamens, gloxinias, and other plants with soft, hairy leaves. Water those plants from the bottom.

Watering from the Bottom

Place your pot into a dish pan, bowl, or sink of tepid water that reaches to just below the pot's rim. Let the

Misting periodically improves humidity. To protect plants from water sitting on their leaves, hold a card over the leaves, and mist the base of the plant.

pot absorb water until the surface soil looks and feels wet. Depending on the plant size, this may take 15 minutes to an hour. Remove the pot and allow excess water to drain.

Once a month, give all of your plants a good soaking. To do this, fill a sink or a pan with water and set the containers in the water. The water should be deep enough to reach just below pot rims. If the soil is dry, air will bubble out of the soil as water displaces it. When air bubbles no longer appear on the soil surface, remove the containers, and let the excess water drain.

Heat and Humidity

Most houseplants like average home temperatures of 70° to 78° F with a drop of 10° at night. (Exceptions are noted in the plant profiles, beginning on page 108.) The daily temperature difference helps plants manufacture sugar, which fuels their growth. Some plants, such as cyclamen and amaryllis, prefer cooler conditions. If you have cold winters and drafty windows, protect window plants by placing a sheet of material, such as poster board, between them and the windowpanes.

Humidity is a measure of the moisture in the air. Most homes have a humidity level of 30 to 40 percent, which is fine for most houseplants. Some plants, such as ferns and philodendrons, prefer higher humidity. Others, such as snake plant, prefer lower humidity.

Plants release water through their leaves in a process called *transpiration*, and they give off moisture more quickly when the air is dry. If they lose water faster than they can replace it, their foliage becomes thin and depleted-looking. Also, the hotter the temperature, the faster the air dries out.

Strong growth and firm leaves are two indications that the humidity is at the right level for your plants. Spindly growth and limp leaves usually signify too little moisture in the air. Keep houseplants away from hot radiators, hot-air vents, and drafts.

Misting. On hot summer days, mist plants lightly with water between 11:00 a.m. and 1:00 p.m. In the winter, central heating can drop humidity to an arid 20 percent. So try to keep the humidity more in balance with that of the summer months by employing a room humidifier or by

USING FERTILIZER SPIKES

1 Use a dowel to poke a cylindrical hole into which a fertilizer spike can be placed.

2 Insert fertilizer spikes into dowel holes to furnish food to the plant gradually.

misting the area around the containers and soil surface between 6:00 and 8:00 p.m. every other day. *Caution:* Do not mist the leaves of soft- or hairy-leaved plants, such as African violets, begonias, cyclamens, and gloxinias. Water can permanently damage their foliage and leave unsightly spots that won't wash off.

Air Circulation

Good air circulation helps retard the proliferation of insects, such as mealybugs. In fact, you should let in fresh air from outdoors as much as possible. In the winter, when the air is drier inside than outside, ventilation helps maintain adequate humidity. Open a window slightly whenever the weather is not too frigid, or be sure there is sufficient ventilation near the plants. However, do not let cold air blow directly on your plants because cold air can damage them. When it's really cold outside and impractical to open a window, use a small fan to circulate air.

In summer, air conditioning is a boon for houseplants. Most houseplants wilt in torrid weather, but air conditioning perks them up. Be sure not to let the cold air from the air conditioner blow on the plants directly. Otherwise, plant leaves may wilt or turn yellow and then fall as a result of excessive moisture loss.

SYNTHETIC FERTILIZERS

Liquid   Granule   Spike   Powder

Fertilizer

Plants need three major nutrients for health: nitrogen (for vigorous growth and good leaf color), phosphorus (to grow strong roots and produce seeds and fruit after flowering), and potassium, or potash (to help them absorb other nutrients and resist disease). The labels on fertilizer containers indicate the percentage of each of the three major elements, in the order listed here. For example, a 10-10-5 fertilizer contains 10 percent nitrogen (N), 10 percent phosphorus (P), and 5 percent potassium (K). The rest of the material in the bag is

RIGHT *The croton has grown too wide for its container. Trim the outside growth to give the plant more room.*

FAR RIGHT *The groomed plant is now properly centered and has a more pleasing shape.*

Four Rules for Houseplant Feeding

❀ *Be sure the soil is moist.*
❀ *Start feeding when plants are 2 to 4 inches tall, usually about three to five weeks after seeds germinate. Because their new roots are too young to absorb nutrients, never feed seedlings.*
❀ *Feed only healthy plants. Sick plants can't absorb nutrients.*
❀ *Do not overfertilize. Forcing a plant into growth by excessive feeding will weaken or kill it.*

inert fillers, included to make it easier to give plants the right amount of fertilizer and to apply it evenly. A 10-10-10 or 20-10-10 formula is best for most houseplants, but follow guidance for specific plants given in the plant profiles.

Natural Fertilizers

Natural, or organic, plant foods are excellent sources of nitrogen, and are better than synthetic fertilizers because

TRIMMING STRAY BRANCHES

1 Trim away errant branches to keep your plant healthy and attractive. Prune straggly branches that detract from the plant's form. To avoid tearing tissue, always cut at an angle.

2 Cover open wounds at the base of the plant with horticultural charcoal. This speeds healing by sealing cell walls and keeping disease-carrying fungus and bacteria out.

Pruning shears and scissors keep your houseplants neatly groomed. You can trim most of your plants using the scissors, but you'll need the pruners to cut through woody stems, such as those of the jade plant.

they add organic matter to the soil and their nutrients are released gradually. Cottonseed meal, fish emulsion, bloodmeal, and composted steer and cow manure are all organic nitrogen fertilizers available at nurseries and garden centers. Fish emulsion is sold in bottles and the other fertilizer types are sold in bags.

There are other organic materials that supply phosphorus and potassium, as well as organic blends that contain sources of all three nutrients. With the exception of fish emulsion, organic fertilizers do not smell bad; they have a clean, earthy smell. However, organic fertilizers take more time to release their nutrients than synthetics do.

Again, there's no need to use plant foods formulated for specific plants.

Synthetic Fertilizers

Synthetic plant foods come in the form of granules, tablets, liquids, and spikes. All are dissolved in water. Spikes are the most convenient to use. Granules are also easy because you simply sprinkle them on top of the soil and then water them in. Liquids are convenient because they allow you to feed and water at the same time, while powders can be messy. Tablets frequently do not disintegrate or spread well, and timed-release fertilizers may release too much fertilizer.

Trimming & Grooming

Most houseplants need trimming, grooming, and some training. (Exceptions include cacti and most succulents, orchids, and bromeliads.) Trimming involves removal of old branches to encourage fresh growth and improve overall health and vigor. Trimming also involves

Remove dead flower heads as soon as you notice them. Deadheading allows the plant to devote its energy to growing and staying healthy rather than producing seeds.

A spent flower has been cut from this tricolor bromeliad, leaving the red bract from which the flower stalk grew. Many bromeliads flower once, then die. Look for "pups," or offsets, from which to propagate new plants.

removal of decayed areas, which can attract fungus. Grooming involves picking off dead leaves and flowers and keeping the soil surface free of debris.

Trimming

Winter trimming could stimulate growth in dormant plants before their normal growth season. Therefore, spring is the best time to trim plants. Follow the plant's natural growth habit. For example, some plants grow in a rosette—a cluster of leaves arising from a central point. Others have a bushy, branching habit, and still others are vertical growers. Observe your plants from a distance to determine their natural growth habit.

When trimming to improve shape, remove damaged, diseased, and misshapen growth. Cut back long stems growing at odd angles using pruning scissors or shears. Use stronger pruning shears or a sharp knife to cut woody branches. After cutting, sterilize the scissors or knife to kill any disease organisms by running a flame under the blades or cleaning them with alcohol.

Cover open wounds with charcoal from a burned match to seal any open cells and keep out fungus. After you trim

All plants rest. *Orchids, like many flowering plants, need time to rest between blooming periods. The orchid at left is resting, indicated by its slowed or stopped growth. Resting plants usually need less water. The orchid at right is actively growing and has sent out a bud.*

plants in the spring, let them rest. Keep the soil barely moist for a few weeks; then resume watering as usual.

Grooming

Groom plants about three times a year. Get rid of any yellowed leaves and decayed flowers because they invite insects and disease.

Grooming also involves cleaning the outside of the container of any scum, algae, or other dirt with hot water and a sponge. Dirt can harbor bacteria that harms plants. Using a stiff brush, scrub off encrusted fertilizer salts.

Gently wipe the foliage of all plants, except those with fuzzy or hairy leaves, with tepid water once a month to remove insect eggs and mites.

Resting

Like people, plants need to rest to restore their energy. Most plants rest at some time of the year. While resting, plants grow much more slowly than usual or not at all, and flowering plants stop setting buds.

Plants from different climates rest during different seasons. Plants from the Northern Hemisphere tend to rest when it's winter in that part of the world. Plants from the Southern Hemisphere, such as African violets, are more likely to rest in spring or summer north of the equator, because that's winter in their homeland. Also, for wild plants in warm climates, dormancy comes during the dry season, and growth resumes with the return of rain. Even though your houseplants may be far removed from their native habitats, their cycles of growth remain the same.

Most plants need less moisture or none at all when they are resting. The rest period is usually short, approximately three to five weeks. Many plants take a little rest after they flower. However, some plants will produce heavy foliage growth after blooming.

Your plants will indicate when they want a rest by their declining vigor. They will stop growing, and they may look a little faded or just tired. When you see the signs, gradually reduce watering, and stop feeding the plants. If you are unsure whether a plant is ready to rest

and may need daily watering. Fertilize plants that are actively growing now. Protect plants from hot sun by means of a sheer curtain or window screen. Provide good humidity and ventilation—houseplants do not thrive in a stuffy atmosphere.

When temperatures exceed 85°F, mist plants several times a day to reduce heat at their surfaces. Inspect for insects at this time of year as well. (See Chapter 7, for information on coping with insects and disease.)

Fall. In the fall, when days can fluctuate between warm and cool, water attentively, giving each plant the amount it needs. Plants such as gingers and some orchids are now in a semidormant state, so stop feeding them. *Remember:* Never try to force resting plants to sprout new growth. At this time, let the soil become somewhat dry but not caked between waterings.

Taking Plants Outdoors in Summer

Many houseplants enjoy and really benefit from a summer vacation outdoors. In early summer, when the nighttime temperatures no longer drop below 60°F, you can safely move tropical houseplants outdoors.

Before you move plants outside, prune those that need it. Set pots on a shady porch or patio, or in shady parts of the garden. To reduce watering frequency, you can sink the pots into the ground or even transplant them in the garden. Shade and even moisture are important because houseplants will not be able to tolerate direct summer sun.

LEFT *Protect plants from the full strength of the sun when you first move them outside. Even geraniums, which thrive in the sun, need to be gradually acclimated. Start with plants in the shade. Then in a few days move them into diffuse light and finally into full sun.*

or having a problem, consult its profile to see whether the plant is likely to rest at this time of year.

Seasonal & Vacation Care

The seasons influence when plants grow as well as when they rest. Most houseplants do the majority of their growing in spring and summer, so this is the time when they need the most water. Repotting of old plants is generally best done in February and March, just when they're coming out of dormancy. This way the plants have moderate weather to resume active growth. To help ready your plants for the upcoming warmer months, repot them in fresh soil; supply adequate humidity; and water regularly to keep the soil evenly moist. (See "Potting," page 71, for more information.)

Summer. During the summer months, when most plants are growing actively, give them the moisture they need. (See Plant Profiles, beginning on page 108, for information on specific plants.) Certain plants, such as columneas and some begonias, need plenty of moisture at their roots

Whiteflies *have gathered on the underside of a geranium leaf. See Chapter 7, for remedies.*

If slugs and other soil-dwelling pests are problems, slip a piece of old pantyhose over the bottom of each pot to keep critters from crawling in through the drainage holes. Water and fertilize your houseplants—indoors and outdoors—as recommended in the plant profiles. Most plants are growing actively at this time of year.

Bringing Plants Indoors

In late summer, as days begin to grow shorter, begin preparing your houseplants for the move inside. Pinch back plants that have grown leggy. Repot plants that have outgrown their containers, giving them a larger pot and fresh soil mix. As summer draws to a close, before the weather turns cool—and certainly before there's even a remote possibility of frost—bring your houseplants indoors. Don't forget to bring in clay pots, which crack in freezing temperatures.

Northern gardeners should begin this process around Labor Day, while in the South and along the West Coast, the plants can stay outdoors until later in fall. To avoid shocking the plants, move them when the temperature outdoors is close to the temperature indoors.

Pests. Examine the plants carefully for signs of insects and disease. Especially check tender new shoots, the leaf axils (where leaves join stems), and undersides of leaves—all places where pests like to congregate.

In addition to inspecting for the pests themselves, look for evidence of their presence, such as sticky honeydew on leaves, fine webbing in leaf axils, and on shoot tips, black sooty mold, and stippling or chewed edges of the leaves and flowers. If you do see evidence of pests, take appropriate action, as recommended in Chapter 7, before bringing the plants back indoors.

To check for soil-dwelling pests, sink each pot in a bucket of water nearly up to the rim, and let it soak for 15 minutes. Saturating the soil should drive any pests to the surface. Remove the pests, and let the pots drain.

Just to be safe, for a week or two after bringing the plants back indoors, keep them in a separate room from any plants that remained indoors. Check frequently for signs of infestation before placing them with other plants. You don't want problems to spread to the rest of your houseplants.

A pebble tray provides a good means of raising the humidity around plants. Rather than water each plant individually, you can simply water the pebble tray, from which the plants' roots absorb water as they need it. Be careful to keep the water level below the top of the pebbles, so the pots don't sit in water.

Gravity-powered slow waterers will take care of larger plants while you are away. Simply fill the container with water, and insert the perforated long spike into the soil. The water will gradually trickle into the soil, providing steady moisture. This device works best with moisture-loving plants.

Place a plant on bricks in a tub of water before you go on vacation. Wrap damp paper towels or peat moss around the pot to slow the evaporation from the soil to the porous pot. This contraption keeps plants moist for five to seven days.

This slow-watering plant container has a reservoir from which water is slowly drawn upward to the roots. Filling the reservoir is as easy as watering a plant.

Your Vacation

Your weekends away do not need to be a problem for your plants. To prepare your plants, thoroughly water medium-size and large containers in the morning, right before you leave. Then mist the leaves. Under these conditions, plants should stay moist for up to five days.

Up to a Week. The soil in smaller containers dries out quickly, so group small pots in a watertight metal bin or plastic tray 5 to 6 inches deep with a 2- to 3-inch-deep layer of pebbles in the bottom. Pour water into the bin or tray until it just reaches the top of the pebbles, and then set the containers on top. Wrap and pack peat moss, paper towels, or newspaper around the outside of the pots, to within 2 inches of the rims. Dampen the wrapping, which will continue to absorb moisture from below and help slow the evaporation of moisture from the soil in the pots. This also helps maintain desired humidity levels above the soil, keeping small plants moist for five to seven days.

A bathtub or shower stall is a good place for small and medium-size containers while you're away. Set the containers on bricks placed in 2 to 4 inches of water so that the water level just reaches the top of the bricks.

A capillary mat provides a simple means of keeping plants watered for a few days. Capillary attraction in the soil and roots draws water upward as needed, defying gravity in a phenomenon known as capillary action.

CHAPTER SIX

Propagating Houseplants

Purchasing houseplants is just one way to acquire them. Once you have a few plants in your home and have learned how to deal with their idiosyncrasies, you will undoubtedly want to have more.

An inexpensive way to grace your home with plants is to grow them from seeds or propagate them from your existing plants. The table on page 98, "Propagation Methods & Hints," lists methods of propagation that are most effective for specific plants. The table also includes cultivation tips to help you successfully raise your plants. Propagating your own plants is fun—it gives you a wonderful sense of creation while saving you money, and it is fairly easy to do.

LEFT *Propagating plants* from stolons, or runners, as shown trailing from this spider plant, is one of many easy options for increasing your plant collection.

ABOVE *Square peat pots* separate easily.

Peat pots, available round or square, can be filled with sterile medium. They are equally suited to starting seeds and rooting cuttings, as shown here. Seed pellets, which look like biscuits in a tray, are used to start seeds.

Propagating with Seed

Starting houseplants from seed takes time and patience, but it's worth it. There is a sense of accomplishment in growing your own plants from scratch.

Containers

Seed can be sown in all sorts of containers, ranging from special terra-cotta pots, peat pots, and seed pellets to recyclables, including egg cartons, plastic storage boxes, and aluminum trays from frozen foods. Any container you use for growing seed should be 4 to 5 inches deep, with drainage holes in the bottom; you can use an ice pick to poke out drainage holes.

Terra-Cotta Pots. Terra-cotta, or clay, pots are attractive, inexpensive, and easy to use.

Peat Pots. To use peat pots, which are made of compressed peat, soak the pots in water, fill them with soil, and insert a few seeds. When leaves appear, transplant the pots into larger containers, making sure the rims of the peat pots are completely buried. It's a good idea to tear their sides when transplanting to ensure that roots can grow. Transplanting with peat pots reduces shock by minimizing damage to tender new roots.

Seed Pellets. Seed pellets, or disks, are even easier to use: simply add water and insert the seed. The pellet expands and becomes the container. When leaves appear, transplant the plant along with the expanded pellet into a larger container with soil. Again, tear or cut the sides of the pellet to ensure that the roots can easily reach surrounding soil.

Recycled Containers. If you use a recycled container to start seeds, be sure to disinfect and rinse it thoroughly—containers for seed starting need to be clean. Recycled containers are less convenient than peat pots or pellets, but they're free.

Covered Units. You can purchase special seed-starting and propagation units that come with their own covers. Some of them also supply bottom heat. They are available by mail order.

SEED PELLETS

TOP *Seed pellets expand when watered. Then the pellets become containers.* **BOTTOM** *Use a pair of tweezers or a folded piece of paper to place the seeds in the pellet.*

Perlite

Soil

Sand

Horticultural Charcoal

Humus

FAR LEFT *Square peat pots* make starting plants easy.

LEFT *A satisfactory houseplant medium* contains the following ingredients: soil, humus, horticultural charcoal, sand, and perlite.

BELOW *The seed* has germinated and the seed leaves (cotyledons) are up.

BOTTOM *True leaves* have appeared.

Growing Medium

Use a sterile medium, such as disinfected soil, vermiculite, perlite, sand, sphagnum moss, or a combination that drains well and retains moisture. Or use a commercial seed-starting mix. Garden soil and old potting soil may contain disease organisms and a fungus that causes "damping-off," which kills seedlings. Fill the containers with the soil mix you wish to use, to about ½ inch from the top. Then spray the medium gently with water until it is moist, but not soggy, all the way through. If the seeds are large, ⅟₁₆ to ¼ inch, press them about ¼ inch into the medium. If the seeds are too small for you to handle individually, sprinkle them on top of the medium, and then scatter a thin layer of sterile soil over them. Spray the medium again, very gently, to moisten the top layer of soil, and place the container in a shady spot where the temperature is a warm 72° to 78°F.

Humidity

To increase humidity, make a little greenhouse over the container. To do this, prop a layer of plastic wrap or a plastic bag over a framework of four sticks inserted into each corner of the soil. The greenhouse effect will retain enough humidity to keep the growing medium moist, which is essential. Check the medium every day to be sure the seed is

not receiving too much moisture. If that is the case, the inside of the plastic will be wet. If so, remove the plastic for a few hours each day so that air can circulate around the seedlings. If the medium feels dry, mist it with water.

Temperature

The correct temperature is crucial for germination. Low-voltage heating cables laid in the soil are excellent because they maintain a constant gentle temperature of 70° to 78°F. Heating cables are available at many nurseries and garden centers.

Or if you have an older refrigerator, place the seed tray on top; the warm air from the coils behind the unit will rise to the top, providing bottom heat. Never place containers on top of a radiator because the heat cycles from too high to too low.

Germination

Depending on the plant, seed takes several days to several months to germinate. When the first tiny green shoots appear, supply more air by removing the plastic tent for most of the day. The first pair of seed leaves,

or cotyledons, are generally round or oval. True leaves are usually the second set of leaves a seedling develops and have the mature plant's characteristic leaf shape. Discard the tent when true leaves sprout. Give the seedlings more light, and be sure that through the entire germination period the growing medium remains uniformly moist but not wet.

Transplanting & Repotting

When seedlings display their true leaves, remove weaker plants using a pair of tweezers, or nudge them out of the medium using a pencil to give the sturdier seedlings more room to grow. Work carefully to avoid injuring the delicate roots of nearby seedlings.

Transplanting. When the plants are large enough to be handled, remove them from their starter container, and plant each one in a separate, 2-inch pot in a sterile, packaged houseplant soil. Handle them by the seed leaves, not by the true leaves, stems, or roots. Young seedlings are delicate, and it's easy to damage the stems or true leaves, which could interfere with future growth. Think of the cotyledons as baby teeth. They are temporary and will soon be replaced by the true leaves.

As you transplant the seedlings, be careful not to disturb the rootball. Be sure to plant them in room-

GERMINATING SEEDS

1 Fill a clean plastic tray with sterile medium. Use a piece of wood to make rows.

2 Sow seed according to directions on the seed packet, using a folded sheet of paper.

3 Cover seed lightly with soil, using a trowel. This step is optional.

4 Trickle water slowly over the seedbed until the medium is evenly moist.

5 Cover with plastic to retain humidity. Remove once a day to allow some air in.

6 When seedlings have two to four leaves, move to a 2-inch pot.

Transplanting *can occur when seedlings are sturdy enough to handle. This basil seedling has two distinct types of leaves: its first leaves, or cotyledons, and the second set of leaves, or true leaves. The seed leaves are round and the true leaves are long and oval, resembling the leaves of the mature plant. Use a pencil to gently nudge the seedling out of the pot. Always handle seedlings by their cotyledons, never by the true leaves or stem, which can easily be torn.*

temperature soil and to water them with warm water. Cold water can shock the plant; hot water will scald it.

Next, put the newly planted pots in a terrarium or other moisture-retaining enclosure for several days to allow the plants to recover from transplant shock. Do not let the soil become overly moist or overly dry. Check the moisture level by poking your finger into the soil. When the soil doesn't give and feels dry below the surface, it's time to water. Keep the soil evenly moist.

Repotting. When the seedlings are a few inches tall, repot them again. The ideal container diameter for most young houseplants is 3 to 4 inches. Later, when the plant outgrows this container, you can repot it in a larger pot. For this more permanent potting, use a packaged soil mixed with humus or sand, as described under "Potting" on page 71.

Vegetative Propagation

There are other ways to start plants besides planting seed. Vegetative methods of propagation produce new plants from plant parts. These new plants are genetically identical to the parent.

Vegetative propagation is the only way to reproduce hybrids, which do not "come true"—meaning they cannot be exactly duplicated—from seed. For the most part, vegetative propagation is easier and faster than starting plants from seed.

Planting Offsets and Runners

Among the simplest ways of producing new plants is to divide offsets and runners from the parent plant. Many plants produce offsets, which are small duplicate plants that grow from buds at the crown of the parent plant. Other plants produce aboveground runners, called stolons, from which tiny plants emerge.

Plants such as agaves and bromeliads and some gesneriads bear offsets at the plant base. When these offsets are 2 to 4 inches tall, cut them off, and root them in soil.

Plants, such as spider plants and flame violets, bear runners. To produce new plants from either of these, cut the connecting stem, as shown below, and insert the new plant in soil where it will root and grow. Another method is to plant the baby plants in pots of soil and let them form roots before you sever them from the parent plant.

Repot plants *when they outgrow their containers. Transplant seedlings into 2-in. pots, then into 3- or 4-in. pots, and later into larger pots. The plant shown here at different stages is schefflera, not basil.*

You can propagate runners *by placing the young plant in a prepared pot of soil in a semi-layering method. Leave the runner attached to the mother plant for a few weeks; then cut it from the parent.*

PROPAGATING BY DIVISION

Division is a method of separating a plant that forms a clump of stems into two or more smaller plants. This is a good technique to use when you don't want to put a plant in a bigger pot. (See pages 98–99 for suitable plants.)

The first step in dividing a plant is to remove it from its pot. See "Repotting," page 70, for information on unpotting plants. Next, shake some soil from the roots so that you can see the crown, the point at which the roots meet the stem. Look for natural divisions in the clump of stems. Pull the plant apart into sections, or use a sterile, sharp knife to cut it apart where the natural divisions occur. Sterilize your knife by passing it over a flame or dipping it in rubbing alcohol. Make sure each division has ample roots to support the top growth.

After dividing the plant, gently tease away more soil from the roots. Cut away any roots that are dead (brown at the tips) or damaged. Immediately pot each plant in fresh soil so that the roots do not dry out. It isn't necessary to dip roots into water first if you repot divisions right away.

If the plant grows from tubers, such as dahlias or tuberous begonias, or from rhizomes, such as rhizomatous begonias, divide it by cutting apart the clumps of swollen roots. To propagate orchids, divide the pseudobulbs, or thick stems that arise from the rhizome at intervals. Try to give each division at least three pseudobulbs.

Another way to propagate plants by division is to place them in a tall glass of water. Keep the glass on a bright but not sunny window ledge, and change the water weekly.

To increase the humidity, put a plastic bag loosely over the division (see page 90). When the division shows one- or two-inch long roots, remove it from the water.

Dip the newly formed roots into hormone powder. Plant the rooted division in a two- or three-inch container of sterile potting medium. Keep the soil evenly moist, and put the cutting in a warm place (between 75° to 80°F).

Dividing Most Plants

1 *Grasp an overgrown potted plant at the bottom, and locate natural divisions in the plant by viewing them from the top.*

2 *Remove the plant from the pot and then gently pry apart each division.*

3 *Fill new pots with fresh soil, and plant one division per pot.*

Dividing a Bromeliad

1 This crowded bromeliad needs to be divided. Remove part of the plant by cutting through the rootstock using a sterile knife.

2 After lining a clean pot with shards to provide adequate drainage, fill the pot with fir bark or a soil-and-bark mixture.

3 Firm the potting medium by gently pressing down the soil with your fingertips and adding more if necessary. Don't over pack the soil.

Dividing an Orchid

1 To divide an established orchid, grasp part of the plant and cut using a sterile knife, leaving at least three pseudobulbs per division.

2 Fill the new pot with fir bark or soil-and-bark mix.

Dividing an African Violet

1 To divide an African violet, grasp the plant with two hands. Then gently pull the root mass apart.

2 Transplant each division into a new pot filled with soil.

Propagating with Cuttings

Taking Tip cuttings

Stem, or "tip," cuttings and leaf cuttings produce new plants exactly like the parent. To take a tip cutting, remove a stem 3 or 4 inches from the tip.

Then cut below a leaf node, and remove bottom leaves. For most plants, spring is the best time for this. (See pages 98–99 for suitable plants.)

Plants with little top growth and woodier stems, such as this plant (*Cordyline terminalis*), can be reproduced by rooting sections of stems in a warm, moist soil mix.

To root stems, fill a container with 3 or 5 inches of medium. Dip the cut end of the stem in rooting hormone powder, and insert the cutting about 2 inches into the medium. Cover the container with a clear plastic tent to provide the high humidity that cuttings need to form roots.

Taking Tip Cuttings

1 *Select a healthy overgrown plant. Pinch stems to remove cuttings, or use a sterile knife.*

2 *On a wooden board, prepare the tip cuttings for potting.*

3 *Dip ends of cuttings in commercial rooting hormone powder.*

4 *Place each cutting in a separate pot. Insert wooden sticks, and place a plastic bag loosely over the cuttings. Keep the plastic loose so air circulates within the plastic tent. Remove the tent whenever condensation develops. Keep the soil moist. Roots will grow, and the plants will be ready for potting in larger containers in two to three weeks.*

Keep the growing medium evenly moist, and set the container in a warm, 75°F, low-lit location. Tug gently on the cutting every few days to see if it has roots. When the plant resists your gentle tug, roots have formed. Transplant the rooted cutting into a 3-inch container of sterile growing medium, as described on page 86.

Taking a Sansevieria Leaf Cutting

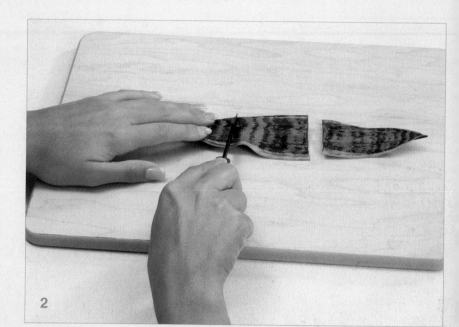

1 *To propagate a sansevieria from leaves, use a sharp sterile knife to remove a leaf at its base.*

2 *On a wooden board, cut the leaf into 2-in. sections.*

3 *Fill a pot with soil, and insert the sections about halfway down into the soil. Note: insert the tip section cut side down. Then water and keep the soil moist.*

PROPAGATING WITH CUTTINGS, CONT'D

Leaf Cuttings

Like tip cuttings, leaves and pieces of leaves can be cut and inserted into pots of soil to root and produce new plants. The new plants grow from the leaf blade itself. (See pages 98–99 for suitable plants.)

First, remove a healthy leaf still attached to a portion of stem. Then you can either cut the leaf into pieces or use the whole leaf. Cover the leaf with a clear translucent cover. If you don't have a commercial cover, you can use a plastic bag or an inverted glass jar. Place the covered container in a warm, low-lit spot for a few weeks.

As shown on the next page, you can place certain leaf cuttings horizontally on vermiculite. Rex begonias, kalanchoes, and African violets can all be propagated this way. After cutting across the leaf veins in several places on the underside of the leaves, lay the leaves—right side up—flat on the vermiculite. Rooting plantlets will soon appear along the cuts and will at first obtain their nourishment from the mother leaf. When you can handle the new plants easily, cut them from the parent leaf, and pot each one separately in soil.

Taking Leaf-Section Cuttings

1 You can make new plants from pieces of leaves. After removing a leaf from an established plant, place it on a wood board, and cut the leaf into triangular pieces. Multiple cuttings can be taken from one leaf as long as each has veins.

2 Insert the pointed ends of the cuttings halfway into a sterile medium in a tray. Lightly water the cuttings, and place a plastic cover over them. In a few weeks, after the leaves emerge, put the new plants into individual pots.

Taking Whole-Leaf Cuttings

1 Select a healthy leaf and cut it from the base of the plant using a sterile knife. Be sure to keep the stem attached.

2 Place the leaf upside down. After removing the stem, use a sharp knife to cut across the veins on the underside of the leaf.

3 Place the leaves upside down in the potting tray, and pin each leaf to the medium using a hair pin.

4 Gently water the medium, but avoid wetting the leaves. Cover them with a dome to retain adequate humidity.

5 In a few weeks, when baby leaves emerge, remove the dome. Place the tray in a warm spot, and keep the medium moist.

6 Transfer young plants to pots filled with fresh soil. Young plants generally like snug quarters.

PROPAGATING BY AIR LAYERING

Plants with woody stems that tend to grow lanky and lose their lower leaves with age, such as rubber trees and dieffenbachias, are best propagated by air layering. With this method, you need to wait six to nine months for new roots to form.

Don't throw away the old plant. Cut the stem back just above a bud. Place the plant in a warm spot, and keep the soil moist. In a few weeks several new shoots will emerge. Good candidates for air layering include dieffenbachias, dracaenas, ficus, and swiss cheese plant.

1 Remove the lower leaves on the main stem. Using a sharp knife, cut on a diagonal partially through the stem. Note that the cut is made directly below a leaf node. Place a toothpick in the cut to keep it open.

2 Place a plastic tent around the open cut, and then fill with moist sphagnum moss. Tie one end shut. Be sure the moss forms a compact mass around the cut before tying the other end of the plastic.

3 When you can see roots forming within the plastic ball, sever the stem at the base.

4 Remove the plastic, and then place the rooted air-layered stem in fresh soil in a pot. Water thoroughly.

PROPAGATING BULBS

Plants that grow from bulblike structures (including bulbs, corms and rhizomes) are easy to propagate; they already contain all necessary nutrients to produce a new plant. You just need to provide water and warmth. After the plants bloom, allow the foliage to gradually turn yellow and die by cutting back on water; this allows the bulb to gather food through its leaves to be stored for the next year's growth. Remove the leaves after they die, and place the pot in a cool (60°F), dry place and keep the soil barely moist. In the spring, repot the bulb in fresh soil.

FAR LEFT *A rhizome, or swollen root, is placed in soil and partially covered before being watered. Curcuma grows from a rhizome.*

LEFT *Place curcuma in bright light, and continue to water. A new plant will emerge after a few weeks. Bloom occurs when the plant matures after a few months.*

Planting Bulbs

1 *Plant healthy bulbs in a mix of equal parts potting soil and sterile medium, such as vermiculite.*

2 *Water moderately, and place the container in a warm area with bright light but not direct sun.*

FORCING BULBS FOR WINTER COLOR

You can add color to your indoor garden during the drab days of winter by forcing bulbs into bloom. Forcing causes bulbs to flower before they normally would outdoors.

Start the process in autumn. Buy the best-quality bulbs you can find. When you pick out bulbs, examine them thoroughly. You want bulbs that are firm and solid, with no mold, soft spots, or physical damage. Store tender bulbs in a cool location with good air circulation. Store hardy bulbs in the refrigerator. Even hardy bulbs will not survive in the freezer. Lacking the insulating protection of soil or snow that they receive when planted outside, bulbs will succumb to frostbite.

It takes 8 to 12 weeks to force bulbs into bloom, so plan ahead. Plant your bulbs in 5- to 6-inch-diameter pots filled with a well-drained, porous medium, such as a mix of equal parts potting soil, peat moss, and sharp sand. Use pots with drainage holes. A conventional 6-inch pot will accommodate three daffodils or hyacinths or five to six tulips. Smaller bulbs, such as crocuses or netted iris, can be forced in a 5-inch bulb pan (a pot that is wider than high).

Pots. Scrub the pots using a stiff brush to remove dirt, algae, and salt buildup. Soak them in a solution of one part chlorine bleach to nine parts water. Rinse well. Soak clay pots overnight in clear water so the walls will not draw moisture from the potting mix after the bulbs are planted.

Planting. Most bulbs can be planted with the tips exposed. Don't bury them completely unless noted in the table opposite. Set them so that the soil level will be about ½ inch below the rim of the pot. Plant as many bulbs as will fit in the pot, leaving about 1½ inches of space between them. Water to thoroughly moisten the soil mix. Cover the pots to keep out light.

Special bulb-forcing pots allow the bulb shoots to grow out the sides. These pots give the bulbs plenty of fresh air, which they need.

Location. Place pots of hardy bulbs in a cold location with temperatures of 35° to 45° F. If you expect below-freezing temperatures, insulate the pots by covering them with shredded leaves or a blanket. During the cold period, the roots will grow. Place pots of tender bulbs, such as florist's anemone, in a cool location, where the temperature is 45° to 55°F.

Water and Light. Check the pots weekly to be sure the soil remains moist but not wet. Do not fertilize. When the chilling period is over, bring the pots into bright light to produce flowers. Most bulbs do best in a bright but rather cool location indoors. Water to keep the soil evenly moist.

To layer bulbs for forcing, put large bulbs such as daffodils near the bottom of the pot. Cover them with soil. Add smaller bulbs on top and cover them with a layer of soil.

Tips for Forcing Bulbs

Name	Temp./Weeks of Cold	Notes
Florist's anemone *Anemone coronaria*	45–50°F for 6–8 weeks	Soak tubers before planting until they're soft enough to dent with a fingernail.
Dutch crocus *Crocus* cultivars	35–45°F for 8 weeks	Water sparingly until plants are fully grown. Then keep evenly moist.
Freesia *Freesia* cultivars	50°F for 8 weeks	Plant corms deep enough to just barely, but completely, cover them. Plants need 10°F temperature drop at night.
Hyacinth *Hyacinthus orientalis*	45–50°F for 8 weeks	Easiest of the hardy bulbs to force; can be forced in water or soil.
Netted iris *Iris reticulata* *Iris danfordiae*	35–45°F for 8 weeks	Plant 2–3 inches deep and 2–3 inches apart.
Corn lily *Ixia* cultivars	50°F for 8 weeks	After forcing, rest bulbs over the summer, and force again next season.
Enchantment lily *Lilium* 'Enchantment'	60°F for 3–4 weeks	As plant grows, feed monthly with an all-purpose fertilizer.
Paperwhite narcissus *Narcissus papyraceus*	No cold period needed	Can be forced in soil or a pebble-filled bowl of water. Practically foolproof.
Narcissus and daffodils *Narcissus* cultivars	35–45°F for 12 weeks	Plants do best in cool temperatures of 60–65°F.
Persian buttercup *Ranunculus asiaticus*	50°F for 8 weeks	Soak tubers before planting until they're soft enough to dent with a fingernail.
Tulips *Tulipa* cultivars	35–45°F for 12 weeks	Plant bulbs with tips ½ inch deep. As plants grow, give them bright light but no direct sun.

PROPAGATION METHODS & HINTS

Plant	Method	Hints
Abutilon × hybridum (flowering maple)	Tip cuttings, seed	Needs ample humidity
Acalypha hispida (chenille plant)	Tip cuttings	Needs good humidity
Adiantum tenerum (maidenhair fern)	Division	Easy
Aechmea species (vase plant)	Offsets	Easy
Aeschynanthus speciosus (lipstick plant)	Tip cuttings, runners	Subject to damping-off
Aglaonema commutatum (Chinese evergreen)	Division, stem or tip cuttings	Easy
Aloe species	Offsets	Easy
Anthurium andraeanum (flamingo flower)	Division	Dust ends of cutting in hormone powder
Aphelandra squarrosa (zebra plant)	Tip cuttings, seed	Cut plants yearly to prevent leggy growth
Asparagus densiflorus (foxtail fern)	Division	Easy
Aspidistra elatior (cast iron plant)	Division	Easy
Asplenium nidus (bird's nest fern)	Division	Easy
Begonia, all types	Leaf cuttings, division	Needs ample humidity
Billbergia species	Offsets	Easy
Calathea makoyana (peacock plant)	Division	Subject to damping-off
Caryota mitis (fishtail palm)	Division, offsets	Slow growing
Cattleya cultivars	Division	Easy
Chlorophytum comosum (spider plant)	Runners	Grow in water
Cissus discolor (begonia vine)	Stem cuttings	Easy
Clivia miniata (kaffir lily)	Division	Divide in late summer
Codiaeum variegatum var. *pictum* (croton)	Stem cuttings, seed	Easy
Coleus cultivars (painted nettle)	Tip cuttings, seed	Needs ample humidity
Columnea species	Tip cuttings	Sometimes unsuccessful
Cordyline terminalis (ti plant)	Division	Easy
Cryptanthus species	Offsets	Easy
Dieffenbachia amoena (dumbcane)	Tip cuttings or air layering	Layering best
Dizygotheca elegantissima (false aralia)	Tip cuttings	Difficult to start
Dracaena species	Division	Easy to start
Epipremnum aureum (pothos)	Tip cuttings	Very easy
Episcia species	Stem or leaf cuttings	Needs ample humidity

***Note:** See Plant Profiles for propagation methods for plants not listed here.*

Plant	Method	Hints
Euphorbia milii var. *splendens* (crown-of-thorns)	Tip cuttings	Easy
Euphorbia pulcherrima (poinsettia)	Stem cuttings*	Will root in water
Ficus species (fig or rubber plant)	Air layering	Usually successful
Guzmania lingulata	Offsets	Easy
Gynura aurantiaca (purple velvet plant)	Tip cuttings	Temperamental
Heliconia species	Division	Easy
Hoya carnosa (wax plant)	Tip cuttings	Difficult
Kalanchoe blossfeldiana (starfire kalanchoe)	Seed	Difficult
Maranta species (prayer plant)	Division	Subject to damping-off
Medinilla magnifica (pink grape plant)	Stem cuttings	Difficult
Monstera deliciosa (Swiss cheese plant)	Stem cuttings, air layering	Layering usually successful
Neoregelia carolinae	Offsets	Easy
Nephrolepis exaltata (Boston fern)	Division	Easy
Oncidium species (dancing lady orchid)	Division	Easy
Paphiopedilum species (lady slipper orchid)	Division	Easy
Pelargonium cultivars (geranium)	Stem cuttings	Dust ends of cutting in hormone powder
Peperomia species	Stem or leaf cuttings	Easy
Philodendron species	Tip or stem cuttings	For most types, just place cutting in water
Polypodium vulgare (polypody)	Division	Easy
Saintpaulia cultivars (African violet)	Leaf cuttings	Easy
Sansevieria trifasciata (snake plant)	Division; leaf cuttings	Division easy
Schefflera actinophylla (umbrella tree)	Tip cuttings	A bit difficult
Scindapsus	Tip cuttings	Easy
Spathiphyllum species (peace lily)	Division	Easy
Streptocarpus rexii (cape primrose)	Leaf cuttings, division	Very easy
Syngonium podophyllum	Stem cuttings	Easy
Vriesea species	Offsets	Easy
Zantedeschia	Separate bulbs	Easy
Zebrina pendula	Tip cuttings	Will root in water

*****Note:** *Wear gloves when handling Euphorbia because the sap can cause a rash.*

CHAPTER SEVEN

Problems: Symptoms & Cures

Today, improved growing conditions at suppliers increase the likelihood that the plants you bring home will be pest and disease free. Pest and disease problems are most likely to develop when plants are growing in unfavorable conditions or are weakened by poor care. Because inappropriate growing conditions lead to stressed plants that are more susceptible to pest infestation and disease, the best defense is to provide optimal growing conditions. Make sure your plants receive the right amount of light, moisture, humidity, and fertilizer, and that the indoor temperatures are suitable for each plant.

LEFT *Use a magnifying glass* to inspect your plants for insects. Look closely at the tops and bottoms of leaves.

ABOVE *Soak new plants* in water to bring insects to the surface.

POOR CARE: SYMPTOMS & POSSIBLE CAUSES

Plants that are yellowing and losing leaves aren't necessarily succumbing to a disease or being attacked by pests. Poor care, or cultural practices, may be to blame. Plants showing physical problems may need soil with better drainage, a different watering schedule, increased humidity, or just more fresh air. When there are multiple possible causes, change just one condition at a time to isolate the problem.

Symptom	Possible Causes
Leaves are spotted brown or yellow	Heat too high; humidity too low; not enough fresh air; soil too dry or too wet
Leaves have yellow or white rings	Water too cold (requires room-temperature water)
Leaves drop	Temperature extreme; water too cold; humidity too low
Leaves are pale, growing weakly	Light insufficient; heat too high; too much fertilizer
Plant grows slowly	Soil drainage poor; plant resting
Buds drop	Humidity too low; temperature extreme; shock from draft
Plant collapses	Temperature extreme; root rot from poor drainage
Leaves are dry and crumbling	Heat too high; humidity too low
Leaves wilt	Soil too dry; heat too high
Stems are leggy and weak; leaves are sparse	Light insufficient

RIGHT *Spotted leaves* suggest various potential problems: heat too high, humidity too low, not enough fresh air, or soil too dry or too wet. Change the conditions one at a time to be sure of the cause.

BELOW RIGHT *Insufficient light* caused this plant to reach awkwardly toward the sun and grow leggy stems with sparse leaves.

Leggy, Reaching Plant

Inspecting for Symptoms. You can avoid serious problems by inspecting plants for signs of disease or insects. To detect insects, examine the tops and undersides of leaves. Examine new shoots for distorted growth and for yellowing or discolored leaves. Look for webbing in leaf axils, stickiness on stems, and insects themselves.

Wilting Plant

Lack of water and humidity or excessive heat, or both, have caused this plant to wilt.

Most diseases are caused by either bacteria or fungi, both of which enter a plant through minute wounds or natural openings such as leaf pores. Once inside the plant, bacteria and fungi multiply rapidly and start to break down plant tissue.

When a plant shows evidence of insects or disease, isolate and treat it for at least a month to contain the problem. In the case of an insect infestation, wait a few more weeks before returning the plant to its usual location; this is to ensure that no eggs are hatching new generations of pests.

Insect Control

Insects tend to attack plants that are growing in less-than-optimal conditions. Houseplants are sometimes attacked by pests that like the hot, dry conditions found in homes during the winter. To prevent problems, provide plants with fresh air, increase room humidity, and keep the temperature between 65° and 75°F. Occasionally open a window a bit. Also invest in a humidifier, and lower your thermostat a few degrees.

Try to keep insects from entering your home on a new plant. Examine new plants carefully. Insects hiding in soil or on the undersides of leaves can be difficult to see. As a precaution, soak newly purchased houseplants in a tub of water up to the pot rim for a few minutes. This will bring insects in the soil to the surface so you can dispose of them. If some of your houseplants spend the summer outdoors, check them carefully before bringing them back inside.

Inspect all of your plants regularly for signs of insects. Some insects have preferred locations. For example, mealybugs and aphids lurk in leaf axils and on the under-

sides of leaves. Thrips inhabit soil, and scale generally cling to the stems at the lower part of a leaf.

Plants with thin, delicate leaves, such as calatheas, are more susceptible to insects than thick-leaved plants. Succulents are seldom attacked by critters because their leaves are thick and tough skinned.

Home Remedies

Even with the best of care, the strongest plants may occasionally be attacked by insects. Often the best defenses against houseplant critters are traditional home remedies. Always test any treatment on a few leaves before applying it to the whole plant. Before panicking and resorting to harsh chemicals, try physical controls or the home remedies described below. Or, if you have a heavily infested plant, it's often better to dispose of it in a sealed plastic bag.

Hand Picking. If you see insects, use a toothpick or tweezers to remove them, and then destroy them by dropping them into a container of soapy water. Remove any dead or diseased leaves. Clean your tweezers and scissors with rubbing alcohol, or pass them over a flame so you don't inadvertently carry the insects from one part of the plant to another.

Damp Wiping. Wipe plant leaves, both top and bottom, with a cloth dampened with clear water. This eliminates many insect eggs and discourages pests that like dry conditions.

Water Spray. To dislodge a small number of pests from a plant, try a simple blast from your kitchen sink sprayer or

FAR LEFT *Swab tobacco tea* on leaves to get rid of scale or mealybugs.

LEFT *Sticky traps* are used to catch flying insects, such as whitefly, that have attacked houseplants.

MEET THE INSECTS

Pests

Insects may be able to gain a foothold on your plants, despite good cultural practices. They can ride indoors with new plants, or they may lie dormant in the soil until the conditions are right for them to emerge. Ongoing inspection and good growing conditions will help you prevent a few insects from becoming a major pest problem.

If you discover harmful insects on your plants, try physical remedies first, such as picking them off by hand or wiping them off with a damp cloth.

If these benign physical methods don't work, try the home remedies described on page 103. Before you resort to commercial insecticides, consider throwing out the plant and replacing it. Try insecticides only as a last resort, and be sure to follow label instructions carefully.

Hint: To keep treasured plants going, continually propagate them. Then, if an older plant should develop a problem, you will still have its offspring.

Scale are tiny, *oval-shaped, soft-bodied immobile insects protected by a hard shell. These insects suck plant sap, leaving plants sticky and causing yellowing.*

Spider mites *are tiny arachnids that suck the sap from leaves or flowers, leaving plants with yellow blotches and causing leaf loss. Look for spider mite webbing between leaves and stems. These pests love hot, dry conditions.*

Ants *themselves do no damage, but some herd aphids for the honeydew they excrete and may transport plant disease.* ***Aphids,*** *as shown here, are one of the most bothersome plant pests. These green, black, or red insects pierce stems, leaves, and buds, leaving plants weak with stunted or deformed leaves and blooms. They often cluster in leaf axils, along stems, and on the undersides of leaves.*

Whiteflies *are tiny, mothlike insects with greenish larvae that suck leaves, causing yellowing and leaf loss. Adult whiteflies flutter around like snowflakes when an infested plant is shaken.*

Mealybugs *are small, white, cottonlike insects that form colonies and destroy plant tissue. Infestation can lead to plant wilt, yellowing, and leaf loss. Look for mealybugs along tender new shoots and in leaf axils.*

Beneficials

Not all plant insects are bad. Some are beneficial in the indoor garden and on houseplants that seasonally go outside. Though few people may want insects inside their homes, ladybird beetles (ladybugs) and their larvae, lacewings and their larvae, tachinid and syrphid flies, and praying mantids all eat insects that feast on houseplants. Beneficial insects may hitchhike into your home on new plants or gain access through open doors or windows. If you find beneficials on your houseplants, you may prefer to move them outdoors, but don't kill them.

Tachinid (left) and syrphid flies (below) are members of separate families with larvae that prey on aphids and scale. Although this tachinid resembles a bee and this syrphid resembles a yellow jacket, neither stings. Some family members instead resemble houseflies.

Larva

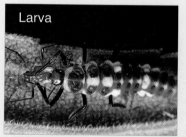

Adult

Ladybird beetles (ladybugs) are usually bright orange-red with black spots or black with red spots. They eat the eggs and young of aphids, scale, and other soft-bodied insects. Ladybug larvae somewhat resemble tiny, flat alligators. They are even more voracious than adults.

Praying mantids, so called because of their "praying" stance, dine on many plant insects, including beneficials. Depending on the species, an adult praying mantid, may range in size from 1 to 4 inches.

INSECTICIDE USE & STORAGE

Always follow the manufacturer's directions carefully. Insecticides are both plant- and pest-specific and so should be used only on the plants and pests listed on the label. There is no such thing as an all-purpose insecticide. If your plant or pest problem is not included on the label, the product is not intended to treat it. In addition, adhere to the general guidelines below:

✳ Always use insecticides outside or in the garage with the door open. It is not wise to use insecticides in the house, where they will linger in the air. Avoid inhaling fumes or dust from any insecticides, even organics. Wear a face mask and goggles when using powders.

✳ Insecticides labeled "organic," or "natural," are dangerous nonetheless. Take all of the same precautions with organic insecticides that you would take with synthetics.

✳ Apply insecticides out of direct sunlight. Many insecticides begin to break down when exposed to light, thereby losing their effectiveness. This is especially true of organics.

✳ Be sure the soil is moist before you apply the insecticide—otherwise the plant will not be able to absorb it.

Whether you decide to use an organic or synthetic insecticide, carefully follow the directions on the package for use, storage, and disposal. Repeated doses are usually necessary to eliminate all insects, so you will need to keep the products on hand. Be sure they're stored safely—in locked cabinets—out of the reach of children and pets.

---

bathroom showerhead. Also start misting your plants every other day. This may not sound like a high-tech solution, but spraying plants regularly will deter many insects that prefer dry conditions.

Soap Treatment. Clean more heavily infested plants with soapy water. Use a mild dishwashing liquid that has no whiteners, fragrance, or other additives. Squirt 2 teaspoonfuls into 1 gallon of water, and carefully wash the plant. Pay special attention to the undersides of leaves and the base of the leaf where it attaches to the stem. If this seems too tedious, cover the soil with aluminum foil, hold the plant by its base, and plunge the foliage into the soapy water. This soapy solution will also deter aphids and mealybugs.

As a preventive measure, spray plants once a week with a solution of soap and water. Rinse any plant washed with soapy water well using warm water 10 minutes after the soap treatment.

Insecticidal Soap. If a larger amount of insects are present, try an insecticidal soap. Made of sodium or potassium salts, insecticidal soaps are effective against many household pests and are not harmful to people or pets if they are used at the recommended dosage. Still, it's best to restrict your use of these products. Frequent use of chemical controls encourages pest populations to develop higher resistance. (Everyone knows about cockroaches; they have evolved such resistance to insecticides that they are jokingly referred to as

the only family likely to survive a nuclear blast.) Follow the package directions, and use these products with caution.

Rubbing Alcohol. To kill aphids, mealybugs, and scale, dab them with a cotton swab soaked with rubbing alcohol. Repeat applications every two to three days. This method takes a little time, but it is effective. Use this technique with caution. Covering the whole leaf damages the plant tissues.

Disease or not? *Spots on the geranium leaf (top) and begonia leaf (bottom) are not symptoms of disease. Possible causes are too much heat, direct sun, or fertilizer burn.*

Tobacco Tea. Tobacco is just as bad for insects as it is for humans. Use it to rid your plants of scale. To make the tea, steep tobacco in water for several days. Dip a cotton swab in the tea, and dab the insects. *Caution:* Keep this highly toxic tea in a sealed jar out of reach of pets and children.

Plant Diseases

Fortunately, houseplants that are well cared for rarely develop diseases. Houseplant diseases are mainly caused by bacteria and fungi. Bacterial diseases tend to be more of a problem in greenhouses than in the average home. As a matter of fact, most plant bacteria are actually beneficial, helping plants absorb nutrients from the soil.

Fungi, on the other hand, are fairly common problems for houseplants. Like bacteria, fungi enter a plant through a wound or natural opening or by forcing their way into a plant's stems, leaves, or flowers.

Fungal Diseases

Fungal spores are carried by wind, water, air, and tools. Fungi multiply rapidly in damp, low-light conditions. In fact, moisture and low light are essential to their reproduction. Plants and soil that remain too wet for too long invite problems.

Botrytis and other fungal diseases once constantly plagued houseplants, but not any longer because many plants today are bred to be disease resistant. Such diseases usually occur in a greenhouse or garden room full of plants, where the humidity might be too high or where conditions are otherwise favorable for diseases to take hold. Spots, rusts, mildew, and streaks on leaves are some signs that diseases are at work. Soft roots, wilts, and rots are other symptoms.

Botrytis Blight. If a gray, moldy growth starts to cover the leaves, stems, or flowers of a plant, botrytis blight may be the cause. This disease thrives on plants that have been overfed, overwatered, or overcrowded. Start by cutting off the affected leaves or stems. Decrease the water, and stop fertilizing. Divide the plant, or trim off some shoots to give it more room. If the outdoor temperature is not bitterly cold, open a window. Or install a fan near the plant to circulate the air.

Powdery Mildew. White, fuzzy growth that later turns brown is a sign of powdery mildew. Cut out all of the affected parts, and improve air circulation, as mentioned above.

Also, powdery mildew can be treated with a solution of baking soda and water, just as outdoor gardeners treat roses affected by powdery mildew. Mix 1 tablespoon of baking soda and 1 tablespoon of horticultural oil in 1 gallon of water. The oil helps the baking soda stick to the leaves. Spray the affected plant completely.

If you remove plant parts damaged by disease or work around infected plants, wash your hands and sterilize your tools to prevent the spread of disease.

Preventive Measures

The best defenses against plant diseases are a clean environment, proper growing conditions, and fresh air.

Try using horticultural charcoal to deter fungal disease, mildew, and many bacterial diseases. Purchase horticultural charcoal at nurseries, or you can simply use ashes from your fireplace. Sprinkle the charcoal or ash onto the leaves of affected plants.

Powdery mildew *on African violet is caused by poor air circulation. Cut the leaf off at the base of its stem. Then improve air circulation around the plant.*

This plant is not diseased. *Insufficient water or too much fertilizer has burned it. Cut off the damaged leaves; water the plant thoroughly; and mist.*

CHAPTER EIGHT

Plant Profiles

The houseplants described in this second part of the book are widely available. Here you'll find traditional houseplants, such as Boston fern and philodendron, as well as a host of comparative newcomers—we've added over 50 new plants for this edition. If you'd like to purchase any of these plants but don't find them at your retailer, inquire about ordering them.

The author has personally grown all plants described in this book. He directed the photography of most plants in this section as well as the step-by-step photos in the first part of this book. He decided not to include some plants often regarded as houseplants, such as agaves and pileas, because they didn't perform well indoors.—The Editors

The Family Arrangement

Plants profiled on the upcoming pages are arranged within two subsections. Each subsection groups the plants alphabetically by the family common name, such as Begonias, Cacti, and Ferns. Within each family, the plants are arranged alphabetically by the scientific name for the genus and species. The first subsection, beginning on page 112, covers the major families—those that include the vast majority of houseplants. The second subsection, beginning on page 195, features excellent houseplants from families that contain a much smaller portion of readily available houseplants.

Yet there's a more practical reason for the two subsections. Where possible, it allows the grouping of plants from major families on whole pages and two-page "spreads," thereby helping you see the similarities and differences within families and genera (plural for genus).

The Profiles

Each profile includes the kinds of information shown on the next page. Here's more on growing factors:

Light. Although all growing factors mentioned below work together, light should be your first consideration in placing a plant.

Soil. Most plants grow well in all-purpose potting soil. Packaged houseplant soil generally contains all the nutrients plants need. Yet some plants prefer a richer soil, which you can supply by adding sterile humus (compost) to your potting soil. Also, many cacti and succulents like a mix of potting soil and sand. Bromeliads and orchids grow better when planted in fir bark.

OPPOSITE *Orchids,* such as this Dendrobium, *are among the most popular houseplants.*
RIGHT *A cascade of color in a hanging basket combines blue lobelia with yellow tuberous begonias, golden bidens, and red and pink petunias.*

Sow seeds *that are large enough to easily handle one or two at a time into flats, cell packs, peat pots, or other containers of moist potting mix.*

Carefully cover *seeds that don't need light to germinate by sprinkling fine, loose, moist potting mix over them to the correct depth.*

Temperature & Humidity. Most plants adjust to average household temperatures of 70°F or higher with a drop of about 10°F at night. Exceptions are noted in individual profiles.

Water. Soil kept evenly moist usually works best. Some plants like a little less water in winter and when resting, such as after blooming. You'll find these preferences noted.

Fertilizer. Most of the profiles include a recommended fertilizer ratio for Nitrogen (N), Phosphorus (P), and Potassium (K), expressed in that sequence on packaging as percentages of the entire mix, thus: 20-10-10 or 10-10-10 for general-purpose fertilizer.

Fluorescent lamps *provide ideal light for seedlings. Use daylight tubes or a combination of cool white and warm white, and keep the seedling tops a few inches below the lamps. Adjust the height of the containers as the plants grow, always keeping them no farther than 5 inches from the leaf tips.*

How to Read the Plant Profiles

Aroids (*Araceae*)

Family common name

Family scientific (botanical) name (*See the family descriptions in Chapter 1, beginning on page 11.*)

Common name *used by most plant sellers*

Scientific (botanical) name *The first word is the genus, which usually contains a collection of similar species. The "✕" symbol means that this plant is a hybrid, resulting from crossbreeding of different plants. The species name follows the genus. The genus and species names are conventionally shown in italic. For detailed definitions of these terms, see the "Glossary," pages 216-217.*

Light needs

Soil and water needs

Temperature needs

Fertilizer needs

Cultivar *is short for cultivated variety (not found in nature) and is expressed within single quotation marks.*

The photograph *may show a mature plant or an immature plant that looks more like young plants you'll find at retailers. When immature plants are shown, consult the text for a description of the full-grown plant.*

aka *is short for "also known as." Scientific nomenclature changes as research reveals new plant relationships. Thus older references and some retailers may list this plant as Caladium bicolor. In this case, the "C" is the abbreviation for Caladium, referring to its mention in preceding text.*

At-a-glance highlights *include probable maximum heights, as follows:*

Small: to 18 inches
Medium: to 36 inches
Large: 36 inches & taller

Meaning *that these plants are grown mainly for their foliage. Many foliage plants will bear flowers under favorable conditions.*

Propagation method (*See Chapter 6, beginning on page 82 for propagation methods.*)

Fancy-leaved Caladium

Caladium ✕ hortulanum
(aka *C. bicolor* and other botanical names)

✳ **Medium size**
✳ **Likes moderate light**
✳ **Easy to grow**

Fancy-leaved caladiums are showy foliage plants with heart-shaped leaves in different combinations of red, pink, white, with various shades of green. There are hundreds of hybrids. Caladiums are grown from frost-tender tubers.

Caladiums thrive in moderate light. Grow in an all-purpose potting soil kept quite moist during the growing season. The plants prefer warmth, with nighttime temperatures of at least 65°F. Feed with 10-10-10 fertilizer every two months during the growing season but not at all when dormant (mostly in winter). Start new plants from tubers.

Good cultivars: 'Pink Beauty', 'Rosebud', 'Frieda Hemple'

Acanthus Family (*Acanthaceae*)

Zebra Plant, Yellow Plume Plant
Aphelandra squarrosa

✻ **Cheerful yellow flowers**
✻ **Handsome foliage**
✻ **Good small- to medium-size plant**

Hailing from South American tropical forests, zebra plant has green leaves dramatically ribbed with white. A plume of yellow flowers with bright yellow bracts appears at the top, usually in summer. The plant grows upright to 24 inches and can get leggy.

Zebra plant appreciates a bright location and grows well in standard all-purpose houseplant soil. Keep the soil evenly moist except in midwinter, when the plant needs a month-long rest. Keep the soil only barely moist at this time. Feed monthly with 20-10-10 plant food (except during the midwinter rest), and repot yearly in fresh soil. Prune when the plant gets too leggy. Propagate new plants from cuttings.

Zebra Plant, Yellow Plume Plant

Firecracker Flower
Crossandra infundibuliformis

✻ **Popular medium-size houseplant**
✻ **Striking orange flowers**
✻ **Needs bright light**

In its native environment in southeastern Asia, firecracker flower can develop into a large bush. As a houseplant, though, it rarely grows taller than 30 inches. The attractive orange flowers pop out one after the other; hence, the common name. In spring, the flowers make this plant worth the careful cultivation it requires.

Grow firecracker flower in a bright window. Use a small pot of standard all-purpose houseplant soil. This plant requires precise watering and feeding, so keep the soil evenly moist. Feed monthly with 20-20-10 fertilizer, and repot in fresh soil every second year. Start new plants from stem cuttings.

Firecracker Flower

Nerve Plant
Fittonia argyroncura

✳ Lush appearance
✳ Minimal care
✳ Tolerates shade

Nerve Plant

Nerve plant is an old reliable originally grown in Peru at high elevations. It does well with little care in the home. *Fittonia argyroncura's* flat, papery oval leaves are netted with white veins. This is a compact plant that grows quickly, but it remains decorative even when it becomes large. Let soil dry out between waterings. Will tolerate shade, but needs warmth and high humidity. Can be used in baskets, and is also suitable for terrariums. Buy mature plants for their decorative effect. Feed four times a year with 10-10-5. Stem cuttings root easily.

Mosaic Plant
Fittonia verschaffeltii

✳ Pretty veined foliage
✳ Excellent for small windowsills
✳ Tolerates moderate to low light

Mosaic Plant

This subtly beautiful Peruvian native deserves greater recognition. Compact, it grows to about 24 inches and makes a handsome display in a hanging basket. The name mosaic alludes to the fine reticulation, or network, of veins in the foliage—pink to reddish stripes that crisscross the deep green leaves in a netlike pattern.

Grow mosaic plant in standard all-purpose houseplant soil kept evenly moist all year. Use a small pot because the plant grows best when potbound. Repot when roots extend from the drainage holes. Feed monthly with 10-10-10 fertilizer. Propagate new plants from cuttings.

Hemigraphis repens

Hemigraphis repens

✳ Unusual, undemanding plant
✳ Thrives in bright light
✳ Grows in small pots

This new introduction to the Acanthus family features small, metallic-toothed leaves and tiny, white flowers. This plant is lacy and delicate and the dark-green leaflets create an eye-catching effect. *Hemigraphis repens* is a good plant for a sunny spot and grows easily. It is also undemanding and generally not troubled with insects. The plant has a bushy appearance and blooms with numerous flowers in the summer. *Hemigraphis* likes plenty of water, and can actually be grown in a watery environment such as a fountain or terrarium. It also makes a good hanging basket. Propagate from cuttings. Use as a fill-in with other plants. Feed every other month with 10-10-5.

Acanthus Family (*Acanthaceae*) cont'd

Polka Dot Plant

Hypoestes phyllostachya (aka *H. sanguinolenta*)

❋ **Small and attractive**
❋ **Good window plant**
❋ **Colorful foliage**

A fast-growing plant from Madagascar, polka pot plant is a good choice for a bright windowsill. The common name, "polka dot," derives from the pink spots sprinkled over the foliage.

For greater visual impact, combine two plants in one container. Grow in standard all-purpose houseplant soil, and allow the soil to dry out between waterings. The plant tends to get leggy, so cut back the stems to encourage a bushier, more compact form. Feed monthly with 10-10-10 fertilizer. Start new plants from cuttings.

Polka Dot Plant

Shrimp Plant

Justicia brandegeana (aka *Beloperone guttata*)

❋ **Long-time favorite**
❋ **Medium size**
❋ **Easy to grow**

The shrimp plant has curved, shrimp-like spikes of pinkish or yellow bracts for most of the year. This plant is bushy and can grow as tall as 36 inches if left unpruned. It makes a good window plant.

To develop the best color, provide a bright location with some direct sun. Use standard all-purpose houseplant soil, and keep it evenly moist, except in winter when watering can be decreased somewhat. Feed monthly with 20-10-10 fertilizer. Shrimp plant becomes leggy if you don't prune as needed; cut back the stems to keep the plant compact and bushy. Repot annually in fresh soil. Propagate new plants from stem cuttings.

Shrimp Plant

Lollipop Plant, Yellow Shrimp Plant

Pachystachys lutea

❊ **Bright yellow flower spikes**
❊ **Good small table plant**
❊ **Requires minimal care**

With its bright yellow spikes topped with tiny white flowers that peek from overlapping yellow bracts, lollipop plant (*Pachystachys lutea*) looks very much like its close relative, yellow shrimp plant (*Beloperone guttata*). The difference is that Pachystachys' leaves are larger and its spikes grow upright rather than arch to one side. Pachystachys, from pachys, means thick or large, (as in pachyderm), and stachys means spike. Grow these plants in bright but indirect light, in standard all-purpose house-plant soil. Keep the soil evenly moist all year, and feed monthly with 10-10-10 fertilizer. Prune the stems when the plant gets leggy. Propagate plants from stem cuttings.

Lollipop Plant, Yellow Shrimp Plant

Purple Spike

Purple Spike

Porphyrocoma pohliana

❊ **New and desirable variety**
❊ **Grows in a small pot**
❊ **Handsome table decoration**

This new member of the Acanthus family, recently arrived from Panama, is a handsome, lush plant with lavender flowers that bloom periodically throughout the year, purple-red bracts, and dark-green leaves with silvery veins. Purple spike grows in a compact, bushy form and can be quite appealing when mature. Use it with other plants for the best visual effect. Purple spike needs bright light but minimal care. Keep soil evenly moist. Can grow tall. Feed monthly with 10-10-5. Propagate from cuttings.

Acanthus Family (*Acanthaceae*) cont'd

Purple False Eranthemum
Pseuderanthemum atropurpureum

✳ **Good accent plant**
✳ **Grows in small pot**
✳ **Good for aquariums**

This new introduction from Polynesia is an upright-growing plant that reaches heights of approximately 12 to 18 inches. The leaves of mature plants are variegated with purple or green and white, and add bright color to a plant grouping. Their vertical growth and color make them good background plants. The plant likes moist soil and bright light. It can be used as an aquarium plant or in hydroponic gardens because it can tolerate wet conditions. It is not susceptible to insects and is easy to propagate by cuttings. Keep leaves clean with a damp cloth. Feed four times a year with 10-10-5. It is recommended that you purchase this plant in its mature state.

Purple False Eranthemum

Ruellia Colorata

Ruellia Colorata
✳ **Unusual plant**
✳ **Grows slowly**
✳ **Needs light to bloom**

A native of South America, *Ruellia colorata* has lanceolate (spear-shaped) leaves. There are many Ruellias, but this particular variety is quite good for the home. The plant can reach a height of 14 inches when mature, and makes a handsome, bushy appearance that looks great in basket plantings. With full sun and warmth, Ruellia will yield red flowers from fall until spring. Keep soil barely moist. Sometimes susceptible to mealy bug attacks. Provide feedings of 10-10-5 every other watering. Buy mature plants, and prune once or twice a year to keep them compact and bushy.

Sanchezia Speciosa

Sanchezia speciosa (aka. *S. nobilis*)

❊ **Medium-size to large plant**
❊ **Fine attractive leaves**
❊ **Easy to grow**

Warm-climate gardeners know sanchezia as an outdoor plant, but it grows well indoors, too. This pretty and undemanding foliage plant from Ecuador has green leaves with prominent yellow veins. Sanchezia is shrubby in form but can be kept under control with light pruning. Grow sanchezia in bright light in all-purpose potting soil. Keep the soil evenly moist all year, and mist the leaves regularly—this plant likes moisture and high humidity. Feed monthly with 10-10-10 fertilizer. Propagate new plants from stem cuttings.

Sanchezia Speciosa

Persian Shield Plant

Persian Shield Plant

Strobilanthes dyerianus

❊ **Stunning foliage**
❊ **Medium-size, compact grower**
❊ **Great room accent**

This lovely foliage plant has fine-toothed leaves in a unique purple-green combination that commands attention. Pale blue flowers occasionally appear, but this plant is usually grown for its striking foliage. Persian shield plant looks great on any desk or table, and can grow vertically to 30 inches. Grow in a temperate location in bright but indirect light. Use a standard all-purpose houseplant soil kept evenly moist in warm months and somewhat drier in cool months. Do not mist the leaves. Feed quarterly with 10-10-10 fertilizer. If the plant gets straggly, cut it back. Repot only when the plant is potbound, usually about every second year. Propagate new plants from stem cuttings.

Amaryllis Family (*Amaryllidaceae*)

Kaffir Lily
Clivia miniata

✳ **Dependable spring bloomer**
✳ **Striking flowers**
✳ **Medium size**

In spring, Kaffir lily produces a cluster of vivid orange, trumpet-shaped flowers with yellow centers above strap-shaped, glossy, deep green leaves.

This plant prefers to be out of direct sun and tolerates low light. It thrives in cool temperatures. Grow in a large pot of rich, humusy soil, and keep the soil evenly moist all year. Kaffir lily likes to be potbound and can be grown in the same pot for many years. Instead of repotting, topdress with 4 inches of new soil every year. Feed quarterly with 20-10-10 fertilizer. Propagate new plants by division.

Kaffir Lily

Amazon Lily

Amazon Lily
Eucharis × *grandiflora*

✳ **Medium size**
✳ **Lovely fragrant white flowers**
✳ **Easy to grow**

Amazon lily bears fragrant white, star-shaped, lily-like flowers on erect stems. The leaves of this 30-inch plant are large and glossy dark green.

Grow Amazon lily in a somewhat sunny space with moderate temperatures in rich, humusy soil. Use a small container because the plant does best when potbound. Keep the soil evenly moist until the plant finishes blooming. Let the bulb dry out for a month or so; then start routine watering again. The plant may rebloom in a few months. Fertilize with 10-20-10 plant food every month, except when the plant is resting just after it finishes blooming. Propagate new plants by division. See Chapter 6, page 95, for tips on growing bulbs indoors.

Fireball, Catherine Wheel

Haemanthus katherinae (aka *Scadoxus multiflorus ssp. katherinae*)

❋ **Fine for cut flowers**
❋ **Stunning bright red blooms**
❋ **Small, easy to grow**

This South African plant produces a sphere of small, starlike red flowers on an erect stem. The bulb can be started at almost any time of year, and flowers bloom about nine months later.

Fireball likes bright light and average household temperatures. Grow in a 6- to 8-inch pot, in rich soil, and leave the tip of the bulb exposed above the soil line. Water fireball moderately, and increase watering as the stem grows so that the soil stays evenly moist. Feed once or twice monthly with 10-10-10 fertilizer. After flowering, stop watering the bulb to allow the plant to rest. After about six months, repot in fresh soil so it blooms again. Fireball is difficult to propagate at home; to start new plants, buy new bulbs.

Fireball, Catherine Wheel

Amaryllis

Amaryllis

Hippeastrum cultivars

❋ **Great gift plant**
❋ **Medium size, with huge flowers**
❋ **Easy to grow**

The original species of Amaryllis from South America has given rise to dozens of cultivars in a range of colors, including red, pink, orange, salmon, white, and streaked. The flowers—some 7 inches across—bloom just a few months after bulb planting.

Plant the bulb with the top half above the soil line in a pot just large enough to hold it. Grow in a bright location with some direct sun, in all-purpose potting mix. Water sparingly at first; then keep the soil evenly moist when growth appears. After flowering, cut off the thick flower stalk, and let the leaves grow for a few months to nourish the bulb. Gradually reduce watering so that the leaves turn brown and die back. Stop watering, remove the dead leaves, and give the plant a dry rest. Store the bulb in a paper bag in a dark, dry place. In two months plant it again in fresh soil.

Aralia Family (*Araliaceae*)

Finger Aralia,
False Aralia

Finger Aralia, False Aralia

Dizygotheca elegantissima
(aka *Schefflera elegantissima*)

❋ **Graceful appearance**
❋ **Large, vertical plant**
❋ **Easy to grow**

This Pacific Island native is popular in the indoor garden for its lacy, airy grace. It is actually a small tree, capable of growing to a height of 48 inches. The slender leaflets can range in color from coppery red to green, and are arranged in a circle around the tops of the stems so that they resemble fingers. Aralia is easy to grow if given good routine care. Supply with bright light and sustained moisture at the roots. Grow aralia in standard all-purpose houseplant soil. Feed monthly with 10-10-10 fertilizer. Propagate from cuttings.

Ivy

Hedera canariensis

❋ **Favorite ivy**
❋ **Decorative leaves**
❋ **Easy to grow**

Ivy

Hedera canariensis, a popular member of the ivy family, is an attractive, upright grower that branches as it matures. It makes bright decoration against the brick walls in a plant room, and grows well in baskets or trained in topiary forms. Don't try to grow ivy in a warm room; coolness and humidity are the keys to its success. Give plants bright light rather than sun. Soak soil, then let dry, then soak again. Give the plant an overhead spraying in the sink at least once a week, and an occasional soapy wash to keep plants free of aphids and spider mites. Do not feed. Propagate by cuttings.

English Ivy

English Ivy

Hedera helix

❋ **Great trailing plant**
❋ **Many hybrids available**
❋ **Easy grower**

With its lobed leaves and lush growth, English Ivy has long been a household tradition. Today there are countless hybrids, some with plain green leaves, others with foliage variegated with yellow or creamy white. Ivies make good room accents. Provide bright light and well-drained all-purpose soil that is kept evenly moist but never soggy. Feed quarterly with 20-10-10 fertilizer. Propagate new plants from leaf or stem cuttings.
Good cultivars: 'Gold Dust', 'Glacier', 'Curlilocks.'

Ming Aralia
Polyscias fruticosa

❊ **Versatile and decorative**
❊ **Heart-shaped leaves**
❊ **Easy to maintain**

Ming aralia is a graceful plant from Polynesia with attractive, crinkled foliage. Its botanical name, Polyscias, means many-shaded, a reference to the luxuriant foliage of this family. Ming aralia can grow to a height of 30 inches, but can be kept small through frequent trimming. It grows in full sun or heavy shade, but is quite happy in a north window. Grow Ming aralia in a small pot of standard all-purpose houseplant soil kept evenly moist. Feed monthly with 10-10-10 fertilizer. Maintain warm temperatures because ming aralia does not tolerate cold well. Propagate new plants from cuttings.

Ming Aralia

Ginseng

Ginseng
Polyscias guilfoylei

❊ **Delicate appearance**
❊ **Grows easily**
❊ **Overlooked species**

*Polyscias guilfoylei,*commonly known as ginseng, resembles a small tree. This handsome plant has upright growth that can climb to 24 inches. Variegated leaves make these desirable plants that add color to the home. While young, ginseng's small, heart-shaped leaves make it a fine addition to dish gardens and terrariums. It requires north light and evenly moist soil. Feed every other watering with 10-10-5. Propagate by cuttings at any time.

Aralia Family
(*Araliaceae*) cont'd

Balfour Aralia

Polyscias scutellaria 'Balfourii' (aka *P. balfouriana*)

❋ **A handsome, tall vertical plant**
❋ **Small round leaves**
❋ **Good foliage plant**

Polyscias balfouriana has roundish, slightly cupped leaves with scalloped edges. Balfour aralia likes medium light, but will tolerate full sun for several hours a day. Keep moist at all times and mist daily. Fertilize every 14 days with a mild solution during active growth. Clean leaves monthly with warm water. Water and feed less during winter. Grow Balfour aralia in standard all-purpose houseplant soil. Feed quarterly with 20-20-20 fertilizer. Propagate new plants from tip cuttings.

Good cultivars: 'Marginata', 'Pennockii'

Balfour Aralia

Variegated Umbrella Plant

Variegated Umbrella Plant

Schefflera actinophylla 'Variegata'

❋ **Handsome variegated leaves**
❋ **Large plant**
❋ **Easy to grow**

This popular plant is a good addition to the indoor garden. Its oblong leaflets are graceful looking, and the plant brings a hint of the tropics into a home. Its branching habit and shiny green leaves edged with white distinguish it from the typical green scheffleras. It tolerates a range of conditions and makes a good room accent. Schefflera is sometimes listed by the genus name Brassaia.

Grow umbrella plant in bright light with no direct sun. Pot it in standard all-purpose houseplant soil, and keep the soil evenly moist. Feed quarterly with 20-10-10 fertilizer. If the plant gets too leggy, cut the lower stems. Propagate new plants from cuttings.

Aroids Family (*Araceae*)

Amelia Chinese Evergreen
Aglaonema 'Amelia'

❋ **Handsome foliage**
❋ **Medium size**
❋ **Easy to grow**

Attractive green foliage mottled with lighter gray-green makes 'Amelia' an enduring houseplant favorite. This tropical foliage plant is very durable and can survive dim light, drafts, and dry air . Grow 'Amelia' in bright light but not direct sun, in all-purpose, well-draining house-plant soil. Keep the soil evenly moist all year. Feed monthly with 20-10-10 fertilizer. 'Amelia' tolerates temperatures as low as 55° to 60°F. Propagate by division. This plant is toxic, so keep it away from kids and pets.

Amelia Chinese Evergreen

Camilla Chinese Evergreen
Aglaonema 'Camilla'

❋ **Tolerates neglect**
❋ **Medium size**
❋ **Easy to grow**

Camilla Chinese Evergreen

Both beautiful and durable, 'Camilla' is variable in leaf color. This Southeast Asian native was introduced in 1856 and grows to about 30 inches.

Grow the plant in bright light but not direct sun, and use a standard all-purpose potting soil. Keep the soil evenly moist, and feed twice a month with 20-10-5 plant food. Repot annually. Propagate new plants from stem cuttings.

Good cultivars: 'Silver Queen', 'Silver Spear'

Shield Plant
Alocasia × amazonica

❋ **Exotic appearance**
❋ **Striking foliage**
❋ **Medium size**

From tropical Asia, this dramatic plant features large arrow-head-shaped leaves floating atop tall stems. The showy, velvety

Shield Plant

green foliage often has contrasting copper, gray, silver, or red veins. Shield plant may go dormant if chilled or allowed to dry out. However, after a few months it will resume growth.

Provide bright light (but not direct sun) and warm temperatures. Add a little peat moss to the potting mix, and keep it evenly moist. Feed monthly with 20-10-10 fertilizer. Repot annually. Propagate by division.

Aroids Family (*Araceae*) cont'd

Black Velvet Alocasia

Alocasia 'Black Velvet'

✳ **Small to medium-size plant**
✳ **Dramatic foliage**
✳ **Survives cool temperatures**

This robust hybrid of Asian heritage grows to 24 inches. The leaves, on short stems, have a striking greenish black sheen.

Grow 'Black Velvet' in all-purpose potting soil kept evenly moist (but not soggy) all year. Do not overwater. Avoid getting water on leaves; otherwise they will spot. The plant can withstand some coolness, but nighttime temperatures should never drop below 50°F. Repot every second year. Feed monthly with 20-10-10 plant food. Propagate new plants by division.

Black Velvet Alocasia

Copper Alocasia

Copper Alocasia

Alocasia cuprea

✳ **Small to medium-size plant**
✳ **Attractive foliage**
✳ **Survives cool temperatures**

The arrowhead-shaped leaves of this native of Borneo are an outstanding burnished copper color. This alocasia grows slowly to 20 inches tall and is a good plant for a desk or table.

A low-light northern-window exposure is ideal for this plant. Grow copper alocasia in a mix of equal parts fine-grade fir bark and all-purpose houseplant soil. Keep the soil evenly moist, never too dry or too wet; otherwise the leaves become limp. Feed once a month with 10-10-10 fertilizer. Copper alocasia will withstand temperatures to about 55°F, and that's lower than most alocasias can handle. Propagate new plants by division.

Green Goddess Alocasia

Alocasia 'Green Goddess'

❋ Medium size to tall
❋ Likes low light
❋ Exquisite heart-shaped leaves mottled with light green and dark green

With large heart-shaped leaves on tall graceful stems, 'Green Goddess' is an exotic plant that grows to 36 inches. The rich green foliage shaded with green-black commands attention.

Grow the plant in a somewhat low-light location with temperatures above 60°F. Keep the plant out of drafts, which cause the leaves to fold. Use a humusy soil that drains well; add extra humus to all-purpose potting soil as described in Chapter 5, beginning on page 62. Keep the soil evenly moist all year except in winter, when the soil can be allowed to go somewhat dry. Feed only in spring and summer with 20-20-20 plant food. Propagate by division.

Green Goddess Alocasia

Flamingo Flower

Flamingo Flower

Anthurium cubense

❋ New variety of Flamingo flower
❋ Large plant
❋ Decorative foliage and flowers

Anthuriums are now available in a spectrum of leaf color and make fine houseplants. From Central and South American jungles, Flamingo flower produces "lacquered" blooms in winter and spring that make superb indoor decoration. This plant needs a potting mix of half standard soil and half fine-grade fir bark to insure perfect drainage. Grow in a shaded location and keep soil moist. Better not try them unless you can provide warmth with 80-percent humidity. Feed four times a year with 10-10-5.

Aroids Family (*Araceae*) cont'd

Tailflower

Anthurium hookeri

❋ **Medium size**
❋ **Fountainlike form**
❋ **Grown for foliage**

This species from the West Indies has large heart-shaped leaves that form a fountain shape. Although seldom encountered in retail stores, it is available if you make enough inquiries. It makes a worthwhile edition to the indoor garden. A compact plant, it grows to about 30 inches in diameter.

Tailflower likes a low-light location, such as a north window, and good air circulation. Grow the plant in a mix of equal parts fine-grade fir bark and potting soil kept evenly moist all year. Good drainage is essential; otherwise the plant can develop root rot. Feed quarterly with 20-10-10 fertilizer. Propagate new plants by division.

Tailflower

Flamingo Flower

Anthurium scherzerianum and *A. andraeanum*

❋ **Medium size**
❋ **Long-lasting flowers**
❋ **Excellent cut flower**

The flowering spathes of flamingo flower can last an astounding six weeks. Many hybrids are available, with flowers in a variety of warm colors. Originally from Costa Rica, the plant is now widely grown in Hawaii. It is the most popular houseplant in the genus.

Grow flamingo flower in bright light in an all-purpose potting soil. Keep the soil evenly moist. Provide good ventilation, and feed monthly with a 20-20-10 fertilizer. Repot annually. Grow new plants by division.

Good cultivars: 'Southern Blush' and 'Lady Jane'

Ivy

Fancy-Leaved Caladium

Caladium hortorum hybrid

❋ **Fine indoor growth**
❋ **Many varieties**
❋ **Great indoor color**

Caladiums are superlative plants both outdoors and indoors and come in numerous varieties to please everyone. They are a large family of 20- to 30-inch plants with stunning foliage. The paper-thin, heart-shaped leaves are white, pink, red, or olive-green, and many shades in between. Provide shade and warmth, and water well during their growing season, generally from April until October. Caladiums prefer 60 percent or higher humidity. Feed during the summer with 10-10-10. In fall, when leaves die down, gradually reduce amount of water. When growth has completely stopped, remove tubers from pots, dry them out, and store in paper bags at 60°F for two to three months. Then repot, one tuber to a 5-inch container. Although you can buy mature plants at nurseries, it is easy and fun to start your own. In summer, Caladiums look great in shaded windows.

Fancy-Leaved Caladium

Fancy-leaved Caladium

Caladium × hortulanum
(aka *C. bicolor*)

✳ **Medium size**
✳ **Likes moderate light**
✳ **Easy to grow**

Native to Brazil, Caladiums are grown from frost-tender tubers. There are hundreds of hybrids. Fancy-leaved caladiums are showy foliage plants with heart-shaped leaves in different combinations of red, pink, and white, with various shades of green. Caladiums thrive in moderate light and grow in an all-purpose potting soil. Keep soil moist during the growing season. These plants prefer warmth, with nighttime temperatures of at least 65°F. Feed with 10-10-10 fertilizer every two months during the growing season, but not at all when dormant (mostly in winter). Start new plants from tubers.

Good cultivars: 'Pink Beauty', 'Rosebud'

Fancy-leaved Caladium

Hilo Beauty Colocasia

Hilo Beauty Colocasia

Colocasia 'Hilo Beauty' (aka *Alocasia 'Hilo Beauty'*)

✳ **Compact growth, medium size**
✳ **Colorful foliage**
✳ **Highly recommended**

The colocasias are sometimes considered inappropriate for the indoors because of their large leaves and sprawling growth habit. However, 'Hilo Beauty', a recent hybrid, has smaller leaves mottled green and yellow, and its slow, compact growth—to about 24 inches—makes it more suitable for most homes.

Grow 'Hilo Beauty' in standard all-purpose house-plant soil kept evenly moist all year. Place it in a bright but not sunny location, and feed quarterly with 10-20-10 fertilizer. This is an outstanding foliage plant because the leaves are borne on erect stems and create a beautiful picture. Propagate this plant by division.

Aroid Family (*Araceae*) cont'd

Camille Dumbcane
Dieffenbachia picta 'Camille'

❋ **Large plant**
❋ **Colorful foliage**
❋ **Many available cultivars**

Dumbcane is native to the tropical Americas. Characterized by splashed, speckled, and splotched foliage—white on green, yellow and green, shades of green—this dieffenbachia offers bright, vibrant, colorful leaves in a host of variegation patterns. All parts of the plant are poisonous and cause the mouth and tongue to swell if chewed; hence the common name. Keep it away from small children and pets. Grow dieffenbachia in bright light with an all-purpose potting soil that drains readily. Feed monthly with 20-20-10 plant food, and keep plants in a warm location away from drafts. Repot in fresh soil every second year. Start new plants from cuttings.

Other good cultivars: 'Tropic Snow'; 'Exotica' and its variants

Camille Dumbcane

Exotica Dumbcane

Exotica Dumbcane
Dieffenbachia picta 'Exotica'

❋ **Medium plant**
❋ **Handsome patterned leaves**
❋ **Easy to grow**

With beautiful broad leaves splotched yellow and green, 'Exotica' grows to about 30 inches tall from a central trunk. This excellent, compact plant can tolerate neglect.

'Exotica' likes an evenly moist, standard all-purpose houseplant soil. Put the plant in a bright but not sunny location, and feed it monthly with 10-20-10 fertilizer. Propagate by air layering.

Tropic Snow Dumbcane

Dieffenbachia 'Tropic Snow'

❋ **Medium size**
❋ **Handsome foliage**
❋ **Easy to grow**

Tropic Snow Dumbcane

With broad leaves patterned in green and white, this dieffenbachia is attractive and popular. It is compact, rarely growing more than 36 inches.

Plant 'Tropic Snow' in standard houseplant soil, and keep it evenly moist all year. Place it in a bright but not sunny area, and feed with 20-20-20 plant food every fourth month. Wipe leaves occasionally with a damp cloth. Propagate by air layering.

Marble Queen Pothos

Epipremnum aureum 'Marble Queen' (aka *Scindapsus* and *Philodendron*)

❋ **Good vining plant**
❋ **Bushy appearance**
❋ **Grows fast**

Marble Queen Pothos

With green heart-shaped leaves handsomely splashed with white on long trailing stems, this pothos cultivar either climbs or trails. Support the stems on a piece of bark or a trellis inserted into the soil, or grow the plant in a hanging basket. Pothos tolerates almost any indoor conditions, but for optimal growth give it bright light, and keep the soil evenly moist. Trim back overlong stems, and feed twice a month with 20-10-10 fertilizer. New plants root easily from cuttings.

Other good cultivars: 'Wilcoxii', 'Golden Pothos'

Satin Pathos

Satin Pathos

Epipremnum 'Satin'

❋ **Vining plant**
❋ **Gorgeous foliage**
❋ **Easy to grow**

Referred to as an *Epipremnum* (its scientific name) or a pothos (its common name), 'Satin' is a new introduction. Offering beautiful, satiny gray-green heart-shaped leaves, it grows slowly to 24 inches and is compact in habit.

Grow 'Satin' in a bright location. Plant it in a standard all-purpose houseplant soil, and be sure drainage is good. This plant does not tolerate overwatering. Feed quarterly with 20-10-10 plant food. A fine new edition to the pothos family, sure to become a traditional favorite, 'Satin' grows best in a small pot. Propagate from tip cuttings.

Aroid Family (*Araceae*) cont'd

Emerald Gem Homalomena

Homalomena rubescens 'Emerald Gem'

❋ **Small to medium size**
❋ **Lush decorative plant**
❋ **Handsome foliage**

The parent species of this attractive aroid cultivar with heart-shaped, dark green leaves is native to Java. 'Emerald Gem' tends to grow in the shape of a compact bouquet. This is a lush foliage plant that has been overlooked and has only recently become widely available. The heart-shaped leaves are especially desirable, and the plant stays compact.

Grow 'Emerald Gem' in dappled sunlight, in a rich potting soil kept evenly moist. Feed quarterly with 20-10-10 fertilizer. Wipe the leaves occasionally with a damp cloth to keep them clean. Repot infrequently; the plant dislikes having its roots disturbed. Propagate by division.

Emerald Gem Homalomena

Swiss Cheese Plant

Swiss Cheese Plant

Monstera deliciosa

❋ **Very large when mature**
❋ **Ideal for large tubs**
❋ **Generally easy to grow**

When young, this plant has smooth leaves. But as it matures and the leaves grow larger, the leaves develop deeply cut edges and wide holes, inspiring the nickname, "Swiss cheese plant". The slashes, holes, or cuts in the huge leaves enable them to withstand strong winds and heavy rains in their native Central America jungles. Mature plants can reach 8 or more feet in height, with leaves up to 18 inches long.

Grow this plant in a bright but not sunny location. Provide a large tub of standard all-purpose houseplant soil that drains well, and give the plant plenty of water. Use a trellis for added support. Feed monthly with a 10-10-10 fertilizer. Keep the plant away from drafts, and wipe the leaves using a damp cloth occasionally. Topdress with fresh soil once a year, and repot the plant only when it is potbound. Propagate from stem cuttings or by air layering.

Good cultivars: 'Albovariegata' and 'Laceleaf'

Nephthytis

Nephthytis hybrid

❋ **Small plant**
❋ **Handsome bronze foliage**
❋ **Easy to grow**

Striking broad, bronze foliage is the main asset of nephthytis, which is sometimes included in the genus Syngonium. But nephthytis is only a distant cousin to the plants in that genus, and there is little family resemblance.

Give nephthytis a bright, but not sunny location, and pot it in standard houseplant soil. Keep the soil evenly moist, and fertilize with 10-20-20 every month. Propagate by division.

Nephthytis

Philodendron

Philodendron

Philodendron squamiferum

❋ **Medium size**
❋ **Fine bushy philodendron**
❋ **Handsome hanging plant**

This attractive philodendron, with handsome lobed green leaves and fuzzy stems, is a slow grower that needs little attention.

Grow the plant in a bright but not sunny location. Plant it in a standard all-purpose houseplant soil. Let the soil dry out between waterings; the plant dislikes soggy conditions. Wipe leaves using a damp cloth occasionally to best display the glossy green foliage. Feed monthly with 10-10-10 fertilizer. Propagate by division.

Xanadu Philodendron

Philodendron 'Xanadu'

❋ **Medium size**
❋ **Needs minimal care**
❋ **Slow growing**

'Xanadu' is a recent introduction. Unlike the familiar trailing philodendrons, this handsome cultivar grows upright, to 30 inches tall, with shiny green lance-shaped leaves. It eventually resembles a bouquet of leaves.

Give this low-maintenance plant bright light without direct sun, and grow it in a standard all-purpose houseplant soil. Keep the soil evenly moist all year. Feed monthly with 20-10-10 fertilizer. Start new plants by division.

Xanadu Philodendron

Aroid Family (*Araceae*) cont'd

Domino Peace Lily
Spathiphyllum 'Domino'

✳ **Medium size**
✳ **Attractive foliage**
✳ **Fine vertical growth habit**

This beautiful new spathiphyllum cultivar has attractively mottled white-and-green lance-shaped leaves. 'Domino' grows to about 30 inches tall and achieves an elegant upright appearance.

To maintain the foliage variegation (contrasting colors within the leaves), this cultivar needs more light than the plain-leaved species. So grow this plant in bright light but not direct sun. Use standard all-purpose houseplant soil kept evenly moist except in winter, when the plant can be allowed to dry out somewhat. Feed quarterly with 20-10-10 fertilizer. Propagate by division.

Domino Peace Lily

White-flag Plant

White-flag Plant
Spathiphyllum floribundum

✳ **Large plant**
✳ **Rarely attacked by pests**
✳ **Easy to grow**

Spathiphyllums offer white flowers, consisting of a slender spadix surrounded by a hoodlike spathe, somewhat similar in structure to those of their aroid cousins, the anthuriums. From Colombia and South America, spathiphyllum species include several undemanding, adaptable houseplants that grow to 38 inches. They tolerate low levels of light. There are many cultivars to choose from.

Spathiphyllums prefer a bright location without direct sun. Plant them in standard all-purpose potting soil kept evenly moist except in winter, when it can be allowed to dry out somewhat between waterings. Note: This plant will not flower if it is not kept moist. Topdress yearly with fresh soil, and feed plants once a month with 20-20-10 fertilizer. Propagate by root division.

Good cultivars: 'Marion Wagne' and 'Mauna Loa'

Arrowhead Plant

Syngonium podophyllum

❋ **Medium-size climber**
❋ **Elegant**
❋ **Easy to grow**

Arrowhead Plant

The tropical syngoniums (sometimes called neph-thytis) are attractive, generally small plants that are bushy but vining. There are many hybrids offering colorful foliage.

Arrowhead plant is fast growing and easy to culti-vate. It prefers bright light without direct sun but will adapt to lower light. Give it well-drained soil kept evenly moist all year. Feed once a month with 10-10-10 fertil-izer. Support the climbing stems with a small trellis in the pot, or grow the plant in a hanging basket. Grow new plants from cuttings.

Good cultivars: 'Emerald Gem', 'Imperial White', 'Frosted Valentine'

Angel's Wings

Xanthosoma lindenii (aka *Caladium lindenii*)

❋ **Medium size**
❋ **Decorative white-marked leaves**
❋ **Easy to grow**

Marble Queen Pothos

This plant from Central America has attractive large white-veined leaves and grows to about 30 inches. Seldom encoun-tered at retail stores, this plant deserves more attention. If you don't find it at your plant store, you can inquire about ordering it.

Xanthosoma does best in a bright but not sunny loca-tion. Give it a small pot of standard houseplant soil kept evenly moist all year. Feed this plant monthly with 10-10-10 fertilizer. Propagate by division.

Zamioculcus zamifolia

Zamioculcus zamifolia

❋ **Overlooked plant**
❋ **Decorative**
❋ **Good accent plant**

Hailing from East Africa, this Cycad-looking plant has thick rhizomes and stalks of small, dark, wavy leaves with yellow veins. It bears small flowers at its base. Although it is not often seen, it is a worthwhile plant to add to your collection. It likes somewhat dry soil and will tolerate shade. This plant is relatively pest free and very robust. Propagate from leaves. Feed four times a year with 10-10-5 fertilizer.

Aroid Family (*Araceae*) cont'd

Golden Calla Lily
Zantedeschia elliottiana

❋ **Small to medium size**
❋ **Pretty, colorful flowers**
❋ **Easy to grow**

Most small calla lily cultivars available today grow to 20 inches and have large, oblong leaves. Many splendid short-stemmed flowers consisting of a slender spadix surrounded by a smooth hoodlike spathe are produced on each plant. Calla lilies grow from bulblike structures called rhizomes and are easily started almost any time of year. They are generally available around Easter.

Keep this calla in a bright, somewhat sunny location while it is growing. Wet the soil until water drains from the bottom of the pot. It's time to water when the soil is dry an inch down. Use a rich soil, but there's no need to fertilize. After blooming, rest it for three months; then repot rhizomes in fresh soil.

Golden Calla Lily

Pink Calla Lily

Pink Calla Lily
Zantedeschia rehmannii

❋ **Small to medium**
❋ **Lovely pink flowers**
❋ **Easy to grow**

This charming plant from South Africa has handsome green leaves and pretty pink flowers with the classic calla lily form. Other color forms are available in pastel shades as well as classic white. The plant is easily grown from a rhizome and is now available in supermarkets at holidays.

Grow the pink calla in a bright location, in humusy soil that drains readily. Keep the soil evenly moist. Plant rhizomes any time you find them for sale; flowers appear in 6 to 8 weeks. Do not feed the plant. Propagate from rhizomes.

Begonia Family
(*Begoniaceae*)

Cleopatra Begonia
Begonia 'Cleopatra'

❋ **Large basket plant**
❋ **Stunning foliage**
❋ **Tolerates low light**

Handsome, colorful maple-shaped leaves make this begonia a favorite. It's also an excellent hanging plant, growing to 36 inches in diameter. Small pink flowers are borne in clusters in summer, but the foliage is the asset. Use this plant to brighten dim corners of rooms.

'Cleopatra' grows in moderate light. It likes standard all-purpose houseplant soil kept evenly moist all year. Trim back the stems occasionally to keep it compact. Feed monthly with 20-10-10 fertilizer. Propagate from leaf cuttings.

Cleopatra Begonia

Reiger Begonia

Reiger Begonia
Begonia × *hiemalis*

❋ **Medium size**
❋ **Many flowers**
❋ **Easy to grow**

Reiger begonias bear abundant blooms in a range of bright colors—yellow, red, and orange—akin to tuberous begonias. These compact, bushy plants grow from a corm (bulb) and reach 20 inches tall with dark green leaves. Reiger begonias are often sold as gift plants.

Give Reiger begonias a bright location with some sun. They need evenly moist all-purpose potting soil. Unless you provide thorough drainage, the plants will soon perish. Most Reiger begonias are used as temporary plants—expect them to last six months or so. To keep them growing, repot in fresh soil annually. Feed semi-annually with 10-20-10 fertilizer. Reigers are difficult to propagate, so purchase new plants from suppliers.

Begonia Family (*Begoniaceae*) cont'd

Kewensis Begonia
Begonia 'Kewensis'

❋ **Grows quickly to 40 inches**
❋ **Handsome dark green foliage**
❋ **Lovely hanging plant**

Striking angel-wing bronze foliage creates a dense-leaved halo of color around this choice hybrid. Small white flowers appear in spring and summer. The mature plant is stunning on a tabletop or trailing in a hanging basket.

Keep in bright light for maximum leaf color. Grow in standard all-purpose houseplant soil that's kept evenly moist. Feed monthly with 10-10-10 fertilizer. Propagate by division.

Kewensis Begonia

Red-leaf Begonia
Begonia hybrid

❋ **Excellent medium-size hanging plant**
❋ **Lovely red foliage**
❋ **Easy to grow**

Red-leaf Begonia

Rounded, red-hued leaves are this begonia's main asset. Plant in a hanging basket, and the somewhat pendant stems will trail attractively. Red-leaf begonia grows rapidly to 30 inches in diameter and requires little care.

Place Red-leaf begonia in a brightly lit location out of direct sun. Grow in standard all-purpose houseplant soil that drains readily. Keep the soil evenly moist all year. Red-leaf tolerates both cool and warm home temperatures. Feed quarterly with 10-10-10 fertilizer. Propagate by division.

Iron Cross
Begonia masoniana

❋ **Many varieties**
❋ **Handsome foliage**
❋ **Easy to grow**

This plant from Southeast Asia has a dark cross on the leaves, making it a desirable and unusual addition to your home. They look their best when massed three plants to a pot. Few begonias require exacting care and the Iron Cross is no exception. It thrives with little attention. Do not overwater, although the plant does like humidity. Do not get water on leaves as they spot easily. Feed with 10-10-5 four times a year. Propagate new plants by pressing leaves in soil.

Iron Cross

Angel-Wing Begonia

Begonia hybrid

❊ **Medium size**
❊ **Many flowers**
❊ **Handsome in baskets**

The canelike stems of angel-wing begonias cascade gracefully from hanging baskets and grow to about 30 inches. The leaves are shaped like angel's wings and may be light or dark green, solidly colored, or spotted with white. During warm months, angel-wing begonias bear masses of small flowers.

Most angel-wings need a sunny location and plenty of water. They don't do well in drafts. Grow in all-purpose houseplant soil. Feed with 20-10-10 plant food. Maintain a vigil for insects. Propagate from leaf, stem, or tip cuttings.

Angel-wing Begonia

Picotee Begonia

Begonia 'Picotee'

❊ **Medium size**
❊ **Long-lasting flowers**
❊ **Many flowers**

With long-lasting, profuse blooms that come in many colors, this easy-to-grow Reiger begonia is a houseplant favorite. Even small plants bloom.

Grow 'Picotee' in a bright location in rich soil. Feed twice a year with 20-10-10 fertilizer. Keep the soil evenly moist during bloom time. After blooming, the plant needs a rest period, so water sparingly then. 'Picotee' generally blooms again in about three months. Propagate by division.

Picotee Begonia

Begonia Family (*Begoniaceae*) cont'd

Rex Begonia
Begonia Rex-Cultorum hybrid

❋ **Compact habit, medium size**
❋ **Exquisite colorful foliage**
❋ **Moderate light**

Sometimes called tapestry plants because of their exquisite foliage, rex begonia hybrids have been favorite houseplants for decades. There are now hundreds of hybrids. The wing-shaped foliage has irregularly notched or ruffled edges and is streaked, veined, and splashed with combinations of silver or various shades of green, pink, rose, red, maroon, purple, brown, or black. The plants grow to 24 inches.

Grow rex begonias in bright to moderate light in a rich soil. Keep the soil evenly moist, and fertilize twice a year with 10-10-10 plant food. Avoid getting water on leaves, or they will spot. Start new plants from leaf cuttings.

Rex Begonia

Wax Begonia

Wax Begonia
Begonia Semperflorens-Cultorum hybrid

❋ **Small plant**
❋ **Many flowers**
❋ **Tolerates neglect**

Today's wax begonias flower freely in white and in many shades of red and pink. (Older varieties were small and not too attractive.) The waxy leaves come in burgundy, bright green, dark green, and variegated with white. For quick color the wax begonia is tough to beat, and some varieties are almost everblooming indoors. Plants are small, so you should grow several in a decorative pot for greater impact.

Grow wax begonias in a bright location in rich soil kept evenly moist all year. Feed monthly with 10-10-10 fertilizer. Trim back the foliage occasionally, and keep plants out of drafts. Propagate by division.

Maple-leaf Begonia

Begonia superba 'Rana'

✳ **Large plant**
✳ **Handsome foliage**
✳ **Easy to grow**

The unusual reddish brown foliage of the 'Rana' maple-leaf begonia makes it one of the handsomest in this huge family. A tall, upright plant, it has a decorative appearance for interiors. The pink flowers borne in winter are another asset.

Plant 'Rana' in evenly moist all-purpose soil, and place it in an airy location with some sun. Feed quarterly with 10-10-10 fertilizer, and prune away lower leaves as the plant matures. Produce new plants by division.

Maple-leaf
Begonia

Bromeliad Family (*Bromeliaceae*)

Urn Plant

Aechmea fasciata

✳ **Medium size**
✳ **Long-lasting floral bracts**
✳ **Good room decoration**

With stiff, arching leaves that have undersides frosted with silvery scales, urn plant is the most popular bromeliad. Like its cousin, silver urn plant (shown on page 140), urn plant has a crown of pink bracts that lasts for months surrounding tiny blue flowers. Most kinds of urn plant have frosted mottled-green foliage.

Grow urn plant in a bright location, and pot it in fine-grade fir bark. Keep the plant's "urn" filled with water, and change it weekly. Keep the fir bark slightly moist. Maintain moderate temperatures, and do not fertilize. Two misconceptions about this and other bromeliad are that putting an apple inside the urn will make them bloom and that insects will gather in the urn when grown indoors. Neither is true. Propagate from offsets.

Urn Plant

Bromeliad Family (*Bromeliaceae*) cont'd

Silver Urn Plant

Aechmea chantinii hybrid

❋ **Large plant**
❋ **Long-lasting floral bracts**
❋ **Easy to grow**

Urn plants originated in South America and are named for their "urn" of leaves that catches water. Their genus name, *Aechmea*, is derived from the Greek, meaning "spear point." Indeed, the plants have stiff, pointed leaves and tiny blue flowers surrounded by pointed, stiff pink bracts.

Grow urn plants in a bright location but out of direct sun. The plant does best in a mix of equal parts potting soil and fine-grade fir bark kept evenly moist. Always keep the "urn" of the plant filled with water, and change it weekly. Do not fertilize. Maintain moderate temperatures that never drop below 55°F at night. Keep the plant in its pot until the flowers fade, and then let it die naturally. Start new plants from offsets.

Black Velvet Alocasia

Variegated Pineapple Plant

Variegated Pineapple Plant

Ananas cosmosus 'Variegatus'

❋ **Dwarf to large varieties**
❋ **Novelty plant**
❋ **Not easy to grow**

Spanish conquistadores discovered the pineapple plant in South America in the early 1700s, and European royalty enjoyed eating the sweet, exotic fruit. Pineapple plants are slow growing and fussy about conditions. Variegated pineapple plant, shown here, has leaves colored in a blend of green, cream, and sometimes red. It bears blue flowers and nonedible bitter red fruit. The species' standard size is large and spiny when mature, so also look for the dwarf species, *Ananas nanus*, which grows to about 15 inches tall.

Grow pineapple plants in fine-grade fir bark, and keep the center of the plant filled with water. As with other bromeliad, change the water in the urn every week. This plant is fussy about cultivation, but is an attractive novelty. Propagate from offsets.

Fantasia Bromeliad

Billbergia 'Fantasia'

❊ **Medium size**
❊ **Long-lasting flower crown**
❊ **Easy to grow**

This bromeliad hybrid appears frequently in collections because it is free flowering and easy to grow. It has a purple-and-red inflorescence, or flower cluster, and leaves mottled with cream. This tube-shaped, vertical plant grows to 30 inches tall. Although not as spectacular as some bromeliad, it is dependable.

Grow 'Fantasia' bromeliad in fine-grade fir bark, and keep the medium evenly moist but never soggy. Do not fertilize. Provide a bright location out of direct sun, and keep temperatures above 50°F at night. Propagate from offsets.

Fantasia Bromeliad

Earth Star

Cryptanthus and hybrids

❊ **Small plant**
❊ **Colorful foliage**
❊ **Easy to grow**

The plants in the genus *Cryptanthus* are small (to 14 inches in diameter). New cultivars constantly appear, one more colorful than the other. Grow these plants for their crinkly leaves. 'Tricolor' has the star-shaped rosette form and slender leaves that are strikingly tri-colored: green, white, and pink.

Earth stars respond to basic care. Give them bright light without direct sun to fully develop the foliage color. Pot earth stars in equal parts potting soil and fine-grade fir bark, and grow them in small pots because the plants like to be potbound. Keep the soil evenly moist, and fertilize quarterly with 20-10-10 fertilizer. Start new plants from offsets.

Earth Star

Bromeliad Family (*Bromeliaceae*) cont'd

Orange Star Bromeliad
Guzmania lingulata 'Orange Star'

❋ **Medium size**
❋ **Long lasting floral bracts**
❋ **Easy to grow**

From South America, the genus *Guzmania* comprises some 70 species, many of which are stellar houseplants. 'Orange Star' grows in a rosette, almost fan-shaped, form to about 24 inches across. Orange bracts that stay colorful for five months encircle the small, white, true flowers in the plant's center.

Guzmanias like a bright location out of direct sun. They thrive in a mix of equal parts fine-grade fir bark and potting soil. Keep the medium evenly moist, and change the water in the urn weekly. Do not fertilize. Plants bloom once and then die, but produce many small offsets, which you can propagate.

Orange Star Bromeliad

Rana Bromeliad
Guzmania lingulata 'Rana'

❋ **Medium size**
❋ **Elegant appearance**
❋ **Colorful at bloom time**

Rana Bromeliad

This new *Guzmania* hybrid has somewhat larger flower heads than the species, and its fine green foliage grows in an attractive rosette. The plant grows to 30 inches tall. It thrives under the average temperature and humidity conditions of most homes and rarely needs attention. Wipe the leaves using a damp cloth to keep plant healthy.

Give 'Rana' a bright location out of direct sun. Plant this bromeliad in fine-grade fir bark, and keep it evenly moist. Keep water in the plant's center, and remember to change the water weekly. Propagate from offsets. See Chapter 6, "Propagating Houseplants," page 82, for detailed instruction on dividing offsets from bromeliad.

Poker Plant
Guzmania zahnii

❋ **Medium size**
❋ **Compact fountainlike growth**
❋ **Easy to grow**

The tall flower spike of this handsome small plant from Brazil rises from the plant's center covered with tiny yellow flowers. The plant stays in bloom for many weeks and makes a good table accent. It grows to 24 inches across.

Grow in a bright location out of direct sun. Plant in fir bark, and keep the medium evenly moist all year. Keep plant's center filled with water, and change the water weekly. Do not fertilize. Propagate from offsets.

Poker Plant

Striped Neoregelia

Neoregelia carolinae forma *tricolor*

❋ **Medium size**
❋ **Stunning color**
❋ **Easy to grow**

This South American bromeliad appeared in cultivation about 1940 and created a sensation with its handsome multicolored leaves and bright-red flower bracts. The leaves—striped with green, creamy white, and pink—grow in a compact rosette to 28 inches. At bloom time, the leaves near the plant's center turn bright red. Best of all, this plant is easy to grow. Display it on a low table, so its striking colors can be seen easily.

Provide a bright sunny location. Grow the plant in a mix of equal parts fine-grade fir bark and potting soil, and keep the mix moderately moist all year. Feed twice a year with 20-10-10 fertilizer. Propagate from offsets, which form at the base.

Striped
Neoregelia

Royal Burgundy
Bromeliad

Royal Burgundy Bromeliad

Neoregelia 'Royal Burgundy'

❋ **Medium size**
❋ **Extraordinary leaf color**
❋ **Easy to grow**

Unlike many other bromeliad, neoregelias are grown primarily for their handsome leaves. This decorative hybrid has burgundy-colored foliage and grows to about 36 inches tall. Because it needs little attention, this is a good bromeliad for beginners.

Give 'Royal Burgundy' a bright location with some sun to produce good foliage color, and plant it in fine-grade fir bark. Water sparingly so that the planting medium is barely moist all year. Keep the center of the plant filled with water, and change the water monthly. Start new plants from offsets.

Bromeliad Family (*Bromeliaceae*) cont'd

Blushing Bromeliad

Neoregelia hybrid

✽ **Medium size**
✽ **Handsome foliage**
✽ **Fine interior decorative plant**

This *Neoregelia* from Brazil has stunning leaves blotched green and red. Growing in a rosette form, the plant has the tubular central urn typical of bromeliad and grows to 30 inches tall.

Give this bromeliad a place in bright light but without direct sun. Use a potting medium of fine-grade fir bark. The root system is small, so water sparingly, keeping the bark barely moist all year. Keep the plant's urn filled with water, and change the water weekly. Do not fertilize. Start new plants from offsets.

Blushing Bromeliad

Fingernail Plant

Neoregelia spectabilis

✽ **Medium size**
✽ **Leaves bright red at center**
✽ **Easy to grow**

The center and tips of this Brazilian native's leaves turn scarlet at bloom time, the tips inspiring the painted fingernail image in the common name. Small violet flowers are hidden deep in the center.

Grow in bright conditions, near east- and south-facing windows. Pot in fine-grade fir bark, and keep the bark evenly moist. Do not fertilize. The plant does best in normal household temperatures that never drop below 60°F. Propagate from offsets.

Fingernail Plant

Plume Bromeliad

Tillandsia cyanea

✽ **Small to medium size**
✽ **Handsome pink bracts**
✽ **Easy to grow**

Plume Bromeliad

With a low rosette of narrow green leaves and a pink plumelike flower stalk that bears large, short-lived violet-purple flowers, plume bromeliad commands attention. This Ecuadorian plant was once available only in a large size, to about 40 inches. Now there are dwarf cultivars to 10 inches.

Grow this plant in a bright location out of direct sun. Plant in small pots in fine-grade fir bark. Keep the bark medium-moist, but never soggy. Maintain normal household temperatures. Feed twice a year with 20-20-10 fertilizer. Propagate from offsets.

Tufted Bromeliad

Tillandsia ionantha

❋ **Small epiphytic plant**
❋ **Colorful foliage**
❋ **Easy to grow—even foolproof**

Forming a tiny fountain of grayish green leaves, the center of which turns blood red at bloom time in summer, this little bromeliad is not to be missed. It's an epiphyte, meaning that its roots take moisture and nutrients from the air rather than from soil. Like other epiphytes, this one grows best wired to a piece of wood. It grows to only about 4 inches in diameter and is a fascinating conversation piece.

Tufted bromeliad needs a sunny place and does best when misted with water almost daily. It does not grow well in a pot. Instead, choose a piece of branch or wood of some type to support it. Wire the plant in place; eventually it will take hold. Do not fertilize. Start new plants from offsets.

Tufted Bromeliad

Yellow Poker Plant

Vriesea hybrid

❋ **Grows easily to 30 inches**
❋ **Beautiful yellow plume-like flower heads**
❋ **Dramatic color**

This *Vriesea* hybrid bears an exotic tri-colored yellow flower head on which the inflorescence, or flower cluster, stays fresh for many weeks.

Grow yellow poker plant in a bright, somewhat sunny location. Pot it in fine-grade fir bark. Keep the center of the plant filled with water, and be sure to change the water weekly. Do not fertilize. Propagate new plants from offsets.

Note: Flower heads remain in color for many weeks and, in time, dry naturally on the plant. The flower heads can then be cut and used in long-lasting dried flower arrangements.

Yellow Poker Plantaq

Bromeliad Family (*Bromeliaceae*) cont'd

Poelmanii Flaming Sword
Vriesea poelmanii

✳ **Small to medium-size plant**
✳ **Fiery red flower bracts**
✳ **Colorful for months**

A large, fiery red, narrow plumelike flower head makes this bromeliad from South America a popular choice. The plant grows to about 24 inches.

Grow flaming sword in a sunny location, and pot it in fine-grade fir bark. The plant will also grow on a chunk of tree branch or a slab of bark. Water frequently in warm weather, and keep the central urn of the plant filled with water, but change it weekly. Feeding is not really necessary, but the plant likes good ventilation. Start new plants from offsets that form at the base of the plant.

Blushing Bromeliad

Flaming Sword

Flaming Sword
Vriesea splendens

✳ **Medium size**
✳ **Long-lasting flower head**
✳ **Easy to grow**

Flaming sword bears a distinctive reddish orange sword-shaped flower cluster on an erect stem. This plant has been popular since the late nineteenth century, and today there are countless hybrids.

Flaming sword can tolerate low light but does best in bright light. Pot it in fine-grade fir bark, and keep the bark evenly moist all year. Like other vrieseas, flaming sword prefers warm conditions in which the temperature never drops below 60°F at night. Keep the center of the plant filled with water, and change the water weekly. Propagate from offsets.

Other good species: *V. × mariae, V. schwackeana*

Cacti and Succulents (Various Families)

Desert Rose

Adenium obesum

✳ **Medium size**
✳ **Pretty pink flowers**
✳ **Easy to grow**

The unusual treelike shape and clusters of handsome pink flowers in summer make this succulent particularly desirable. Desert rose has an attractive branching growth habit and grows to 30 inches. It deserves to be more widely used in homes.

Grow desert rose in bright light in a mix of equal parts potting soil and sharp sand. Keep the medium barely moist all year—this plant does not tolerate overwatering. Feed quarterly with 10-10-10 fertilizer. Don't attempt to propagate new plants at home; instead, purchase them from suppliers.

Desert Rose

Peanut Cactus

Chamaecereus sylvestrii (aka *Echinopsis chamaecereus*)

✳ **Small plant**
✳ **Fine red flowers**
✳ **Easy to grow**

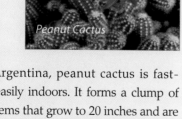

Peanut Cactus

Originally from Argentina, peanut cactus is fast-growing and blooms easily indoors. It forms a clump of branching, columnar stems that grow to 20 inches and are covered with soft spines. On a young plant, the stems resemble peanuts. Orange-red flowers appear in summer.

Place peanut cactus in a warm, sunny location. Grow in a mix of equal parts sharp sand and potting soil kept evenly moist. Use small pots for best growth. Feed twice a year with 20-10-10 fertilizer. Repot the plant only occasionally, because it takes time to recover after being disturbed. Propagate from offsets.

Jade Tree

Crassula ovata (aka *Crassula argentea*)

✳ **Medium size**
✳ **Leaves resemble small pieces of jade**
✳ **Easy to grow**

This wonderful bushlike plant grows to 30 inches or more over time. If given enough light, jade plant bears small whitish flowers in summer. Large plants in decorative containers are quite attractive.

Grow in a bright location, and pot in standard houseplant soil. Keep the soil somewhat dry all year. Feed quarterly with 20-10-10 fertilizer. Occasionally clean the leaves using a damp cloth. Propagate from leaf cuttings.

Jade Tree

Cacti and Succulents (Various Families) cont'd

False Rose
Echeveria hybrid

❋ **Small plant**
❋ **Handsome roselike growth**
❋ **Easy to grow**

Many echeverias have flowers resembling small open-faced roses in shades of pink or yellow. This unnamed hybrid has bronze gold leaves in a small rosette to 12 inches across. It's perfect as a table decoration and doesn't need much attention.

Grow in a mix of equal parts sharp sand and potting soil kept barely moist all year. Keep in bright light but out of direct sun. Feed quarterly with 20-20-10 fertilizer. Propagate from offsets.

False Rose

Orchid Cactus
Epiphyllum spc.

❋ **Great flowers**
❋ **Crawling plant**
❋ **Nice active**

Orchid Cactus

These large hanging plants, mostly epiphytic, grow to 4 feet when grown as natural trailers in baskets. If staked and grown upright, they reach 20 inches. Grow this cactus for its fine, large flowers. The leaves are spindly and unattractive, but the flowers are beautiful. They are famous for evening blooms of red, pink, purple, or white, with peak color in May and June. Hybrids have also been developed for day bloom.

Keep plants pot-bound and in a bright window. They need space. Keep them well watered all year, but never let them dry out. Take cuttings in spring for new plants. Feed with 10-10-5 every other month.

Crown-of-thorns
Euphorbia milii

❋ **Thorny medium-size plant**
❋ **Small red flowers**
❋ **Blooms in winter**

This unusual-looking poinsettia relative from Africa commands attention, especially in winter, when it blooms abundantly. Dense and shrubby, the plant has thorny stems but offers fine green color and red, pink, or yellow flowers.

Grow near a bright window. Plant in a 6- or 8-inch pot, and use equal parts sharp sand and potting soil. Keep the mix evenly moist all year, especially during the fall. Keep water away from the leaves. Feed quarterly with 20-20-10 fertilizer, and never allow the temperature to drop below 60°F at night. Propagate from stem cuttings.

Crown-of-thorns

Gymnocalycium baldiana

❋ **Small and pretty**
❋ **Needs little care**
❋ **Good dish plant**

Gymnocalycium baldiana

This interesting desert cacti is a real curiosity and nice if you are looking for a plant that is different from others in your cacti collection. It grows to 12 inches, with red, white, yellow, or chartreuse flowers that usually open in spring and summer. Grow in full sun in sandy moist soil. Grows on its own and needs little care. Feed four times a year with 10-10-5. Group with other cacti and succulents. Propagate by offsets, and beware of spines.

Wax Plant, Porcelain Flower

Hoya carnosa

❋ **Very large**
❋ **Available in many improved cultivars**
❋ **Easy to grow, thrives on neglect**

Wax Plant, Porcelain Flower

The wax plant is really a vine with deep green succulent leaves and clusters of waxy, honey-scented white to pale pink flowers with red crowns, which may drip nectar. The plant needs time to adjust when you bring it home, but don't give up on it, for it may not bloom lavishly until two or three years old.

Wax plant needs full sun to bloom and blooms best when potbound. Don't remove the stem, or spur, on which the flowers have been produced because it's the source of next season's bloom. Grow in standard all-purpose houseplant soil. Water plentifully in spring and summer but not as much in winter, when the soil can be allowed to become quite dry. Propagate from stem, leaf, or tip cuttings taken in spring.

Felt Bush, Velvet Leaf

Kalanchoe beharensis

❋ **Medium size to large**
❋ **Interesting leaves**
❋ **Tolerates neglect**

Mostly native to Madagascar and Africa, this kalanchoe is dubbed teddy bear plant because its thick leaves are softly fuzzy. Decorative year-round, it can grow to 40 inches.

Plant in a bright location. This plant needs a somewhat sandy soil, so add some sharp sand to standard houseplant soil. Water evenly all year, but keep the soil dryish, never allowing it to become very wet. Keep water away from leaves, or they will rot. Feed every third month with 10-10-10 fertilizer. Propagate from leaf cuttings.

Felt Bush, Velvet Leaf

Cacti and Succulents (Various Families) cont'd

Starfire Kalanchoe
Kalanchoe blossfeldiana

✳ **Small plant**
✳ **Available in several colors**
✳ **Can bloom twice a year**

With succulent green leaves and pretty bunches of red, orange, yellow, or beige flowers that bloom twice yearly, starfire kalanchoe is a winning houseplant.

Provide bright light. Grow in a 6- or 8-inch pot of standard all-purpose houseplant soil. Keep the soil evenly moist except after bloom. Then, in order to force another flush of flowers, decrease watering and do not fertilize for at least six to eight weeks. This kalanchoe likes average household temperatures. Start new plants from stem cuttings.

Starfire Kalanchoe

Dinner-plate Kalanchoe

Dinner-plate Kalanchoe
Kalanchoe thyrsiflora

✳ **Medium size**
✳ **Exquisitely colored leaves**
✳ **Highly recommended**

The succulent greenish gray, red-tinged leaves of this unusual-looking plant from South Africa are as large as dinner plates. This plant grows to 24 inches tall and offers a lot of color.

Dinner-plate kalanchoe thrives in bright light. Plant it in a potting mix of equal parts houseplant soil and sharp sand. Keep the medium evenly moist, but do not overwater. Feed quarterly with 20-10-10 fertilizer. The plant tolerates temperatures down to 55°F at night. Because propagation is difficult at home, purchase new plants from suppliers instead.

Globe Cactus
Mammillaria celsiana (aka Mammillaria muehlenpfordtii)

✳ **Small plant**
✳ **Globe-shaped**
✳ **Easy to grow**

Sculptural and globe-shaped, this durable Mexican native is covered with short yellow spines. In summer, purplish red flowers appear. Globe cactus grows to only 4 inches tall and about 5 inches in diameter.

Grow globe cactus in a bright window. If the plant receives sun, it may reward you with rosy blooms. Plant in a mix of equal parts potting soil and sharp sand; keep the medium just moist, never really wet or dry. Feed every three months with 20-10-10 fertilizer. Propagate from offsets.

Globe Cactus

Pachyphytum Plant
Pachyphytum species

✳ **Medium size**
✳ **Bright green succulent leaves**
✳ **Easy to grow**

This handsome, slow-growing succulent has pale green, almond-shaped, thick leaves. A compact plant, it grows to 30 inches tall and looks good in a hanging basket. If you don't find this plant when shopping, inquire about ordering it. It's a reliable performer that survives neglect.

Pachyphytums need dappled sunlight. Plant in standard all-purpose potting soil that drains well. Allow the soil to dry out between waterings. Feed only twice a year, in spring and summer, with 20-10-10 fertilizer. Propagate new plants from stem cuttings.

Pachyphytum Plant

Cacti and Succulents (Various Families) cont'd

Ball Cactus
Parodia penicillata

❋ **Small plant**
❋ **Orange-red flowers**
❋ **Easy to grow**

From Argentina and Bolivia, this globular plant with light-colored spines sports handsome orange-red flowers in summer that emerge from the top of the "ball" but last only a few days. This 6-inch cactus makes a good table or desk accent.

Grow in a sunny location in equal parts potting soil and sharp sand that drains well. Keep the medium somewhat moist but never soggy. Feed twice a year with 20-10-10 fertilizer. Propagate from offsets.

Ball Cactus

Easter Cactus
Rhipsalidopsis rosea
(aka *Hatiora rosea*)

❋ **Medium size**
❋ **Spring blooming**
❋ **Abundant flowers**

Easter Cactus

Nineteenth-century plant collectors discovered this plant in the rain forests of South America. It does its ancestors proud. Easter cactus is a stellar performer that produces dozens of small cerise flowers in spring. Growing to 24 inches high, these plants have gracefully arching stems composed of flat oblong segments. This is a jungle cactus, not a desert type, so it needs different growing conditions than those required by cacti from arid environments.

Grow Easter cactus in bright light but out of direct sun. Pot in organically rich soil that contains some humus. Water the soil evenly all year, but decrease watering for a few weeks after blooming to let the plant rest. Keep humidity high by misting with water daily. Routine care will bring another bloom of flowers in a year's time. Feed monthly with 10-20-10 fertilizer. Propagate from cuttings.

Crown Plant

Crown Plant
Rebutia hybrid

❋ **Delightful red flowers**
❋ **Small grower**
❋ **Needs sun**

Also known as the fireball cactus, this is a small gem. It is a round globe that in summer sports tiny red flowers making it a very desirable indoor plant. Grow in sun. These desert species require more water than most cacti except in winter when they can be grown cool (55°F) and somewhat dry. Although small, this is a tough plant that sometimes bears flowers twice a year. Dwarf varieties are available. Propagate by cuttings.

Keep soil somewhat dry and feed only twice a year with 10-10-5.

Pencil Cactus

Rhipsalis species

❉ **Medium size**
❉ **Succulent, pencil-thin leaves**
❉ **Easy to grow**

These exotic-looking jungle cacti have slender upright or trailing stems, that look best in hanging baskets. In their native habitat, these epiphytic plants grow directly on tree bark.

Provide pencil cactus a location with dappled sunlight, similar to the light filtering through overhead trees in a jungle. Plant in equal parts potting soil and fine-grade fir bark kept just barely moist all year. Do not overwater. Feed quarterly with 20-10-10 fertilizer. Propagate by division.

Pencil Cactus

Christmas Cactus

Christmas Cactus

Schlumbergera × *buckleyi* (aka *Zygocactus*)

❉ **Small to medium-size plant**
❉ **Seasonal blooms**
❉ **Easy to grow**

Formerly included in the genus Zygocactus, Christmas cactus graces homes with lovely blooms in time for the holidays. This plant was developed in cultivation and is not found in the wild. Over 200 named cultivars are available, blooming in shades of red, rose, pink, and purple, as well as satiny white. The arching, branched stems are made up of flat, jointed segments with smoothly scalloped edges.

Christmas cactus prefers reasonably bright light from an eastern exposure, with a bit of direct sun in winter. Plant in a mix of equal parts potting soil and fine-grade fir bark, and keep the medium evenly moist all year. The plant does best in normal household temperatures and needs cool nights (to 55°F) for buds to develop. Feed monthly with 20-10-10 fertilizer. You don't need to keep the plant in the dark to encourage blooming. Keeping it away from artificial light at night for a few months prior to the holiday should be sufficient to promote flowering. Propagate from cuttings.

Cacti and Succulents (Various Families) cont'd

Thanksgiving Cactus

Schlumbergera truncata

❋ **Small to medium-size plant**
❋ **Seasonal blooms**
❋ **Easy to grow**

Thanksgiving cactus is epiphytic, growing on trees in the jungles of Brazil. In fall, multitudes of brightly colored red, rose, or pink flowers bloom at the tips of the stems.

Thanksgiving cactus needs bright light from an eastern exposure, with some direct sun in winter. Plant in a mix of equal parts potting soil and fine-grade fir bark, and keep the medium evenly moist all year. Provide normal household temperatures. Feed monthly with 20-10-10 fertilizer. To promote Thanksgiving flowering, keep away from artificial light at night a few months prior to the holiday. Propagate from cuttings.

Thanksgiving Cactus

Donkey's Tail

Donkey's Tail

Sedum morganianum

❋ **Medium-size to large plant**
❋ **Cascading leaves**
❋ **Easy to grow**

The weight of this plant's succulent leaves causes mature branches to cascade like a donkey's tail. The stems of young plants are upright. If conditions are right, the plant bears small pink flowers.

Grow donkey's tail in a mix of equal parts sharp sand and potting soil, and keep the mix just barely moist. Provide full sun from a south window. Avoid placing the plant in drafts. Use a hanging container so that the stems can trail over the sides. Feed every two months with 20-20-10 fertilizer. Donkey's tail is difficult to propagate under home conditions. Buy new plants from suppliers.

Starfish Flower
Stapelia gigantea

✳ **Medium size**
✳ **Bizarre malodorous flowers**
✳ **Handsome sculptural form**

Like many succulent houseplants, starfish flower is native to South Africa. It caused a sensation when first presented for sale in the mid-nineteenth century. The star-shaped flowers are large—to 7 inches across—luridly colored and generally malodorous. Compact, the plant rarely grows more than 24 inches tall. With its handsome, dark green, grooved high columns, it's a fine plant for a windowsill. The flowers droop and usually appear in summer.

Grow starfish flower in a sunny spot. Grow in equal parts fine-grade fir bark and potting soil. Keep the medium barely moist all year; do not overwater. Feed quarterly with 10-10-10 fertilizer. Propagate by division.

Starfish Flower

Torch Cactus

Torch Cactus
Trichocereus candicans (aka *Echinocereus candicans*)

✳ **Large plant**
✳ **Columnar**
✳ **Slow grower**

From Argentina, this columnar cactus with yellow spines grows to 40 inches. It rarely flowers indoors and is used like sculpture. Many varieties are available, all similar in appearance.

Grow in a bright location, in all-purpose houseplant soil. You can add sand, but do not grow the plant only in sand. Keep the soil barely moist. Feed monthly with 10-10-10 fertilizer. Purchase new plants from suppliers.

Euphorbia Family (*Euphorbiaceae*)

Chenille Plant

Chenille Plant

Acalypha hispida

❋ **Excellent medium-size plant**
❋ **Distinctive**
❋ **Needs regular care**

Chenille plant thrives in a large container, producing unusual strings of tiny pinkish red flowers on and off throughout the year.

Provide a brightly lit location, with sun in winter. Grow in standard all-purpose houseplant soil, and feed monthly with 10-10-10 fertilizer. Provide high humidity and moderate temperatures. Propagate from cuttings.

Snow Bush

Breynia nivosa

❋ **Overlooked plant**
❋ **Decorative fern-like leaves**
❋ **Impossible to kill**

Snow Bush

Lacy and delicate this plant adds much beauty. Its pendent fern-like leaves are laced with white, earning it its name. This variety grows to 18 inches, making it an excellent vertical accent. It grows quickly and is fine for shady indoor places. Keep soil moist. Watch for insects. In the same family with croton, poinsettia, tapioca. Propagate by suckers or cuttings.

The small leaves and stems can be pruned if necessary. Feed with 10-10-5 monthly.

Croton

Croton

Codiaeum variegatum var. pictum

❋ **Medium-size to large plant**
❋ **Colorful foliage**
❋ **Needs some attention**

This sun-lover from Malaysia and southern India is known for its brightly colored foliage in various shades and combinations of green, red, orange, yellow, pink, and white.

Plant crotons in a large pot of standard all-purpose houseplant soil. Keep the soil evenly moist all year, and feed every other week with 20-10-10 fertilizer. Propagate from cuttings.

Croton

Codiaeum variegatum var. ebumeum

❋ **Fine for indoors**
❋ **Colorful foliage**
❋ **Many varieties**

There are dozens and dozens of crotons, one prettier than the other. All do well indoors. Striking multicolored foliage makes these splendid accent plants that grow to 3 feet or more. Foliage form varies, and colors run from pale yellow to pink, orange, red, and brown, with many shades of green, as shown here. To grow these well, give them attention. Set them where there is good air circulation and 2 to 3 hours of sun. Keep soil evenly moist, except in December and January; then decrease watering somewhat. Maintain high humidity, to 70 percent, by misting. Watch out for red spider mites. The sap of the plant stains, so wear gloves when handling. Seed capsules explode. Leaves are excellent for arrangements. Propagate from cuttings. There are countless cultivars. Feed four times a year with 10-10-5.

Croton

Poinsettia

Euphorbia pulcherrima

❋ **Great medium-size to large seasonal plant**
❋ **Glowing red bracts**
❋ **Needs a dark period for 10 weeks to rebloom**

Poinsettia

A Mexican native, the poinsettia is the traditional Christmas gift plant. Its "flowers" are really leaflike bracts that surround tiny yellow and green true flowers. Traditionally red, cultivars now come in white, pink, or streaked red and white. The plant lasts several weeks indoors and may grow to 48 inches. Most are discarded when the color fades, but rebloom is possible. Here's how: grow in a bright but cool location, with daytime temperatures of 65° to 70°F, dropping no lower than 50°F at night. Use standard all-purpose houseplant soil that drains readily. Keep soil evenly moist until leaves start to fall, and then water sparingly. Do not fertilize. In late March or early April, cut back severely to 6 inches, and repot in fresh soil. In summer place the plant outdoors in a shady location. After Labor Day, bring the plant inside. To initiate new buds, provide 12 hours of darkness every day for about 10 weeks prior to the holiday. Propagate from cuttings. *Caution:* The plant is poisonous, so keep it away from pets and children. Also the sap of euphorbias can cause a rash.

Ferns (Various Families)

Lacy Maidenhair Fern

Adiantum tenerum

❋ **Small plant**
❋ **Graceful**
❋ **Somewhat difficult to grow**

With delicate, lacy, light green fronds on wiry arching stems, lacy maidenhair fern is a handsome, decorative plant from Mexico and Venezuela. It has been grown indoors since the mid-nineteenth century.

Provide a bright but not sunny location. Pot it in humusy soil, and keep the soil evenly moist, never too dry or too wet. Fertilize three times a year with 20-20-10 plant food. Propagate by division.

Good cultivars: 'Wrightii', 'Pacific Maid'

Lacy Maidenhair Fern

Bird's Nest Fern

Asplenium crispum

❋ **New variety**
❋ **Handsome crinkled leaves**
❋ **Very decorative**

This is one of the unusual ferns having scalloped crisp leaves that form a fountain-like appearance. These handsome 14 to 30 inch ferns add interest to the indoor garden with their fresh shiny green fronds that are parchment thin and clustered around a center. Add chopped fir bark to the standard soil mixture. Grow in full light and keep soil evenly moist; provide 50 percent humidity. Mist often and watch out for scale. Do not overpot as this variety likes to be rootbound. Feed four times a year with 10-10-5. Propagate by offsets or spores.

Bird's Nest

Bird's Nest Fern

Asplenium nidus

✳ **Medium-size to large plant**
✳ **Impressive when mature**
✳ **Easy to grow**

Bird's nest fern produces a crown of smooth, shiny fronds with a hollow and funnel-shaped center, somewhat like a bird's nest. This native of New Zealand, tropical Asia, and Polynesia can grow large—to 4 feet in diameter—but generally stays closer to 2 feet indoors.

Grow bird's nest fern in moderate light. Use a rich potting mix of equal parts soil and humus in a large container. Keep the soil evenly moist all year. If you summer the plant outdoors, protect it from slugs and snails. (Use a snail bait without metaldehyde.) Feed every month with 10-10-5 fertilizer. Repot every third year. Propagate by seed (spores) or buy new plants.

Good cultivar: 'Elegance'

Bird's Nest Fern

Tree Fern

Blechnum gibbum

✳ **Medium size**
✳ **Stiff green fronds**
✳ **Durable fern**

Also known by the botanic name *Blechnum occidentalis*, this fern from New Caledonia flourishes in the home with little care. A favorite from Victorian times, it grows slowly to 30 inches.

Plant in equal parts soil and fine-grade fir bark kept evenly moist. Place in a bright location, and feed semiannually with 20-20-10 plant food. Propagate by division.

Tree Fern

Holly Fern

Cyrtomium falcatum

✳ **Medium size**
✳ **Graceful**
✳ **Can take neglect**

This Asian native has attractive deep-green fronds with leaflets shaped like holly leaves. Unlike some ferns, it does not shed. At 30 inches,

Holly Fern

holly fern's compact size makes it ideal for many rooms.

Grow in bright light. (It will grow in dimmer conditions but won't do as well.) Plant in standard all-purpose houseplant soil, and allow the soil to dry out between waterings. Feed semiannually with 20-20-20 fertilizer. Keep holly fern out of drafts. Propagate by division.

Good cultivar: 'Rochfordianum'

Ferns (Various Families) cont'd

Rabbit's Foot
Davallia trichomanes

❋ **Good fern**
❋ **Can take dryness if necessary**
❋ **Creeping roots**

The rabbit's foot fern has been a traditional favorite houseplant for years and deserves its popularity. It is a slow grower that needs little care and prefers small pots. Rhizomes appear like rabbit's feet, thus its common name. The ferns have lacy fronds and brown or gray surface rhizomes. Grow in bright light and keep soil evenly moist. Mist foliage frequently. Put mature plants on pedestals so that the full beauty of the pendent graceful fronds can be appreciated. Good hanging-basket plant. Feed four times a year with 10-10-5. Resents overwatering. Propagate by division of rhizomes; cut them into sections and partially bury in sand.

Rabbit's Foot

Japanese Shield Fern
Dryopteris erythrosora

❋ **Medium-size, compact plant**
❋ **Bright green color**
❋ **Elegant appearance**

Seldom seen indoors, though it makes a fine houseplant, this slow grower has a neat branching habit and graceful appearance. It is native to China and Japan.

Grow in moderately bright light without direct sun. Pot in humusy soil that drains well, and keep the soil evenly moist. Feed quarterly with 10-20-10 fertilizer. Propagate by division.

Japanese Shield Fern

Hart Leaf Fern

Himionitis arifolia

✳ **New variety**
✳ **Small and decorative**
✳ **Good table plant**

This dwarf fern from Mexico, with smooth sword-like fronds and leaves on short stalks that become more pronounced as the plant grows, is sometimes called the strawberry fern. This is an unusual fern for home growing and is seldom seen, but it is worth the space. Highly recommended. Buy mature plants. Use several to a pot for best appearance. Generally pest free. Propagate by leaves.

The plant needs evenly moist soil. Feed every other watering using 10-10-5 fertilizer.

Hart Leaf Fern

Strap Fern

Strap Fern

Microsorum spc.

✳ **New variety**
✳ **Handsome foliage**
✳ **Easy to grow**

With a creeping trunk and strap-shaped leaves or feathery foliage, these long-lived plants require little care. This plant grows on its own and soon fills a pot with shiny bright-green leaves. They thrive firmly potted in rich soil with some peat moss and sand. Peak growth is in spring and summer, so water heavily then but reduce watering at other times; however, never let soil get really dry. Provide bright light, and keep foliage clean by wiping leaves with a damp cloth once a week. Ferns benefit from a summer outdoors where they can enjoy warm showers. It can tolerate shade if necessary. Pests rarely bother these plants. Feed four times a year with 10-10-5. Propagate by cuttings.

Ferns
(Various Families) cont'd

*Nephrolepis
'Lemon Tree'*

Nephrolepis

❋ **Fast growing**
❋ **Popular fern**
❋ **Hearty**

This fern is a fast-growing native to the American tropics and subtropics. This plant is a delicate looking plant with small leaves. Its common name, Lemon Tree, comes from its stature when mature, appearing somewhat like a small lemon tree. Give the plants winter sun, but provide shade in summer. Keep soil evenly moist, but avoid overwatering. In addition, water large plants by submerging the pot up to the rim in a sink of water for about an hour once a week. Ferns benefit from warm rains when temperatures outdoors are above 50 F. Propagate from runners taken from the base of mature plants. Feed with 10-10-5 every four months.

Fluffy Ruffles Boston Fern

*Nephrolepis exaltata
'Fluffy Ruffles'*

❋ **Medium-size to large plant**
❋ **Lovely in a hanging basket**
❋ **Grows in bright light or shade**

*Fluffy Ruffles
Boston Fern*

The classic Boston fern species, which originated in Africa, remains a favorite. Today there are innumerable cultivars, including 'Fluffy Ruffles' (shown). These cultivars are sturdier than the species. Some can grow to 60 inches in diameter with arching fronds. The one drawback is their tendency to drop leaflets, which can look untidy.

Grow in a bright location without direct sun, and use humusy soil—add extra humus to standard all-purpose houseplant soil. Feed twice a year with 20-20-20 fertilizer. For best results, repot annually in fresh soil. Propagate by division.

Another good cultivar: 'Dallasii'

Timii

Timii Nephrolepis

Nephrolepis exaltata 'Timii'

❋ **Small to medium-size fern**
❋ **Fine table accent**
❋ **Easy to grow**

This Boston fern cultivar is small—rarely growing over 30 inches—and its fronds are similar to those of the Boston fern but somewhat bushier. This graceful plant makes a lovely accent on a table or desk.

'Timii' likes a bright but not sunny place. Plant this fern in a well-draining soil rich with organic matter. Feed a few times a year with 10-20-10 fertilizer. Start new plants by division.

Button Fern

Pellaea rotundifolia

❋ **Small plant**
❋ **Low growing, trailing**
❋ **Easy to grow**

With arching, trailing fronds composed of small, round, green leaflets, this New Zealand native has a tropical look.

Grow in bright light without direct sun. Button fern needs good drainage, so add some perlite or sand to the soil mix. Keep the soil moist, but avoid overwatering. Feed monthly with 20-20-10 fertilizer. Repot every second year in fresh soil. Propagation from spores is difficult. Instead, purchase new plants.

Button Fern

Cabbage Head Fern

Cabbage Head Fern

Polypodium vulgare (aka Polypody)

❋ **Medium size to large**
❋ **Compact growth**
❋ **Lush green fronds**

A fast-growing plant with large scalloped leaves and, when mature, fuzzy brown rhizomes, this fern is native to Europe, eastern Asia, and North America. It can grow to 48 inches. If you have the space, cabbage head fern makes a striking room accent in a large decorative container.

Grow this fern in moderate light, and pot it in a mix of equal parts fine-grade fir bark and potting soil. Keep the soil evenly moist all year. Feed monthly with 20-10-10 fertilizer. A difficult fern, this one dislikes drafts and overwatering. Propagate by division.

Ferns
(Various Families) cont'd

Cretan Brake Fern
Pteris cretica

❋ **Small fern**
❋ **Decorative accent**
❋ **Easy to grow**

Cretan brake fern fronds are small and may be multicolored or striped with silver, as well as plain green. Originating in the tropics, this fern serves well as a spot accent. Many small ferns are mistakenly called Pteris, so before you buy, be sure you get the plant you want; ask for it by botanic name. There are dozens of cultivars, and most need minimal care. The species grows in a somewhat fountainlike form to about 20 inches. Cretan brake fern is a nice small plant.

Grow Cretan brake fern in bright to moderate light without direct sun, in a rich, humusy soil. Keep the soil evenly moist all year, and feed every other month with 10-10-10 fertilizer. Start new plants by division.

Cretan Brake Fern

Pteris cretica 'Lemon Tree'

Pteris cretica 'Lemon Tree'

❋ **New variety**
❋ **Small and pretty**
❋ **Likes water**

This is another of the Pteris class of ferns. This one has become popular because of its frilly foliage and ease of growth—good background plant. It is relatively new to the market and a nice addition to the indoor garden. Give it sun in the winter, but shade in summer. Keep soil evenly moist. Mist foliage frequently; the plant thrives in about 50 percent humidity. They will occasionally attract mealybugs, which could cause a problem, but for the most part, they are not bothered by insect. Propagate new plants by division. Feed four times a year with 10-10-5.

Leather Fern
Rumohra adiantiformis

❋ **Medium size**
❋ **Attractive leathery green fronds**
❋ **Good hanging plant**

Leather Fern

Leather fern is a tough, robust plant. The fronds can grow to 36 inches, and the plant has an airy appearance. It provides a refreshing change from the common Boston fern. As it matures, it looks better in hanging baskets.

Grow in a bright window. Use a mix of equal parts potting soil and humus, and keep it moist all year. Feed monthly with 20-20-10 fertilizer. Propagate by division.

Gesneriad Family (*Gesneriaceae*)

Lipstick Plant
Aeschynanthus species

❋ **Large trailing plant**
❋ **Lovely flowers**
❋ **Tolerates neglect**

There are many species and cultivars of aeschynanthus, some with blackish green leaves, others with bright green leaves; some have red flowers, and others have brownish red or orange flowers. The tubular blossoms, resembling lipstick in a tube, inspired the common name for this plant. The trailing stems grow to 48 inches.

Grow this plant in a bright location with some direct sun, especially in winter. Plant in all-purpose potting soil, and keep it evenly moist all year. Provide good air circulation. Feed about once a month with 20-10-10 fertilizer. Propagate from cuttings.

Lipstick Plant

Button Columnea

Button Columnea
Columnea arguta

❋ **Large, excellent trailer**
❋ **Abundant flowers**
❋ **Dense foliage**

If you come across this spectacular performer from Central America, buy it. With small button-shaped leaves and orange flowers that appear for six months on stems growing to 48 inches long, this exotic, elegant trailer should be displayed in a hanging basket.

Grow button columnea in a bright, airy location. Water about three times a week and feed monthly with 10-30-10 fertilizer. To encourage blooming, provide a three-week winter rest by reducing watering and not fertilizing. The plant does well in average house temperatures that never drop below 50°F. Propagate from cuttings.

Gesneriad Family (*Gesneriaceae*) cont'd

Flame Violet
Episcia cupreata

✳ **Small trailer**
✳ **Blooms in spring**
✳ **Likes warmth**

This South American native has leaves that combine shades of deep green, mahogany, brown, and copper, with contrasting veins of silver or light green. Tubular flowers in red, yellow, orange, and pink bloom in spring.

Place flame violet out of drafts, near a bright window. Use standard all-purpose soil that drains readily. Keep the soil evenly moist, but avoid wetting the leaves. Feed monthly with 10-30-10 fertilizer. Grow in a small pot. Repot every second year in fresh soil. Propagate from cuttings or offsets.

Good cultivars: 'Acajou', 'Cygnet', 'Emerald Queen'

Flame Violet

Goldfish Plant

Goldfish Plant
Nematanthus gregarius (aka *Hypocyrta nummularia*)

✳ **Medium size**
✳ **Bright shiny foliage**
✳ **Easy to grow**

This Central American plant has trailing stems to 30 inches long, lined with glossy deep green oval leaves. The pouchlike orange flowers resemble goldfish and generally bloom during warm months.

Grow goldfish plant in a bright location, ideally an east window. Pot in standard all-purpose potting soil. Water freely all year except in winter. Feed monthly with 20-20-10 plant food, except when the plant is resting. Generally, it goes dormant in winter and after flowering but eventually starts growing again. When the plant rests, withhold fertilizer, and cut back on watering until new growth begins. Grow in a hanging basket. Repot every second year. Start new plants from stem or tip cuttings.

Good cultivars: 'Tropicana', 'Black Gold'

African Violet
Saintpaulia cultivars

❋ **Small plant**
❋ **Longtime favorite**
❋ **Flowers in many colors**

Miniature, dwarf, and standard-size African violets come in many flower types and colors and may grow in a neat rosette or have trailing stems. Flowers may be single, double, edged with white (picotee), fringed, or star-shaped. Flower colors may be blue-violet, purple, pink, dark red, and white, as well as bicolored. Grown from nine species found throughout Africa, today's hybrids all have the typical cup-shaped, somewhat hairy leaves and clusters of small, pretty flowers. Given enough light, they bloom practically year-round.

Provide African violets good winter sunlight (and bright light in summer) and night temperatures above 55°F. Pot in standard all-purpose potting soil that drains well, and feed monthly with 10-10-10 fertilizer. Let the soil surface dry a bit between waterings. Avoid spilling water on leaves, or they'll spot. Propagate from leaf cuttings.

African Violet

Gloxinia

Gloxinia
Sinningia hybrid

❋ **Medium size**
❋ **Stunning large flowers**
❋ **Excellent gift plant**

The large, ruffled, trumpet-shaped flowers of gloxinia come in a stunning range of colors—violet, cardinal red, purple, pink, and white, some edged, blotched, or streaked with a contrasting color. The blooms are carried on slender stems above a rosette of large, broadly oval deep green leaves. Gloxinia hybrids are descended from a plant native to South America. Their dramatic flowers open in spring, but good care can keep them blooming indoors for several months. Given a cool, dark, dormant period, the tubers may rebloom, but most people use gloxinia as a seasonal plant and then discard it.

Grow Gloxinia in bright but filtered light in a location near a south or east window covered by a sheer curtain. Pot in all-purpose potting soil, and feed weekly with 10-20-10 fertilizer. Keep the soil evenly moist while the plant is growing and blooming. Here's how to make the plant rebloom: When growth stops, withhold water until the foliage dies. Remove leaves, and store the tuber in a cool, dry place. Barely moisten the soil every few weeks. When you see new growth, repot the tuber in fresh soil. Leave only the sprout exposed, and place the pot in bright light. If your gloxinia originally grew from a tuber, it may not go dormant.

Gesneriad Family (*Gesneriaceae*) cont'd

Temple Bells
Smithiantha speciosus

❋ **Unusual small to medium-size plant**
❋ **Pretty orange-red flowers**
❋ **Impressive mature specimens**

With small, pretty flowers that bloom off and on throughout the year, this handsome but often over-looked plant grows to about 24 inches.

For this gesneriad, a bright location is ideal. Use an all-purpose potting soil that drains readily, and keep the soil well watered. If the plant is allowed to dry out, it quickly succumbs. Feed monthly with 10-10-10 fertilizer. Propagate by division.

Temple Bells

Streptocarpella Cape Primrose

Streptocarpella Cape Primrose
Streptocarpus hybrid (*subgenus Streptocarpella*)

❋ **Medium-size hanging plant**
❋ **Small purple flowers**
❋ **Bushy growth**

Flowers in shades of violet and purple bloom off and on year-round on plants in this trailing hybrid. Mature plants grow to 30 inches in diameter.

Grow in bright light, in a hanging basket. Pot in humusy soil that drains readily. Keep the soil moist, and feed monthly with 10-10-10 fertilizer. The plant sends out errant stems, but light pruning keeps it handsome. Propagate by division.

Cape Primrose
Streptocarpus hybrid

❋ **Small plant**
❋ **Colorful flowers**
❋ **Likes moderate temperatures**

Cape Primrose

The trumpet-shaped flowers of Cape primrose are borne on slender stems above a cluster of fairly large fuzzy leaves. Flower colors of this native to South Africa and Madagascar now range from purple, mauve, and pink to white. Cape primroses are fine decorative plants, with one flower following another in early spring to summer. Compact hybrids rarely grow higher than 18 inches.

Grow Cape primrose in a bright location with plenty of winter sun. Pot in a well-drained all-purpose potting soil. The plant can tolerate temperatures as low as 55°F at night. Fertilize monthly with 10-20-10 fertilizer. Propagate by division or leaf cuttings.

Good cultivars: 'Bright Eyes', 'Dark Shadow', 'Fireworks', 'Midnight Flame', 'Moonlight', and 'Nightingale'

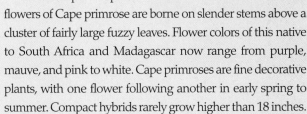

Ginger Family
(*Zingiberaceae*)

Orange Tulip
Costus curvibracteatus

* **Medium size**
* **Pretty little orange flowers**
* **Handsome bushy growth**

If you want tropical beauty, buy this ginger relative. It is densely covered with handsome green leaves arranged in a spiral pattern around the stem. At the stem tips, small orange flowers bloom periodically through the warm months. A decorative plant well suited to indoor culture, orange tulip is becoming more widely available from mail-order suppliers.

Provide sunshine, water, and moderate temperatures. Use all-purpose potting soil, and feed monthly with 20-30-10 fertilizer. The plant dislikes being disturbed, so keep in the same pot for several years. Topdress annually with fresh soil. Propagate by division, or purchase new plants from mail-order suppliers.

Orange Tulip

Crepe Paper Flower
Costus cuspidatus (C. igneus)

* **Medium size**
* **Brilliant flower display**
* **Easy to grow**

Crepe Paper Flower

This Brazilian native offers dramatic fan-shaped orange flowers, with a crepe paperlike texture, that bloom in winter, one a day. With handsome dark green foliage, the plant grows to 30 inches tall.

Grow in a bright but not sunny location, and pot in standard all-purpose houseplant soil. Water evenly all year. Feed at every other watering with 10-20-10 fertilizer. Propagate by division.

Siam Tulip
Curcuma alismatifolia

* **Small to medium-size plant**
* **Exotic flowers**
* **Easy to grow**

Siam Tulip

Flowers of curcuma are usually pinkish violet and very pretty, set off by dark green leaves. Siam tulip makes a fine pot plant and can also be used as a cut flower. The parent species is native to Thailand.

Start rhizomes in spring for summer bloom. Plant in well-drained humusy soil, and place in bright light. Do not feed. Purchase rhizomes from suppliers to start new plants.

Ginger Family (*Zingiberaceae*) cont'd

Java Tulip
Curcuma species

❋ **Small to medium-size plant**
❋ **Exotic flower head**
❋ **Tuliplike foliage**

Java Tulip

This beautiful plant is a spectacle in bloom, with pink bracts hiding tiny yellow and violet flowers. Two of the most popular common names for this plant are Java tulip and hidden ginger.

Grow in a bright but not sunny location. Use humusy potting soil. Keep the plant well watered in the warm months. During cool months, starting around November, decrease watering to allow the leaves to die back naturally so that the plant can rest for three months. Repot the rhizomes in fresh soil each year. Purchase new rhizomes from suppliers.

White Dragon Butterfly Ginger
Globba winitti 'White Dragon'

❋ **Colorful medium-size plant**
❋ **White butterfly flowers**
❋ **Fussy about conditions**

White Dragon Butterfly Ginger

This pretty ginger is from Thailand. Recently available commercially, it grows to about 30 inches tall and has a sprawling habit.

Butterfly ginger is somewhat temperamental and sensitive to drafts and cold. Provide bright light in a warm and somewhat humid location. Grow in humusy soil that drains readily, and keep the soil evenly moist all year. Feed bimonthly with 20-10-10 fertilizer. Purchase new plants from suppliers.

Resurrection Lily

Resurrection Lily
Kaempferia rotunda

❋ **Attractive medium-size plant**
❋ **Exotic appearance**
❋ **Handsome foliage**

Native to India, the resurrection lily is cultivated in Java for its edible roots, but in North America it is used as a decorative indoor plant. It has white flowers and a handsome fountainlike growth habit. Its dark green leaves are splotched with darker green. The plant grows to about 36 inches tall.

Grow resurrection lily in a sunny location, in humusy, well-drained soil. Keep the soil evenly moist, and feed quarterly with 10-20-10 fertilizer. Purchase new plants from suppliers.

Lily Family and Relatives (*Liliaceae*)

Aloe
Aloe bellatula

❋ **Medium-size to large plant**
❋ **Orange flowers**
❋ **Easy to grow**

This fine aloe from South Africa has narrow, spiky, succulent leaves with toothed edges. In the warm months the plant bears long stems topped with small orange flowers.

Grow aloe in bright light. Use all-purpose potting soil that drains readily. Keep the soil evenly moist all year. Feed quarterly with 10-10-10 fertilizer. Because this aloe prefers not to be disturbed, repot only when the plant outgrows its pot. Propagate from offsets.

Aloe

Healing Aloe, Medicine Plant

Healing Aloe, Medicine Plant
Aloe vera (aka *A. barbadensis*)

❋ **Small to medium-size plant**
❋ **Popular healing plant**
❋ **Tolerates neglect**

Juice from the succulent leaves of this native of the Canary Islands is widely used to heal minor burns and soothe abrasions. With fleshy, green leaves edged with small spines, aloe is not spectacular to look at, but it is widely grown, especially in kitchens, because of its healing sap. Breaking or cutting a leaf releases the clear, gel-like sap, which may be applied directly to the skin and is used in many lotions.

Grow in bright light but not direct sun. Pot in standard all-purpose houseplant soil, and keep the soil evenly moist all year. Fertilize monthly with 20-10-10 plant food. Propagate from offsets.

Lily Family and Relatives (*Liliaceae*) cont'd

Foxtail Fern
Asparagus densiflorus 'Myersii'

❋ **Medium size**
❋ **Compact**
❋ **Easy to grow**

This South African native is compact, and growing upright, it looks neater than its better-known relative, the sprawling asparagus fern. Foxtail fern and asparagus fern are close cousins of the edible asparagus.

Attractive and easy to grow, foxtail fern likes dappled sunlight. Pot in all-purpose potting soil, and keep the soil somewhat moist all year. Feed every other month with 20-10-10 fertilizer. Occasionally pinch back stems to keep the plant bushy. Propagate by division.

Foxtail Fern

Cast Iron Plant

Cast Iron Plant
Aspidistra elatior

❋ **Handsome medium-size plant**
❋ **Tolerates low light**
❋ **Difficult to kill**

Few respectable Victorian homes with plants were without a cast iron plant in the parlor. The plant grows slowly in a compact clump of elongated shining dark green leaves that may eventually reach 3 feet tall. Unattractive purple-brown flowers may appear at the base. The plant survives low light and doesn't require a lot of water. Originally from China, cast iron plant is depicted in ancient Chinese paintings.

Grow in moderate to low light; the newer variegated forms need somewhat brighter conditions. Plant in a large pot in standard all-purpose houseplant soil. Keep the soil evenly moist except in winter, when the plant rests, and when soil can be allowed to become somewhat dry. Feed monthly with 20-10-5 fertilizer. Propagate by division.

Good cultivars: 'Milky Way', 'Variegata', 'Variegata Exotica'

Cast Iron Plant

Aspidistra 'Milky Way'

❋ **Lush green**
❋ **Plumes of flowers**
❋ **Green all year**

Finally a new variety *Aspidistra*, the old Victorian favorite with long dark-green leaves. This plant is called 'Milky Way' because of its spotted leaves. The 24-inch-tall foliage is sometimes complemented by sprays of purple-brown flowers hidden in the foliage. This plant needs sun. Grow several plants to a pot for a good display. Allow the soil to dry out between waterings; feed every four months with 10-10-5. Split crowns carefully for new plants.

Cast Iron Plant

Bottle Plant, Ponytail Palm

Beaucarnea recurvata (aka *Nolina recurvata*)

❋ **Large plant**
❋ **Unusual structure**
❋ **Tolerates cool temperatures**

If you forget to water this Mexican native, it maintains itself. It can store water for months in its swollen stem. The bottle-shaped stem (also compared to the shape of an elephant's foot) is adorned with a cluster of long, narrow ribbonlike arching leaves sprouting from the top. Indoors the plant grows to about 4 feet tall. Outdoors in mild climates, it can reach 6 feet.

Grow bottle plant in dappled light, and plant it in standard all-purpose potting soil. Allow the soil to dry out between waterings. Feed twice a year with 20-10-10 fertilizer. Keep potbound for best growth. Propagate from offsets.

Bottle Plant, Ponytail Palm

Lily Family and Relatives (*Liliaceae*) cont'd

Variegated Spider Plant
Chlorophytum comosum cultivar

❋ **Medium size**
❋ **Striped beauty**
❋ **Trailing habit**

The handsome trailing spider (or airplane) plant from South Africa has been a favorite houseplant for decades, and the variegated cultivar shown is also popular. Spider plants need little care. The arching slender leaves are striped creamy white and give an airy appearance. The plant sends out miniature plantlets, called runners, on trailing wiry stems.

Spider plants find homes in many offices, apartments, and dormitory rooms because it can be neglected for days without suffering ill effects. Grow in a somewhat sunny location, and use all-purpose potting soil kept evenly moist. The plant grows best when potbound. Feed four times a year with 20-10-10 fertilizer. Propagate by rooting the small, pendant runners that emerge.

Variegated Spider Plant

Orange Stem
Chlorophytum ordhidearea

❋ **New variety**
❋ **Handsome leaves**
❋ **Very desirable**

This is one of the newer *Chlorophytum* available. It has a a fountain-like growth with lush green leaves and contrasting orange stems. Mature specimens bear tiny white flowers on tall, stiff stems in winter. Don't cut off the flowers as leaf clusters will form. These fine 36-inch-tall plants can be neglected and still survive. Strong ropelike roots store water, a safety measure if you forget the plants. Place in large pots because roots quickly fill containers. These are excellent plants to display in baskets. Provide plenty of light, and let soil dry out between waterings. Feed four times a year with 10-10-5. Propagate by removing stem runners, by division, or by cutting plants apart with a sharp knife.

Orange Stem

Ti Plant

Cordyline terminalis

❊ **Medium-size to large plant**
❊ **Handsome colorful leaves**
❊ **Fast grower**

This relative of the *Dracaena* clan has handsome foliage. Mature ti plants are striking and make a great corner accent in a cachepot.

Grow ti plant in a bright location in well-drained humusy soil that you should keep evenly moist. Keep this plant out of full sun to avoid burning the foliage. Feed quarterly with 10-20-10 fertilizer. Repot only when it is potbound; the plant dislikes disturbance. Propagate from stem cuttings.

Ti Plant

Dwarf Pineapple Dracaena

Dwarf Pineapple Dracaena

Dracaena deremensis 'Compacta'

❊ **Medium size**
❊ **Attractive foliage**
❊ **Easy to grow**

Aptly named, pineapple dracaena has shiny green leaves that resemble a pineapple top. One among the vast number of available houseplants in the genus *Dracaena*, this one grows to 20 inches. It differs from most dracaenas because its leaves grow in a tight pineapple shape, compared with the open growth habits of other dracaena.

Grow in bright light, in standard all-purpose houseplant soil kept evenly moist all year. Feed quarterly with 10-20-10 fertilizer. The plant grows well on its own, so you don't need to fuss over it. Start new plants by division.

Lily Family and Relatives (*Liliaceae*) cont'd

Dracaena 'Janet Craig'

✳ **New variety**
✳ **Handsome variegation**
✳ **Easy house plant**

Dracaenas are a genus of excellent African plants that can survive harsh conditions, and 'Janet Craig' is perhaps the most popular because of its graceful growth and ease of culture. The dark-green lance leaves are usually banded white or yellow. Most are large plants that can grow to 60 inches. Give plants good light, but not sun, and keep soil evenly moist. Keep leaves shiny by wiping with damp cloth every month. Do not use liquid shining compounds. Don't let water accumulate on leaves because it can cause spotting. Small plants can be used in a dish garden. Group several on a table or desk for decorative accent. Propagate new plants from stem cuttings.

Dracaena 'Janet Craig'

Red Wine Corn Plant

Red Wine Corn Plant

Dracaena fragrans 'Red Wine'

✳ **Large plant**
✳ **Striking foliage**
✳ **Easy to grow**

The erect, slightly arching leaves of the corn plant are broad and pointed. 'Red Wine' has interesting maroon and green leaves. Another popular cultivar, 'Massangeana', has one or more yellow stripes down the center. Hailing from Africa, corn plants can grow to 60 inches tall. As they grow, the woody stem elongates, creating a treelike effect. Corn plants are undemanding and long-lived.

Grow in a bright location, and use a standard all-purpose houseplant soil that drains readily. Feed monthly with 20-20-10 fertilizer. Occasionally wipe foliage with a damp cloth to remove dust. Repot in fresh soil every second year. Purchase new plants from suppliers.

Other good cultivars: 'General Pershing', 'Lindeni'

Rainbow Dracaena

Dracaena marginata 'Tricolor' (aka D. cincta 'Tricolor')

❋ **Medium-size to large plant**
❋ **Handsome foliage**
❋ **Grows slowly**

When rainbow dracaena was introduced to the houseplant trade in the late 1980s, its tricolored foliage caused a sensation. The narrow, swordlike green leaves are striped creamy white and edged in red. As a bonus, this beauty survives neglect, and adds a sculptural effect to the indoor garden. Mature plants are available and can grow to 60 inches.

Grow in a bright location with some sun. Pot in standard all-purpose houseplant soil kept evenly moist. Feed monthly with 10-10-10 fertilizer. Propagate from cane cuttings or by air layering.

Rainbow Dracaena

Variegated Dracaena

Variegated Dracaena

Dracaena warneckii

❋ **Large plant**
❋ **Decorative leaves**
❋ **Easy to grow**

As a lily this is a hard plant to beat for indoor growing and has been a favorite for years. It thrives almost on its own, but it does need good light to look its best. This plant has white 24-inch leaves with a green center stripe. As with the 'Janet Craig', opposite page, plants can grow to 60 inches. Give the plants good light, but not sun, and keep soil evenly moist. Don't let water accumulate on leaves; it can cause spotting. Grow in large pots. Feed with 10-10-5 every other watering. Create new plants from stem cuttings.

Spotted Ox Tongue Plant

Gasteria bicolor var. liliputana

❋ **Small plant**
❋ **Desirable succulent**
❋ **Slow grower**

Spotted Ox Tongue Plant

This stemless rosette of succulent, tongue-like, spotted leaves is the smallest of the genus gasteria, growing only to about 6 inches tall. Native to South Africa, the plant makes a good table accent.

Spotted tongue plant grows easily in bright light and thrives in a potting mix of equal parts sharp sand and potting soil. Keep the soil just barely moist all year. Avoid splashing water on leaves; otherwise they will become blemished. Feed quarterly with 10-10-10 fertilizer. Start new plants from offsets.

Lily Family and Relatives (*Liliaceae*) cont'd

Silver Squill

Ledebouria socialis (aka *Scilla socialis, S. violacea*)

❋ **Small plant**
❋ **Attractive foliage**
❋ **Easy to grow**

From South Africa, this compact 24-inch plant has small blue-violet flowers that appear periodically set off by succulent green leaves spotted with silver. Silver squill is available through mail-order nurseries, often still sold under its former genus name, *Scilla*.

Grow this plant in a bright location, and pot it in standard all-purpose houseplant soil. Keep the soil barely moist all year. Feed quarterly with 10-10-10 fertilizer. Start new plants by tuber division.

Silver Squill

Song of India

Pleomele reflexa

❋ **Fast growing**
❋ **Needs little care**
❋ **Many varieties**

This *Pleomele* is a handsome, compact plant with rosettes of striped green and golden-yellow leaves. The plant bears white flowers. This robust medium grower—up to 30 inches—is new to cultivation and looks good when mounted on a pedestal. Song of India grows slowly and is generally not bothered by insects. Feed every other watering with 10-10-5. Propagate new plants from cuttings.

Song of India

Spineless Yucca

Yucca elephantipes

❋ **Medium-size to large plant**
❋ **Good floor accent**
❋ **Tolerates low light**

Spineless yucca is somewhat compact as yuccas grow, topping out at about 48 inches indoors. With spineless sword-shaped green leaves on a thick trunk, the plant is a good green accent where most other houseplants fail because it tolerates low light.

Grow in moderate to bright light in standard all-purpose houseplant soil kept evenly—and barely—moist all year. Feed quarterly with 20-10-10 fertilizer. This plant is also available as a mature specimen growing to 60 inches. Propagate by division.

Spineless Yucca

Mulberry Family (*Morceae*)

Weeping Fig, Banyan Tree
Ficus benjamina

✽ **Large treelike plant**
✽ **Likes humid rooms**
✽ **Easy to grow**

Weeping fig has been a favorite houseplant for decades. The plant can grow tall and looks like a small tree, but it generally stays at about 40 inches indoors. The leaves are shiny green, and the form of mature plants is canopylike. Weeping fig has a reputation for being touchy, because it drops a lot of leaves if it doesn't get enough humidity.

Grow weeping fig in a bright but not sunny location and a humusy well-drained soil. Feed quarterly with 10-20-10 fertilizer. Propagate by air layering.

Weeping Fig, Banyan Tree

Braided Fig

Braided Fig
Ficus benjamina

✽ **Unique medium-size to large plant**
✽ **Handsome room accent**
✽ **Slow grower**

Some nurseries sell this fancier version of the standard weeping fig. Its trunk is braided to create a unique stem. Braided fig was a trendy houseplant and quite popular some decades back; it has begun reappearing at plant centers. This handsome plant grows to about 36 inches and has a leafy crown.

Grow braided fig in a bright, airy location in standard all-purpose houseplant soil kept evenly moist. Feed quarterly with 10-20-10 fertilizer. Repot only when necessary. Keep this plant and weeping fig out of drafts. Purchase new plants from suppliers.

Mulberry Family (*Morceae*) cont'd

Ficus Benjamina

Ficus benjamina 'Silver Cloud'

❋ **New variety**
❋ **Handsome foliage**
❋ **Clean foliage with damp cloth**

These are almost perfect houseplants with diversified foliage and growth. Lacy and delicate, this ficus makes a handsome appearance indoors and adds a delicate look to a garden. Some have broad leathery 12-inch leaves. Plant even large specimens in small pots. Occasionally wipe foliage with a damp cloth to keep it shiny, but avoid clogging leaf pores with oil or special leaf-polishing preparations. Grow plants in bright light, and keep soil evenly moist except in winter when they can get along with less moisture. Humidity levels up to 70 percent are best for this plant. Feed plants about four times a year with 10-10-5. Propagate from leaf cuttings or air layering.

Ficus Benjamina 'Silver Cloud'

Variegated Fig

Variegated Fig

Ficus benjamina 'Variegata'

❋ **Medium-size to large treelike plant**
❋ **Fine variegated foliage**
❋ **Easy to grow**

This popular cultivar offers a canopy of handsomely variegated pale yellow and green leaves. It has a lacy appearance and more charm than the standard weeping fig.

Grow in bright to moderate light, even though the plant also grows well in low light. Pot in standard all-purpose houseplant soil. Feed monthly with 10-20-10 fertilizer. This plant needs little attention. Start new plants from stem cuttings.

Burgundy Rubber Plant

Ficus elastica 'Burgundy'

* **Large plant**
* **Good color**
* **Easy to grow**

Rubber plants are bold, tropical, and treelike and have large, green, oval leaves. In their native Asia, rubber plants become sizable trees. When cut, they bleed a sticky white sap. In the home, rubber plant grows to 36 inches, making a strong vertical accent. There are numerous cultivars.

Grow in moderate light, in standard all-purpose houseplant soil kept evenly moist. Wipe the leaves with a damp cloth occasionally. Feed only in spring and summer with 20-10-10 fertilizer. Propagate by air layering.

Other good cultivars: 'Decora', 'Variegata', 'Doescheri'

Burgundy Rubber Plant

Variegated Creeping Fig

Variegated Creeping Fig

Ficus pumila 'Variegata'

* **Small to medium-size plant**
* **Tiny-leaved beauty**
* **Easy to grow**

This diminutive, slow-growing vining member of the genus ficus has great charm. The variegated cultivar's small buttonlike green leaves are edged with yellow. To train the plant vertically, place a small trellis in the pot for it to climb. This is an easy plant to grow, and the variegated leaves make it a good addition to home gardens.

Grow variegated creeping fig in a very bright location. Keep this plant in a small pot; it does best when the roots are slightly crowded. Pot it in a well-drained all-purpose houseplant soil. Keep the soil somewhat dry all year. Feed quarterly with 10-10-10 fertilizer. Propagate from cuttings.

Orchid Family (Orchidaceae)

Stefan Isler Orchid

× *Burrageara* 'Stefan Isler'

❋ **Medium size**
❋ **Colorful orange-red flowers**
❋ **Winter bloomer**

This fine hybrid is a cross between × *Vuylstekeara* and *Oncidium*. Obtain from orchid suppliers. It grows to 24 inches tall, flowers freely, and blooms twice a year with good care.

Grow in bright light, in medium-grade fir bark kept evenly moist all year. Provide warmth. Nighttime temperatures should never drop below 55°F. Feed monthly with 10-30-20 fertilizer. Propagate by division.

Stefan Isler Orchid

Guatemalan Orchid

Guatemalan Orchid

Cattleya guatemalensis
(aka *C. deckeri*)

❋ **Medium size**
❋ **Stunning flowers**
❋ **Tolerates cool conditions**

This orchid from Guatemala bears a cluster of bright pink flowers in autumn, reaching a compact 30 inches. The plant grows easily. When "orchidmania" beset England during the 1860s, this species was a prized possession, and breeders have used it ever since then to produce hybrid Cattleyas of similar flower color.

Provide a bright, somewhat sunny location. Nighttime temperatures can drop to 55°F. Pot in medium-grade fir bark kept evenly moist all year. Feed quarterly with 20-30-10 fertilizer. Start new plants by division.

Corsage flower

Cattleya hybrid

❋ **Medium size**
❋ **Dramatic, long-lasting flowers**
❋ **Tolerates neglect**

Corsage flower

Orchids bear colorful flowers that last for weeks. With thousands of Cattleya hybrids available, orchids have become America's favorite houseplant. The Cattleya flower is now available in all colors, except black.

Grow in a bright but not sunny location, and pot in medium-grade fir bark. Provide even moisture, but allow the plant to rest for two months with little water. Feed monthly with a 20-30-20 plant food, except when resting. Propagate by division.

Wildcat Orchid

✕ *Colmanara* 'Wildcat'

❋ **Medium size**
❋ **Fine yellow-brown-white flowers**
❋ **Available from orchid suppliers**

This excellent hybrid flowers freely in winter and grows to just 24 inches tall.

Provide a bright location. Grow in medium-grade fir bark, and keep well watered all year. Provide minimum nighttime temperatures of 55°F. Propagate by division.

Wildcat Orchid

Jill Katalinca Orchid

Jill Katalinca Orchid

Cymbidium 'Jill Katalinca'

❋ **Large vertical plant**
❋ **Handsome large flowers**
❋ **Needs attention**

From the genus *Cymbidium*, native to India and China, comes this spectacular 48-inch hybrid, bearing large colorful flowers profusely on tall scapes. It makes good cut flowers but needs careful attention.

Provide bright sun in winter and somewhat low light in summer. Unlike most orchids, Cymbidiums need cool temperatures to initiate flower buds. Provide about six weeks of nighttime temperatures in the 50s. Grow in medium-grade fir bark kept evenly moist during active growth. Reduce watering in fall, and keep the plant potbound. Feed monthly with 10-20-10 fertilizer. If you can't get this orchid to bloom, apply a layer of ice cubes to the growing medium once a week for about six weeks. It works! Propagate by division.

Orchid Family (Orchidaceae) cont'd

Stars 'n' Bars Orchid

× *Degarmoara* 'Stars 'n' Bars'

❋ **Medium size**
❋ **Large, colorful, long-lasting flowers**
❋ **Easy to grow**

This hybrid is a robust grower with brown and yellow flowers in a bar pattern.

Provide bright light without direct sun. Plant in fine-grade fir bark kept evenly moist all year. Feed quarterly with 10-30-20 fertilizer, and don't fuss over the plant—it grows on its own. Propagate by division, or purchase new plants from suppliers.

Stars 'n' Bars Orchid

Antelope Orchid

Antelope Orchid

Dendrobium antennatum

❋ **Medium size**
❋ **Fine small white flowers**
❋ **Long-lasting blooms**

This pretty species from New Guinea was introduced in England in the mid-nineteenth century. There are several hybrids, two of which are shown here. Antelope orchid has erect stems to about 24 inches and small, fragrant flowers in a variety of colors. The flowers have twisted petals shaped like an antelope's horns. This orchid commands attention. In spring, it bears many flowers.

Provide bright light, and pot in medium-grade fir bark kept evenly moist. Average household temperatures suit this plant fine. Feed monthly with 10-20-10 fertilizer. Start new plants by division.

Topaz Dendrobium

Topaz Dendrobium
Dendrobium bullenianum

✳ **Dependable medium-size plant**
✳ **Sometimes semideciduous**
✳ **Available from orchid suppliers**

A handsome orchid, not easy to find, but worth the search, this Dendrobium has stunning orange flowers borne in clusters from bare branches. The plant grows to 24 inches tall. Its sprawling stems become striking when the plant blooms in October.

Easy to grow, this orchid likes a bright, sunny location. Pot in fine-grade fir bark kept evenly moist all year. Feed quarterly with 20-30-20 fertilizer. Propagate by division.

Epidendrum Stamfordianum

Epidendrum Stamfordianum
Epidendrum stamfordianum

✳ **Compact, medium-size plant**
✳ **Bears hundreds of tiny flowers**
✳ **Easy to grow**

Native to Central and South America, from Guatemala to Venezuela, this species bears a bountiful crop of small red-and-yellow flowers on graceful stems. A mature plant with hundreds of flowers makes quite an impression. A longtime favorite of hobbyists, this orchid will grow well without pampering.

Provide a bright location, and plant in medium-grade fir bark. Water thoroughly, but allow the medium to dry out between waterings. The plant tolerates night-time temperatures as low as 55°F. Propagate new plants by division.

Dancing Lady Orchid

Dancing Lady Orchid
Oncidium maculatum 'Paolo'

✳ **Decorative medium-size plant**
✳ **Long-lasting fragrant flowers**
✳ **Easy to grow**

This orchid is a hybrid of *Oncidium maculatum*, which comes from Mexico and Central America and is a parent of many fine varieties. In nineteenth-century England, the species was prized. Here the original small-flowered species has been hybridized to create a plant with large flowers that bear the brown-and-yellow markings typical of Oncidiums. A pretty, compact plant, this one grows to 30 inches tall.

Provide this orchid with a bright, somewhat sunny location. Pot in medium-grade fir bark kept evenly moist all year. Keeping the plant in a small pot should force it to bloom. Feed quarterly with 20-10-10 fertilizer. Propagate by division.

Orchid Family (Orchidaceae) cont'd

Sharry Baby Orchid
Oncidium 'Sharry Baby'

❋ **Medium size**
❋ **Perfumed flowers**
❋ **Dependable bloomer**

This recently introduced orchid bears wands of highly scented flowers that last for weeks. Foliage is sometimes spotted red (not indicative of disease), and the plant grows to a compact 30 inches. It is easy to grow and blooms twice a year.

Grow this plant in a bright location in medium-grade fir bark kept moist all year. Feed quarterly with 20-30-10 fertilizer. Repot only when necessary—the plant dislikes disturbance. Propagate by division.

Sharry Baby Orchid

Lady Slipper Orchid

Lady Slipper Orchid
Paphiopedilum insigne

❋ **Medium size**
❋ **Decorative flowers**
❋ **Grows in low light**

Native to the Himalayas at elevations to 6,000 feet, this orchid not surprisingly tolerates cool temperatures and has been hybridized extensively because of its cold tolerance. The plant grows to 24 inches tall and bears green-brown-yellow pouchlike flowers, typical of lady slippers, on an erect stem. The blooms last for weeks.

Provide this plant with bright light, but no direct sun. Pot in fine-grade fir bark. Water evenly all year, and feed four times a year with 20-10-10 fertilizer. Propagate by division.

Red Sky Lady Slipper Orchid

Paphiopedilum 'Red Sky'

❋ **Decorative small to medium-size plant**
❋ **Flowers last for weeks**
❋ **Easy to grow**

This decorative hybrid orchid bears a lovely maroon-and-green flower on an erect stem with a distinctive maroon top. Its exotic appearance stunned British gardeners in the late 1800's. The leaves are mottled, and the plant is small, growing only to about 20 inches.

Provide a bright but not sunny location, and plant in fine-grade fir bark. Keep evenly moist, and feed twice a year with 20-10-5 fertilizer. Repot only when necessary. Propagate by division.

*Red Sky Lady
Slipper Orchid*

Lady Slipper Orchid

Paphiopedilum sukhakulii

❋ **Medium size**
❋ **Long-lasting exotic flowers**
❋ **Tolerates some coolness**

This handsome orchid hails from Thailand and grows to 10 inches tall. Borne on erect stems, the single flowers are multicolored—spotted and banded in greens, browns, and tan. They appear in autumn or winter.

This orchid likes a warm location and moderate light. Plant in fine-grade fir bark kept evenly moist all year. Grow in a small pot to encourage bud formation. Feed monthly with 10-20-10 fertilizer. Propagate by division.

*Lady Slipper
Orchid*

Orchid Family (Orchidaceae) cont'd

Moth Orchid, Dogwood Orchid

Phalaenopsis hybrid

❋ **Small plant**
❋ **Attractive foliage**
❋ **Blooms last a month or longer**

There are thousands of hybrids of these wonderfully reliable orchids from Java, Southeast Asia, and the Philippines. The elegant arching wands of flowers are easy to coax into bloom. There are solid, striped, or spotted flowers in several colors. The nickname comes from the Greek phalaina, meaning moth, and aptly describes the shape of the blooms. Moth orchids also make good cut flowers.

Provide a bright location, in clay pots of medium-grade fir bark kept watered all year. Feed with 10-20-10 orchid fertilizer every third week. Repot in fresh fir bark every 18 months. Propagate from offsets that form around the base of the plant.

Moth Orchid, Dogwood Orchid

Moth Orchid

Moth Orchid

Phalaenopsis hybrid

❋ **Medium size**
❋ **Dozens of flowers**
❋ **Easy to grow**

Originally from the Philippines, this fine moth orchid bears plenty of flowers. It was introduced to the West in England about 1830. The flowers are small and yellow and appear in winter or spring. The plant grows to 24 inches tall with large oar-shaped leaves. Moth orchids are adaptable, resilient houseplants and a good choice for beginners.

Provide bright to moderate light and temperatures ranging from 55° to 80°F. Pot in medium-grade fir bark, and keep the medium moist but never soggy. Fertilize with 10-20-10 plant food every three months. Propagate from offsets.

Orange Cattleya

Sophrolaeliocattleya Hazel Boyd 'Sunset'

❋ **Medium size**
❋ **Long-lasting exquisite small flowers**
❋ **Easy to grow**

This beautiful orchid is a hybrid of three popular genera: *Sophronitis*, *Laelia*, and *Cattleya*. It bears lovely small orange and red flowers in typical cattleya form. Plants grow to 30 inches and bloom freely, sometimes twice a year.

Grow this plant in an airy, bright, somewhat sunny location. Plant in medium-grade fir bark kept evenly moist all year. Provide normal household temperatures. Feed quarterly with 20-30-10 fertilizer. Propagate by division.

Orange Cattleya

Orchid Lily

Orchid Lily

Spathoglottis plicata

❋ **A true orchid**
❋ **Easy to grow**
❋ **Nice vertical accent**

This lovely and exotic orchid variety grows readily with little care. The fine glossy leaves are complemented by small purple flowers that bloom in summer. It can be grown in soil that is kept evenly moist all year. This fine plant can withstand shade. It is, generally, insect free. It is particularly lovely when used in groups. The Orchid Lily is a favorite with orchid growers. Feed every fourth watering with 10-10-5. Propagate by division.

Winter Orchid

Winter Orchid

Zygopetalum crinitum

❋ **Medium size**
❋ **Dramatic fragrant flowers**
❋ **Winter bloomer**

From tropical and South America, this handsome orchid has flowers that are a combination of brown and blue—and fragrant. Plus, they bloom in winter. The plant grows to 30 inches, with papery thin green leaves.

Grow winter orchid in a somewhat bright, cool area. Use medium-grade fir bark kept evenly moist most of the year. Feed monthly with 10-30-20 fertilizer, except during the month after flowering. Also decrease water then. Propagate by division.

Palm Family (*Palmae*)

Fishtail Palm
Caryota mitis

❋ **Large tropical beauty**
❋ **Interesting, ragged-edge leaves**
❋ **Dark green fronds**

Native to Southeast Asia, the popular fishtail palm is a decorative beauty that sometimes grows to 72 inches indoors. If you have the room, a well-grown plant is a beautiful sight, becoming lush and handsome as it matures. What's more, the fishtail palm can survive neglect and still look good. It needs vertical space.

Grow this plant in a bright but not sunny location. Pot in a large container with standard all-purpose houseplant soil kept evenly moist all year. Average household temperatures are fine. Repot it only when the roots grow from the bottom of the pot, and trim the leaves, which tend to turn brown at the edges. Feed this palm monthly with 20-20-10 fertilizer. Propagate from offsets or by division.

Fishtail Palm

Bamboo Palm

Bamboo Palm
Chamaedorea erumpens

❋ **Large plant**
❋ **Best palm for home conditions**
❋ **Easy to grow**

The Palm Family is large, but only a few species can tolerate home conditions. Bamboo palm does beautifully indoors, growing to 60 inches tall. Its canopy-type growth is especially attractive when used to fill in a corner. The plant's fronds are dense, and its stalks are stout.

Grow bamboo palm in a bright but not sunny place. Pot in standard all-purpose houseplant soil kept somewhat dry all year. This easy-to-grow palm adapts to both cool and warm household temperatures. Feed quarterly with 20-10-10 fertilizer. Propagate by division.

Butterfly Palm

Chrysalidocarpus lutescens

✴ **Medium-size to large plant**
✴ **Graceful form**
✴ **Easy to grow**

The fronds of this Madagascar native are slim and airy, and the plant has a fountainlike form. Butterfly palm grows to 40 inches and makes a good corner accent.

Provide a bright location. Grow in standard all-purpose potting soil kept evenly moist, never too dry or too wet. Feed quarterly with 20-20-10 fertilizer. Occasionally trim the bottom leaves, which can become straggly. Propagate by division.

Butterfly Palm

Chinese Fan Palm

Licuala grandis

✴**Large, graceful plant**
✴**Attractive in a decorative tub**
✴**Easy to grow**

When mature, this palm is a picture of grace. Its fan-shaped leaves are carried on tall stems. From New Guinea, the plant grows slowly to 48 inches tall.

Chinese Fan Palm

Provide bright light without direct sun. Grow in a large decorative tub filled with humusy soil that drains readily. The plant tolerates cool evening temperatures as low as 55°F. Fertilize monthly with 10-10-10 plant food. Propagation is difficult under home conditions, so purchase new plants from suppliers.

Lady Palm

Rhapis excelsa

✴**Large plant**
✴**Attractive mature specimen**
✴**Easy to grow**

This graceful plant may be the best potted palm. It bears fanlike fronds on tall canelike stems. Lady palm has often been depicted in paintings in its native China.

Lady Palm

Grow lady palm in a large container with standard houseplant soil kept evenly moist all year. The plant tolerates moderate to low light. Feed with 20-20-10 fertilizer every three months. Repot lady palm every fourth year, and topdress it with fresh soil annually. Propagates easily from offsets.

Spiderwort Family (Commelinaceae)

Brazilian Wandering Jew

Callisia repens

❋ **Medium-size to large plant**
❋ **Small attractive leaves**
❋ **Easy to grow**

This plant is related to the tradescantias, which share the wandering common name. Attractive but over-looked, this dense trailing plant has small dark green leaves and is quite beautiful in a hanging basket. The stems can reach 48 inches long.

Grow in a hanging basket in bright to moderate light. Pot in standard all-purpose houseplant soil kept just moist, never soggy or dry. The plant likes good air circulation. Feed monthly with 10-10-5 fertilizer. Because this plant is difficult to propagate at home, you should purchase new plants from suppliers.

Brazilian Wandering Jew

Moses in a Boat

Moses-in-a-boat

Rhoea discolor variegated

❋ **New variety**
❋ **Low growing**
❋ **Very colorful foliage**

This small plant from Mexico is, unlike most of its cousins, a dwarf and never grows over 14 inches—see opposite page. This plant has lovely variegated and multicolored leaves, and little white flowers enclosed in boat-shaped bracts. It grows slowly into a bushy plant. When watering, keep the water off of the leaves. Feed four times a year with 10-10-5. Grow new plants from cuttings.

Moses-in-a-boat, Moses-in-the-cradle

Rhoeo spathacea (aka *Tradescantia spathacea*)

❋ **Small to medium-size plant**
❋ **Tolerates low light**
❋ **Easy to grow**

This plant from Mexico gets its common name from the small white flowers tucked inside the boat-shaped bracts at the plant's base. The plant grows to about 20 inches tall, in a clump of stunning green and purple leaves. This is a popular plant because it is so easy to grow, has a compact shape, and tolerates low light. Indoor gardeners have grown this plant for decades.

Grow Moses-in-a-boat in bright to moderate light, without direct sun. Pot it in standard all-purpose houseplant soil kept evenly moist all year. Except for watering, the plant needs little attention to thrive. Feed quarterly with 10-10-10 fertilizer. Propagate by division or from stem or tip cuttings.

Moses-in-a-boat, Moses-in-the-cradle

Purple Heart Plant

Purple Heart Plant

Setcreasea pallida
(aka *Tradescantia pallida*)

❋ **Small accent plant**
❋ **Tufted leaves**
❋ **Easy to grow**

Though not a spectacular plant, purple heart is easy to grow and makes a pleasant small-table accent. The green leaves have purple undersides and grow in bunches along sprawling stems. Small pink flowers, as shown, may appear at stem tips in summer.

Grow purple heart plant in bright light to develop full coloration of the leaves. The plant can tolerate lower light, but then the foliage will be more green and less purple. Pot in a small container filled with humusy soil that drains readily. Keep the soil moderately moist all year, never too dry or too wet. Purple heart tolerates cool or warm household temperatures. Feed this plant quarterly with 10-10-10 fertilizer. Propagate from leaf or tip cuttings.

Spiderwort Family (Commelinaceae) cont'd

Purple Heart
Setcerasea purpurea

✳ **Overlooked plant**
✳ **Great decoration**
✳ **Highly recommended**

The Purple Heart from Brazil is one of several *Setcerasea* species. Named because of the color of the leaves when in sun, the plant bears tiny orchid-like flowers periodically. This busy-looking plant has dark green arrow-shaped leaves and can tolerate shade if necessary. They have good color and provide a nice architectural look. They thrive when grown in small pots filled with loamy, moist soil. They can also be grown in water. Propagate from cutting, or buy mature plants and feed every other watering with 10-10-5.

Purple Heart

Wandering Jew

Wandering Jew
Zebrina pendula (aka Tradescantia zebrina)

✳ **Medium size**
✳ **Long-time favorite**
✳ **Fast-growing for hanging basket**

Numerous plants from Mexico and Central America share this common name. Some have greenish leaves; others have white-and-green striped foliage; and still others are striped with white, purple, and green. This species has green or purple leaves striped with creamy silver tops and purple undersides. It needs little attention to grow lush and vigorous.

Grow this plant in bright to moderate light, in standard all-purpose houseplant soil. Keep the soil evenly moist all year—the plant needs no rest period. Average household temperatures suit it fine. Trim stems when they start to get leggy. Feed every two weeks during active growth with 10-20-10 fertilizer. Propagate from cuttings.

Other Families

As explained on page 109 of the Plant Profiles, this subsection presents excellent houseplants from families that contain a much smaller portion of houseplants commercially available than the previous subsection does. As in the preceding profiles, here you'll find the plants arranged alphabetically by the family common name. Within each family, the plants are arranged alphabetically by the scientific name for the genus and species, which is a convention in gardening publications.

Reminder: There is another good reason for having two subsections in the Plant Profiles. In most cases, it allows the grouping of plants from major families on whole pages and multiple two-page spreads on preceding pages, thereby helping you see the similarities and differences of plants within families and genera (plural for genus).

In this subsection, you'll find anywhere from one to three representatives from each family. Whenever there is more than one plant represented from a given family, you'll find them on the same page or the same two-page spread for easy comparison.

Amaranth Family (*Amaranthaceae*)

Joseph's Coat
Alternanthera hybrid

✳ **Very decorative**
✳ **Small plant**
✳ **Easy to cultivate**

If you like colorful plants, you will delight in this perennial from the South America tropics. This small decorative foliage plant has a rainbow-colored leaf pattern and pretty diminutive white flowers. For best results, grow on a south-facing windowsill and keep the soil on the dry side—but provide 50 percent humidity. Propagate from cuttings. Feed every other watering with 10-10-5. Propagate by cuttings.

Joseph's Coat

Red Plume

Red Plume
Celosia plumosa

✳ **Overlooked plant**
✳ **Nice flowers**
✳ **Grows easily**

The red plume plant is so named because of the striking vertical red plume. The leaf color varies on this compact annual that can be grown indoors. The combination of red and green, along with its growing shape, make this a good accent plant. Try grouping several together to make an interesting display. To grow, keep the soil evenly moist. This plant does best in good light, but it will grow in a shaded area. The flowers make attractive dried arrangements. Red plume is easily raised from seed. Feed four times a year with 10-10-5.

Araucaria Family (Araucariaceae)

Norfolk Island Pine

Norfolk Island Pine
Araucaria heterophylla (aka A. excelsa)

✳ **Treelike, large plant**
✳ **Needlelike green leaves**
✳ **Slow grower**

From Norfolk Island in the South Pacific, this plant grows tall outdoors but stays about 48 inches indoors. It has a handsome growth habit, with tiers of needle-covered branches, though it is not a pine.

Grow in bright light. Average household temperatures are fine. Plant in a large container in standard all-purpose houseplant soil that drains readily. Keep soil evenly moist, but water sparingly in the winter. Mist occasionally. Feed quarterly with 20-10-10 fertilizer. The plant dislikes disturbance, so topdress with fresh soil each year instead of repotting. Purchase new plants from suppliers rather than propagating.

Aucuba Family (Aucubaceae)

Gold-Dust Plant

Gold-Dust Plant
Aucuba japonica

✳ **Compact medium size**
✳ **Handsome foliage plant**
✳ **Easy to grow**

From western Africa, the gold-dust is a compact, slow-growing foliage plant with green leaves dusted with golden yellow spots. These bushy plants grow to about 30 inches. Most of the numerous cultivars thrive in home conditions.

Grow in a bright airy location. Pot in standard all-purpose houseplant soil with excellent drainage. Keep the soil evenly moist all year, never too dry or too wet. Feed quarterly with 20-10-20 fertilizer. Propagate by division.

Banana Family (*Musaceae*)

Parrot Plant
Heliconia psittacorum

❋ **Large vertical accent**
❋ **Beautiful orange-red flower bracts**
❋ **Handsome lance-shaped leaves**

Heliconia is a large genus from Brazil in the same family as the banana plant. Plants called *Heliconia psittacorum* can lead to confusion because many different plants are listed with that scientific name. Several fine cultivars are available. Parrot plant has vertical stems sheathed with green leaves and tall spikes topped with exotic orange-red floral bracts that resemble those of the bird-of-paradise (*Strelitzia reginae*) but is a far more amenable houseplant. It grows to more than 48 inches and can be moved outdoors in summer.

Grow in a bright location, in a large pot of well-drained all-purpose houseplant soil. Keep the soil evenly moist all year. Heliconias thrive in warm conditions but will tolerate nighttime temperatures as low as 55°F. Feed monthly with 10-10-10 fertilizer. Propagate by division.

Parrot Plant

Flowering Banana

Flowering Banana
Musella lasiocarpa

❋ **Overlooked for the house**
❋ **Give plenty of water**
❋ **Different and lush**

For something different, grow a banana plant indoors. It will not produce fruit, but *Musella* adds a colorful note to the indoor garden with its colorful leaves and handsome yellow flowers. Give it plenty of room to grow, and plant in a tub. It is dormant in the winter months, so keep soil barely moist at that time. Although tropical by nature, the plant can withstand temperatures down to 48°F. Insects will not bother this plant. Feed four times a year with 10-10-5. Propagate by suckers.

Bignonia Family (*Bigoniaceae*)

China Doll Plant

Radermachera sinica

❊ **Medium-size to large plant**
❊ **Attractive treelike shape**
❊ **Easy to grow**

Introduced in the 1980s, China doll plant took the world by storm. This Southeast Asia native has shiny green leaves and grows to a treelike 40 inches. It is a good alternative to the somewhat temperamental ficus plants.

Grow in bright light, in standard all-purpose houseplant soil. Water sparingly all year. Feed monthly with 10-10-10 plant food. Propagate from tip cuttings.

China Doll Plant

Velvet Plant

Composite Family (*Asteraceae*)

Velvet Plant

Gynura sarmentosa

❊ **Colorful leaves**
❊ **Small plant**
❊ **Best in genus**

This popular ornamental plant, which is also available in a variegated form, is known for its large, finely serrated purple leaves. Velvet plant's dramatic color adds a decorative indoor accent. The plant grows rapidly to 30 inches. Gynura likes sun, frequent watering, and about 70-percent humidity. This is an unusual plant; the foliage almost glows with color and its orange flowers make a nice counterpoint. Keep soil moist, but avoid getting water on leaves. Feed every other watering with 10-10-5. Propagate by cuttings.

Cycad Family (*Cycadaceae*)

Sago Palm

Cycas revoluta

❋ **Medium size**
❋ **Can grow to 36 inches across**
❋ **Survives neglect**

This slow-growing Java native belongs to one of the oldest known plant families. It resembles a conifer and forms a trunk similar to a palm, and it needs little attention to thrive.

Sago palm needs bright light and standard all-purpose houseplant soil kept evenly moist all year. Repot only when necessary, about every third year. Purchase new plants from suppliers.

Sago Palm

Dogbane Family (*Apocynaceae*)

Dipladenia

Mandevilla × amabilis

❋ **Excellent large basket plant**
❋ **Stunning flowers**
❋ **Easy to grow**

Hailing from Brazil, this stellar plant bears large cerise flowers with yellow throats almost year-round. The plant is vining and can quickly grow to a height of 48 inches. Flowers are borne on fresh growth, so occasional pruning stimulates blooming.

Grow in bright light and pot in a large container of standard all-purpose houseplant soil. Feed monthly with 20-10-10 fertilizer. In winter, let the soil dry out somewhat between waterings so that the plant can rest. Propagate from cuttings.

Good cultivars: 'Alice du Pont', 'Magic Dream'

Dipladenia

Dogbane Family (*Apocynaceae*) cont'd

Trumpet Plant
Allamanda (Dwarf)

❋ **Robust plant**
❋ **New dwarf variety**
❋ **Lovely yellow flowers**

Allamandas are mostly evergreen climbers from Brazil with green leaves and waxen, tubular flowers. Alamanda is usually a large plant, but this new dwarf variety grows to only 18 inches and produces lovely yellow flowers. Flowers appear in summer and make a handsome accent in the indoor garden. Give Trumpet plant full sun and plenty of water during growth, as well as 30 to 50 percent humidity. In winter, keep soil barely moist. Prune back in spring to keep in bounds. Occasionally bothered by insects so use necessary precautions. Feed four times a year with 10-10-5. Propagate by soft wood cuttings.

Trumpet Plant

Wishbone Plant

Figwort Family (*Scrophulariaceae*)

Wishbone Plant
Torenia fournieri

❋ **Fine flowers**
❋ **Dense foliage**
❋ **Good in small pots**

Wishbone plant features bright green, serrated leaves and pretty tricolor flowers in a wishbone shape. This handsome plant can add a colorful bouquet of blooms throughout the year, although it is at its peak in the summer months. Bushy and lush, wishbone can grow to a height of one foot if given plenty of bright light. Provide lots of water and loamy soil. Trim plant occasionally. Feed with 10-10-10 every other month, and 10-10-5 four times a year. Grow new plants from seeds.

Gentian Family (*Gentianaceae*)

Persian Violet, German Violet

Exacum affine

* Compact plant
* Pretty purple flowers
* Easy to grow

Growing to 14 inches, this bushy little plant has waxy leaves and small purple flowers with yellow centers. Although not spectacular, it makes a charming table accent. Or you can mass several for greater impact as a display for interiors. Persian violet is widely grown for gift-giving at holiday times. This plant has a lovely fragrance.

Grow in bright light, in well-drained all-purpose potting soil. Plant in a small pot, and keep the soil evenly moist all year. Do not fertilize. As the plant becomes straggly, take tip cuttings for new plants, and discard the old plant. (See Chapter 6, page 90 for instructions on taking tip cuttings.)

Persian Violet, German Violet

Geranium Family (*Geraniaceae*)

Geranium

Pelargonium × hortorum

* Large plant with colorful flower heads
* Favorite indoor and outdoor plant
* Hundreds of varieties

Blooming in shades of red, pink, and white, geraniums are tough to beat. But as permanent plants they are difficult to keep for more than a few months. The Pelargonium × hortorum hybrids, which most gardeners know as geraniums, are popular both as houseplants and as outdoor summer annuals. They are sometimes called zonal geraniums because the leaves of some cultivars are marked with dark, circular "zones."

Provide plenty of light and direct sun for best blooming. Plant in fast-draining all-purpose potting soil. Keep in small pots. In large pots, plants tend to get leggy and need pruning. A winter rest is needed, so water sparingly then. Feed monthly with 20-10-10 fertilizer, except during the winter rest. Propagate from stem cuttings.

Geranium

Grape Family (*Vitaceae*)

Begonia Vine
Cissus discolor

❋ **Small to medium size plant**
❋ **Handsome foliage**
❋ **Easy to grow**

Begonia Vine

This beautiful vine has arrowhead-shaped leaves of silver, green, purple, and pink.

Grow in a bright but not sunny location, in humusy soil that drains readily. Keep the soil evenly moist all year—it's temperamental about watering. Feed monthly with 20-10-10 fertilizer. Pinch back leaves to encourage bushier growth. Propagate from stem cuttings.

Grape Family (*Vitaceae*)

Kangaroo Vine
Cissus rotundifolia

❋ **Grows with low light**
❋ **Old favorite**
❋ **Upright plant**

Kangaroo Vine

Cissus rotundifolia is a handsome upright plant that deserves more attention by home growers. A semi-succulent, these ambitious trailers climb to 5 feet or more unless pruned. They are among the easiest vines to grow in an indoor planter, basket or bracket, thriving even in an apartment. Kangaroo vine has rounded, glossy leaves. Grow in sun or shade, and allow soil to dry out between waterings. Repot every year or two; they thrive in fresh soil. Do not feed. Propagate by cuttings or division.

Hydrangea Family (*Hydrangeaceae*)

Hydrangea
Hydrangea macrophylla

❋ **Bountiful flowers**
❋ **Medium-size gift plant**
❋ **Excellent temporary decoration**

Hydrangea features large round flower clusters 8 to 10 inches in diameter. Cultivars have flowers that last six weeks in pink, blue, red, or white. Purchase hydrangeas in spring or summer—the normal blooming season.

This plant likes bright light and evenly moist soil. If too dry, the plant quickly dies. Do not fertilize. Start new plants from stem cuttings.

Persian Violet, German Violet

Loosestrife Family (*Lythraceae*)

Cigar Plant

Cuphea hyssopifolia

❋ **Give plenty of water**
❋ **Needs light**
❋ **Seldom seen but worth the space**

This plant from Mexico grows into a small bush with dense foliage. It blooms in summer but is short lived. This is a good accent plant for indoor beauty. If too dense, trim judiciously. Needs warmth. Plant in small pots of loam. Feed cigar plant when it blooms in summer, but do not feed in winter. It is usually not bothered by insects. Use cuttings to propagate the plant.

Cigar Plant

Madder Family (*Rubiaceae*)

Cape Jasmine

Cape Jasmine

Gardenia jasminoides
(aka *G. augusta*)

❋ **Compact medium-size plant**
❋ **Fragrant flowers**
❋ **Attractive foliage**

Egyptian Star Cluster

Pentas lanceolata

❋ **Good medium-size plant**
❋ **Colorful flowers**
❋ **Many cultivars**

Egyptian Star Cluster

This plant is a native of China. Although difficult to grow, it is a favorite with hobbyist because its creamy white flowers can deliciously scent an entire room.

Cape jasmine and its cultivar 'Radicans' need time to adjust to new surroundings when you bring them home. Provide a location in bright light without direct sun. To avoid bud drop—the most common gardenia problem—avoid drastic temperature changes. Also, provide more humidity during the winter. Keep the soil evenly moist, and feed monthly with an acidic fertilizer. Gardenias are difficult to propagate at home. Instead, purchase new plants.

Native to Africa, these plants grow to 36 inches and have clusters of star-shaped flowers in spring through summer. The flowers can be yellow, pink, red, or orange.

Grow in a sunny location, in sandy soil. Keep the soil evenly moist all year. If the soil dries out, the leaves will drop, but avoid overly wet soil as well. Feed monthly with 20-10-10 fertilizer. Propagate by division.

Mallow Family (*Malvaceae*)

Flowering Maple

Abutilon × hybridum

❋ **Pretty bell-shaped flowers**
❋ **Large vertical plant**
❋ **Difficult to grow**

This plant has maplelike leaves variegated with white in some cultivars. A favorite houseplant for over 100 years, flowering maple has been much hybridized and can grow to 48 inches. The lovely bell-shaped flowers come in shades of red, rose, orange, pink, and yellow. The plant wilts quickly without proper watering.

Grow in a sunny spot, and use a houseplant soil that drains readily. The plant must never be dry or too wet. In hot weather it may need watering every other day. Do not fertilize. Provide warm temperatures, and cut back the stems occasionally. Propagate from cuttings.

Flowering Maple

Prayer Plant

Maranta Family (*Marantaceae*)

Prayer Plant

Calathea majestica 'Roseolineata' (aka *C. ornata* 'Roseolineata')

❋ **Medium size**
❋ **Beautifully marked leaves**
❋ **Easy to grow**

Prayer plant, a relative of Peacock plant, is so called because the leaves close at night like hands folded in prayer. This pretty cultivar grows to 28 inches tall.

Grow in bright light, in humusy soil that drains well. Keep the soil evenly moist all year; allow it to dry somewhat in the winter. The plant needs average household temperatures. Feed quarterly with 10-10-10 fertilizer.

Peacock Plant

Calathea makoyana

❊ **Excellent medium-size plant**
❊ **Colorful foliage**
❊ **Easy to grow**

Caltheas are a stunning group of plants with many cultivars. The bold leaf markings of the Peacock plant make it a great choice for a shady room. It prefers light shade in summer and brighter light in winter, but keep out of direct sun to avoid dulling the color of the leaves. Caltheas love misting when possible. Keep the compost moist in the summer. Brown tips will let you know that the humidity is too low. Use an all-purpose houseplant soil kept evenly moist. Repot every year, and feed monthly with 20-20-10 fertilizer. Propagate by division.

Peacock
Plant

Prayer Plant

Prayer Plant

Maranta roseo picta

❊ **Best color**
❊ **Handsome foliage**
❊ **Keep out of sun**

It is tough to beat Maranta as a houseplant. There are several varieties and most have colorful leaves. When mature they make a handsome bouquet. Ornamental foliage and fast growth at north windows give these plants a top spot on the desirable list. Keep soil moist; 50 percent humidity. Plants thrive in 4- or 5-inch pots and where there is good air circulation. When resting time comes in late fall, cut away old foliage; leave the more recent foliage. Resume watering in early winter. Likes to be fed 10-10-5 every other week. Propagate by division at repotting time or using leaf-stalk cuttings.

Maranta Family (*Marantaceae*) cont'd

Stromanthe sanguinea

✻ **Unusual plant**
✻ **Good vertical accent**
✻ **Will grow in shade**

Native to South America, Stromanthe is sometimes known as *Calathea discolor*. It grows to four feet tall and adds drama to any indoor garden. Stromanthe features bracts and white and red flowers. It has glossy green leaves that are variegated with red and have red undersides. This is a new offering at nurseries that is seldom seen but certainly should be grown more indoors. Stromanthe is an undemanding plant that likes evenly moist soil and is not troubled by pests. Easily propagated by division. Feed four times a year with 10-10-5.

Stromanthe sanguinea

Melastoma Family (*Melastomceae*)

Pink Grape Plant
Medinilla magnifica

✻ **Large, handsome plant**
✻ **Pendant flower heads**
✻ **Easy to grow**

This plant bears large, drooping clusters of pink flowers and bracts, followed by long-lasting purple berries. Another species, *M. myriantha*, is similar in appearance but somewhat smaller and with pink berrylike flowers. This tropical shrub grows to some 48 inches and sports, thick-veined green leaves and pendant flower scapes in summer.

Grow in bright light. Use a humusy potting soil kept quite moist in warm months, somewhat drier the rest of the year. Provide high humidity. Feed twice a month with 10-20-10 fertilizer. Repot only when necessary—about every second year. Propagate by division.

Pink Grape

Milkweed Family (*Asclepiadaceae*)

Dragon Flower
Huernia kewensis

✳ **Striking, starlike flowers**
✳ **Exotic appearance**
✳ **Can grow without water for weeks**

Native to South Africa, the dragon flower is a small succulent with prostrate green stems, tiny leaves, and large funnel-shaped purple flowers. The flower has an unpleasant odor, so grow as a curiosity. An oddity of nature but worth the space because of the large star-like flower that hugs the edge of the pot. Allow the soil to dry out between waterings. Use small pots for bloom production. Do not feed. Propagate from cuttings.

Dragon Flower

Madagascar Jasmine

Madagascar Jasmine
Stephanotis floribunda

✳ **Large plant**
✳ **Intensely fragrant flowers**
✳ **Vining growth habit**

In the summer months, this vining Madagascar jasmine responds well to cool conditions and bears a profusion of highly scented waxy white flowers that brighten any indoor garden. The flowers are often used in bridal bouquets.

Grow in a bright but not sunny location. Pot in standard all-purpose houseplant soil, and provide a support for the vining stems. Feed monthly with 20-10-10 fertilizer. Keep the soil evenly moist for most of the year. In winter decrease watering somewhat, but never allow the soil to become dry enough to cake. Madagascar jasmine needs nighttime temperatures of 55°F to set buds. Propagate from runners..

Mint Family (*Labiatae*)

Flame Nettle
Coleus spc.

❋ **Favorite old plant**
❋ **Colorful foliage**
❋ **Group several in a pot**

Old-fashioned favorites, coleus are easy-to-grow plants valued for their colorful foliage of plum, red, pink, green, or yellow. There are dozens of coleus, all with handsome variegated leaves, so the decision is strictly based on personal preference. Grow in a bright place, water every second or third day, and they will grow luxuriantly. If you put coleus outside in summer, you will be rewarded with blue flowers. Watch for mealy bugs. Grow several in a pot. Do not allow to dry out. All coleus like feeding every month with 10-10-5. Cultivars appear frequently. New plants from seed.

Flame Nettle

Painted Nettle

Painted Nettle
Coleus blumei (aka *Solenostemon scutellarioides*)

❋ **Fast-growing small plant**
❋ **Colorful foliage**
❋ **Easy to grow**

Coleus is often planted as an outdoor annual in shady gardens, but it also grows well indoors. The foliage is colorful, and there are some 200 different hybrids with leaves of varying shapes and sizes in many combinations of colors. The plants are generally good for only a season, but tip cuttings root easily to create new plants.

Coleus likes bright light and a humusy, well-drained potting soil. Keep the soil evenly moist, neither too dry nor too wet. Feed every few weeks with 10-20-10 fertilizer. Pinch off flowers to keep the foliage in better condition. Tip cuttings root easily in water or soil.

Swedish Ivy
Plectranthus australis

❋ **Medium size**
❋ **Handsome trailer for a hanging basket**
❋ **Easy to grow**

This old-time favorite, with dense green, scalloped leaves, needs little care to thrive. Provide bright to moderate light, ideally with a bit of morning sun. Pot in standard all-purpose houseplant soil. Keep the soil evenly moist except in winter. Never allow the soil to become dry. Feed quarterly with 10-10-10 fertilizer. Wipe the leaves occasionally with a damp cloth. Prune when needed to control shape—the plant can grow quickly. Propagate from stem cuttings.

Swedish Ivy

Swedish Ivy

Swedish Ivy
Plectranthus fruticosa

❋ **New variety**
❋ **Handsome foliage**
❋ **Good window plant**

Plectranthus, a close relative of coleus, comes from the Pacific Islands. It typically features waxy, scalloped leaves on trailing stems and pretty little flowers on and off throughout the year. Swedish ivy has a busy appearance and variegated leaves that make it appear like a small bouquet. These plants are nearly foolproof to grow and are worth space at a window. Grow in either light or shade and keep soil evenly moist. Fast growing; good for baskets. Feed every other month with 10-10-5. Propagate by seeds sown in spring or by cuttings at any time.

Morning Glory Family (*Convolvulaceae*)

Sweet Potato Vine
Ipomea batatas

❊ **Easy to grow**
❊ **Vining**
❊ **Good in hanging basket**

Many of us remember growing traditional sweet potato plants as children by putting a potato in a jar of water and watching it sprout. This very pretty new variety is still fun for children to grow. *Ipomea batatas* features ovate, light-green leaves and makes a striking appearance in the indoor garden. This plant grows fast and needs occasional pruning. With its trailing habit, sweet potato vine makes an excellent windowsill plant. Keep water level halfway up plant and do not feed.

Sweet Potato Vine

Baby's Tears

Nettle Family (*Uritacaeae*)

Baby's Tears
Helxine solieria

❊ **Keep evenly moist**
❊ **Grow near window**
❊ **Will grow indoors with minimum care**

Helxine solieria is native to Corsica and Sardinia. It has a moss-like creeping habit with lush green leaves or place in a basket as a trailing plant. It spreads rapidly and likes warmth and plenty of moisture. A great plant for indoors providing good color; it can also be used outdoors as ground cover at the base of large plants. Do not feed. Propagate by cuttings.

Panama Hat Family
(*Cyclanthaceae*)

Panama Hat Plant
Carludovica palmata

* **Excellent as a pot plant**
* **Unusual and decorative**
* **Needs bright light**

The Panama Hat has fan-shaped palm leaves with cylindrical leaf stalks, which are fairly uncommon in the palm world. A common landscape plant in tropical climates, it also makes a great indoor decoration. Panama Hat needs warmth and protection from wind, lots of moisture, and good drainage. Buy mature plants. Do not allow to dry out. Propagate by cutting. Feed four times a year with 10-10-5.

Panama Hat Plant

Trailing Peperomia

Pepper Family
(*Piperaceae*)

Trailing Peperomia
Peperomia obtusifolia

* **Medium size**
* **Attractive foliage**
* **Sturdy trailer**

From the jungles of Mexico and northern South America, trailing peperomia comes in many varieties. Grow in bright light, and plant in all-purpose houseplant soil. Too much water causes problems and too little stunts growth, so keep the soil evenly moist. Propagate by division or by taking cuttings.

Pepper Family (*Piperaceae*) cont'd

Common Peperomia

Peperomia scandens

❋ **Medium size**
❋ **Old-time favorite**
❋ **Easy to grow**

This bushy, somewhat sprawling plant can become large, and it grows quickly to 36 inches. The attractive oblong, succulent leaves come in variegated as well as plain green forms. Common peperomia needs little care to thrive.

Grow in bright light, and plant in standard all-purpose houseplant soil. Keep the soil evenly moist all year. Feed monthly with 10-10-10 fertilizer. Start new plants from tip cuttings.

Common Peperomia

Primrose Family (*Primulaceae*)

Florist's Cyclamen, Shooting Star

Cyclamen persicum

❋ **Colorful flowers**
❋ **Small seasonal plant**
❋ **Innumerable hybrids, including miniatures**

Growing to a compact 24 inches, these free-flowering plants with decorative foliage generally bloom in fall and winter. Cyclamens grow from a tuber and are usually gift plants used as table accents that are discarded after blooming.

Grow in bright light, and plant in standard all-purpose houseplant soil. Keep the soil evenly moist—never let it dry out. No fertilization is necessary. Purchase new plants rather than attempting propagation.

Florist's Cyclamen, Shooting Star

Rose Family (Rosaceae)

Miniature Rose
Rosa chinensis 'Minima'

❋ **Small cousin of garden roses**
❋ **Range of flower colors**
❋ **Seasonal plant**

Miniature roses are diminutive versions of their larger outdoor cousins. Of the hundreds of hybrids, most are derived from Rosa chinensis. The plants usually grow about 14 inches tall.

Give miniature roses bright light and standard all-purpose houseplant soil. Keep the soil evenly moist. It is not necessary to fertilize the plants, because they are usually discarded after blooming. Purchase new plants from suppliers.

Miniature
Rose

Saxifrage Family (*Saxifragaceae*)

Strawberry
Begonia

Strawberry Begonia
Saxifraga stolonifera (aka *S. sarmentosa*)

❋ **Small trailing plant**
❋ **Grows well indoors**
❋ **Moderate light**

This native to Japan and China is neither a strawberry nor a begonia. The common name derives from the runners that trail from the plant, similar to those on a strawberry plant, and the leaves, which have the same general shape as those of some begonias. This plant grows to about 14 inches high in bright to moderate light. Pot in standard all-purpose houseplant soil kept evenly moist all year. Feed every month with 10-10-10 fertilizer. Propagate from runners.

Selaginella Family (*Primulaceae*)

Moss Fern
Selaginella krausiana

✳ **Unusual appearance**
✳ **Grows easily**
✳ **Shade loving**

From Central America, Moss fern is a member of the Selaginella family, which are small, ferny plants that are excellent for terrariums and dish gardens. Some are attractive hanging plants, others are creepers good for covering the soil of larger plants. We don't see this plant often grown indoors but it does make a handsome addition to the indoor garden and mature plants can be quite handsome. Grow in shade; soak soil, and let dry out between waterings; 50 percent humidity. Avoid water on foliage; it causes rot. Apply 10-10-5 every month. Propagate by cuttings.

Moss Fern

Crassula spc.

Stonecrop Family (*Crassulaceae*)

Crassula spc.

✳ **Tolerates dryness**
✳ **Many varieties**
✳ **Striking foliage**

Native to Africa, crassulas make ideal house-plants. Due to their fleshy leaves and stems, they tolerate low humidity and moisture. Some have gray or blue foliage; others are green. Several have branching stems, many produce low rosettes of leaves. Bright light or full sun suits them; let soil dry out between waterings. Feed only in summer with 10-10-5. Keep evenly moist. Crassulas are usually not bothered by insects but are occasionally attacked by mealy bugs. Propagate from seed, stem, or leaf cuttings.

Sunflower Family (*Compositae*)

Wax Vine
Senecio macroglossus

❋ **Medium size**
❋ **Unusual ivy-type vine**
❋ **Easy to grow**

Wax vine is a vigorous plant with fleshy leaves that are more pointed than those of English ivy. It is handsome and needs little attention to thrive.

Grow Wax vine in bright light, in standard houseplant soil. Keep the soil evenly moist except in winter, when you can leave the soil barely moist. Feed monthly with 20-10-10 fertilizer. Propagate from cuttings.

Wax Vine

Lantana

Verbena Family (*Verbenaceae*)

Lantana
Lantana camara

❋ **Colorful flowers**
❋ **Easy to grow**
❋ **Small plant**

Lantata camara is a shrubby spreading plant with yellow, lavender, or orange blooms. It is generally used as an outdoor plant, but also does well as a houseplant and becomes loaded with flowers in summertime. Place in sun; give plenty of water in summer. In winter, after flowering, cut plants back and grow somewhat dry. Several varieties grouped together makes a nice bouquet effect. Feed every month with 10-10-5. Propagate by cuttings or seed.

Glossary

Air layering. A propagation method for plants with woody stems.

Amendments. Organic or mineral materials, such as peat moss, compost, or vermiculite, used to improve soil.

Axil. The angle at which a leaf joins a stem.

Bract. A modified leaf or leaflike structure that often embraces a flower bud and opens with the flower. Bracts occur at the base of the flower stem and may be part of the flower head. Usually small and green, some bracts, such as those of poinsettia, are mistaken for flower petals.

Bud. A protrusion on a plant stem that develops into a flower.

Bulb. A fleshy underground structure from which a flowering plant develops. The term *bulb* is often used loosely to refer to corms, rhizomes, and tubers, as well as true bulbs.

Cachepot. A decorative plant container without drainage holes.

Come true. When an offspring plant grows to be identical to its parent, it is said to *come true*. The only way to ensure that a hybrid plant comes true is to vegetatively propagate it, such as by cuttings or division.

Corm. A fleshy underground structure from which a flowering plant grows. Curcuma grows from a corm. See *Bulb*.

Cotyledon (pronounced *cot-l-EED-n*). The first leaf or pair of leaves a seedling sprouts; also called *seed leaves* (usually round or oval).

Crown. The junction of roots and stem, usually at soil level.

Cultivar. Short for *culti*-vated *var*-iety. A plant variety developed in cultivation, rather than occurring in nature.

Culture. General plant care. Good culture results in optimal growing conditions.

Cutting. A plant part (usually a stem or leaf section) removed and rooted to grow a new plant.

Damping-off. A fungal disease that attacks seedlings and causes them to collapse.

Daylength. The number of hours of daylight that a plant receives in a 24-hour period.

Day-neutral plants. Plants that do not require a particular daylength and will flower at various times of the year. See *Daylength*.

Division. A propagation method that separates a plant into two or more similar pieces, each with at least one bud and some roots.

Epiphyte. A plant that is not rooted in soil. Epiphytes grow on other plants and obtain their nourishment and moisture from the air.

Exposure. The intensity and duration of light a plant receives.

Fir bark. A potting medium in which orchids and bromeliads are often planted.

Forcing. Causing a plant to flower indoors ahead of its natural blooming time.

Genus (plural: genera). A closely related group of species sharing similar characteristics and probably evolved from the same ancestors.

Germination. The sprouting of a seed.

Habit. The characteristic shape, or form, a plant assumes as it grows.

Horticultural charcoal. A clean by-product of burned wood. Applied to plant wounds, it decreases the chances of diseases starting there. Also used to keep water fresh.

Humus. The fibrous residues of decomposed organic materials in soil. Humus provides nutrients and helps the potting medium drain.

Hybrid. A plant resulting from cross- breeding of parents that belong to different varieties, species, or genera. Seeds of hybrids often do not come true but revert to the traits of one of the parent plants. See *Come true*.

Leaf cutting. A propagation method that stimulates cut pieces of leaves to grow roots.

Leggy. Weak, elongated growth, usually caused by insufficient light.

Long-day plants. Plants that require long days to set buds, meaning that they bloom in summer, when days are long.

Mist. To spray a plant with water droplets. This cleans foliage and adds humidity to the plant's environment.

Native. A plant that occurs naturally in a particular geographic region.

Node. The point along a stem from which a leaf or roots emerge.

Offset. A new plant that forms at the base of the parent plant. Most bromeliads reproduce from offsets.

Peat moss. Partially decomposed mosses and sedges mined from boggy areas and used to improve the texture of a soil.

Perlite. Heat-expanded volcanic glass used to lighten potting mediums and create space for air particles.

Photoperiod. See *Daylength*.

Potbound. A plant with a root mass that has grown too large for its container. The overgrown roots take on the shape of the pot, grow in circles, and may strangle the plant.

Potting medium. The material in which a plant is potted.

Potting mix. A blend of growing mediums for container-grown plants.

Propagate. To create more plants.

Pseudobulb. A swollen organ through which orchids reproduce.

Repotting. Transplanting from one container to another, usually to a larger container.

Resting period. The time when a plant's growth naturally slows, often after flowering.

Rhizome. A horizontal underground stem from which a new plant can grow. See *Bulb*.

Rooting hormone. A liquid or powder that encourages cuttings to root.

Rootball. A plant's combined mass of roots and soil.

Rosette. Foliage emerging from a central cluster.

Runners. A slender arching or trailing shoot that emerges from a mature plant. New plantlets form along the nodes of the shoot.

Scape. The flower stalk arising from the center of a plant.

Seed leaves. See *Cotyledon*.

Seed pellet. An organic, manufactured disk that expands when watered to become a seed container.

Seedling. A tiny new plant that has grown from seed.

Shards. Broken crockery used in the bottom of pots to aid in drainage.

Sharp sand. A coarse sand used as a potting medium and often sold as builder's sand.

Short-day plants. Plants that will not bloom unless they receive enough hours of darkness each day.

Sow. To plant a seed.

Spadix. A flower spike protected by a spathe. See *Spathe* below.

Spathe. A leaflike hood protecting the spadix. The peace lily flower is surrounded by a spathe.

Species. A group of plants that shares many characteristics and can interbreed freely.

Specimen plant. A large plant often displayed on its own or in a prominent position.

Spike. An elongated flower cluster, with individual flowers borne on short stalks or attached directly to the main stem.

Standard houseplant soil. A commercially available blend that provides ample drainage and air yet doesn't dry out quickly.

Stem cutting. A propagation method that stimulates root growth from the cut end of a stem.

Sterile medium. A soilless mix used for germinating seeds and rooting cuttings.

Stolon. A stem that produces a new plant at its tip.

Succulent. A plant with fleshy, thick foliage that retains moisture.

Tip cutting. A propagation method that employs the cut tips of leaves to stimulate root growth.

Transplanting. The process of replanting a plant in new soil.

True leaves. The second pair of leaves that emerge on a seedling. These leaves have the distinctive shape of leaves of the mature plant.

Tuber. A fleshy underground structure from which plants emerge. See *Bulb*.

Urn. A water-holding, vase-like shape formed by leaves in bromeliads; also called a *vase*.

Variegated. Foliage that is marked, striped, or blotched with a color or colors other than green.

Variety. A variant of a species that is the result of natural mutation.

Vegetative propagation. Producing new plants from parts of a parent. The resulting plants are genetically identical to the parent plant.

Vermiculite. A mica product used in potting mixes. It retains water and releases it as the surrounding soil dries.

Index

Photo Credits

Unless credited below, photos by David Van Zanten.
Page 1: Friedrich Strauss/Garden Picture Library **pages 5–6:** both Andrew Addkison **Page 10:** Friedrich Strauss/Garden Picture Library **page 11:** Alan & Linda Detrick **page 12:** *top left* Eric L. Heyer/Grant Heilman Photography **page 14:** *top left* Jerry Pavia **page 17:** *left* Erica Craddock/Garden Picture Library **page 18:** *left* Michael & Lois Warren/Photos Horiticultural *right* Frank Nikolaus/KW/OKAPIA/Photo Researchers, Inc. **page 22:** *bottom left* John Glover/Garden Picture Library *bottom middle* and *right* Lynne Brotchie/Garden Picture Library **page 24:** Friedrich Strauss/Garden Picture Library **page 26:** *top* John Glover *bottom left* Jerry Howard/Positive Images **page 27:** Crandall & Crandall **page 28:** *top* Ann Kelley/Garden Picture Library *bottom* Friedrich Strauss/Garden Picture Library **page 29:** *top* Mayer/Le Scanff/Garden Picture Library *bottom* Steven Wooster/Garden Picture Library **page 30:** *bottom left* Mayer/Le Scanff/Garden Picture Library *bottom right* Crandall & Crandall **page 31:** *bottom middle* Eugene Mopsik/H. Armstrong Roberts **page 32:** *top* Jennifer Deane *bottom* Jane Grushow/Grant Heilman Photography, Inc. **page 33:** *left* Mayer/Le Scanff/Garden Picture Library *right* Alan & Linda Detrick **page 34:** *top left* Linda Burgess/Garden Picture Library *bottom left* A. Teufen/H. Armstrong Roberts *right* Crandall & Crandall **page 35:** A. Teufen/H. Armstrong Roberts **page 36:** Telegraph Colour Library/FPG **page 37:** Lynne Brotchie/Garden Picture Library **page 38:** *top* Elyse Lewin/Image Bank *bottom* Jennifer Deane **page 39:** *left* Crandall & Crandall *right* Michael S. Thompson **page 40:** Crandall & Crandall **page 41:** *left* Howard Rice/Garden Picture Library *right* Alan & Linda Detrick **page 42:** *top* M. Barrett/H. Armstrong Roberts *bottom* Rion Rizzo/FPG **page 43:** *top* Mayer/Le Scanff/Garden Picture Library *bottom* Lefever/Grushow/Grant Heilman Photography, Inc. **page 44:** *left* Steven Wooster/Garden Picture Library **page 45:** *left* Jose Luis Banus-March/FPG *right* E. Alan McGee Photo Inc./FPG **page 46:** *top* Jessie Walker *bottom* Peter Gridley/FPG **page 47:** *left* A. Teufen/H. Armstrong Roberts *right* Lynne Brotchie/Garden Picture Library **page 48:** *top left* Jennifer Deane *bottom left* K. Rice/H. Armstrong Roberts *right* Telegraph Colour Library/FPG **page 49:** *top* Larry Lefever/Grant Heilman Photography, Inc. *bottom left* J. Shive/H. Armstrong Roberts *bottom right* A. Teufen/H. Armstrong Roberts **page 50:** *top* Mel Watson/Garden Picture Library *bottom left* Patricia J. Bruno/Positive Images *bottom right* John Glover **pages 52–53:** Friedrich Strauss/Garden Picture Library **page 54:** *top* Alan & Linda Detrick *bottom* Friedrich Strauss/Garden Picture Library **page 55:** *top left* and *bottom* Friedrich Strauss/Garden Picture Library **page 56:** *both top* Friedrich Strauss/Garden Picture Library *bottom* Alan & Linda Detrick **page 57:** *bottom left* Lefever/Grushow/Grant Heilman Photography, Inc. *bottom right* Friedrich Strauss/Garden Picture Library **page 58:** *top* John Glover **page 60:** Alan & Linda Detrick **page 65:** John Glover/Garden Picture Library **page 66:** John Parsekian **page 67:** *top* Rita Buchanan *middle* and *bottom* John Parsekian **page 68:** *top* courtesy of Lee Valley Tools *bottom* courtesy of Charley's Greenhouse Supply **page 69:** *top left* Patti McConville/Image Bank **page 71:** *top* Jessie Walker **page 72:** *top* American Phytopathological Society **page 77:** *bottom right* Runk/Schoenberger/Grant Heilman Photography, Inc. **page 79:** *top* Horticultural Photography *bottom* Brian Carter/Garden Picture Library **page 81:** *bottom right* courtesy of Charely's Greenhouse Supply **page 82:** Crandall & Crandall **page 85:** *both* courtesy of Lee Valley Tools **page 87:** *top* John Parsekian **page 96:** *left* Friedrich Strauss/Garden Picture Library *right* Dutch Gardens **page 100:** Friedrich Strauss/Garden Picture Library **page 102:** *top left* American Phytopathological Society *right* Crandall & Crandall **page 103:** *right* Friedrich Strauss/Garden Picture Library **page 104:** *top* J.S. Sira/Garden Picture Library *middle left* Noah Poritz/Macro World/Photo Researchers, Inc. *middle center* Jerome Wexler/Photo Researchers, Inc. *middle right* J. H. Robinson/Photo Researchers, Inc. *bottom* Holt Studios/Photo Researchers, Inc. **page 105:** *top* M.T. Frazier/PSU/Photo Researchers, Inc. *middle left* Grant Heilman Photography, Inc. *middle center* Dwight Kuhn *middle right* Louis Quitt/Photo Researchers, Inc. *bottom* Dwight Kuhn **pages 106–107:** all American Phytopathological Society **page 108:** Alan & Linda Detrick **page 109:** John Glover **page 110:** *top left* Jane Legate/Garden Picture Library *top right* John Glover *bottom* Neil Soderstrom **page 118:** *both bottom* John Glover/Garden Picture Library **page 119:** John Glover **page 125:** *bottom* Andrew Addkison **page 126:** *top left* Friedrich Strauss/Garden Picture Library **page 134:** *left* Jerry Pavia **page 136:** *bottom* Andrew Addkison **page 138:** *both bottom* Neil Soderstrom **page 140:** *top* Michael & Lois Warren/Photos Horticultural *bottom* Mayer/Le Scanff/Garden Picture Library *inset* J.S. Sira/Garden Picture Library **page 141:** *right* Michel Viard/Garden Picture Library **page 143:** Michael & Lois Warren/Photos Horticultural *top left* Roger Hyam/Garden Picture Library *top right* Andrew Addkison *bottom* Vaughan Fleming/Garden Picture Library **page 144:** *top left* Andrew Addkison *top right* C.G. Maxwell/Photo Researchers, Inc. **page 150:** *top* Lefever/Grushow/Grant Heilman Photography, Inc. **page 152:** *left* Andrew Addkison **page 153:** *bottom* Neil Soderstrom **page 154:** *bottom* Frank Nikolaus/KW/OKAPIA/Photo Researchers, Inc. **page 156:** *top left* Derek Fell **page 159:** *bottom left* Jerry Pavia **page 160:** *top* Andrew Addkison **page 162:** *top left* Andrew Addkison **page 163:** *top* Derek Fell *bottom* Jerry Pavia **page 164:** *bottom left* Andrew Addkison **page 167:** *top* John Glover **page 168:** Friedrich Strauss/Garden Picture Library **page 172:** *top* Howard Rice/Garden Picture Library *bottom* Brigitte Thomas/Garden Picture Library **page 173:** *bottom* Alan & Linda Detrick/Photo Researchers, Inc. **page 178:** *top right* Andrew Addkison **page 182:** *bottom right* Neil Soderstrom **page 195:** *top* Steven Wooster/Garden Picture Library *top inset* Michael & Lois Warren/Photos Horticultural *bottom inset* J. S. Sira/Garden Picture Library **page 197:** *bottom* Andrew Addkison **page 205:** *top* Michael & Lois Warren/Photos Horticultural **page 207:** *top* Andrew Addkison *bottom* Juliet Greene/Garden Picture Library **page 208:** *bottom* E.R. Degginger/Photo Researchers, Inc. **page 212:** *top* Derek Fell *bottom* Lefever/Grushow/Grant Heilman Photography, Inc. **page 214:** *bottom left* Friedrich Strauss/Garden Picture Library **page 215:** *bottom left* Andrew Addkison

Have a home gardening, decorating, or improvement project? Look for these and other fine Creative Homeowner books wherever books are sold.

An impressive guide to garden design and plant selection. More than 900 color photos and illustrations. 320 pp.; 9"×10"
BOOK #: 274610

A comprehensive guide to growing over 100 types of roses. Over 280 color photos. 176 pp.; 9"×10"
BOOK #: 274061

Lavishly illustrated with portraits of over 100 flowering plants; more than 500 photos. 208 pp.; 9"×10"
BOOK #: 274032

A guide for getting the most from your garden year-round. Over 1,000 photos. 320 pp.; 9"×10"
BOOK #: 274013

Complete guide to creating a gorgeous landscape. More than 350 photos. 208 pp.; 8½"×10⅞"
BOOK #: 274154

Home landscaping guides that cover seven regions: Mid-Atlantic (274544); Midwest (274390); Northeast (274625); Southeast (274771); Northwest (274351); California (274273); Texas (274483). 400 illustrations each.

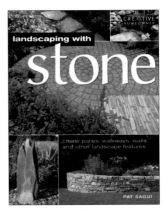

A step-by-step guide for incorporating natural stone in a landscape. More than 350 color photos. 224 pp.; 8½"×10⅞"
BOOK #: 274172

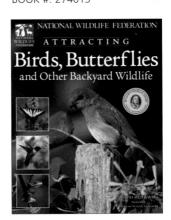

Wildlife-friendly gardening practices. Over 200 color photos and illustrations. 128 pp.; 8½"×10⅞"
BOOK #: 274655

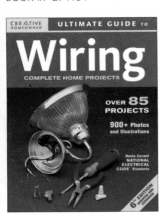

New, updated edition of best-selling house wiring manual. Over 700 color photos. 320 pp.; 8½"×10⅞"
BOOK #: 278242

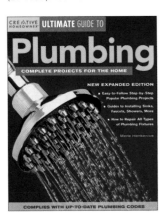

The complete manual for plumbing projects. Over 750 color photos and illustrations. 288 pp.; 8½"×10⅞"
BOOK #: 278200

How to work with space, color, pattern, texture. Over 400 photos. 224 pp.; 9¼"×10⅞"
BOOK #: 279679

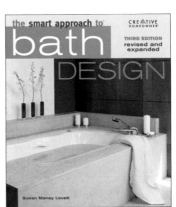

All you need to know about designing a bath. Over 260 color photos. 224 pp.; 9¼"×10⅞"
BOOK #: 279239

For more information and to order direct, visit our Web site at www.creativehomeowner.com

GARDENING / HOUSEPLANTS

COMPLETE Houseplants

FEATURING OVER 240 EASY-CARE FAVORITES

Include houseplants in your decorating to provide style, color, and texture to all the rooms of your home. Don't know where to start? *Complete Houseplants* can make you an expert by supplying

- Complete growing and care information for all of the most popular species of houseplants
- Expert tips on displaying, fertilizing, watering, grooming, and propagating houseplants
- Over 480 color photos and illustrations

Jack Kramer is the author of over 100 books on gardening, including the *World Wildlife Fund Book of Orchids*, as well as dozens of magazine articles. He has researched the growth habits of thousands of houseplants, including those in this book. He is a resident of Naples, Florida.

Safest Methods for Pest and Disease Control

Tips for Dividing Container Plants

Best Types of Soil and Fertilizers

CREATIVE HOMEOWNER®
creativehomeowner.com

ISBN 978-1-58011-397-7
90000
EAN
9 781580 113977

$19.95 US
$21.95 CAN

CH #274820